THE NEEDLE IN THE BLOOD

SARAH BOWER

Proudly published in 2007 by
Snowbooks Ltd.
120 Pentonville Road
London
N1 9JN
www.snowbooks.com

Cover design by Gilly Barnard, Snowbooks
Image from The Bridgeman Art Library
The Fox and the Crow, illustration from 'The Fables of Bidpai' (vellum)

ISBN: 1-905005-39-3
ISBN 13: 978-1-905005-39-0

A catalogue record for this book is available from the British Library.
Printed and bound in Great Britain by Cox & Wyman Ltd., Reading, Berkshire.

Acknowledgements

Many people have contributed to the making of this book. My warmest thanks are due first and foremost to Emma Barnes and Gilly Barnard at Snowbooks, also to Mary Allen, Bernardine Coverley, Mary-Jane Cullen, Patricia Duncker, Sara Fisher, Sue Fletcher, Ryan Gattis, Christina Johnson, Paul Magrs, Sarah Molloy, Andrew Motion, Ingrid Perrin, Michele Roberts, and not forgetting Mark, Guy and Hugh for their forbearance and unfailing optimism.

For my mother, who made it all possible

"Has the pen or pencil dipped so deep in the blood of the human race as the needle?" *Olive Schreiner, "From Man to Man"*

"What shall I say of Odo, Bishop of Bayeux?...In this man, it seems to me, vices were mingled with virtues, but he was more given to worldly affairs than to spiritual contemplation." *Orderic Vitalis, "Ecclesiastical History", Book IV.*

THE NEEDLE IN THE BLOOD

EPIPHANY

14TH OCTOBER 1066

The voice doesn't sound like his, though he can feel its vibrations in his throat. It sobs and growls, bellows and screeches like a cacophony of demons. *My name is Legion for we are many.* Odo is afraid he's lost his reason, but if the rumours are true, and William is dead, it might be better to be out of his mind. If Godwinson finds him.

"You said this couldn't happen," he yells, in this voice like a cracked bell. The air is thick with smoke where fire-tipped arrows have set the grass smouldering. "You were the Wrath of God. How could you die?"

He has let the reins go, one hand trails the borrowed sword, the other is clasped around the amulet he wears, the Tear of the Virgin, William's gift. *He has lost his shield. Fool. Lost his shield? What sort of soldier is he?* God's *soldier, he is God's soldier.*

His horse plunges down the ridge, shouldering its way past crowds of men on foot, stumbling over corpses and hummocks of maram grass, slipping on churned earth, slimy with blood and spilt guts. Disorientated in the pall of dust and smoke, the animal rears to avoid a kneeling peasant trying to prise a severed hand from the hilt of a sword. Norman? Saxon? Which side of the line is he? Doesn't matter. The main thing is to stay in the saddle, clear of the melee of men on foot hacking and pulping one another. Heels down, weight forward, squeeze with the thighs, at one with the animal.

Perhaps *he* is dead, not William, and the din battering his hearing, the sting of tar and horse sweat and burning fat in his nostrils, the eerie sense of being both in the thick of it yet watching himself from somewhere else, perhaps this is hell. He is a prince of the Church, which is inclined to make a man assume he is immune from hell, but he knows now that he has never truly believed it. Nothing is certain but uncertainty.

His eyes smart, full of tears, or sweat, or blood, he cannot tell. His helmet is a vice, branding the rings of the chain mail hood beneath it into his temples and the tonsured crown of his head. It's possible he has been wounded, he can't remember, but there is such a pain in his heart. Yet it is still beating. He can hear it, feel its rhythmic rush and suck. Arrows drumming against leather shields. Silence. Reload. The whistle of quarrels from bowstrings. Instinctively he turns the horse broadside to the archers, to shield himself, and ducks behind its neck. Screams of fallen men and horses. Other men and horses. So he is still alive. A voice in his head taunts him: *Which is more than this horse will be if you don't move. Horse, shield, what next?*

Over to his right he can hear the Saxon war cry: *Goddemite*, God Almighty. The men in the front line on top of the ridge shake their shields in time with the chanting. The sun is out now, burnishing blood and weapons, gilding the smoke pall. The iron rims and bosses of Saxon shields flash in the corner of his eye. To the left the Norman response, William's motto: *Dex Aie*, God aid us.

Except that God is not helping them. God has taken William from them.

"Why?" he shouts, raising his eyes heavenward. "Tell me, I'm Your anointed priest. Make me understand."

His horse stumbles to a halt among a group of young knights

whose armour is as pristine as their white, beardless cheeks. He can measure their inexperience by the shock in their eyes as they look at him. Look to him, identifying him by the hauberk of woven leather he wears over his mail. Courting disaster, William had snorted. Being myself, he had thought.

"Is it true, My Lord?" asks one, scarcely audible above the din. "That the Saxons have broken through and Duke William is dead?"

He blinks away the tears, the blood, whatever it is, brings his gaze into focus on the boy's pleading face. He removes his helmet, pushes back his hood and runs his hand through his hair, matted with sweat. He finds the odour of his own body reassuring as he raises his arms, familiar, human. Not the perfume of a soul mounting to heaven nor the reedy scent of a ghost. He smiles, he hopes, his parched lips cracking, his jaw aching. He only knows he has succeeded when he registers the effect of his smile on the young knights. It is a well-rehearsed smile, companionable, disarming. It usually serves him well. The young knights look relieved. They can trust him, he is the Duke's brother, his confidant, he will know what to do.

He looks around the battlefield, seeing it suddenly as though he were a bird flying overhead, mapped out below him like a diagram in a text on military strategy. He sees footsoldiers from Harold Godwinson's right flank pouring down the ridge like water from a broken dam. They are in pursuit of the panicking Bretons who were supposed to hold the Norman left. Fucking Bretons, maids and milksops the lot of them, they'll pay for this. A low hillock rises some way to the west. Gathering the reins and coaxing his horse into the centre of the group of boys, he beckons them closer, so they will be able to hear him above the noise of the battle. The horses stamp and snort and jostle one another, fighting for space. One thing they never tell you is how crowded a battlefield is.

"Look." He points at the Bretons and the pursuing Saxon *fyrd*, hoping the boys cannot see their faces from here. "See the Bretons over there, the ones who look as though they're retreating. They're not. They don't listen to rumours. They're leading Godwinson's men right into a trap. They're going to drive them up that rise and surround them. You men go to their aid. Quick as you can."

The young knights look where he points. They pause, nerving themselves for the fray, then one of them shouts,

"Bishop Odo," his voice lurching up the scale from adolescent croak to childish falsetto, "it's the Duke!"

Odo looks. The sun glances off swords, shields, armour, harness, arrowheads. Blinded by gold and iron, he raises one hand to shield his eyes. The gesture seems to take forever, as though the gulf between will and action is unbridgeable.

Then he sees a knight on a black war horse, bareheaded, his hair glowing like a firebrand as the wind catches it. William. And behind him, the Frenchman, Eustace of Boulogne, flamboyantly moustached, bearing the Papal standard. Odo catches his breath, realising as he does so that he has been holding it for several seconds. The sudden inrush of air makes him dizzy.

William laughs as he draws rein and leans forward in the saddle to punch his brother's shoulder. Odo prays he will not feel him shaking. He clenches his hands, one over the other around the pommel of his saddle, to steady them, afraid he might revive the demons if he tries to speak. That if he does not cling to his saddle he will find himself on his knees in the mud, clutching at William's stirrup, whimpering like a child unable to throw off a nightmare.

"You've a face like curds, little brother. Did you think I was dead too? They shot my horse out from under me, that's all. They can't touch me, I told you, God won't allow it." William pauses. The smile vanishes and his mouth forms an obstinate line. The gaze he fixes on Odo is as blue and unstoppable as a glacier. "I am His Vengeance. Never forget it."

"No, Your Grace. I thank God you are unhurt."

"Time enough for that later, Odo. Shall we get on? I should like to put an end to this business before nightfall." And he is the no-nonsense general again, a bulky, reassuring figure on his tall horse, trusting God but reliant on no-one but himself.

The young knights ride after the Saxon *fyrd*, whose pursuit of the Bretons is already unravelling as Odo has predicted. *Dex aie*, they chant, *Dex aie, Dex aie, Dex aie*. Watching them, Odo has an idea. To begin with it seems too simple so he says nothing, but tests it in his mind for weaknesses. And finds none.

William and Eustace gallop on down the Norman line. The gold cross on the Papal banner glitters as the flag snaps in their wake. William waves his helmet in the air as though he has already won a famous victory. When he reaches a spot directly opposite the apple tree up on the ridge where Godwinson's personal standard flutters, the Fighting Man looking more like a dancer, he draws rein and bows. The unmistakable red hair falls over his forehead, catching the autumn sunlight.

For a measure of time that might be a second or might be forever, there is neither sound nor movement among the Saxons on the ridge. Their shield wall traces the contours of the high ground and behind it they are invisible. Then a single javelin thuds into the churned earth, yards short of William but close enough to unsteady his horse. The spell is broken. William crams his helmet back on his head, raises his sword and begins the charge up the hill, Eustace at his shoulder.

Odo gives certain puzzling instructions to units of cavalry under his command, but all are men who have been promised much in exchange for their support and they do not question him. Twice during the remainder of the day they feign retreat as he has ordered, drawing off troops from the Saxon side and then surrounding them, and so crucially weakening their force.

Odo himself fights beside his brothers, as he has been taught, with the club that is the weapon of priests, having no cutting edge. He stands in his stirrups to make best use of his height, and lays about him, twisting his upper body this way and that, throwing its weight behind the blows. He is aware of nothing but the working of his body, the linkage of muscles from groin to waist to shoulders and arms, the flexing of joints in wrists and elbows, sweat running between his shoulder blades, the flow of the horse between his thighs. He splits skulls, cracks open breastbones, splinters vertebrae. A fragment of memory comes to him later, a strange and shaming impression that he was thinking, not of the lives of the men he killed and maimed, nor even of his own life, but of Tacitus' Agricola: "...*atque ubi solitudinem faciunt, pacem appellant.*"

He is everywhere in the battle, yet he is off the field, changing horses behind the lines, when news reaches him of the death of Godwinson.

"Shot in the eye, My Lord," says the page with relish, eyes shining in his grubby face. What is he? Ten, eleven maybe. Shortly to become a squire, dying to be a knight.

"In the eye, eh?" Good, fitting, though surprising it should be fatal. Blinding is how poachers are punished. Odo winks at the boy. "Thank you for your news, boy. Go safely. No, wait." He wants to give the boy something, out of gratitude for his good tidings. He feels he has not shown sufficient elation. The fact is, he is worn out. All he feels is relief, and a desire to sleep.

"My Lord," says the boy. Odo fishes inside his hauberk and unclasps the brooch fastening the neck of his shirt. It is silver and amethyst, Celtic workmanship. He hands it to the boy, noting how warm it is to the touch. The boy beams as he takes the bishop's gift, a little too quickly perhaps, afraid that it might be withdrawn.

"For your pains, boy. Now off you go with your news."

The boy runs off, grinning, and is soon lost to view among the tents.

Odo mounts, takes helmet and shield from his squire, and a mouthful of gritty water from the skin the young man offers him, and rides off westward at an easy canter. It is almost sunset, and the dead cast long shadows on the trampled ground. The last residue of fighting has moved away from the Norman lines to the far side of the ridge so that the shouting, the clash of arms, are muffled by distance. Crows flap lazily into the air as he passes. Camp fires are beginning to flare, their glow competing with the bloody remains of the sun pushing between the horizon and the canopy of cloud stretched above it. The homely scent of woodsmoke overlays the stench of carrion.

It's over, he thinks. *We've won. William and Robert and I have won. I've won. I've won.* He tries to savour the moment, but his mind runs on. This is only the beginning. There will be so much to be done. Roads must be laid, fortifications built. There must be churches and abbeys, laws and inventories. Forests must be cleared and wildernesses claimed. The might of Christ will drive out wood sprites and water nymphs, His light will shine in the darkness. There will be order. Today they have dug a foundation only.

And now he is thinking of home, of his palace in Bayeux, of the plans for his great new cathedral of Notre Dame spread on the table in his dark, empty hall, weighted down with an assortment of plates and goblets, and a mottled pink stone Adeliza found on the seashore, years ago. Now he will be able to complete it, once William has kept his promises.

He finds William, together with Robert and several other lords, close to the tree where Godwinson had raised his standard at the beginning of the day. How long ago? Six, seven hours at least, to judge by the sun. Feels like more, feels like less. The men are staring at the ground, contemplating something. A corpse, naked, recently mutilated. Only now does he notice the shockingly intimate, meaty smell of butchered men. His gorge rises as he approaches. Sweat breaks on his top lip, saliva floods his mouth. He removes his helmet, pushes back the hood beneath it and wipes his mouth with the back of his hand, notes he needs a shave, hopes he isn't going to throw up.

"Shot in the eye, I was told," he says, drawing rein. His horse, unnerved by the stench, tosses its head and dances beneath him. He pulls its ears and talks nonsense to it until it settles.

"Might have been. We haven't found the head yet," says William.

"How do we know it's him, then?"

"She says it is." William nods towards the tree. Now he notices the women standing in the shade of its gnarled branches. There are four of them, Saxons, two ladies of high rank from their dress, and two others he supposes to be ladies in waiting.

"She?"

"Godwinson's whore. The young one. You know her, don't you? The other's his mother for God's sake."

Odo gives a grim laugh. "How does she know? The part she's most familiar with is missing, as far as I can see."

William shakes his head. "Marks on the body known only to her, she says. How would I know? But that's his standard lying beside him. That'll do for me. The women want him for burial."

"Will you let them?"

"No."

The head is found. Some joker has stuffed the penis into its mouth, but the eyes are intact. Darkness has fallen when William gives orders for the remains to be taken to the beach and buried. Odo does not accompany the burial party. Godwinson has no need of a priest, William tells him, and Odo does not argue with him. Godwinson swore to uphold William's claim to the English throne, swore on holy relics from Odo's own church, fought alongside William against Conan of Brittany, and then grabbed the Confessor's crown before the old man was cold in his grave. The thought of his oath, his raw boned hands resting on the delicate reliquary shrines, makes Odo feel defiled. Of course Godwinson has forfeited his right to Christian burial.

Odo sleeps soundly, in his tent pitched on the battlefield beside those of his brothers. When his servant removes the mail shirt that shields his body from neck to knee, he feels as though he is floating on a cushion of air as he slips into unconsciousness. The moans of the wounded and dying do not disturb him, nor the cold seeping into his bones. The blood dries on his face and beneath his fingernails. Corn gold stubble grows along the sweep of his jaw. He does not remember his dreams.

ODO'S SMILE

ALL SOULS 1066

"Tomorrow," says the messenger, on one knee before the great chair beside the hearth where King Harold used to sit, his voice a little unsteady. The word ripples around the hall. Heads bend towards one another, a swing of plaits, a brush of sleeves, as the women murmur together, round eyed with fear and fascination. Tomorrow. Tomorrow. Tomorrow. They hand the word along, one to the next, like a hot coal. Trudy lets out a little shriek and collapses onto the bench alongside the oak table running down the centre of the hall. One of the others pours wine for her from a chased silver jug, but she dashes the cup aside with the back of her hand.

"I'm not drinking that," she says, "it's French."

"French, my dear, not Norman." It is the first rational remark Lady Edith has made in two weeks. "Drink up," she continues, her words sounding hollow from the depths of the king's chair, falling into the tense hush which has descended on the hall like pebbles into water, "and bring a cup for this man here. He looks in need of it. Where is Gytha?"

"Here, madam." Gytha steps from behind her mistress' chair, set apart from the Saxon women by her small bones and raven's wing hair, though they all turn expectantly towards her like flowers to the sun. *It's a miracle*, thinks Gytha, smiling at Lady Edith, *it must be. A sign. They will stop the Bastard here, in Winchester, the seat of the old kings.*

The messenger rises and bows, then drifts towards the table where Trudy holds out a cup of wine with her usual dimpling and eyelash batting. Edith Swan Neck leans forward in her lord's chair and grasps Gytha's hands in her own, the skin still with a rusty tinge, black crescents of blood congealed beneath the nails.

"You must go to the gate for me," she says, then, addressing herself to the messenger, adds, "Where will the Duke enter?"

"By the West Gate, I believe, madam."

Edith nods. "Yes, that is the way from Hastings. We came that way ourselves when...after..." Her high, pale brow knits in a bewildered frown. Taking her hands from Gytha's, she holds them up in front of her face and examines them, twisting them slowly palm to back, as though the end of her sentence might be written there.

There is the end of everything, thinks Gytha, stabbed by despair as Lady Edith's face seems to close up again, the spark of reason extinguished as she contemplates her beloved lord's blood still staining her hands. There are no able-bodied men left in the city, and what could a mob of women, children, old men and cripples hope to achieve against William of Normandy's army? She has seen what it is capable of, on the ridge between Caldbec Hill and Telham Hill which the Bastard's men now call Senlac, the Lake of Blood. In that at least, Gytha agrees with them. You could not imagine such butchery if you had not seen it, and as there are no words adequate to describe the smell, or the slip and squelch of their feet among blood and offal, or the clamminess of dead flesh on a damp autumn evening as they turned over corpses in an attempt to identify the king and his brothers, she and Lady Edith are bound by a conspiracy of silence.

"Send someone else, madam," she pleads. "You need me to take care of you." No-one who was not there can possibly understand Lady

Edith's retreat into madness, her absolute refusal to wash Harold's blood from her hands or change the gown whose hem is stiff with gore. It is all she has left, not even a grave to put flowers on, thanks to William Bastard.

Edith shakes her head. "You must bear witness, Gytha, you must see it through. You will not be afraid?"

"No, madam." Not of the Normans marching into Winchester, only of being separated from her mistress. And yet, she asks herself, what is there to fear? Everyone she has ever loved has been wrenched from her, and somehow, she has survived. Perhaps that is what she should fear. Survival.

"Bring the children to me," commands Edith suddenly. The women exchange doubtful glances, then look to Gytha, all at once, synchronised like mummers in a play.

"The children are in Ireland, madam. Don't you remember? King Harold sent them there, before he left for Yorkshire, to King Diarmait."

"Ah yes, yes, of course." It is plain she remembers nothing, perhaps not even her children's faces. She says these things from time to time, dredging up phrases from happier days without any sense of their meaning.

Gytha sleeps fitfully and wakes before dawn, though she can tell morning is close by the rustle of the doves and chickens roosting in the eves of the hall. She sits up, rubbing the backs of her calves to drive out the hard cold of the earth floor. Since their return from Senlac, and Lady Edith's refusal to leave the King's chair, they have given up retiring to her bower, where they had mattresses of wool and straw to sleep on, and have made do with the hall. As her eyes adjust to the thinning darkness, she becomes aware of shapes moving towards the king's chair, where Lady Edith dozes, slumped against one of its carved arms. She jumps to her feet to intercept them, her heart lurching into her throat as though it has been thrown free of her chest wall by the force of her movement.

"Who's there?" she demands in an urgent whisper. Have they come already, the Bastard sending some men stealthily ahead of his main force to take Edith and find out from her where Harold's sons are hidden?

"Just me," replies Trudy.

Gytha sighs with relief. "God you gave me a shock. I thought you were a Norman."

"We thought we'd try and get her changed while she's still half asleep," says another voice. Malfrid. Always easily led.

"What?"

"Oh don't sound so shocked. That dress is beginning to stink."

"You won't lay a hand on her. You thought I'd left already, didn't you? You thought I'd be gone for good. Well, Trudy, I'll tell you something. If you try to do anything against my lady's wishes, I shall know about it. And if they kill me, I shall haunt you till your teeth turn black and your hair falls out." She fingers her dark plait. "You know I'm a witch, don't you? You know I mean what I say?"

"All I know is you're as mad as she is." Trudy's response is tart, but there is an uncertain note in her voice which reassures Gytha her threat has struck home.

To be certain, though, before she leaves the house she wakes the slave, Skuli. Hunchback he may be, but he is strong and fiercely loyal to Lady Edith, who stopped his mother drowning him as a baby.

"Stick to her as if you were in the same skin, Skuli," she orders him. "Whatever happens."

Rape. That's what they all believe, the sullen crowd gathered before Winchester's West Gate, in the square where the tax men usually collect the duty on beasts brought into the city for market. It's clear from their faces, fear mixed with impotence and embarrassment, and the round eyed children, clinging to their mothers' skirts, who don't understand but just want to look at the soldiers. But Gytha, from her vantage point on the gate tower roof, sees something much worse.

Did Lady Edith already know what the Queen Dowager intended, how easily she would give away Winchester, her home, seat of government of both her husband, Edward of blessed memory, and her brother, Harold? That she would turn out to be a greater whore by far than her brother's concubine?

Up here, Gytha is almost on a level with the queen where she stands on the walkway above the great gates, suspended between past and future, gazing down imperiously at the Bastard's upturned face and upturned lance, her choice made. She looks every inch the queen, richly dressed, not a hair out of place beneath her jewelled coronet and sheer linen veil, though no-one attends her but a couple of pages and a single lady-in-waiting, no-one who might detract from the drama of this moment, this solitary moment in which she holds the keys of England in her perfectly white hand, the iron ring which binds them poised over the point of William Bastard's lance.

Behind her, the crowd in the square shifts and mumbles, malevolent, fearful, bored and uncomfortable in the drizzle which clings to their clothes and hair. Before her the Bastard's army, drawn up in motionless ranks, their faces lost beneath the helmets they wear with nose pieces angled down almost over their mouths. To Gytha they look like an army of skulls, more dead in their rigid immobility, their leather and mail blackened by the rain, than any blood bright Saxon corpse she saw that day on the field at Senlac. Three of which were the bodies of Queen Edith's brothers, Gyrth, Leofwine and Harold, the King. As she leans out over the parapet and drops the great iron ring of keys over the point of the Bastard's lance she looks as though she has forgotten that.

Couching his lance, the Bastard lets the keys slide to the ground, where they are retrieved and handed to him by a footsoldier stationed there for the purpose. Then, at a signal from one of their officers, the Normans commence a rhythmic beating of weapons on shields, accompanied by chanting in French. The massive thud of iron on leather shivers the air like the heartbeat of an angry god. It shudders through Gytha's bones, making her wrap her arms around herself as though to hold her frame together. *Dex aie,* the Normans chant, *Dex aie, Dex aie, Dex aie.* From inside the walls a single voice is raised in defiance.

"God help you go fuck yourselves!" shouts a man who understands their language. A fair few do. The Confessor himself had Norman blood in him after all and the Channel, though treacherous, is not wide. Now, though, is not the time to advertise one's Norman connections, and while the crowd obviously applaud the speaker's sentiments, Gytha sees several doubtful looks cast in his direction. She wonders if the Bastard understands English. Not that he will have heard that single, reckless yell above the din of his triumphant army. So many of them. He must have emptied every house and hovel in Normandy of its able-bodied men to pack his ships and swarm across England like a plague of black ants.

She longs to run back to Lady Edith's house, to the comfort of its familiar rooms whose fine hangings will keep out the Normans as they keep out draughts. Even now Lady Edith's power seems unassailable; seated in the King's great chair before the hearthstone, still wearing the gown she wore as she knelt in the mud and gore on Senlac Ridge, she is all England's defiance concentrated in one frail form.

"Well?" the Bastard had asked, his voice harsh and unexpectedly thin for such a big, barrel chested man.

"Yes," she had replied, stretching out her fingers to touch the bloodied torso just below the left nipple, her tone as cool as meltwater, "that is My Lord the king. Here, you see, is the strawberry mark over his heart. He used to joke that it was his bullseye. Perhaps your archers need a little more practice, Your Grace." Forcing the Bastard to look, to take in his army's handiwork, the head severed, one leg gone below the knee, the genitals hacked away to leave a mushy hollow surrounded by blood soaked hair. Even Countess Gytha, King Harold's redoubtable mother, nearly vomited, and her lady-in-waiting fainted dead away, even the men with the Bastard hung their heads and cleared their throats and broke a sweat despite the creeping cold of an October evening.

Gytha herself felt as though her head had floated off her shoulders and her bowels turned to water. It was not so much the mutilation of King Harold as the sheer scale of the destruction, bodies and parts of bodies strewn everywhere, twisted, torn, open-mouthed as though they had been about to speak when they were struck down. A chorus of screams and groans from the wounded, the sad, exultant cawing of the crows circling in the bloodshot eye of the setting sun, awaiting their turn. She knows death, of course she does, who does not, but before this she knew only its quiet face, blue-lipped or sunken-cheeked on a pallet, turned to a wall, its mess hidden beneath the sheets. But this, well, this was so showy.

Lady Edith, however, treated it all with lofty indifference, continuing to gaze at her lover as though he were still as he used to be, laughing and golden with eyes as blue as the sea in summer, leaving the Bastard no choice but to do likewise.

Now the Bastard knocks three times on the gates with the tip of his lance. He has only to walk his horse forward with the lance pressed against them for the gates to swing open on their well oiled hinges, the crowd inside dividing, stumbling back over their own feet to clear a space in the centre of the square. As the Queen turns to watch, William of Normandy, distinguishable by the gold coronet encircling his helmet, flanked by two of his senior officers and their standard bearers, rides into the city of Winchester, the great hooves of his war horse dancing nervously over the earth where lie the bones of generations of the kings of Wessex. The horse knows the power of their ghosts even if its rider cannot feel it.

His soldiers have stopped their chanting now, as they form up to follow their lord into the city, and his entrance is greeted by a silence as pervasive as the drizzle blurring the grey November sky, that sings in Gytha's ears like an echo of the chanting and shield-beating. Waiting until his advance guard are through the gate and deployed in a cordon around the citizens who have turned out to witness his arrival, the Bastard raises his right hand to command their attention. Peering down into the square, Gytha sees the fair, ruddy-faced English behind the cordon like a rich, lively tapestry drained of its vibrancy by a dark frame.

"Unhelm," says the Bastard to the group of men surrounding him. "Let these people see we are men like them."

The Bastard's companions appear to doubt the wisdom of his order. Gytha sees heads turn, towards each other, towards the crowd from which a few ragged jeers escape in response to the Bastard's words. Only one man follows his lord's example without a moment's hesitation, raising his arms to lift the helmet from his head and hand it to his squire, pushing back his mail hood and running a hand over his tonsured crown. His movements are deliberate, exaggerated, like those of a mummer, whose every gesture has some precise and particular meaning. He smiles, turning this way and that so everyone can see his smile, broad, sensual, with his mouth turned down slightly at the corners so he seems to mock himself. Don't worry, says his smile, all this is only for a moment, for a day. We are players on the stage for an hour or two. The blood is not real, the corpses will get up and walk off between scenes, you will find Death in the ale house later, with a mug and a plate of cheese, his mask hung around his neck like a hood.

People smile back, as though they cannot help themselves. At once the atmosphere becomes more relaxed. The rest of the Bastard's lieutenants remove their helmets, though none of them has a smile as disarming as that of the bold cleric. Their expressions veer from the supercilious to the faintly embarrassed. Even as the Bastard, who does not even attempt to smile beneath his shock of hair as red as Judas', addresses the people, their eyes remain drawn to the man with the tonsure and the curls almost as fair as an Englishman's.

Gytha is not impressed; she has seen that smile before and, like a survivor of the smallpox, she is proof against its charm. At dinner, in Lady Edith's great hall, softened by wine and candlelight, its warmth flowing into Lady Edith's eyes as he listened to her craft some witticism. Later, when he cast away his lute saying he was too drunk to play, and played ill enough when sober, and Earl Harold must finish his song without accompaniment. Broadening as Lady Edith retorted that if Earl

Harold must finish so bawdy a song, she would withdraw her ladies to her bower, as some were maids and should not be encouraged to set their sights on so merry a widowhood, lest no man would then be brave or foolish enough to marry them.

On the battlefield, as he glanced across to where she stood beneath the dead apple tree with Lady Edith and Countess Gytha, leaning to exchange words with the Bastard, ugly, guttural French words, then bursting into laughter.

The smile of Odo of Bayeux, the Bastard's brother.

"I wish you to know I come in peace," says the Bastard in his disappointing voice, his English heavily accented. Bishop Odo nods for emphasis. "This city was the seat of my revered and beloved kinsman, King Edward, may he rest with God." The Bastard crosses himself. His lieutenants do likewise, though the bishop also contrives to bow his head in an instant of prayer. "Generations of your kings lie buried here, guardians of a fine system of government which I swear now, before you all, as the latest in that line, to uphold and protect, and to build on as God grants me power." The Bastard exchanges a glance with his brother, almost as though looking to him for approval, then backs his horse up a little, leaving the stage to him.

Bishop Odo uses no fine words, though his English is far more fluent than his brother's, but confines himself to facts, to the dull, administrative business of an occupation. A curfew will be imposed at dusk, he tells the crowd. No citizens will be allowed beyond the walls for any purpose, though the country people will be allowed in on two days of the week to sell their beasts and produce. A governor will be appointed who will fix prices and tariffs and take responsibility for law and order. He does not expect the people to notice many changes to their everyday lives – some subdued jeering at this, ignored by the bishop – but two important alterations to the laws of the Witan will take effect immediately. All slaves will consider themselves free forthwith and King William has further decreed that, as he respects God as the sole arbiter of life and death, there can no longer be recourse to capital punishment in England.

"We are not ogres," he concludes, after a pause, turning his horse so that people on all sides can see his face, candid, sincere, perhaps the merest trace of irony in the white lines scored by sun and laughter at the corners of his eyes, "but we believe a society can only flourish if it has just laws, properly upheld. As the pretender Godwinson was punished for his treason, so will those be punished who transgress the law."

He looks as though he is about to say more, but at that moment a small child, apparently attracted by the gold and silver discs decorating his horse's harness, darts out between the soldiers in the cordon and lunges for the largest, brightest roundel at the centre of the chest strap. The startled animal rears, and though the bishop quickly regains control of it, trying to force it back on its hind legs before the flailing front hooves can come down on the child, he is hampered by the men behind him. In the crowded square, there is no space into which he can safely manoeuvre the thrashing animal. The little boy, intent on the shiny ornaments, leaping to reach them, stretching out his arms, blinded by their glamour, has no idea of the danger he is in.

A hoof strikes the side of his head. Gytha hears a soft, sickening thud, though she knows it is impossible; the sound of a child's skull cracking is too small to be heard above the shuffling and murmuring of the crowd. The boy crumples, bare, skinny legs folding like broken sticks beneath his body. For a split second it looks as though the bishop is about to fling himself out of the saddle in person in an attempt to drag the child to safety.

Then, as those close by realise what is happening and surge towards the child, pushing out a bulge in the cordon, the soldiers caught off guard, staggering against the wave of fury and panic behind them, he thinks better of it. Instead, he and the rest of the Bastard's officers bunch protectively around their lord. Perhaps, if he had dismounted, made some attempt to save the boy, however futile, he might have won them over, shown them he was a man like the rest of them, moved by the instinct to protect a child. If he had put them before the safety of his brother. But it is too late.

A woman breaks from the crowd, screaming, wailing like a wood sprite fleeing the tree fellers. The soldiers push her back. She stumbles, but collects herself and tries again.

"My baby!" she cries, "my baby!" over and over again. The words slice through Gytha, colder than the rain; tears stand scalding in her eyes. My babies, cries her heart in unison, my babies. She slumps against the parapet, gouging her nails into the lip of the wall until the remembered pain in her womb is driven out by the rough stone grazing her hands. The mother hurls herself again and again at the cordon, arms raised, fists clenched, her mouth gaping open, reckless in her grief and desperation. Her child lies quietly, on his side, his knees drawn up to his chest as if he is asleep.

Bishop Odo, breaking from the group of men surrounding the Bastard, begins to shout orders above the rising din, the crowd roaring and boiling behind the cordon. More men run into position to reinforce it, but it is clear they cannot hold the mob back for long. Their anger swells and binds them, transforming them into a single, raging force against which the bishop's smooth words will break as easily as the child's skull. For a brief, exhilarating moment Gytha thinks, *they'll do it, we'll do it, we'll throw them out.*

Then suddenly, a Norman pikeman loses his nerve and runs his weapon through the woman, who clutches at her belly before doubling over, casting one, last look of reproachful astonishment at the bishop before she falls. The crowd stills, the roar dies away as hundreds of lungs swell with sucked-in breaths, hundreds of hearts miss their beats with shock, hundreds of eyes, round and brimming with disbelief, turn to their neighbours and then to the bishop, grim and white faced as the marble faces of long dead Romans still sometimes turned up from the soil during ploughing. The child, they understand, was an accident, but this is murder.

Gytha, still gripping the parapet, its stones digging into her palms, mortar crumbling under her fingernails, looks to Queen Edith. Surely she must do something, say something, remonstrate with the red

28

haired savage on his black horse, impassively watching his brother lose control. But she does not move, it is as though she is tied to the spot by invisible bonds, silent as if the Bastard had personally strapped a scold's bridle to her head. Her expression, moulded by years of training and rigid restraint, gives nothing away, yet, as Gytha watches, she stoops slightly to wipe the tears from the cheeks of one of her pages with her immaculate sleeve. It is all that is left to her as the history her surrender has set in train starts to unwind in the square below.

Norman soldiers are now pouring through the gate, but far from intimidating the citizens, their arrival seems to reignite the flame of rebellion temporarily doused by the cold horror of the grieving mother's murder. Gytha's human tapestry begins to unravel as the crowd finally bursts through the Norman cordon and turns on the soldiers, pitting fists and walking sticks, stones and dinner knives against the Bastard's army, love and rage against implacable efficiency. Women gather up their children and flee back down the main thoroughfare, to seek sanctuary in the priory whose precinct faces the square at the opposite end of the street. The old and infirm, and the early wounded trailing a slime of blood, struggle away down the many narrow alleys and passageways winding between the jumble of buildings bordering the square. The Bastard's men will not pursue them in among their own shadows and secret shortcuts.

Bishop Odo, still conspicuous by the fatal flamboyance of his horse's harness, still bareheaded, though his brother and the rest of his officers have by now retrieved their helmets from their squires, glances up at Queen Edith, exchanges brief words with the Bastard, then spurs his horse into the affray, shouting more orders to the soldiers, kicking away his assailants with his spurred boots, fending off the more determined with a hefty, nail studded club as well as a sword. His saddle, marvels Gytha ruefully, must be some kind of portable armoury, his harness a chain of pennies for dead men's eyes. Does he, she wonders, bother to carry the Sacrament with him also, or is he not that kind of bishop?

The Bastard dismounts, and to her horror, Gytha sees him

disappear into the gate tower directly below her, accompanied by several of his men. Stupidly, she had believed herself safe up here, high above the square and concealed behind the parapet of the wall. But if he intends to come up here looking for the Queen, she cannot help but be discovered. She could go to the queen, to whatever protection her status and her two pages can offer, but there is little love lost between her and Lady Edith, whose three sons by King Harold she has always seen as an impediment to the ambition of the Godwins for legitimate kingship. She would as lief hand Gytha over to the Normans as protect her against them. Her only other alternative is to make her way around the walls in the opposite direction in the hope of finding her way down by some ladder or stairway not yet occupied by William Bastard's troops.

Hoisting her skirts, she begins to run, stumbling over the rubble-strewn surface of the parapet, dodging around the ramshackle shelters which have made their appearance over the years, temporary homes to the watchmen, with their makeshift hearths, pots and tripods, and the telltale scatterings of straw which can be hastily kicked into a bedding mound once the officer of the watch's back is turned. Though her feet are bruised through her fine calfskin shoes, she is scarcely even out of breath before a voice hails her from within one of these rough huts.

"Help! Help me." An English voice. She ducks without hesitation under the lopsided lintel. As her eyes become accustomed to the gloom inside she can make out a face, a glimmer of pale skin in the feeble light from the doorway, a glint of an eye, a dark scribble of beard. But something is wrong; the features seem to stand in the right alignment to one another, yet the face itself is not where she would have expected a face, but resting on the floor, one cheek pressed into curious undulations by its lumpy surface.

"I fell you see," says the man. Gytha begins to see. The stranger is lying on his side, stranded on account of the fact that the half of his body in contact with the floor has only bandaged stumps of arm and leg, no leverage to get him back upright, too painful no doubt for him to roll himself over. Though she feels sympathy for him, she cannot help laughing, and her laughter is like the mob in the square, because once it has escaped she cannot stopper it up again, it spills from her like ale from a leaking spigot, washing away the sight of the little boy falling under the bishop's horse, the awful, helpless anguish of his mother, the white-lipped fury of the bishop hacking and clubbing his way through the mob in the square as though the disaster were somehow their fault.

"I lost my limbs at Hastings," says the man indignantly, but there is laughter in his voice also, as well as pain, and she can feel the twinkling of his eyes through the dusty dark.

"These Normans have brought us all very low, sir," she responds, wiping tears from her eyes, kneeling at his head and pushing him into a sitting position. "How did this happen?" He sucks in his breath sharply. She thinks he must be in great pain from his injuries.

"I was on a stool, then I leaned to get my drink from the floor beside me and overbalanced."

"But what are you doing here all alone?" she asks indignantly. "How did you get up here in the first place?"

He gives a dismissive shrug. "My brother is a guard. He lets me live here. My wife went back to her father when I...well, I'm no use to a woman like this, am I? So here I am. My brother went off early to watch the Normans arrive."

"Then he'll have seen more than he bargained for. One of their horses kicked a child and killed it and now the crowd has turned ugly and I'm afraid there will be a great deal of blood spilled."

"I wondered what was going on. There seemed to be a lot more noise than I would have thought, seeing how the Queen told us all to receive them in peace. I sometimes wonder if it was worth fighting them at all. Perhaps we should just have stood aside and let William Bastard in. After all, what difference does it make to people like us who's king?"

"We must fight. King Harold has sons living, we must fight for them if nothing else. We cannot simply sit by while they trample our children to death and steal from us and…"

"Alright." He raises his one hand in a gesture of surrender. Gytha feels herself blushing. Her tongue was always her curse, Adam said so, and her mother before him, worrying that a girl such as her, with only a modest dowry and such quick wits, would never get a husband. Well, she got Adam, and tried to be a good wife and keep her wits to herself, and was left with Adam's debts for her pains.

"I'm sorry. I saw it, you see, that great horse about twice the size of any I've ever seen. The child's head couldn't have been much bigger than its shoe. And the man riding it never even drew rein." Why the lie? Why conceal the identity of the rider? She has a sense that, in some curious way, the story is her own, not to be shared, that it has for her a special power and meaning, that the name of Odo of Bayeux is a spell too potent to be uttered aloud. Nonsense. The accident was witnessed by hundreds of people. What makes it so special to her? She is tired, overwrought; she must return to Lady Edith. But what will she tell her? "Come now, let me lift you. They'll be sending their own men up here soon. You must try to find your brother."

"I have a crutch somewhere. It slid out of reach when I fell. If you find that and wedge it under the stump of my arm I can manage."

"How will you get down from the wall?" she asks, casting about for the crutch which she finds lying only a few feet away.

"There's a ladder close by. I can hop down it. You'd be amazed what I can do."

Gytha smiles at him. "I'm sure I would."

She helps the man to stand, then props the cross piece of his crutch as gently as she can in his armpit. Though he winces, he makes no protest and sets out briskly enough, ducking under the lintel, covering the ground surprisingly quickly, his stump swinging like a bell clapper between his crutch and his good leg. She follows him out onto the parapet. The smell of smoke reaches her along with shouts and cries, the nervous whinnying of horses and a ragged whistling of arrows, the smoke striking a hot, acrid note beneath the pervasive odour of wet wood and the stale beer-breath of the stranger as he turns to her.

"They set fires to contain riots," he explains, sniffing the air. "I've seen it. Rings of fire around the crowd, as if it's a scorpion and will sting itself to death."

"And I suppose they take great care with firebreaks, so they are not deprived of the spectacle of the scorpion's suicide," says Gytha bitterly. "It seems our new king is surprisingly pernickety about killing. Oh my God." She stops, instinctively grasping the stranger's good arm. Heavy footsteps clatter towards them, running, spurs jangling, breathless, shouted exchanges in French. "They're here."

The two Normans look as surprised to see Gytha and the maimed man as she is horrified to come face to face with them. Rounding a bend in the wall, they skid to an uncertain halt, exchange doubtful looks and begin muttering to one another in their barbarous language. Though Gytha cannot understand their words, she can tell from their gestures they are debating something to do with her companion. Whether or not to kill him most likely. One of the soldiers slides his hand towards the dagger in his belt.

"No! *Non!*" she yells, thrusting herself protectively in front of the invalid. "Can't you see he's a cripple?"

The soldiers shrug, look blank.

"*Blesse, blesse,*" pleads the man, gesturing at his stumps with his one good hand, but the Normans look unimpressed. Now both have their daggers drawn and are advancing on the crippled Saxon, yet he has done them no harm, lying helpless in his eyrie on top of the wall. And he clearly cannot defend himself against them. She could not forgive herself for standing by and letting them kill him, yet she has no weapon, and she is a small woman, no match for two well-fed Normans. A woman. Of course she has a weapon, the most powerful of all.

"Go, quick as you can," she whispers to the man as she lets go his arm and steps forward, hips swaying, pushing back her cloak with one hand to reveal the line of her breasts beneath her gown. Though loose, the wool is very fine and falls close to the curves of her body.

Swallowing her fear, licking her dry lips, she lets a smile spread slow as a summer sunset across her mouth.

By the time she arrives back at Lady Edith's house the city is quiet again, its rabble of low buildings squatting sullenly beneath a false twilight. There is no wind to disperse the smoke from the fires set by the Normans around the square, and it hangs, settling over roofs beneath the weight of the rain, loitering in back streets and the narrow alley by which Gytha makes her way, squeezed between the city wall and the back courts of the merchants' houses lining the main street.

It was not so bad, she reflects as she wades through the smog, coughing, scarcely able to see more than a step in front of her. No worse, really, than lying in the marriage bed with Adam, stiff backed, eyes squeezed shut as he toiled above her, his cock rasping in her dry fanny, his sweat soaking the front of her night gown. At least the soldiers were quick and she didn't have to sleep beside them afterwards or wake to their sour morning lusts. At least by these acts she has saved a life, rather than creating a new death, another baby too weak to survive. At least, if a child were to result from what she has done, she might strangle or drown it without demur; her body already knows well enough what it is to be tricked out of a baby to suckle. She touches the bronze and enamel locket she wears, a gift from Lady Edith last Christmas, and thinks of the four twists of dark, downy hair she keeps inside it. How it can be that God should have so punished her for submitting to her duty as a wife, yet inflict no sense of guilt upon her for what she has just done?

Opening the narrow gate, she slips from the alley into Lady Edith's back court and squats behind the moult house to take a piss, grabbing a handful of straw to clean between her legs. She cannot enter Lady Edith's presence still sticky with Norman spendings. As she rises and straightens her gown she hears a clatter of hooves and harness, and voices. Men's voices. French voices. She shakes her head. She must be mistaken, her ears still full of the hot, panting breath of the soldiers, playing tricks on her. She is exhausted, wanting nothing more than to warm herself beside the fire in her lady's company, to tell her tale then drowse with a cup of mulled wine while her clothes steam gently dry and someone picks out sad tunes on a lute. But the voices come again, a string of words, a sudden bark of laughter. Harness jangling. A splash. She will have to get away from here.

And the family of the dead woman and child? The wounded left lying in the square? For they will have been left; on Senlac Ridge the Bastard gave no thought to the English dead and injured. Those whose houses have been burned or pulled down to make firebreaks, their bowls and drinking horns scattered in the street, looms and spinning wheels and children's toys smashed for kindling? Can they get away? Besides, where can she go? This is her home now, she belongs to her mistress body and soul. Whatever the Bastard has in store for Lady Edith, that is Gytha's fate also. She must go on, find what she will find. Crossing the yard, dizzy with the flutter and jolt of her heart in its bone cage, she pushes cautiously at the rear door to the hall.

She need not have feared anyone would notice her. The hall is in uproar, Norman soldiers swarming over its treasures like ants at a picnic. Rolled tapestries, jewel chests, sacks clanking with plate and silverware are being carried out into the main courtyard by a procession of men wearing green tabards over their mail, decorated with golden wolves, heads lowered, tails straight behind them like dogs on a scent. Two wrestle with the ungainly bulk of King Harold's great chair. Neither Lady Edith nor any of her women are anywhere to be seen. Nothing but men, armed, spurred, some with blood-streaked faces, calling out to one another in voices harsh with greed and contempt, sudden explosions of derisive laughter as they hold gowns up against themselves, pursing their lips and wiggling their hips like tarts. Like me, Gytha realises, with an uprush of loathing and horror for what she has done.

All the lamps and candles have been lit, but remain untended, puddling oil and tallow on to the polished surface of the great oak table, too heavy to move, she supposes, or doubtless they would have their great, grimy paws on that too. Tapped barrels drip wine and ale, split grain sacks spill their contents among the floor rushes, a pair of hounds play tug o' war with a venison haunch. The smoky glare has transformed the hall, Gytha's home for the only happy time of her life since childhood, into a vision of hell. But then, hell is all she deserves now.

And in the midst of it all, Odo of Bayeux, pacing up and down trailed by a wake of scribes and page boys, a grey brachet with anxious, yellow eyes close at his heel, dictating letters in a dizzy mix of English, Latin and French, snaking and swooping from one to the other with diabolical ease, describing extravagant gestures with his jewelled hands as he speaks. Once again, Gytha is reminded of a mummer. Is he so vain, so assured of his own importance, that he believes the world his stage? He looks briefly towards the door where she is standing, peering around its edge. For a second he seems to be looking directly at her, and she is resentful of how desperately tired he looks, with honey brown eyes from which everything appears blanked out, every spark extinguished. A look like that should be the prerogative of the vanquished.

Then she panics, but instead of retreating from the wedge of light falling through the open doorway she freezes. He must see her, he is scarcely ten paces away, and yet he does not. The devil knows what he does see, but it isn't her.

"*Fermez*," he says to no-one in particular, with a slight shiver and a weary wave of his hand towards the door. As one of his attendants hurries to do his bidding, Gytha snaps back into reality and slips away, back across the yard and out into a narrow lane leading down between Lady Edith's compound and the rear wall of the priory hospice to the main street. The priory is the place to go; the prior will know what to do, and she will be safe there. She can rest overnight and decide what her next step should be in the morning. She is wet and worn out, cold to her bones, with nothing in her mind but a longing for somewhere warm and dry.

Emerging from the lane, her way is blocked by a covered cart. More of the bishop's loot, no doubt, but no, she can hear voices, women's voices, low and anxious, then a sudden cry, piercing, anguished.

"His heart! Where is his heart?" A slap. Some French. Gytha shrinks back against the hospice wall. Then the unmistakable boom of Skuli, whose malformed spine has deepened his chest into a kind of sounding box so his voice echoes around inside it.

"You take your hands off her, you ugly Norman c..." Silence. Peering around the edge of the wall, Gytha sees Skuli sink to his knees in the muddy wheel ruts, hands clutched to his chest as though in passionate prayer, except that the haft of a Norman pike protrudes between them. As he falls forward, his killer kicks him.

"*Cochon*" he spits, before turning his attention to the gaggle of women clustered beside the cart, herded together by two more Norman soldiers with weapons drawn.

"His heart!" Again that anguished wail from Lady Edith. Gytha starts forward out of the shadow of the wall. The soldiers' backs are turned. They do not see her, but Edith does, and for a second her eyes clear. She shakes her head, so slightly it might easily be mistaken for a tremor of fear or cold, flicks one hand at Gytha as though wafting away a troublesome insect, mouths a single word, "No."

She has gone too far. One of the soldiers throws a quick, sharp glance over his shoulder. Holding her breath, Gytha steps back against the wall, putting her foot down as slowly as she dare, toe to heel, like dancing. It seems to take forever.

"*A qui parles toi?*" growls the soldier.

"The King, of course." Edith gives an inane giggle.

The soldier shrugs. "*Foue comme une hase,*" he says to his companion, making a circular motion with his hand beside his temple. Then, "In," he says in English, prodding Trudy, who is nearest to him, with the point of his pike. She screams, echoed by one or two others. The women cluster around Edith, who stands her ground. The soldier shrugs, leans his pike against the tailgate of the cart, then picks up Trudy and bundles her inside. At this, Edith holds out her hand for assistance, almost as though inviting her captor to walk her in to dinner, and climbs onto the back of the cart followed by the rest of her women. For a second, Gytha's heart is empty of everything but love and admiration for her mistress, the way she keeps her dignity intact, snatching a last, small victory from this catastrophic defeat. Then the soldiers close and bolt the tailgate, one of them slapping it twice with the flat of his hand to signal the carter the women are all aboard.

Whatever Lady Edith ordered, Gytha cannot simply let them go like this, dragged off to whatever fate Bishop Odo has in store for them like a load of pigs to market. Yet she is Lady Edith's woman, sworn to serve, not to question, though it is more her nature to question than to serve. As she struggles to force some order into her thoughts, to stop the maypole dance in her head, the cart creaks into motion and begins to pull slowly away. *Now, it must be now.* A couple of steps, a jump, that's all. But she cannot. Her legs buckle and she sinks down, trembling like a frightened dog, into the mud of the track, her back scraping against the hospice wall.

Everything. Home, honour, the joy of living there was in Lady Edith's cornflower blue eyes and the laugh King Harold used to say sounded like a wood pigeon's love call. He has taken everything, packed it up in a wet cart and dragged it down into the vortex of his greed. If she lives, she will find him and kill him.

By the time she comes to herself night has fallen, bringing with it the total, almost solid dark of winter. Her hands clamped around her knees are the merest bone white glimmer. Only as she clambers unsteadily to her feet and feels the weight of her soaked clothes pressing down on the backs of her shoulders is she certain her body still exists. The rain has stopped and a wind has risen which seems to drive every cold, wet fibre of her gown into her flesh like a tiny cheese wire. The sodden rope of the braid down her back threatens to break her neck. Such beautiful hair, Lady Edith used to say, watching Gytha comb out the dark, glossy coils. Her own was fine and fair, soft as feathers against her long, white neck.

Was? Is. She cannot be dead. They had it from the bishop's own mouth, from the Bastard's brother himself, that there would be no executions. They will send her into exile, surely, to Ireland perhaps, where she has kin, where she can set up a new court and work for her children's future. She will want Gytha then; Gytha is her favourite. She will spend tonight in the priory church, and tomorrow she will set about finding her mistress.

Tonight. Night. A curfew will be imposed at dusk, the bishop had said. If the Normans catch her now they are bound to run her through first and ask questions afterwards, and she will only be reunited with Lady Edith in heaven. And not even there, after what she has done. But her motives were good. What matters most to God, thought or deed? A sudden blast of noise, laughter, raised voices, a dog barking, as the door to Lady Edith's hall swings open, light leaking dimly through chinks in the compound fence to illuminate the ruts and puddles in the lane. Gytha shrinks back against the hospice wall, sidling cautiously towards where the lane opens into the street alongside the priory gatehouse. What does not seem to matter to God is the fate of the English.

She hears footsteps approaching on the other side of the fence, then silence. The night is so quiet under the curfew she can hear the man breathe, heavily, as though he has eaten and drunk to excess. She holds her own breath, her back pressed against the hospice wall, wishing she might simply dissolve into it, wet flesh into sodden plaster, bones to lath. Urine splashes into a puddle, the footsteps move away again, she lets her breath go in a long, shaky sigh and creeps out into the lane where she knocks stealthily on the priory gate and whispers her claim for sanctuary.

The church is packed. Entire families have established little encampments, barricading themselves behind stacks of their possessions. Some who were in the square sit alone and silent, hugging their knees to their chests, staring into the dark spaces between pools of smoky, orange tallowlight. Others huddle together, passing round casks of ale, noisily denouncing the occupation, inflaming one another as though their brave words are sticks rubbed together to make fire. A group of girls and young men sidle around each other, taking advantage of the unusual circumstances and the preoccupation of their elders to have unchaperoned conversations. Flurries of words and giggles are whipped up like dust devils and as quickly die. Hands touch then start back as if burned. Looks flicker, blushes flare. The wounded have been laid out in the choir, where the monks tend them, unhurried, unquestioning, sure in their knowledge that all this is less than a blink of God's eye, that golden Harold Godwinson and William Bastard, for all their grand titles, all their virile swagger, are no more or less to God than the sparrows in the rafters or the spiders whose webs they have pulled from the corners of the church to staunch bleeding.

Finding herself a little space behind a pillar, wrapping herself in her cloak, Gytha falls into a deep, exhausted sleep, lulled by the warmth of the bodies around her, by the mundane domesticity of crying children, smells of tallow and wet wool, the monks performing the night offices in whispers, crammed into the little space left to them around the altar. She does not awake until after Prime, as bread and water are distributed, with a little milk for the children, and rueful jokes are cracked about the feeding of the five thousand. Then the monks, who are the only people who can quit sanctuary without fear of arrest, set about emptying pisspots, taking wet clothes to be dried over their laundry fires, foraging for food and news of friends and relatives on the outside.

Immediately after Terce, a knocking comes on the west door of the church, reverberating around the suddenly silent nave. Mothers hush their children, conversations tail away, even the wounded cease groaning as the prior unbars the door to reveal the Bishop of Bayeux in the full regalia of his office, his mitre on his head, the jewels in his gold crook and the cross borne behind him winking in breezy winter sunlight. The weather is so transformed it is as though the world outside the church has somehow become somewhere else during the long hours of that miserable night.

Bishop and prior converse in Latin, though Gytha, quietly unlacing her shoes and rolling off her hose to give her feet a chance to dry in the sun which strikes warm through the windows in the lee of the wind, can understand enough of what is said to know that the prior stands his ground and refuses to let the bishop enter sanctuary, for he may be a bishop in Normandy, but here he is a soldier and an enemy of the people of Winchester. To which the bishop responds good humouredly that God makes no distinction between one side of the channel and the other, that heaven forbid he should violate sanctuary, but that he has come to guarantee the safety of those who will leave, as King William has need of the church for his coronation. More follows, the prior's tone shifting from hostile, to dubious, to grudging capitulation while the bishop's remains equable and reasonable, his words shaped by the smile which never leaves his face.

After half an hour or so, the prior allows Bishop Odo to enter the church. He stands just inside the door, attended by several clergy, and informs his audience that they have his word as a servant of the Church and brother to the King that the privileges of sanctuary will be respected and they need have no fear for their safety as long as they return immediately to their homes.

And he is as good as his word. Cautiously at first, but with growing confidence, families bundle up their belongings, retrieve their young people from the mischief of the night, and their old from mumbling corners, and make their way back to hovels and houses, or for some, sifting dunes of ash, charred posts poking up like rotten teeth. No-one is arrested, no-one robbed, no-one even jeered at by William Bastard's soldiery.

Drifting in the wake of those with somewhere to go, someone waiting for them outside, Gytha hesitates to leave the priory precinct. Still barefoot, she flexes her toes against the hardening ruts of the yard and lifts her face to the sun, letting its brightness scour her heavy eyelids, hoping it might enlighten her as to what to do next.

"What now?" she asks the ash tree in the centre of the courtyard, seating herself on the circular bench the monks have fashioned around its trunk while she draws on her hose and fastens her shoes. Keys pirouette down from its branches and slip through the slats of the bench. *Too close*, thinks Gytha, kicking one away, *a new tree can never grow there.* She cannot stay in Winchester, thinking of that smiling Norman lord dreaming his avaricious dreams in Lady Edith's bed, eating at her table, keeping his horses in her stables and his falcons in her mews. She will return to the Convent of Saint Mary of Egypt. Yet if she does that, if it is even possible to travel as far as Colchester now, how can she ever find out Lady Edith's fate? Then again, if she stays here, behind these locked gates and walls swarming with Norman patrols, how can she ever help her? The tree has no answers; the tree is driven by its own imperatives. The monks and lay brothers going about their daily work glance at her curiously but none stops to speak. She is no longer the sort of woman with whom Saint Benedict would think it suitable for a monk to have a conversation, and clearly, in some subtle fashion, in the tilt of her chin perhaps, or the way she points her toe to tie her shoe, it shows. Rising from the bench, she brushes down her clothes and sets out into the city. At least she has a good gown, a warm cloak and serviceable shoes. And her locket. It is more than many people have this morning.

With no particular aim and nowhere to go, she finds herself drifting with others, first in ones and twos, swelling to a steady stream as they near the old royal palace, towards the court Bishop Odo has set up in the palace compound to hear the cases of the rioters. He is already sitting when she arrives, flanked by a number of other high ranking Normans, on a bench elevated above the defendants, their witnesses and advocates, and the crowd of onlookers, crowded on to the flat bed of a hay wain. Their standards snap and glitter behind them, the bishop's golden wolf seeming to gallop across his green field for the sheer joy of sun and breeze. William Bastard and Queen Edith, whose guest he is, watch the proceedings from beneath an awning erected over the entrance to the great hall to protect them from the weather.

Apparently indifferent to hunger or thirst, or the bite of the November wind, Bishop Odo remains on the bench for all the hours it takes to hear the arguments and pronounce sentence. He gives equal weight to every plea and doles out penalties accordingly; his justice is severe, but no-one can call it unfair. Where there is doubt, witnesses are called and the bishop consults with his fellow lieutenants, even, on occasion, with burgesses of the city. People exchange looks of bewildered disappointment, they shrug and spread their hands helplessly. The spirit of rebellion is slipping down an ice floe of fairness; the bishop is ruthless in leaving it no foothold.

Among those sentenced is the soldier who ran through the mother of the dead child with his pike. Condemned to one hundred lashes, he is bound hand and foot to a wheel and the punishment carried out in front of the widower and other witnesses from among the burgesses and portmen. Accounts of this beating race from mouth to mouth faster than fire running before a wind. Not a strip of skin left on his back, they say, the white of his backbone plain to see. None could watch without turning away, not even the Bastard himself. No, corrects someone, that's not right. The bishop watched; they say he never even blinked. Well, blinked perhaps, he must have done, but he never flinched. *If the dead child had been his own son*, thinks Gytha, fascinated and repelled in equal, bewildering measure, *it would have made no difference*. Though she doubts his blood is hot enough to make a son. Her hatred rises against the wall of his impassiveness like a high sea storming a breakwater, endlessly smashing and reforming itself. Everything, she tells herself again, as though reciting her catechism, he has taken everything, just as Adam, with his bad debts and dead babies, did before him.

But Adam died, and his death delivered her freedom, of a kind. Repudiated by Adam's family because she had failed to give him an heir, unwelcome in her father's house now that he had made a new marriage to a woman near her own age, she had become a lay sister in the Convent of Saint Mary of Egypt, where she discovered her small, deft hands possessed an exceptional skill in embroidery. This had brought her to Lady Edith's attention, but that was not the whole of it. Lady Edith was sweet and kind and a generous mistress, but what underlay Gytha's happiness in her service was the knowledge that she possessed this unique talent which did not depend on her being someone's daughter, wife, mother, servant, but solely on being herself. It is the one treasure no-one can take from her.

What, she wonders idly, enjoying the weak warmth of the sun where she sits in the lee of the wind, believing that if she does not think about her problems a solution will present itself, might she have to gain from Bishop Odo's death? Fruitless speculation. He is well guarded, and well able to defend himself, as she has seen, and he looks as strong as a horse. She is powerless against him, and this realisation sharpens her hatred more, seasons it with frustration, brings angry tears to her eyes. Only when people turn to look at her does she become aware that she is weeping aloud, for butchered Harold and mad Edith, for the stories of dragons and princesses her mother took to her grave, and the ghost lives of her children, the empty spaces in the world which will never be filled. Fleeing the court, all the curious stares boring into her back, she believes her heart is broken. But it can't be, it hurts too much for a dead thing.

SERVICE

AFTER EPIPHANY 1067

Agatha feels as though she is in the eye of the storm, standing in the courtyard of the Convent of Saint Justina the Virgin, watching snow meander out of a lowering sky. Both familiar, this rutted yard of frozen puddles and sodden straw with its low buildings humped beneath the snow, yet strange to Agatha, who has not set foot outside the convent since joining its community fifteen years ago. She watches the way each snowflake follows its individual course to earth to merge with the rest, effaced, but essential. *A good analogy*, she thinks, *for the soul's yearning towards oblivion in God*; she will use it in teaching her novices.

Behind the walls surrounding her, a whirlwind of sweeping and dusting, polishing and scouring, has broken out in preparation for the bishop's visit. Saint Justina's being a house of little significance, despite its connection with the ducal family, his pastoral visits are infrequent. Its sisters are not drawn from families able to provide generous dowries, it possesses no important relics. Unless, thinks Agatha sometimes, she herself may be counted a relic. Comparing herself to the novices in her charge, the pink girls bursting like ripe fruit with tears of ecstasy or homesickness, blushing and giggling at confession, she feels sufficiently desiccated, revered rather than loved, more myth than flesh and blood. The Duke of Normandy's odd sister, put away in this obscure place for reasons only she now knows, since the old Abbess' death. Only she, and Bishop Odo, who gave her to Saint Justina's.

Where is he? The water in her basin is growing cold, she can no longer feel her feet. How long since the portress ran to Sister Prioress who ran in turn to Mother Abbess, who then sent word to Sister Jean-Baptiste, as Agatha is known in the convent, that the bishop's party had been sighted and was expected within the quarter hour?

"You will greet His Reverence," Mother Abbess instructed her. "According to his letter, it is you he has come to see. You will offer the water for washing."

"Yes, Mother." Always, yes, Mother. She glances at the Abbess standing beside her. Though her face is invisible behind the damp folds of her hood and veil, Agatha knows what she is thinking. She mistrusts Sister Jean-Baptiste, nobly born, well educated, so beloved by those who have served their novitiate under her that they all seem to keep in touch with her. On the days when letters are permitted, they arrive for Sister Jean from all over Europe, once, even, from the Holy Land, from a house said to stand in the shadow of Mount Sinai itself. Sister Jean was the one they asked to stand for election when the old Abbess was dying; her current superior only holds her position by default, because Sister Jean said she was unworthy. Bishop Odo was asked to intercede. Bishop Odo replied that his noble sister knew her own mind.

Agatha sighs; Mother Abbess darts her a reproving glance; Agatha makes a short prayer for patience, which God answers by carrying the muffled thud of hooves on snow and the jangle of harness to her ears. The two nuns, and the novice waiting beside Agatha with the towels, turn their heads sharply towards the gate.

I have seen something wonderful, something marvellously surprising in this wet, wretched island of bogs and haunted forests. It made me think immediately of you, dearest sister, and of a service you might do for me.

The words he wrote to her, in his own hand, in the note accompanying his letter to the Abbess, in which he requested, with all courtesy and every expectation of being obeyed, an audience with his beloved sister and daughter in Christ, Jean-Baptiste, and that the enclosed message be given to her. *A service you might do for me.* She knew he would ask one day.

She does not recognise him at first, among the small party of armed men who trot single file through the gate and reassemble in the courtyard. Although it is only a short time after Sext, the afternoon is dark and flares have been lit in the courtyard, sending gigantic shadows of men and horses leaping up walls and across the snow, the play of light and shadow confusing the eye. She looks for a mule, for episcopal dress, with a tiny trickle of dread, insistent as water dripping from the thatch over the kitchen, whose fires have melted the snow. What does it mean when you cannot recognise your own brother, your favourite brother, the person you love most in all the world?

Then a figure detaches itself from the rest, taller perhaps, but dressed the same, in short cloak and mud-spattered leather gaiters. As he approaches the women, he pauses suddenly, as though he has forgotten something, to unbuckle his sword from its belt, a task which seems to cause him some difficulty and is eventually completed for him by a second, shorter, older man she recognises as her brother's servant, who takes the sword and stows it in a saddle scabbard. Odo then pushes back his hood to reveal his tonsure and the familiar contours of his face with its strong bones and seducer's smile.

"You are welcome, My Lord," says Mother Abbess, curtseying, as Agatha steps forward with her bowl of water.

"I am glad to be here. The God of Moses has thrown all His box of tricks at us on the journey save fire and pestilence. I will save your gentle ears any account of the sea crossing."

So why has he risked it? wonders Agatha, handing the water bowl to the novice and taking a towel to dry his hands. As she performs this service, she realises why he struggled with his sword. His left hand is badly bruised and splinted at the wrist. Though she is tender and careful with him, he cannot repress a hiss of pain as she dries it. Yet she observes no swelling; it is not a recent fracture, just poorly tended, probably beyond proper healing.

"Thank you, Sister," he says, exchanging with her the briefest of glances, teasing, affectionate, before she lowers her eyes and kneels with the others to kiss his ring and receive his blessing.

As they go indoors, he addresses himself to the Abbess. He has brought gifts from England. Some plate come by in Winchester, a pair of particularly handsome gold chalices from the island of Saint Columba, etched with designs in knotwork, a pleasing crucifix set with agates, a vial of water from the pool at Bethesda. The carcass of a boar they were lucky enough to kill en route and some flagons of a liquor made from honey by which the English set great store. The King? The King, God be praised, is in excellent health and spirits. And now, by Mother Abbess' leave, time is short and he has urgent business with his sister while the horses are rested and his men refresh themselves.

Agatha accompanies him to the room normally set aside for lay guests. It has a larger fireplace than the nuns' parlour, and more comfortable furniture, and she has been given permission to light some candles, though only tallow; beeswax candles are kept strictly for the great festivals and the Feast of Saint Justina. By their smoky light she examines him with concern.

There are new lines on his face, deep grooves gouged from cheek to jaw, and grey peppering the light brown curls fringing his tonsure. The fine skin beneath his eyes is blue tinged and puffy, like the skin of a bruised plum. He has lost weight since she last saw him and his complexion, beneath its superficial weathering, is pallid.

"What happened to your hand?" she asks, as if his answer to that might contain replies to all the other questions she feels forbidden to ask.

"A horse fell on me."

Agatha crosses herself. "Then you are lucky to be alive."

He shrugs.

"And you look thin," she persists, shrewish in her anxiety. She expects him to protest, but he does not.

"There has been some fever among the troops. I was not seriously affected, thanks be to God."

"Troops? Surely you are not still with the army? I thought the fighting would be done by now."

"Done?" He repeats the word as though it is in a language he does not understand. He pauses, massaging his wrist. "It's like trying to press air out of a bladder. As soon as we manage to put down one rebellion, another breaks out somewhere else. Always just beyond our reach, in some pathless forest or the far side of a river without fords. Or at least, none marked on the maps we have. The roads the Romans left are ruined, some say deliberately. William may have bribed or bludgeoned their thegns into submission, but these people don't take account of their lords the way it's done in Normandy."

"So our brother's coronation was not universally welcomed. We had heard as much." She gestures towards a chair and, though he does not sit himself, he grants her permission to do so.

"Which?" he asks, "Winchester or London?"

"Wasn't one enough? Did he harbour some doubt after all about what he was doing?"

"Winchester was Godwinson's capital. London is the better place strategically, but Winchester has political significance. I...he...we..."

"No need to explain. I dare say you will never unravel one from the other. It is London I am thinking of. We heard all sorts of rumours. Rioting, fires. Is any of it true?" she asks, smoothing her habit over her knees and folding her hands in her lap. The smell of wet wool is added to the mingled scents of tallow and lavender and the whiff of the stables.

"It was nothing, a misunderstanding. The Saxon thegns set up some ritual shout or other, the custom, apparently, at their king makings. Our guards thought there was going to be a riot and set fires to contain it in the usual way. They had it under control within the hour." He stands in front of the hearthstone, pinpoints of fire reflected in his eyes. She fears the element of fire may have gained the upper hand in him, drying the blood that gives him his normally sanguine temperament. That would account for the fever and the weight loss, the sense she has of a man devoured from within, the skeleton burning beneath the skin.

"You know," he says, "at the coronation, when I did homage to William for Kent, and I knelt and put my hands between his, I felt something between us, some force, like lightening. I really believed we were invincible, that if we had done this, we could do anything. Less than a hundred years since Rollo embraced Christianity, and now his descendant is made a Christian king. Like Charlemagne."

"I guessed that might be his reason for choosing Christmas Day. Such a dull man, but so good at the grand gesture. Or was that, perhaps, your idea?"

He gives her a tight, enigmatic smile. "I wished only to please God, though He has shown us little sign since that He is on our side. I had expected it to be easier."

"Surely you of all people haven't fallen into the trap of confusing the easy way with the right one, Odo."

They are interrupted by a servant who brings food and drink, and waits to serve the bishop, but Odo dismisses her.

"I will wait on His Reverence," says Agatha, though Odo shows no sign of interest in the meal she has so carefully arranged for him, the cheese and bitter apples she knows he cannot get in England, the brandy usually dispensed only to the sick. He crosses to the window and peers out, rubbing away the frost with his sleeve.

"I have very little time," he says, pacing the room, picking things up and putting them down, forgetting his injured hand and wincing when he tries to bend his fingers. His prowling makes even this room seem small, the early dark closing in around them, swallowing the candlelight. "I must tell you about the Byrhtnoth hanging."

"The what? Who is Byrhtnoth? Odo, please sit down."

He does so, but on the edge of his chair.

"Well?" she prompts. "If you have so little time, you must tell me about the hanging. Is this the marvellous and surprising thing you wrote to me about?"

"I saw it in the abbey church at Ely, an odd place. The local people call it an island, though it stands on a marsh, not water. Shall we say it aspires to be like Mont Saint Michel, but fails. For one thing, their churches admit scarcely any light, as though they are loathe for God to see what goes on in them. They're pagans, Agatha, for all their Saint Augustine and Saint Cuthbert and Bede's History. I have seen images of the Norse gods on their altars and everywhere odd little shrines stuck with blood and feathers." He shivers and stretches out his hands to the fire.

"Odo, has something happened to you? I do not know you like this." No, not strictly true. She has seen him this way twice before, torn between the risk and its consequences, between love and duty, and both times it was William's doing.

He frowns, his mouth working, whether to form words or keep them back she cannot tell. "I...dream..." He shakes himself, like a dog shaking off water. "No, nothing has happened to me, just a touch of fever as I said. This hanging. It's not woven, the style is more like... embroidery on clothes or vestments...except for the colours. No gold, no purple."

"No gold? I would have thought you would have wanted plenty of gold, Odo."

"You miss the point, Agatha. It's a story, a chronicle in pictures, about the Earl Byrhtnoth, who was some sort of tribal leader in East Anglia about a hundred years ago. When he was killed, his widow apparently made this work as a memorial to him and gave it to the abbey. It's on a long strip of, I don't know, linen I suppose. It hangs around all four walls of the church, like a frieze. You see it by torchlight, and the figures seem to leap out at you, so real I kept my hand on my sword hilt, I half believed some warrior was going to jump down from the wall and revenge himself on me for William's triumph." He gives a sheepish laugh.

"I notice you have taken to wearing a sword."

"All pictures of this Byrhtnoth and his people, fighting, feasting, holding councils, even love making," he goes on, choosing to ignore her reproof. "It seemed to me to unfold like life does, some stages orderly and clearly seen, others obscure, muddled, contradictory. That's why it doesn't want gold. It's the story of a life, a real life. There's a commentary, but it's in English. I've set myself to learn to speak the language, but they make their letters strangely so it's difficult to read. It doesn't matter, though, the pictures speak for themselves. Wonderful pictures, ordinary people, so the artist didn't have to conform to the conventions."

"Of representing the saints, for example? No haloes, no eyes raised to heaven? If you have one leg shorter than the other or a nose shaped like a bottle, the artist can show it? I begin to see what you mean."

"None of the constraints of holiness." Their eyes meet and they exchange smiles of understanding.

"And it set me thinking," he goes on, "that it would be an excellent way to record what we have done."

"Surely a chronicle would have more permanence. Or a poem. You could be Turpin to William's Roland. Your strip of linen sounds perilous to me. It could rot in the sun, be eaten by mice, anything. Looked at back to front."

"Perhaps, but so can a book, and whoever reads books, other than a handful of monks and scholars? A hanging could be displayed anywhere…"

"Big enough."

"Big enough, I grant you. My idea is that it should have a permanent home in Bayeux, in the new cathedral, but it could travel. And be seen and understood by anyone, lettered or unlettered, Saxon or Norman. And it has the merit of simultaneity, like real life, the good and the bad balancing one another. It seems to me that's impossible to achieve in books, where you see only one page at a time. Books tell, pictures suggest."

"Couldn't that be dangerous? If you want to be sure people understand events from your point of view?"

"Only if we had something to hide." He pauses, as though expecting some response, then goes on, "So, I shall take you to see this Byrhtnoth hanging, and then you'll understand what I want."

A sense of dread creeps over Agatha like a chill. The fire has settled to a dull glow and the room, outside its penumbra, is almost in darkness. She stirs the embers and piles on fresh wood. Perhaps she has misunderstood.

"Why must I understand it, Odo?"

"Didn't I say? You are to design it for me. That is the service I wish from you. I've considered it all ways round, and you're the obvious choice. You have the gift of representation. You can join my household so that I can recall and describe events for you whenever we can snatch a few minutes. Longer periods are difficult, as you can imagine. Then, when the design is ready, who better to seek out embroiderers with the skills I need? The King's sister, and a religious, you can gain access anywhere. I will make sure you have all the authority and money you need."

"Wait, Odo, wait! I can't do it. I can't leave here. I haven't been outside this place for fifteen years. I no longer know how the world works. And just because I used to enjoy drawing as a child doesn't mean I can succeed in a task such as you envisage. You must find someone else. English needleworkers are supposed to be some of the best in the world. Surely you can find someone better than me in England to design and execute your hanging."

"You haven't understood me properly, Agatha. Of course there are people skilled enough in England. There's a strong tradition in Canterbury, I've discovered, which will no doubt be very useful to us..."

"Ah yes, your new seat of power. Tell me, how does a Norman bishop feel recast as a Saxon earl?"

"I have hopes of more."

"More, Odo? Are you not lord of half our brother's new kingdom already? Must you have all his toys?"

"Not land, Agatha, the Archbishopric. Can't you see me as Archbishop of Canterbury?"

She shakes her head in exasperation. Is nothing ever enough for Odo? It is clear William plays on this hunger of his, keeping him close with promises like a falconer training a young bird with titbits, but she thinks it must be an uncomfortable alliance, however much they love one another. "He would be mad to concentrate such power in one pair of hands." Especially yours, she adds to herself. "What about Lanfranc? Surely he stands to gain also?"

Odo gives a dismissive wave, pulling in a sharp breath between his teeth as the shards of bone grind together in his wrist. "What did Lanfranc do besides go and talk to the Pope? I preached the campaign and gave a hundred ships full of armed men and horses. Besides, Lanfranc will never leave Caen. He's already turned down Rouen. Why should he want Canterbury? It's even further from his beloved Alps. Now, this hanging. The reason I need you is this. You're the one person I can tell everything to. We're so close in age it sometimes feels to me as though we're twins. We have everything in common, even William. Especially William. We're the ones he's made the most difference to, aren't we?"

She nods, forced to acknowledge the truth of this. Because of William she has bent her will to the Rule of Saint Benedict and hobbled her imagination with the discipline of prayer.

"Talking to you will be like talking to myself. Because it isn't simple, and if I'm to make a true record, I can't make it simple. I can't do it without you. Do you understand?"

"Not really, but it's true I owe you a service, and English earl or no, you're my bishop, so I must do as you bid me. But Odo..."

"Yes?"

"What if, in the world...what if...?"

"You will be strong, as you always have been. I have never known

54

a woman more determined to resist temptation, nor man neither, come to think of it. I have faith in you, Agatha, I always have, or I would not have taken your side against William over the matter of your marriage . Now, I want to leave before nightfall, so go and make yourself ready."

She has little to pack, and spends most of the time he allows her for preparation at prayer in the chapel. She prays for obedience, that she might submit to his will, the will of her bishop, God's representative on earth, with joy. She prays for strength to resist the world's temptations, and the vision to distinguish what is good from what is the Devil dressed in angels' wings. But her prayers become entangled, because in saving her from the marriage William had arranged for her, Odo effectively condoned her sinful instincts, granted her absolution without confession and placed his own soul in as great a peril as hers. It is true what he says, that they are so alike as to be almost the same person in two skins, but she fears this likeness may not be the strength he seems to think it is.

CHOICE

LAMMASTIDE 1068

Two days after William Bastard arrived in Winchester, he was gone again, and his brothers and his chief lieutenants with him. After a hasty, shamefaced coronation service conducted behind closed doors, the blood of the wounded rioters still marking the floor of the choir in patches of faded rust, they set off for London, leaving behind a garrison in the charge of a knight from Calvados, a vassal of Bishop Odo, who had, apparently, an English wife. Not that this seemed to give him any sympathy for the English. He closed the city, taking sole charge of bringing in food supplies, which he then sold at exorbitant prices, keeping the best back for his own table and those of his officers.

Forced to abandon any plans she might have had to return to Colchester, Gytha sought refuge in the households of men who had been loyal to King Harold and friends to Lady Edith. But, as winter hardened and food became scarcer, their welcome wore out. Neither her skill with a needle nor her devotion to her mistress carried much weight with people forced to come to an accommodation with their new overlords in order to put bread in their children's mouths. There was no hard news of the fate of lady Edith or her children. Some said they had been sent into exile, some that they had been executed in spite of the grand assurances of the Bishop of Bayeux back in November, some that Lady Edith had run mad and been locked in a convent. Gradually, the truth ceased to matter, and Edith and her children, like King Harold, began to fade into folklore, flesh metamorphosed into the words of tales and songs, myth dressed in memory's clothes.

One night, shortly after Epiphany, unable to sleep for cold and hunger, Gytha rose, pulled her cloak about her shoulders and stepped quietly out of the ladies' bower of the household she was staying in. Her teeth chattered in the icy air, and her legs shook, so weakened was she by always deferring to her host's family and housecarls at mealtimes, often giving up most of her portion to the children. But the hard light of the stars seemed to hold her together, she swallowed the frost down into her belly and it gave her strength, the strength of being part of the frozen earth beneath her feet, welcomed back from whence she came. Dust to dust. She knew death was stalking her, awaiting his chance. Slowly, with arms outstretched as though to embrace a lover, she turned to face him.

But death had a woman's eyes with blank, lustreless dilated pupils like holes in her face. Her body was spatchcocked against the woodpile beside the kitchen house, a gleam of exposed thigh pale in the starlight, shaken by the thrusts of the man fucking her like a dead rat worried by a dog. Gytha tried to turn away, but the woman's gaze held her. She was captivated by its indifference, the sense that no-one actually inhabited the body submitting to the man, now spent, after a moment of inertia straightening his tunic and placing something which looked like a hunk of bread in the woman's open palm. And remembering the two Norman soldiers up on the wall, she realised there was a way to stay alive, to keep the memory of Harold and Edith golden and feed her hatred for Odo of Bayeux.

She rents one of the cells behind the city bathhouse. On her earnings she could afford a room of her own, even a modest house, set herself up in a small way as a courtesan, with regular gentlemen who would disguise payment as gifts, but she has no wish for this work to become entwined with the rest of her life. One-Eye Peg made that mistake, they say. A great beauty in her day, she entertained thegns and merchants and city burgesses, had even bought herself a burial plot under the priory nave. But when she was caught attempting to procure an abortion, none of her high connections could save her from a stoning. Those who remember say her punishment was all the more fierce because half those who sat in judgement on her had also lain with her. So now, scarred and toothless, with a dragging leg and a puckered hole where her right eye used to shine with love, she begs outside the bathhouse, permitted to remain there by the burgesses as a warning to others, or perhaps as a sop to their consciences.

Gytha sees her work as something which happens in the interval between heartbeats, the space between breaths, temporary and marginal, nothing to do with the woman inside her skin. She keeps only what she needs to survive, money for rent and fuel, and new soles for her shoes, cloth for a spare gown and a winter cloak, enough food to preserve the illusion of fecundity in the swell of her breasts, the rise of her belly, the sweep of her hips. The rest she gives to the priory for the maintenance of orphans, going there at dusk with her hood drawn close about her face so she will not be recognised, leaving her gifts of money and food, and the occasional piece of jewellery, with the porter.

She is popular and can charge highly for her services because she knows herself to be barren. The first month after her congress with the soldiers, when she did not bleed, she feared the worst. But then a second month passed, and a third, and though she remained clean, she experienced none of the symptoms of pregnancy and supposed her fertility ended, carried away like Lady Edith in her cart or Harold's corpse washed out to sea. She had heard of it before, in women who had suffered sudden shocks, and knew it to be widespread during famine years, though then the problem would usually right itself when food was plentiful again.

She has no regrets, for what did a quickening womb bring her but pain overlaid with heartache? At least she does not have to take the precautions the others take to ward off conception. She does not have to swallow bees or drink her clients' urine, or smear her women's parts with tincture of honey and excrement. No hopping seven times on her left leg after the act for her. The men are not obliged to withdraw and spill themselves on her belly, in the air which, even accounting for the steam from the baths, kills men's seed with its dryness. She does not try to incite them to ejaculate into orifices forbidden by the Church, unless, of course, that is their preference and they are prepared to pay for the indulgence. She is uncomplicated, and that is what the men like in these days full of rumour and rebellion. They find her indifference irresistible, a challenge they rise to again and again, but never surmount.

Even the kind ones are brutes, writhing and panting on top of her, crushing the air out of her lungs, with their little cries of triumph as they squirt their seed into her useless womb. She will never look at their faces, flushed, contorted, self absorbed, or the tight little smiles with which they rearrange their clothing, hand over their gifts of money, or a joint of meat, some yards of cloth, a modest jewel their wives will not miss, and scuttle away. If she allows herself to indulge the contempt she feels rising in her like bile, she fears it may dilute the hatred she cherishes for William Bastard's rapacious brother.

Sister Jean-Baptiste arrives at the end of a busy day. Hot summer afternoons are good for business. It is the sort of weather that sets the fleas jumping and brings customers to the baths, and what man of affairs, languorous from the steam, skin tingling from the ministrations of the attendants with their brushes and wash cloths, wants to return too quickly to his stuffy counting house or gloomy hall, or the constraints of a nagging wife in her bower? Gytha is lying stretched out on her bed, alone for the time being, the lacing at the front of her dress loosened, her arms crossed behind her head, remembering a story her mother used to tell her, about the Emperor of Rome and his dream of a maiden.

In her half waking, half sleeping state she can hear her mother's voice perfectly clearly inside her head, its Welsh song rising and falling as though she were sitting at Gytha's side and not dead in childbirth for twelve years.

And when he awoke neither life nor being nor existence was left him, for the maiden he had seen in his sleep. Not one bone-joint of his was there, not the middle of a single nail, to say nothing of a part that might be greater than that, but was filled with love of the maiden.

She cannot keep the regret out of her voice when she hears the footsteps hesitate on the far side of the curtain covering the open side of her cubicle. Such vivid memories come only rarely.

"I'm alone. You can come in." She sits up, pulling her laces tighter as she does so, pushing up her breasts which are still full and firm but not set as high as the new fashion dictates, though she is bound to admit, grudgingly, that the close fitting Norman style of dress suits her better than the loose Saxon tunic. "It's a penny up front, and I shall weigh it, mind. No clipped coins."

"I am glad you place a proper value on your services. We are all precious in the sight of God."

Gytha looks up in astonishment to see the nun standing at the foot of her bed, immaculate in black habit and white veil, the plain wooden crucifix lying flat against her chest. She is smiling, which unnerves Gytha further, the powdery, ageless skin around her eyes folded into little, sharp pleats. There is something familiar about the smile, with its ironic, downward turn. Gytha finishes lacing her dress, trying discreetly to pull the neck a little higher, wishing she had roused herself to wash after the last man left. The nun meanwhile appraises her with the candour of a dealer assessing the soundness of a horse, registering, Gytha feels, a great deal more than outward appearances. She then shifts her gaze to take in their surroundings, the narrow space between the rough planks partitioning Gytha's cubicle from the ones on either side of it, the plaster flaking from the damp rear wall, furnished with nothing but the bed and a stool that doubles as a nightstand.

"Functional," she comments, "not unlike my own cell really."

"The comforts I offer are rather less demanding than the consolations of religion, My Lady."

"Good," says the nun, as though admiring a deft piece of needlework or a subtle parry of the sword, "very good."

A Norman, a newcomer to judge by her accent, and well born. What does she want here? She is clearly not one of those dispatched from time to time by the burgesses to make sure the women are not diseased, dispensing pious platitudes with their herbal ointments and potions, not expecting miracles.

"You can understand me, then," the nun continues. "I'm afraid I have not yet mastered your language as well as I should like."

"I understand you."

"Good. You are Aelfgytha? From the manor of Colchester?"

"Yes," she replies cautiously. How does this Norman nun know who she is, and what can she want of her?

"Then I am glad to have found you. It has not been easy. May I sit?"

Gytha jerks her chin in the direction of the stool, at the same time shifting around on the bed to face the nun, leaning against the wall with her knees drawn up in front of her. The nun sits, straight backed, hands folded in her lap as though she were in chapel. Hugging her knees, Gytha waits. In the next door cubicle, cries of passion have been replaced by murmured conversation, rustling clothes, the chink of money changing hands.

"I hope your daughter is well again soon," she hears her neighbour say as her client leaves.

"I should introduce myself," resumes the nun. "I expect you are thoroughly confused by now, wondering why a nun from Normandy should be chasing around the south of England looking for you."

"I wonder very little nowadays, My Lady. It serves no purpose. I remember those who thought the comet last spring portended well for King Harold."

"You are wise, Aelfgytha. Some in Falaise, where I come from, believed it heralded the Second Coming."

"You'd know more about that than I would, My Lady."

The nun gives her a shrewd look. "I am pressed for time. My Lord, the temporal lord, that is, whose business I am on, is not a man who appreciates being kept in suspense. Briefly, my name is Jean-Baptiste, and I am on a commission for the new Earl of Kent, who is my brother and commanded an army in the recent crusade."

"Crusade? Is that what you people think you were doing? Crusading? Why, it seems to me you've done nothing but burn down our churches since you got here. There's nowhere left for a pious Christian to worship. Even Canterbury Cathedral, so I hear. I suppose that was your Earl's doing?"

"My Earl, as you call him, had not yet been invested with his earldom when the cathedral burned down. He had probably never set eyes on Canterbury. You would do well to remember that Archbishop Stigand was under interdict when he crowned Harold of Wessex. Perhaps the fire was sent from God." The nun's calm is unassailable. "Opposition is always more effective if you get your facts straight." Gytha gives a sulky shrug. "The Earl rendered the King great service during the...invasion, and wishes to keep a record of his achievements. Which is where you come in."

"It seems improbable to me that your mighty earl should need to send all the way to Winchester for a whore. Are there no brothels in Canterbury? Does he not draw a shoal of concubines in his wake as most great men do?"

"But you were not always a whore, were you, Aelfgytha?"

"Your people made me one. What I was before can be of no interest to you."

"Many have suffered to put King William on his throne, and not all Saxons. There is no point in pitying ourselves." A sudden bitterness in her tone makes Gytha look up. Briefly, their eyes meet in a flicker of mutual understanding. But the moment passes and, stung by the nun's patronising words, Gytha gropes for some clearer way to explain her feelings.

The Normans are like the men she does business with. They do not see her as a woman, as a daughter, a mother, a wife, a whole person to be cherished or punished for her uniqueness. To them she is just a hole in which they bury themselves, the price of a few seconds of oblivion. When the Bastard looked out to sea and envisaged the island he aimed to conquer, what did he see? Land, that was all. Farm land, building land, forests for hunting. Not people, not the Anglo Saxons, or the Celts or the Danes or any of the rest who made up their ancient, intricate communities where Christ and Thor, and even Jupiter supped from the same dish. Stone he saw, but not churches or moot halls, or the mysterious ruins of Roman temples and villas crumbling on empty hillsides like petrified echoes. Gold he saw, but not the way the master jewellers wrought it to frame dark sapphires or milky moonstones, or needlewomen like herself could transform gold thread into the rising sun, or the halo of a saint, or the glint in the eye of a lover contemplating his lady. What he saw, the Bastard with his Judas hair, was simply the reflection of his greed. But she cannot say this to the Norman nun, the Earl of Kent's sister, so she keeps silent.

"You have nothing more to say?" queries Sister Jean-Baptiste. "Then let me explain what I want of you. As I said, the Earl seeks a memorial of the invasion, and please, for now, let us not debate the wisdom of his desire. The desires of great men are facts, are they not, like the weather or the hours of light and dark? There is nothing we can do to change them. His idea is that this should take the form of an embroidered hanging depicting all the events leading to the coronation of King William. I have drawn up the design for the work, and now I am looking for the best needlewomen I can find to execute it." She pauses.

Is she waiting for some acknowledgement of her compliment, Gytha wonders. Well, let her wait; she plied her needle in Saxon houses, for Saxon noblemen and their churches; the Normans made her the whore she is now, who does not even trouble to darn her hose.

"The abbess at the Convent of Saint Mary of Egypt in Colchester told me how the late Earl of Wessex's concubine singled out your work for special praise on a visit to the convent," Sister Jean continues, "and how she then took you into her household. So I came here to Winchester to find you. Though it has not been easy. You have hidden your tracks well. Most people I made enquiries of told me all Edith Swan Neck's women went into exile with her."

Exile. Thank God, oh, thank God she is still alive. "She is not dead then?" She cannot keep her relief out of her voice. Hearing it, the nun gives her a quick, warm smile, which makes her look younger, less severe. "Where is she? Do you know? Is she in the charge of your Earl?"

"Alas, I know nothing more than my enquiries after you have turned up. But there is generally a kernel of truth in rumour so it seems likely she is not dead."

Gytha slumps back against the wall. "Rumour, never anything but rumour."

"Well you may be sure of one thing, and that is, she is not in Winchester. Perhaps if you will come to Canterbury with me you may learn more outside these walls."

"My Lady, I'm sure I should be flattered by your attention and yes, I was a good embroiderer, but that is all in the past. Nowadays I'm just a whore. I'll tickle your Earl's cock for him, for a price, but not his vanity. I have little enough to be proud of, let me at least take pride in being a Saxon." Sister Jean-Baptiste raises her eyebrows at this. Gytha, with her small stature and dark colouring, looks nothing like a Saxon. "Now I must ask you to leave. I have work to do."

"I think not. It's late and I can't hear anyone outside. I am offering you respectable, reliable employment for years to come. You will have a sound roof over your head, regular meals, and the protection of one of the most powerful men in England, who has even stood regent for the King."

"The work I have now is reliable, Sister, if not respectable. A good deal more reliable than embroidery, if I may say so, the one being merely a luxury, the other – as men would have it – a necessity of life."

"I have seen the chasuble that captured Edith Swan Neck's attention, Aelfgytha. God bestowed a great gift upon you. It is your duty to use your talent wisely."

"And who's to say I don't?"

"Oh, really. Now you are talking like a child. Besides, this is not a work of mere luxury. It is to be a chronicle of sorts, an account of important events to hang in a cathedral. For people to see and learn from."

"A cathedral? But I thought you said…"

"The Earl is also a bishop, in Normandy."

Gytha feels the blood grow still in her veins. When she opens her mouth to speak, she realises she has been holding her breath for several seconds. Everything has fallen away, the world is suddenly nothing but the nun and herself, the question hanging on her lips, the knowledge the nun has which may be everything or nothing. "Where?" she asks, sounding as casual as she can.

"Bayeux," replies Sister Jean-Baptiste pleasantly. "He is building a new cathedral there. He envisages this embroidery hanging in the nave." The nun continues to speak, but her words are nothing but background noise to Gytha, merging with voices and footsteps outside, hurrying to be indoors before dark, or the shuffled rearrangements of bodies in the neighbouring cubicles. Bayeux. The word hammers in her head like the ringing of the curfew bell. Obviously Lady Edith's hangings were not enough for him, then, and his greed has given her her chance. The little room is stuffy and reeks of sweat and semen. She begins to feel faint, separated, as though she is looking in on herself from outside.

"What about this hanging then?" she asks, as soon as she can trust her voice, struggling to keep her tone light, casual, non-committal. "I hope it will be truthful. I refuse to sew lies. Besides, a lot more people will see it than would read a chronicle. Your Earl will get caught out quicker than a tale teller when he changes the words."

"You will come then?"

"Is it up to you?" If he has any say in the matter, then he may already be aware of her identity, which will make her task harder. "I would have thought he would want to make the choice himself, if this hanging is so important to him."

"He has entrusted the task to me entirely. I am to choose."

Choice. There has never been any choice for a woman, not since Eve chose the serpent. Of course she will go with Sister Jean-Baptiste, though not for any reason the sister could dream of. She nods.

The nun stands up and holds out her hand. "Good. That's settled then. I stay tonight at the priory. Come there tomorrow at Prime and we will set out for Canterbury." Sister Jean-Baptiste's grip is sinewy and dry, though her hand feels as delicate as a songbird in Gytha's.

They make slow progress on the first day of their journey. Traffic throngs the narrow road, heavy grain wagons rumbling between fields and mills, forcing their party off the track and into the woods and meadows bordering it, bands of old men and boys with scythes and flails balanced on their shoulders following the harvest, the usual assortment of barefoot friars, peddlers, prostitutes. If she catches a girl's eye, Gytha smiles her recognition, but rarely receives anything other than a scowl or a blank stare in return. Without the white cockade of her profession pinned to her hood, they do not know her, and eventually she stops trying, riding with eyes cast down like a respectable woman.

Rain has fallen overnight, transforming baked earth into syrupy mud which clings to their clothes and faces and makes the horses slip and lurch uncomfortably. Several times they have to wait while their escort help to free stuck wagons, laying mats of brush or sheaves of straw beneath the wheels. Nor does it aid their progress that Sister Jean-Baptiste insists on stopping every three hours to say the daily offices, despite the advice of the commander of their escort that they're sitting ducks for all manner of outlaws on the quieter stretches of road.

"Nonsense," she retorts. "It is the King's boast that a man may travel the length and breadth of England with a crock of gold in his breast and remain unmolested, and I believe him."

She doesn't, of course, following her travels with Odo the previous year, noting down the account he gave her of the invasion as he toured his new manors, sitting in council, inspecting the rolls, holding courts, tithe bargaining with suspicious abbots, attempting to explain the obligations of frankpledge to bewildered villeins. Everywhere stamping the authority of his new seal, which showed on one side the Bishop, his face bathed in saintly benevolence, his hand raised in blessing, and on the other, the Earl, armed, mounted, holding an unsheathed sword.

When William appointed him regent, she remained unobtrusive among the crowd of sycophants and fortune hunters, watching the King embark for Normandy with his train of Saxon hostages. She saw how, when the brothers kissed, rivalry vied with love in the gesture. Odo, standing alone, ankle deep in the cold, grey sea, the hem of his cloak floating out behind him as the Mora diminished to the size of a great insect crawling across the water, was engaged in something much more complicated than a public display of fraternal affection and feudal obligation. Looking towards home, his dream of a cathedral, his library, his school, his son, with the great, wet weight of England at his back, he wrestled with the question, what if. What if William never returned? None of them, not his brother, Robert of Mortain, not Fitzosbern, with whom Odo was to share his regency, must see it on his face.

Sketching out her designs in makeshift accommodation in the half built castles at Dover and Rochester, she too fell prey to what if, after Odo had ridden in pursuit of the turncoat Eustace of Boulogne, whose vanity in his descent from Charlemagne had made him easy prey for whatever flotsam the tide of William's success had left in its wake. What if Odo were killed? Would his hanging too, like that of Earl Byrhtnoth, become simply the doting memorial to a fallen hero sewn by the women he left behind? But he came back, and Eustace fled to France, and after her experience of the aftermath of that revolt, she will not be deflected from her religious duty by the prospect of a gang of half starved villeins on the run from their overlords.

Gytha never prays with her, even at the main daily office of Vespers, but Agatha, not wishing to antagonise her latest recruit, makes no comment. She is grateful for Gytha's change of heart, she had feared she would be unable to persuade her to join in the fabrication of Odo's memorial, and though she had the means of coercion at her disposal, she was loathe to use them. Gytha's skill must be freely given if she is to bring to Odo's hanging the same lovely spontaneity Agatha noted in the chasuble stitched at the Convent of Saint Mary.

As they converse along the road, she finds herself growing to like her companion, though not with the disquieting affection that leapt into her heart when she first saw Margaret in her father's house, eyes cast down and blushing as she held out an embroidered shift for Sister Jean's inspection. Margaret smells of fresh baking and orange blossom, and her plump, freckled forearms covered with fine red blond down make you want to stroke them. Gytha, with her awkward cleverness, her words like cats fighting in a sack, does not inspire such gentleness, more a sense of common identity. In other circumstances, Agatha wonders if she might have ended up living as Gytha has been living, in the margins of society, like a spark thrown off a Catherine wheel. She feels at ease with Gytha, and senses that Gytha too is beginning to relax in her company, albeit cautiously, every friendly remark framed by some reminder that they are enemies, more divided than united by their common purpose. But who is she reminding, Agatha wonders. Agatha, or herself?

Towards None on the fourth day, Sister Jean calls a halt at a point where the road passes through a woodland clearing, the track temporarily losing itself in close bitten grass where the horses have to tread carefully to avoid rabbit burrows. Rabbits, like stunted hares without grace or magic or silver in their fur, forever escaping their warrens and ruining vegetable plots, another unwanted Norman invader. Gytha walks into the woods to stretch her cramped muscles, enjoying the cool, green light filtering through the trees, the silence hardly touched by the soft scurrying of unseen creatures in the undergrowth. She takes off her shoes, burrowing her toes into the forest floor, sensing through her worn hose the different textures of grass spikes, damp leaves, pine needles, beech mast, inhaling the sharp earth scent released by the disturbed vegetation.

Suddenly, to their mutual astonishment, a man erupts from the bushes only yards away from her. He has a bow slung across his chest and around his neck the carcass of a deer, tongue lolling, feet neatly hobbled. He is breathless and at the sight of Gytha goes very pale, his face reflecting the green light of the sun through leaves. Gytha flushes. How foolish she must look, wandering aimlessly in the woods with her shoes in her hand and her hose damp. Then turns cold at the thought of what will happen to him if he is caught.

"I haven't seen you," she says quickly. He gives a curt nod, and a grimace that might have been a smile, and runs on before Gytha can warn him that he is heading straight for Sister Jean and the Earl's men. She wants to run after him, but she will never be able to keep up in her bare feet, and by the time she has put her shoes back on it will be too late. She watches him disappear again among the trees. How can she help him anyway? The road is in the king's peace and the woods on either side the king's also. He will be shown no mercy where the king's deer are concerned; the road is crawling with royal patrols, he is bound to be caught sooner or later.

By the time she emerges from the wood, the poacher has been taken, two men holding him by the arms while another secures the deer carcass to one of the packhorses. The man stands passively, as though submitting to the inevitable, but between Sister Jean and the escort commander it seems to be a different story. They are arguing, in low voices but with obvious ferocity, the commander's face and neck flushed, Sister Jean drawn bolt upright in front of him, quivering with anger the way birch trees do in the lightest of breezes. As Gytha watches, she reaches into the flat leather wallet suspended from her girdle and withdraws a folded parchment with a showy seal appended to it. The officer makes a stiff bow and, crossing to his men, gives them their orders.

The two soldiers holding the poacher drag him towards the edge of the clearing, his legs buckling under him, his feet scuffing the grass. Another unclips his horse's reins and uses the length of leather to bind the poacher by his wrists to a tree. He then takes his knife to the hem of the prisoner's shirt, hacking away a sufficient length of it to act as a blindfold. Gytha cannot believe what she is seeing. The Normans are usually so particular about sticking to the rules, yet here is the Bastard's own sister openly flouting his law. Or perhaps the law has no currency where poaching the Bastard's own deer is concerned. She tries to catch Sister Jean's eye, but the nun never for a moment looks away from her victim.

Gytha hurries across the clearing to the officer, where he stands beside a young archer crouched on the ground sorting through a quiver full of arrows.

"Is she mad?"

The officer looks close to answering her before he remembers his position and turns away impassively.

"Sister," pleads Gytha, "this man is unshriven. At least you should fetch him a priest."

"Is he secure?" asks Sister Jean, approaching the group beside the tree.

"Yes, madam."

"Then know this," she says to the prisoner. "This is not the King's justice but his sister's. You will thank me for it in heaven."

The young archer fits his chosen arrow into his bow, takes aim, draws back his firing arm and, on a sign from his officer, releases his shaft. Sister Jean crosses herself and begins a recitation of prayers for the dying, though all Gytha can hear is the whistle of the arrow, ending in an abrupt squelch as it hits its target. It is a good shot; the poacher sags against the tree without uttering any sound other than the sigh of his breath being knocked out of his body. Gytha has never witnessed an execution before. She cannot look away as a thin, dark trickle of blood appears at the corner of his slack mouth, like something he meant to say before it was too late.

"If I'm not mistaken, there's a priory not far from here. Take him there for burial, and the venison for distribution to the poor."

Agatha knows how it looks, but she has no intention of explaining herself, even though she regrets the way Gytha withdraws into hostile silence, refusing any longer to ride at her side but trailing several, sullen yards behind so the escort is forever having to drop back to keep an eye on her. She has acted as common sense and her conscience dictate. What else could she do? If she had released the man, he would have been picked up by a royal patrol in no time. If she had handed him over to the proper authority herself the result would have been the same. A summary trial. Blinding, possibly the loss of a hand. William, of his piety, forbids the taking of life by any but God and contents himself with humbler punishments. The man is better dead. This way he is not condemned to a life of begging. His wife, if he has one, is free to marry again. His children will not starve. Her reasons are sound, yet she feels they imply criticism of Odo, the architect of William's laws, so she will keep them to herself.

Canterbury castle is a disappointing place, mean in comparison with Winchester, a simple, shabby motte and bailey construction protected to the south east by the remains of the Roman wall and on the town side by a new double palisade. Glancing up at the bailey tower through the blur of rain, Gytha forms the impression that the motte on which it stands is about to dissolve, bringing the bailey sliding down into the outer court where it will sink into the mud. The new earl must find it very mean in comparison with Lady Edith's house she thinks with satisfaction, wondering how many more of Lady Edith's possessions apart from herself have ended up here.

The bailey thatch is in need of attention, and the bailey itself affects the eye strangely due to the fact that four new windows, about twice as wide as the customary shot windows, have been cut into it half way up its height. Private apartments for the Earl, says one of their escort in answer to her query, holding her mule as she dismounts. Private apartments. She has never heard of such a thing. Not even King Harold and Lady Edith had private rooms, though their bed stood on the opposite side of the hearth from where the rest of the household and its guests slept, and the curtains were a double thickness of wool, in winter at least.

They leave their mounts at the guard house and Sister Jean leads her across the outer ward to what appears to be the only stone building in the compound. The bailey is of wooden construction, most of the buildings around the outer ward, bakehouse and kitchen, blacksmith, fletcher, mews, stables, sties and byres, of wattle and daub. It is the oddest building Gytha has ever seen, two storeys high with a tower at one end of it, like a Norman church with its watchtower. It has no windows overlooking the ward at ground floor level, but the walls of the upper storey seem to be made entirely of glass. Even in this water logged light she can see straight through from one side of the building to the other, to a further square of grey sky divided into patchwork by lancets so fine they are scarcely visible. It is as though the roof, tiled rather than thatched, hovers over the building on a cushion of air.

Sister Jean takes a latch key from the bundle hanging from her girdle and opens a wicket set in a wide, iron bound door at the opposite end of the building to the tower.

"What is this?" Gytha shivers. She's soaked through and her bones ache from the journey. She is a poor horsewoman, more accustomed to walking.

Agatha does not reply. She is happy to let the building speak for itself. It is, to her mind, beautiful and purposeful, not a stone laid but in the service of the embroidery, which she intends also to be beautiful and purposeful. She shows Gytha into the entrance hall. Tall windows, their arches decorated with chevrons, carved and brightly painted in the

Earl's livery of green and gold, give a cloistered effect. The shutters are battened against the rain but the hall is brightly lit by flares in wrought iron wall brackets. The stone of the walls, where visible, is smooth and so pale that it seems to take on completely the smoky orange glow from the flares. The walls, however, are almost entirely covered with pictures.

Some are charcoal sketches on vellum, mostly palimpsests showing blurred ghosts of their previous uses beneath the fresh drawings, others are painted on linen but unframed, their raw edges curled and fraying. So striking are they, so alive in the warm, flickering, uncertain light, that Gytha is indignant at the careless way they have been pinned up, a prey to dust and light, or the first gust of wind strong enough to rip them from the walls. They make little sense to her, showing scenes as varied as ploughing and ship building, the preparation of a banquet, a hunting party, a farmer among his vines, but it scarcely matters. They have, not beauty exactly, but a sense of authenticity that makes many works she has seen, meticulously painted, lavishly gilded, seem dead in comparison. Peering at the images as they shimmer into view, she can smell the turned earth, hear the sucking and sighing of waves and the hammering of shipwrights, taste the grapes, the way the sweet juice bursts into the back of your mouth when you press the fruit between tongue and teeth until the skins split.

"These are extraordinary. I wonder they aren't taken better care of."

"So you are a connoisseur of pictures, are you?" Sister Jean-Baptiste is leading her down the hall, but slowly, sensing her absorption.

"You don't need to know anything about art to know these are special. I've never seen anything to resemble them."

"Thank you. Although I must confess the style isn't completely original. My brother showed me a hanging in Ely Abbey that uses similar motifs for buildings, trees and the like. I think it is typical of the work of your countrymen. And there's a Pentateuch in the library at St. Augustine's Abbey here that I found most inspiring."

"These are yours then? For the hanging? They're very good." What a pity they will go to waste when Bishop Odo dies. As he will, as soon as Gytha can find the means. When God gives you a talent, an opportunity, you must use it. You have no choice.

Sister Jean-Baptiste halts before a door which she opens and stands aside for Gytha to enter. She finds herself in a dormitory containing a row of narrow box beds, each with a linen chest at its foot. The room is dark, with no natural light other than what trickles into it from the hall through a series of narrow apertures close to the ceiling. A fire burns in a brick hearth at the far end of the room, smoking a little from rain finding its way down the chimney. So that is what the tower is. Gytha has heard of chimneys, but she has never seen one before. She is sceptical of their usefulness. Surely the heat of the fire must all be sucked up the great stone chute without ever warming the room it stands in.

A deep half barrel stands before the hearth. *A bath*, thinks Gytha, feeling the longing in every cold, battered bone of her body, like the ones Adam used to make as a sideline to his coopering business, copper lined for waterproofing and insulation. They had sold quite a few of them, to the monasteries, merchants' households and the like. She turns back towards Sister Jean-Baptiste.

"But there don't seem to be any fighting scenes."

"Oh there are, I assure you. But battles are like the tip of a pyramid. One has to consider all the negotiations, misunderstandings and fallings out that lead to them, and the practical preparations. And remember that ordinary life continues to flow on around them. You are not the only one to be concerned with the truth, Gytha. Now, look at you, you're wet through. Here is a bed for you, a straw pallet only, I'm afraid, but clean. I will send in the servant to help you bathe, but don't undress yet. The men will be on their way from the bakehouse with hot water. You will find fresh clothes in the chest."

"A straw pallet only," she mutters to herself, mimicking Sister Jean's strong Norman accent as she gives the pallet a cautious prod. As if she was used to sleeping on anything else. And this at least is covered with a clean blanket, the wool fulled for warmth, a welcome luxury as the beds are clearly only intended for a single sleeper. Bishop Odo must either shit gold or not have the sense he was born with where spending it is concerned.

She peers inside the linen chest and sees, but does not touch, a starched linen cap, carefully folded undergarments and a dress of some dark, demure stuff beneath them. She crosses to the fireside and looks into the barrel, and it is indeed a bath, with a little crossbench, waiting to be filled.

As if on cue, the door opens and a girl enters, followed by a man carrying two iron cauldrons of hot water suspended from a yoke.

"You must be Gytha." She is perhaps sixteen or seventeen, a tall, big boned girl with pale, freckled skin and a mass of red gold curls pushing against the cap, identical to the one in the linen chest, balanced on top of them. *Like a dove sitting on a bush*, thinks Gytha.

"Are you the servant?"

"Me? No, I'm Margaret. My sister Alwys and I are embroiderers here. Sister Jean said to make sure you were alright. She always sends us packing when she comes back from a journey, so she can look at what we've been doing in peace, she says."

The man empties the water into the bath and takes his leave, lingering fractionally too long in the doorway. Gytha turns away, folding her arms tight across her breasts. She hates being trapped in this body that speaks a language at odds with that of her rational mind, a language so rich and complex she shrinks from the effort of translation.

"No need to wait for Leofgeat," Margaret is saying, "I'll help you. She's got a sweetheart in the bakehouse. I imagine they're dallying over the next batch of hot water. You might freeze while true love burns on the other side of the ward."

"Is it love bakes the bread and warms the water here then?" Gytha unpins her cloak and sits on the edge of her bed to remove her shoes and hose. Her feet, the skin mud stained and puckered from the wet, look like something that has been hidden under a stone.

"Hardly," says Margaret, testing the temperature of the water with her elbow. "Art," she says, straightening up and smoothing her skirt over her broad hips and round, child's belly. Her dress is of the same dark grey stuff Gytha has seen in her own linen chest, a shapeless tunic like a nun's habit, with a girdle to match from which Margaret has a thread box hanging. "Sister Jean never tires of telling us that art is the master here. Apparently it's not our skills as needlewomen, nor hers as designer, nor even the Earl's as...whatever he's good at."

Looting, thinks Gytha, *killing, imposing curfews, inflicting floggings, bundling defenceless, grief-stricken widows into carts and packing them off into oblivion. Not art, not the beautiful images pinned to the walls outside.*

"It's all art," continues Margaret. "Come on now, before the water gets cold. The others will be here in a minute."

"Others?" Gytha has pulled off her dress and, her clothes being so wet, her shift has come with it, leaving her naked. She bows her head, shaking her hair forward so that it covers her breasts, notices that her garters, stiff with water, have left livid wheals in the pads of flesh just above her knees. "What others?"

"Oh, some of the others who stay here. There are some local women who embroider vestments and things for Saint Augustine's, but the rest live here, in the castle. Alwys is coming, and Emma who's...well, you'll see, and Judith. She's a thegn's widow and never lets us forget it. We sleep in this dormitory."

"Like nuns yourselves."

"Sister Jean seems to have very particular views about us sharing beds, but we do when it gets so cold you'd rather be kicked all night than freeze. Would you like me to wash your hair for you?"

The water is hot enough to make her gasp as she slides into it, sitting a little gingerly on the crossbench, and to bring out goosebumps on the parts of her back and shoulders that remain exposed. Steam envelops her, warm tongues of water lap her aching backside and the tender skin on the backs of her thighs chafed by the saddle. Her toes tingle as the blood begins to flow back into them.

She tips back her head to wet her hair. "Why not?"

"You have such lovely hair." Margaret kneads Gytha's scalp with camomile and thyme until she feels as though a new skin is being pulled over her head. "I wish mine was straight."

"Nettle is good for straightening hair. Pound it into a paste, comb it through and leave it overnight." Gytha closes her eyes, surrenders herself to the pummelling, to the soothing gurgle of water and smells of the herbs blending with woodsmoke and hot copper. Even when she hears the door open again, and the rustle of floor rushes disturbed by several pairs of feet, she feels too lazy to be curious.

"I'm just rinsing her hair," says Margaret to the newcomers, "then we'll get her dry and dressed."

"I'm not an invalid," says Gytha idly, "I can dress myself."

"It's just something we like to do," says a strange voice, "to help make you one of us." Gytha bridles at the imperious tone. She sits up straight and opens her eyes.

The speaker is taking clothes out of the linen chest at the foot of Gytha's bed and laying them out. Gytha notices that her own small bundle of possessions has been relegated to the floor and her old clothes handed to the servant, Leofgeat, who is even now pushing them into the fire with a long poker, grumbling that the cloak is too wet to burn properly. A pile of towels has been placed beside the tub. Gytha signals impatiently to Margaret to hand her one, which she wraps around her hair, and another, with which she covers herself as she steps out of the tub.

"How can you know that I want to be one of you?" she asks. "Or that you want me to. You know nothing about me. And why is she burning my clothes? I never said anyone could burn my clothes." Unaware of how she looks, with her hair scraped back from the strong upward sweep of her cheekbones and her dark brows arched, she feels foolish and powerless, clad only in a towel and smaller than the rest of them.

"Well, you're here, aren't you?" The older woman straightens up, having completed her tirewoman's duties with the removal of a pair of dark blue hose from the chest. Indigo dyed, Gytha notices, expensive. The woman has the spare bones of a well bred horse, with pale, prominent eyes and a pursed, loveless mouth. "None of us has to be here. This is not a house of correction." She makes no reference to the burning clothes.

"After what I've seen of the mistress of this house, I wouldn't be so sure of that. I'd like to see how she'd react if any of you tried to leave." She unwinds the towel from her hair and shakes it down well below her waist.

"What do you mean?" asks the horsy woman. With a short, bitter laugh, Gytha sits on the end of the bed closest to the hearth and crosses her legs, exposing strong calves scattered with dark, silky hair. Welsh legs, her mother used to say, good for climbing hills. She looks from one to the next. Besides Margaret, Leofgeat and the horse faced woman, there are two others in the room, though Gytha has to double check this with herself because one of them, at first, and even second, glance is identical to Margaret. The sister, Alwys, she assumes, not surprised that Margaret failed to mention their being twins. Twins are nothing to boast of, even boys; Alwys' and Margaret's father was likely very grateful to have found them a place in an earl's household, even a Norman earl, even this Norman earl. It is only when she concentrates that she can tell them apart by minor variations in dress and the fact that Alwys' hair is a shade darker and a little less curly than her sister's.

The other is a mousy creature with lank hair and sallow skin bearing the pits of small pox. She also has a vigorous tic that wrenches her chin round towards her left shoulder. The muscles in the right side of her neck are oddly thickened and corded as a result. In repose, if you can call it that, she keeps her hands thrust deep into the pockets of a linen apron she wears over her dark grey dress. With this variation, all the women are dressed in the same dark tunics and white caps as Margaret. The horse faced woman has a key hanging from her girdle. *She's the one to watch, then*, thinks Gytha, Sister Jean-Baptiste's journeywoman. Judith, the thegn's widow.

"I mean, if you cross her, she might just have you shot."

"Shot?" says Margaret. "Don't be silly."

"From what I've seen, she doesn't have much respect for human life, even by Norman standards." And she tells the women the tale of the executed poacher.

A resentful silence settles over them. Everyone wishes Gytha had kept her shocking story to herself. Now they know they are prisoners. *Me and my big mouth*, thinks Gytha, *me and truth*. A self destructive relationship if ever there was one. She should carry a sprig of myrtle under her tongue, to curb its talkativeness.

"Nothing she does surprises me any more," says Alwys. "She makes us bathe once a month, whether we want to or not. You can only get out of it by saying you've got your monthly visitor. She even offered to teach Meg Latin. What would Meg need to know that for? If you ask me, she's mad."

"It's not her fault, though, is it?" says Margaret. "It was wrong of the Earl to expect her to be able to design the hanging. Women's minds aren't suited to that kind of work. I expect it's the strain of having to behave like a man."

"And she truly is the King's sister?" asks Gytha.

"Yes," Margaret replies.

"She and the Earl are his half brother and sister," says the horse faced woman. "They have the same mother."

"Judith's our authority for these things, our Book of Genesis," Margaret teases. "She's the only one of us ever to have set eyes on the Earl. He hasn't been here since any of us arrived. Judith's husband used to be something high up at court."

"King Harold's court," adds Judith, seeing the expression on Gytha's face, unaware its fall is due to the discovery that the Earl is absent from his castle rather than anything to do with her husband. Gytha's plans are going to have to wait.

"What happened to him?" she asks, wondering if she might have known him. He might well have sought refuge from a harridan like

Judith in the relaxed atmosphere of Lady Edith's household.

"He was killed just before Hastings. He was on his way to meet the King when his party was intercepted by Norman raiders."

"And yet you're here? Prostituting yourself to the Bastard's brother? Why?"

Judith's face remains impassive, though its expression seems to become more set, as though she has assumed a mask of herself, and her neck and ears flush a deep, dull pink. Margaret stops brushing Gytha's hair.

"Obviously you can't be expected to understand these things. The Earl came to me as a man of honour. He had known my husband slightly. He praised his valour and loyalty, knightly qualities in any gentleman, he said, whether he be Saxon, Norman or the Emperor of Byzantium. He understood I was skilled at fine needlework. He explained his vision to me, that he wished to make a faithful record of the actions of great men at a turning point in history. For the enlightenment of those who come after them. He thought my rank and experience would help to bring balance to the work, and that his sister would be grateful for a companion of equal status in whom to confide. He promised to make good all the damage done to our estates during the occupation, swore on the Cross to keep my husband's lands under his personal authority until my work here was finished. He even sent me some of his own men to help me get in the harvest. I believe it would have dishonoured Emeric's memory to refuse his offer."

"You dropped into his palm like a ripe plum, Judith. He'll look after your estates so he can marry you off to one of his vassals once he's finished with you himself. That's what men do with us women, they take what they want and hand us on like batons in a relay. Only the high born ones dress it up by talking about honour and reciting poetry."

"Oh, so she is one of us now, is she?" laughs Margaret.

"You're pulling my hair. Here, give me the brush. If you carry on like that I'll be bald."

"He quoted Virgil," says Judith doubtfully.

"'*Quid faciat laetas segetes, quo sidere terram uertere, Maecenas*'."

"You know Latin?" All eyes upon her now, except for the servant, Leofgeat, who is on her way to the door with a pile of wet towels. Even the one with the tic falls still. Damn. That was stupid. Nobody here must know, or even guess, her connection with King Harold.

"No, not really." She gives a dismissive shrug. "I was once in a household where the lord liked to read aloud to us in the evenings. For our improvement, he said, though personally I think it was to make us fall sound asleep so that he and my lady could enjoy one another's company undisturbed. I have a gift for remembering words, that's all. I'm not sure what it means, I just know it's something about farming."

"Why are you here, then," asks Judith, her composure recovered as Gytha found herself wrong footed, "if you're so set on defying the Normans?"

"Me? Oh, I had no choice. Now, I'd like to get dressed before I freeze all over again. I doubt even the Earl's handpicked men could be harvesting on a day like this."

The women carry her new clothes to the hearthside. Gytha unwinds her towel and stands naked in the guttering firelight, shadows licking her body, seeking out its curves and hollows, bringing roses to her skin. Outside, rain continues to lash the building, drumming on shutters, clattering against the great workshop windows, and now the wind has got up, and snarls around corners, sniffs under doors. There is a hiatus, a confusion in their ritual, as the women look at Gytha and note the line of dark hair running down the centre of her belly, forming, with her private hair, an arrow, or a tree uprooted and turned on its head. A mark of promiscuity, of otherness, of demonic knowledge.

Then, shaking her head as though trying to dislodge a disturbing dream, Alwys says she will fetch the man to empty the tub, while her sister hands Gytha her underclothes. The spell is broken. The woman with the tic, who is mute, Margaret whispers, and called Emma, helps to bind Gytha's hose with perfectly steady hands. Judith and Margaret pull the grey gown over her head and lace the sides. Finally, Emma offers her an apron like her own.

"We don't usually bother," says Margaret. "Emma only wears hers so she can keep her hands in her pockets to stop them shaking. Don't you, Emma?"

Emma smiles apologetically. Not simple as well as mute, then. Gytha takes the apron but returns it to her linen press; the apron is the badge of Emma's courage. Gytha will find something else.

Now," says Margaret, taking a step back, "let's take a look at our new novice."

Alwys returns and the women gather round Margaret, staring frankly at Gytha, who stands beside her bed, now identical to them in her plain tunic. Yet each of them is acutely aware of something hidden, panting in the shadows like an animal at bay. The sexual authority of her little waist and broad hips, the curve of breasts and thighs suggested by the fall of the fine wool, is like another presence in the room; a satyr exulting in the gift of permanent erection, a cunt carved on a church doorpost to ward off the Devil. Nobody says a word.

"Is something wrong? I should braid my hair but it isn't dry yet." She winds her hair into a rope and coils it on top of her head, only to let it fall again.

"Perfect," says a voice from the doorway. How long has Sister Jean been standing there? "Perhaps you would like to see our workshop now." She feels, as she follows Sister Jean along the hall and up the stairs to the workshop, as if she has forgotten something. But what is there to forget? The white cockade, somewhat squashed? The locket? Let them stay hidden in her bundle, for now. What she needs to remember will not be forgotten.

ODO'S DREAM

ADVENT TO SAINT STEPHEN'S DAY 1070

Gytha winces as she pushes her needle through the stretched linen. She cannot withhold a sharp intake of breath, making Margaret glance up at her. Margaret is acutely aware of everything Gytha does or says. She feels that, having been the first of the women to meet her on her arrival in Canterbury, she and Gytha are bound by a special tie. Sister Jean is always chopping and changing the pairings of embroiders at each frame, probably, Gytha says, in part for the same reason that she advocates sleeping singly, but Margaret wishes she could always work with Gytha. She is content with Alwys, of course; they have done their sewing together since they were little girls, sitting with their mother and the other women of the household, practising their stitches on worn out shirts while their elders mended, patched, hemmed or embroidered. But Gytha is different. She is as bold and funny as a boy, always telling jokes that make Judith's ears turn pink and her thin lips purse as though she has drunk verjuice. Yet she is mysterious, shying suddenly and inexplicably at questions most people would answer without a second thought.

"Chilblains," Gytha says. "We must be in for snow." She looks out of the window, across the narrow strip of garden separating them from the outer palisade, and up at the sky, which seems almost to be in the room with them, kept out only by sheer walls of glass. Dirty pink cloud hangs low and swollen. The light has a grudging quality. "We shall be finishing early today." They work only during the hours of daylight. Candles are forbidden in the workshop because of the risk of fire.

"My brother Tom used to get chilblains. Our stepmother would cover his hands in goose grease and oil of henbane. It made him smell like a jakes." She giggles. "And he was so particular about his looks. He was very good looking." Her eyes shine.

Margaret prattles about her dead brothers as though they were still alive, just away on a journey perhaps, or grown up and making independent lives for themselves far from home. She seems to feel no sense of loss. Is it, Gytha wonders, that she is somehow protected by the presence of her twin, or because she had years in which to get to know them? Not days, or even hours, before their spirits deserted her.

"I hate the winters here," Margaret continues, as though Tom has never been mentioned, "there's nothing to do."

Gytha knows what she means. Though the work of the household goes on around them, they are not part of it. They are observers, as though their windows were frames around a picture or a tapestry. In the outer court today, for example, pigs are being slaughtered. Their squeals and the raised voices of the slaughterers, the barking of excited dogs and wickers of nervous horses reach them muffled by the glass. They cannot smell the blood as it is drained off into barrels where it will be left to thicken for making black puddings, but only their own, for someone is always menstruating and, as no-one is pregnant or nursing, Sister Jean sees no reason for this to excuse them from work.

"What about that blond boy from the garrison? Can't you pass the evening teasing him after dinner? I saw him looking at you all doe eyed when you were coming back from Mass this morning." From these same windows, foreshortened, in the world on the other side of the glass, attempting to pinch Margaret's waist before Sister Jean sent him packing. Gytha does not go to Mass.

"Oh, it's Advent," says Margaret dismissively, though she is blushing, blotches of scarlet suffusing her freckles and clashing with her hair. "I never trust boys in Advent or Lent." The longest periods of fasting and abstention prescribed by the Church, which Gytha used to look forward to when she was married, though not when she was whoring and had to take on the work pious wives could lay aside.

"Gytha, are you married?" asks Margaret, glancing up then quickly affecting deep concentration on her work.

"Widowed."

Margaret waits, carefully couching down the rump of a horse, laying a second run of stitching over the ground to achieve a density of texture such that, in patting the chestnut hindquarters, you might almost raise dust and feel real horse hair. They are so close, on either side of the narrow frame, less than the width of a man's stride, that she can see the grain of Gytha's linen cap and hear, almost feel, her breathing as she continues to work but does not elaborate on the subject of her marriage.

Margaret sleeps next to her in the dormitory, with Alwys at her other side, and has taken to creeping in beside her on cold nights, curling her soft, blowsy body around Gytha's little frame. She knows Alwys feels left out, but Alwys is the younger sister, by the width of a nail their father says, holding his finger against the side of a burning candle, so she will have to get used to being on her own because Margaret will marry first.

She and Gytha wash each other's hair at the monthly baths, when Gytha applies the nettle paste and wraps Margaret's head in a warmed towel to make it work more quickly. Every time Margaret unwinds the towel, her hair is as springy as before, but every month her dream of straight, silky locks is rekindled and they try again. After all, Alwys' curls do not frizzle like hers do, as though they have been singed; Alwys' hair cascades, like water stained red by running over rocks with iron in them. Gytha's attentiveness makes Margaret feel like a separate person, not just one of the twins, part of a set like a pair of matching candlesticks or a couple of hounds. Tom had the same knack, a special way of looking at her, always standing up for her when she and Alwys fell out. He made her feel unique. Though she is ashamed to admit it, she has always missed Tom more than the others, but now Gytha has come into her life, she has begun to feel less lonely.

Margaret has learned that cats make Gytha sneeze, and that she sews with her left hand, but little more. Gytha never talks about her life before the invasion the way the other women do, though occasionally she will make some remark about the work she is doing which intrigues Margaret. Once she said, as she worked the wing feathers of a falcon, laying dense rows of ochre inside a terracotta outline, "King Harold always carried his hawk on his right wrist, you know. Obviously Sister Jean is unaware of it. I'll change the next one round."

"How do you know that?" demanded Judith, seated opposite, her sharp nose fairly quivering with curiosity.

Gytha shrugged. "I suppose you must have told me, you were at court."

Judith continued to stare at her intensely, but Gytha shifted her attention back to her work as though their exchange was already forgotten.

Now she says, "I'm still alive and still whole. Being alone is best. Think of your poor parents, Meg, four sons dead and two daughters sent into slavery. Or Emma, taken away from her husband and children. How many is it?"

"Five, I think, but it's hard to tell if she misses them. You see things too much in black and white. I'm not a slave, slavery's illegal now, isn't it? And thankfully, my parents aren't so far away that I couldn't go home if I needed to."

"You're as bad as Judith. Pass me some more of that blue will you? I'm running short."

Margaret twists round to reach the wooden stand behind her, from which skeins hang from dowel pegs set in the cross pieces, and unwinds a length of the blue grey wool Gytha is using. A similar stand is beside each frame, each with eight pegs to carry skeins of each of the eight colours the embroiderers are using: terracotta red, blue woad, a deep blue-black derived from indigo, sea-green and sage-green, ochre yellow, yellow weld and a dark, yew green produced by over-dying. Gytha finds it curious, remembering the procession of Bishop Odo's soldiers stripping Lady Edith's hall of its treasures, that the materials for the hanging should be so plain. No silk thread or baudekyn, no gold or silver wires to cut and roughen the fingertips, just simple running stitch, wool on white linen, like making tablecloths.

"Enough?" queries Margaret before cutting the thread with the small bone knife hanging from her girdle by a plaited leather thong.

"You believe you're free, but your father wasn't really given any choice in the matter, was he?" Gytha continues, pausing to suck the end of the wool to a point so she can thread it through the eye of her needle. "When Sister Jean came to call on his new Norman lord with her royal warrant and her royal blood, I imagine his lordship rolled over like a puppy to have his belly tickled by our mighty and mysterious Earl. Look at you. What are you? Nineteen, twenty? You should be married and raising a family of your own by now, not cooped up in here day after day." She stabs her into the fetlock of a Norman war horse. "Mary Mother of God, my hands are cold."

A fire blazes in the hearth set into the chimney breast, a larger version of the one in the dormitory, the crackle of seasoned logs punctuating the murmur of conversation among the women, but little heat escapes into the room. In considering the design of the building, Bishop Odo's first concern was clearly to preserve his hanging from smoke and fire rather than to keep the embroiderers warm.

Sister Jean has a plan, on parchments, pasted together into a long strip, laid out on her work table beneath the north windows facing the courtyard, its top edge carefully measured and annotated. Gytha looks at it, when the rest are at Mass, but it is always changing. Every morning there is something different, a newly scraped bare patch or the addition of some figure or marginal design. She almost believes fairies come during the night and meddle with it. She can read enough Latin, thanks to her years as a lay sister and then in the household of Lady Edith, who was an educated woman, to decipher the captions Sister Jean has added to some of the images, but many are not captioned and in others the words are ambiguous.

The mystery is compounded by the way Sister Jean makes them work. The embroidery does not follow the order of the plan, nor any order recognisable as that of the events they have all lived through. One day horses falling in battle, the next King William and his brothers commissioning ships to be built; a morning on Saxon peasants pursued by Norman knights wielding whips, an afternoon on the exploits of Harold fighting alongside William against Conan of Brittany, heroically rescuing a man from drowning in a river writhing with giant eels. Some days working upside down before switching sides with your partner and seeing the strange world of wool and linen the right way up again. These partnerships also are ever changing, the women switching from one frame to another as they complete a figure or a scene.

They are a small group, only eighteen women who meet Sister Jean's exacting standards, working at nine frames set up on trestles in front of the great south facing windows. The frames, about half the length of a tall man, might just accommodate four workers each, but Sister Jean does not seem disposed to seek out any more. Clearly the quality of the work matters more to her than the speed of its completion. Gytha also suspects that her choice has been limited by the fact that much of the north of the country remains too dangerous for anyone but the army to enter.

Everyone prefers to work with the outlines sketched in charcoal on the linen right way up, but Gytha is less insistent than most. She has plenty to occupy her thoughts when she is defeated in her efforts to understand the intentions of the design. Dwelling on her intention to have her revenge on the bishop, as though by ceaselessly thinking about it she is somehow moving her plan forward, she goes over and over in her mind what she knows of the castle, its weak spots and hidden places, the access to the private apartments, the aspect of their windows. It is pitifully little. The women's movements are strictly circumscribed by Sister Jean, to keep them well apart from the garrison, Gytha supposes. Apart from going to chapel and taking their meals in the great hall in the bailey, they rarely leave the atelier.

Most of what they know of their surroundings is framed by the great workshop windows. Even Gytha cannot help but marvel at them, these sheer glass cliffs supported by lancets so fine and pale you would think they must crumble beneath the weight of glass. The walls of the workshop seem to be made of light, taut and insubstantial as a held breath. Sometimes she wonders whose vision they were, the bishop's or his architect's. Sometimes she catches herself off guard, revelling in their sparkle and purity, the unblemished panes couched flat in their leads, the flow of light lying cool as water against her eyes or, when the sun is out, warm as a lover's hand in the small of her back.

Slowly, often imperceptibly, it seems, the bolts of virgin linen shrink and the lengths of completed embroidery grow, carefully pleated into shallow baskets lying beside each frame, but the slowness reinforces Gytha's sense of dislocation. Here in Canterbury she had believed she would be able to find out Lady Edith's fate, that she would be at the core of her loathing for all things Norman. Yet the man who is the focus of her hatred is never here, the rumours of his whereabouts slipping through her fingers like wet fish. He is in London, or Normandy, or Rome. He has led an army to the north or a deputation of clergy to Flanders. He is like a sprite, this earl-bishop, a thing of shadows and whispers, a spell, a fever of the brain.

Yet the embroidery is real enough, the wool stinking of the sheep's piss used to set the dyes, the linen taut as drumskins in the frames, men and horse, ships and city walls emerging from the tangle of needles and thread and charcoal lines as the world came out of Chaos. Though a great deal more slowly. It can take a week or more to complete a single suit of mail, overlapping the stitches so densely that you can almost imagine the woollen replica would offer as much protection as the real thing, building up ring by ring the fishscale effect that sometimes reminds Gytha of accompanying her father to the early morning market, his great red, gentle hands lifting the gills of the fish to test their freshness. And you can eke out the process further by snapping needles, knotting threads, rubbing out Sister Jean's guidelines so mistakes ensue and have to be unpicked.

Last winter, Gytha lost track of the time she and Margaret spent embroidering the image of a Norman abbey called, according to Sister Jean's legend, Mont Saint Michel, its dainty arches balanced on a folded hill of sage green and ochre, its roof ridged with yellow gold, a place impossible outside the imagination of God yet built by these two, with their aching backs and smarting, fingers stiff with cold, their tips swollen with chilblains like overripe plums. Even if they could work the complete cycle of the hours, without stopping for food or rest, the project might take so many years its patron would be in his grave before it was complete. With only the most subtle of interruptions, Gytha knows, letting her sleeve smudge the outline of a hunting dog as she threads her needle, it need never be finished.

"Attend me." Agatha is standing at the lectern where she often reads to the women to help pass the hours. She elbows the cat off the lectern and brushes stray fur from Horace's Odes, in her own, somewhat rough Anglo Saxon translation, before opening a parchment and smoothing it out before her. "I have received a letter from the Earl," she continues, "in which he tells me it is his intention, by the grace of God and King William, to hold Christmas court here at Canterbury this year. Naturally he regrets that he will not be with the King at his mid winter crown wearing, but is acutely aware that the King's business has kept him out of Canterbury for almost three years and that his estates in Kent require his attention. My lord looks forward particularly, he writes, to inspecting what he calls his tapestry." She looks up with a conspiratorial smile. "My Lord's grasp of the refinements of needlework is, I fear, somewhat tenuous." There is a murmur of obsequious laughter from one of the Saint Augustine's women, but the rest remain silent.

Agatha continues, "He expects, God willing, to arrive here by the Feast of Saint Thomas and will stay at least until Saint Stephen's Day before beginning a tour of his manors."

Not long, thinks Gytha, slowly laying down her needle, but long enough. Her hand moves to the little bone knife hanging from her own belt, just as Margaret's does. If it could cut the underhung venison they had been given at the day meal yesterday, it will surely serve to cleave the pampered flesh of a bishop from his bones. All she needs is a dark corner of the hall, a narrow space of mud and shadow between the buildings in the outer court, a moment off guard. And she knows just how to catch a man off guard.

What then? When it is done? She gives a mental shrug of the shoulders. It does not matter. She has been dead inside since the moment she collapsed, paralysed with fear, against the wall of the priory hospice in Winchester, and watched her mistress carried off in a wagon as though she were no more than the cups and plates and tapestries from her hall. Where her heart used to be is only the desire for revenge, her veins are threaded with hate, burning like hot wires. Let them do as they will with her body, she has no further use for it.

"Might it be possible for me to speak to the Earl about my estates, do you think, Sister?" Judith is asking, in the tone she keeps for Sister Jean, intended to remind listeners that she and the King's sister are equals.

Agatha gives her a tolerant smile. Gytha is looking very pale, she thinks, hoping her workshop will not be decimated by sickness by the time Odo arrives. This will be the first time he has set foot in the atelier since overseeing the installation of the windows and she is anxious that he should be pleased by what he sees. His trust in her still terrifies her. Often she feels as though she is not quite in control of the embroidery, as though it is growing in unanticipated ways, like a child rebelling against the authority of its father.

"His lordship takes a close interest in the management of all his business, Judith," she replies. "I do not think you need be concerned that he will have neglected to ensure your husband's holdings yield all that they should."

"It's for my grandsons in Denmark, you see..." Her words tail off into a lame silence as Sister Jean's smile freezes.

Odo is in no mood for Christmas. His damaged wrist aches in damp weather, a nagging pain that gnaws at the edges of consciousness, leaving him irritable and frustrated with his physical limitations. He is approaching the age when a man's blood starts to thicken and slow his body down; his inclinations and his abilities are increasingly at odds. The journey from London has been intolerably slow, the road sometimes a quagmire and sometimes a frozen sea of ruts and craters. He prefers to travel light and quickly, in the company of small groups of knights and men at arms. Certain journeys, however, have purposes in addition to that of leaving one place and arriving safely at another. They are freighted with significance.

The really heavy wagons left several days in advance of the main party, carrying wine and provisions, furnishings, tableware, several litters of pups too young to make the journey on foot, and Master Pietro, the Italian pastrycook whose girth reassures Odo as to his professional skills but makes riding a practical impossibility. Odo's hawks travelled in a specially designed cart, a wheeled cage containing a perch for each bird, though their handler had to sit in its bed and endure being shat on by the unsettled birds. Further wagonloads of Odo's personal effects, his clothes and jewellery, his sacramental plate, as well as his treasury and various official seals, all under heavy guard, set the pace for the main party. This was as carefully orchestrated as any of William's public crown wearings, and served a similar purpose. After conquest comes occupation, says William.

Odo himself, surrounded by the lords and senior clergy of his entourage, his standard bearer at his shoulder and his midget, Turold, beside him on one of the tiny ponies William discovered in Scotland, rode at the centre of the procession, preceded by a body of knights and his personal praetorian guard in his new green and gold livery. A seemingly endless trail of cooks, varlets, concubines, laundresses, body servants, chaplains, huntsmen, dogs, horses and their handlers, brought up the rear. Outside every town or village en route, the entire party ground to a halt as the varlets were sent ahead to strew the way with brush and straw to make the going easier, and alert the people to the impending spectacle. The musicians would be assembled and thrust up front to provide an accompaniment to their lord's progress and entertain the spectators. Balanced on the shaggy back of his pony, the dwarf would perform rolls and handstands. Odo had also devised other distractions; the release of white doves from baskets, the distribution of wheat loaves or silver pennies stamped with his image as Earl of Kent. This is the part of the planning he enjoys, for the rest he relies on Osbern.

Osbern, who holds no official status in the household other than that of being Odo's body servant, nevertheless understands its workings so intimately that he acts almost in place of the chamberlain. He directs his master's relocations with a strategic skill and attention to detail at least as thorough, thinks Odo, a little disconcerted, as his own. Throughout these progresses he is invaluable, able to conjure billets from the most unpromising communities. He can cajole the surliest prior into letting them overrun his hospice and is equally accomplished in shielding his master from the worst excesses of obsequious vassals who seem only too pleased to let their households go hungry and bedless in order to accommodate the Earl and his entourage.

The rigours of the journey are not the source of his wretched humour. On the whole, it has gone well. There have been no attempts at robbery, no broken axles. The onlookers tended to be sullen, but not openly hostile as has happened in the past; no blood has been shed. The enfolding warmth and good odours of meat roasting in his own kitchens after days on the road do not account for his lassitude as he sits in his winter parlour above the kitchen and Osbern directs the unpacking around him.

Lanfranc is the problem. Everything he wrote to Agatha is true, but Lanfranc is the real reason he is not spending this Christmas with William. He still feels stunned by William's decision to appoint the Lombard to the Archbishopric. He had been so certain of his brother's mind, and so certain that, even if offered the appointment, Lanfranc would refuse it, as he has steadfastly refused everything William has tried to lavish upon him other than the abbacy of Caen, that he had never even thought to articulate his expectation. But now, suddenly, unexpectedly as a crossbow bolt from out of the sun, this fissure has opened up between them. William, his duke and benefactor, the older brother he adores and looks up to beyond the power of words to express, has let him down.

Surely he was the obvious choice, already combining his ecclesiastical responsibilities in Normandy with his lay lordships in England, and with an administration established in Canterbury. If William wished to ensure a minimum of papal interference in the government of the church in England, how better to do it than to combine church and state in the person of a single man, and that man his brother and close confidant, and one of his strongest supporters in his English venture? Fluent in the language, moreover, and well versed in English culture and mores. By bestowing the See of Canterbury on a member of his own family, William would have sent the clearest possible message to the English about the concentration of power both spiritual and temporal in the person of their new king and the men of his blood.

And then, in the spring, when Thomas, formerly a canon of his own cathedral in Bayeux, came to England to be made Archbishop of York, William had said, casually, over the welcome feast at Dover, with his mouth full of roast pigeon,

"I'd like to delay the consecration for a month or two. I've asked Lanfranc to take on Canterbury, but he can't be here before the summer. It would send out the right message if Thomas' consecration was reserved to him. I hope you agree, Odo."

"Lanfranc?" he demanded, almost choking on his own food. "Lanfranc? He'll never come."

"Why do you think that? The delay is only while he puts his affairs in order at Caen. He has given his word, and Lanfranc does not go back on his word. Besides, I have ordered it."

"I thought he was your friend. I suppose a king must command even his friends."

"Beware, brother." And immediately he understood William's decision. Lanfranc was discreet, diplomatic. He remembered his station the way a dog remembers a rabbit hole. Whereas he himself, though just as good a jurist, just as persuasive and possibly a better administrator, was also flamboyant and restless, cursed with a passionate imagination which sometimes blinded him to things as they were. His understanding brought him no peace, it only embittered his disappointment, but he was wise enough to dissemble and couch his objections in terms of pure political expediency. William had greeted his protests with smiling disbelief.

"You, Odo? It was never in my mind. You are my Justiciar, you guard me against all comers along the south coast. Splendour of God, man, you even rule in my place when I'm overseas. Are there no bounds to your ambition?"

"I want only what is best for Your Grace," he had replied, laying his knife carefully beside his plate, suddenly not hungry. "I haven't once failed in your service nor questioned your decisions since I was a boy. You cannot doubt my loyalty, but I am your brother, which I think gives me the right to speak freely. Lanfranc is a churchman through and through. If it comes to it, he will support the Pope against you."

"You disobeyed me once only, as far as I can remember, and I forgave you then, as I forgive you now. Tell me, Odo, this business with Lanfranc, what is it all about? Did he have you beaten once too often when you studied at Bec? Or perhaps not often enough. He is my friend, and a man of the utmost virtue and integrity, without whose good offices, I might remind you, we probably wouldn't be here at all. It wasn't until he went to Rome and got us the Pope's backing I was able to raise an army."

"You had my ships, William, a hundred of them and all the men they could carry. I didn't wait to be told what to do by the Pope. I risked my soul to fight beside you. I didn't skulk in Normandy saying my prayers or loiter behind the lines with my altar boys like Coutances. *Ja bon vassal nen ert vif recreut.*"

William had embraced him then, with tears in his eyes, pressing his greasy mouth to Odo's cheek, and Odo found himself fascinated once again by how easily words came to him, billowing out of him like a smokescreen to conceal his feelings.

"And you are a good vassal, the best. And my gratitude is beyond measure, Odo, as I hope I have always shown. Here, drink. This is really very good." Offering Odo his own cup, the rim carefully turned so that he must place his lips over the imprint of his brother's. Odo drank.

"Lanfranc may be my friend," went on William, "but you are my flesh and blood. Which is why I don't want to see you torn between Rome and me. We are one, Odo. Let it remain so."

Of course it is so, he had wanted to shout, it will always be so. He has adored William since the moment he first set eyes on him, himself a boy of ten or eleven years, William then eighteen, tall, powerfully built, the shock of red hair blazing in the dim light of the great hall at Conteville. Since his father said,

"Here is your brother, Odo, Duke William of Normandy," and had then fetched him a good clout about the head because he stood gaping and forgot to kneel. And William had laughed and hugged him, pressing his smarting cheek against the hard body beneath its leather hauberk, and said,

"I have brought you a merlin, Odo. I'm told you like to hunt. So do I. We will hunt together."

His own hawk. As if he were a man, not just a boy kicking about among the varlets. As if the young duke, god-like in his glamour, heroic as Roland in his feats of arms and narrow escapes from his enemies, were admitting him to the pantheon.

As for William, he keeps his feelings close, as though they were his most dangerous enemies, but Odo knows how much he is needed. Weaving and shouldering his way through the press of people in the hall on his arrival, sidestepping a nasty altercation between one of the castle dogs and a hound he had brought with him from London, he had noticed that the clerk to whom he usually entrusts his correspondence with his brother was already waiting for him, a bulging satchel slung across his shoulder.

"My Lord." Osbern is hovering in front of him with a surcoat of yellow silk edged with ermine draped across his outstretched arms. "Will you dress for the ladies now?"

Odo passes his hand across his face, as though trying to erase his bitter recollections from his features. "Yes," he says, "but not that, not for Sister Jean's women."

He is soberly dressed, in a long tunic of deep blue trimmed only with squirrel, when he leaves his apartments in the bailey and, descending the motte cautiously to avoid slipping on the steep, muddy slope, passes through the gate in the inner ward on his way to the atelier. His only concession to outward show is the gold pectoral cross set with pearls and sapphires. Osbern has certain notions about how men should dress to please women, and his instincts are often, in Odo's experience, shrewd. The women Osbern is thinking of, however, bear no resemblance to Agatha and her group of quasi-nuns. He has been amused, when approving accounts for payment, to note that she has purchased cloth similar to that used for making monastic habits for her women's clothes, their livery. Snow is falling briskly; flakes catch in his hair and sting his newly shaved tonsure.

Entering the building, he sends the page ahead to announce him to his sister and waits in the hall, strolling up and down its length, looking at the mass of sketches and cartoons pasted to the walls, stopping frequently to peer at a particular piece of work. Many of them he has seen before, but not all, and even those he has have been thrust to the back of his mind in the intervening years, so it is like seeing them as new.

More than that, seeing them as though he himself is someone different.

Here, a little smudged and grimy with ash from the torches on the wall, is an image of himself, round cheeked and boyish looking, blessing the feast they held to celebrate their landing at Pevensey. Memory, imagination, the way events are changed by the process of translation from one person to another, all peel away to nothing like the layers of an onion. What's real? The tables made of shields balanced on scaffolding poles, the Roman fort looming against the sky as the light drained away, the ill grace with which the men set to reinforcing it, exhausted, hungry and still hampered by their sea legs. But where's the sand sticking to the food or the sharp onshore wind that bit off his prayers as he uttered them? Where is the fear sucking his still nauseous stomach up against his ribs whenever he looked at William, eating heartily, cheerfully likening himself to Caesar, who had also lost his footing and fallen, when disembarking on the coast of Africa? How can Agatha ever have imagined he was smiling like that? Or that they had time to bake bread? At least she has left out William's fall from the *Mora*, that sickening, incredible moment when everyone who witnessed it united in yearning to be able to wind back time, to erase such an omen from the record. Perhaps he never told her about it, he can't remember.

"So, my dear lord, all these pictures and I find you studying yourself." There is just enough humour in that dry tone to soften the blow, though not to deflect it from the target. Odo blushes.

"I wasn't..."

"Welcome home." Agatha kneels to kiss his ring. The wrist, as she had predicted, has healed badly, the bone now lying at an odd angle. He raises her to her feet and enfolds her little frame in his arms, then holds her away from him.

"You look well, thank God."

"I am. Now that we are settled here, this work keeps me out of the world and out of trouble just as well as the Rule of Saint Benedict. Although the sisters are a mite more unruly."

"Are they, indeed?"

"Nothing I can't handle, though there's one…But the women aren't your concern. You're here to see your 'tapestry'."

"And I've come to you before seeing to any other business. There's a queue of petitioners half a league long in the hall, they tell me, and Hamo says my knights are putting up too many tents in the court so he can't move the garrison out. I don't know what he's afraid of. Perhaps he thinks Archbishop Lanfranc has designs on my earldom."

"And my servant, Leofgeat, whose husband works in the bakehouse, says your fancy Roman pastrycook is likely to get his sweetbreads battered if he can't keep his hands to himself."

"D'you think I could hide out here among your seamstresses till Saint Stephen's?" Laughing together, they climb the stairs to the atelier.

Despite the snow clouds and the early beginnings of the winter dusk, he is momentarily dazzled as Agatha holds back the curtain and he steps into the workshop. It is like a concussion, no, more a glimpse of heaven. He had not forgotten the windows; the slender lancets of creamy Caen stone, the fine tracery of lead, the lights flawless as diamonds conjured from fire and sand, shine in his memory. He had just forgotten the physical impact of beauty, how it makes the pulse race and the blood sing. His life at William's court, always in the company of soldiers and politicians, has become mean and narrow. He hears nothing but dispatches and petitions for his patronage, talks of nothing but the last campaign or the next rebellion, the clearance of a road here or the construction of a fortification there; even the mystery of the sacraments has been soured for him by the thought of Lanfranc. Enthralled by the expanse of white sky reflecting the snow covered earth back at itself, he gasps, like of a man in the throes of passion, making the women look up from their work.

He will not know her, Gytha reassures herself, of course he will not, after so many seasons, so many towns occupied, halls looted, women and children killed. But if she lets him see her face he will recognise her loathing, sleek and fattened on its own bile, like the serpent endlessly consuming its own tail. She busies herself with the little page, making sure he has his feet properly on the hearth where his shoes stand the best chance of drying, then returns to her stool with her head bowed and her face turned aside. He will think her modest and seemly, if he thinks of her at all.

"Attend me," Sister Jean orders the women, coming to stand beside her brother, the top of her head reaching just below his shoulder, "here is our lord and patron, the Earl of Kent." Gytha notices how carefully Sister Jean announces his title, as though she is not yet quite used to it, her Norman tongue struggling with the Anglo Saxon *earl*. Stealing a glance from the corner of her eye, Gytha sees him incline his head slightly towards the women, a gesture of teasing charm. Stools scrape along the floor, releasing the perfume of the dried lavender strewn among the rushes, as the women stand and bow. Emma almost falls; she lunges at her frame to prevent herself, but it wobbles on its trestles and would have overturned had not her sewing partner, on the other side, reached out to steady it. Bishop Odo watches this pantomime with a puzzled frown.

Briefly, he glances in Gytha's direction, and once again she has the sense of not being seen. It is her failure to bow he notices, not her. Then he whispers something to Sister Jean, who nods and they smile at each other, the same downturned smile, the same humorous crinkling of the eyes at the corners.

"Will you inspect the embroidery, your grace?" Sister Jean enquires.

"That would please me very much."

"You may sit," she instructs the women. "Resume your work." Then, turning to her brother, she asks, "where will you begin?"

"Here, I think," he decides, striding across the workshop to Emma's frame. He stands behind Emma for several minutes, his expression shifting from relief to wonder as he observes how still she becomes once her needle is in her hand, and the excellence of her work, the faces she embroiders which have almost more life in them than the flesh and blood she emulates with needle and thread.

As Judith sees him heading in her direction, she lays down her needle, rises once again from her stool and kneels to kiss his ring, all in a single, fluent movement. *Every inch the courtier*, thinks Gytha, bowing and scraping to some man or other from the moment she could walk.

"May I speak, madam?" Judith asks Sister Jean.

"Please," says the bishop.

"Thank you, My Lord, you are very gracious. It is the matter of my estates, My Lord..."

"His grace has no time for such trifles now, Judith."

"It's alright, sister." The gaze he fixes on Judith glows with sincerity. "All that I have promised will come to pass, madam, I assure you. Now...where next?"

As he turns away, Gytha sees the light extinguished, snuffed out by hard indifference.

"Here, I think," he concludes, advancing on her and Alwys. Gytha lays down her needle across the image of Earl Harold swearing fealty to the Bastard, her hands trembling too much to continue. He is so close, neither armed nor surrounded by guards, just himself, a man like any other, with veins that can be emptied, lungs punctured, heart broken. Her wait is nearly over, all the patient hours and days and years of bones that ached with the yearning for vengeance and eyes seared by the images of his triumph have come to a halt this snowy afternoon. She folds her hands in her lap and bows her head. She thinks of Christmas; her time, like Mary's, has almost come.

A half remembered scent of rosemary and sandalwood envelops her as he leans over her shoulder to inspect her work, his gaze coming to rest on the image of Harold, hands outstretched to touch the reliquary shrines, the city of Bayeux rising steeply behind the Bastard on his throne. The scent makes her dizzy, her palms begin to sweat.

She has been working for many days on Earl Harold's hands; Sister Jean often chooses her for the most intricate work. But, inexplicably, this time she has been unable to follow Sister Jean's drawing. On the shrine closest to Duke William, the one to which the duke points and

Harold's gaze is directed, instead of the flat of his palm, he rests only two fingers, the others curled under in a fist, just as if he were pointing back at the duke, accusing him of something. Perhaps the light was poor, or the charcoal smudged. She offered to redo her work, though she knew Sister Jean would let it pass; she does not want her great design transformed into a soiled rag of unpicked stitch holes.

But he won't, he has an eye for detail, he lets nothing pass. He will have Gytha dismissed. Her chance will have passed before even coming into being. Like the lives of her children. She picks up her needle; if she cannot have the man himself, she can at least indulge herself in the small pleasure of stabbing his image right in front of his eyes. That will not be lost on him either. And perhaps, who knows, it may work the way stabbing wax dollies or burning straw men works. There are all kinds of ways of procuring a man's downfall.

"You have made Bayeux very pretty," he remarks, an edge to his voice which makes it sound as though the prettification of Bayeux is some kind of misdemeanour. "Quite a fairy city."

Gytha stares at the scene, needle suspended, eyes raking the outlines of charcoal and wool. Where is he? Surely he is there. This is his city, the shrines come from his cathedral. Surely he was present to deliver the *coup de grace*. They are such great hunters, these Normans, with their acres of forest suddenly off limits to people who have depended on its bounty for generations. Surely he must have been in for the kill.

"If I had drawn it as it is," Sister Jean replies, "I doubt it would have impressed the eye as you would wish."

But he is not there. No sign of him, not a smudge or a shade that might be made to resemble him. Not a ghost, not a trace. Gytha lays down her needle again with a sigh of vexation.

"You may carry on working," says Sister Jean. "His lordship wishes it."

"His lordship is in my light."

Although the normal low hubbub of the workshop has already been silenced by Bishop Odo's presence, now the silence thickens, settles over the women like a fog as their breath freezes in their chests and their hands fall motionless over their work.

The bishop stares at Gytha, disbelieving, expectant, as though waiting for her to repeat herself so he can be sure he heard her aright. Sister Jean raises her eyes to heaven, her lips moving as she offers up a silent prayer. Suddenly he smiles. Perhaps her prayer has been answered.

"Forgive me," he says to Gytha, who glares back at him as though she has failed to detect the touch of sarcasm in his tone.

As the other women sit with eyes downcast, as modesty dictates in the presence of a man who is not a relation, Gytha thinks of each of them in turn. Of Judith and her exiled grandsons, of Emma torn from her family and Meg and Alwys and their four dead brothers. Of herself and her skill with a needle, and how he has appropriated even that from her for his own ends. Summoning all their losses into her eyes, she gives stare for stare.

Until Bishop Odo's smile fades, and, turning smartly on his heel, he stalks out of the workshop with Sister Jean and the little page hurrying behind him.

"Well really," says Judith once they are out of earshot, "there'll be no chance of my talking to him about my estates now."

"Oh shut up, Judith," snaps Margaret.

Alwys shakes her head in wonder. "He didn't know what to say to you." She looks across at Gytha, her green flecked eyes round as patens. "You beat him, Gytha."

Gytha shrugs. "Women have their tongues, men have everything else." But inside she is exultant. A victory, a victory, chants her heart, though her mind tells her it is only a small one, and the real challenge will be to build on it.

"God forgive me, but damn, and double damn." Agatha slams the door to her parlour and leans back, pressing her palms flat against the sturdy panels to stop her hands shaking. "I'll get rid of her, Odo, I'm so sorry.

I can't imagine what she was thinking of."

He is standing with his back to her, apparently studying the drawings and wool samples on the worktable beneath her parlour window, shuffling them about beneath his fingers. Agatha is irritated by the gritty whisper of parchment against the fine coating of sand from her caster. "No," he says, his voice uncharacteristically hesitant.

"Well, she would be a great loss. With such small hands she is second to none when it comes to very fine stitching. If you don't mind..."

"I thought I'd get used to it," he interrupts, turning to face her, "the hatred in their eyes. Or that they'd come to hate us less once they realised we meant to abide by law and order. But I haven't, and they don't. Just some little jade of a seamstress with a sharp tongue, and look how she affects me." He is her little brother again, his honey brown eyes full of hurt and bewilderment. I'm to be a priest, he had protested, sitting beside her on the bank of the moat at Conteville, putting his hands over hers to correct her hold on her fishing rod, William is sending me to Bec. Can't you stop him? This is where I belong. Sweeping out his free arm to embrace the rambling house with its tangled string of yards and gardens, its orchard and pasture, the village and its common full of tethered goats, beehives and stiff-legged chickens, fringed with cultivated strips of green and brown and the silky silver of bean plants. Of course not, she had replied, casting her line again, William is like winter. Harsh, inevitable, to be endured.

"I'll not have any of the women in my atelier 'affecting' you, Odo." She narrows her eyes at him. "You were first among those advising William to take this course of action, you should have considered what it would mean for you. For all of us."

"It is God's will William should be king of this place. The Blessed Edward promised it. How should I stand by and let Godwinson have it by deceit?"

"Oh, God's will is it, bishop?"

"Sarcasm is unseemly in a woman," he snaps.

"There are a great many things in me that are unseemly in women," she snaps back. "You must take me as you find me, or pack me off back to Saint Justina's."

Suddenly he smiles. "How could I possibly do that, when you have created such a wonder for me up there?" He glances up in the direction of the workshop above them.

"Oh, Odo, do you really think so? I can hardly judge for myself, being so close to it day and night." Her eyes sparkle; despite the chill in the room, smelling familiarly of damp stone and cold incense, there is a touch of pale pink in her cheeks. Her excitement is endearing, and it is justified, and he meant what he said, but there is something more.

He has never seen the like of it before, excelling even Earl Byrthnoth's hanging in its artistry and vitality. It is, so far as he can tell in its current, fragmented condition, a faithful reproduction of all that he told Agatha during that first summer, more faithful, perhaps, than he intended. War horses, for example, are never gelded, everyone knows that, there's no need to show it quite as explicitly. The narrative is everywhere punctuated by exquisite fairy castles and fabulous beasts, the multi-coloured sea and the knotted, muscular trees reminding him of the stone columns growing in the nave of his new cathedral, branching out to support the vaults whose soaring arches will bear his worship straight to the ear of God.

Yet it is more than the sum of these things, and that disturbs him. There are elements he cannot grasp, lying beyond his recollection or control and affronting his sense of order. They are connected with his feelings on entering the atelier, his unrestrained joy in the windows coupled with an obscure sense of threat aroused by stepping into this community of women. The issue of celibacy does not preoccupy him the way it seems to vex the Cluniac reformers, but the life of the warrior priest does not bring him into contact with women very often nowadays; William, having once captured his Matilda, sees no need for women. A distraction, no more use than music, or that moth eaten collection of Ovid his hare-brained little brother always has his nose stuck into. He smiles inwardly, hearing William's harsh, somewhat high pitched voice in his memory, suddenly sensitive to an emptiness at the heart of his life, and to how the women are beginning to fill it with the richness of their own experience.

"I think," he says, groping after words that will express his feelings without causing offence to hers, "that it has a life of its own."

"I don't know what you mean."

"I'm not sure I do." In the ensuing silence, as he tries to marshal his thoughts, the household chapel bell begins to ring for None. Agatha's servant comes in with a basket of wood to lay a fire in the brazier. *At last*, thinks Odo, who cannot understand why his sister continues to live as though she were still in the convent. Agatha crosses herself and murmurs a brief prayer. Odo bows his head. She then goes to a table beneath the narrow window overlooking the garden, unearths an hour glass from among the piles of notes and sketches and wool samples, and turns it over. The servant lights the fire and excuses herself.

"It's familiar, of course," he continues slowly, picking his way through his impressions, holding out his ringed hands towards the nascent flame, "but at the same time I feel like a stranger looking at it."

"Perhaps it's the distance of time."

"Partly, maybe, but also, yes, I think what I mean is this. First I told you what I remembered, and you turned my memories into sketches, and now the sewing women are turning your sketches into something else again. Everyone adds a layer until the original becomes unrecognisable. Like wrapping a surprise for a child."

"Had you thought that maybe your memory isn't reliable? In my experience, it's often the events we swear to ourselves we'll never forget that vanish soonest."

"But there are elements in what I've seen today that I've never experienced. In Judith's work, for example. God, that woman! She's shown a horse drawing a plough in one of her borders. I've never seen a horse drawing a plough. I can't imagine such a thing. Why risk a horse's wind like that instead of using oxen?"

"Perhaps because there were no oxen, Odo," says Agatha quietly. "That scene is taken from Judith's memory, not yours. Foraging parties from your army had taken all the oxen from her farm for meat. The horse was her husband's war horse. He was killed in a raid, as you know. Judith was never going to ride a great brute like that, so she made the best use of him she could. I take full responsibility. Naturally it can be changed if you so desire. One layer you missed out, though. The effects of what I've seen and heard, watching you enforce the will of God, as you put it."

Odo shrugs. "I am bound to do so, as God's servant and William's."

"Oh William, your eyes are full of stars where he is concerned. You know there are those less smitten with our brother than you are who call what you do terror and the gratification of lusts."

"Are you mocking me, Agatha?" His expression is searching, almost doubtful.

"Do I smile? I had better be careful if I am, in case my head ends up hanging from a castle gate like those of the Dover conspirators."

"That was so long ago I can hardly remember what I did." He fiddles with his rings.

"Three years. Shall I remind you?"

Many of Eustace of Boulogne's rebels had fallen from the cliffs as they fled, drowned or hacked to death on the jagged rock face. Odo had their bodies retrieved from the beach, their heads cut off and hung from the castle walls as a warning to any others who might consider plotting against his brother or himself. He remembers the way the little flags of skin at the edges of their severed necks fluttered in the autumn winds as they dried. He used to mutter words from the Requiem Mass under his breath whenever he passed them. Sometimes, when he is at Dover, he still does.

"There's no need. Now I must go, I have work to do. But I can come again? Any time?"

"Of course. Do you intend to preach tomorrow? I should like the women to hear you."

"Probably not till Christmas Eve. I shall be very busy until the festival. I intend only to preach then and Christmas morning Mass. I'm sure two of my sermons will be enough to have you all praying for my departure."

"False modesty. You speak well, and you know it. I expect Archbishop Lanfranc is fearful of an empty church on Christmas morning, with one of his star pupils performing just up the road."

"Lanfranc has nothing but the ruins of the old cathedral to preach in. If they flock to me it'll be because I can provide a roof over their heads so at least they can doze off in some comfort while I ramble on."

"Oh he's started building, didn't you know? They began house clearances as soon as he got here, and went on digging out the foundations until we had some very heavy rainfall about a month ago, around your saint's day, that put paid to it for this year."

"So he'll be afloat in an outsize waterhole, preaching from a boat like Our Lord at Galilee will he?" says Odo, trying to keep his voice light and unconcerned. House clearances, he'll give Lanfranc house clearances. "Well maybe I could hold Mass in the bailey and call it the Sermon on the Mount. Now I really am going. I must find Hamo." He'll keep his petitioners waiting just a little longer while he and Hamo, his castellan, go through the rolls to find out exactly who owns what around the site of Christ Church.

"You know what we could do," he adds, pausing on his way out of the door. "When it's finished, we could copy it, do it properly, with silk, and gold and silver thread. As many times as we like. One for all my houses."

"What?"

"The hanging, of course."

"Odo, when it's finished, I'm going home. Remember what you said? It needs no silk or gold."

"You're quiet tonight," says Margaret, speaking into the darkness in the general direction of Gytha's bed. It's late, and the fire has died right down, leaving the dormitory in almost complete darkness. Gytha, whose hair is so thick, tends to sleep with her head uncovered so there is not even the pale smudge of a cap to locate her by. During the lengthening lulls in the women's conversation, the silence of the snowbound castle is absolute. "I thought you'd have a lot to say about our Earl." Margaret waits, the rest wait. No reply. Gytha is asleep. Her sleep is untroubled. He is here now, the time of waiting is over. God has kept her alive for a purpose; once she has fulfilled it, she can go to her children.

The Feast of Saint Stephen dawns bright and frosty, and Odo decides to delay his departure to enjoy a day's hunting in his forest bordering the Stour. A noisy, high spirited party, attended by foresters, huntsmen, falconers, and a cartload of servants to dispense two cartloads of food and wine clatter out of the city by Wincheap Gate just as the sun clears the castle keep. The change in the weather has raised everyone's spirits, after a nativity celebrated mainly indoors due to days of relentless snow and wind. As many as could be accommodated abandoned their tents in favour of the bailey, and Odo was thankful for his private quarters, however cramped, wedged as they are between the great hall and the main bedchamber over it. At least he has been able to pass his nights in relative peace, with only his dogs and Osbern for company, away from the mass of sleepers above and below him, snoring, farting, fucking, talking in their sleep. Though he makes it his business to know who lies under whose quilt and what they say in their sleep.

Overcrowding, wet feet and clothes, stinging eyes and sore throats for everyone as the wind made the fire in the great hall back up, and the effects of too much rich food and wine, have led to several displays of unseasonable bad temper. Two knights fought a duel over a perceived slight to the pedigree of one man's falcon. The loser had his nostril slit, the wound becoming infected and slow to heal, and has now sworn to have vengeance on the man who thus disfigured him. The resolution, Odo fears, will cost him time and money he can ill afford, but he can afford quarrels among his vassals even less.

The pleasure of dancing was marred by the fact that the damp, smoky atmosphere put the music frequently out of tune. Master Pietro, laid low with a chill, had been unable to make his eagerly anticipated contribution to the Christmas table, a disappointment which did nothing to improve Odo's humour, already bleak as a result of his discovery that Lanfranc has overstepped no boundaries in clearing the site for his new cathedral. All in all, Christmas was about as enjoyable as he had anticipated.

By High Mass on Christmas morning, his throat was so badly affected by smoke that he could not speak above a whisper and had to have his sermon delivered for him by one of his chaplains, who read in an incantatory monotone that effectively killed every phrase so carefully wrought to convey the joy and mystery of Christ's birth. Odo felt isolated and misunderstood in his attempt to share the meditations that had drifted like visions through his mind as he observed the Christmas Eve vigil, alone, kneeling on the beaten earth floor of the chapel, entranced by the pain in his knees and back and wrist, and the cold that seemed to freeze the blood in his veins. Joy is such a simple thing, he explained to his puzzled clerk as he walked up and down his parlour after Lauds, flexing his stiff joints, hands thawing around a cup of hot, spiced wine. It isn't angels praising God or kings bearing gifts, it's relief from pain, it's a new baby with a monkey face and a cry like a seagull, it's being warm, and safe, and not alone. My lord, what shall I write, the clerk had asked. Leave your materials, he had replied, I'll write it myself.

This morning joy is exchanging mitre and crook for a well balanced bow and a cap with a pheasant feather in it. Joy is pulling the cold, pure air into the back of his throat and feeling it work on the inflammation like a cold compress on a sprain. Joy is this good horse under him, so responsive to the slightest pressure of knee or thigh he thinks it knows what he wants before he knows himself, and the eager panting of his favourite dogs at his heels.

When they reach the edge of the chase, the party splits into smaller groups, some to try their hawks in stretches of open country, some to pursue boar and venison in the verdure. Odo prefers the latter; hawking in winter is hard sport for little reward. As if in vindication of his choice, he has been following the forester scarcely more than ten minutes before the dogs catch the scent of something, the huntsman unleashes them, and they're off in pursuit, trusting to the horses to find their footing as they hurtle through the undergrowth. The wind laughs in Odo's ears and pinches his cheeks with teasing fingers. The drumming of his horse's hooves on the hard ground vibrates through his body with the rhythm of a dance. He is one with the animal, ducking and weaving around tree roots and low hanging branches, every nerve and sinew alive and alight with the exhilaration of the chase. He opens his mouth and lets out a long whoop, for the sheer pleasure of hearing his voice. It is not only by the recitation of prayer that you praise God.

"A stag, My Lord," pants the forester, coming abreast of Odo in a clearing. Odo checks his horse to match the other's pace.

"Then I shall try a shot at him here, I think."

"Very good, My Lord." The forester and Odo's huntsman ride out of the clearing. Odo and his squire wait among the trees at the edge of it for the hounds to flush the stag into the open. Holding his horse with his left hand, Odo uses his teeth to pull the leather guard over his right. Surveying the territory, he decides to take the shot on foot. His aim will be steadier that way, and the clearing is large enough to give another member of the party plenty of opportunity to bring the animal down should he miss or merely wound it. He kicks his feet clear of the stirrups as his squire charges his bow, and waits, listening to the huntsman's horn, trying to envisage from the cracking of branches and the hounds giving tongue the pattern of the stag's flight. Hunting, his father used to tell him, is all a matter of second guessing your quarry, and not underestimating its cleverness.

The snow lying so thickly plays tricks with sound, sometimes muffling, sometimes amplifying it, so that for all his experience and concentration, he is taken completely by surprise when the stag crashes into the clearing not ten yards away from him then stops, panting hard, its delicate legs quivering with exhaustion. It appears unaware of the men. There is no wind and the cold and snow have deadened their scent. Now, he tells himself, don't dismount, get the shot in now. He leans to take the bow from the squire. A fragment of sunlight, glancing through the bare branches, strikes one of its iron reinforced tips. The stag's attention is caught. To Odo, it seems as though, for the space of a heartbeat, the creature, shivering in its sweat darkened skin, looks him straight in the eye, then takes flight into the woods on the far side of the clearing. He doesn't think, doesn't even take the time to thrust his feet back into his stirrups before galloping in pursuit, across the open ground, in among the trees, the light flashing in his eyes, the blood pounding in his ears like waves on a shore, mind become body as he fights to stay in the saddle, to hold his bow steady, not to lose sight of the prey. He'll have the stag, he will have it, no matter what it takes.

Light. Not the winter sun, more than the sun, stronger. The windows. As if a fist of divine light has punched its way through the windows. Shards of glass. Scattered diamonds. Fist across the jaw. Kick in the kidneys. A scream. Then nothing. Not even darkness.

Though darkness surrounds him by the time he recovers consciousness, and cold stars flicker through the tree canopy, lending an eerie glimmer to the snow covered ground. He is lying on his back. He feels terribly drowsy, but freezing. Must find a warmer place to sleep. He lifts his head. So far so good. Levers himself stiffly upwards until he is resting on his elbows, but when he tries to sit, pain engulfs him, washing from the small of his back into his abdomen. He leans over and vomits, and faints again.

The next time he awakes it is still dark, but the moon is up and it feels much warmer, although the snow still lies and crunches loudly beneath him as he climbs cautiously to his feet. His horse is nowhere to be seen and he has no idea where he is, but he is no longer in pain so nothing else matters. He starts to walk, quickly falling into a rhythm, covering the ground in long, even strides. The snow does not impede him, he does not slip or catch his footing in brambles or rabbit burrows. It's like floating. *I'm walking on water*, he thinks madly, and laughs aloud, his laughter ringing around the silent, frozen forest.

He has no idea how long he has been walking when he finds himself in an assart, at the centre of which is a rough hut whose thatch pokes up untidily against the oval of a three quarter moon. Approaching the hut, he looks for a doorway but cannot find one, only a small, heavily shuttered window. At the rear, he discovers the hut has a short extension, so that the overall shape of the building is a stunted L. He finds a door at the end of the L and, pushing it open, steps into a chapel. A tiny chapel containing nothing but a rough hewn stone altar bearing three wooden crosses and some stalks of honesty in a pewter jug, and before the altar a wooden footrest curiously worn at the centre into two wide, shallow indentations. It is only when he kneels that he realises it is worn into the shape of knees, and how it receives the supplicant as a cushioned chair might receive a man who has been all day in the saddle.

All this he sees by the light of the moon shining through the chapel door.

"Forgive me. I do not wish to interrupt your prayers, but you might close the door behind you. The night is extremely cold."

The voice of an old man, a little querulous, but strong, and speaking good Norman French.

"Where are you?" Odo demands, looking around the bare little room.

"Close the door and you will see."

Odo rises from his knees, bows to the altar and goes to close the door. When he turns back into the chapel, a thin beam of yellow lamplight pierces the darkness from somewhere behind the altar. Of course.

"You are an anchorite," he says, approaching the small window, identical to the one in the front wall of the hut except that this one opens on to the chapel rather than the outside world. From here the anchorite, sealed into his cell, is able to listen to divine office and receive communion. Although it looks to be a long time since any services were held here.

"In a manner of speaking, though I tired of dispensing advice to lovesick youths and ointments for bunions and the like. So I moved out from the town to this spot. Now those who find me are only those who have real need of me."

"How do you live?"

"By gifts, as always. Those whom I help bring me gifts of food and wine. Some give their time to cultivation."

"I bring you nothing, Father."

"You have no need. I live in your forest. This assart is your gift."

"How do you know me?"

"How could I not know you, kneeling there in your armour like a young knight keeping his first vigil?"

"But Father, I am unarmed. I have been hunting merely. And I am not a knight but a man of God like yourself."

"Well, well. My eyes must be worse than I thought. It seemed to me that you were quite the knight, all glinting mail and gold spurs and a sword belt full of rubies."

Odo presses his hands cautiously to his midriff. "Perhaps it is my blood you see, old man. I fell from my horse. I lost consciousness for a time, I think. I was trying to find my way back to my companions when I came across this place. I don't know what happened to my horse."

"God aid, you boys are all the same."

God aid? God aid is William's motto. "Who are you, old man?"

"My name does not matter, and nor does yours. I am the King's man as you are. You are one of the sons of Herleve de Conteville. You have her face."

"She had blue eyes."

"Nevertheless, you have her face. She is dead then?"

114

"For several years. And my father also. May God have mercy on them."

"I will pray for their souls. But first we must concern ourselves with more practical matters. It is late, and very cold, and you have no horse. You may sleep here, in the chapel, and be on your way in the morning. You will find the prayer stool makes a serviceable pillow."

"Thank you, Father. Though I should warn you, I am given to nightmares. My servant complains that I often wake him, crying out in my sleep."

"Dreams should not be ignored. Consider Pilate's wife."

"If Pilate had not ignored his wife, Christ would not have died for our salvation."

"If she had not dreamed, Pilate would never have known that he was God's chosen instrument."

"An interesting view."

"An heretical one, you mean, yet no less deserving of consideration. But you are in no state for philosophy. I see your eyelids drooping and you are as pale as a saint. Tell me your dream. It will help you sleep."

"Very well, then. This is my dream. I am riding through a battlefield. It is the hour of Compline near enough, and the field is bathed in red. The grass is stained with the blood of the fallen, their white faces and their armour reflect the setting sun. The sky above the horizon, where the sun rests, is white as bone, as though it too has bled to death. No birds sing, no-one breathes, the planets are silent. My horse and I are the only living things in the universe. My horse is black, there is a low hill away to my right and this too is black, and on top of it the black silhouette of a leafless tree, the branches all twisted in one direction by the labour of the wind.

"As I draw closer to the hill, I see four women standing beneath the tree, two tall and fair, one dark, one with her head covered. As I draw abreast of the hill, the younger of the two fair women detaches herself from the rest and comes down the hill towards me. She is dressed in white samite. Her hair flows over her shoulders and down her back to her waist. Her eyes are as blue as summer and her lips have the texture of rose petals. She moves among the corpses as though she is wading in the sea, her skirt floating around her ankles. She comes towards me smiling, holding out her arms to me, so I reach down and lift her into the saddle in front of me. She lays her head against my breast, I hold her tenderly about her waist, and a phrase comes to me: *you are more precious to me than my own son.*

"Overwhelmed by love for her, I take her to my bed. I carry her in my arms. She weighs no more than a child. I lay her gently down on furs and sheets as fine and white as the membrane of an egg, and when I lie beside her and feel the length of her body against mine, cool and smooth, I believe I am in paradise. I kiss her with all the fondness and fervour my heart is capable of. I run my hands along her flanks and...and then nothing.

"In a panic I pull back the sheets. The bed is drenched dark red with blood. The woman's body is severed, torn apart at the very top of the legs. I see the ragged ends of veins still pulsing and pale marrow oozing from the great bones of her thighs. Her sexual organs are gone, nothing left but the little triangle of hair, tight, sticky curls. I am eaten up with horror, not at what I am looking at, but because, despite her mutilation, I still want her, and I feel cheated. This makes me mortally afraid. I scream out in my fear, and I think this is what wakes me. I wake soaked in sweat, feeling as though a furnace is burning inside me. Even on a night such as this I have to get up and stand naked at the window to cool myself. Then I do not sleep again."

For a long time the anchorite remains silent. Odo peers anxiously through the little window, but the hermit's lamp is shining in his eyes and he can see nothing but a vague impression of an unkempt beard and a gleam of moist lips. The window is too small to reveal the whole of the man's face.

"Help me," he pleads, tears beginning to prick his eyes.

"You have helped yourself, boy, though it would be unwise to be complacent. Who knows what the Devil may have in store for us?"

"I can resist the Devil if I can sleep."

The anchorite gives a short, knowing laugh. "Ah the arrogance of those in the prime of life. In the end, you know, we are all like Saint Peter. We betray what is dearest to us and to God. But sleep now, My Lord, and I will watch and keep the Devil at bay for tonight at least."

BLOOD LETTING

AFTER EPIPHANY 1071

"Come," calls Lanfranc. A young monk pokes his head around the door to the Archbishop's parlour.

"My Lord Archbishop, Brother Infirmarer says you should come quickly. The patient is waking up."

"Good news indeed, brother." The Archbishop smiles, which makes him look less like an Old Testament prophet. "Thank you for your pains in coming to me. Shouldn't you be in the refectory at this hour?"

The young man looks at his superior with affection. The Archbishop has been tugging at his beard again, a habit he has when thinking. Grey hairs scatter the papers on his desk.

"Return to your meal, boy. I can find my own way to my own bed chamber, I think. Has the physician been sent for?"

"My Lord has his own physician with him, Your Grace."

Leaning against the sickroom door, Lanfranc lets the warmth seep into his bones. He has another cold; no matter that he has lived nearly half his life in the northern damp, he still spends every winter feeling as though his head is stuffed with wool and his nose has no skin left on it. Although he has subdued his will to the Rule of Saint Benedict, he has never been able to persuade his body it belongs anywhere but in the sweet, pure air of the Alps. Even now, if he shuts his eyes, he can almost believe the scents of the herbs burnt to purify the air around the sick man are really the perfumes of mountain pastures, new grass, rock rose, melt water. His surrender is brief, unnoticed by the infirmarer or the doctor, the one holding the patient's head as he tries to coax him into a sip of borage tea, the other stooped intently over a chamber pot.

"The urine is much improved, Your Grace." The doctor stretches his arms with a self satisfied air.

"Then we must thank Saint Artemios for his intercession. Brother Thorold, how is our patient? I'm told he's regained consciousness."

"You may speak with him yourself, Your Grace, but go carefully, a step at a time. He is still somewhat confused."

"Thank you, Brother. You are most considerate. Now, perhaps it would be best if you left us. My Lord bishop shouldn't be taxed with too many visitors all at once. You too, doctor, if you please."

When they have gone, Lanfranc draws up a stool to the bedside. Odo's eyes are closed, and the left side of his face remains badly swollen and discoloured, but when Lanfranc takes his hand, the pressure is returned.

"Well, brother, you gave us all quite a fright."

Frowning with the effort, Odo opens his eyes. The whites are startlingly yellow. *Wolf eyes*, thinks Lanfranc, rather pleased with the analogy. The wolf is Odo's emblem, a gold wolf on a green ground, predatory, cunning, a creature of the ancient dark.

"Where's the anchorite?" He turns his head in Lanfranc's direction, wincing as his jaw makes contact with the pillow. "Where am I?" He has spoken in French. Lanfranc, who is more comfortable in Latin, nevertheless replies in his own execrable vernacular.

"You are in my house. You have been here almost two weeks,

unconscious or raving. Though I hesitate to appear disloyal to my infirmarer, or critical of your doctor, I think it is only God's providence and the strength of your own constitution that have pulled you through. You took a terrible fall."

"Two weeks?" His voice is weak and hoarse; the stiff jaw makes him slur his words like a drunkard. He tries to swallow but has no saliva. Lanfranc dips a sponge in the bowl of tea cooling on the nightstand and uses it to moisten Odo's parched lips; Odo pulls a face. "The King..?"

"The King has been informed of your accident and that you are in my care. It's the dead of winter, nothing will spoil while you recover. I will send a messenger to His Grace today to tell him you have regained consciousness. I've no doubt he'll be very relieved. As am I."

In this Lanfranc is in earnest, the more so because, when he had first laid eyes on the injured man lying on a litter in the great court of Christ Church Abbey, his lips and fingernails blue with cold, his swollen face encrusted with dried blood and vomit, his first thought had been that Odo's death would make his job easier. It would set him free to concentrate on the subjugation of the English church to the king's authority without always having to look over his shoulder to see what Odo was up to along the shared borders of their secular power.

And his second was this, that a world without Odo would somehow show less of the wonder of God's creation and more of its order and predictability. Odo has always had this effect on him, since he was a boy of eleven, forever disrupting classes at Bec. It might be a toad tactically released from his sleeve just as Brother Damian, who taught rhetoric and was of a nervous disposition, walked past his desk. Or an unorthodox, but irrefutable, response to a question of doctrine. Nothing has changed, except in degree; it remains unwise to turn one's back on Odo, though now you are more likely to feel a sword between your shoulderblades than a toad around your ankles, and lose the contents of your treasury rather than an argument. And, absurdly, end up admiring the charm with which he defeated you.

In remorse for his uncharitable thoughts, Lanfranc had locked himself in his room, this room, where he had scourged himself until his blood flowed then put on a hair shirt beneath his robe which he had sworn not to remove unless or until his old pupil made a full recovery. He had then, while keeping vigil at the sick man's bedside, composed a letter to Pope Alexander, begging to be released from his Archbishopric and to be allowed to return to Caen. He has not the strength for this work, he is too easily corrupted. He must save himself from becoming like the man on the bed.

"There was an anchorite," Odo says again, his voice a little stronger now. "He gave me shelter. I got lost. My horse... The anchorite must be thanked. Provisions. Something for the chapel."

"I know of no anchorite. My wardens found you, unconscious, in a part of my chase that borders yours, near the Dover road. It seems you were caught across the face by a branch and thrown. My men found your horse later, wandering with a quarrel in its neck. It looks as though your bow must have discharged when you fell. The animal had to be destroyed. I'm sorry. The doctor diagnosed severed bruising to the kidneys. Luckily your jaw was not broken. He has been bleeding you daily to cure the jaundice." The two men exchange sceptical looks. Odo glances at the backs of his hands. As well as looking as though they have been stained with turmeric, each bears several small cuts in varying stages of healing. "Your sister has been here every day," Lanfranc continues. "I offered her lodgings, but she said she could not be spared from the workshop." He pauses, as though he has thought better of what he was about to say and is looking for something to fill the gap. "When you're stronger I can show you my plans to rebuild the cathedral. Now I think you should rest. Shall I remove this?" Lanfranc picks up the bowl of tea.

"Thank you."

At the door, the Archbishop turns back. "Odo..."

"Yes?"

"I somehow have the feeling your fall was providential, that we have been circling around one another like a couple of fighting cocks since August. There is a great deal we should discuss, when you feel strong enough."

Odo smiles, a tight, lopsided smile, careful to avoid splitting his cracked lips any further, but says nothing, and by the time Lanfranc has shut the door on him, his eyes are closed once more. He is sad about the horse.

By the time Odo's recovery is sufficiently far advanced for Brother Thorold to allow him out of bed, there is a mood abroad in the Abbey, carefully concealed from the Archbishop, that the Bishop of Bayeux has outstayed his welcome. He has imported his own cook and his personal servant, as well as a miscellany of pages, his dwarf, three musicians and two favourite hounds and their handler, with each of these impositions insisting, sweetly but firmly, that they are necessary to the speedy restoration of his health. He has taken over all the Archbishop's private apartments, except his chapel, which is currently serving as abbey church, to accommodate his household, although, to Brother Thorold's horror, the dogs are allowed to sleep on his bed. The Archbishop's bed, worries the infirmarer, wondering if he dare make known to the bishop his concerns for the Archbishop's health and dignity if he has to sleep in the monks' dormitory for very much longer.

Brother Thorold and Odo's physician wrangle with chilly courtesy over his treatment, but Osbern is a particular bone of contention. While his devotion to his lord is commendable, and hints at aspects of Odo's character not immediately obvious to those charged with his care, his undisguised contempt for the Abbey's domestic arrangements is stinging. He had been shocked by his first sight of his master on arrival at Christchurch, but more by the fact that Odo was unshaven and dressed in the plain, black habit of a Benedictine than by his loss of weight or the bruises still discolouring his cheek and jaw. He had sent novices scurrying for soap and water and clean linen with an arrogance at least equal to his lord's, and before long the bed chamber was so imbued with Odo's favourite perfume that Brother Thorold, bringing arnica to treat his bruises, wished he could avoid breathing the air for fear of corruption.

Odo himself is bored and uncomfortable. His body has been made a battleground, pulled between doctor and infirmarer as though they are contenders in a tug of war. Lanfranc's private apartments are furnished with the kind of pious simplicity Odo discarded without regret twenty years ago, when summoned from school in Bec to take up his bishopric. Most of Archbishop Stigand's library having been destroyed in the great fire three years ago, there is little to read. Lanfranc will not be able to begin to restore the collection until he has a building fit to house it. Perhaps Odo himself will commission a manuscript out of gratitude for Lanfranc's care. A gospel, a book of hours? Perhaps a medical text would be appropriate in the circumstances, Galen, or the infidel Avicenna, of whom he has heard that he memorised the entire writings of Aristotle and could write while riding a camel. What does a camel look like? How can it be made to accommodate an escritoire? He envisages a sort of hunch backed horse, and wonders why anyone should want to ride such a thing.

He is also becoming wary of Lanfranc's hospitality. Despite the confines of his sickroom, he is aware of tensions in the abbey community. He is certain Lanfranc is equally conscious of them, yet he seems in no hurry to let his guest leave. Though Odo insists he is well enough to go home, that his recovery would progress more quickly if he had his own bed to sleep in, Lanfranc prevaricates. He feels it would be inadvisable for a man who has been so badly hurt to travel in this weather; he is afraid Odo might take another fall when it is so icy underfoot, and Brother Thorold fears the effects of a chill on his injured kidneys. Very well, Odo concludes, he will play for them, for now, he will be the spoilt prince, the degenerate priest. Let them think he believes himself unassailable behind the curtain wall of William's authority.

But it is a sensible precaution to put his own man in the kitchens and to keep his dogs close at hand. The three musicians brought from the castle have all served with him under arms, and no-one should make the mistake of believing that Osbern's devotion to his person extends only to its comfort and adornment. Razors are not the only blades he wields with accomplishment. Odo knows Lanfranc is wearing a hair shirt, and he knows why. They have been neighbours and rivals for many years, Odo in Bayeux, Lanfranc at Caen; they know one another like father and son. Better, in fact, in his own case, thinks Odo, who never saw his father again after he was sent to Bec. Lanfranc, on the other hand, is as persistently and inconveniently present as his conscience. The idea of his conscience as a venerable greybeard in a hair shirt amuses him, though it does not make him smile; smiling remains painful.

On the morning of the Feast of Saint Agnes the city awakes to a thaw. Melting snow drips from the thatched roofs of the buildings in Mercery Lane and lies in wide puddles in the Buttermarket, reflecting the pale blue sky. Gytha and Leofgeat make their way through streets crowded with people abroad for the sheer enjoyment of one another's company and the tenuous warmth of the sun. They greet one another with the conspiratorial camaraderie of those who have shared a great ordeal and lived to tell the tale. They have survived another winter and spring is round the corner. No-one worries about wet feet or muddy hems. No-one thinks of February, the coldest month, almost upon them, when the birds drop frozen from the sky and the dead sleep in the outhouses, waiting until the ground is soft enough to bury them. No-one remembers it is still almost two months to the spring equinox and the beginning of a new year.

"It looks as though the earth's got holes in it," says Gytha, stepping around a puddle, "and you can see right through to the other side."

Leofgeat gives her an uncomprehending stare, blank as the sky itself and Gytha wishes she'd held her tongue. She's as jumpy as a virgin on her wedding day, swinging wildly between terror and elation. Here it is at last, the chance she has looked for, waited for, dreamt of for so long she can scarcely remember a time when it did not form the background to everything she said or thought or did. But what if she fails? There will be no second opportunity, he is bound to make sure of that. And if she succeeds? If, when his guards run her through, or she gasps her last in some dank cell, blind and starving with only the rats and cockroaches to witness her passing, his is the first face she sees in hell? Will that be her fate, to be bound to him for eternity? As they pass through the gate into the abbey close she has the sense of having stepped off the end of the world, into the unknowable. She almost stumbles when she finds there is still earth beneath her feet.

The abbey masons are taking advantage of the good weather. Sounds of stone chipping reach their ears from the leather clad lodges clustered around the edges of the cathedral building site like piglets round a sow. The air in the precincts smells of stone dust, cold and peppery. Two men, stripped to the waist and running with sweat despite the sun's weakness, toil at a pump to speed up the drying out process; they pause in their work to cast an eye over the women. Gytha draws her hood closer over her head, but Leofgeat, newly pregnant and proud of her little belly and swelling breasts, lifts her chin at a coquettish angle and smiles at them. Gytha remembers that feeling, that sense of exultation in her womanhood, the way men responded to her fecundity, the way Adam couldn't keep his hands off her, despite the rules about lying with a woman during pregnancy; the memory clenches her womb like a cramp, and she hurries past, shielding her body with the flat, leather scrip given her by Sister Jean.

"I don't feel well enough to go out of the house today," she had said when Gytha, wondering what mark she had overstepped this time, answered the summons to her parlour. "I should like you to take Lord Odo's letters to him."

"I'm sure Lord Odo will not wish to see me, madam." Sister Jean must be sicker than she seemed. Had she forgotten entirely how Gytha stood up to Lord Odo before Christmas, how he cut short his examination of the work because of her outspokenness? "Why not simply send word that you are ill today and will go again when you feel better? After all, if I go, my share of the embroidery won't get done."

"Ah, but it will. I want you to take this with you." She picked up a parchment from the table beside her, folded so Gytha could not see what it contained, and handed it to her. "It's a new drawing. I don't want to go any further without My Lord giving his opinion. I want you to bring his view back to me. Also, these letters are from the King and the Archbishop of York. He'll want to see them straight away." Her pale face, the nose scarlet with blowing, softened. "He's chafing at the bit. He's not a good patient, I'm afraid. Some new company may improve his temper."

"But mine, madam? Send Judith. She'll have a better idea how to attend to his lordship than me."

"Oh, come, Gytha. All women are nurses, as all men are like children, given to recklessness and feeling sorry for themselves. It always falls to women to tidy up the mess. Some can make entertaining conversation as well."

Clearly she had not forgotten, so what was her intention? Then again, what did it matter? All that mattered was this chance to get close to him while he was still weak, to slip her little knife into the soft flesh between his ribs, up, twisting, into his heart, to carve a channel in that stony organ and fill it with the sweetness of her revenge. There might never be another. Why was she stalling? Merely for the pleasure of the chase? Had she become so vindictive during the years of waiting?

She took the scrip and went to find Leofgeat, who was to accompany her with a batch of delicacies from Master Pietro to aid his lordship's recovery.

They announce themselves at the gate and are shown into what is normally the Archbishop's office, where Osbern meets them. He recognises Leofgeat from previous visits and, after a cursory examination of her basket, sends her to the kitchens.

"And you are..?" He turns disdainfully to Gytha.

"Aelfgytha," she replies curtly. "I'm one of the embroiderers. Sister Jean is unwell and asked me to bring my lord's dispatches in her stead. She has sent a note. Here." Gytha pulls the bundle of documents out of her scrip and sorts through them until she finds the one bearing Sister Jean's seal. Osbern flicks his eyes back and forth along the lines of writing, thankful the seal is clear enough for him to be certain the note does come from Sister Jean. All he has managed to understand is that the woman said she was sent by Sister Jean.

"Wait," he tells Gytha.

The wait seems interminable. Looking out of the window behind the Archbishop's desk, she is certain the angle of the sun, shining through sample cuttings of stained glass ranged along the sill, has altered completely before Osbern returns. Sunlight patterns the surface of the desk with rubies and topaz. Surely they have slid a thumbs' length along its edge already. The day will be over before it has begun at this rate.

"I have spoken to my lord," says Osbern, in hesitant English, as he re-enters the room. At last. "He is not pleased, but he will see you. Follow me. He is up, but still in his chamber."

"I am to go in alone?" It is not the impropriety of it she questions, but her luck.

Osbern gives her a long, considering look. She casts her eyes down, trying to look demure.

"He's a priest, mistress," he says, "and sick."

And soon, very soon now, he will be dead.

As saints are wafted to heaven on clouds of incense, Gytha has come to believe she will be carried down to hell on a tide of that perfume. Not incense. Not blood or shit or fear, or arnica for bruises. Rosemary and sandalwood. Always rosemary and sandalwood. Feeling like a Christian entering the circus, she plasters a smile to her face.

"Good day, My Lord. I thank God to see you looking so well." And indeed she does. It would have been galling in the extreme to be cheated of her quarry by a hunting accident.

"Do you, mistress, do you indeed?" He sits facing away from the door, in a chair close to the brazier on the hearthstone. He turns stiffly towards her, as though his back is causing him pain. The hound which had its head in his lap when she came in slinks away to hide under the bed. The same yellow eyed beast she saw in Winchester, or its descendant.

"Of course, My Lord, I am not entirely without charity."

"And like every charitable woman, you devote time to visiting the sick. Thank you for taking my sister's place. I hope she is not seriously indisposed."

"A head cold, that's all. She blames it on the change in the weather." She keeps her tone clipped, neutral.

How well his sister understands him, what a perfect morsel she has tossed into his den, flesh succulent, but enough bone to keep his teeth sharp. He extends his hand, but she does not kneel to kiss his ring, merely stands in front of him, clutching her scrip. Her hands, he notes curiously, are shaking. The ring slips down towards his knuckle and he pushes it back impatiently with his thumb.

He is thinner, and his hair has grown longer, curling over the collar of his loose, dark gown. His face is somehow unveiled, the bones bold and delicate within the web of muscle, thrown into relief by the work of draught and flame. *He looks like an angel*, she thinks, *a tired angel, worn out with watching over mankind, an angel who can never blink nor turn his head away, trapped in his own nature.* She finds herself smiling at him. Looking at him, she realises, gives her a sense of joy, the same pure, arbitrary joy that comes with watching swallows at sunset or feeling snow on her eyelashes.

Determinedly, she summons other memories, images of his men stripping Lady Edith's hall, of Lady Edith holding out her hand to the soldier in charge of loading the cart, her back turned rigidly on the body of Skuli folded into the mud. Yet punctuating them is always the recurring memory of Odo's face as he ordered the hall door closed, a mask of exhaustion, not a spark of triumph or a glint of avarice that she can recall.

She is bewitched. He knows her intent and has called up some demon to infest her mind and deflect her from her purpose. She must do it now. Now, while she is still lucid enough to know what power he is exercising. She takes a step forward, curling her fingers around the haft of her knife, reassured by its solid familiarity.

"You have letters for me?" he prompts. Perhaps she is more touched than clever, he speculates, watching unreadable expressions chase each other across her face like clouds running before a wind. *Sometimes,* he thinks, reflecting on Turold, his dwarf, *it is hard to tell the difference; both lie outside the main way, in the margins.* It would be disappointing, though. Clever women are bracing, like new wine or a ride along the beach early on a winter's morning.

"Oh...yes." Letting go the knife, she rummages in the scrip and hands him the bundle of letters. "And this." He has beaten her, beguiled her with his angel's face. Instead of simply unhooking the knife from her girdle and driving it into his body, she has let herself become encumbered with the fastenings on the satchel, the bundles of documents with their festoon of dangling seals. "A new drawing Sister Jean would like your opinion on," she adds crossly. He raises his eyebrows at this, but shows no inclination to unfold it, putting everything in a pile on the low table beside his chair.

"Take off your cloak," he orders her. "I think it too warm in here today, but Brother Infirmarer insists on burning his concoctions to keep the air pure, so the fire is never out."

She tightens her grip on her knife, focuses her concentration on the smooth bone handle, its warmth, the way it has worn over the years to fit her hand. "I mustn't be long."

"But you must at least wait until I have looked at the drawing? If you are to take my opinion back to your mistress?"

Her mistress? Sister Jean is not her mistress. Not as long as Lady Edith lives. Perhaps she was right to stay her hand after all; perhaps he might give away some clue as to her ladyship's fate if she listens carefully enough to what he has to say.

He does not intend to stare at her as she removes her outdoor clothes, but he cannot help himself. She has the supple grace of a seal, as she pushes the cloak back from her shoulders, then stoops to gather it up before it falls to the floor. The way her breasts rise and flatten as she lifts her arms, the slenderness of her waist and her rounded hips entrance him. She wears her chaste uniform as though she is Venus adorned in nothing but her hair and a cockleshell. His mouth goes dry, his mind blank as he tries to think about something else. *Pater noster, qui es in caelis, sanctificetur nomen tuum...* Words. What use are words?

He clears his throat. "Sit," he commands, indicating a stool facing his chair across the hearth. She sits, sweeping her skirt under her, her hands following the curve of her buttocks in a gesture of such unconscious loveliness he begins immediately to cast about in his mind for some pretext to make her rise and sit again. If he touched her hand, he wonders, would he feel what she felt, the warm flesh beneath the wool of her gown, the stretch of her sinews? *Adveniat regnum tuum.*

This is not what Agatha anticipated. He knows Agatha and her cerebral games, dry as her wit, as her papery skin and the homilies she delivers to her novices. Like anyone rehearsed in the art of rhetoric, she marshals her facts selectively, and it would be Gytha's acid, rebellious tongue not her physical attractions that would have persuaded her to send Gytha to him in her stead, give him his chance to get even. She expects Gytha to talk, not simply to be. "Tell me what is going on in the world," he says, as soon as he can trust his voice. "I am so confined here I am even excused my religious observance. I keep pleading with Brother Infirmarer to let me go for a walk, but he thinks it's too soon."

"Surely, My Lord, you need neither my account nor the evidence of your own eyes to know what is going on in the world." Let him talk if he wants to; she has nothing to say.

"A picture is made of many brushstrokes, mistress, or should I say, many stitches?"

Yet she cannot help herself. "But only one design, which is the truth at its heart."

"Are you sure of that? Is there no role for interpretation?"

"You are a bishop, your grace. You of all people must know there is only one right way." If God brings her safely through this, she swears she will take a vow of silence.

"And they told me you were not religious, Gytha."

His tone is light, but there is a serious enquiry at the back of it, a probing bass note which makes her feel she has been found out. The situation is running away from her, she is losing touch with her purpose. "Let me tell you about the hanging, My Lord," she says, rising. "I really must not be much longer. Sister Jean was anxious to have your view of the drawing as soon as possible." She picks it out of the pile on the table at his side and thrusts it in front of him. He takes no notice, he looks only at her, his gaze disconcerting, devouring, an angel consumed by his duty of praise and contemplation.

A murderer, and a looter, and probably a rapist, and certainly a man for whom the right way is always the one which suits him best.

"Then I must not rush my consideration of it, must I?" His tone is languid, teasing, which makes her feel she is being patronised. "Talk to me while I look at it. Amuse me. They tell me my favourite stallion bit the marshal. Is it true? I gather one of the grooms took quite a beating for it. Do sit down again. It tires me to have to look up at you so."

Eventually, she does as she is bidden, but this time fails to smooth her skirt under her, out of spite, he imagines, as though she is aware of the effect it had upon him.

"Sister Jean stayed up half the night with the boy herself, My Lord, poulticing his injuries against infection."

"Women are always so sentimental. I suppose she thought the boy shouldn't have been beaten?"

"If she did, I doubt it was due to her being sentimental."

"Then we must agree to differ. I can't imagine what else urges her to these occasional forays of hers against the rule of law."

Gytha remembers the poacher. "She does not believe the law is always right. I respect her for it."

He does not reply immediately but looks at her, as though trying to make up his mind about something, then gives a curt nod of his head, an approving nod, she thinks, the gesture of a man who has tested a horse's fetlock and found it sound, or bitten a coin and found it solid. And she is pleased by his approval, and yearns for a spirit less complicated, with fewer rooms whose doors remain locked against the power of the will.

He starts to unfold the drawing. "So tell me, what's in this drawing she's so concerned about?"

"I don't know, My Lord, I haven't looked. She just asked me to note your comments for her. I am merely to be your mouthpiece."

Mouth. Luscious mouth, lips the colour of overripe redcurrants, when they lose their transparency and the red darkens almost to mulberry. He is gripped by an overwhelming desire to take that full, slightly sulky bottom lip gently between his teeth. What's to stop him? He could just get up, step across the hearth, bend and kiss her. Why not? *Fiat voluntas tua.*

Look at him, holding the half folded parchment as though he has forgotten he has it in his hand. Taunting her, stringing their meeting out because he knows she wants to get away. She feels the light drag of her knife where it hangs from her girdle. "My Lord? Will you look at it now?"

"What?" He frowns and passes his hand in front of his eyes in confusion. "I'm sorry, I was distracted. You know my mind was wandering for two weeks? I sometimes think it isn't quite ready yet to make the return journey. Yesterday I was thinking about camels."

"Camels, My Lord?"

"Wondering what a camel looked like."

"Like a sheep, My Lord, a tall, brown sheep with a long neck and a hump of fat on its back." She strokes her knife, hoping her gesture will look absent-minded, but he does not seem to notice. His eyes, fixed on her face, widen in astonishment.

"You've seen one?"

"I was once a waiting woman in a household whose lord received a gift of a camel from the Holy Land." She pauses to see if he shows any sign of recognition, but sees only his curiosity, hungry and insistent. "The poor thing was very mangy. Its fur was all peeling off like plaster off a damp wall. It died."

He is full of wonder; he feels like weeping with gratitude for his sister's miraculous gift. A woman who has seen a camel, who can describe a camel with the same casual precision with which she might give instructions to the gardener or place an order for a bolt of cloth.

"It sounds as though you have had a much more interesting life than I have. Will you tell me more?"

"Surely you mock me, My Lord?"

"No." But the tone was patronising, ill considered. All this soldiering, he's losing his touch. "I assure you, my interest is genuine." He summons his most charming smile, though even that fails to work its usual magic and she remains unmoved, her lovely lips set in a bitter line.

"Then I shall disappoint you." Disappointment handed on, the only legacy of her life. And will it also end in disappointment, failure, because she is so easily distracted? Keep it brief, just the bare essentials. "My father was a free man with a fish salting business in Colchester. I married when I was sixteen. My husband was a cooper. Now I'm a widow."

"I'm sorry."

"You have no need. It wasn't your fault. My husband died of a flux the year Earl Harold killed King Gryfudd, before you came here." She remembers the year because of her mother being Welsh.

"I had no intention of accepting the blame for your husband's death. Whatever the circumstances."

His shirt is open at the neck. A pulse beats rapidly beneath the skin at the base of his throat. Tender skin, easy to pierce, just above the curious glass ornament he wears, shaped like a tear whose apex marks the entry point.

"I'm surprised you have not married again," he continues.

"My husband left a great many debts."

"And have you no children?"

"None living, My Lord." None living. Such simple words, ordinary as barley porridge or a spinning wheel. Easy words to say, as long as you don't think about what they mean, because, if you do, the pain will rob you of the power of speech.

"Will you snap my head off again if I say I'm sorry? Really. My own son is a great consolation to me, although I see him far less often than I should like. It seems to me we are never so blest in this life as by the love of children."

His son? He has a child? Suddenly she is back on top of the West Gate tower in Winchester, her eyes fixed in horror on the small boy darting out between the soldiers to grasp the bishop's shiny harness. Once again she sees Odo slip his feet from his stirrups ready to throw himself from the saddle, then hears the Bastard's thin, harsh command. *Non, Odo! A moi!* As clear as if he had been standing next to her on the tower. She wonders that she has never remembered it before. "What is his name, My Lord?" she asks. Not that she cares, of course.

"John." His son's name fills him with nostalgia. John. "My sister, your mistress, is his godmother. He is fourteen. He is at school in Liege, although I haven't yet decided if he will take orders."

His wistful indulgence makes her wince. Seven years now since her last confinement, yet the pain never lessens. Feeling the tears well up from that deep, scarred place inside her, she bites her lip, hard enough, temporarily, to supersede one pain with another.

She glances out of the window, which gives on to a neat square of grass bounded by the crumbling west wall of the cloister. The Archbishop's house casts long, dense shadows across the lawn and under the cloister arches, where the brothers, like shadows themselves in their black habits, are gathering to go into church. *Vespers*, she thinks, listening to the bell, and realises that this day of short hours has almost disappeared.

Yet she has made no move, the bishop's white skinned throat remains as unblemished as when she entered the room, his heart still beats with the love of a living son. A tall boy, probably, ungainly, with legs like a stork and curly hair, and a voice that cracks uncontrollably, like a donkey braying. Matthew would have been about that age by now. Matthew. Her firstborn.

"Please look at the drawing, My Lord," she says, with a break in her voice that makes him glance at her with concern. She stares at her hands, at her knife hanging uselessly at her side, his compassion battering down her exhausted defences. She blinks furiously to keep the tears from her eyes.

"Alright," he says gently, and finishes unfolding it. In the waning light, he sees a single figure, a slender, long legged knight sporting a lavish moustache. His shield is stuck full of arrows. In his shield hand he also holds a javelin, but his sword arm is raised to his face, the great fist clenched around another arrow which appears to have entered his right eye. His arms and armour, the knee length mail shirt and pointed helmet with its nose guard, proclaim him to be a Norman, but the moustache identifies him. And his height. These are the details Agatha has remembered, impatient with the technical variations between Norman and Saxon military paraphernalia because she could not see the need to understand them. She has also remembered the curious manner of his death. Except, of course, that she has not. She has merely remembered what Odo chose to tell her.

"The death of Godwinson," he says. "You may tell my sister I am content." He holds out the drawing to Gytha, who takes it from him quickly, almost eagerly. He releases it with a small, sad smile that does not reach his eyes. Had it been anything else, she would not have bothered to look at it. But the death of Harold touches her, so she looks.

"Christ's blood!"

He glances up in astonishment from sorting through his letters. Has she not recently told him she was lady-in-waiting in some great house? This is not generally the way Saxon women of good breeding express themselves. A furious flush suffuses her cheeks. She breathes hard, her hand, holding the parchment at arm's length as though it is contaminated, shakes.

"I beg your pardon, mistress?" He tries to sound like an affronted churchman, but it is impossible to keep the amusement out of his voice. Her eyes, he decides, are the deep, translucent blue of a summer night, and just now they are full of shooting stars. He wonders if he might compose a verse or two, an elegy, after Ovid. "My sister should not have sent you here with this," he says, giving up the pretence at outrage. "I suppose there were men who fought at Hastings who were known to you."

"There were men fought at Hastings known to every woman in England. Not a household but didn't lose someone. I am not so full of my own importance as to let that distress me."

"And you think it was any different for the women of Normandy?" He is stung by her self-righteousness. How many homes has he visited in his own diocese, ducking under the low lintels of cottage doorways or served rye bread and new wine in farmers' halls? How many easy lies has he told to grieving mothers about the inexpressible courage of their terrified sons? No, he did not suffer. Yes, he had plenty of time to make his confession. Naturally he was honoured to die in the Duke's service.

"Yes," she snaps back without hesitation, "it was your choice, not ours. And now this…" Taking a step towards him she waves the drawing savagely in his face. "This…travesty."

Summoning all his self control to stop himself flinching, he asks, "What do you mean?"

"You know damn well what I mean." The devil's beguiling scales have fallen from her eyes now. If he looks like an angel, it is just a trick of the firelight. So what if he has a son? The Bastard himself has sons. They are still butchers, carving up her country and tossing it to their dogs of vassals just as they carved up the body of her king and kicked the pieces off a cliff edge to be picked over by gulls.

"I assure you, mistress, I do not," he says, mild as you please. "Have some wine, calm down and then perhaps you can explain yourself." He attempts to stand, to go for the wine jug on the night table. He could call Osbern, but he is enjoying himself too much.

But as he puts his hands to the arms of his chair to push himself out of it, she lunges forward, slamming her hands over his, the parchment crumpled under her palm, pressed into the back of his hand. She has a mermaid smell, of salt and fish, wind and wet rocks.

She has acted without thinking. Her knife is useless, still knotted to her girdle. But she has teeth and nails, feet, fists, a whole body she can use to kill him, since it is no use for giving life.

Then she notices the jewelled hilt of the dagger he wears in his belt, in a little leather scabbard, not even tied. Balling the parchment in her fist she flings it in his face. Before he can recover himself she lunges for the dagger with her other hand, her fingers curling hard around its hilt, whipping it from its sheath, pressing the point against his throat.

As light and thrilling as a caress. He isn't afraid, not for a moment. He has only to call out for Osbern and his guards to come running. Even without them he is more than a match for her, so small a woman, despite the ferocity of her temper. It is not her sudden fury that throws him off balance, but the force of his desire for her, slamming into him like a blow.

But first, the dagger. He grasps her wrist and twists until she is forced to drop it. Catching it in his free hand, he flings it across the room out of reach, then pushes her aside. As she stumbles he springs to his feet and, gripping her by the shoulders, grinding her flesh against the bone, pulls her up to face him, holding her so close their breath mingles in the tense space between them, and he knows she must feel his arousal. She struggles, tries to twist her arms free, but it is useless; her sleeves chafe and burn against her skin, and she has no doubt he will break her arms if need be.

"So I am not worth an honourable death either," she spits at him.

"What are you talking about?" He intensifies his grip on her shoulders to make her understand he has tired of the game and wants an answer this time. She does not even wince, just stares at him with contempt, then suddenly smiles, a second before bringing her knee up sharply into his groin.

He drops to the floor, his face grey, sweat breaking from his forehead, a delta of pain flowing out from his groin, spreading through his bowels and belly, washing the bile into the back of his throat. He swallows, determined not to give her the satisfaction of vomiting. The dog creeps out from under the bed and dances around him, barking, butting her long snout into his shoulders, trying to entice him to play.

Gytha makes a dash for the dagger, but as she stoops to pick it up, Odo recovers sufficiently to make a lunge across the floor, his body stretched full length, grabbing her ankle and pulling it out from under her. She falls heavily, ribs and knees crashing against packed earth, and lies winded, helpless, as Odo crawls towards her, pinions her with one knee in the small of her back and reaches for his knife, which he then holds against her neck, just above the nape, its point tracing the wave of a tendril of dark hair escaped from her coif. Turning her head sideways she comes face to face with the dog, jowls spread over her paws, eyebrows quizzically arched. Gytha sneezes. As she tries to raise her arm to wipe her nose, Odo twists it up her back until she can almost feel the tearing of sinew, the ball of her shoulder popping out of its socket.

"Enough? Or a little more?" He gives her arm another wrench.

She cries out, giving voice to her screaming muscles. "Enough!"

As he releases her arm and lifts his knee from her back, she feels suddenly cold. Shock, she tells herself, sitting up, flexing her fingers, prodding her shoulder to make sure everything is still where it should be. Her body, as she watches him sheath his dagger, then rock back on his heels and get to his feet, tells her something different, but she refuses to listen to it. She tries to rise, but stumbles over the hem of her gown. He lifts her, his hand beneath her elbow. She fancies she can feel every whorl of his fingerprints through the fabric of her sleeve. As soon as she has regained her balance, she shakes him off as if he were made of fire.

"What's going on, My Lord?...Oh." The commotion has brought Osbern running from the next door room, but seeing his lord and the woman standing close, flushed and panting, he grins and withdraws. Osbern, Odo teases him, guards his lord's morals so fiercely even he cannot always gain access to them.

"Now," says Odo calmly, though he remains pale and somewhat breathless, "tell me what this is all about."

"I saw the King's body," she says, her veins full of ice now, the spark of his flesh against hers doused. "I know he didn't die of a shot in the eye. You have lied. There, I have said it. Send for your soldiers, I'm ready."

"How do you know?" he asks, sounding almost fearful.

"The household I spoke of, with the camel? It was Edith Swan Neck's. I accompanied her when she came to ask for his body."

Silence. Now he will do it, send for his men, or perhaps just break her neck himself with those broad, muscular hands. She closes her eyes, squeezes them shut until she sees tiny, dancing points of light in the darkness. Her children's souls, beckoning her. A weight lifts from her shoulders. She is floating. She opens her eyes.

He has not moved. He stands very still, his arms hanging at his sides. His stillness has an air of impending catastrophe about it, as though he is suspended over nothingness by a frayed rope that will break if he moves.

"Then," he says slowly, as though the words don't quite fit in his mouth, "you have been in my dreams these past four years." Four women, two tall and fair, one dark, one with her head covered. One dark. "I wonder, are you real? Or like the anchorite? Am I going to wake up soon with Lanfranc wagging his beard at me and find Godwinson really was shot in the eye? Or that he's not dead at all and I'm still in Normandy? Maybe I even dreamed William. Did you know that the Romans weren't sure this island existed before Caesar invaded it? I read a lot of Caesar while I was sitting around in Saint Valery waiting for the wind to change. And Tacitus..."

He slumps back into his chair, staring into the fire, no longer, apparently, aware of her presence. God knows what he sees there. He must have suffered some sort of relapse, ranting like a madman about dreams and hermits and Julius Caesar when confronted with her knowledge of his deceit. He is possessed, she is sure of it. Devils live in the hearts of fires; if you stare into them as he is doing you will see their faces, and if you stare long enough they will enter through the eyes and travel straight to the spirit. If a devil takes her she will never find her children.

"I'll call your servant, sir," she says fearfully, hurrying towards the door, fumbling to unfasten her knife before the devil gains the strength to pursue her.

"Wait," he says suddenly, wrenching his gaze away from the fire. "Come back. Were you truly on the battlefield? Can you confirm my dream to me?"

"I don't know, My Lord, I don't know what you dream." And don't tell me, please don't tell me, begs her heart, one hand on the latch, the other still fiddling with the thong fastening her knife. "Let me fetch your servant. You are unwell."

He waves a dismissive hand at that. Looking at him she feels her panic subside a little. He looks more himself again. Perhaps, after all, the fire devil did not have time to jump into his eyes. She stops trying to free her knife, noticing his gaze flick from her hand to her face. He gives her a quick, knowing smile. He is not ill, or possessed, but completely in control.

"Did my sister know all this when she found you?"

"No, My Lord, only that I had been a tiring woman to Lady Edith, on account of my skill as an embroiderer. You might have remembered me, but you did not."

"Men notice women after battles, mistress, not during them."

"Men do not notice women at all, My Lord. What men notice is if their bellies are empty or their shirts need mending."

She could be pretty, he thinks, yet it is the hardness in her that

140

appeals to him; it is probably what he deserves. He starts to laugh, displaying even teeth. "And you call me plain spoken. Come here. Sit down. We will have a drink and decide what's to be done about poor Godwinson."

"Aren't you going to have me arrested?"

"Why? Is that what you want?"

"It is what I expected."

"For now, my main concern is for my tapestry. When it is finished, if you still wish to be arrested, I will see what can be done, you have my word on it."

"You should be more careful of words, My Lord. It's not a tapestry. That's a different thing altogether."

"So Agatha keeps telling me. A detail. Here, drink this, only be warned. Brother Infirmarer insists on adding honey to it. It's abominably sweet." He hands her a drinking horn, the tips of their fingers brushing as she takes it. He watches her drink, the tilt of her chin, the ripple of the muscles in her throat, rosy in the firelight, a little shudder as she swallows the over sweetened drink.

Emboldened by his obvious appreciation, she decides she will try to salvage something from her failure. "Can I ask you a question, sir?" She smiles, feeling herself flush from the fire, the wine, her ridiculous desperation. Her pride.

He looks amused and perplexed all at once. "You can."

"Lady Edith, what happened to her?"

"I have not laid eyes on her since Winchester fell, and that's the honest truth of it." Turning from her he adds, in a more hesitant tone, "I suppose you saw...all that also?"

His day's growth of beard gives the impression that some celestial illuminator has partially gilded his face before stopping work till tomorrow. A half finished angel. She has no more stomach, all of a sudden, for baiting him. "You mean the child?"

He nods.

"That was an accident. It was terrible, but I do not blame you

141

for it. I have no wish to hold you accountable for things beyond your power. To be honest, it's a relief to me to find there are some things beyond your power."

"Thank you." He looks at her sidelong and their eyes meet. She recalls her father, the day her mother died, Adam struggling to tally his figures by a smoky tallowlight. He wears the same expression, of hurt and bewilderment, he makes the same mute, hopeless appeal for an explanation.

Rising from her stool, she replaces the horn in a silver bracket on the hearth. At the same instant, as though by some signal, Odo also stands and, stepping towards her, folds her in his arms, his left around her waist, his right hand drawing her head down against his breast, enveloping her in his perfume. With a sense of blissful relief, she leans into him, and lets him take the weight of all the grief and anger that has wracked her for so long. She closes her eyes, luxuriating in the breadth of his frame, the strength of his arms, the certainty which comes to her that he can absorb it all the way a good shield takes the shock of a lance.

The bones of her skull, beneath her cap and couvre chef, curve perfectly into the cup of his hand. His heart pounds as though trying to break out of his chest, and he wonders if she feels it too. Her lips part slightly and he feels, rather than hears, the soft sigh which escapes her, caressing his fingers as they explore her face. Her strong little hands glide down his back, stroking his ribs like harp strings.

But it's not enough. What he craves is more than she can offer. His emotions, forced out of shape by the imbalance in his body, are too raw for the absurdity of the physical. He isn't ready for knots in laces and stuck belt buckles, for exposure, for saliva, sweat and semen. He's afraid, sick of body and heart as he is, that he wouldn't be capable of making love. He feels too vulnerable to expose himself to Osbern's knowing leer if he asks him to ensure they are not disturbed, and refuses altogether to consider the notion that the bed behind him belongs to Lanfranc. He yearns for an exalted passion, for consummation without the mess, to love and be loved without trying. He's exhausted. He's being childish. He loosens his grip on her and, seconds later, trembling with frustrated desire, she does the same.

She has failed, and she will never have another chance. He will always be on his guard now. Clearly he thought it was her intention to seduce him only in order to finish what she started, and that is why he drew back. Yet he wants her, his body will not let him lie about that. And he did make the first move, he did put his arms around her, holding her with such fierce tenderness that the memory of it tugs at her with visceral sweetness. As she waits to be dismissed she tries to concentrate on breathing, sucking clear air into her lungs, yet the air in this room is as tricky as a marsh, laden with the scents of medicinal herbs, and his perfume, and the sharp, feral heat of his body seeping under her skin.

Odo is sure a host of tiny demons is practising dance steps in the pit of his stomach, wantonly calling his heart to keep changing its tempo. He has loved all kinds of women in his life, modest or strident, demanding or discreet, some beautiful, others who compensated for a lack of beauty with certain rare skills he hardly likes to admit to himself, let alone his confessor. He knows the love of women. It does not feel like this, not dumb and inept and bewitched by dreams.

"The fact is," he begins, "I have this dream, often, sometimes every night for a week or more. Though not, I grant you, since my accident. And you seem to be part of it. The thought had a strange effect on me. No doubt a consequence of my delirium."

"Tell me. Perhaps it will help." He cannot refuse the immense gravity of her expression, where the answers to all his questions seem to be suspended as the fixed stars are in heaven. He thinks, as he begins, that he will not tell her the end of it, but as he nears the point, as he stumbles over his account of the feelings the fair beauty arouses in him, he realises she is already the custodian of his shame, in life as in his dream. She has discovered him in lies and in lust, as he has discovered in her the intent to kill him. One more perversion can only bind them closer. The dream seeping into life. He tells her everything. He rehearses every word he spoke to the anchorite of his delirium, he spares her nothing.

Revolted yet fascinated, her blood cold and dancing, she cannot take her eyes off him. She keeps her fists clenched beneath her chin because she does not know, if she gives her hands their freedom, whether she will try to claw his throat out or wind her arms around him and cover him with kisses. She exults in his pain, it is no more than he deserves, and then her heart goes out to his weakness, she yearns to smooth the lines from his forehead and kiss away the shadows around his eyes. He must feel pain, it is his just desert for what he has done, condoned, lied about. Yet the suffering in this dream may also be a sign of repentance, and if he repents, then the hatred and anger which has sustained her will have nothing left on which to feed. They are together in the power of his dream.

When he comes to the end of his tale, he is leaning forward in his chair, his forearms resting on his knees, twisting one of his rings around and around his finger. The room has grown dark, Osbern conjecturing his master would not welcome his intrusion to light the lamps. The fire murmurs and pops; Gytha scoops a handful of dried herbs out of an earthenware bowl standing on the hearthstone and tosses them into the brazier. She breathes deeply, scents of juniper, thyme, mint and lavender bringing echoes of summer into the late winter afternoon.

"Is it God or the Devil speaks to us in dreams, do you think?" she asks, looking into the fire, the fizz and flare of the burning herbs dancing in her eyes.

"Or our own poor souls released from the constraints of their humanity."

"Which sounds like the same thing."

"Sounds like, but isn't. If the soul were God or the Devil, then we would be sublime, immortal. Instead of just a battleground, as the Manichees have it."

"Perhaps your dream is a battle, My Lord. The black and the white. Love and violence. The woman among the bodies. Life and death."

"Yet it seems to me more of a memory than an allegory, Gytha."

"I don't doubt it. You need to be conscious to play at allegory. Like dice."

"And none of us would consciously think the things that fill our minds in sleep."

"If we did, we wouldn't need to dream. God..."

"Or the Devil?"

"Or the Devil, could speak to us more directly."

"So we have come full circle. Tell me, Gytha, in your opinion, is this dream of mine sent by God or the Devil? Is it of *somnium coeleste* or *somnium animale*?"

She considers him earnestly, a slight frown drawing her brows into a sweet furrow above her nose. "I think it is sent by your guilty conscience, My Lord."

"I have no conscience." He drops his gaze and stares at his hands, at the thin scorings of the infirmarer's fleam like tiny bridges of scar tissue across his veins. As though he has willed it, her fingers reach out to him until their tips brush one of the cuts.

"You do yourself an injustice, My Lord, if you think that, as your dream shows," she says gently. "Confess and be absolved."

"Do you confess?"

"When I had a priest, I confessed to him. But he is dead and the church I worshipped in burned down. I imagine there's some great, dark lump of stone in its place by now. I don't see how God can be present in a stone house. So cold and earthbound, none of the warmth and life there is in wood. I keep my prayers to myself these days."

"Do you think I shall be plagued by this dream forever? Perhaps now I've confessed it to you, it's up to you to grant me absolution."

"Even if it were in my power to absolve you, My Lord, I don't think you have shown sufficient contrition for your sins yet." She keeps her tone light, but she is testing him.

"For what? For lying about Godwinson? Consider. If I asked my sister to record what you and I saw, what do you think it would do for his memory? I know my honour means nothing to you, but how might his suffer if it was allowed to be known that he was cut up like butchers' meat? I made my decision out of charity, out of respect for the man I once knew."

"And looting Lady Edith's house? Bundling her off in a cart with her women as though they were pigs to market? Did you do all that out of respect also?"

A spasm of embarrassment crosses his face; for a second he looks like a boy caught stealing apples, before his expression clears again. "When I remember how Godwinson was foresworn, it would be easy for me to say, alright, let's have the truth in all its grisly, humiliating detail. It's no more than he deserves. And it's not as though my reputation would suffer. It couldn't get much worse. Besides, I didn't kill him, nor did any of my vassals. I've no idea who did. And in dispersing his household I did no more than any sensible man in my position would. Frankly, Aelfgytha, there is little honour on either side, the way it's told to us in songs and stories." He crosses to the window and looks out on the shadowy cloister wall and the square of lawn, blue in the dusk. "They'll be locking up soon."

She twists round angrily. "Do you believe a word you've just said?"

He gives her a rueful smile. "Well, the bit about locking up seems uncontroversial. As for the rest, think what you like. You and I might not believe it, but other people will, the people who only see my tapestry. We have to be practical. I'm not going back to live obscurely in Bayeux. You're never going back to Godwinson's court. The shot in the eye, it's a myth for the present. It greases the wheels, makes things easier. God aid, he died four years ago. It won't make a bit of difference to him, or your poor, mad mistress, wherever she is."

"Or his children?"

"It won't make any difference to them." It is plain from his tone he will not entertain any enquiry as to why not. Two years ago, she remembers, rumours circulated for a while that Harold's elder sons had launched an invasion from Ireland. It was believed they had landed in Wales, but then no more had been heard of them.

"But the truth, My Lord…"

"Is what the victors say it is, I'm afraid. Interpretation, Gytha, do not underestimate its importance. Now, I am tired and I must look at my letters. You may go. You will have an escort back to the castle, and you will please convey my best wishes to my sister and tell her I pray for her recovery." After a pause, he adds, "As regards Godwinson's death, tell her…whatever you like."

With a questioning frown, she sweeps up her cloak to leave, her heels beating a rapid tattoo on the floor. He does not offer his ring to be kissed, and she neither bows nor bids him farewell. Uncertain whether she has won or lost, she has no idea how to conduct herself. All she knows is that she has to escape the tricky, stifling atmosphere of the sickroom, to clear her head and cool her blood. Backward and forward her feelings have gone, like the shuttle in a loom, but in the hands of a poor weaver, so now everything is tangled, the design corrupt and impossible to follow.

Odo smiles at her back. She will say nothing to Agatha about the shot in the eye, he is certain of it, for if she did, she would be forced to disclose a great deal more.

He tells Osbern he will attend Compline. While Osbern dresses him, he reads his letters; he is determined not to think about Gytha, despite the fact that Osbern's studious disinterest keeps her present to him as though she were still in the room. Sometimes he does confide in Osbern, often enough for Osbern to consider it his right and take offence when his lord is less than open with him. But his confidences are not genuine, they are merely rehearsals of decisions already taken, attitudes already adopted. They are like his public confessions. Whatever he may feel the need to confess about this afternoon is far from clear to him yet; it lies in a murky, unexamined corner of his heart.

There, as he breaks the seal on the letter from Thomas of York, to remain. He becomes increasingly bad tempered as he reads, prowling around the room so that Osbern has to perform various feats of agility to divest him of his loose gown and persuade him into a clean shirt. Only when he helps Odo on with his chausses does he manage to keep him still, and then with such a poor grace that, fearful of a cuff on the head before he completes the task, he wishes chausses fitted more easily over the heels. Still, God must be thanked for small mercies; a week ago my lord wouldn't have had the energy for such a display of petulance, and a woman in his bed chamber all afternoon as well. He brushes Odo's long tunic and hands him his Psalter with a smile of satisfaction.

"Fit for Saint Peter himself, My Lord."

"On the contrary, I feel we're giving Saint Peter a good run for his money. I think we shall go home tomorrow, Osbern, I feel so much stronger. And the King has business needing my attention. Make the necessary arrangements."

"Certainly, My Lord."

"And Osbern." He stoops to pick up Agatha's crumpled drawing from the floor, and tosses it on to the brazier where it flares up briefly before crumbling into ash. "Get this room cleared up. I want that revolting sweet wine out of here and the physician's instruments of torture returned to him. He'll have no more of my blood for now."

"No, My Lord."

"Such a beautiful, beautiful night," remarks Gytha and she and Leofgeat make their way back through the town, two men in Odo's livery preceding them. The moon is full, sharp etched in a cold, cloudless sky. An O shaped moon, an Odo moon, open as a mouth for kissing. Beneath it, Canterbury lies bewitched, still and blue and silver.

"Cold." Leofgeat shivers. "There'll be a frost." She shifts her basket to her other arm. "My back aches."

"Give me the basket." Though it is heavy with stone jars of preserved plums from the Archbishop's excellent orchard, and a blood pudding sent by Lord Odo to his sister to aid her recovery, Gytha swings it effortlessly from one hand to the other, striding out to its rhythm as though pulled along by its weight. She starts to sing. She wants to dance. Her bones are full of music. She is reprieved, reborn, a new life beginning, lit by this bright, fat moon. "Look at the man in the moon," she says, "grinning like a jackanapes."

"Just listen to my stomach rumble," Leofgeat complains, "and supper will be long over by the time we get back."

Odo enters the chapel late, attended by two of his pages and Juno. Having read Thomas' letter, he is no mood for appeasement and if he wants to take his dog into church, he will. She attracts no more than a cursory glance, however, from some of the younger novices whose powers of concentration are not yet well developed and for whom Archbishop Lanfranc's exalted guest is a boundless source of lurid speculation. As the hound is just a hound, and the pages boys much like themselves, and the Bishop of Bayeux has neither horns on his head nor a tail behind, they quickly lose interest.

The congregation is singing the first of the psalms, the men's and boys' voices in harmony, swelling to fill the incense fragrant arch of the nave. *If incense had a sound*, thinks Odo, *this would be it*. The plangency of the men's voices makes the air tremble in ecstasy, the purity of the boys' soars to heaven. And hears his own voice, faltering, broken, then gaining in confidence, merged with the rest. *Irascimini et nolite peccare quae dicitis in cordibus vestris in cubilibus vestris complingimini*. Commune with your own heart and be still.

Compline is a short service. Having missed the start of it, he does not feel ready to leave the chapel after the Dismissal and, as the rest of the congregation makes its way to the dormitory for the first sleep of the night, he goes forward to kneel at the altar. No questioning eye catches his; he is not a member of the order nor bound by its rule. His two pages, having received no signal from him, hover at the west door until Lanfranc puts an arm round each, like a hen gathering her chicks, and ushers them out. Juno, not so easily influenced, lies at the altar rail with her head on her outstretched paws, beside her kneeling master.

He does not pray, not in words, but, in the stillness of the Great Silence that will now hold the abbey till Matins, he tries to offer his day to God. He starts with what he can see when he lifts his head and opens his eyes, the rood screen carved with scenes from the Passion, leading the eye up to the tall east window whose stained glass shows Christ coming in glory, though it is a muted and human sort of glory now that night has fallen and only moonlight illuminates it. The acolytes have snuffed out the candles; there is no light in the church but the red pinpoint glow of the lamp burning before the Host. Odo kneels back on his heels, head bowed, hands loosely clasped in front of him, and waits for the cool wings of God's compassion to brush him in the darkness.

But it does not come. All there is in the day now ending is confusion. A woman tries to kill him, and he responds by making love to her, and then shies away like some silly virgin unable to make up his mind. Was that God's intervention? Should he give thanks that he has been turned aside from sin? But fornication is only a venal sin, and besides, neither he nor the woman is committed to anyone else. And besides, if God had intended him to be celibate, surely he would not have given him John. God knows better than most the seductive agony of having a son to love. So what? Guilt about Godwinson? Ridiculous. He sees again the man's great hands with their freckled backs lying on the gold filigree reliquaries beneath their embroidered silk shrouds and feels sick.

"Today is the Feast of Saint Agnes the Virgin, who resisted the blandishments of Rome to dedicate her life to Christ. Do you meditate on Saint Agnes, my son?" Lanfranc. The music of his Latin, the flat of his hand resting lightly between Odo's shoulder blades, the smell of his unwashed, old man's body. He does not answer immediately, he has lost his voice somewhere among all the other voices clamouring inside him. Eventually he says,

"Meditation is too strong a word for it, I think, Father. I am simply waiting for things to make sense."

"Is it not enough for you that your life makes sense to God? Can't you trust him even that far?"

"To be honest, Father, He hasn't given me much cause."

"That is where faith comes in, Odo."

"And if the consequences of faith call faith itself into question? If, in doing what I understood to be my Christian duty, I have fallen from grace?"

"Then your understanding is mistaken."

"So easy to say, Father. We priests, we say these things to our flock every day. We never let them see our struggles, though, do we? Even in confession we hide behind the form of words."

"I will allow, Odo, that in your case the way has been made harder by another's intervention. You should have been allowed to complete your education. Find your vocation in your own time, as I have no doubt you would have done."

"What if is an absorbing question, but not a very useful one. I have a more practical matter I should like to discuss with you before I leave tomorrow."

"I rejoice in your recovery, my son." A clipped, business-like note entering his voice, the edges of his words hard and clearly defined. He cannot allow himself to be seduced for long by the satisfactions of giving priestly counsel; he is an Archbishop now. "Come to me after Chapter in the morning and I shall be glad to hear you. Now I shall leave you to your prayers. I do recommend you give some thought to Saint Agnes."

"Goodnight, Father. God grant you rest."

"And you, my son."

God grants Odo an imperfect rest, filling his mind with Thomas' complaints, William's summons to him to join him in arms as soon as possible to put down an uprising in the Fens; and with half waking dreams of Gytha that seem to brand the shape of her lips and eyes and breasts into his flesh, leaving his blood clinging in his veins like hot oil and his nerves so raw he feels as though his skin has been flayed.

Eventually, as dawn sifts through gaps in the shutters, he rouses Osbern and sends him to the well for cold water in which he douses himself repeatedly until the fire in his body is extinguished and his mind is clear. He dresses soberly and, wrapped in his sable lined cloak, lets himself out of the house.

He walks in the Archbishop's garden, the cold air scouring his lungs, among frost blackened roses with a few scarlet hips still clinging to their branches. He pauses to pick a quince from a leafless bush and tosses the golden fruit from hand to hand as he walks, pearly mirrors of honesty catching and breaking against the hem of his cloak as he passes.

Lanfranc also rises before Prime and summons his personal servant to the bath house to help him remove the hair shirt. It is a slow and painful process. The rough hair-cloth has delayed the healing of the wounds he inflicted on himself by scourging, so that the shirt is now embedded in a sticky mass of blood and putrescence and has to be peeled away from the Archbishop's tender skin like a plaster. Though the servant winces and groans, and has occasionally to turn away from the mess of mortified flesh, Lanfranc, naked but for the shirt and braced against the clammy bath house wall, neither moves nor utters a sound.

As his servant washes and binds his wounds, his mind is fixed on the coming interview with Odo. He has a shrewd idea what direction it will take, for which he is much indebted to one of the cellarer's boys, who overheard a member of Lord Odo's household talking about letters from Thomas of York and saw fit to report his intelligence. God has rewarded Lanfranc's abasement with Odo's recovery; now he must substitute soft wool for hair-cloth, politics for prayer, and resume his temporal mission. The pain is transitory.

They stand in the master mason's tracing house on the site of Lanfranc's new cathedral. A chilly breeze slices through the unglazed windows, setting up dust devils in the corners and swirling the men's skirts around their legs. Odo draws his cloak closer, the fur silky against his neck and jaw. Lanfranc, clad in a white habit embroidered in gold thread, shivers. Odo ignores him; he appraises the older man's solid, square body and is satisfied that Lanfranc has no need of his pity or his cloak. The masque of frailty is merely the opening performance in the play they are about to enact.

"Let me show you the designs for the corbels in the nave," says Lanfranc, riffling through the heap of dust covered parchments on the long worktable beneath the windows. "I find them most amusing. You see? Caricatures of members of our community here. You'll recognise Brother Thorold. And the Prior. And this, I fear," pointing a finger whose joints are swollen with rheumatism, "is me."

Odo can see immediately that the likenesses are wickedly truthful, and in other circumstances might be amused by the mason's cheek and impressed by his skill, but this morning Lanfranc's delaying tactics only irritate him, and this irritates him further because he knows it's what Lanfranc wants. He must not lose his temper.

"Your Grace, I must speak to you about Thomas of York." Wishing his Latin, though fluent, had the same elegance and precision as Lanfranc's.

"And what touching Thomas is so important to you?" Lanfranc rolls up the drawings.

"He writes that you have refused to consecrate him until he makes you a written profession of obedience."

"Not me, Odo, but the See of Canterbury. It would be most presumptuous to exact such an oath to my person."

"Frankly, I think it unacceptably presumptuous anyway. As far as I can understand, there is no precedent for York taking second place to Canterbury. York's independence goes back more than three hundred years." Odo starts to cough; after the long silences of his recuperation, his voice has lost the strength for argument.

Lanfranc waits for the fit to pass before asking, "May I ask why you are involving yourself in this matter?"

"Thomas was a canon of my cathedral in Bayeux, as I'm sure you're aware, Your Grace. I sponsored his education. He approached me for advice. As his spiritual father. Which I am still, I suppose, as he remains unconsecrated."

"But you have no ecclesiastical jurisdiction in England, Odo. It is none of your business." He fixes his sharp, dark gaze on Odo. "Walk with me a little. I am afraid we shall be in Master Paul's way if we stay in here. Take my arm," he says as they leave the tracing house and begin to make their way around the boundary of the building site, treading cautiously on the slippery, rubble strewn surface, stopping occasionally to peer into the craftsmen's lodges and watch the stone carvers and carpenters at work.

"We're like a couple of old men," he remarks, "me with my rheumatism and you with your back. Propping each other up." They pause to watch one of the carpenters planing a length of oak, delicately arched like the rib of a ship. "How old are you, Odo?"

Where is he going now? Patience. "Thirty four my last saint's day," he replies after a pause; it had been his mother's business to keep track of his age.

"Mmm." He looks at Odo speculatively, tugging his beard. "You look older. And I am sixty." Is he, or is it just the age he chooses to be, a neat, round number, not young, not senile? "Yet I am building for the future here and you look to the past. This tapestry of yours. A commemoration, is it not? You see, what Gregory III promised to Archbishop Egbert of York three hundred years ago is irrelevant. It's past. We must go forward."

"Surely the past, Your Grace, is our foundation. Otherwise why did you school me in the classics and the Old Testament when I was at Bec? Didn't you expect me to learn from them?"

"Yes, Odo, not to swallow them whole like a snake with a rabbit. You disappoint me."

"Well I've always done that, haven't I?" The swish of the plane along the curve of the wood grates on his ears, his eyes are full of sawdust. He turns away from the carpenter's lodge, though Lanfranc keeps hold of his arm, preventing him from moving on.

"Only because your ability is so great. You are capable of anything. William knows that. That is why I am Archbishop of Canterbury and not you. I am capable merely of carrying out the will of the king and, I trust, of God."

A bell begins to toll, marking the next office of the day. Odo looks up at the sky; the wind drives rags of dirty cloud across the sun which has already reached its short zenith. He wants to conclude this business and be on his way. The carpenter lays his plane aside and composes himself for prayer before eating his midday meal. Lanfranc slips his arm out of Odo's and drops to his knees in the mud and sawdust. Odo, whose only prayer is that his exasperation with this pantomime of modesty and obedience will not show on his face, does likewise, feeling the cold seep through his clothes as Lanfranc recites the *Deus in adjutorium*. God is merciful, and Lanfranc contents himself with this portion only of the office of Sext before rising, brushing himself down and resuming their walk.

"Regarding Thomas," Odo begins again. "If you reject history as a justification for his autonomy, let us consider the fact that he was appointed directly by His Holiness. We are not talking about some provincial abbot here. You, on the other hand, have only my brother to thank for your elevation. It is an English affair."

"Nevertheless," says Lanfranc with a bitterness which takes Odo by surprise, "one of which His Holiness is in full support. I am not an ambitious man, Odo. Your brother alone could not have persuaded me to leave Caen to take up this responsibility. Indeed, I refused him, despite the fact that he is probably my best friend. I am here only on the direct orders of our Holy Father." He gives a short laugh. "Another unruly pupil."

"Can you prove this? Do you have letters? You have not been to Rome for your *pallium*."

"Do I have to prove it? Is there no honour between us?"

"As I see it, this is a matter of law. Law must be proven, as you yourself taught me. There must be precedents, and witnesses. Until you can produce these, I shall urge Thomas to swear no oath."

"And I shall not consecrate him until he does. I assure you I have the King's support in this. The King understands that the Church in England must be gathered under a single head, just as the people are gathered under him."

"But who's tune are you dancing to, Lanfranc? William's, or the Pope's?"

"Why God's, of course. It is very straightforward for me. I do not wear a bishop's hat on one side of the Channel and an earl's coronet on the other. You should consider the consequences of your actions more carefully, Odo."

"Oh I do, Lanfranc, believe me, I do." Odo turns and walks away, his long cloak swirling about his heels, covering the ground a great deal more quickly now he is free of the older man. Lanfranc makes no attempt to follow him, but returns by a different route to the refectory, reflecting serenely that he is going to be in trouble with his servant for making such a mess of the white gown. He is not worried by Odo's clever questions and Delphic oratory. His duty is clear, as the Holy Father pointed out to him in his astonishingly speedy rejection of Lanfranc's request to be allowed to return to Caen. Odo is merely a temptation, and he has always been dispiritingly strong at resisting temptation.

"A warm welcome, sir," says Osbern. They can still hear the hubbub in the castle wards, muffled by the fine Flemish tapestry now covering the parlour window against the onset of the evening's cold. The entire household turned out to welcome him, from Hamo and his lady and two sullen little daughters to the smallest spit boy from the kitchens. Everyone smiled and congratulated him on his recovery, some pressing the flanks of his horse or hanging on to his stirrups as though he were a hero returning from the wars. Planks of wood strewn with fresh straw had been laid over the worst puddles in the courtyard, newly cleaned out so that it smelt more of damp earth than manure for a change.

The well had been decorated with ivy and winter jasmine, and Countess Marie awaited him there with a bowl of mulled wine. Leaning down from his horse to take it from her caused him a moment's anxiety. In order to enable him to ride, Osbern had bandaged his midriff so tightly he was not sure he could bend without losing his balance. He was also wary of coming into contact with his pommel, after the additional injuries inflicted by his encounter with Mistress Gytha. Countess Marie, however, is a tall woman and held the bowl up high, averting disaster.

He drank the health of all of them, lifting the bowl in every direction, but particularly towards Agatha and her embroiderers clustered outside their door like a flock of wood pigeons. But not Gytha. *Why? Where was she?* Realising her absence, a pain shot through him more sudden and intense, and unexpected, than any in his ribs or kidneys or his jaw when he smiled. But at least, he told himself with a gallows grin, appropriate to one of his bruised and aching parts.

"As warming as a fire built entirely of kindling, I think, Osbern," he replies. "Now for pity's sake get these bandages off me. I can hardly breathe."

Osbern undresses him and removes the bandages, which he rolls and puts away discreetly in the bottom of the linen press. Odo has orders to join the King in Ely as soon as possible, to put down a rebellion of the East Anglians. There can be no question of damaging rumours about his fitness.

"Give me my dressing gown, then you may leave me to rest. I shall dine in hall tonight. Come back in an hour. No, on second thoughts, ask Lord Hamo to attend me, and a scribe." Messengers must go out to his vassals no later than the morning ordering them to join him for the expedition to Ely.

Good, loyal, efficient Hamo with his pasty, pockmarked face and his Gascon harridan, the Countess Marie, whose marriage Odo himself had blest days before they embarked for England, though in Odo's opinion, the only good thing to come out of Gascony is its horses. It is lucky he knows his lord's vassalage almost as well as his lord does, because this evening Odo is curiously and uncharacteristically absent-minded about who owes what in knight service and how long everyone is likely to need to assemble their forces.

"My Lord," he ventures, after pointing out for the third time that Ursulin FitzHugh is already in East Anglia and that therefore there is little point in ordering him to attend a muster in Canterbury, "should you be undertaking this campaign? Shall I go in your stead?"

Where is she? Why was she not there to welcome him? Could she be ill? Dead? "Hamo, you're a good man, but I assure you I'm fine, just a little tired. Besides, I need you here. I have been considering replacing this castle. It's inadequately fortified and damnably uncomfortable."

How dare she have the gall to snub him? When he has been generous enough not to have her clapped in irons for attempting to murder him? Women. Whatever you give them, it is never enough.

"Yes, My Lord."

"There's a suitable site just beyond Worthgate, with the Roman walls to the southwest and the river to the north, roughly. There's nothing much there at the moment, a few small houses and a church. To Saint Mildred, I think. The houses can come down and we'll put another church in the castle ward. I'd like you to get things started, plans, land clearance, foundations and so forth. Find me a good, plain mason. No artistic temperament. I want to see the keep up by All Souls."

"Possible if we use local stone, My Lord, rather than bringing it in from Caen as you did for the women's house."

"Fine."

But how would she excuse herself to Agatha? Has she told Agatha the truth? How else could she account for the fact that she no longer had the drawing? If she has, will Agatha be grateful to get her back, with her small hands so skilled at fine needlework, or will she account him a contemptible fool for letting her go?

"My Lord, there is just the matter of cost."

"If the money isn't available, Hamo, levy a tax. We aren't in a famine or anything, are we, and my people cannot expect me to defend them entirely at my personal expense? If there's resistance, you hold my seal and command the garrison. You know what to do."

"Right, My Lord. That just leaves de Mortimer."

Perhaps she was there after all, and it was just that he failed to see her because of her small stature, "De Mortimer?"

"For the muster, My Lord. Only a dozen knights and their people, but as he's not more than a day's ride away from your northern border, well situated to reinforce you if necessary. I suggest you send to him to stand in readiness in his own manor, rather than bringing his force here."

"Eminently sensible. See to it, Hamo."

Nonsense. Of course she wasn't there. He saw Agatha, didn't he, and she is of a similar height? He will go to the atelier as soon as he finishes his business with Hamo. No, he won't. It isn't for him to go begging to her. But it would be only natural, expected, that he should want to see how the work has progressed during his absence. After dark? When he can see so much more clearly in the morning, by daylight?

Once Hamo has bowed his way out, Odo goes through to his bed chamber where Osbern is laying out his clothes for dinner in hall.

"Leave me."

When Osbern has retired, he lies on his bed, cheek resting on his folded arms, staring into the darkness, feeling his back ache, feeling like a lovelorn adolescent. Feeling a fool. Feeling sorry for himself.

Feeling, he realises, lonely. He has never been, is never, alone. He is surrounded by his household, his priests, his soldiers, his vassals at every waking moment, dressing, eating, shitting. Fucking..? Thinking, reading, ruling his world. More often than not he is in the company of the King, from whom, the chroniclers tell him, he is inseparable. Even as a tiny boy he shared a bed, first with Agatha, later with Robert. Now Osbern sleeps outside his door every night, or on the other side of the hanging which partitions his tent, close enough for his breathing to lull Odo to sleep, certainly close enough to be the one who holds him until his teeth stop chattering when his nightmare visits him. Even now, in solitude and darkness, God is watching him.

Except that he has no sense of it. The crowds have dispersed from the wards and it is so quiet. No rustle of angels' wings, no muffled laughter, no-one standing between him and himself. He feels abandoned by everyone. By William and Lanfranc in their reforming zeal. By Agatha, who cannot read his mind after all. By God.

But Gytha cannot leave him, she is inside him, she is his, because he dreams her. Except that he does not; he has been free of his nightmare since recounting it to the anchorite. The anchorite. The anchorite must be found so that Odo can reclaim his dream, and her.

"Osbern!" he shouts as he returns to the parlour, running his hands over his face and through his hair as though trying to rid himself of the maudlin humour clinging like spiders' webs in an unused room.

Osbern hands a tray of wine and drinking horns to a small boy from the buttery summoned for the purpose, and bows, flapping his hands behind his back at the boy in a gesture of dismissal. "My Lord?"

"Send the verderer to me. Straight away. I must speak to him before dinner. Then you may dress me."

FABLES

LENT 1071

He sends no page to announce him this time. He does not have to. The women can hear the clank of his spurs as he runs up the stairs. Sister Jean breaks off in the middle of reading Aesop and hurries to meet him.

"This is an unexpected pleasure, My Lord. I thought you would be gone by now." The household has been on a war footing for weeks. The shields have been taken down from above the high table, leaving pale ghosts of themselves on the plaster, the heavy mail hauberks have been unpacked from their boxes, the swords and javelins sharpened. Every day the outer court has been occupied by a queue of nervous war horses waiting for the farrier, and several people have been kicked or nipped, passing too close to the highly strung animals.

"Any minute." The din in the outer court is rising with the delay. Horses snicker, harness jangles, dogs bark, the occasional laugh, full of bravado, rises above the rest. "I...I wanted to take a last look. To have this work fresh in my mind to compare with the Byrhtnoth hanging when I see it again."

He has decided to give her one more chance. He has come to

the atelier every day while waiting for the muster to assemble. Every day. Loitering about on some pretext or another, talking to Agatha about matters he knows she has perfectly well under control, such as the supply of wools, the consistency of dyes, the danger of fire if the women are allowed to have extra braziers. He knows he has driven his sister to distraction with remedies for Margaret when she had an inflammation of the eye, a present of Saint Agatha cakes from Master Pietro for the women to share on the day they commemorate the saint's martyrdom, some needless nonsense about a mistake he has spotted in the embroidering of a bridle, which no-one but he is ever likely to notice. Yet he could not help himself, he was powerless to keep away.

And she has never once looked at him. Even now, she is the only one who does not raise her head as he comes in, but continues to sew as though not even the Trump of Doom could distract her. If he were to cross the room and stand, looking over her shoulder at what she is doing, breathing in her mermaid smell, she would simply sit motionless, her hands folded in her lap, her head demurely bowed, exposing the downy nape of her neck with its scribble of dark hair escaped from her cap, and wait. Whatever comment he might make would elicit nothing more than a low "Yes, My Lord," or "No, My Lord," or possibly a "Thank you, My Lord," if he tried to win her over by praising her work.

She has no right to treat him this way when he has exercised such forbearance. She may have served Edith Swan Neck but when all's said and done she's no more than a common little whore, and a whore's tiring woman before that. Oh yes, he knows all about her now. He has extracted the information from Agatha by degrees during these waiting days. Information is a commodity he understands well, the conditions in which it proliferates, how to harvest it, its uses and its resale price. Yet this information has somehow turned on him. The knowledge of her whoring has served only to draw him in more deeply.

The thought of other men fucking her, of men fucking her for their pleasure, of the wishful thinking men indulge in with whores, obsesses him. It is like the gap left by a drawn tooth, a bloody mess you must always be poking your tongue into. When he thinks of her now, that is how he sees her, servicing her clients in some steamy, sordid little cell, her skin slippery with sweat, her hair sticking to her face, and he feels sick with lust, lying in his gut like an indigestible meal.

When he does not think of her, he thinks of nothing. The only embassies to which he pays proper attention are the daily reports from his verderer, always the same, always nothing. Every evening his heart lifts at the prospect that today they may have, must have, found some trace of the anchorite. Every evening, when Osbern shows the man in to him, he can tell immediately from the mournful, slightly wary set of his countenance that they have not. The rational half of him knows they never will, that the anchorite is a mirage, conjured by fever, but he cannot give up looking. Remember Brutus, whose dream island he is now living on, enduring the very real vagaries of its climate and the dangerous eccentricities of its people.

His confessor, clearing his throat, his ears turning scarlet, speaking in a strangled whisper, suggests that solitary vice, in moderation and for the sole purpose of averting the excessive accumulation of seed, which can contaminate the blood, is forgivable. But he doesn't want solitary vice, or moderation. Or forgiveness.

"Perhaps this will interest you, My Lord," says Agatha, leading him towards the frame where the twins are working, next to Gytha and Emma. She notices how his glance repeatedly flicks in their direction, understanding, probably better than he does himself, how he is ensnared. Margaret sits there too, blithely oblivious to the effect she has on Agatha, like a serene red and white cow, smiling her merry smile in response to some remark of her sister's.

He stands for long minutes, contemplating the scene stretched on the twins' frame, without once looking up. There he is again, the tall knight with the arrow in his eye, but no longer dramatically suspended in empty space. He is flanked by a standard bearer, although the standard carries no clearly identifiable arms. It may be a dragon, the Godwinson emblem, or a fox, or a wolf. Anything really. A mounted Norman soldier canters behind him, and beneath the horse's front hooves a footsoldier, mutilated by the Norman's sword. The whole scene carries the legend, *Hic Harold Rex interfectus est*. Harold the King it reads, and it is impossible to say to which of the two dying men it refers.

"I see," he comments loudly, "that Mistress Gytha gave a full and frank account of our discussion about Godwinson's death." She must acknowledge him now.

But if she does, he does not see it, because just at that moment, Alwys, who has been attending to him rather than her work, snaps her needle and tears the middle finger of her right hand with the sharp stub, letting out a little shriek, distracting him. He is mesmerised by drops of dark, bright blood falling on to the white linen, next to a tiny headless man with large hands, toppling to his death in the lower margin, beneath his executioner's feet. He stares at it, certain it reminds him of something, until Agatha, bustling about with a bowl of water and strips of bandage, elbows him out of the way so that she can attend to Alwys' wound. Nobody notices Margaret wince, sucking her own middle finger as though it, too, is bleeding.

By the time Alwys' wound has been bound and the needle replaced, the moment in which Gytha might have said something, or even merely met his eye, has passed. He moves on, stopping to exchange courtesies with Judith and to ask one of the Saint Augustine's women how the community feels about the appointment of a new abbot. He himself is overjoyed that it is to be Scolland, another man from Bec like most of Lanfranc's appointments, but one whom Odo remembers for the warmth of his compassion, a priest more concerned for the plight of a sinner than the correct form of granting absolution. He hopes for an ally in Abbot Scolland. He then returns, pausing to satisfy himself that the damage to Alwys' finger is not serious, to the position to which he is becoming hopelessly accustomed, standing behind Gytha.

He is going away to war. True, these risings seem to have become almost routine over the years, but they are no less deadly for that. He could be horribly maimed, or held to ransom for years. He might die. Suddenly it is unthinkable he should face these possibilities without holding her in his arms again, feeling the imprint of her body on his like a shield, or a sense of hope. Why is he hesitating? She belongs to him anyway; if he were to order her into his bed now, this instant, the only people with any right to complain would be the army waiting for him in the outer ward, in the squally March wind, the munitions carts sinking slowly into the mud.

"Mistress," he says, sounding horribly nervous and peremptory, "a word, if you please. Privately."

She cannot reply. Her heart seems to be stuck in her throat. Her palms are sweating. It is the same whenever he enters the atelier; she doesn't look at him, tries to avoid speaking to him, yet her body responds to everything he does, every nuance and inflection of his speech, every one of those looks he darts at her. She marks them all. She lays down her needle, wipes her hands on her skirt and pushes back her stool. As she rises, she becomes acutely aware of how close to her he is standing. The air between them seems to take on shape and substance. All conversation ceases; she hears nothing but the rhythmic jangle of his spurs and the knocking of Emma's stool against the floor as she begins to twitch. All eyes are on them as they walk out of the workshop, passing Sister Jean's long worktable on one side and the row of frames on the other, Gytha preceding Odo, who holds back the curtain for her at the head of the stairs. Even Alwys stops fiddling with the bandage around her finger.

Gytha has no idea where to go. Even though the hall is empty, the door is open on to the courtyard where his army waits. The curiosity of the other women presses around them like a crowd at a fair. The only privacy is to be found in the women's dormitory, or Sister Jean's parlour, where she also sleeps. Is she destined always to meet him in rooms where there are beds? She turns at the bottom of the stairs

"Where..?" but her question remains unfinished. Taking her chin between his thumb and forefinger, he tilts her face towards him and kisses her mouth, sealing in the rest of her words with his lips. Struggle, she tells herself as he parts her lips with his tongue, resist this foreign, treacherous thing, but in the realm where his kiss is possible, where nothing exists but his kiss, the rules are different and her body won't obey. She clings to him, her arms around his bowed neck, her fingers entangled in his hair, and kisses him back, hard and hungry, her tongue learning from his, a sinuous, sensuous dance. Her body arches itself against him. All her senses are flooded with him, the hot, salty smell of his skin mingling with the familiar perfume and the faint residue of the pig grease they use to rustproof armour, the play of bone and sinew as he wraps his arms around her, the surprising, minty taste of the cardamoms he chews to freshen his breath, the gorgeous pressure of his erection just above her pubic bone. His eyelashes curl, like his hair; a man in whom nothing is direct. His mail shirt brands small rings into her skin beneath her dress, though she feels no pain but the famished ache of lust between her thighs. She is disbelieving when, eventually, he draws back from kissing her, dazed to find they are still separate people, not fused irreversibly in the furnace of that kiss.

"I only meant to talk to you about the camel," he murmurs. She frowns, but her mouth smiles and she licks her lips, tasting bruises.

"The camel?" Oh fortunate camel, to be in Gytha's mind, in Gytha's lovely mouth.

He straightens up but continues to hold her, hands clasped in the small of her back. "A favour for a soldier on the eve of battle."

"Another one?" Her fists are loosely curled against his chest.

"One of anything is never enough." He sounds hoarse, breathless, as though strangled by desire. She strokes his throat, holding her fingertips against the pulse that beats there like a moth trapped beneath the skin. Then they kiss again, watching each other with hungry eyes, until they are distracted by some commotion outside in the courtyard, horses whinnying, the stamp and slip of hooves, raised voices.

"It's time I was going." he says, making no attempt to disengage himself, breathing the words into her mouth.

"What about the camel? You'd better tell me quickly, or they might leave without you." Giggling. Delicious conspiracy.

"Shall I let them? And stay here with you?" He strokes her breast, the tips of his fingers tracing the hard bud of her nipple beneath her gown. "With the bed curtains drawn and Osbern guarding the door?"

She feels as though her bones and sinews and all her organs have dissolved into a hot, languorous fog. Her voice, brittle and teasing, seems to come from somewhere else. "I would have thought you'd spent enough time confined to bed recently, my lord." She fences, she fends. "Now, what about the camel?"

"Will you embroider me one? So I can see what it looks like?"

She laughs and shakes her head. "Whatever you wish."

"I have the notion now that I shall ask for it as a lady's favour, instead of a sleeve or a pennant or what have you. Something to carry with me into battle and keep under my pillow at night."

"But I can't possibly do it now, there isn't time."

He smiles, though sadly, at her stricken expression, and strokes her cheek, savouring the realness of her skin, the crazing of tiny veins beneath its whiteness, the fine lines bracketing her mouth. "There'll be other wars, don't doubt it. Give it to me next time."

"I pray you live to see a next time, My Lord."

"If I have your prayers, Gytha, then I am sure no harm can come to me." Nevertheless, he fishes his glass amulet out from the neck of his shirt and kisses it. One of anything is never enough.

"What is that, My Lord?"

"This? It's called a Tear of the Virgin. It has a splinter of the True Cross inside. See?" He holds the charm towards her, extending the chain to its limit. She takes it between thumb and forefinger, tilting it to the light until she can see the tiny dark filaments at the heart of the glass drop. It feels warm from its place next to his skin. This, and her prayers, a fragile defence. "William gave it to me at my consecration."

William. Here she is, nestled against the still beating heart of the Bastard's brother, the man she swore to kill. How easily her body has betrayed her, let her forget him laughing with his brother over the mangled corpse of King Harold, dictating to his scribes as his men bundled Lady Edith off God knows where and stole her possessions. For all she knows, his apartments are decorated with Lady Edith's tapestries, his rooms lighted by her silver candlesticks. She doesn't move, but he senses some change and holds her closer.

"It's alright," he reassures her, "I'm sure nothing's going to happen to me."

"Your men are getting impatient, sir, and Sister Jean will be after me if I don't go back upstairs." She struggles to free herself but he won't let her go.

"A last kiss?" he begs.

"Come back safely, My Lord." She pushes at his chest, gently, steadily, until he releases her with an uncertain laugh.

"One more thing," he says, turning at the foot of the stairs.

"Yes, My Lord?" She has already started back towards the workshop. Although she pauses, she remains facing away from him, fists clenched at her sides. He fancies she is trembling slightly.

"Why did you not come out to greet me when I returned from Christ Church? It is the custom, you know, when your lord has been away for some time."

She raises one hand, rubbing distractedly at the back of her neck. "I..."

"Yes?"

"I could not. I was not ready...to see you again so soon."

"Yet it was you who brought me home."

The gentleness of his tone, the swoop from lordly arrogance to something almost humble, makes her turn to face him. She feels she owes him an explanation, but what can she tell him? That she is ashamed of her behaviour, that she regrets having failed in her mission? Better to say nothing than to tell a lie.

He waits, watches how she looks around, everywhere but at him, as though the words she wants may be hidden somewhere in the hall, behind the open door or in the curled corners of the drawings pinned to the walls and rustling softly in the wind.

"It's all wrong," she says eventually, "this is all wrong."

Again that brief, uncertain laugh. "We shall see," he says.

And is gone, into the embrace of men and horses, tactics, map reading, muddy roads, comfortable words for the dying.

"God speed," she murmurs as the door closes behind him, and crosses herself, something she has not done for years. She hears the clatter of hooves and armour, the creak of cart wheels, the squelch of feet in mud as she climbs the stairs to the atelier. They'll follow the old wall north and go out of the Quenin Gate, she thinks, the way she would go if she were going home. Returning to the workshop, she glances out of the windows over the outer ward, unable to help herself. Of course she cannot see him, but she does glimpse his standard, the golden wolf on the green ground, fluttering among the banners of the other knights in his company as they file out of the gate.

"What was that all about?" hisses Margaret as Gytha passes her on her way back to her frame. She sounds like a goose, a silly, plump goose.

"Nothing. A small favour."

Margaret leaves her place under the pretext of collecting wool. "There's none of the green left on our stand, sister," she calls in response to a sharp glance from Sister Jean. Then, "Don't be so cagey," she says to Gytha. "He's sweet on you, isn't he? It's obvious."

They speak in loud whispers. Gytha glances at Sister Jean, who is watching them intently from her lectern, continuing to recite Aesop from memory rather than reading. "You should pay more attention to the feelings you arouse in others, Meg, and less to what his lordship might or might not think of me. Anyway, I'm sure he's completely indifferent to me."

"That's impossible. You're too...I don't know. Anyway, he can't take his eyes off you. And look at the way he's taken to hanging around here, like some moonstruck boy. It drives Sister Jean to distraction, you can tell. What are you going to do about it?"

"Not much I could do if it were true, is there? I'm his to do as he likes with, just as you are. Anyway, if he's gone after Hereward he'll most likely get himself killed and my virtue will remain unsullied."

"D'you really think he might? I wonder what would happen to us if he did?"

"You'd be alright, I'm certain of that."

"Gytha, what are you talking about?"

"Nothing. Just saying you'd be alright. You could...go home to your parents and let your father find you a nice husband."

"Gytha?" Forgetting herself, Margaret lays down her needle, but, catching Sister Jean's eye, quickly picks it up again.

"Yes?"

"What's it like? You know, going with a man?"

It's messy, ridiculous, humiliating, irresistible, painful in all kinds of ways. "My husband did his best to be pleasing." She laughs, a wry puff of air through her nose. "He had a notion there must be pleasure on both sides to make babies." And what is Odo's best? Odo, with his living son. "But...there was a beggar woman I used to see sometimes, with a little child. She'd been a slave in a thegn's household. Her master had had her against her will, and got her pregnant, then, because she wouldn't give up the child to his wife to be raised, had her thrown out of the house in disgrace. I used to wonder how Adam's theory stacked up against that. But I was grateful too. Adam was dim witted, but he wasn't cruel."

"Is he the only man you ever went with?"

"Meg, is your brain over heated? If this is about the Earl, there really is nothing to tell. Did you imagine he'd ripped off my clothes and made passionate love to me on the hall floor while you were all sitting here listening to Aesop?" The pit of her stomach suddenly feels as though it is filled with quicksilver. "He is a bishop, you know," she says, as much to remind herself as Margaret.

Margaret lets out a little shriek of laughter, quickly stifled. She tries to concentrate on her work but can make no sense of the charcoal lines in front of her that she is meant to transform into embroidery. Something is in the air, something confusing, adult, mysterious. She curses the luck that brought her here, to be mewed up in a castle before her time, like Saint Barbara in her tower.

"This is life," Gytha continues, "not a romance."

Margaret doesn't believe her. "Oh well, I don't suppose I shall ever know. By the time the Earl's finished with us I shall be an old maid with no property and I'll have to go back to my parents, if they're still living, or my sister-in-law."

"I didn't realise any of your brothers was married." Gytha is relieved to be able to change the subject.

"Oh, Tom was. He married young. Christine brought a good dowry and Papa said it would do him good to settle down. He was a bit wild." She smiles wistfully. "They were expecting a baby when he went to join King Harold. Christine had a little boy. She called him Tom too."

Odo, the widow maker.

"It's the fear he might have died unshriven," continues Margaret. "It worries me more because his body was never found so we couldn't even be sure of giving him a Christian burial. D'you suppose God makes allowances?"

"I think God makes all sorts of allowances for soldiers."

"Gytha, Margaret." Sister Jean raps on the lectern.

"Sorry, Sister," says Margaret, looping her wool off the stand and returning to her frame.

"Thank you. The next fable is that of the Fox and the Crow. A crow was sitting on the branch of a tree with a piece of cheese in her beak when a fox observed her and set his wits to work to discover some way of getting the cheese.

"Coming and standing under the tree he looked up and said, 'What a noble bird I see above me! Her beauty is without equal, the hue of her plumage exquisite. If only her voice is as sweet as her looks are fair, she ought without doubt to be Queen of the Birds.'

"The crow was hugely flattered by this, and just to show the fox that she could sing she gave a loud caw. Down came the cheese and the fox, snatching it up, said, 'You have a voice, madam, I see; what you want is wits.'

"What do we understand from this? That flatterers are not to be trusted."

Margaret gives Gytha a meaningful look. "See. She's noticed too."

Gytha continues to sew. Chain mail. Only now does she begin to feel the bruises on her breasts and upper arms.

She cannot sleep, her mind plodding a treadmill of its small stock of memories of Odo, the discomfort of her bruises dissolved in the encompassing ache of guilt and frustration. She fears he will be killed, she fears he will not. She is relieved it went no further, yet feels the promise of his body pressed against hers as distinctly as her linen shift bunching and tangling as she tosses and turns. She tries to imagine becoming his mistress, but it is beyond imagining. She conjures visions of him out of the darkness, his hands, his mouth, his doe eyes, the weight of his body - *what does he look like, feel like, naked?*; and remembers in a flood of mortification that he is a bridegroom of the Church. And her enemy. As grey light begins to filter through the window shutters, she abandons all attempts at sleep. Pulling her cloak around her shoulders, she creeps out of the dormitory, drawn to the workshop and the view from the great windows. Somewhere to breathe, to be alone and think.

Dawn has already reached the workshop. The sky in the east is the colour of opals and the tips of the palisade are touched with the first, tentative, rose gold light of the sun. She walks slowly down the length of the room, feeling the knots and splinters of the floorboards under her bare feet, breathing the solitude of cold ash and cat's piss, running her hand over the embroidery frames, feeling expectancy in the taut stretched linen from which figures emerge like Adam from the dust.

She stops at random, and quickly recognises Emma's work in the face of a soldier riding to Bosham with Harold at the beginning of his ill-fated embassy to Duke William. The face that seems to foresee how it will all go wrong, looking far ahead of the homely scenes of prayer and feasting and dogs being carried into the ships by patient men with their skirts kilted up to the buttocks, seeing shipwreck and false promises. Emma has a real gift for faces.

Why did Harold go to Normandy when he did, when it was obvious the old king had not much longer to live? In Lady Edith's household it was understood that he went to negotiate with William for the release of hostages. Yet the Normans say he carried King Edward's confirmation of his promise of his throne to their Duke. That would explain his journey, but not why he would swear fealty to the Bastard. He and his brothers had the Witan in their pockets; there was no doubt they would elect him king when the time came. He must have been tricked, duped by the Judas' Hair from the moment he fell into the hands of that pirate, Ponthieu, forced off course by a storm in the Channel. Do the Normans even have the weather on their side? Dear God, it's all so unfair.

Yet now, looking at Harold's entourage boarding their ships, she finds herself remembering Odo's bitch, Juno, and thinking how the scene with the dogs would delight him, how it is probably derived from Sister Jean's experience of life in Odo's camp rather than anything she has been told about King Harold. She turns her back on the frame and leans her elbows on the smooth stone sill to watch the sun rise. Through Odo's windows.

Just then, the cat, which has been asleep on the lectern as usual, decides her day is beginning and jumps down. The copy of Aesop falls to the floor on her tail, the loose pages fluttering after it, making her squawk and run for the stairs.

Gytha only starts to read, in her painstaking way, so she can return everything to the lectern in order. The book is, of course, in Latin, primitively illuminated so that she cannot rely on the illustrations to show her which fable is which. Foxes look like wolves, crows like eagles and men like monkeys. The loose leaves are transcriptions of the Latin text, each line alternated with an English translation.

Sister Jean has made many translations, of everything from Ovid to Archbishop Lanfranc's much acclaimed new commentary on the Epistles of Saint Paul. But this is not in Sister Jean's hand, nor, to judge by its erratic layout, that of a professional scribe. The letters are boldly made and easy to read, but often the lines are not very straight and are frequently interrupted by marginal notes and glosses in French which Gytha cannot understand. The translation, she thinks, is also better, more subtle and less literal, than Sister Jean could manage, made by somebody with a greater facility in the nuances of the English tongue.

The more she reads, the more certain she becomes of the translator's identity. She can feel his hand forming the letters, the play of muscle and bone beneath the skin, the pressure of his square-tipped fingers on quill and sand caster. She sees the light catching in his jewellery and the gold hairs on the back of his hand as it moves over the parchment. She hears the scratch of the nib and the long silences in between, tense with thought. And, knowing him, is drawn into the reading as though into his mind, her lips shaping the words he has made, oblivious to everything but the precarious thrill of falling, past Aesop's creatures in their Babel Tower of morals, through the sheets of linen stretched out to break her fall, through the sparkle of shattered glass, like Lucifer falling through the floor of heaven.

At the end of The Fox and the Crow he has written, *'The moral of this story is...'* then something in French, then *'...that you must know you can stomach lies before you swallow them'*. Which gives her an idea, a kernel, an embryo she will nurse. This one will not die.

She listens avidly to Sister Jean's readings from Aesop, sizing up each tale to see if it will fit the mould of her idea. Her sleepless nights, whenever Odo will leave her alone, when, perhaps, he sleeps himself and does not dream, are peopled by Aesop's creatures, the smooth talking fox, the vain crow, the frog and the mouse running a three legged race from drowning, the lion made foolish by childlessness. The darkness around her seethes with them, as though her thoughts have taken physical form. The air rustles and whispers, pads across the floor on bare feet, murmurs her name.

"Gytha. Are you awake?"

"Alwys? What is it?"

"I thought you were awake. I didn't want to disturb Meg."

"What's wrong?"

"It's my finger."

"Your finger?"

"The one I pricked the day the Earl left."

The day the Earl left. *A full and frank account of our discussion about Godwinson's death.* Oh, of course. Lord Odo has had a change of heart, Sister. He would like to tell the truth now. Surely he could see how easily she has compounded his lies with her own. What a myth they have created between them, what a bond of dreams and make believe.

"I'd quite forgotten. Sorry."

"I don't think it's right." A note of genuine fear in her voice refocuses Gytha on the present. "It's all swollen up and throbbing fit to burst."

Gytha gropes under her bed where she keeps a stub of candle and a flint. Glancing into the darkness in the direction of Margaret's bed, but detecting no sign the other twin is awake, she whispers, "Come out into the hall and let's have a look at it." They go out, closing the dormitory door softly behind them. Gytha strikes the flint against one of the few patches of wall not covered with pictures and, by the light of the candle, examines Alwys' finger. It looks like a half cooked sausage, the skin stretched and shiny, on the verge of splitting. At the tip, where the needle entered, it is crimson. "Cold water," she says with a confidence she does not feel, "I'll go to the well. You get back into bed. I might be a little while, I shall have to get Sister Jean up to unlock."

Agatha is not asleep when the knock comes on her parlour door. She is kneeling at the prie dieu in her bedroom, contemplating the image of her patron saint hanging above it, oddly animated by the warm, flickering light of a candle. The saint, chastely clutching the flaps of redundant skin over the bloody gashes where her breasts used to be, seems to be laughing. Her mouth gapes more in a grin than a grimace, her shoulders heave with mirth. Is this, thinks Agatha, the best she can do with her prayers, make the saint laugh? She wishes she could see the joke. Cupping her hands over her own shallow breasts, she wonders if the solution can truly be so simple; she would do it if it was. *It is better for thee to enter into life halt or maimed, rather than having two hands or two feet to be cast into everlasting fire.* For the saint perhaps, the victim of cruelty, tortured by the lover she had spurned. But what defence of virtue is there for the victim of Margaret's cheerful indifference? How can she fight an enemy who does not even know she is one?

Having no servant to attend her at night, she answers the door herself, half expecting, half dreading to find Margaret standing there, conjured up by the demon of her mistress' perversion. But it is not Margaret.

"Gytha? Is all well?"

"Sorry to disturb you, madam, but Alwys is complaining of her finger, the one she pricked. It's very swollen and I wanted to get some cold water to bathe it. Can I have the key so I can go to the well?"

It isn't difficult to see how she has bewitched Odo, with her bold eyes, her red lips and black brows and the hair falling as heavy as water below her waist. But it would be disappointing to find she had set out to do it deliberately.

"Come in," she says.

"I just need the key, madam. I needn't disturb you for long. I'm sure it's nothing serious."

"Then it can wait a minute or two. Sit. Please." Her tone is not to be gainsaid.

Gytha, unfamiliar with the layout of the parlour, looks around in the gloom for somewhere to sit.

"I wanted a word with you in private. Now is as good a time as any since we're both wide awake."

The chair she finds is severe, its arms carved with open mouthed, sharp toothed beasts which bite into Gytha's palms. But it is outside the circle of light cast by the single candle, which Agatha has put down on a low table in front of her empty hearth, and that makes Gytha feel easier.

"Yes, Sister," she says. There is a pause. Agatha, like a skinny ghost in her white shift, seems to float across the room as she paces back and forth. Eventually she says,

"Be careful."

"I beg your pardon?"

"Don't pretend you don't know what I'm talking about. Odo...the Earl...enjoys female company, but he is not...influenced by women. Do not imagine that you have found a way to gain power over him."

Power. The very mention of the word makes her wonder what others see in her that she does not see in herself. "I don't, madam," she says, the right reply and the true one for once in accord.

"And do not forget his calling. His love is not his own to give."

And the son? John? "Correct me if I'm wrong, madam, but the Earl is merely a clerk. He is not in orders, not sworn to celibacy."

"No, but it is expected among the higher clergy, as you are well aware."

"Nor poverty, it seems," Gytha continues. "Clearly he is cautious in what he swears to, for fear of being tempted to break his word. He is very strong on the solemnity of oaths."

"As you know, Gytha, I've a fondness for your clever tongue. But sometimes it tires me."

"Then speak plainly, madam, and I can do likewise. Then we can get this over and done with and attend to Alwys. What should I be careful of? What do you think has transpired between the Earl and me? Tell me, and I'm sure I can set your mind at rest. I do not think you will find that the balance of power between us has changed." Oh no, not even if Hereward, bereft of everything but his sword arm, kills him.

She has been over it so many times. She has analysed each move, every word spoken, considered every alternative, every meaning both obvious and hidden. She has missed nothing, not the tiniest catch in his voice or the faintest falter in his gaze. She looks at Agatha, now perched on the edge of the table, and Agatha's face twists beneath her gaze. A starveling smile stretches her lips, her pale eyes strain. She hugs herself close.

"Perhaps you should tell me," she says, "as you have no confessor."

When Gytha lived in the convent, she was aware of certain friendships more than usually intimate and exclusive. She was neither shocked, nor surprised, nor envious of them. In her experience, love is a scarce enough commodity in this world and she attaches no blame to those who take it where they find it. She does not feel unlucky, merely unworthy. She is no elegant, high-waisted Edith Swan Neck or sweet natured Meg. She has wit and common sense, but these do not inspire love, and she could not hold on to her children, no matter how fiercely she loved them. She feels more pity for Agatha, with her self imposed restraints and her vigilant conscience, than for herself, for whom no such effort of will has ever been necessary. Until now, cautions her heart, until now.

"There's nothing much to tell, madam. His lordship kissed me. Just a kiss, the sort of silly impulse men have before they go off and get themselves killed. I'm sure by the time he comes back, God willing, we shall both have forgotten all about it. It meant nothing." As she says this, she believes it, and suddenly everything seems simple. He might have picked any one of them; he only chose her because of her knowledge of the camel.

"Well, perhaps not," says Agatha.

You're wrong, says Gytha's heart, you know you are. It changed everything.

She takes the key to the wicket and goes to fetch the water. It is a beautiful night, cold and clear, the stars seeming close enough to touch in a moonless sky. Most nights the stars are small and distant, indifferent to earth as they sing their songs to heaven, but tonight they are gathered round, peering down at humanity, expecting something. She leans against the well parapet and looks up. Somewhere a dog howls, answered by whickering from the stables. Footsteps crunch along the Roman walls as the soldiers on watch change position. Are the stars out wherever he is, looking at him with the same close scrutiny? Does he feel it? Or maybe it's raining, cold rain angling under tent flaps, needling him awake. What does he do when he can't sleep? Talk to that sinister servant of his? She wonders if his nightmare has returned, what is a day's journey from here for an army. She is so small and ignorant. She shivers, shaking off all the useless questions, and starts to wind up the bucket from the well, the splash of water in the shaft echoing loudly in the quiet ward. Steadying the bucket against the parapet, she fills the jar she has brought with her for the purpose, then lets the bucket go, the winch handle spinning as the rope unwinds, the crash as it hits the surface of the water far below, the water leading its own life, hardly disturbed, hardly depleted. Nevertheless, she apologises to the well sprite for disturbing its rest before going back inside.

In the dormitory, everything is in uproar. Everyone is awake, lamps are lit, Sister Jean has been summoned and is kneeling over Alwys who lies shivering beneath her bedclothes, her face drawn in tight with pain, sweating dark patches into the pillow. Margaret, so pale her freckles look blue in the half-light at the edge of the candle's glow, stands behind Sister Jean, holding a shallow bowl, a towel over her arm, the way the servants in hall offer the diners above the hearth water for washing. Judith grips Emma by the shoulder in an attempt to keep her still; she has already knocked over one candle, the tallow now drying in fatty lumps among the singed floor rushes. How long has she been gone, Gytha chides herself, dreaming of stars and water like a lovelorn maid?

She sets the jar down beside Sister Jean, who nods her acknowledgement but does not take her eyes off Alwys.

"Margaret," she says, and Margaret stoops so Sister Jean can dip a cloth in the bowl, wring it out and dab at Alwys' forehead and temples with it. Gytha smells roses, summer sweet. Then Alwys begins to heave, her throat arched, the muscles around her mouth working.

"She's going to be sick." Gytha grabs the bowl from Margaret as Sister Jean turns Alwys on to her side. A thin stream of greenish bile pollutes the rosewater. Margaret turns away abruptly.

"Are you alright, dear?" asks Sister Jean, darting Margaret a quick look, behind the prevailing drama the perpetual awareness of the other, like the bass note in music, that feeling of being tugged by invisible strings whenever the other moves or speaks, or even breathes in a changed rhythm.

"I'll deal with this," says Gytha, taking the bowl to empty on to the garden.

"What hour is it, d'you think?" Sister Jean asks her when she returns.

"Around Matins I should guess, madam. Still pitch dark anyway."

"I shall send to Christ Church for their infirmarer. I don't think this should wait till daylight."

Gytha takes her place beside the sick woman as Agatha goes to order the officer of the watch to send one of his men to fetch Brother Thorold.

"What's wrong with her? Why does she need the infirmarer? I'm frightened."

"I'm sure Sister Jean is just being careful, Meg, she wouldn't want you to be upset."

"You see, if one of us gets hurt, sometimes the other one feels it too."

Gytha pulls Alwys' blanket up to cover her injured hand and

muffle its smell. Alwys moans. The swelling has spread, the little tear made by the needle split and gaping like an idiot's grin, oozing blood and pus on to the bedclothes. "Go back to bed," she says to others. "There's nothing more to be done until Brother Thorold gets here. We should just try to keep her cool."

Margaret dutifully dips a clean napkin in the water jar, folds it and lays it across her sister's brow. Gytha watches her, touched by her tearful conscientiousness. To distract her, she asks, "Who's the eldest?"

"I am, by half the width of a fingernail, our father says." Seeing Gytha's puzzlement, she explains. "The time it takes for a candle to burn down half the width of a nail."

"Ah, I see." Gytha smiles. "It must be confusing, having that special closeness, and having to be ashamed of it at the same time."

"We used to try to pretend we weren't."

Looking from one to the other broad, freckled face, each for its own reason pale as the bed caps from which their irrepressible hair springs, Gytha's smile broadens.

"I know," says Margaret, "but the bishop granted our father permission to put our mother away on grounds of adultery and marry again, and we were afraid we'd be sent to a convent too."

"None of the girls in Winchester had twins that I can remember." Gytha's tone is reflective, as if she has forgotten she has an audience, but though she and Margaret have been speaking in whispers, the dormitory is quiet and their voices carry.

"Girls?" queries Margaret, and at the same time Judith says, "I knew it. I saw the cockade among your things when Sister Jean brought you here."

"Cockade? Gytha, you weren't, you didn't..?" Margaret starts to giggle, Alwys forgotten as she delves into the lurid possibilities of Gytha's past. Judith has loosened her grip on Emma, but Emma remains quite still.

Gytha takes the cloth from Margaret, dips it in the water jug and bathes Alwys' temples. The girl mutters, then screams as some involuntary movement of her arm brings her blanket in contact with the poisoned wound. Gytha calms her with soft shushing noises, then removes her bed cap and, sliding her hand beneath Alwys' head, lifts her hair clear of her sweating neck. "They say war is full of surprises. But in my experience it isn't. We do what we can to survive, the same things people always do to survive. It seems we can't help ourselves."

Judith emits a sceptical snort.

"Anyway, Meg," she continues, with an air of putting an end to the conversation, "there was a time when I knew a lot of women who slept with a lot of different men, and none of them had twins, so where does that leave the notion that two babies means two fathers? Probably thought up by some husband too mean to provide for them."

Judith returns to her bed, her head at a precariously haughty angle on her long, scrawny neck. Emma sits down on Margaret's bed, a grimace which might be a smile or simply the effect of guttering lamplight crossing her pockmarked face. How strange it is, thinks Gytha, the relationship between body and soul, like that between a man and his house. Just as he successfully repairs a hole in the roof, a window shutter breaks loose or a wall begins to bulge. Unpredictably, sometimes keeping the elements at bay, sometimes broken and reformed by them.

"Gytha?"

"Yes, Meg?"

"Does the Earl know?"

Does he? Has he wondered how she bridged the gap between Lady Edith's house and his atelier? Of course he knows. Sister Jean must have told him. And she has been so foolish, so naïve, as to believe he might have some genuine feeling for her. She is no more to him than a horse or a parcel of land. Probably less than a horse, in fact, certainly less than a field of good barley or a well defended manor. Just a little Saxon whore. Worth her board and lodging, though, since she can embroider as well, cosset his pride as well as his cock.

"I hope whatever the Earl knows has gone to his grave with him by now."

Agatha knows what is in store for Alwys, and that nothing she can do with rosewater or poultices or herbal teas for fever will make any difference. She learned a great deal about the pathology of wounds during her travels with Odo in the summer after the Conquest. She goes from the guardhouse to the chapel, where the priest and his deacons are saying the night office. Only a miracle can save Alwys' hand, and Agatha's one hope for a miracle is to confess. She will confess everything, everything she has thought and felt since first setting eyes on Alwys and Margaret in the mourning gloom of their father's house, the self pity and salacious curiosity in which she wallowed while the poison worked its rotten magic in Alwys' finger and Saint Agatha laughed.

The altar candles gutter as she opens the chapel door and slips inside on a draught of night air, then strengthen again when she closes it, splashing waves of buttery light up the whitewashed walls to catch in the gilded ceiling vaults. Although it is unusual for anyone else to attend Matins when the Earl is away, it is not unheard of, and the priest continues to sing the office without faltering. Agatha identifies immediately, with affection, the lines from Saint John for the Feast of Saint Joseph. *There was a man sent from God whose name was John.* And almost as quickly is seized by a pang of exclusion, knowing herself to be utterly unworthy of the name she chose when she made her profession, unworthy then, as now. She cannot give testimony of the light as John was sent to do.

She approaches the altar and prostrates herself, arms outstretched so her body forms the sign of the Cross on the beaten earth floor. The priest glances sidelong at her and falls silent. He is a timid man, this priest, a man well suited to be left in charge of the spiritual needs of a household whose lord is absent. His timidity confuses him as to who has a prior claim upon him, God or Saint Benedict. Lack of sleep and the effects of the Lenten fast do not help matters. Saint Benedict seeming somehow closer at hand than God, he elects to see the long office of Matins through to its conclusion. Perhaps the words will give comfort to the Earl's sister, or at least offer him some guidance as to how to approach her, so exalted a person in such a position.

"I implore you, Sister," he interrupts when, the office completed, she begins her confession, her forehead patterned red and white by the uneven floor, dust clinging to her habit. He raises his hands to his face as though trying to ward off an attack. "Go no further. Remember who you are. We are not alone here." He glances round at his two deacons, who continue to prepare for Lauds, studiously ignoring his plight.

"Of course we are not alone, Father," snaps Agatha. "We are in God's house and God is with us. As for me, I am simply a daughter of Christ who wishes to make confession. You have a duty to hear me and absolve me. Bless me, Father, for I have sinned. I have entertained lustful thoughts of a girl in my charge. I have abused not only her trust but the teachings of the Church in matters of procreation. And now the rottenness in my heart has found a way to manifest itself in the flesh, not my flesh but the flesh of the innocent..."

The priest lets out a whimper of panic. "Only thoughts, Sister?" he enquires, clinging to a vestige of hope. One of the deacons is trimming a candle, releasing an oily scent of cold beeswax.

"Thoughts, Father, of a specific nature."

"Providing you are clear in your mind as to the sinfulness of these thoughts, Sister, I do not think it will be necessary to elaborate on them."

"But I feel that it is, Father, if I am to be truly absolved." Odo kissing Gytha, herself kissing Margaret. How do they work, the kisses of lovers? How do their tongues intertwine? Do their teeth collide? What connections do their bodies make while their mouths are fused?

"There is a danger in detail, Sister. The female imagination is too easily inflamed, lacking in intellectual discipline. I fear that by recounting your thoughts you will revive the feelings they engendered and thus fall deeper into sin. I will absolve you of whatever is in your heart. That would be best."

"It would be a shoddy compromise, Father. And at the risk of adding the sin of pride to my burden, to condemn me for a lack of intellectual discipline is complete nonsense."

"It is my bishop's directive in matters of this sort."

"Who is your bishop? Is it not Lord Odo?"

"No, Sister, it is Archbishop Lanfranc."

"Ah, Lanfranc, who spent his youth in the law schools before making his profession. A lot Lanfranc knows about women. But still, I cannot expect you to disobey your bishop. I will make my confession in general terms, and I will recommend that you set me the hardest penance permissible, and that you report me to the proper authorities if you believe, when I have finished, that I have committed any crime."

The relief on the priest's face drains away at the prospect of having to report Lord Odo's sister for any crime, let alone one so heinous and unnatural as she is hinting at, and he is unable to do more than nod his agreement, a muscle twitching in his jaw. Agatha's conscience is pinched by remorse. She has been harsh; the fast is taking its toll on her temper also. But she cannot afford to treat the priest sympathetically. Unless her concentration remains focused on her sins, she has no chance of saving Alwys. What is this decent man's discomfort compared to Alwys' life? Or Odo's great work of art?

She confesses, going into as much detail as she is able before a series of small gasps from the priest warn her that she is overstepping Lanfranc's boundaries. He absolves her, but the penances he sets her are perfunctory, determined more by the status of her person than that of her sin. Absolved, but not resolved. She remembers the scourge lying beneath her bed; she will perform her prescribed penances but add to them the scourge. She hears voices at the gate heralding the arrival of Brother Thorold and the lay brother who assists him but, intent on her own purpose, she leaves it to the guard to escort him to the door of the atelier and slips quickly, shadow-like, through the wicket before the formalities of gaining entry to the castle are complete.

The scourge is dusty, its three knotted tails laced with cobwebs.

So much the better. She strips herself to the waist, takes the shaft of plaited leather firmly in her right hand and lays the scourge over her left shoulder to her back. She continues, lashing the same place over and over until she has attained a rhythm that is hypnotic, until the skin yields and parts and her blood begins to flow, and the yearning so long held in check forces itself out of her in great, rib cracking sobs.

How long before the knocking on the door finds its way through to her consciousness? She clutches her habit around her shoulders and goes to answer. It is Gytha, who takes in her dishevelled clothes and hot, red eyes but makes no comment.

"Brother Thorold thinks it would be best to move Alwys out of the dormitory, Sister. He wonders if he can bring her into your bed chamber."

"Yes, yes of course. Ask him to give me a few moments."

Gytha nods and goes. She cannot help Agatha any more than she can help herself.

In mid afternoon Brother Thorold calls Agatha in to the sick room for a consultation, after which Agatha puts on her outdoor clothes and sets off in search of Hamo, who is away supervising the land clearance for the new castle. Agatha goes on foot, the distance across Wincheap Green being hardly worth the saddling of a mule, but when she finds Hamo she envies him the height of his horse, elevating him above the pall of smoke swirling about the site and out of the eye line of the sullen, uncomprehending huddle of the dispossessed, watching their homes fired and their livestock scattered by the Earl's men. Hamo himself looks no happier than his men or their victims, but then, he never does.

"My Lord," says Agatha, dispensing with courtesies, "I have need of your assistance."

"I am at your disposal, madam," he replies with a small bow.

"I need a good swordsman. Accurate."

Sister Jean's request presents Hamo with some difficulty. "The best men are on campaign with Lord Odo," he says, "but I expect I can find someone."

"Not squeamish." They both survey the men firing the marked houses with pitch flares, faces grimy with soot and scored by streams of sweat, Odo's green and gold livery dulled as though it too has been tempered by flame. "And available immediately." She follows Hamo's gaze until it settles on a burly young man with tow coloured hair who seems to be parleying with the people who have been evicted. The helpless, reluctant way he hovers on the edge of the group does not fill Agatha with confidence, but she has no option other than to trust Hamo's judgement. Hamo nods towards the young soldier.

"That one," he says. "He has good reason to be grateful to be removed from this duty. He's got a girl with a baby living in this quarter. That's why he hasn't gone after Hereward. Couldn't have kept his mind on the job. Good enough otherwise. Hey, Fulk."

He spurs his horse forward among the smouldering wreckage, the horse's ears flicking nervously as sparks fly before the wind, until he is close enough to Fulk to make himself heard. Agatha, eyes smarting, watches as Fulk listens to his orders, nods and begins to walk away from the rest of the group. Immediately a young woman, clutching a bundle of rags which Agatha presumes must be the baby, darts out from among them and begins to follow him. A tall girl, but very thin, with jutting cheekbones and fine, pale hair that seems to reflect the cold sun shining above the smoky glow of the fires. Fulk turns and tries to argue with her, but she is not to be deterred. He ignores her studiously as he presents himself to Agatha.

He has been in the Earl's service since he was a boy, having travelled from Normandy in his retinue as a groom. He knows the Earl as well as any man in his position can know a man like the Earl, but this is the first time he has seen Lady Agatha up close. A lot of stories circulate about what goes on in my lady's atelier, all the more colourful for the fact that it is off-limits to everyone except Lady Agatha, the Earl and the embroiderers. Most of the men call it Odo's brothel, some of a more superstitious turn of mind mutter darkly about needles, and image making, infidels and the presence of identical twins. Witchcraft, they murmur, crossing themselves discreetly. Fulk is not an imaginative man, but there is more than enough in his mind to make him nervous as he bows to Agatha.

"I hope you are as strong as you look, Fulk," she says, appraising him. "I'm afraid what I require of you will need a strong stomach as well as a good sword arm."

"I'll do my best, madam."

"Where are you taking him? You can't take him. What am I to do?" It is the girl, her baby cradled in the sharp angle of one arm, clinging to Fulk's sleeve with the other hand. Hamo removes one foot from the stirrup and kicks her aside, his spur catching in her shawl and tearing it before he manages to disentangle himself. Agatha presses her lips together, forcing the words she might have spoken back down her throat. She must think only of Alwys, but perhaps compassion may have a practical use here. She has no time to become embroiled in Fulk's domestic difficulties.

"Is he the father of your child?" she says to the girl. Doubt flickers across her face as she looks at the nun, but her voice does not waver when she replies. "Yes, mother."

"And you are homeless?"

"I hadn't much to begin with, and they've shooed off my chickens and broken my loom..."

"Very well, you may come with us." She glares at Hamo. "I will find you work and lodging in the castle. On my own responsibility. But we must make haste."

As they make the return journey, Agatha explains to Fulk what will be required of him. He is horrified; he's a soldier not a butcher of women. But he makes no protest, feeling his Freya's arm through his and her full, milky breast bouncing against him as they walk.

Little work is being done in the atelier. A few of the Saint Augustine's women, who do not know Alwys well, are seated at their frames, but most have joined the other group and are standing around, bent together like saplings tied to form the ribs of a bower, consoling themselves with gossip. They know Sister Jean has gone out looking for Lord Hamo, and they are certain they know why. Margaret is with her sister. Gytha, who is only distracted by the sudden silence which greets Sister Jean's return, is still reading Aesop.

"How is she?" asks Judith, unable to anticipate anything from Sister Jean's expression. Sister Jean shakes her head.

"Gytha," she says, "may I speak with you a moment?"

Gytha closes the book and follows Sister Jean out of the workshop, feeling all eyes on her back. Again.

"Why me?"

"She knows you. You won't panic. I can't send Leofgeat, not in her condition, and I can't do it myself because someone has to keep an eye on Margaret."

After what Margaret has told her, Gytha is forced to acknowledge the wisdom of this, whatever Sister Jean's true motive. "What will happen to Alwys?"

"That depends."

"I suppose it does."

The silence is unbearable as they walk down the stairs to the door, past the drawings, the terrified faces of conquered and conquerors, the palaces and ships, the burning houses and horses with broken necks.

"You seemed very absorbed in Aesop," says Agatha suddenly. "I wasn't aware you could read so well."

"I can't really. I was never taught, just picked it up as I went along."

"You have quick mind. Your curse, I think. My brother made that translation, you know."

"Lord Odo?" Gytha asks, for the sake of feeling his name on her lips, its moon shape in her mouth.

"Of course. Literature couldn't be said to be one of Robert's talents." She smiles and pauses, then says, "I'm sorry, Gytha. They're in the Great Hall. They needed a large table."

The bell is ringing for Vespers as Gytha enters the hall through the wicket in the main door, and Brother Thorold and his lay brother are saying their prayers. He will be praying somewhere, she thinks, if he's still alive, kneeling on the wet earth among tents and cooking pots, or the cold floor of a woodland church, or a cushion in the chapel of a great house thrown into turmoil by his arrival. Praying for victory, for courage, that lances will not splinter nor bowstrings snap, for safe deliverance from the coming night. For her? She would like to hope so, would like to be able to pray for him.

She waits for them to finish beside the great double doors, locked now in case anyone in the household has not heard the news and comes to hall expecting dinner. Torches flare in all the wall sconces and a good fire burns in the hearth at the centre of the hall. The long handle of a cautering iron protrudes from the fire and rests on a trivet on the hearthstone. Smoke dawdles in the ceiling space, winds among the posts and beams supporting the Earl's apartments, before drifting out around the leather curtains that have been hung at the windows to thwart the curious.

The figures in the hangings, the hunting scenes, illustrations of scenes from the *Chanson de Roland,* the great painting of King William investing his brother with the arms of his earldom on the wall behind Odo's place at high table, seem galvanised by fire. The hart leaps, the dogs race, heroes do battle against the Infidel, the King's hands fumble with buckles. The furniture is laid out as if for dinner, the high table on its dais forming one side of a square of long trestles, with spaces at the corners for kitchen and buttery staff to serve. Such a pretty scene, such extravagance of light and warmth for the woman lying on the table opposite the doors, like a joint of meat ready for carving, oblivious to it all.

The two monks rise from prayer and Gytha crosses the hall to join them. Fulk is also there, solemn and tense, testing his sword blade against his thumb; she had not been able to see him before, with the bright hearth between them.

"What would you like me to do, brother?" she asks.

The chapel bell has fallen silent and the service of Vespers begins with the psalms. There is a large congregation, people drawn to church by a pervasive sense of foreboding. Lord Hamo and his wife and daughters are present, as are Judith and Emma, Agatha and Margaret. Margaret seems close to fainting, swaying from time to time against Agatha's shoulder. Agatha struggles with her burden, but it is hers to bear and she does not look for help. Freya is there, with her sleeping baby swaddled against her chest in strips of clean linen, and several of the Saint Augustine's women prepared to risk returning home after dark to pray for Alwys. One of Hamo's little girls, sensitive to the cold smoke drifting over the wards from the site of the clearances, has a coughing fit, causing the priest to lose his place and Marie to dart a sharp, anxious glance at her daughter. For each of these daughters she has already lost a son.

Brother Thorold folds clean napkins and wedges them beneath Alwys' injured hand. He works methodically but gently and Alwys, who seems to be unconscious, does not react as he lifts her arm at the wrist and packs the napkins underneath. The lay brother, who must maintain the pressure on the veins, consults quietly with Fulk about how close to the wrist he can grasp them without endangering his own fingers. Gytha sits on a bench opposite the men, close to Alwys' head. She has a bowl of rosewater next to her, and a barber's strop, the thick leather oiled and gleaming. From time to time, she strokes Alwys' fine, tight curls back from her forehead. The smell of the wound is unmistakable in its almost familiarity, its wrong side of the blanket relationship to the smells of sex and childbirth. Brother Thorold has made the right decision.

"We remember in our prayers our sister, Alwys. Christ who triumphed over the torments of the Cross, have mercy upon her. Pour the balm of

Your healing upon her and restore her to health. Amen."

"Amen."

Brother Thorold gives the strap around Alwys' upper arm a last tug, as though tightening a girth. He pours wine from a small flask over Alwys' wrist, skin and the napkins under her hand, which are stained purple. The lay brother braces himself, then bears down with all his weight on a point two or three inches above her wrist, his thumbs feeling expertly beneath the tendons for the blood vessels to be blocked off. Fulk, his face glistening with sweat, gives his hands a last wipe down his tunic and picks up his sword.

The priest pronounces the dismissal, then looks up at his congregation and says, "Any who wish to are welcome to stay and keep vigil." Nobody stirs.

Fulk squares his balance on the balls of his feet, adjusts his grip and raises the sword above his head. Gytha tries the strop again, but Alwys will not bite on it. Her mouth is slack, eyes closed; surely, God be praised, she is completely unaware of what is about to happen to her. Brother Thorold nods. Fulk brings the sword down, blade flashing through torchlight. Gytha keeps her eyes on Alwys' impassive face, which she dabs from time to time with rosewater. There is a muffled thud and the rosewater shivers in its bowl as the sword, slicing through sinew and bone and bloody napkins, makes contact with the table.

It could be Odo's body, a Saxon sword hacking through Odo's arm. Oh God, dear God, please...

In the chapel Margaret screams and falls to the floor where she lies on her back, eyes staring, legs twitching under her grey skirt, her left hand clutched in her right as though if she does not hang on to it, it will float off up into the vaults, with the cherubs and gargoyles carved on the roof bosses. The priest turns from the altar, two small acolytes who have come in to light the lamps stop what they are doing, open-mouthed, the elder of Hamo's daughters starts to jump up and down in an effort to see over the heads of the adults.

Fulk drops his sword and vomits over his shoes. Gytha, wrapping her hand in a cloth soaked with rosewater, pulls the cautering iron out of the fire. Brother Thorold takes it and applies the disc of red hot metal to Alwys' stump. A loud hissing and the smell of charred flesh set Fulk retching again. A dog, overlooked in a dark corner, venturing out to investigate the smell of cooking, sniffs at the severed hand lying among the floor rushes then, wrinkling its nose at the stench of putrefaction, retires into the shadows.

The congregation crowds around Margaret. Agatha, kneeling, cradles her head in her lap.

"It's the falling sickness," says Judith. "We need something to stop her swallowing her tongue."

Agatha says nothing, but darts the priest an accusing glance, as though it is his fault. Yet if his absolution was not perfect, it can only be because her confession was not heartfelt.

"Here." Marie withdraws a stout wooden pin from her hair and offers it to Judith. Her husband watches her as she walks towards the altar, the black hair escaping from her couvre chef and snaking down her back towards the strong buttocks beneath her Flemish wool gown. Judith depresses Margaret's tongue with the pin, wedging it firmly between her teeth, then holds her legs as the priest starts to intone prayers for the casting out of devils. Hamo's wife returns to his side, bundling her hair back beneath her veil. Unnoticed, Freya slips away as the baby begins to stir, starfish hands curling and uncurling, nuzzling her tiny, suckling mouth towards her mother's breast.

Alwys lies peacefully asleep in Sister Jean's bed. Brother Thorold has given her poppyseed for the pain, and she is unlikely to wake now before morning. Her fever is down and the bandages around her stump still clean and fresh smelling. Brother Thorold, satisfied with her progress, has returned to Christ Church. Margaret also sleeps, dreamless and exhausted, while Agatha lies awake in Alwys' bed next to her sister's, listening to the light snores, the rustlings and sudden mutterings of the sleeping women around her, trying to distinguish the sounds Margaret makes from the rest. She thought this would come to her, like learning to walk or speak, and now her throat aches with grief that it did not, reminding her that her love is not natural, like learning to walk or speak.

Fulk and Freya lie among the sleepers in the hall. Alwys' blood has been scrubbed from the table and Fulk's vomit from the floor. They lie facing one another, with their daughter between them, Freya's knees drawn up against Fulk's thighs. Dogs nose softly among the remains of a late dinner.

When the priest rises for Matins, as usual on his way to chapel, he sticks his head round the door to the bakery to wake the baker's boy and tell him it's time to light the oven. The boy, sluggish and yawning in the cold and dark, throws the bloody package on to the fire with the rest of the fuel, without noticing it.

Marie is restless. Hamo would not let her go to sleep with the women after making love to her, and she finds his presence constricting, sprawled over three quarters of their bed at least, it seems. She lies on her back, arms tucked stiffly into her sides, listening to the sporadic coughing of her younger daughter in the adjoining room. *It's the smoke*, she thinks, *just the smoke*. But unease seeps into her heart the way the English cold soaks her Gascon bones. Unable to settle, she shakes Hamo awake.

"I want to have the chapel washed."

"Mmmm," he replies sleepily, "on Palm Sunday. We always do."

"Before. Tomorrow. What happened in there at Vespers, it was the

Devil's work. I think it must be exorcised also."

"Go to sleep, woman. Things'll look different in the morning."

In the workshop Gytha shivers and chafes her hands to stop them stiffening. She sets her candle carefully beside the frame where Harold's embassy to Normandy is depicted, smiling again at the far sighted soldier and the dogs that must be kept dry. She then carries Aesop across from the lectern and balances it on the edge of the frame, though when she opens it, part of it rests on the linen itself and obscures Harold's entry into the church at Bosham. She takes a stub of charcoal from Sister Jean's worktable and begins to draw on to the linen in the empty bottom border.

Beneath the scene where Harold holds a banquet before embarking for Normandy, she draws a pair of hounds licking their paws. Or a pair of wolves perhaps. Then, as the diners begin to board the ships, a crow sitting in a tree, dropping a morsel of cheese from its beak into the waiting jaws of a fox. Although the fox has a thin, whippy tail, more like a wolf. The predator, the law breaker. Usurper of the golden lion king.

She begins to sew.

Yet Aesop says, in the Fable of the Wolf Who Reigned, that the lion gave up his throne willingly to the wolf.

FLOOD

NATIVITY OF THE BLESSED VIRGIN MARY 1071

Odo is taking a bath, soaking in warm water, fragrant with his perfume. He has spent the afternoon with Hamo, inspecting the foundations for the new keep. No rain has fallen since harvest, and he feels as though the dust is everywhere, even under his eyelids and coating the back of his throat. Now his long body is sprawled as far as possible in the beaten silver tub. Eyes closed, neck cushioned by folded sheets, he listens to Turold the dwarf picking out a tune on the citole, the notes of music mingling in the steamy air with the swish and bubble of water every time he moves. He dozes, considers idly that he is hungry, and glad the trouble in the bakery seems to have been sorted out. *What was that all about?* he wonders, hardly aware of the sudden commotion erupting in the parlour adjoining his bed chamber, raised voices muffled from his hearing by the heavy arras hanging across the doorway. Nothing to do with him, he thinks comfortably, Osbern can sort it out. It's a pretty tune, he'll get Wulfric to teach it to him, he'll amuse himself setting words to it. He starts to hum, pleased with the acoustic effect of the high sided bath, irritated when Osbern appears from the parlour.

"My Lord," he says firmly, "that woman's here. I've tried to send her packing but she won't take no for an answer."

"What woman?" he asks, though he knows perfectly well. There's only one woman who won't take no for an answer, and he has been deprived of her company for far too long, in the bloody, bog-ridden shambles of Ely, and he wants to hear her name spoken.

"You're the only one he'll listen to," Margaret had said, her voice a pleading whine, her eyes full of tears. Since her fit in the chapel during Alwys' amputation she has been well enough physically, but changed, shaken. "If he sends Alwys away, what will she do? No-one will want her."

"Sister Jean should speak to him." Gytha stabbed her needle into the linen, but Gytha was shaking so with rage there was no point in her continuing to try to embroider. She looked across at Alwys, rocking the babies with her foot, top to tail in their crib, as she and Freya wound wool into odd, three handed hanks. Late afternoon sunlight washed through the great windows and broke around them, over Freya's glassy hair, Alwys' pacific smile and the two babies' curled, sleeping fists. It was as if all Margaret's blithe self confidence had flowed into her sister, though Alwys, talking in undigested chunks of Psalms and Bible stories, would doubtless say it was the Holy Spirit. Should she tell them what Lord Odo intended? It would mean nothing to Alwys, but Freya had some spirit, even if she had thrown in her lot with one of his men.

Freya had quickly made herself indispensable to the atelier. As Leofgeat's pregnancy advanced with the summer, Freya took over her duties while Leofgeat waited out her goose month, still and swollen, her child's kicks now plain to see beneath the clothes stretched tight across her belly. When her pains began the midwife was away attending another birth so Freya said that she would be happy to sit with Leofgeat. After all, she said, she had given birth herself only recently, and she had had an aunt who was a midwife in York. Gytha had dreaded this duty falling to her. She was certain her attendance would have put the evil eye on the baby so it would not live, and Leofgeat's love, like her own, be buried alive alongside the tiny bones and papery skin swaddled in a winding sheet.

Whatever knowledge Freya had, however, it turned out not to be enough. Towards the end, Leofgeat's screams and curses could be heard clear across the castle wards. They shuttered all the windows on the courtyard side of the atelier, but it made no difference, and the women waited, in a tense, wincing silence, broken only by Alwys singing to Freya's baby, Thecla. When the bell rang for None, Sister Jean gathered them together in prayer, the women kneeling around her in a semicircle, reciting their responses by rote, for each the same words expressing a different supplication. For an end to pain, for a new life, for courage, for love, for abstinence, for the dead. Some crossed their fingers behind their backs and thought of spells they knew had worked for a neighbour, a sister, a woman in the next village. Margaret remembered words Gytha once spoke to her: *this is life, not a romance.* Agatha thanked God, and Odo, for her deliverance and, opening her eyes briefly, saw Margaret, grasping Gytha's hand, and considered the cost. Odo gave, God exacted the price. Gytha saw souls behind her tight shut eyes, bright souls floating like scraps of silk caught up by the wind, twisting and turning through shafts of sunlight. Keep them safe, she prayed, don't let them forget me.

Freya came back then, with Leofgeat's son in her arms. He was a good, sturdy boy, she said, as proudly as though he were her own, with a lusty cry and a strong suck. He would live, but there had been nothing to be done for Leofgeat. He was a large baby, and Leofgeat had torn inside giving birth to him. She had lost too much blood. Gird was out of his mind with grief and refused to see the child, so Freya had brought him with her. She had more than enough milk for two. As his father would make no decision on the matter, she had decided to call him Leofwine, for his mother.

Everyone living in the castle suffered with Gird. It was natural enough for those few who had known his wife to mourn her, but the discontent of the rest lay closer to their bellies than their hearts. It was Gird's responsibility to prepare the bread dough for the household. Every afternoon he mixed the dough during Vespers and left it to prove till Compline. After Compline he prepared the loaves: rye for below the salt, wheaten for high table, oven bottom cakes as broad as upturned plates and small, sweet rolls to be glazed with honey or apricot conserve for the ladies, then covered them all with sheets of muslin, as tenderly as he might tuck a child into bed, and left them by the warm oven to rise until Matins when the fires were lit.

When Leofgeat died, the dough stopped rising. Perhaps the tears Gird wept over his work slaked it until it was too thin. Perhaps the chill of his misery infected the air in the bakehouse so that it was never warm enough to activate the yeast. Weeks passed. The young pages became desultory in their practice at arms, the men of the garrison grew mutinous, even the dogs lay dry nosed and panting, their bellies distended to bursting point by feasts of unleavened bread handed furtively under the tables in hall. Then one day during the barley harvest Freya carried Leofwine out of the castle, on a visit, she said, to her mother, to show her the baby. Agatha, who understood Freya had lost her family during the harrying of York, was briefly puzzled before a problem with a batch of needles put the matter out of her mind.

On Freya's return, she took the baby to the bakehouse, where his father was preparing his dough on the long wooden counter, smoothed and worn to a shallow basin by years of kneading and folding. She said nothing, merely stood in the doorway with Leofwine on her hip, but something drew Gird's attention away from the dough and towards the pair of them, the young woman holding his child. He left his work and gathered up Leofwine in his floury arms. He tossed him in the air and kissed him, from the soft crown of his head to the tips of his prehensile baby toes. He carried him around his domain, showing him flour sacks, rolling pins, some weevils and a dead mouse, the maw of the bread oven behind its great iron door.

Freya shrugged when he thought to ask about the leather pouch full of coloured stones hanging around Leofwine's neck. A gift, she said, bring him to me when he's hungry. The name is good, Gird had called after her, thank you, and went back to his kneading and folding. When bread was broken next morning, everyone remarked on the lightness of the loaves, everyone hung their noses over them and inhaled the warm, doughy smell. Sweet as a baby's breath, they said. Only the dogs were disappointed with the lack of bounty from the tables.

Though the rest of the household were thankful for the small miracle of the bread, Alwys, since her accident, had been absorbed by a much greater miracle of her own. She had never felt the slightest twinge of pain from her stump. Sometimes she experienced ghostly visitations from the absent hand, tingling fingers, a sensation of grasping, dreams in which she was whole of body yet lame of spirit. She knew she would triumph over these bodily deceptions, that holiness entered her when Fulk hacked off her hand, filling her bones with light. That she could no longer embroider to a standard acceptable to Sister Jean perturbed her not at all. She passed her days serenely, doing small jobs in the atelier, soothing the babies with cooings and snatches of song she said Our Lady used to lull the Christ Child.

Then Margaret, coming up beside Gytha as they were leaving the workshop one evening at Vespers, whispered that the Earl intended to replace Alwys. The intensity of her reaction surprised her as much as it did Margaret. She felt betrayed. How could he? Making love to her one minute, casting aside her friends like a suit of worn out clothes the next? What harm was Alwys doing, what difference could she possibly make to him? It was not as though providing bed and board for a single crippled woman would tax the charity of a man as wealthy as Odo. But Margaret had it on good authority. Sister Jean had told her.

"Go and see him," urged Margaret next morning. "Get him to change his mind."

Very well, she would go; she would not be made a fool of.

He has been back in Canterbury for two weeks, but she has not spoken to him, and only seen him at a distance, in hall or crossing the outer ward on his way into or out of the castle. The only sign she has that he has remembered her existence at all is the cryptic message he sent her in a letter to Sister Jean during the summer. He asked her to inform her women that the King, with God's help, had defeated the rebel, Hereward, and then he asked about the camel.

"'Mistress Gytha will know what I mean'," Sister Jean quoted, with a bemused expression on her face. Gytha sent no reply, because she cannot write and had nothing to say to him fit for the ears of a scribe, or Sister Jean. Because she has done nothing about the camel, preoccupied as she has been with her fables. Because of Alwys.

She happened to glance out of the windows overlooking the courtyard one morning, and saw him mount his horse and lean down to take a hawk on to his wrist from his squire, saw him talk to the bird, holding her up close enough for his breath to ruffle her feathers, and scratch her breast. And look up briefly at the window where Gytha was standing. And see her. And ride out of the gate.

Waiting here now outside the entrance to his apartments, her way barred by two men at arms with pikes crossed in front of her, she doubts she can change his mind about anything, even if she can gain access to him. But the guards have made her angry, the knowing, contemptuous way they look at her. Besides, how could she face Margaret if she failed even to speak to him?

"I want to see his lordship," she announces, straightening her back and tilting her chin defiantly, though the top of her head is still scarcely as high as the point where the men's weapons cross. Perhaps she could duck underneath and make a run for it.

"And you are..?" sneers one.

"From the atelier." The two men exchange a doubtful glance, but mention of the atelier clearly has some effect, for one of them slips through the parlour door, and a few seconds later reappears with the servant, Osbern.

"His lordship is bathing, but he will see you. Come back in a little while."

"I will not. You know me, Osbern." She lowers her chin a little and darts Osbern a coquettish glance from beneath her thick, black lashes. Funny how there are some things you never forget. "You have seen me before." Osbern nods. "So let me enter. I doubt his lordship will object."

This must be the end. She remembers the dagger, the flash of gems, the smooth balance of the haft as she closed her fingers around it. Her wrist burning as he twisted the blade from her grasp. Something she was unaware of until now, a vision of Osbern's face appearing around the door to Archbishop Lanfranc's bed chamber. She waits, thinking of her children, for the long point of a pike to enter her. How will it feel? A sharp pain or a dull one? How will she know when she is dead?

"Very well. Wait in the parlour. I'll tell him." The soldiers stand aside and she follows Osbern inside.

"Hand me a dry sheet," he says to Osbern. He dismisses the dwarf with a wave of his hand, climbs out of the tub and turns himself about in front of Osbern to enable his servant to dry him. As Turold lifts the arras on his way out of the room, Gytha strides in past him.

"Mistress!" exclaims Osbern, fumbling in his haste to cover his lord's nakedness with the drying sheet.

"Leave us," commands Odo, taking the sheet from his servant and tying it himself with unhurried nonchalance. Go on, then, his body says to Gytha, look, it's what you want, isn't it? *Isn't* it?

"I see I did you no permanent damage, then, My Lord," she remarks, trying to sound flippant.

He laughs. "I should engage you instead of my physician if you can make a diagnosis on so cursory an examination, mistress."

"Except that you might find it hard to trust me with a bleeding knife." For once her sharp tongue works for rather than against her; as long as she can keep the rational part of her mind to the fore, she can pretend not to notice the beast writhing and moaning in her belly, the beast that wants to lap up the shadows pooling behind his collarbones and lay its cheek against his naked chest, and shudders in ecstasy at the memory of his kiss.

"I have trusted you with matters even closer to my heart than the blood in my veins," he says, abruptly soft and serious, a slight, but insistent, inclining of his head compelling her to meet his eyes. It is like being dazzled by the sun. Then, peeling her gaze away, she finds herself dazzled a second time by her surroundings.

She has never seen such opulence. Not even in Lady Edith's house were there such rugs and hangings, silks napped like velvet, colours to dazzle and bemuse the northern eye, attuned to greys and browns and watery blues. Even the window ledge is scattered with silk cushions, marigold and peacock blue, and the windows hung with tapestries rather than the painted hides that served as curtains in Lady Edith's house. With such objects surrounding him, what could he possibly have wanted with her mistress' treasures? Perhaps to furnish one of his lesser houses? A man who owns more than four hundred manors must have many houses to equip. Or perhaps it is merely a habit with him, to strip and move on, the way locusts demolish cornfields or his brother ravaged the Vale of York.

Book chests bound in gold and ivory lie beside his richly curtained bed, some with the books spilling out of them. She frowns. She is accustomed to see books locked and chained to library shelves, not spread about a room with such abandon. For all the glinting haloes and angels' wings she glimpses in their rich illuminations, there is something diabolical about such wantonness with words. She looks away from their dense texts and jewelled bindings, towards a prie dieu of polished walnut bearing a devotional work in a silver filigree cover and...a clumsily made wooden statuette of a saint in bishop's cope and mitre, garishly painted, the fiddle head of his crook snapped off, a chip in his halo. This makes her glance enquiringly at Odo, trying not to notice the pattern of hair on his chest, lying flat against his skin in damp whorls, like links of embroidered mail.

"My patron saint," he says, watching her with mild amusement. She drops her eyes. "Hideous, isn't it? But it has sentimental value. John carved it. It goes everywhere with me, that's why it's in such a state."

"My Lord?" She will not be distracted a second time by his son.

"Yes, Gytha."

"I want to ask you something."

"And I thought you'd come to scrub my back."

"I'm serious."

"So am I."

"Is it true you intend to make Alwys leave? You can't. Where would she go? What can she do? And Margaret might go too, or at least not be able to work, so you'd lose two…"

"Gytha." His hands on her shoulders, shaking her almost. How is he suddenly so close to her? Which of them has moved? How white his skin is, where the sun never touches it. Not even a fleabite. "Be quiet." Mouth over hers, smothering her words, sucking out her anger like snake venom, licking it away. Tongue of flame.

One fire extinguished, another lit. This is what he has waited for, why he has held off from speaking to her until the uncertainty gnawing at him would evaporate in the heat of his desire. During the whole of the Ely campaign, though he planned tactics with William and Fitzosbern, deployed troops, fortified camps, gave stirring speeches, was the first man to set foot on William's causeway across the marsh, he felt he was only acting the part of the King's lieutenant. His true self was the lover, biting his pallet through the June nights of not quite darkness in a torment of doubt and frustration, riding out sometimes without even Osbern to protect him, to rage at the moon like a mad wolf.

Not a word, he would yell, not a bloody, fucking word, even when he sent her a direct enquiry. His worst enemy would treat him with greater courtesy. Who does she think she is? Just a whore, replied the moon, just a cunt to poke like any other. One of a kind, argued the moon's reflection in the marsh, misted and pierced by spikes of grass. Precious, unique, remember her lips, that stern arch of her brows, her breasts, her little waist, remember her tongue, agile as a good sword in the hands of a master. Tread carefully as the prince hunting the sleeping beauty in her citadel of briars.

Even now, he does not know how she will react, but he can no longer help himself. He must have her whatever the cost, yet he is as gauche as the boy who fathered John with Adeliza. His hands refuse to work properly. They shake and fumble as though his brain can no longer control them. He tears at her clothes, the drab tunic, the plain linen shift, the underthings Agatha insists on for the women. At some point she trips, over her hose, over the edge of a rug, who knows, and falls, hitting the side of her head on the bath, but neither of them notices. He drops to his knees in front of her, the towel slipping from his hips, pinning her to the floor with one hand against her breastbone, pushing her legs apart with the other. Touches her heart's dance, the skin high up the insides of her thighs almost too soft to feel.

Everything is going wrong. If this is the price of his compassion for Alwys, then she is better equipped to pay it than any of the other women, but there is no call on her to enjoy it, no reason why her body should respond as it does, opening, sucking, salivating at the taste and feel of him, forgetting even to breathe as she drinks him in. Her fingernails do not try to claw him away, but dig into his back, pressing him closer, branding him. Her legs entwine themselves around his waist, pulling him down into her with a violence that makes him cry out. Incomprehensibly, in his own language, with an intensity that makes her open her eyes to see him looking at her, his gaze sweet with lust, but mixed with something unexpected.

She had thought to see her own hunger reflected there, but she sees something else as well. A withholding, an apprehension, a terror even. Remembering the mistress of his dream, she smiles a little. Then frowns as he drives deeper inside her, tearing her open as Adam did, except that what he penetrates is not some token membrane but the door to her heart.

Her frown is the sweetest, most poignant thing, a sudden drawing together of her fine, dark brows to some point of introspection he longs to reach. He wants, needs to hurt her. Fucking her, he is punishing the other men. With every thrust into her he slays one of them, her husband, the sower in stony ground, the men who paid her, sowers by the wayside. His passion will make her fertile, he will give her children who live, make her happy, make her his. His. *Possessio mea.* How he will love her.

At the end of the line of men awaiting the little martyrdom is himself. Father, son, unruly spirit, emptied into her.

She relaxes her grasp on him a little, but only a little, and turns her face into the hot, damp skin of his neck. She does not think she can bear to have him any further from her than this, resting now inside her as his breathing slows down and his heart reclaims its normal rhythm, separated from her by nothing more than a slick of sweat.

"D'you think Aristophanes is right?" she mutters. Absorbed in the physical sensation of her breath stirring the tiny hairs on his skin, the words do not immediately make sense to him; even after his brain has sorted them out, they make very little sense to him. Lifting himself on his elbows, he smiles down at her, marvelling at how lovely she is, with her dark hair spread out around her flushed cheeks and the way her breasts lie like tears of flesh, slightly to her sides.

"Aristophanes?"

"Yes. The theory of perfect wholes."

He is moved, not so much by her sentiment as by the way she has got it wrong. He loves the way she knows halves and parts and fragments of things, as though her mind is like a block of stone, waiting for the sculptor to free its images. One day he will tell her it was Plato, turning aside from his pursuit of love's final mysteries to enjoy a joke, who put the words into the mouth of Aristophanes, and that Plato is now known only by Apuleius' translation, and how sad it is, how frustrating, to be able to feel the living pulse of the Greek inside the Latin and yet have no means of freeing it. Though perhaps there may be something in the notion that lovers bound in perfect communion can challenge even the power of God.

He hugs her close, cupping one hand behind her head, her hair slipping like water through his fingers, then shivers. The room has grown cold, the darkness now almost total beyond the window shutters and the brazier burned down for lack of attention. He can feel gooseflesh creeping up his back and his wrist beginning to ache.

"Let's get into bed." He rolls off her and stands up.

It is then he notices the blood on his genitals. He looks at her in panic, in the same second that she sees him, sits up and stares at her own thighs similarly smeared with whorls and contours of blood.

"Is it your time?"

"No."

No, of course not, he would have noticed. "Don't move." He fishes in the tepid bath water for a wash cloth and cleans himself, quickly establishing that it is not he who has sustained any injury. Wrapping himself in his dressing gown, which he finds on a chair beside the bath, he takes the cloth and kneels in front of her. Parting her legs gently, his fingertips butterfly kisses on the tender skin inside her thighs, he mops away her blood and his semen, realising that the combination makes the carnage look worse than it is. She has the languid look of a rose about to drop, her lips swollen, tendrils of hair stuck to her forehead and temples, eyes dreaming beneath half closed lids.

"It's cold, I'm sorry," he says, stroking the cloth over her thighs and the tight, matted curls of her private hair and all the precious, secret, hidden parts of her. "Oh dear God, what have I done to you? Are you in any pain?"

She feels no pain, only a syrupy heaviness, a vestigial trace of him inside her, the working of his fingers beneath the cloth. "I'm alright. I'm sure it's nothing. I feel..." She gives him a wise smile. "Wonderful." He tosses the cloth back into the bath but remains kneeling in front of her like a penitent, his stricken gaze taking in her torn clothes and the bruise beginning to swell like a storm cloud on her temple, hers fixed mischievously on the renewed stirring of his sex, which she encourages by stroking him with the tips of her toes.

"You must rest," he says, slightly anguished, moving out of reach of her foot, "and I shall have the physician sent for."

"No, I don't need a doctor."

"But someone must attend you."

"Freya, then," she says, lying back with her arms folded behind her head, gazing up at the ceiling whose beams are decorated with the ubiquitous green and gold chevrons. "Sister Jean's new servant. She has some knowledge."

He raises his eyebrows at this, but lets it pass. "Alright, I'll have Osbern send someone to fetch her. Can you stand?"

"Of course I can," but, weak with wanting him again, she has to let him take her weight. Her legs buckle like those of something newborn, the distance to his bed seems immeasurable. She leans against him as he pulls back the bed curtains, lazily admiring the deep blue damask, yellow lined, embroidered in gold with moons and stars, the signs of the zodiac and feather tailed comets. He lifts her, holding her against his heart, her cheek branded by the brocading on his gown. She feels her own smallness, her lightness, how nearly nothing she is.

"It'll make you sneeze," he says of the arctic fox coverlet on his bed, the colour of newly skimmed cream.

She laughs. "No, it's only living things, not dead fur. Cats and dogs and so on."

"Ah." He lays her on the high bed and tucks the bedclothes around her with all the tender solicitude of a child's nurse.

Then he tells her he must dress and go to hall, where a bevy of clergy are waiting to dine with him and submit a dispute over land title to his adjudication, a complicated matter, he explains, trying to look apologetic, involving liability for repairs to a grange and the translation of relics of a saint whose name he cannot remember. He is sorry, really sorry, he says, sitting down on the bed and kissing her bruised temple, but it will probably be late before his business is concluded. She pouts, runs a teasing finger along his collarbones and around the tight circles of his nipples, but she can see from the slight crinkling of the skin at the corners of his eyes how much he is looking forward to the argument.

"Osbern," he shouts before she has a chance to protest that she is content, has no need of company, would, in fact, appreciate a little time alone before Freya is sent for. She thinks about her blood, darkening the gold brown hair where his penis now nestles demurely. What has he done to her? What has given way inside her after so many years?

Osbern appears, silently and promptly, from the other side of the arras.

"My Lord?"

"I must get dressed, Osbern. And," waving his hand in a gesture designed to take in the bath full of cold water, the torn clothes and bloodied rug, the woman in the bed, "sort all this out, will you? Oh, and Osbern, keep the dogs out."

Gytha, enfolded in the vast warm space of Odo's bed, cosseted by his feather mattress and pillows soft as clouds, the piles of quilts, the fox fur coverlet pulled up to her chin, nevertheless watches Osbern at work with the close interest of a fellow professional. She notes with approval, and not a little admiration, the way he never looks at her, behaves, indeed, as though she cannot possibly be there. He must notice her teeth marks in Odo's shoulder, the scratches on his back, but if he does, nothing in his demeanour shows it. Perhaps it is not unusual. She recognises, with a pang of nostalgia for her own former life, the comfortable intimacy which exists between lord and man, born of the years that Osbern has been about his master's person, far more years than she was granted with her beloved Lady Edith.

Her eyes follow Odo, sitting, standing, turning himself about in Osbern's competent hands, his mind no doubt running on how best to settle the dispute to be laid before him, running, perhaps, a little on her. As Osbern smoothes the plum coloured chausses over his master's calves, pulls his shirt over his head, laces his crimson tunic, buckles his girdle and lifts the stiff, brocaded surcoat on to his shoulders, she understands that this relationship has a closeness, a depth of physical intimacy that a man in Odo's position can achieve with no-one else, not even a wife were he permitted one.

She feels the prick of foolish tears behind her eyes, but cannot turn away, captivated by every move of her lover's body, her concentration so focused on him that she can sense how his clothes feel against his skin, the warmth of fine wool, the linen crisp and cool, the sudden, sharp scraping when Osbern accidentally draws the comb over the tonsured part of his scalp. It is the only mistake Osbern makes and, although not punished, it is not overlooked, eliciting from Odo a sharp hiss of pain before he waves the comb away and holds out his wrists for the pair of wide gold cuffs set with red amber he has chosen to complete his adornment. The cuffs shimmer through her tears, their clasps lock, one after the other, fat, well-oiled clicks.

Finally Odo himself selects a crucifix from a stamped leather jewel case on his dressing table, a lavish affair of gold set with garnets to represent Christ's wounds and a crown of tiny jet thorns. He kisses the crucifix and hangs it, on its ruby studded chain, around his neck, then goes to his prie dieu where he kneels in silent prayer for several minutes. Osbern moves quietly about the room, cleaning razors, folding clothes, shutting chests and boxes and comb cases, stoppering crystal bottles. As though, thinks Gytha, their perfumes are like exotic wild animals, rare and dangerous. He bundles up discarded clothing and wet towels and stokes the brazier, normally jobs for lesser servants, or the smallest pages, but these are unusual circumstances and gossip, like fire, is only a comfort until it runs out of control.

Gytha watches Odo, thinking he himself is a prayer, her prayer, with the soles of his shoes so neatly together and his hair curling into a drake's tail at the nape of his neck and his body so straight and strong, bearing the stigmata of her teeth beneath all the layers of linen and wool and gold embroidery.

He finishes his prayers and comes to sit beside her on the bed, taking one of her hands between both of his. She turns on her side and curls up with her knees under the bedclothes pressed against his thigh.

"Tell me what you pray for."

He looks reflective, does not answer immediately, so she is afraid she has overstepped some boundary she was unaware of, then says,

"That God will remind me of the name of this saint whose relics we have to discuss, before it becomes clear to everyone that I don't know it. You seem to have a saint under every bush in this country."

"Oh, we are very holy people, My Lord."

"So why did I lately come upon a shrine to a Saint Venus? Can you unravel that puzzle for me?"

"I could, My Lord, but you have to go down to dinner." She gives a laugh like the splash of water, deep underground. He kisses her, chastely, on her forehead, because if he kisses her laughing mouth he knows he will not go. "Osbern will take care of you, and Saint Odo, and Freya, of course. And later, perhaps we can pray to Saint Venus together. Promise me you won't try to get up." He rises, Osbern hovering at his back with a clothes brush. "Oh, and Gytha, my sweetheart," he says, as though it is an afterthought, "I never said Alwys had to go, just that my sister had my leave to find a replacement for her as an embroiderer. It's all a matter of interpretation."

Now he has gone she tries to be angry, but she feels too weak. There is not enough room inside her for anger, yet he has cheated her, no, worse, outwitted her. She will leave, but she has no clothes. All the women have a spare set of everything, she will ask Osbern to fetch hers, but she does not know how. Osbern, by ignoring her so completely, even the imprint of her teeth in his master's flesh, has made her uncertain she exists for him at all. Perhaps she cannot speak to him, her voice will not work, or her words will come out jumbled into nonsense, or he will simply be unable to hear her. She and Osbern, each in a separate sphere of Odo's life, speaking different languages, each condemned to a fixed orbit, unless he chooses to lift them out of it. Everything comes back to Odo, and the cycle of rage and rebuttal begins again.

She will get up, borrow his clothes if need be. God knows, he seems to have enough of them. In her idle inventory of his room she has counted at least half a dozen clothes chests, all exhaling clouds of camphor and lavender. She will go back to the atelier and tomorrow she will continue work on her fables. Yet how can she? How can she simply walk into the women's dormitory as if nothing has happened, as if her body is not pierced by his as clearly as the linen stretched on the embroidery frames is pierced by his memories. Besides, his bed is warm and comfortable, holding the template of his sleeping self in all its folds and feathers, and she isn't confident the bleeding has stopped completely. He is right, she should rest, allow herself to be taken care of.

She must have slept, for when she opens her eyes the clutter of objects in the room is lost in shadow, only a pool of light from a single candle on the nightstand showing her the figure of Freya, her back protectively curved as she offers her breast to one of the babies. Gytha does not look long enough to identify which, although even with her eyes squeezed shut she cannot now deny the soft, wet sucking of the child's mouth on Freya's nipple, nor the smell of milk resting uneasily in the air of this room which, for all its opulence, is a man's room. Her body responds as though caressed by ghosts, her nipples harden and her womb clenches, repeating their unfinished catechism. She turns away from Freya, drawing her knees up to her chest, making herself into the smallest possible target for grief.

She aches for Odo, with a rush of elation that he is flesh and blood, sweat and substance, divided from her only by the floor of this room; if she listens carefully, she can probably distinguish his voice from among the babble drifting up from the hall below. Missing him is in time, not eternity.

"Are you awake?" asks Freya, shifting the baby to her other breast. Gytha opens her eyes and turns reluctantly back towards her. It's Freya's baby, she thinks, Freya's little daughter.

"Can I get you something? Water? Something to eat? The manservant said to ask." She looks around the room. "No shortage of anything, is there? Makes you wonder what he wanted with my few bits and pieces. It's the second time it's happened to me, you know. My family came from York originally. Fled down south after the harrying. You've never seen so much of...nothing, after the Bastard finished with us. He even had all the farm animals slaughtered, far more than they needed to eat, and just left them to rot in the fields."

Gytha makes no reply, and Freya considers her thoughtfully. "The page said you'd been taken ill. When I came...I met the Earl on the stairs. He said you'd asked for me specially. He said...He looked..." she gropes for the right word, "panicky," she concludes with satisfaction.

Gytha smiles. "He was all for summoning his physician, as if I hadn't lost enough blood for one day."

Freya looks up sharply at this and Thecla, sensing her mother's distraction, grizzles a little. "I hope he would not bleed you for women's troubles in this month. It can only be done with the sun in Scorpio."

"That's why I asked for you. I was sure you would know what to do. I remember how you took care of Leofgeat and the baby."

She tells Freya everything. Freya listens attentively, nodding from time to time, sighing occasionally when Gytha struggles for words to reduce this act of love and wonder and violence to a medical conundrum. Chastened, Gytha tries to see herself as Freya must see her, as a puzzle, a set of physical organs to be defended against the effects of emotional chaos, and begins again. When she stumbles to the end of her account, Freya lays the baby down on the end of the bed, straightens her clothes and folds back the covers to examine Gytha. Thecla sneezes as she turns her head towards her mother and the fur tickles her nose. Freya laughs besottedly, but stops when she sees Gytha's face. Gytha longs to say it's alright, but it isn't, so she says nothing.

Freya presses Gytha's belly with cool, knowledgeable hands. She inserts her fingers between Gytha's legs, asking as she turns her wrist whether she feels any pain. Here? Or here? Her tone is detached, as though she is a shopkeeper asking what weight of cheese or length of linen.

"Not pain exactly," says Gytha, struggling to name what she does feel, this opening, melting sensation, sweet and visceral. Freya suddenly straightens up, wiping her hand on her skirt. She gives Gytha a quizzical, almost conspiratorial, look.

"I can't find anything wrong with you, nothing your lover doesn't have just as badly at any rate."

Her *lover. Her* lover. "What do you mean?"

Freya picks up her daughter and sits back down. "That you're smitten with lust just as strong as he is."

"And how do you know what he feels?"

"Everyone does. Except you, it seems. He's carried your image in his eyes as long as I've known him face to face, and it looks fixed, as though it was there a long time before I had the chance to see it."

"It will pass."

Freya frowns. "You sound almost as though you wish it. On the contrary, you should make sure you hold on to him."

"He's my enemy, Freya." Gytha sits up, shaking her hair out of her eyes, hugging her knees. "I wonder you don't understand that, after what you told me earlier."

"They're here to stay, Gytha, and they're not all bad. Just people like the rest of us."

"Odo isn't people like the rest of us. He's the Bastard's brother. For all we know, the harrying of York was his idea. My...they do say most of the Bastard's ideas are his."

"And my Fulk is in his personal service. Be sensible."

"I'm afraid. What will happen to me?"

"If you play your cards shrewdly, you'll become rich enough to fart through silk and pick your teeth with gold." Freya leans and kisses her sleeping daughter's head. "I can help, you know. Binding spells, love potions, that sort of thing."

Gytha reaches out and squeezes her hand to silence her, quickly withdrawing it as her fingers brush against the baby's cheek. "One thing, perhaps," she says, thinking of the blood, the familiar, though long forgotten, dragging sensation in the pit of her stomach. "I can't have a child."

"You don't like children, do you?" The accusation stings like sparks from a fire in a high wind. "Children would be a good idea. Make sure he had to go on paying out even after you've grown old and fat and he's moved on to fresh pastures."

"I can't."

"Suit yourself. You could try this," Freya suggests, "it works for some women. Take a piece of thread from your clothes, or a hair from your head's best. Tie a knot in it and put it somewhere in the bed. Shouldn't be difficult to hide it in a bed this size. It will tie up the neck of your womb and stop his seed getting in. You must say these words whilst you tie the knot." She leans and whispers in Gytha's ear.

"Thank you," she says, "I'll do it now."

"No. When you're thinking of him, of bedding him."

When is she not thinking of him? When was she ever not thinking of him? Wincing slightly, she pulls a strand of hair from the top of her head and knots it deftly, just as she knots threads at the back of a piece of embroidery, to make a neat finish.

It is late when he comes back to her, stepping carefully around the inert form of Osbern, rolled in a blanket on the threshold to his bed chamber.

"You can go to sleep now, Osbern," he whispers.

The fire is out and the room is cold. He takes off his clothes unattended, and feels his way to bed in pitch darkness, guided by familiarity and the sound of Gytha's breathing. He crawls, shivering, under the covers and snuggles up to her, curling his body around hers, her back to his chest, her hair catching in the chain of his amulet. He is so relieved to find her still there. He had not been sure she would be.

He has tormented himself with the question, in the part of his mind not engaged in the sharp delights of the evening's legal and theological arguments. He has stipulated terms, driven bargains, made small compromises and subtle changes of emphasis. He has sent his guests on their way satisfied, full of fine wine and excellent food, each one thinking he has won a victory, each one convinced he basks in the bright, narrow beam of the Earl's special favour. Yet his heart was not in it, his heart was lying here all along, beating against her ribs. Of course she's here, she belongs here.

He thinks he will lie quietly beside her, emptying his head, letting his heartbeat slow to keep pace with hers, until he sleeps. He thinks he will look at this new and wonderful situation in the morning, and that daylight will show him the ways in which it is going to change his life. But his body has other ideas. His body burns. He tosses and turns about the bed in search of places where the sheets are cool, but his nerves are strung so tight that even the bland caress of linen sets them humming with desire. He wakes her, though when he shakes her shoulder, she turns to him so promptly he wonders if she was ever asleep.

Afterwards, they lie fused together in a long, sweating silence, wondering at the changes they find, back in their own skins, as they cautiously flex fingertips, stretch arms and legs, draw breath into their lungs. Gytha feels as though her bones have melted. Her throat aches, her sinews sing like harp strings. She cannot remember a man who kept his eyes open and looked at her as he fucked her, any man who has made love to her as Odo has, with that insistent, questioning gaze fixed on her. Do I please you? How? Where? Here? What are you thinking? How do you feel? If? When? Nor has he left the bed, or turned his back on her and withdrawn into sleep, but lies now with his arms around her and her knees trapped between his, stroking her back and shoulders until they fall together into a shared dream.

Their passion overflows them, spills out of them, it floods the room, washes through the castle, carrying away walls and guard posts, stables, mews, armoury, brew house, chapel. Page boys and altar boys, cooks and priests, gossiping laundresses, soldiers, dogs and horses are swept up in it. The flood is littered with splintered fence posts, lumps of sealing wax, upturned helmets, wooden spoons, barrels, basins of fizzing yeast. It smashes the atelier, sets Agatha's drawings bobbing on its surface like gulls riding out a storm, it rips the embroidery from splintered frames and drags the linen sheets in its wake. Hanks of wool tangle with rusting crossbows, illuminated letters from holy books wink like gems beneath love's sparkling surface. Waves break on Norman beaches and wash around the foot of William's great tower by the Thames.

And their bed becomes a ship of fools.

"You were talking in your sleep," she whispers as, sensing she is watching him, he opens his eyes and looks at her through his curling lashes.

"Was I? What did I say?"

"I don't know. It was all in French. What were you dreaming about?" She touches his brow, close to his hairline.

"You know. You were in it with me."

Her fingers trace the v-shape of the veins in his forehead where his seed is made. A smile spreads over her face as she runs her hand down his neck and shoulder and flank, over his hip and into the warm fold of flesh between the top of his thigh and the parts where the seed is stored.

The life of the castle goes on around them, yet seems curiously suspended. There is nothing unusual in the fact that Hamo sits in Odo's great chair, with its arched back and gilded heads of gryphons carved into the arms; except that Odo is not absent, and everyone who comes to transact business before Hamo knows it. Hamo's decisions are valueless, transitory, liable at any moment to be overturned. Everyone keeps one eye on the castellan and one on the stairs to the Earl's apartments, expecting to see him descend as he usually does after Terce, threading his way through the crowd of messengers, petitioners, clerks looking for preferment, knights seeking places for their sons or husbands for their daughters, smiling, grasping a hand here, touching a shoulder there, exchanging a word about the price of wool or the prospect of game. They hunger for his charm, the ease with which he makes things happen, they mill around the foot of his staircase, only reluctantly moving forward in the line leading to Hamo.

Each morning it is the same. The door to Odo's apartments opens and all eyes, even those of the dogs with their enquiring brows, are raised in hope, then hope expires in a great, concerted sigh, when Osbern appears and makes his way stiffly through the crowds to his daily assignation with the stewards of pantry and buttery to inform them that no, his lordship will not dine in hall tonight. His lordship is not to be disturbed. He remains…indisposed.

Osbern is furious. What is he supposed to say? Any rumour of a prolonged indisposition is bound to be unsettling to that great mass of people whose security depends on the Earl's person, and who in turn owe him their service only so long as he can protect them. On the other hand, what mischief might His Reverence the Archbishop make of hearing that the Bishop of Bayeux was choosing to neglect his public duties in favour of a mistress? Osbern does not doubt the ability of such news to fly across the Alps to Rome with the speed of winged Mercury, and he doubts not at all how it would set the Archbishop pulling out his beard by the handful. He takes particular care to evade the strained expression of the chaplain, who has been attempting to gain an audience since Odo's return from East Anglia, on an urgent matter of family business, he says. He notes that the messenger from Rome is still there, calmly paring his fingernails in a corner out of the press.

The atelier, away from the public eye, the censoring proximity of the Earl's apartments at the head of the stairs, buzzes with gossip, much of it orchestrated by Judith, who wastes no time in telling the women of Canterbury about the white cockade she saw among Gytha's possessions. Alwys takes no part in it, and nor does Freya, though the rest, knowing she has been up to the Earl's apartments since Gytha's disappearance, do everything they can to engage her.

"Gytha is quite well, is she?" asks one, full of casual sympathy, as she comes for wool to reload one of the stands.

"Is it true the Earl keeps books up there?" queries another. Men of the Earl's stature usually employ clerks to read books for them.

Margaret is in agony, torn between curiosity and the fear that, if something bad has happened, she is at least partly to blame. Eventually, just before Vespers on the second day, she goes to Sister Jean's parlour.

"I do not think you should have stopped work just yet," says Sister Jean, standing at the door, wearing that familiar expression of disapproval which seems to Margaret to pull all her features down towards a point just beneath her chin, as though they have been knotted together like the strings of a child's bonnet. "I have not heard the Vespers bell."

"Sorry, Sister." She curtseys. "But I'd just finished a horse and it didn't seem worth starting anything else, and I wanted to talk to you before Vespers." But only just before Vespers, so Sister Jean cannot detain her as she occasionally does, rambling on about something, or someone, she calls "the tenth muse", and Saint Augustine's letters to his sister.

"You had better come in then." She steps aside to allow Margaret to enter. As usual, there is no brazier lit, and the room smells cold and musty, the way old people smell, which is odd, because Margaret doesn't think Sister Jean is much older than the Earl, though she looks it, being so thin and spare. "What is it you want to talk to me about?" She does not invite Margaret to sit and remains standing herself, beside the table under the window, which is covered with papers, pens, inkpots, pebble-shaped lumps of charcoal, squiggles of wool and candle stubs.

"It's Gytha."

"I thought it might be."

"It's not fair, Sister, the things they're saying, and I feel bad about it because she only went to see the Earl about Alwys and now, well, he's...taken her prisoner."

Sister Jean gives a faint, chilly smile. "Is that what you think?"

Fiddling with a twist of hair that has escaped her cap, Margaret stares at her feet, feeling the blush creep up her neck and face as though she is being immersed in hot water.

"My brother is not in the habit of imprisoning women, Margaret, I do not think he generally sees the need, although perhaps, for political reasons, where the woman concerned has wealth or influence..."

"Then..?"

"I think we may safely assume Gytha is with his lordship of her own free will."

"So..?"

"And that the gossip in the workshop contains at least a kernel of truth." Her bitter tone shocks Margaret. This is not her customary acerbic humour but something more intense, reminding Margaret of the fierce resentments that used to blow up between Alwys and herself and their brothers. As though she is envious of Lord Odo and Gytha, yet why should she be? Presumably she did not have to become a nun.

"Sit down," she commands.

"But Vespers..." The flat note of the chapel bell, which has a crack in it, is clearly audible across the courtyard.

"No matter if we miss it. It will happen again tomorrow." Sister Jean lights a taper from a tinderbox lying on her table and stalks about the room lighting candles. "He's a fool, and selfish with it," she mutters eventually, as though she has forgotten Margaret is there.

"Perhaps he loves her, madam," ventures Margaret, for whom romantic love is an excuse for any kind of boldness.

Pausing in front of her, Sister Jean strokes her cheek with dry fingertips. Margaret shrinks instinctively from the caress, and is immediately annoyed with herself. She doesn't want to put Sister Jean off now, just when the conversation is becoming interesting.

"You're not a child any more, Meg," she says, a little more kindly. "It's time you stopped seeing life as a romance." What a coincidence; exactly the same thing Gytha said before the Earl went to Ely. She and Sister Jean, both busy denying what seems to be going on right under their noses. "Lord Odo's heart is not his own to dispose of. It is pledged to the King and ultimately, to God. They are both jealous masters."

Margaret feels suddenly cold and shivery, as though she has the beginnings of chill, or someone has walked over her grave. She has never properly considered before just who Sister Jean and Lord Odo are. The brother and sister of the King, the Conqueror. Danger enters the room with this thought, and the determination to tell Gytha what Sister Jean has said. To warn her.

Odo loves Gytha with every part of his body. He makes love to her with his eyes and fingers, his lips, his tongue, his arms and toes and neat, clean teeth. He eats and drinks her, leaves his skin beneath her fingernails. His greed for her makes her feel as precious as all the rare and beautiful things surrounding them. She is mined, melted and cast like gold, blown like the finest Venetian glass. Her skin is illuminated like vellum, brushed with colour and papered with gilt, polished like gemstones. She floats in an ether of bliss, yet something is wrong, there is a fly in the nectar, a niggle of mortality in heaven, of time in eternity. No lover could give as generously as he does as though, having taken everything from her, having even appropriated her skill with a needle, he now feels bound to try to fill the empty space inside her. But if he fills her with himself, if he gives so relentlessly without being able to receive acts of love from her in return, then she will cease to exist just as Lady Edith and her children, and her household treasures, have ceased to exist, dissolved in the boundless mass of everything he owns.

Why does he shy away from her advances? Is it some unfathomable treaty he has negotiated with God concerning the boundaries of sin? Is it that they have completely misunderstood one another, their intuitions scrambled by desire? The question swells between them until she feels it must be lanced, whatever poison may be contained in the answer. She tears herself away from his kisses, his salty skin, his incomprehensible French endearments, unlocks the circle of his arms and sits up, pulling back the curtains on her side of the bed to reveal a wedge of the room, its treasures lit by the honey glow of autumn afternoon sunshine. *Apple picking*, she thinks desperately, gulping down air, her throat full of sadness, and the oyster harvest, at home, in the rich, iron-smelling mud.

A sob escapes her, and then there is no stopping her tears.

"Gytha? What is it?" His voice, tender with anxiety, the shape of her name on his tongue, almost melts her, but when he sits up and tries to put his arms back around her, she wrenches herself away. She has to say something, she owes him that much, but she has no idea where to begin. It is like trying to speak a different language. When she doesn't reply, he takes her by the shoulders and turns her to face him. Her cheeks shine with tears, her nose is running, and he begins to lick her clean, his tongue moving strong and gentle over her face, smoothing her hair out of her eyes.

"Stop it," she says, holding him away from her.

"Tell me, then." He leans against the high back of the bed, arms folded behind his head. The light splashes his face and chest, gleams in his three days' growth of beard and the dark blond hair curling in his armpits. She wants to say it doesn't matter, but it does.

"Why..?" she begins, and stops.

He turns briefly to look at her, then averts his gaze and fixes it on the steepled outline of his feet beneath the bedclothes, composing his face into the neutral mask he wears to hear confessions.

She rocks uneasily, hugging her knees up to her chin. "Why are you like you are? In bed?" A flicker of a puzzled frown, quickly extinguished. He will neither help her nor hinder. "You give so much, but you don't let me give anything back. That's not the way to love."

"You give me...your pleasure. Perhaps it's just that you can't possibly be aware of how you make me feel. Held. Cared for."

"What I do without awareness is surely of little value compared to what I can achieve with it. Now I see through a glass darkly?"

He laughs at this, throwing his head back against the pillows. "Is this how you make love to a bishop? By bringing theology into the bed chamber? I fear Saint Paul would not approve."

"Don't try to deflect me. It's not the bishop we're talking about here but the man. You're holding out on me. Don't try to deny it. I know. Everyone I have ever loved has been taken from me. I know what it feels like." She stops rocking and looks at him, drawing his eyes, drawing it out of him. He sits up straight. He prises one of her hands from around her knees and plays with her fingers, their tips scarred and reddened from the years of pushing her needle through the taut, resistant linen, winding them between his own. It is a long time before he answers her.

"Are you saying, then, that you love me?" She blushes, she tries to withdraw her hand but he tightens his grip and she gives up. "Answer me," he demands.

"I...don't know."

"Because I love you. I'm sorry if that's not what you want to hear, if you think it imposes too much of a burden on you, and God knows, it was never my intention, but it's happened and there seems to be nothing I can do about it." He gives a nervous laugh. "What was it Ovid said?" He translates, but poorly, which irritates him, though he doubts she would notice. "'Then I submit, Cupid. I'm your latest victim, standing here with my hands raised.' And my love has made me jealous."

"Jealous?" She gives an incredulous laugh. "Of me?"

"Of the men. Those men. I can't bear to think of what you did with them. I don't want to know what you know."

So her past is not hidden from him, yet what he has done with his knowledge is not what she would have expected. "I didn't think you were aware of that part of my life."

"I made Agatha tell me. After your visit to Christ Church."

"You know what they say about a little knowledge, My Lord. If you wanted my life story, you should have asked me for it."

"I did try. You told me it wasn't interesting."

"It wasn't. But it happened, it's part of me. If you find it... distasteful, then it would be best to take this no further."

"Is that what you want?"

"I don't know. Everything I have to do with you is so contradictory, it's hard to know what I want."

"And if I said I'd try to be more...to overcome this delicacy, would you know then?" He guides her hand down between his legs, but she removes it, with a small, sad smile, and sits apart from him, hunched over her knees, with the sheet drawn up to her breasts. He waits. Briefly he thinks of the petitioners no doubt waiting in his hall, trapped on their seesaw of hopes and disappointments, and sees himself as part of a great pyramid of waiting, decisions endlessly deferred, men growing old listening to the empty spaces between heartbeats, with Gȳtha the goddess at the pinnacle, arbiter of all their fates. Well, he has spent a lifetime waiting on the whims of deities of one sort or another.

As he watches her, she seems to soften, her shoulders relax and she turns to him with a smile. Does she love him? Is she pleased that he loves her? "Ovid," she says. "Did you know he was a favourite of King Harold?"

"Really?" He does not quite manage to keep the cynicism out of his voice; everything he has won in this country seems to have been at the expense of Harold Godwinson, his incompetent double dealing tarnishes it all.

"Yes. He and my lady were especially fond of the poem about the dinner. In the *Ars Amatoria,* I think it is." Her hands begin the quick, darting gestures she uses when something excites her. He thinks he will explode with love. "All those instructions for secret communications to deceive the poor, cuckolded husband. Or, in their case, wife."

"The *Amores,*" he corrects.

"Pedant," she teases.

He makes a rueful face, acknowledging the truth of her accusation. "'The language of eyebrows and fingers with annotations in wine.' So if I see you stroke your cheek at dinner, I shall know you're thinking about me?"

In reply, she pinches the lobe of her ear between her thumb and forefinger.

"Ah, I've made you angry."

"Yes, you have rather. I can't make my past life disappear, so how

224

can I stop you being jealous? And besides, consider the circumstances that led to my becoming a whore."

He winces.

"You would prefer me to dress it up in prettier language?" she goes on, her voice rising. "Just as you do when you talk about carrying out the wishes of King Edward? Or punishing a man who dishonoured himself by going back on his word? Perhaps I should make an embroidery of it, a new set of bed hangings to...inspire you."

"Enough!"

Her cheeks are flushed, the shooting stars have reappeared in her eyes, he is mesmerised by a little pulse beating furiously beneath the creamy skin of her neck. The depth of her anger mortifies him, yet he marvels at her ability to scythe through to the truth of things. It hurts him inexpressibly to be the object of such a rage, but he wants it to last forever because it makes her so beautiful. But then, everything makes her beautiful.

She considers him for a moment, weighing something up in her mind, then,

"Alright," she says calmly, kneeling, letting the sheet slip away from her, climbing between his legs. She winds her arms around him and kisses his mouth. His chest hair grazes her nipples, she feels him stir and harden against her thigh and desire floods her once more from her throat to her knees. "Lie down," she commands, then, lacing her fingers between his and pinning his hands by his sides, starts to kiss his body, sliding her tongue over his breast, under his ribs, around his navel, measuring the tilt of his pelvis. He flinches slightly as she takes him gently in her mouth, but then he is sunk below thought, in a place where there is no Ovid or Godwinson or broken promises, nothing but the deep lake of her hair spread over him, the caress of her lips and tongue and the barest, most tantalising graze of the tips of her teeth. Ecstasy. Sin. How is that possible? But he wants children, longs for children. A dynasty. Waste.

He holds her close, pressing her cheek against his chest, her hair snaking over his skin, so that she feels rather than hears his answering chuckle, a teasing vibration through the bones of her skull. Then how he freezes, the mechanics of it, the tensing of muscles, the locking of joints, the remorseless thud of his heart.

"Is that what you would do," he asks, "with them? To avoid... consequences?"

She sits up, wiping her mouth with the back of her hand. "Consequences, Odo? Do you mean babies? How could you?" and before he can defend himself, "Osbern," she calls. No response. "OSBERN!"

"He won't..." but he does. He appears from the other side of the arras, looking straight through her at Odo.

"My Lord?"

"Have Mistress Gytha's clothes brought, Osbern" he says wearily.

"And water, Osbern, please. I'm thirsty," adds Gytha. Odo translates.

"Yes, My Lord."

Odo gets out of bed and pulls on his dressing gown. He picks up a hand mirror from the dressing table. Looking at his reflection in the polished silver oval, he runs a hand through his curls, his unshaven tonsure, over the growth of beard smudging his jaw, and frowns.

"How long?" he asks.

"I don't know."

They wait almost like strangers until Osbern returns with her clothes and a jug of water, saying nothing, exchanging tight smiles if they happen to catch one another's eye as he paces about the room, picking things up and putting them down. What he terms love, then, she thinks, is too fragile to survive even the oblique light of late afternoon, the ringing of Vespers which makes him start and look guilty. It is not the same as her love, which has survived four deaths and ten years of famine. She has bled for love, been transformed by it, restored and purified. For him, like everything, it is words and pictures.

"Shall I be your tiring woman?" he asks, watching her struggle to fasten the laces down the back of her dress. He would have helped her sooner, but was prevented by her self-containment as she rolled her dark blue hose over her calves and thighs then tied her garters, straightening each leg in turn, pointing each toe; as she stood and slipped her shift over her head, hiding her body from him with an abruptness that shocked him.

"Thank you." She turns one way then the other as he threads and ties the laces, relaxing as she feels the competence of his hands. "You're good at this, aren't you?"

"I have three sisters, remember, four if you include my father's daughter from his first marriage. I've had plenty of practice. There were never enough maids to go round on feast days."

She smiles at him over her shoulder. "Even for Sister Jean? I can't imagine her taking a lot of trouble over her dress."

"Oh she was quite different when she was a girl. She loved dancing."

"What happened?"

"Nothing, really. She still does love dancing. Now, turn round. Let me look at you."

She turns and he looks, trying to see beneath the drab gown all the glowing colours he has conjured from her flesh, the golds and apricots, pinks and peaches, the blue patterning of her veins, her nipples the colour of mulberries.

"You should have some other clothes," he says.

"Why?"

"You know why. You can't go back to the atelier."

"I can, Odo, I want to."

"What?"

"I want to finish something."

"I'm sorry."

"That I am keen to go back to work for you? I thought you would be glad."

"For what I said. It was unforgivable. If I try not to think…about the past, will you stay?"

"You can't be jealous of phantoms, Odo, they're not real." She puts her hands on his shoulders and stands on tiptoe to kiss his forehead, and leaves him, sweeping past Osbern on his way into the bedroom with water and towels for shaving.

"Will you see the man from Rome before dinner, My Lord? He's been waiting for three days."

She slips into chapel towards the end of Vespers, during the *Magnificat*, closing the door as quietly as she can and standing at the back. She has not set foot in a church since she prayed for King Harold in Lady Edith's household chapel on the eve of the battle at Senlac. Staring at his butchered remains not twenty four hours later, she convinced herself that God had been deaf to her prayers yet again, and resolved it would be the last time. Now what is she to make of His plan?

She watches the priest perform the rite of incensing the altar, but sees Odo in his vestments, the hands that have worshipped her swinging the censer, and feels that she is incense, infinitely precious and insubstantial, curling, floating, high above the congregation among the gilded angels gazing down from the roof. The words she has heard sung so often they have almost ceased to have any meaning, now slice through her with a terrible, deceitful clarity. *Quia fecit mihi magna, qui potens est.* For he that is mighty hath done to me great things. *Esurientes implevit bonis.* With good things hath he filled the hungry. Words branded on her wilful flesh, chiselled into the paving stones on the road to damnation. But if she is to burn with Odo, what use has she for salvation?

As the plain chant ends and they kneel for the prayers, she notices she is kneeling beside Margaret, and sees what she must look like in Margaret's astonished, fearful, fascinated eyes. Even though she has dressed her hair in plaits hanging either side of her face, rather than putting it up under her cap as she usually does, the bruise on her temple remains ill concealed. She has neither eaten nor seen daylight for how long? *Three days*, she thinks, *maybe four*. Her eyes are huge and feverish above her sharpened cheekbones, she has to press her hands together ardently to prevent them from trembling. She is hollowed out, fire runs in her veins, her bones are moondust, she will live on nothing but her lover's tears and smiles.

Yet he is not in church, he is, she supposes, attending to whatever business he has been neglecting these past three days, and she has to parry the prurient stares, the unspoken questions, the way people freeze when they come near her as though she has the plague, alone. As soon as the service is over, she takes refuge in the dormitory, knowing the rest of the women will being going to hall for the evening meal. She cannot sit there among the clerks and squires and Countess Marie's women, watching him chat and charm, making people laugh at high table as though the earth has not somehow slipped sideways on the pillars that support it over the abyss. How can she bear Margaret's simpering expression when the squire, Guerin, pauses on his way up the hall to do some errand for his lord to pinch her waist? Or the way Judith sucks up to the Countess' Gascon ladies? Or any oblique remark from anybody about the best treatment for bruises.

When they return to the atelier to prepare for bed she pretends to be asleep. She can sense Margaret's longing to talk to her but, though she shifts her position to make room for the big girl to climb in beside her, complaining of the cold, she says nothing. There is nothing to say, no words yet invented which would not mock and demean the transaction of hearts that has taken place between her and Odo. Holding herself still, forcing herself to breathe the even rhythm of sleep, she thinks about Aesop's Fables to take her mind off the ache in her temple, the pins and needles in the arm trapped beneath her, and the questions that seem to be crowding behind her ribs like prisoners rattling the bars of a cell. Her own fables, she realises, as the bell tolls for Prime and the women begin to stir beneath their blankets, will be her last testimony to the life which died with Harold Godwinson.

THE FEAST OF SAINT ODO

SAINT ODO'S EVE TO SAINT ODO'S DAY 1071

Odo's shoulder is already beginning to throb as Osbern rubs a foul-smelling decoction of old wine and the root of Solomon's seal into the bruise. He will be thirty five years old tomorrow, the Feast of Saint Odo; it really is time he gave up jousting for sport.

"That should disperse the blood and stop the skin discolouring, sir. I'm sure nothing's broken but perhaps your physician should take a look, just in case."

Odo grimaces. "I think I'll leave well alone."

"As you wish, My Lord."

Odo prods the injured area cautiously with his fingertips, feeling for swelling or broken skin, for changes she will notice the next time she kneels beside him on his bed and removes his clothes, slowly and lovingly, as though unwrapping a longed for gift.

It has been six weeks. As Osbern dressed him after she had gone, leaving the reproachful imprint of her lips on his forehead, he was so preoccupied, he could not seem to understand what Osbern wanted of him when he asked him to raise his arms, or turn this way or that, or sit while Osbern fastened his shoes. Like a half grown boy not in control of his body, he fumbled the clasps holding his cross chain to his shoulders, knocked John's figure of Saint Odo off his prie dieu when he knelt to pray.

Feeling faint and somehow separated from himself, he could not concentrate on prayer. For hours, days, until he reminded himself how she had taken pleasure in him. He had not imagined the way her body was wracked with pleasure and her cunt clenched around him like a strong fist, how she held him as though she wanted to climb right inside his skin. How nearly she had admitted to loving him. To hold her, he must go to her; with the reminder of his physical presence, he was certain she would be unable to resist him.

He went to the atelier. He stood behind her, breathing in her scent of salt and camomile and the sharp smell of the wool which the dyers soak in sheep's piss to set the colours. That translation he had made of Aesop for Agatha lay open in her lap, his words, sprung from his mind, his mouth, his hand guiding the pen, gathered in the slack of her skirt, between her slightly parted thighs. He smiled broadly, though only Margaret, at the opposite side of the frame, had the benefit of it. When Gytha finally turned to look at him, he rubbed the side of his nose with his finger, hoping she would remember their conversation about Ovid.

He was barely half way across the outer ward when she caught up with him, panting a little, her cheeks flushed, eyes cast down beneath their thick, black lashes. His only acknowledgement was to shorten his stride to match hers. He had no idea what he might say if he opened his mouth, no idea where it might end if he were to take her lightly by the elbow, as a gentleman should, to guide her around puddles or piles of horse dung. The hour was close to None; the only person in the hall was a spit boy turning a hog's carcass over the fire, so absorbed in whatever pictures he could see in the flames, leaping as fat sputtered into them, he never noticed Odo and Gytha climbing the stairs to Odo's apartments.

He dismissed his servants, but without waiting for them all to leave, gathered her into his arms and kissed her, long enough to know he was right, she was as hungry for him as he for her. Yet when she pulled away from him, he thought only the space of time measured by a single heartbeat had passed.

"I missed you."

"You could have come sooner."

"It's only been two days."

"Really?"

"I still love you. I didn't imagine it."

"And are you still jealous?"

"I try not to think about it. I fill my mind with you as you are now, not then, or in the future. To be honest, now is as much as I can cope with."

She made no reply to this, but took him by both hands and led him through to his bedroom. "Lie down," she said and, when he started to undo his belt, shook her head and repeated her command. Bemused, he obeyed, watching her, his arms folded behind his head, as she removed her cap and let down her hair, running her fingers through it, shaking it down her back to her buttocks. Then she bent to unlace her shoes, the hair falling forwards, dark, glossy coils catching on her breasts as she straightened up.

She knelt beside him on the bed and began to undress him. She worked methodically, starting with his shoes, his belt, smiling to herself as she laid his jewel-handled dagger on the nightstand. She made him sit up and raise his arms as she pulled his tunic and shirt over his head, then removed his chausses, working them skilfully over his erection. He reached for her with a groan, but she shook her head and pushed him away, saying nothing, as enigmatic as Emma, the mute.

Then she began to run her hands over his body, lightly at first but gathering force, stroking and squeezing his flesh like a potter moulding clay, making him her own. When she touched his flanks he doubled up with laughter.

"Ah," she said triumphantly, "ticklish."

She has set a pattern for their encounters. Every time, this is how they begin. She strips him naked and explores him, telling him the story of his body, which is not the story of the body he knows, consecrated to God and to William. She tells him that the way the hair curls on his chest reminds her of embroidering chain mail, and that one day, she supposes, it will turn as grey. That the skin on the insides of his knees and elbows is so soft it is almost impossible to believe it belongs to the same body as the callouses on his hands. His navel, she says, is as deep as the first joint on her index finger, and she is unsure whether to trust a man with curly eyelashes. She tastes iron in his mouth when she kisses him, of swords and the nails on the Cross, and the sea in his seed. His earlobes feel like velvet and his penis, when hard, is silky as a mushroom cap. He is unique, and the way she loves him is unique, learned from him and not from other men.

He is relieved she was not here to witness his defeat this afternoon, though he was not thrown and managed to deflect the worst of the blow, turning his horse's head as his opponent's lance collided with his shield, the shock fizzing through his arm and shoulder and jaw, exploding behind his left eye. She was away in the castle somewhere with Freya and the dressmaker from Rouen, putting the finishing touches to her gown for this evening's feast. That is some consolation at least, for two broken lances and his wounded pride. And the other man is what he would term a professional, travelling round Europe from tournament to tournament, making his living by winning prizes. His squire has already been to Odo's tent to lay claim to horse, shield and a purse in lieu of the splintered lances. Wincing as Osbern draws his shirt sleeve back over his arm, he wonders what kind of dancing partner he is going to make. Still better than his brother Mortain or his fat nephew Curthose.

"Will the King be there?" she had asked him, thoughtfully testing the length of primrose yellow silk between her fingers.

"William doesn't particularly enjoy feasting. But he's sent me a gift, a Life of Saint Odo with three new miracles." He was glad she was too absorbed in examining the fabric to notice his expression.

As Osbern eases him into the rest of his clothes, he hears raised voices outside the tent. *Another man down*, he thinks ruefully, though the English are not usually so responsive an audience, more interested in the pie sellers and the acrobats who do balancing tricks on the lists between bouts than the jousting knights themselves. Well, what can you expect of a people who fight on foot with axes like a rabble of serfs and think football is a game for gentlemen? Then suddenly the commotion is closer, the hide hung across the entrance to the tent shivering as a body seems to stagger into it before regaining its balance and moving away.

Drawing his knife from the belt Osbern is about to fasten around his hips, Odo steps forward and pulls back the hide in a single, rapid movement. He comes face to face with a man as tall as himself, whose strange, green eyes, dense and luminous as enamel slipped over silver leaf, are disconcertingly familiar. Though big, the man is gaunt, no match for the two guards standing with long pikes crossed to bar his way. He is a Saxon by his colouring and the style of his sandy moustache, worn long and without a beard.

"Who are you, man? How did you get here?" asks Odo in English.

"God is watching you, Norman."

"Not through your eyes, I think." He replies with a confidence he does not feel, appraising the stranger's long cloak of lambskins so white they seem to glow from within, making the glitter of the standards fluttering around the tournament ground seem tawdry by comparison. "Get rid of him," he tells his guards, "then report yourselves to your commander for a flogging, and have him send me some more competent protection."

The intruder struggles, his chest pushing against the crossed pikes. He is stronger than he looks. Odo raises his dagger to the man's throat.

"Don't think I won't use it," he warns, and as the man straightens up, and lifts his arms in a gesture of surrender, draws its point, almost in a caress, down over his breastbone, cutting open his threadbare shirt.

He gags, almost drops the knife. The smell is terrible, like rank meat. His dagger has cut, not only the shirt, but a wad of filthy bandages underneath. The man's chest is densely scarred, whorls and roundels like contours on a map, purple and angry red, some weeping thick yellow pus. The pikemen shy away in disgust as Osbern, casually threatening, tossing his own knife from hand to hand, comes to stand beside his master.

"Do not pity me, Norman," sneers the intruder. "I am beyond harm. I was dead, but rose again."

"Dear God in heaven." Odo crosses himself, with his left hand, his amethyst catching the hard winter sunlight falling through the tentflap.

"You think holiness resides in a stone, priest?"

Arrow wounds, he realises, beginning to understand. He gives the Saxon his best self-deprecating smile. "As the saint says," he says, switching to Latin, "'since the world began life has betrayed those who placed their hopes in it.'"

"Then you know me, Norman. Be on your guard, you will see me again." And before any of them are aware of it he has gone, swallowed up by the crowd which closes around him as though he had never been.

"You look very pale," whispers Agatha as he takes his seat beside her for the rest of the tournament. "Where were you? What took so long? Are you really hurt? You should give this up, you know, a man of your age."

"Getting my injuries seen to, and no, they're not serious and yes, I should give it up. Stop nagging and tell me what I've missed. I got waylaid by some hedge preacher pretending he was Saint Sebastian." His had been the last bout on horseback and they have moved on to hand to hand combat; the English, he notes, glancing across to where Agatha's women sit like a row of magpies, are taking more notice now.

"Saint Sebastian?" queries Agatha. "How odd. You didn't miss much. The last pair fought with maces. Dull, all brute force and no skill.

Saint Sebastian was probably more entertaining. This is better, though one sided. You see the one on the right, in the leather and mail, his grip's all wrong. He'll tire quickly."

He laughs, then sucks in his breath sharply as the air jerking through his body jars his shoulder. "You should have been a man, Agatha."

"Yes." She continues to stare at the men fighting, but they are just a blur, flashing blades, dust clouds, a few grunts and the remorseless clang of iron on iron as if she were condemned to sit in a smithy all day. How noisy it must be on a battlefield, she thinks, stealing a sidelong glance at Odo. He knows, of course. He has spoken to the priest. There are so many things they cannot speak about, yet he ought to understand.

"I was thinking," he says, "that I might arrange a marriage for Margaret once the tapestry's finished."

"Embroidery," hisses Agatha. "How many times do I have to tell you?"

The man with the faulty grip stumbles and drops to his knees. A ragged cheer goes up from the crowd. Odo slaps his thigh three or four times in appreciation, then, to the accompaniment of excited oohs and aahs, the man struggles up again and the fight resumes.

"Shall we have a bet on it? I'm not sure I agree with your assessment."

"Really, Odo, are you not deep enough in sin by taking part? Must you gamble as well?"

He shrugs. "You know me. Anyway, what do you think? My squire, Guerin. His prospects are good. Some land in the Cotentin, enough to keep the crippled sister as well. And he can't take his eyes off her."

He has guessed. Who else could it be? Stuck up Judith? Emma with her twitch? Mad, maimed Alwys? Gytha? This is his way, to trick and tease. She suddenly remembers a time early in their childhood, before William, before Bec or Saint Justina's, when he crept up behind her and pushed her into the moat at Conteville.

Then, of course, dived in himself to pull her out and talked Maman out of beating her for ruining her clothes.

"Will his family agree? Will hers?"

"Her father is my vassal, and I dare say he'll be relieved to get rid of a daughter who will be well over twenty and another one who's good for nothing. As for his, I'll make sure Margaret brings a good dowry. Good enough to make them think of her as if she were my daughter."

"Will Guerin wait?"

"He can't marry before he's knighted, and that won't be for a year at least. He hasn't seen sixteen summers yet."

At which age, Odo had already been a bishop for three years. Lucky Guerin, not to have his decisions made for him by William of Normandy.

Odo's gaze is challenging. There is no way out, it tells her. She struggles until her muscles ache to keep the smile on her face. There is a surge in the crowd as the man with the faulty grip brings the flat of his sword down conclusively across the back of his opponent's neck, sending him sprawling. When he does not move, a couple of his servants run in from among the tents clustered around the ends of the lists to drag him from the field. Each takes hold of an ankle; the man's head bumps over stones and hummocks of grass. The victor bows to the raised platform where Odo and Agatha are seated with Hamo and his family and Odo's birthday guests.

"You'll have to excuse me," says Agatha, trying to rise, but he stops her, his hand clamped over hers where she has rested it on the bench to push herself up.

"No work today. I forbid it."

She sighs, he relaxes his grip and rubs his shoulder. "Why didn't you come to me?"

"Because you were in Ely. Or dead, for all I knew. Because…well, what would be the point in confessing to you?"

"I'm a priest."

"And up to your neck in sin yourself."

"Aren't we all?"

"You know what I mean. Tell me, when did you last confess?"

Four men enter the lists, two armed with swords and two with the curious double-headed axes favoured by some of the English.

"This will be bloody," he says, then suddenly turns to look at her, full on, his eyes wide. "I love her. It's not a sin."

"Yet if I love, it is? Even though I have never laid a finger on the girl, never even spoken to her, well, not in language she would understand anyway. Whereas you…"

"You know there's no comparison. The love of men and women is ordained for procreation."

"Priests are ordained to love God."

"She is…my way of loving God."

"Then perhaps you should consider leaving the Church. If William will let you, of course."

It is unthinkable. Sent to Lanfranc's school at Bec when he was eleven, he can scarcely remember a time when his life was not dominated by the canonical hours, fasts, festivals, rules of dress and demeanour, the sacraments. Even in the breach he honours them. Even in his readings of the classical philosophers, he is looking for glimpses of the One True God, Father, Son and Holy Ghost. Outside the Church there would be no love.

Gytha's eyes follow the path of candlelight from the mirror, as it breaks and spills over Freya's glassy hair and is reflected back again. She is not yet ready to look at herself. She holds out one arm in front of her and admires the way the wide yellow sleeve falls back to reveal the close fitting emerald green underdress. She turns her hand in front of her, whitened and softened with baths of milk and scented oils, as though it belongs to someone else, then smoothes it over the gown, where it hugs the rise of her belly like a second skin, the skirt flaring where Freya will fasten the girdle set with citrines and freshwater pearls around her hips. So much silk, so many stones. She looks through the mirror, over the reflection of her shoulder, at the green satin slippers, embroidered with pearls and gold thread, aligned under a chair like miniature soldiers awaiting battle orders. *Footsoldiers* she thinks, beginning to giggle.

"Just look at yourself, madam," says Freya, leaning from behind to pass the girdle around Gytha's body, "what is there to laugh at?"

Gytha swallows her laughter and lets her eyes move slowly away from the shoes until they meet themselves, silvery, blurred as though by tears, looking out from the polished surface of the mirror. Where am I, she asks herself, where am *I*? Who is this woman with gold in her hair and the eyes of a mermaid? She looks for herself for a long time, until Freya has buckled the girdle, arranged Gytha's overskirt so the rich brocading beneath is set off to best advantage, and adjusted her neckline the better to show off her breasts and shoulders.

She looks for herself until Freya is beginning to cast anxious glances towards the adjoining door between this, Odo's solar, which has been made over, for this evening, into a dressing room for Gytha, and the winter parlour where he will by now be waiting. But there are so many selves. Peeping through the legs of the adults is the little girl growing up on oysters and fish head broths, the silver black estuary and stories of Celtic princes consumed by passions for faeries, dream princesses, virgin-skinned witches with wits honed like shark's teeth. Here is the bride wreathed with ivy and almond blossom, carried to her bridegroom's house on the shoulders of tall young men who only yesterday were little boys she used to go digging for sandworms with; and here the young wife, earnest, hard working, awkward and disappointed in her husband's arms. The mother she will not look at, nor the ghosts whose tiny hands clutch at her skirts. Here is the lay sister sewing her tears into altar cloths, and here she, not Freya, dresses her lady for love, taking her time, exchanging charged glances in mirrors while my lord waits in the next room. The whore; ironically the only time in all her life that she ever slept alone in her curtained cell. And backwards, and forwards, to the dark woman of Odo's dream. That is all she is, why her reflection wavers and fades in front of her as though she is watching herself drown. She is Odo's dream.

She turns away from the mirror, crosses to where her shoes are waiting under the chair, and pushes her silk stockinged feet into them.

"Am I ready?" she asks Freya.

Freya's gaze is careful and critical. She steps forward and makes a small adjustment to Gytha's veil, a fine tissue of gold beneath which her hair hangs in a single thick braid, then nods her satisfaction.

"I'll tell his lordship he can come in, shall I?"

"No, one more minute." She has noticed, among her day clothes folded over a chair, the flat package tied with red ribbon. "I must hide the camel. Freya, can you take it into the bedroom and...slip it under my pillow?" My pillow? But Freya, taking the package, does not seem to notice.

Gytha shivers. Despite the fire, the extra rugs and thick hangings at the windows, the solar, with its large windows overlooking the Roman walls and the country to the south, is draughty, and she is used to woollen clothes. She knows silk holds warmth, but somehow it does not feel as though it does; this dress feels as though it is still hanging on the dressmaker's dummy, or as though there is no heat in her body it can absorb. With a dizzying sense of unreality, she sees the door to the winter parlour open and Odo come in, resplendent in yew green velvet embroidered with hunting scenes in gold thread, gems and pearls enough to decorate the effigy of a saint in a cathedral. He takes her hands and holds her at arm's length, appraising her.

Possessio mea.

"Turn round for me," he says, letting go one hand and turning her by the other as though they are dancing. "You are absolutely beautiful. Here, I have something for you." Loosing her other hand, he reaches into the close fitting sleeve of his tunic where, she now notices, something is hidden, a jumble of hard edges pulling the fabric out of shape. As he pulls, a glittering snake uncoils itself from his sleeve and curls up again in his palm.

240

"I've heard tell of snake charmers," she says, "mystics who can make snakes docile with music."

He laughs. "And did Harold Godwinson have one of these wonders as well?"

"Thankfully not. I think I would have been mistrustful of it."

"Then I shouldn't regret my gift is not a snake charmer?"

"A gift, My Lord? Surely we should be giving you gifts tonight."

"You do, Gytha, you know it." He takes a step towards her. "Every day."

"Please, My Lord. You'll make me blush."

He has lifted the bright snake to her throat and is reaching his hands around the back of her neck to clasp it.

"Careful of my veil," she admonishes, "Freya has rearranged it I don't know how many times."

"A snake charmer would be more original," he says, "but then, lovers aren't very original are they? There seem to be so few ways to express love. So, we say, I love you, and give binding ornaments." She says nothing as she turns to marvel at the necklace of emeralds and diamonds whose cold fire burns in the silver mirror, because she has no words to describe the sensation of such a jewel next to her skin. Will it corrode in the brine for salting fish, or will its lights be extinguished by mud? Will it throttle her? She puts up her hand to touch it, but her fingers encounter his instead, sliding away from the necklace, along the crest of her shoulder.

"You know the virtue of emeralds?" he asks. "They are for good fortune and constancy in love. They are the stone of Venus."

"Ah, that excellent saint," she teases.

"As you know, I am trying hard to master the variety of your saints." He lightly squeezes her fingers. "The gold was mined in Wales. I thought you would appreciate that."

Perhaps, if she holds on to that knowledge, the necklace may come to seem like hers.

This is a nightmare, a dream of excess of the sort you might fall prey to if you go to bed hungry. There is too much of everything, not a square inch of the bleached linen cloth spread over the high table that isn't covered by a dish of food. Venison haunches marinated in red wine with cloves, fowls stuffed teasingly one inside the other, starting with swans and bustards, ending with ortolans and quails, squirrels' legs fried in sweet batter and pasties of songbirds crowned with tiny, gilded beaks. There are wild boars, and tame rabbits kept in cupboards in the kitchen, force fed herbs and corn. Dishes of peas in cream and parsnips stewed with saffron accompany them, dried figs and apricots from Acquitaine are washed down with sweet muscat wine from Provence. Everything is served on gold and silver platters, except the cheeses, displayed on slabs of marble so heavy it needed six little pages in Odo's livery to carry them into the hall. The jewels in the wine cups wink mockingly in the light of hundreds of beeswax candles, all green and gold.

And where is Odo? Gytha feels sick. Her skin beneath the layers of clinging silk is clammy, sweat trickling down her sides and between her breasts. She wonders, trying to count the weeks, if she is about to start bleeding again, or if, God forbid…No, forget it, it's far too early to tell.

Robert of Mortain, seated on her right, keeps leaning across her at the slightest provocation, belching stale wine in her face, grinning so she can see shreds of meat stuck between his teeth. Next to him, his thin, sour faced wife is absorbed in poking a stick down her throat to make herself vomit. Bishop Geoffrey of Coutances regales her from the far side of Odo's empty chair with accounts of the sexual prowess of his prize bulls. No doubt he considers this fit conversation for a mistress. Beyond him sits Sister Jean, but she cannot catch her eye, her slender, upright form completely obscured by Coutances' jovial bulk. Every time she smiles at Countess Marie, the countess tilts her chin archly and looks away, so she gives up.

He said he wouldn't be long, that he wanted a quick word with Thomas of York in private, Thomas being so recently back from Rome where he had been with Lanfranc to receive his pallium from the hands of the Holy Father himself. He had bitten her earlobe gently and gone outside. Hours ago, it seems.

"…covered the heifer from Charente five times between Sext and Vespers," Coutances is saying.

"So tell me, my dear?" says Mortain, almost dropping a handful of quail's eggs down the neck of her gown, "this hanging of Odo's. Am I represented in it?"

Her beautiful gown. She could cry. "You are, My Lord, twice that I can recall."

"And have you made me a great hero?"

What she would really like to do is climb on the table, stamp her feet and tell them all to go away. "You must ask Lord Odo if he will let you see it. Who am I to judge who are heroes and who are not?"

"By Jove, no wonder he has taken to you so, you even talk as he does."

She nods and smiles and fixes her gaze on the far end of the hall, where the women are sitting, a soothing patch of grey and white, scarcely discernible beyond the forest of lights. If only she could go to them, sink back down among them as a fish drops to a riverbed, scooping out a rest for itself among sand and shale and cloudy water. But until the tables are moved for dancing, she is trapped, and that will not happen until Odo gives the word. She is a dragonfly in his net.

"Just look at those sleeves," says Judith. "Did you ever see anything like them? And it's all silk, isn't it? I've never seen a silk dress before. Twice its weight in silver, silk costs, you know."

"She looks a proper lady," comments Margaret thoughtfully, remembering the odd comments Gytha used to drop regarding King Harold. "I always did think there was something about her, some reason she'd never tell us anything about herself. I wonder…"

"Oh really. Put a silk frock on a sow and you women would call it a lady. You know very well why milady Gytha has kept her past life a secret, and you'd do well to give a little thought to what she's done to get a gown like that."

But what Gytha has done, what she and Lord Odo do, is a source of fascination rather than revulsion to Margaret, a hazy tableau, seen through veils, of featureless nakedness and long, chaste kisses. She yearns for a lover of her own, not the squire, Guerin, with his clumsy hands and kisses like being licked by an affectionate dog, nor like Lord Odo, of course. He will soon be old, and looks as though he might run to fat if he did not spend so much time hunting and jousting and fighting wars, and she could not possibly make love to a man with a tonsure. She wonders if perhaps the Church requires its servants to shave their crowns in order to make them less attractive to women and therefore less a prey to temptation. Tonight, though, by the light of more candles than there are stars in heaven, full of rich food and unwatered wine, the Earl, in the short tunic which flatters his long legs, seems to her to be a prince worthy of his princess.

"Oh don't be bitter, Judith. I think they're lucky to be so in love."

"Love, if that's what you want to call it, doesn't put the pot on to boil. Never did. It can't last. He's a charmer, the Earl, cold as charity, I'd say. I wouldn't want to lie in Gytha's bed."

"Well, she doesn't, does she?" retorts Margaret, giggling, not a little pleased with her wit and sophistication.

Agatha feels as though she has been split in two. She is one half ears, listening gravely to the man on her left, the steward of one of Odo's estates in Essex, complaining that he cannot persuade his wife to come to England for fear of drowning in the Channel, and one half eyes, straining to see to the far end of the hall where Margaret is sitting. It is easier now the last carcass has been lifted off the spit and the fire at the centre of the room is being allowed to die down so the revellers will not burn themselves when dancing. Perhaps it is the heat; sweat prickles her scalp beneath her close fitting headrail, making her wonder if she will have to cut her hair again this year after all. Perhaps, she thinks, with a sharp stab of something which may be hope or desolation, she will have Margaret cut it for her.

There he is, the boy Guerin, seated opposite the women, leaning at full stretch across the board, his forearms resting either side of his plate, fingers outstretched towards Margaret. She only has to pick up her cup to brush their tips with the back of her hand. As she watches, Emma has one of her convulsions, knocking over a cup of wine and sending its contents flooding across the board to soak Guerin's sleeves. He starts back, laughing as Margaret jumps to her feet, takes one arm and then the other and dabs at them with the front of her skirt.

"What do you suggest, Sister?" asks the man from Essex.

Swimming? "Prayers to Saint Elmo. He is the patron saint of sailors."

Margaret's full, round breasts sway in front of Guerin. Scarlet creeps up his neck like the spreading pool of wine on the table. Agatha's eyes suddenly start to play tricks. She can see under the table, the glimpse of Margaret's creamy flesh between her garters and the raised hem of her skirt, the hard mound in the boy's groin. Her stomach knots. She pushes her plate away, swaying forward slightly as she does so, catching sight briefly of Gytha around Geoffrey of Coutances' embonpoint. Their eyes meet. Now you know, Agatha tells her with her eyes, now you really know what it means to depend on Odo. Then they are distracted by the Countess of Mortain vomiting over a hound chewing bones at her feet. The countess smiles, Gytha looks relieved as Robert pours himself another drink. *He deserves better*, thinks Agatha, *William owes him more*. It would not occur to him to petition William himself so she will speak to Odo. Tonight, as soon as he comes back in. She will not look at Margaret, or even think about her, at least not until she is alone in her room with the consolation of her scourge.

Odo gazes up at the white moon veiled by the haze of his breath, stars glittering in a perfectly clear sky the colour of his mistress' eyes. Though he has eaten little, he feels as though he may burst with joy. Everything is coming together as he wishes. On his desk lies a letter from John, in a round, hesitant schoolboy hand from which he sees traces of his own emerging. John tells him of his delight in the wit of Horace and his admiration for the stoic wisdom of Cicero; that he has found a manuscript of the Song of Roland in his school library and wonders, is it really true that his uncle the King had his minstrel perform the song to the troops before they went into battle on Senlac Ridge? Oh yes, the wretched man managed a couple of stanzas before an arrow hit him in the throat. William felt it had the desired effect on morale. But he will not tell John that.

Thomas is nervous. Odo knows it from the way his piss comes in fits and starts, so he is still at it minutes after Odo himself has finished and rearranged his clothing. Odo has been informed of everything that transpired in Rome; he has a sharp man in the Vatican, a minor clerk in the office of the Papal Vice-Chancellor, well placed to observe but remain unnoticed. He is content with the outcome, though it will do no harm to string Thomas along for awhile, to remind him where power lies in their relationship.

"Well, Tom," he says as Thomas finally finishes his business, smoothing his new purple cassock back into place. The wool is very fine, hardly in accordance with the sumptuary laws for the clergy, a small matter in Odo's view, but he lets nothing go to waste. "Will you walk with me a little way?"

"As your grace wishes."

"Please, Thomas, less formality. We are not in council this evening and besides, you are an Archbishop now."

Thomas clears his throat, a strangulated gargle. "Not yet consecrated, your grace."

Odo says nothing. It is quiet here, after the roar of conversation in the hall, no sound but the hunting whistle of a barn owl and the occasional footfall or murmured exchange between the guards on the Roman wall. He slips his arm through Thomas' and leads him towards the wall, whose flints gleam like fishscales in the moonlight. He can feel Thomas shaking.

"You seem nervous, Thomas." His voice is full of concern. "Why should this be? Is there something you know that I don't?"

"I very much doubt it."

"And you are right. I make it my business to know everything. And what I don't know doesn't come to my attention because it has no importance. Do you understand me, Thomas?"

"I'm not sure."

They walk along the wall, Odo exchanging a word with each of the guards. Thomas stops as Odo mounts a firestep and stands, arms leaning on the parapet, looking out into the darkness. A light wind is blowing in from the east, smelling of frost and the sea. No lights are visible beyond the city walls, no sound reaches him but the breathing of the wind and a sudden bark of laughter as two of the guards exchange a joke.

"Join me," he says, shifting his position to make room for Thomas. "Over there, on the hill," Odo continues, pointing to his left, "is Saint Martin's Church, where the blessed Augustine stopped to pray before entering the city to begin his ministry to the Angles. Nearly five hundred years ago, yet there is still so much left for Christian men to achieve in this land." He smiles warmly at Thomas' profile as Thomas strains his eyes into the darkness, though his mind is wrestling with images of Odin and Sleipnir, blood and feathers, mud that breathes and a man with dry eyes but weeping wounds. "And you and I, brothers in Christ, fellow countrymen in a foreign place, old friends, are in danger of falling out over a form of words."

Thomas shifts uncomfortably.

"I will choose to believe that you intended all along to tell me about your oath to Lanfranc, Thomas, or perhaps you assumed I would already know? You did not intend to keep it from me, did you? No, of course not. And indeed, why should you? What have you to be ashamed of? You have done well."

"Well, your grace?" Astonished, relieved, wary, grateful.

"Well, Thomas. You have sworn allegiance to Lanfranc's person. You have not suborned York to Canterbury nor bound yourself to Lanfranc's successors. Lanfranc is a lot older than us, Tom. He can't last forever. I am well pleased." He brushes Thomas' back with the flat of his hand. He is well pleased indeed, recalling his conversation with Lanfranc last February. *It would be most presumptuous to exact such an oath to my person.* Lanfranc's very words.

"There is still the matter of the three bishoprics, your grace."

"But our Holy Father is sending us a legate to guide us in that matter, and I am sure, when Cardinal Deacon Hubert sees the evidence I have assembled to support York's claim, he will agree with me that Archbishop Stigand seized control of those bishoprics without any legal justification. Don't worry, Tom, we shall see off Lanfranc yet. Join me at Prime tomorrow morning, will you, and let us pray for God's continued guidance in the matters before us."

"As you wish, your grace."

"Come, then, let us go back indoors."

At last. Is it Gytha's imagination or do even the candles seem to burn brighter as Odo re-enters the hall? Perhaps it is only the current of cold air from the door, dispersing the fug of smoke which has accumulated under the roof, only the wind making the little flames flicker. His eyes seek her out as he claps his hands for the servants to clear the tables and drag them aside to make room for dancing. He is her anchor, the focal point at the centre of the milling confusion of guests and servants, dogs, musicians, a man with a large spotted cat on a chain which makes the ladies scream and hoist their skirts out of reach as it passes, snarling, a singer gargling noisily to prepare his voice. She feels like the cat herself, exotic and strange, a transitory entertainment. What is a bishop's mistress but an anomaly as bizarre as a bearded lady or an air-breathing fish?

Striding up the hall to take his place beside her in his high backed chair, skirting a gaggle of pages struggling to bear away one of the great marble cheese platters, past the spotted cat as though scarcely aware of its existence, he looks flushed and well pleased with himself.

"What dance shall you have, sweetheart?" he asks, taking her hand and bowing over it.

She meant to chide him for deserting her, but she is too relieved at his return to be angry and besides, it is his saint's day they are celebrating, and he has given her this beautiful gown and the stones so cool against her throat in the steamy heat of the hall. And he calls her sweetheart in front of all these high born folk, counts and countesses, knights and bishops, and Sister Jean. "A circle dance," she says, "as it's close to Saint Catherine's day, and I know no dances associated with Saint Odo."

"No, nor do I. He was a bishop and a statesman, I suppose he didn't dance much."

"It doesn't seem to stop you, My Lord."

"I have such a beguiling partner. History doesn't record that Saint Odo was so lucky. Come now, let us stand up or the others will get impatient. *Jump at the Sun*," he calls to the musicians, and the drummer begins to strike the beat as the dancers form themselves into circles of six.

They dance circles and lines, fours and pairs, until Gytha is dizzy, the hundreds of candle flames blurred to a single pulse of light behind her eyes, her feet in the new shoes burning as though she is dancing on coals. Then, seeing how tired she is, Odo sweeps her up in his arms and carries her to his great chair, where he sits her on his knee while they watch the man with the spotted cat make it juggle with a ball, then hear a long tale of King Arthur's war against the Emperor of Rome, during which she falls asleep with her cheek against his heart.

It is almost dawn before the party breaks up, and then only because Odo, longing for a little time alone with Gytha before he has to go to Prime, dismisses the musicians, the storyteller, the dwarf, the jugglers, the man with the cat and the man whose dogs can walk on their hind feet, saying there will be no-one fit for feasting the next night if they do not get some rest. The hint is taken and the guests dispose themselves for sleep, some in the hall, some in the great bedchamber, one couple among the flour sacks stored behind the bakery where it is warm and secluded. Odo tells Osbern and Freya they will not be needed. He and Gytha will be one another's body servants.

But she does not come to his arms as he expects, setting her agile, embroiderer's fingers to work on his clasps and buckles and laces. She sits on the edge of the bed, removes her shoes and begins to massage her feet.

"I've become unused to dancing," she says.

"Then we must remedy it." He holds out his arms to her. "Come here, dance with me now. There is still music in my head."

She gives a tight, sad smile. "There is nothing but throbbing in mine, My Lord."

"Then shall I let your hair loose?"

In reply she reaches up to unpin her veil herself, then pulls her braid over her right shoulder and begins to undo it.

"Alright," he says with a resigned sigh. He folds his arms across his chest and rests his weight against the dressing table. "Tell me."

"How could you go off and leave me like that?" She fiddles angrily with her hair.

"Leave you? I told you I had to speak to Thomas. It was important. I wasn't gone so long, and surely my brother waited on you."

"Oh he would have done, if his wife hadn't been sitting next to him. They despise me, Odo. The men think they can use me for sport and the women won't speak to me. It's no good." She has stopped trying to unbraid her hair and sits staring at her hands, lying palm up in her lap. "Just look at my hands!" She jumps to her feet and crosses the room towards him, holding them up in front of his face. "I could soak them in milk and almond oil from now till Kingdom come but I'd still have these scars."

Taking her hands in his, he rubs his thumbs gently over her fingertips, feeling the fine, raised lines scored in them by years of working with gold and silver wire. "And if you didn't, they wouldn't be your hands and I wouldn't love them as much." He lifts them to his lips but she wrenches them away. "That's all that matters to me. I thought you felt the same. Why did you wait till now to say all this?"

"I couldn't...not in front of all those people. Besides," she adds sulkily, "I didn't want to spoil your party."

He gives her a sceptical look, but says nothing.

"Odo?"

"Yes?"

"When you go to court at Christmas, what will become of me? What will I do? Go and sit in the workshop in my fine dresses? Stay cooped up in these apartments like some pet bird from Africa? Where will I sit in hall? I'm not the chatelaine here, Countess Marie is. Then Sister Jean takes precedence. Who am I, Odo?"

He picks up the lamp and carries it through to the parlour, stepping over Osbern rolled in his blanket on the threshold, and returns almost immediately with a sealed document in his hand. "This is a title deed, made out in your name, see?" He points to Gytha's name at the head of it, the capital A adorned with flourishes. "It relates to the manor of Winterbourne in Essex, only a small place with a couple of hamlets, but the house is comfortable and the land is good there. It has a decent wool flock, and a mill. And I suppose it will be a kind of homecoming for you, though I'm afraid it's nowhere near Colchester. Anyway, I've decided to give it to you, so you will be relieved of all these worries about precedence and what to do while I am away. You can simply...sit in your hall and read my love letters." He gives a brief, bashful laugh. "The steward of Winterbourne is my guest here for the feast. I will introduce you to him tomorrow."

"Do you think," she asks after a chilly pause, "that you can make me into a lady simply by dressing me up as one? Keep your land. It's of no interest to me. There is nothing I yearn for in Essex, I assure you. Give it back to the man you took it from if you have no further use for it. You said you loved me just as I am."

"Beside the point," he says, in what she thinks of as his business voice. "I'm not sentimental where land is concerned, Gytha. I would have explained this properly tomorrow, but as you seemed so anxious about being left alone here at Christmas, I thought it might help to set your mind at rest. So let me explain now. You are my mistress. All these people here know it, before long the whole country will, the King and his court, Lanfranc. They will know in Normandy, Burgundy, France, Anjou, Rome. Maybe even Constantinople. And don't try to shrug it off. That's not modesty, it's naiveté. There will be a great deal of interest in you, because you're mine." He pauses, putting the deed down on his dressing table and pushing it towards where she is standing. As she neither speaks nor shows any interest in the deed, he goes on, "A man like me has no friends, only flatterers, debtors, and enemies. I could be assassinated, or killed in battle, and then what do you think would become of you? Well, I don't have to tell you, do I? You saw what happened to Edith Swan Neck. And say we have children, how would it go for them? Ask William. He knows all about being a fatherless bastard. So you see, I've decided to make over this property to you to safeguard you and my children. I am a practical man, Gytha. The fief is yours, you have no option, the legalities are already set in motion. I dare say you'll find it easier to accept with a good grace."

"And…if there are no children? What then?"

"You think I would value you less?"

"It has been my experience thus far, and that of most women. I expect you would leave me for someone younger, with more chance of bearing you healthy sons." She twists her hair into knots. "Then what?"

"I won't leave you."

"How can you be so sure?"

"You know how. My dream."

"It was a dream, Odo. At best a disturbance of the mind brought on by the emotions of battle."

"You should take dreams more seriously. Did you not know this island of yours was predicated on a dream of Brutus, in which the goddess Diana told him of a land beyond Gaul, surrounded by sea? To me, my dream was a promise. It binds us as surely as if the priest had bound our hands with his stole. I will never leave you, Gytha, I cannot, however sorely you try me. And you do try me." He gives a rueful laugh. "You do question everything so. Can you not be content?"

He's right, Freya's right, they are all right. She knows perfectly well why Marie and the Countess of Mortain acted so coldly towards her. They are jealous. Neither of them was dressed in silk or wearing such fine jewellery. She should be content, she will try. She goes and puts her arms around him, suddenly conscious of how late it is, how her feet ache and her head throbs as the effects of the wine wear off. The lamp sputters and goes out, making them aware the night is almost over. A glimmer of dawn catches and holds, in their eyes, his glass amulet, her emeralds and diamonds.

"I'm sorry," she says, "my tongue was always my curse. For my next gift, perhaps you should give me a scold's bridle."

"I think," he says, leading her towards the bed, "your tongue has other skills enough to compensate for its sharpness."

Sinking among the quilts and featherbeds, suddenly she struggles up again. "I almost forgot." Supporting herself on one elbow she rummages under the pillows and triumphantly withdraws the flat package bound with red ribbons. "For you."

His face, lined with sleeplessness and the pain from his shoulder, suddenly seems to light up. "What's this?" He unfastens the ribbons and withdraws the piece of embroidery from its wrapping. "The camel." He goes to the window and opens the shutters, turning the camel this way and that in the grey light, feeling the raised texture of the couched and laid work with the tip of one index finger. "What a perfect gift, and so beautifully done. Perhaps I should send you back to the atelier after all."

"It's a small thing compared to emeralds and acres of Essex, but I didn't want you to think I'd forgotten."

"It's a much bigger thing than either," he says, smoothing it out over the fox fur bedspread, then laughs suddenly. "For it will be as precious to me as my little wooden Saint Odo, but far better executed."

Later that morning Odo presides over a High Mass in celebration of his saint. The chapel is so crowded with his household and its guests that even some the most nobly born of the congregation are forced to huddle around the doors, wrapped in their ermine and sables to protect them from the dusty cold. Standing in the vestry as his deacons robe him, he wonders how he will make himself heard and wishes he were with Gytha, whom he left sleeping in his warm bed, her cheeks still flushed with making up their quarrel. He will not see her now until evening, for the men are to hunt after Mass, yet he would far rather eat breakfast with her and talk about her plans for the day, or watch Freya braid her hair, all these inconsequential domestic intimacies which have suddenly acquired such meaning for him.

He had gone into the cold chapel for Prime, unconfessed, unshaven, mentally and physically dishevelled. Once the service was over, he could not remember a word of it, and was certain this was obvious to Thomas, his chaplain and the handful of others present, and was even more, terrifyingly, certain he did not care. He has remained in church since, trying to prepare for Mass, but his thoughts do not seem to be under his control. He has cast his mind over his sermon without improving a word of it. He has made his confession, but it was a partial and inadequate affair, listing only those thoughts, words and deeds which he feels to be sinful, leaving unsaid everything to do with Gytha. He is so mired in his own shifting sense of right and wrong he has forgotten entirely to pray for the peril to her soul.

He watches the two deacons about their work, moved by the reverence with which they take the sacred vestments out of the chests inlaid with ivory crosses in which they are stored, gently shaking and smoothing and brushing before laying them out in the order in which he will assume them: alb, dalmatic, amice, cincture, stole, chasuble, pallium and mitre. The names flow like poetry through his mind. The ritual of clothing, which must be done in the same way, with the same prayers, before every service, calms him as he is transformed from mortal man to priest, from the victim of his senses to the servant of his faith.

But this morning, when he raises his arms to allow the tying of the cincture and beseeches God, *Praecinge me, Domine, cingulo puritatis, et extingue in lumbis meis humorem libidinis,* he falters and is almost unable to continue. Because he does not want the fire of concupiscence quenched in him, he can no longer be satisfied with spiritual passion now that he is in thrall to his earthly love. He wants God and Gytha, but if God makes him choose, he will choose Gytha. Yet he does not believe God will make him choose. God sent him Gytha, in a dream, His preferred means of communicating with his people from Joseph in Egypt to the Holy Virgin.

In the heat of his conviction he steps out of the vestry, the warrior of Christ, to confront his congregation. He has chosen to preach on Saint Odo's dictum that those whom you have snubbed and treated ungenerously in life will be the first to greet you in purgatory and will have the last word on when, if ever, your soul may enter paradise. He chose this text for her, even though he knows she never attends Mass, but he does not want anyone with whom she comes into contact to be in any doubt as to how to treat her. *Possessio mea.*

Not until she kneels in front of him at the altar rail does he realise she is there, and then he doesn't know what astonishes him more, her being there, in church, or the fact that he was unaware of it. He had thought he would always know when she was in the same room, that he would somehow feel the air shift to accommodate her. He is only caught off guard for a second, however, as she lifts her face to him and opens her mouth to receive the Host. She looks not at his hands or the cross on the altar, but directly into his eyes, smiling very slightly as he places the sliver of bread on her tongue. His lips form the words, corpus Christi. Her saliva is on his fingertips, her breath brushes the back of his hand, and these intimacies, watched by hundreds of pairs of eyes yet not seen, not understood, are a sign from God.

PURIFICATION

CHRISTMAS 1071 TO CANDLEMAS 1072

Odo, to his beloved Gytha

In the midst of our festivities, I alone, my darling girl, am sunk in misery.
To see me you would think me the model of priestly virtue and restraint.
I do not eat, because I am sick with longing. I do not dance, because
you are not here to partner me. I do not drink, for fear it will make me
maudlin or indiscreet. I do not tourney because my life is suddenly too
precious to be thrown away in a game. I hear all the night offices because
I cannot sleep. As the poet says, "one in a state of desire loses his reason
for love – he thinks nothing at all of cliffs and rivers; he thinks vigils
are rest and passes plains." When I close my eyes, I can still feel your
body next to mine, your lips, your hands, your breasts, the secret parts
of you I may name in thought and deed but not in word, your breath
like waves whispering over sand. These poor impressions must be my
life until the King releases me and I can return to your side.

Every mile that lies between us is like the unbridgeable gulf between
time and eternity, and time itself seems an eternity here at Gloucester,
where wet snow falls daily from a sky the colour of untempered steel.
I had hoped by now to be able to tell you when I shall be free to leave,
but the King seems determined to keep me here until Candlemas, and

even then I think I must be the very last to quit this damp, overcrowded place. Only this morning, His Grace asked me some question about the wording of the new Charter for London; he believes I have left the matter of inheritance too ambiguous. We will speak again after the Purification service, he then said, peering at me most shrewdly, in the hope that it purifies your thinking.

In the meantime, he and I play endless games of chess and backgammon (for we are better matched than most here), and he chides me for leaving Turold with you at Winterbourne – as if none but he is entitled to be entertained at Christmas time - and tries to tease out of me the source of my seriousness, as though we are bound together on a treadmill of puzzles. But in chess, a bishop may travel farther and faster than a king. William is brave and ambitious, but he is also narrow, there is no romance in his soul. Without jongleurs like Turold – or kin as wayward as me – he has no stories to tell himself. Should I pity him? This may be the season of good will, but I have no pity for any but my own aching heart.

It is as well William cannot read English.

As I breathe, I love you and live only to serve you. I will come to you as soon as ever I can. A thousand kisses.

Odo

His messenger brought her his letter this morning, as one has done every morning since his departure. She has not read them all, because she reads slowly and occasionally he makes mistakes of grammar or idiom which give his English the feel of a foreign language whose meaning she cannot quite grasp. So some of them have been added to the bundle beneath her pillow with their seals still unbroken, and some memorised in part, phrases disjointed, mysterious and beautiful as the fragments of Roman mosaic occasionally turned up by her ploughman. *Never reproach yourself for loving me, never fear,* he wrote on Saint Stephen's Day, *for God made Eve from Adam's rib.* And again: *Why do I keep writing when I know you cannot reply? For the thought of your eyes caressing the pages I have smoothed with my hand and inscribed with my nib. A poor substitute for your warm skin.*

This latest she has read, during her walk to the church of the neighbouring Convent of Saint Eufrosyna, where she has fallen into the habit of worshipping. She hoped it would tell her when she might expect him to join her at Winterbourne, for today is Candlemas, the fortieth day after Christmas, when the court will break up.

The church is full of candles, their flames like shoals of tiny, luminous fish swimming in the murk of a February morning. The air is holy with the scent of stone and incense and beeswax, sweet with the disembodied music of the nuns singing behind the screen which shields them from the view of the congregation. Gytha imagines the golden light of the candles flowing through the church's sturdy lancets, rippling over the newly ploughed soil, and sees it as a small ship in the middle of a petrified sea of damp, dark red earth.

Despite the presence of her steward, and Fulk and Freya and the two babies, and the dwarf, Turold, she has discovered there is no consolation for the loneliness of his absence. Yet her happiness in knowing he will follow only a matter of days behind the messenger who brought his letter, and intends to stay at Winterbourne until the arrival of the papal legate in the spring, is mixed with apprehension. Closing her eyes, the candle flames dancing behind her eyelids, she tries to imagine what it will mean, not to be apart or circumscribed by the need for discretion. Her piety is a lie. What she thinks about in church is not the miracle of Christ's love, but the love of His vicar, Odo. When she takes the Host in her mouth she meditates on the gentle pressure of his fingers on her tongue, his hands cupping the chalice, his voice pronouncing the words, *corpus Christi, sanguis Christi*. During the sermon, she finds herself dreaming her own interpretations of scripture, and that holy writ is becoming, for her, a lexicon for earthly lovers, inscribed in the book of her heart.

For all her early misgivings, her house has seduced her. A long house in the old style, with a separate women's bower, it stands cradled in the rounded folds of its sheep pastures, the demesne holdings spread out in front like a patchwork apron, the stream, a porridge of ice but not quite frozen, winding down the hill behind. She delights in walking around it, touching the furniture, breathing in its orderly scents of beeswax polish, camphor and clean straw, watching the changes in the light spilling through its windows. She loves to stand in her courtyard and survey her byre, her stables, her kitchen, her dairy, the wattle shelter over the stream where the laundry is done, and to know that all these honest, purposeful buildings are hers. The order of the domestic cycle, the milking and churning, cooking and mending, even the care of the two babies, the endless rigmarole of feeding, changing clouts, swaddling and singing to sleep, brings a kind of peace she can lay over her heartache like a poultice.

She opens her eyes, hearing the rustle of the congregation beginning to stir. Everyone stands for the blessing and distribution of candles. She smiles at the faces around her, weathered features softened by candlelight until they are almost indistinguishable from the faces of saints and angels gazing out serenely from the painted church walls. And they smile back, respectful of the handsome widow in her rich, sober clothes, pleased with her modest demeanour and courtesy, and the young man and woman who wait on her and accompany her to church with their two little children. She knows they like the dwarf, because she has caught him occasionally, out of the corner of her eye, cutting discreet capers or pulling comic faces to amuse them during the long, Latin sermons which none of them understands. Of course she is happy. Happiness has these knots in it, like strong wood.

Agatha stands beside Margaret in the procession to carry the blessed candles to the cemetery, glancing at her furtively, looking away before Margaret, or anyone else, becomes aware of her attention. The lights, flickering as the chapel door is opened, animate her placid features and galvanise the coppery springs of hair escaping from her cap. Agatha is aware of her flinching as hot wax splashes her, and longs to take her soft, plump hand in her own and kiss away the sudden pain then peel off the coating of wax from the freckled skin. Perhaps she should offer to carry Margaret's candle, to protect her from burning. She stares at the flame of her own until it fills her vision, and if she looks away, sees its silhouette superimposed on the dark corners of the chapel from which all the lights have now been gathered by the congregation.

They are celebrating the purification of the Blessed Virgin, sealing her virginity in white beeswax and fire. Yet, Agatha asks herself, what are candles compared to the unclouded innocence of this girl, enclosed in the atelier like a virgin martyr in a reliquary? And suddenly it becomes clear to her what she must do. Guerin will not touch her, no-one will touch her. Agatha will give her to God. In the crucible of that milk white body the gold of her maidenhead will be tested and will not be found wanting. She is too good, too pure for human love in all its messy absurdity.

Margaret loves Candlemas, with its sense of beginnings, the presentation of the new baby in the temple, the ploughing and sowing begun at Epiphany, a foretaste of spring in the light of all the candles burning in church and among the graves, a light of hope between black earth and lowering sky. This is when she remembers her brothers, not in the November depths of All Souls but now, when the days have begun to lengthen again, with hope. She knows nothing happens in vain, it is all part of God's plan and God, like Sister Jean, knows the order of the narrative, the purpose of everything in it from the humblest mongrel looking for scraps under the table to the vertiginous loneliness of the King confronting history. God and Sister Jean understand, so Margaret does not have to.

The priest intones the opening line of the anthem and they begin to move forward, following the choir, around the chapel, across the outer ward and through the gate. The cemetery lies beneath a large oak on the far side of the flat expanse of grass separating the castle from the town, where the lists had been set up for Odo's birthday celebrations. The air is dry and icy, almost windless so the candles can burn unshielded. A thin layer of snow crunches beneath their feet, unmarked till now by anything but the delicate tracery of bird tracks. When Odo's hanging is finished, resolves Agatha, she will take Margaret back to Falaise with her. She will be safe there, in the house of women, where Alwys can also be cared for. She will be saved from the world's corruption.

A thin, biting rain has begun to fall. Freya hands Thecla to her father, who tucks the child inside his sheepskin jerkin. Thecla laughs, an exultant bubble of sound rising above the prayers intoned by the priest, and one of the nuns briefly raises her head to smile at the little girl. Shivering, Gytha pulls her hood closer around her face. Her fingers clutching the candle are stiff and aching with cold, but it is more than the wind and rain that has made her shiver. She has a disturbing sensation of being watched, a strange gaze raking the back of her neck, setting her hair on end. It is a relief when the procession starts to wind back among the graves towards the church, forming a queue as each one pauses to cross himself, or kiss the image of the Christ child held up in greeting by a member of the clergy standing at the church door. The queue moves slowly, shuffling forward with heads bowed, the rain soaking through clothes, mud seeping under the soles of shoes. It seems as though they are not moving at all. Behind her, Thecla begins to whine, then to bawl, which seems to trigger a general murmuring of discontent.

When her turn finally comes, she sees what the problem is. Instead of merely bowing to the image, or brushing it briefly with their lips, the worshippers have been kneeling to receive the priest's blessing, each small delay shunting into the next, slowing and sometimes stopping the line. Well she will not. She recoils from pictures of the Child, mocking her with His chubby knees and rosy cheeks, and is annoyed when the priest takes a step towards her, blocking her way into the building. Raising her head to defy him, she finds herself looking into the laughing eyes of her lover, her sadness and irritability purged in a golden glint of mischief. Aware of the people queuing behind her in the rain, she lets her gaze linger for the briefest of moments, but it is enough to take in everything, to soak him up as though she is a sponge, every detail familiar and loved, yet new as the spring about to begin. In his haste to prepare this surprise for her, he has not found time to remove his spurs which poke, muddy and incongruous, from beneath his alb. She frowns at his feet, he grins.

"I rode all night," he whispers as she lowers her hood to receive the kiss of peace, his lips brushing her cheek like a wingbeat. She steps back, but her gaze remains locked to his.

"What about the King's charter?" She tries to speak without moving her lips, so her words come out flat edged as knife blades.

He shrugs dismissively. "Oh, there was nothing wrong with it. He was just...being a king." Enunciating clearly now, in the priestly voice which carries back above the wind to the rest of the congregation waiting among the graves, he continues, "'Behold this child is set for the fall, and for the resurrection of many'." He holds the painted panel at waist height, challenging her to kneel if she is to kiss the Child.

Well, this is as good a way to begin as any. The priest in his spurs, the whore on her knees in her widow's weeds, the painted image of the perfect child between them. As she kisses the Child, the wood seems to dissolve at her touch, moulding itself to the flesh behind, beneath his sacramental robes, the bowl of his pelvis cupping his sex in its nest of dark blond hair, the skin, taut, white, mapped with blue veins. Suddenly the sense of being watched, of being somehow found out, once again creeps up her back. *They know*, she thinks, *they all know; if we stood here as naked as Adam and Eve in the Garden we could not make it any clearer*. She rises too quickly, the blood rushing to her head, suffusing her cheeks, making her stumble. Odo takes her arm to steady her, letting the picture drop at an angle from his other hand, where it hangs between them, a corner digging into her thigh. He makes a play of stifling a yawn.

"I'm ready for my bed," he murmurs, then steps back to let her into the church where the nuns have begun yet another repetition of the canticle of Zachary.

Within days, everything changes. Although he rode from Gloucester accompanied only by a couple of men at arms, in order to travel fast, it is not long before Osbern joins them in a chaos of noise, men shouting, harness jangling, hooves clattering over the little bridge where the stream crosses in front of her gate. The hall seethes with dogs and soldiers, clerks and squires, all jostling for places at table and hearthside sleeping plots. The silver bathtub is hung from a beam in the kitchen building, where people tend to strike their heads against its bevelled edges; a cut or a linear bruise on the forehead rapidly assumes the status of a Winterbourne brand. The great bed is set up in the bower, leaving scarcely room for a linen chest or a brazier, let alone Odo's clothes and books. There are gifts for the babies, rattles, balls, an articulated wooden tumbling man whose joints click as he somersaults over a stick. One day, Odo goes out and reappears with a puppy, the smallest Gytha has ever seen, tucked into his hauberk. The French name for this type of dog, he says, is *terrier,* because it excels at digging rabbits, foxes, even badgers, out of the earth. They quickly discover it also likes biting the backs of ankles and sleeping in Leofwine's crib.

He is never still, pacing around the hall, cracking cardamoms between his teeth, describing great gestures with his ringed hands as he elaborates his plans for her estate. The house must be pulled down and replaced with something more modern. Two storeys, private apartments for himself and Gytha, an integral kitchen with a chimney. A chapel. Bigger stables, a mews. There must be a grain store closer to the mill. Do these English have no concept whatsoever of efficiency? And here, look, they have planted mancorn when it would be better for wheat. He goes on until she feels as disorientated as Thecla and Leofwine when he plays his hectic games with them, tossing them into the air until they scream with terror and delight, pursuing Thecla, who is beginning to crawl, among the legs of tables and chairs, growling like a bear in a forest.

"But I like everything the way it is," she protests gently when they are alone at night, winding her fingers in among the hairs on his chest.

"It could be so much better. I want it to be perfect. Our perfect place."

"Its imperfections endear it to me," she replies, and he folds her in his arms and kisses her, knowing she is no longer talking about Winterbourne.

She has spent her life confined to small spaces, to single rooms and low roofs, cells, a narrow bed, a linen chest, a locket containing four twists of hair. Now she is mistress of an estate, a world whose boundaries she can only just encompass in a day's ride. Odo has enlarged her life immeasurably, and yet he remains larger. He has confided the secrets of his heart and body in her but is as elusive and unpredictable as the gryphons and unicorns everyone can describe but no-one ever seems to have seen.

"I'm the luckiest man in England," he tells her sometimes, but the look on his face when he says it is often complicated; remote, wistful, hungry.

SWANSONG

SAINT AGATHA'S EVE TO THE ANNUNCIATION 1072

Two days after Candlemas, a messenger from Christ Church arrives for Agatha between Terce and Sext. Archbishop Lanfranc wishes to consult her regarding the setting up of a daughter house for women. He craves the opportunity to seek the counsel of an educated and intelligent woman with long experience of living by the Rule. He is obliged to travel to London the following day, to hear pleas in his court at Saint Mary le Bow, and therefore hopes Sister Jean-Baptiste will be free to spend an hour with him this afternoon. Their conversation will give him food for thought on the dreary journey to London.

Agatha praises the Archbishop's proposal. It is her understanding that there was, in former times, a strong tradition of female religious life in England, but that it lapsed somewhat during the rule of Harold Godwinson. She knows that many widows and daughters of the defeated English have sought the veil, and counts it an act of compassion on the Archbishop's part that he should thus consider their welfare. If it pleases His Grace, she will come to him before None, so as to avoid having to travel back after dusk.

Odo's name is not mentioned.

Agatha decides Margaret will accompany her. This invitation is a sign, confirmation that her plans for Margaret meet with God's approval. What better way to begin her education in the Rule than by listening to the discourse of a monk as learned and virtuous as Lanfranc of Bec? And if, as Agatha anticipates it will, the conversation should turn at any point to the matter of Odo and his mistress, well, she will send Margaret to Brother Thorold in the infirmary to beg some of his linctus for coughs and sore chests. By this late in the winter, her own supplies are running low.

Margaret can scarcely touch her midday meal. She has not been outside the castle walls since, she cannot remember when, except for yesterday's procession, of course, and the joust held for Lord Odo's birthday last November, but they don't count. The excitement of going into town, past all the shops and cookhouses, through the Buttermarket with its stalls selling everything from songbirds to sausages, its cock fights and ale counters, is almost unbearable. Not to mention the prospect of seeing the builders at work on the new cathedral, in their short tunics and bare arms. All that male sweat and casual mastery of cranes and pumps, levels and set squares. If she tries to put food in her stomach, she thinks she may explode. Why her? Why not Judith? Of course, Sister Jean would probably have taken Gytha for company if Gytha were here. Has she somehow inherited the wit and worldliness, the air of being surprised by nothing, in awe of nobody, that gave Gytha her unique position in the atelier? Has some element of Gytha rubbed off on her from the years of sharing a frame and washing one another's hair, the way woad or madder might become ingrained in the skin of a dyer? She feels she is at the beginning of some great adventure. She has only to place her feet in the little imprints left by Gytha's green satin dancing shoes to find the way to her own prince.

"I intend that you should be in the room with us while we talk. You will find our conversation instructive," Sister Jean explains as they walk, taking care not to stumble in the frozen ruts of the roads. They pause in the Longmarket while a man tries to drive a large and uncooperative sow through the narrow space between the buildings with their overhanging eaves and bankers open on to the street. Margaret laughs as the sow swerves into a display of game, knocks a truss of partridges to the ground and proceeds to eat them, snuffling and grunting, blood and feathers sticking to her snout.

"But you must keep a modest demeanour. Only speak if spoken to. Do not look His Grace the Archbishop in the eye. Lanfranc of Bec is a great man," Sister Jean continues.

"Not greater than Lord Odo, surely," says Margaret, artlessly, between giggles, as voices are raised between the owner of the sow and the game merchant.

"Different," Sister Jean replies, stamping her feet with cold, or impatience. "Come along. I think we can slip past while the pig is distracted."

They are shown into the Archbishop's private office. The Archbishop raises his eyebrows when Agatha asks if her young companion can sit in on their meeting, but recovers himself quickly and apologises for the lack of space. There is, he explains, no fire as yet lit in his parlour and he fears it would be too cold to be comfortable for the ladies.

"And there," says Agatha, "is one prejudice you must disabuse yourself of, Your Grace, if you are to understand the application of the Rule to women's houses. That we are in every respect less strong than men. The female humour being generally cold and damp, it might be argued that too much warmth or dryness in our surroundings might distract us from the pursuit of the fire of God's love. The airiness of women may serve to make them more receptive to the Holy Spirit."

"Or," counters Lanfranc, waving Agatha into a chair opposite his desk, as Margaret takes her place on a low stool set against the wall beside the door, "it may be that an excess of cold will cause a predominance of the feminine in the humour, thus hindering women from aspiring to the spiritual by causing them to become preoccupied with physical discomforts." He sneezes.

The stool is hard, the plaster behind Margaret's back uneven, and the learned sparring of the Archbishop and her mistress utterly beyond her comprehension. As their discussion continues, ranging over matters as varied as whether or not women religious should undertake physical labour, shave their heads or be permitted mattresses in recognition of their physical frailty, the colour of their habits and the numbers of sets of underwear they should possess, Margaret's attention wanders. Small things distract her, a food stain on her skirt which reminds her that she is, as always, hungry, and sick of eating salt pork and pickles; some scratches on her fingertips make her think about Alwys, and how lucky, yet unlucky, she has been, and that such issues of luck, or fate, or providence, are doubtless real, yet impossible to understand. Margaret has a fondness for horoscopes and, though she dutifully confesses whenever she indulges in improper speculations about the future, she cannot quite give it up. It is as though she needs to do it to reassure herself that she will, one day, when Lord Odo's interminable hanging is complete, have a future; that the minute adjustment in the conjunction of the planets between her birth and Alwys' contains a whole world cut off from Alwys with her hand.

"Excess must be avoided in eating and drinking, but also in abstinence. As the Apostle wrote to Timothy, 'godliness with contentment is great gain'," says the Archbishop. Margaret is at a loss as to what she is supposed to learn from all this. Heaven knows, she has listened to enough sermons in her life. Surely Sundays and the holy days of obligation are enough. She is honoured, of course, that Sister Jean should consider her worthy of an audience with the Archbishop of Canterbury, and that they should trouble to speak in English so she can understand them, but it is not as though she has any vocation to the religious life.

And then she remembers, with a tightening in her chest, that Gytha came here, to this very suite of rooms, with letters for Lord Odo when he was injured, and that she was never quite the same afterwards, both gayer and angrier, and more secretive. Margaret starts to wonder what happened here, and whether, if she looks in the right way, she will be able to see the imprint of those little shoes dancing through the abbey.

"Thank you, Sister, you have been most helpful. You have cleared my mind considerably on these issues. Let me send for some refreshment for you and your companion, and while we wait, tell me your news." Lanfranc tugs at his beard. "Do you expect your brother of Bayeux back from Gloucester soon? I imagine the King's court broke up yesterday."

"His lordship goes to survey his estates in Essex, I believe, Your Grace. I am not sure when we expect to see him again."

"Yes, he has been making reallocations of land in that county, I think."

"I do not concern myself with my brother's business. Your Grace, excuse me, but I have just remembered, there are some things we need from Brother Thorold." Agatha fishes in the pocket beneath her scapular and withdraws a slip of parchment which she hands to Margaret. "Please take this list to him, Meg. If we delay much longer we shall lose the light for our journey home."

How unfair, just when the conversation has finally taken an interesting turn. But a young monk is waiting at the door to guide her through the labyrinth of the abbey buildings to the infirmary, and it is clear from the tense, expectant smiles of Lanfranc and Sister Jean that she has no option but to go. She bows to the Archbishop and arranges to meet Sister Jean outside the chapter house when both have concluded their business.

The abbey is full of quiet activity as monks and servants alike hurry to finish their work before Vespers. Brother Thorold himself is in his dispensary, handing out powders in linen envelopes, little bottles of medicines and pots of salves to a forlorn queue of men and boys, some coughing, one whose hands are cracked and bleeding from eczema. Margaret settles down to wait on a stone bench running along the outside wall, beneath the infirmary windows. The windows are glazed, for Saint Benedict ruled there should be constant consideration for the weakness of the sick and the old, and Margaret cannot help glancing through them in an attempt to distract herself from the cold biting her ears and striking through her clothes as she sits.

She sees a long dormitory, white painted, containing a row of pallets, each with a sheet and a woollen blanket, and a dark wooden cross and a semi-circular basin of holy water nailed to the wall above it. Most of the beds are occupied, but Margaret notices only one of the patients. A tall man, his feet, clad in thick woollen socks, stick out from beneath the blanket. He has very long hair, lying in a coarse, sandy plait over his left shoulder, and his upper lip is overgrown, in the Saxon style, by a heavy moustache. He has extraordinary eyes, bright, yet seemingly opaque, like enamel. Green, of course, she knows they are green, as her own are green, but this opacity is new. As if he knows he is being watched, he turns his head slightly in her direction, but his blank expression never changes and she cannot be certain he has seen her. Perhaps he is blind. That would explain why he never came home. He would have felt ashamed.

"Mistress? I think you are waiting for me?"

"What? Oh, yes, sorry, yes, I have a list...somewhere. From Sister Jean-Baptiste." She looks around distractedly.

"It's here, in your hand," says Brother Thorold, taking hold of one edge of the parchment. Margaret cannot immediately let it go; she has forgotten how her hands work. "Come inside, child, your hand is frozen."

Brother Thorold pauses briefly, her hand in his, looking from it to its companion as though checking something, before leading her into his dispensary, where he pulls up a stool and presses gently on her shoulders until she sits down. Moving quietly and purposefully around the small room, he prepares the medicines Sister Jean has requested, taking down jars and canisters from shelves, weighing and measuring syrups, powders, dried petals and leaves. From time to time he comments on his work. He is sorry, he cannot spare so much vervain; the dry weather has been terrible for coughs. But if there is angelica in the castle garden, Sister Jean may try a concoction of its root in wine.

The girl will speak if she wants to. Perhaps she is in love and querying within herself whether she dare ask him for some potion to work on her lover's affections. She might be wrestling with a vocation, as he himself once did. Perhaps it is simply her age, for though she is clearly a grown woman in the eyes of the world, he can see that in her own eyes, she is still a girl, twin, he guesses, to the one who lost her hand in Lent last year. Didn't Sister Jean say something about a twin, and a curious bout of the falling sickness? Maybe that is the girl's problem.

Eventually, soothed by Brother Thorold's quiet industry, she says, "You have a patient in your infirmary, a Saxon man, not a monk. What ails him?"

"It would not be seemly for me to discuss his symptoms with any but a physician or his relatives."

"But I am his relative," she blurts out. "You see, he is my brother, my eldest brother. Tom. I thought he was dead. Killed at Hastings. We all thought he was dead. He disappeared. No-one saw him again. And now...and now... I know it's him, but...he looks as though he doesn't." She bursts into noisy sobs.

Brother Thorold pours a little wine into a beaker, mixes it with a spoonful of a syrup he uses to dispel melancholy, and offers it to Margaret. The girl is sincere, he does not doubt it, and, if he is honest, his patient's identity is a mystery he would like to have cleared up. Curiosity is a sin, yet without it, how could men ever come to know or understand any of God's creation?

"Calm yourself, child, and tell me everything, from the beginning."

Margaret wipes her eyes and nose on her sleeve. "There is not much to tell, Brother. There were four boys in my family. All went to fight alongside King Harold..." She breaks off and looks fearfully at Brother Thorold, who nods reassuringly.

"He was our king, for a time appointed by God, and now God has seen fit to give us another. Go on."

"Aelfred and Harry were killed at Stamford Bridge, God rest

271

them." She and the infirmarer cross themselves. "And Little Walter, the youngest, on Senlac Ridge. Tom died there also, so we thought, though his body was never found. But time passed, and he did not return home. He has a wife, you know, and a little son he's never seen. So we assumed…"

"Did his 'widow' remarry?"

"Thankfully not. Our new lord, a man called Vital, a vassal of the Earl, I have made a representation of him in the embroidery, talking to Duke William…the King, I mean…"

"You are getting off the point, child," Thorold prompts gently.

"I'm sorry. Lord Vital wished it, but did not insist. Perhaps the absence of a body gave him pause. So Christine has remained unmarried. She lives with my parents. She will be overjoyed to know Tom is alive. They had less than a year together before the invasion, and they seemed very happy. Can I see him now?"

"Be patient."

"I shan't mind if he's blind, none of us will."

"Blind? He is not blind, child, at least not in his eyes. Let me tell you what I know of him, to prepare you. Consider Adam and Eve when the Lord sent them out of the Garden, how some part of them died as the Lord had warned, and yet they were not dead. Sometimes it can be the same way with people even in these latter days.

"Your brother was brought to us a few weeks ago, around Epiphany as I recall. A man who kept his face covered and gave his name only as Martin accompanied him. He was very sick with cold and undernourishment, and to be honest, I did not expect him to live, but he has a strong constitution. For several days he was incoherent, but once he was back in his senses, he told me he was called Sebastian, that he was a second incarnation of the martyr Sebastian, sent to preach the end of the world and the coming of Our Saviour in Glory, and to warn of false messiahs.

"As proof of his identity, he showed me the arrow wounds in his chest, and how they continued to bleed. I had, of course, seen these wounds before during the course of treating him. They were not bleeding, but suppurating due to lack of care and cleanliness. Once I had cleaned them, it became clear they were old scars continually being reopened by some kind of scouring. The original scars might well date back to the time of the invasion."

"What are you saying exactly, Brother?"

"I'm not sure. I have no doubt the man in the infirmary genuinely believes himself to be Saint Sebastian…"

Margaret gives a little cry, quickly stuffing her fist into her mouth to stifle it. Thorold looks into her round, child's eyes and wishes he could offer more straightforward comfort.

"I do not believe he is a fraud," he continues, "though the treatment of the wounds makes me think he has been exploited by people less honest than himself. But child, you must prepare yourself for the fact that he will not know you."

"Surely once he sees me, it will help him remember?" Only yesterday she had called her brothers to mind during the Candlemas service. Surely today's encounter was a sign of God's good intentions towards her. He would not tantalise her with a Tom who was not Tom.

"That is possible, but in my understanding, unlikely. Something very terrible must have happened to make him forget, not only his wife and family, but even himself. You will have to be very patient."

"But he will remember eventually?"

"Only God knows the answer to that, my dear. He and the Evil One are doing battle for your brother's soul, which is the source of his weakness. Our faith tells us that God will win the war, but perhaps not every battle in it. All we can be sure of is that God has His reasons. I will take you in now."

Agatha takes a deep breath, the cold, dry air invigorating after the stuffy atmosphere of Lanfranc's study. She feels as though she has been bled, a fine, sharp blade inserted with precision at the optimum points for leeching information out of her. What she has told Lanfranc during their conversation about Odo is scarcely noteworthy or politically sensitive, except that the Archbishop's avid attention and thoughtful questioning have given her the impression it is. Only circuitously has the subject of Gytha come into their talk. So interesting to meet another of the embroiderers, commented Lanfranc after Margaret's back. I hear you have suffered some depletion of your ranks. Does the work still progress as planned? Yet Agatha is certain that Lanfranc's true intention in bringing her here this afternoon has far more to do with Odo and Gytha than with the administration of convents. Lanfranc is after something.

She bids the Archbishop farewell outside the chapter house.

"Oh, by the way," says Lanfranc, helping her to her feet after she has knelt to kiss his ring, "there's a rumour of plague in one of the villages to the north. Brother Thorold was called there yesterday. He said he couldn't be sure, but I thought it only Christian of me to warn you. The city fathers may well decide to bar the gates if any more are found. I can imagine Bishop Odo would not be amused to find his atelier decimated by disease."

Agatha has lived through several plague outbreaks, as has everybody other than those it has killed. She knows as well as the next person the steps that must be taken to prevent the spread of the disease, one of which is the burning of anything that has been in contact with the sufferers; bowls and drinking vessels, clothing, furniture, bed hangings. If plague enters the castle, Hamo will order the embroidery to be burnt.

As Margaret is not already awaiting her, preoccupied by this new threat to Odo's great enterprise, she makes her way to the infirmary. The bell is ringing for Vespers; she expects at any moment to encounter Brother Thorold and Margaret among the throng of monks and lay brothers heading for the chapel. When she reaches the infirmary, however, she can see shadows moving against the walls in lamplight and hear voices, Brother Thorold's soothing, Margaret's raised and strained, a third, a man's voice she does not recognise. She enters the dispensary, but some sense of trespass prevents her from intruding through the adjoining arch into the dormitory.

Margaret is crouched beside one of the pallets, holding the patient's hand, shaking it from time to time as though to emphasise something she is saying. Brother Thorold stands behind her, balanced on the balls of his feet like a man about to begin a race, his arms half stretched towards Margaret in a gesture of failed restraint. Although Agatha cannot hear what is being said, only the inarticulate murmur of voices punctuated by the occasional cry of "Tom" from Margaret, what she sees is enough for her. With a sense of the gathering frost having reached down her throat and settled around her heart, she realises the man lying on the bed is someone Margaret loves. A man, loved by Margaret. A lover. She retreats from the dispensary doorway and goes to the chapter house where she waits, oblivious to the cold which is nothing compared to the chill inside her.

Despite Brother Thorold's warning, Margaret had expected simply to be recognised, a miraculous falling of scales from the eyes. She had envisaged tears and laughter, rapturous embraces, Tom's delight when she told him about his little boy, Tom striding out of Christ Church at her side, challenging Lord Odo for her freedom, she and Alwys and Tom returning home together to resume their lives as though nothing had ever happened to disrupt them.

But the scales did not fall from those lizard-like eyes, nor the fog clear from his mind. Instead he railed, shouting the Gospel at her as though it were a stick to beat her with, his mouth filled with a holy vomit of false Christs, darkened suns and falling stars. Enough to make her nostalgic for Lord Odo's sermons, through which she generally dozes in a gentle miasma of incomprehension, even when, as he sometimes does, he delivers them in English. Tom forced her to contemplate his wounds, struggling upright and clawing at the dressings on his chest until Brother Thorold intervened, leading her quietly back to the dispensary while he calmed the ward and re-bandaged Tom's chest. Now, seeing Sister Jean waiting for her, straight backed and stern faced, she feels cold and sad, too weary to explain or wonder what to do next.

"Forgive us for keeping you waiting," says Brother Thorold. "My dispensary is always busy at this time of year. Here are the things you asked for." He hands a small bag to Agatha, who peers inside it, seeing nothing, before passing it to Margaret to carry.

"I came to find Margaret, but you both seemed to be very engaged with a patient in the infirmary, so I came away again."

"Yes, he's…" begins Margaret.

"A Saxon man," Thorold interrupts smoothly. "I though it would do him good to have some conversation with one of his own people. His mind is greatly agitated."

Margaret glances from Brother Thorold to Sister Jean. King William's sister. Perhaps Tom has given something away in his ravings that makes the infirmarer believe it wise to conceal his identity. Tom always had that indefinable edge that made people look up to him. Perhaps he was more important in King Harold's army than she had imagined and King William would be displeased to find him still alive. She will follow Brother Thorold's example and say nothing.

"I hope Margaret was able to help."

"God's will be done."

"Amen. Come, Margaret, we must be going. Thank you for the medicines, Brother."

"Godspeed, Sister."

Only when they are in sight of the castle gatehouse does Agatha remember that she never thought to ask Brother Thorold about the likelihood of plague.

"Shall I teach you to play?" Odo, sprawled among a heap of cushions before the hearth, rolls over to face Gytha, wincing as his hip bone makes contact with the sharp limbs of the wooden acrobat. Muttering something into his beard, the dwarf Turold lifts his fingers from the strings of his lute, then lays the flat of his hand across them to quell their reverberations.

"What does he say? Before I learn anything else, I must learn to understand French better. You know what they say, if you would possess another man's soul, know his language." Laying aside the chemise she has been embroidering, Gytha rubs her tired eyes, kneading the lids with her knuckles, then stoops from the settle to pick up the tumbling man and set his limbs straight. "Clumsy," she chides her lover.

"He says I should learn to play myself before trying to teach anyone else."

"He has a point."

"How would you know? Have you ever heard me play?"

"I…" The rest of her sentence is snatched from her by a gust of wind swirling through the hall door, momentarily flattening the flames on the hearth. A tide of dogs surges towards the door and eddies around the newcomer, tales waving, tongues lolling.

"Lord Odo?" His clothes are spattered with mud, his hair, when he removes his cap, plastered to his head with sweat.

Odo pushes himself to his feet, kicking aside the cushions. "Who wants him?" Though the door is closed and the fire has righted itself, his tone makes Gytha shiver. Messengers come and go continuously between Winterbourne and Odo's other spheres of interest, tentacles reaching out to Dover or Rochester, to Bayeux and Rouen, London, Paris and Rome. Some are received openly, the letters from John in Liege proudly shared, the worthy deliberations of his diocesan clergy the butt of affectionate jokes. Some sealed parchments and packages change hands in dark corners, obscured by fogs of whispering, and are locked into strong boxes. Gytha has seen pages of unintelligible squiggles and hieroglyphs she assumes are codes, linings of cloaks slit to reveal caches of precious stones, scarred, swarthy men who speak no language she has ever heard and communicate with Odo by looks and signs, pantomimes which seem to her to parody their own unwritten lovers' communion. This man looks unremarkable in comparison, though he has obviously ridden hard. Why should his arrival provoke the resentful anger she hears in Odo's voice?

"His Grace the King," the messenger replies.

"And what does the King want? It's alright," he continues with a weary wave of his hand, as the messenger hesitates. "There is nothing the King can say that cannot be heard by these present."

"His Grace summons you to London, My Lord, to brief him on the forthcoming council to be held at Winchester."

"Oh, for heaven's sake. The papal legate will not be able to cross the Alps for a month yet at least. If I brief His Grace now, he'll have forgotten everything I have told him by the time we go to Winchester. Come and warm yourself while I compose a reply to his summons. Gytha, see to our guest. Get him food and drink."

Though the royal messenger looks doubtful, he does as he is bidden. Closing the hall door behind her, the last sound she hears is Odo shouting for a scribe.

The scene becomes a familiar one during the next weeks. Every few days a messenger arrives from William, only to be sent packing with some mollifying response from Odo. He will come when the weather improves, when he has news that Cardinal Archdeacon Hubert has left Rome, when the barley is sown, once he is satisfied the stonemason he has employed knows his job. Then one afternoon, returning from an expedition with Freya to hunt for herbs she needs to treat a skin rash that has afflicted Leofwine, she finds Odo seated at the hall table with a man who, by his habit and the fullness of his tonsure, is a clergyman of considerable seniority. Both men look up as the women enter, the stranger grave and watchful, Odo, thinks Gytha, with the expression of a schoolboy caught out in some more than usually serious breach of discipline. She half expects the visitor to untie his cincture and apply its knotted end to her lover's backside, a thought which induces a secret chuckle in the pit of her stomach, a gorgeous glow of mischief between her thighs.

Odo stands, watching her raise her arms to unfasten her cloak and lift it from her shoulders, slipping his arm around her waist as she approaches the table. Her smile of greeting is fixed, a mask. Her lover slides a knowing hand almost imperceptibly downwards until his fingertips lie in the hollow between her hip and the rise of her belly. She rests her head in the cradle of sinew just below his collarbone. The visitor clears his throat.

Sometimes she longs for the world to dissolve to nothing, for all the whispers and strong boxes, the mysterious caches of jewels, the dogs and chickens and milk cows, the children, the quotidian pain of kitchen scalds, scratches and bruises, stiff joints and lost lives, to be whipped up into some great whirlwind, leaving nothing but the two of them, suspended, repeating for eternity the act of union which makes their separateness a miracle.

"Gytha, my darling." All the time with one eye on the clergyman, challenging him to object. "This is Guy de Saint-Omer, a canon of Saint Paul's Cathedral in London. Canon Guy, Aelfgytha, the mistress of this house." He makes the introductions in Latin, their formality emphasised by the slow, careful way he speaks, to be sure Gytha can understand him. "Canon Guy has kindly come to escort me to the King. He would like to leave this afternoon, but I have persuaded him to spend the night and travel fresh in the morning."

Canon Guy forces a wan smile, but will not meet Gytha's gaze; he has the punch drunk expression typical of those who have been subjected to Odo's persuasion. Gytha, her palm resting in the small of his back, almost laughs. With relief that he is not going today, in despair that he will go tomorrow.

"Must you?" she pleads with him later that night, or early next morning. He lies with his cheek resting against her ribcage, his head rising and falling on the tide of her breathing, its rhythm interrupted by her speech, the percussive interrogatives like light blows against his ear. Dawn is finding its way through the bower's wattle window shutters and the dark blue, star scattered bed curtains. *Yes*, he thinks, his fingers idly tracing the line of dark hair below her belly button, burrowing into the moist, glossy bush covering her *mons veneris, yes, I must.* Because William is my king and my brother, and I love him, and he needs me, and I owe him service, and now I have made him angry.

"I could string it out a few more days, I suppose, but Guy won't leave without me. He has made that very plain. It depends how long you can stand his whey-faced prudery."

"Long enough to travel to London with you?"

She is not a stupid woman, far from it, he could not love a stupid woman. But she does not know William. He is no easygoing Harold Godwinson, nor can he be seduced by the shambolic charm of English customs; Odin hanging from the branches of Yggdrasil does not foreshadow Christ's crucifixion in his mythology. He sighs, adoring the way his breath ruffles her hair. "You would not be received."

"No matter, I could stay in your house and see you when you were not at court. If I never set eyes on your brother again it will be too soon for me."

He shakes his head. "If William knew you were there, he would never give me leave of the palace. William and I...it's like a marriage. It works because we show one another the face the other wants to see. He may know almost as much about you as I do, but he would not like to be confronted by you in the flesh, so to speak. He...idealises me."

"And you?" she probes.

"I idealise him. I can't help it, it's a habit of long standing."

"You should beware of confusing love and idealism."

He kisses her, his tongue exploring the whorls of her belly button. "Except in loving God, Who is perfect. And made you." His fingers push deeper between her legs, to a place where there is no William, or, if there is, he doesn't matter. This matters, this woman opening to his touch. God is here, in their bed, their sweat, their tangled sheets, in her eyes and tongue and warm skin, how their seed mingles in her womb, the tears of frustration that sometimes well up in him when he makes love to her because, among all the words he knows, none are adequate to tell her how he feels. And if God is here, what does William matter?

In the atelier, the days pass as they always do. On her saint's day, Agatha grants the women an afternoon off, though she bids them not to stray too far from the castle; she is as anxious to avoid rumour as she is to avoid the plague itself. In hall that evening, everyone eats the little breast shaped cakes, though Gird has not made them as light and melting as Master Pietro did the year before, and Margaret does not appear to notice Guerin pointedly flicking his tongue at a raisin nipple. She has become unusually quiet and preoccupied since her visit to Christ Church; the other women put it down to her being in love, though if she is, Agatha is certain, it is not with poor Guerin.

By the Feast of Saint Valentine, even though Brother Thorold has assured her he has seen no more cases, and must have been mistaken in his initial diagnosis, the risk to the embroidery of an epidemic still prays on Agatha's mind. Except for Margaret, who remains as aloof as a virgin martyr, her women are sillier than ever, sewing hearts and love knots on their sleeves when they should be stitching ships and swords, tucking yarrow leaves and eryngoes beneath their pillows to provoke dreams of love. They giggle in groups, pout and blush and switch their hips at the men of the garrison who do nothing to discourage them, cutting lewd faces on love lanterns made of hollowed out turnips and drawing lots for nonce lovers from a large dish they have set up in the armoury, filled with trinkets to represent each of the women in the castle.

Even Countess Marie is not exempt, so Agatha has been told, her token being a little wooden horse with exaggerated buttocks and a mane of black wool. Will some poor swain draw her company for the feast, wonders Agatha? An emaciated Baptist clad in rabbit skins? With Lanfranc's warning niggling at the back of her mind, she feels like the Baptist, preaching to sand and locusts. A severed breast? A broken heart bound with copper curls?

The atmosphere is hectic, feverish, almost as though Odo and

Gytha are still there, infecting everyone with their lust. The tiniest spark of rumour would be enough to set the place ablaze. Briefly, she contemplates confiding her anxiety to Margaret, until she remembers that Margaret has not suddenly become sensible; it is merely that her lover lies sick in the Christ Church infirmary, rather than playing a masque of lovesickness with cloth hearts and quails eggs.

On the day following Saint Valentine's, she goes to see Hamo. She catches him off guard, before Prime, before the hall has been cleared of sleeping drunkards and other debris of the feast. As she enters the hall, Hamo is picking his way around mounds of snoring cloaks and blankets, frowning occasionally at puzzling combinations of limbs protruding from them. He is clad only in his shirt and chausses, a small page struggling in his wake with his tunic and boots.

"Lady Agatha," he says, resentfully appraising her clear eyes and immaculate white headrail. "How is your atelier this morning? Not such a mess as this, I'll wager."

"Oh, there'll be a few sore heads, I dare say." Her tone, a parody of the barrack room familiarity she learned from her brothers, because she found there was nothing she could learn from her sisters, disarms him. Turning to his page, he takes the tunic and shrugs it over his head, then stands with arms held out stiffly at his sides while the boy buckles his belt. His complexion has the clotted, yellowish texture of curds, his wiry, greying hair stands up on his head, his eyes are small and poached above bags that look as though, if you punctured them, the wine he drank last night would gush out. He will agree to whatever she suggests just to be rid of her.

"I don't wish to detain you long, My Lord, but I am proposing a move which courtesy dictates I apprise you of."

"A move?" Hamo picks up the silver wassail cup from the table and peers into it with distaste; the dregs are full of sodden flakes of roast parsnip. "Hard to imagine that was ever a love potion," he comments as he puts it down again, "saving your presence, Sister. Page, find me something to drink."

Waiting until the page is out of earshot, Agatha continues in a low voice, "The infirmarer at Christ Church thinks he has seen plague, in a village to the north."

"Christ's blood, that's all I need." Hamo runs his hand through his hair, merely redirecting rather than smoothing its turmoil. "Forgive me, Sister."

Agatha makes a gesture of demur. "It's probably nothing. Brother Thorold seemed unsure, and he is an experienced doctor. But to be on the safe side, I have decided to remove the embroidery from Canterbury for the time being. And the women with it, of course. And I must ask you for an escort."

"Well I can't pretend my job wouldn't be easier without your women." He surveys the mounds of tangled forms on the floor around them. *Like Aristophanes' wholes*, thinks Agatha, though perhaps less perfect than Plato envisaged.

"What size escort would you need? I can't spare more than a half dozen at most. Have you told Lord Odo?"

"I sent a message to...to his manor at Winterbourne..."

"That's the place he set his...Mistress Gytha up, isn't it?"

"I understood him to be staying there, but now my messenger tells me he has gone to London, so I do not know if he is aware of my decision or not. Either way, the responsibility is mine."

"Where will you go?"

"To Winterbourne."

"Makes sense. You'll have another hand at the stitching, if he hasn't taken her with him."

"I doubt that. The King is in London."

"I see."

"Well speaking for myself, I'm relieved he's gone." Freya steps back from the kitchen table, holding her rolling pin aloft like a short, thick sword. Gytha gives her a quizzical look as she spoons quince jam into the centre of the ragged pastry circle.

"He always treats you kindly. Probably better than you deserve, with such a sharp tongue on you."

Freya gives her a look whose meaning is unmistakable; she is not the only woman at Winterbourne with an ill-governed tongue. But she says nothing; she may not know her place, but she knows it is too good to risk losing. "It's not his lordship. It's that wretched cook of his."

"Ah, Master Pietro." Laughing, the two women lift opposite edges of the pastry sheet and bring them together. Freya pinches the pasty closed.

"And that's just what Master Pietro was in the habit of doing to my backside. Fulk threatened him with a beating but he burst into tears and went running to his lordship."

"I know. My Lord thought it very funny. He told Pietro that Fulk was the finest swordsman in Normandy and if he valued his extremities he'd lose some weight and get some practice in with a good armourer."

"That's why he stopped, then, and I thought his eye must have alighted on some girl with a fatter arse."

They are distracted by the lowing of an ox and the creak of cartwheels in the yard.

"That'll be Fulk back. I hope the nuns were grateful for the venison." Freya smoothes her hair back from her forehead.

"No more grateful than I am to be rid of it. Odo will have to learn to adjust his hunting ability in line with what storage space we have here."

"Dadadada," says Thecla, stumbling towards the doorway.

"You've got flour on your cheek. Hold still." Gytha leans across to brush away the dusty smudge, holding her fingers briefly against the other woman's cheek. "You're so lucky, you and Fulk."

"Lord Odo won't be gone long."

"Not this time. But don't you see, it'll always be like this. Waiting. He'll always be either just about to go somewhere or on his way back from somewhere. You know the kind of man he is." Glancing towards the kitchen entrance, lit by dusty shafts of early spring sunshine, she says, "I feel like a baby bird trying to fly, rising a little way and falling back again, never getting anywhere."

But Freya isn't listening. "Madam," she calls from the doorway, "It's not Fulk, it's…you'd better come."

It's him, he's back, he's changed his mind. He could not bear to leave her after all. There's been some accident, that's why his party has come back. He's hurt, he's…

Side by side in the kitchen doorway, the two women survey the courtyard. Two oxcarts and an assortment of mules and horses are crammed into the space between the house and its outbuildings. As Freya and Gytha look on, one of the horses, startled by a hen fluttering up from the ground, skitters sideways into the uncovered cart. The oxen stamp and toss their heads, their driver lets loose a string of invective between their ears, the women seated in the cart begin to dismount in a flurry of chatter and complaint, straightening their clothes, dusting themselves down, stretching as they clamber over the tailgate. The other wagon, which is covered, seems to be sinking into the mud.

"I wonder what's in there?" Gytha speculates.

"I think I can guess," replies Freya ruefully, as Sister Jean-Baptiste, leading a fine, white mule, detaches herself from the melee. Freya drops a curtsey, Gytha makes an uncertain bow.

"Gytha, Freya. God be with you." She is immaculate; the dust of the road disdains to cling to her hem or soil her headrail, even her mule's hooves look freshly oiled.

"Welcome to my house, Sister," says Gytha with a confidence she does not feel. Sister Jean nods impassively.

"You must forgive our descending on you this way."

By now all the women except Emma, who is still carefully levering her unruly body over the tailgate, have climbed down from the cart and are making their way towards the house. There is Alwys, kneading her backside with her stump, and Judith's scornful gaze raking the low wooden frontage of the house, its tousled fringe of thatch, a thin coil of smoke unravelling into the pale blue sky. Her contempt brings Gytha's passion for her house boiling to the surface, and she stands proudly at the door to her hall, smiling a welcome as Sister Jean explains why she has come to Winterbourne and the escort begin to unload the embroidery from the covered cart.

"Plague," says Freya. "Well I'm sure Lord Odo will be thrilled to bits to find you've risked bringing plague into this house."

"Be careful," calls Sister Jean, rubbing her elbows as the corner of a frame catches on the tailgate of the cart and tumbles into the mud.

Gytha gives Freya a sharp frown. "Freya, go and look out for Fulk returning. We shall need him to help move the furniture." She is aware of Sister Jean suddenly stiffening beside her, of a pause in the file of women who greet their hostess uncertainly, knowing no better than she does how they should conduct themselves with her. Margaret is standing in front of her, blank-eyed and speechless. "Meg. Oh I have missed you." Only realising as she says it that it is true. Seizing Margaret's hands, she is immediately aware of how thin they have become. Margaret says nothing, merely stands, meek and abstracted, waiting for her hands to be released so she can continue her sleepwalker's progress across the threshold. Gytha lets her go.

"Is she...?" Surely Sister Jean would not knowingly have brought a sick person with her.

"Of course not. I told you, it's a rumour merely, I am just being cautious. I could not bear...how would Odo react if all this work were to be destroyed?" Both women glance towards the cart emptying its cargo into the yard, the rising stack of frames and trestles, the wooden chests which Gytha presumes contain the linen sheets themselves, the wool stands poking up from the mud like strange, stiff saplings. Rubbing her thumbs over her fingertips, feeling the fine ridges of scar tissue there, she wonders how she would feel.

By evening, it is as though the atelier at Canterbury had never existed.

The hall table has been shoved against the wall, directly beneath one of the two windows which light opposite ends of the hall, and is already covered by Sister Jean's master plan, her box of knives and charcoal, and the palimpsests and linen offcuts on which she makes her preliminary drawings and calculations. The frames have been set up between the hearth and the hall door, and Fulk has rigged a makeshift firescreen from deer hides and a broken shield. The sorting and hanging of wools has taken longer than anticipated due to Thecla's insistence on helping. Finally she was distracted by the dwarf, once again left behind when his master went to court, making a bouquet of woollen offcuts disappear then reappear tied together in a single, multi-coloured strand. The carts have been stowed in an empty barn, the mules and oxen turned out, the escort sent on their way, having orders not to be away from Canterbury any longer than absolutely necessary.

As the evening closes in, Sister Jean retires to a secluded corner of the hall where she sets out her devotional objects to say Vespers, while Gytha and Freya collect up all the cushions scattered about the house, splashes of silken colour and elaborate tapestry left like a spoor in the wake of Odo's departure. *Is he also saying his office, in the king's chapel, or that of his own London house, or one of the city's great churches?* She wonders. *Perhaps missing these very cushions as his knees strike cold stone or pitted earth? Or perhaps he is feasting with his brother, surrounded by glistening goblets and golden platters piled with steaming meats and Master Pietro's cakes.*

Gytha has no idea how her household will feed so many guests, especially now they have sent all their surplus game to the sisters at Saint Eufrosyna's. But Freya appears unfazed, rolling up her sleeves in the kitchen, dispatching Fulk to bring in women and boys from the estate villages to help. Hesitating in the kitchen doorway, in billows of steam and gusts of laughter, a thin wail as a spit boy is splashed by hot fat, putting off the moment when she has to join the women in the hall, she feels suspended in a different element. Sounds are muffled, images indeterminate, as though she is peering at them through water. All in the kitchen is fire, which will dry her to nothing if she enters. In the hall is earth, the women sitting on the ground, the gritty, gravely remarks quarried from deep scars of envy, or mistrust, or simple confusion. Water breaks against earth, scattered in rainbows, or soaks into it, becomes indistinguishable from it.

"Good job that tub's gone," she hears from one of Freya's kitchen helpers, and a forest of floury arms rises, hands rubbing brows, laughter ballooning into the yard where she stands, dusk gathering about her, February cold nudging her towards the hall. A path of silence leads her across the room, between the frames and wool stands looming out of muffled firelight, to where the women sit around the far side of the hearth, a crescent of watchful faces in a splash of orange.

"May I?" She smiles, feeling the tension in every muscle. Judith shuffles sideways to make space for her; she sits, cross-legged, smoothing her skirt over her knees, garnet red among the grey, a girdle of plaited silk bound with gold wire whose bright tails coil in her lap. "How was your journey?" Her voice comes to her across a great distance, false, distorted, as though she has spoken through a kerchief or into the neck of a jar. Will they understand her? Will they even hear her?

"Long," says one of the women recruited from Saint Augustine's, who normally, Gytha recalls, goes home at the end of the day.

"We will be as comfortable as we can here, though you will miss your family."

"You'd know all about that," hisses Judith, a whiff of sour breath making Gytha recoil slightly. She folds her hands over her belly to still the ghosts and tries to feel compassion, to see what Judith must see in this Saxon house whose Norman lord is everywhere, in its furnishings, the wine they are drinking instead of beer, the kite-shaped Norman shield guarding the embroidery from the fire. In the dress she is wearing, cut close to the figure in the latest style from Rouen, and the jewels he has presented to her like milestones to mark the stages of their love. But what does Judith see? What are the colours of spite?

"Like Israel fleeing Egypt," says Alwys to Leofwine, cradled in her lap under Turold's watchful eye. Leofwine, who is teething, gnaws on Alwys' stump. "What is the dwarf for?"

"For Lord Odo's amusement," says Gytha.

Judith sits up, tugging her cap straight. "Is he here, then?"

"He is at court. He left the dwarf to keep me company." To guard her, the dwarf who is not a man and Fulk, who notices no woman but Freya.

Women. There will be women in London, exotic, beautiful, witty and wise as the women who used to grace Lady Edith's table, where Odo never noticed her. Stupid. That was then, everything is different now. He trusts Fulk because he understands the exclusivity of Fulk's devotion. Because he feels the same. If he did not, why would he have strung out his departure so, why endure the implacable disapproval of Canon Guy and the undoubted wrath of William? She fingers the ruby pendant hanging from a string of pearls around her neck. She found it after he left, hidden under her pillow with a note and a sprig of dried rue. *Rue for remembrance, ruby for the fire in my blood, pearls for my tears,* he had written. *Pearls for the moon,* she thinks, *the full, bright, beautiful moon of his name.* The dwarf is no consolation, nothing can fill the space he leaves when he goes; it is like the emptiness left inside her by her dead children.

"What can the dwarf do?" It is the first time Margaret has opened her mouth. From the reactions of the other women, all turning towards her with varying expressions of surprise and relief, it is the first time she has spoken for some while.

"Oh, he sings and plays, and juggles a bit. But mostly he likes to remind Lord Odo that he is only a mortal man."

"It's just that there was a dwarf at a fair once who could tell the future."

"Telling the future and telling a great man he will one day come to dust carry quite similar risks," remarks Turold, refilling his drinking horn. Gytha laughs, but Margaret just looks sad.

Sister Jean finishes her devotions as Freya and her team of village women come in with trays of food, and Gytha marvels as greatly as her guests at what they have managed to produce out of nothing but a half-finished quince pasty. It may be Lent, but this is still a great man's household, make no mistake. In the general shuffling around that takes place to accommodate the meal, Gytha finds herself seated beside Margaret. Noticing the big girl makes no attempt to help herself to food, Gytha takes a wooden platter, piles it with mackerel in mint sauce and pike with a pudding in its belly. Freya has adapted seamlessly to my lord's culinary standards, but Margaret, for a girl whose appetite for food was always at least healthy, picks at her plate with as little relish as the sickly Countess of Mortain.

"Come, Margaret," orders Sister Jean, "eat up."

Margaret picks up a piece of bread and tears at it dutifully with her teeth, but she has to make several anguished attempts to swallow, her throat straining and gagging, eyes watering from the effort.

Gytha takes the plate from her and puts it down on the hearth. "Never mind."

Margaret's grateful expression is pitiful. Gytha longs to retreat to her bower, to lie in Odo's bed behind the silk curtains, love's soft footprints all around her in dented pillows and creased quilts. But she will have to give up the bed to Sister Jean, or at least offer to share it with her and Judith, who is also of noble blood, and the thought of sharing that bed with anyone but Odo is unbearable. No, she will sleep here in the hall with the rest of the women.

She rises, which acts as a signal to silence Turold, who has been telling a long, complicated story about a wizard, a magically embroidered robe and an adventurous girl who becomes a pirate. Emma looks disappointed.

"It's late and you must all be very tired. Sister Jean, Judith, I will put my bower at your disposal." She takes a torch from a basket on the hearth, ignites it and escorts the two women to the bower by its smoky, tarry light. Judith's resentment bores into her back; Judith would be happier if Gytha left her something to complain about.

"This is good of you," says Sister Jean, contemplating the great, fur covered bed while Gytha fastens the bower door against a sharp wind now prowling around the courtyard.

"I hope you sleep soundly."

"After four nights of priory hospices or bare earth, I shall at least," says Judith.

"Then I will leave you." Lighting a couple of candles from her torch, Gytha collects a cloak from a hook beside the door.

"Gytha," says Sister Jean.

"Yes, Sister?"

"I have never replaced you, you know. There is a space for you at one of the frames if you want it."

"I...there is a woman in Winterbourne village whose daughter is very sick with a catarrh of the lungs. I intend to visit her tomorrow, to take some medicine my lord's physician recommended."

"Send Freya."

"Goodnight, Sister. I hope you find the bed...comfortable."

Gytha cannot sleep. The wind rises during the night, snapping and snarling around the house, pushing under the door and through gaps in the shutters. Rain batters the walls and hisses onto the hearth through the smoke vent in the roof. Her straw pallet crackles and prickles as she turns from side to side, trying to make herself comfortable. She frets, feeling lonely and responsible, flinching at every creak or crash, every bark or whinny or flurry of cackling from the yard. When Odo is with her, she loves stormy nights, secure in his arms, curtained and cosseted, knowing the ghouls and demons that come with darkness are powerless against the steady beat of his heart. Even when he gets up, to check for broken shutters and fallen branches or calm his horses, the feeling of safety stays with her. Her father used to do the same; several times a night on rough nights she would hear through the plank floor of the loft where she slept, her head inches from salt winds and the rattle of hailstones, her parents whispering together, clothes rustling and the creak of hinges as he went out to make sure of the stacks of salt pans and barrels in his yard. Then she would burrow contentedly beneath her blanket, as though, in his going, he left his watchfulness with her.

But tonight, she is the watcher, her senses strained to encompass the snores and mutters and shufflings of the sleepers around her, the patter of mice, dust sifting through the wind buffeted thatch. A sudden blast of air sends sparks showering out of the hearth; wrapping herself in her cloak, Gytha pads around to the other side to move Fulk's makeshift guard back out of harm's way.

"The Lord has looked on you, Sister, and found you wanting. Praise the name of the Lord." Alwys.

"Shhh," says someone, and though nothing more is said, a pale figure detaches itself from the mound of bedding Alwys shares with her sister and glides towards Gytha among the shadowy angles of frames and stools and stands of wool. It's only Meg, Gytha tells herself firmly, though her hands on the broken shield begin to shake and her bowels feel as though they are being tightened around a winch. Only Meg in her shift.

"Can't you sleep either?" she whispers, gripping the shield tight, but the pale figure makes no response. Weaving its way among the frames, it sits on a stool, where it seems to crumple, to melt and pool like the final extinction of a candle. Sniffs and hiccoughs, then sobs, rise and die away into dark corners.

Resting the shield on the floor, Gytha sits down opposite her old sewing partner, marvelling how her body adapts itself to the low stool, her wrists balanced on the edge of the frame as though she is about to take up her needle and plunge it into the taut linen; she had believed her skin so crammed with new sensations there would be no room inside it for impressions of the old.

"Meg? What is it?"

Margaret lifts her head to find her hot, sore eyes staring at Gytha. Gytha in the flesh, with dark strands of hair escaping from her plait and the laughter lines which bracket her red lips more pronounced than Margaret remembers them. Gytha, whose eyes are deep enough to understand anything. So she isn't dreaming, and the hasty departure from Canterbury, the days of bumping about in the base of a cart followed by silk cushions and mackerel in mint sauce are real. And what Alwys said is real.

"Tell me," says Gytha, in her worn, husky voice that will brook no nonsense. She reaches across the frame for Margaret's hands, and they sit in silence for a little while, their interlinked fingers suspended in the space which tomorrow will once again be crowded with Odo's stories. The wind rattles the shutters and flings raindrops hissing on to the hearth. This is her chance, this lull before the embroidery's clamour begins again.

"Alwys is right. I am wanting," she starts.

She tells Gytha everything. How her brother, her favourite brother, lies in the infirmary at Christ Church, his mind in torment, his soul a battleground for good and evil, his body abused and neglected, and what has she done to help him? Nothing. She has carried on stitching her trees and shorelines as if nothing had changed, as if he were indeed dead. She will as surely burn in hell as Tom with his blasphemies if she does not try to help him. She must see him again, and soon, before he is fully recovered and ready to leave Christ Church. But how? How long does Sister Jean intend to keep them here? Even if Sister Jean would let her go, how could she find her way back to Canterbury alone? What Gytha said all those years ago is as true as it ever was. The women are not free.

Now Gytha says, squeezing her hands, "Tell her. Tell her the truth. She'll be happy for you. Consider how she is with Lord Odo. She knows what can lie between a brother and sister."

"But what if she told the King he was still alive?" She has convinced herself completely that Tom had played some role so vital for King Harold that his survival must be kept secret from the Normans at all costs.

"The King?" laughs Gytha. "I do not think the King would worry one way or the other."

"No," says Margaret in a small voice. It is as though the restless night has been playing tricks with her all this time, transforming tables into dragons or hanging cloaks into ghosts, and Tom into a looming presence of such massive importance she could not see to the edges of it. Now Gytha has lit a lamp, a magic circle of light on whose edges the storm snaps and snarls, and there he is, just Tom, with his laughing eyes and his hair like plaited fire.

Suddenly she hears her father speaking. She and Harry and Aelfred had been caught, during the Lenten fast, stealing preserved medlars from the store cupboard where their stepmother and Hawise, their servant, were stocking food for Easter. The boys had been given a beating and sent to bed supperless, but in Margaret's case, her father had succumbed as usual to the irrefutable logic of the twins; if he punished one, he punished the other, and Alwys had been nowhere near the stolen fruit. Very well, if Margaret would own up, he compromised, she would escape the rod and be permitted a small glass of buttermilk before bed. If all else fails, he had said to her, tell the truth. Gytha is right. She will tell Sister Jean about Tom. Good news is made better by sharing. She gives Gytha a weak smile, rapidly followed by a yawn.

"Go to sleep, now," says Gytha. "I'll come with you to talk to Sister Jean if you like. She should be in a good humour tomorrow after a night's sleep on Lord Odo's featherbed."

The wind and rain have begun to die down and Gytha herself does not return to her pallet but, pulling her cloak close and slipping her feet into her shoes, goes outside to inspect what damage there may have been. She is tired, but her mind races, scrabbling like a hungry rat at half buried scraps of thoughts. She hopes the cold, and the featureless vastness of the cloudy night sky, will act as a balm upon the anger Margaret's story has roused in her.

All these women, their lives, their families, small hopes and ordinary aspirations, wrecked in one way or another by the Normans. But that is not at the root of her anger; at its root is confusion, because she believes Sister Jean is also damaged, in some way she cannot fathom; and the

Queen, who, they say, loves her husband but is compelled by him to spend most of her time alone, in Normandy, mediating between him and their sons; and the little Countess of Mortain with her cheekbones like slivers of glass, her vomit sticks and the way the English cold makes her shiver like a whipped dog. And what of herself, stepping clear of the wreckage on the arm of the man some say is the worst Norman of them all, the architect of the Bastard's ambition, the power behind his throne?

The only man who has ever roused her to passion.

"Mistress Gytha." Fulk appears in front of her. He has a dishevelled, apprehensive expression on his face and a shrivelled, silent piglet tucked into his jerkin.

"What is it, Fulk? Have we had a lot of damage? No-one is injured, I hope?"

"No, madam. It's just that…I'm sorry, madam, what with having to move all the furniture earlier and then Marigold farrowing…" Glancing down at the piglet, he adds, "runt. Might be able to revive it."

Gytha smiles. The revival of runts is becoming something of a competitive sport between Fulk and Odo. Odo has had great success with a piglet, now two or three weeks old and named Melusine, which seems to believe Juno is its mother. "And has it got a name yet?" she asks. "What did you forget?"

"A message, ma'am, from Abbess Biota at Saint Eufrosyna's. She asked if you would wait on her tomorrow…today. After Terce."

"Well. And I thought her holiness was content to accept our charity as long as she never had to contemplate us in our sinful flesh."

"The piglet, ma'am, I'd best get it indoors."

"Goodnight, Fulk."

"Goodnight, madam."

Cloud rolls back from the smiling face of the moon, revealing a litter of broken branches among the cart ruts in the yard, and an empty chicken coop rocking gently on its side in the remnants of the gale. She sets the coop to rights then stands for a moment, smiling back, letting the tension drain from the muscles in her back. Then, realising her feet are soaked, picks her way through puddles back to the house. The men are right to cosset the piglets, they seem to have some healing power.

"You may ask," replies Sister Jean cautiously next morning, when Margaret approaches her, saying she has a request to put to her. Sister Jean is supervising the restoration of the embroidery panels to their frames, checking that none has been damaged on the journey, that they are stretched at the correct tension and display the right points in the narrative. Alwys is busy sorting needles, Freya and the women not engaged at the frames are winding and hanging wool. Gytha is nowhere to be seen, but now Margaret has made up her mind, she needs only the recollection of Tom's blank eyes and suppurating wounds to give her the courage to proceed.

"I wondered how long we might be staying here, Sister?"

"We've hardly arrived, girl. I don't intend returning until I'm sure it's safe to do so."

"Yes, but how long will that be?" Margaret persists.

Sister Jean gives her a searching look. "What's your hurry? Surely you are happy to see Gytha?"

"Of course I am, Sister, it's just that…it's Brother Thorold's patient. I would like to visit him again."

Ice water trickles in Agatha's veins. "He will either have recovered or died by the time we leave here. You should put him out of your mind."

"But Brother Thorold told me he would keep him by until he was back in his own mind. That might take some time, I expect."

Scarcely able to bring herself to look at Margaret's hopeful, childlike expression, Agatha asks, "What is this man to you?"

As Margaret tells her, she feels a tingling in her feet the way she does when she hears a good dance tune. Her brother. Her *brother*. Only her brother. The phrase has the rhythm of a jig.

"Of course you must go," she says. "as soon as we return."

"Could I not go back straight away? Just in case?"

"I'm afraid not." She is kind, but emphatic. "I have no-one to accompany you, and no-one to take your place if you go. But if Brother Thorold says he will keep your brother, then you may rely upon it that he will." Patting Margaret's freckled hands, feeling the ridges of bone beneath her skin, she adds, "Trust in God, Meg, He is merciful."

"If you say so, Sister." Glancing down at the frame closest to her, she recognizes Emma's hand in the face of King Edward on his deathbed, all haggard concentration, his bed hangings like furled sails, waiting to catch the wind for Valhalla. Around him are arrayed a number of unfinished figures, and at the foot of the bed his weeping queen, dabbing her eyes on a fold of her headcloth. Though what she is weeping for, thinks Margaret, Heaven only knows, for he had, they say, never touched her. How can you feel the loss of what you have never had?

Accompanied by Fulk, Gytha sets out for Saint Eufrosyna's soon after Prime. The journey should not take longer than an hour on horseback, but Gytha, despite instruction from Fulk and Odo, remains a cautious horsewoman, and after the storm in the night, there is no telling what state they will find the roads in. They travel mostly in silence, Gytha riding slightly ahead, feeling irritable and nervous. She would have welcomed the opportunity to dress more carefully for this visit, but it was late by the time she and Freya could gain access to the bower where all her clothes are kept.

She chose a gown of fine dark blue wool, but now regrets it; although suitably sober, the indigo dye makes it too rich, too obviously the dress of a wealthy man's mistress playing the part of an honest woman. She wears no jewellery but a tiny, rather battered gold ring set with turquoise and seed pearls which used to belong to Odo's mother and which, having placed on the air finger of her left hand the night before he left her for Christmas, a night of tearful looks and anguished hand holding during the Advent fast, he has forbidden her to remove.

Nevertheless, her shoes are calfskin, her cloak silk lined and her girdle of silver. Abbess Biota's disapproval is already reaching back along the road, in the muddy puddles which splash her hem and the breeze whipping a flush into her cheeks.

When they reach the convent, however, the portress, having accepted Gytha's offering of beeswax candles and duck eggs, tells her it is not Abbess Biota who wishes to see her but another nun, a Sister Cygnea, one who is not in orders but chooses, of her piety, to submit to the Rule. The portress' gaze, properly lowered, reinforces the eloquence of her reproach. Has Abbess Biota set up this meeting as a warning to her irregular neighbour? Clearly this Sister Cygnea has herself at one time been a great man's mistress; it is not uncommon for such women, ousted by younger rivals or exposed by the death of a lover, to seal a pact with a nunnery, to don a habit (though with fine linen beneath) and observe the offices (though not between Compline and Terce). Abbess Biota cannot know that Gytha has sought refuge in a convent before, or that, without Odo, monastic life would hold no terrors for her.

The portress conducts her to a low building of lath and plaster set apart in a corner of the convent garden, overlooking a rose bed whose well pruned stumps poke green wood through packed mounds of manure. Its sharp tang mingles with the scent of applewood smoking up from a narrow funnel in the roof. A cherry tree curves protective branches over the door arch, budding with fat, pink pledges of spring. The portress coughs discreetly at the door and excuses herself.

The occupant is a tall woman, who has to duck her head under the lintel to greet her guest, which she does with a graceful incline of her neck that seems to mirror the arc of the cherry tree. Slender beneath the shapeless habit cinctured tight at the waist, she stands very straight, making no attempt to disguise her height, her white hands with their pearly nails folded over her belly. She smiles; her lips are pale pink, her complexion almost as pale as her headcloth, so tightly wound her smile threatens to escape its bounds. With a low whimper, Gytha flings herself to her knees, embracing the nun's legs, pressing her face into the folds of her habit.

The nun takes her gently by the shoulders and raises her to her feet. "Gytha, Gytha, there's no need for all this."

"Oh, madam," says Gytha, and again, "oh, madam," shaking her head, tears spilling from her eyes and running into the corners of her smile. "What a wonderful surprise," she manages eventually. "It must be a miracle."

"I think not, my dear, merely the triumph of common sense over adversity. I thought you would have guessed, from the name. You have a little Latin, don't you? Cygnea. Swanlike."

Gytha shakes her head, feels her smile spreading foolishly, without her volition, as though it lives independently of the muscles of her face. "Only what Lord Harold used to recite, and then I never understood the half of it."

"And you have learnt no more?" Her tone is searching, her look almost mischievous as she stands aside and gestures for Gytha to enter her bower. She has eyes that would appear intelligent were it not for their doll-like roundness and cornflower blue colouring.

"Why should I, madam?" In her eagerness to take in her old mistress' surroundings, Gytha gives no thought to Edith Swan Neck's question, or her own, disingenuous reply. The room is small, but crammed with beautiful objects Gytha remembers from Edith's house in Winchester. So Odo did not take everything, she realises with a surge of relief, her mistress managed to salvage some remnants of the old life.

"Sit, please." Edith indicates a stool with scrolled armrests and an upholstered seat. As Gytha unclasps her cloak, Edith takes it from her, caressing the fine cloth as she hangs it from a peg beside the door. She herself takes a plain wooden stool, facing Gytha across the hearth where the apple logs crackle briskly.

"How..?" begins Gytha, but simultaneously Edith says,

"I have seen you several times in church."

"I never knew."

"Of course not. I was always behind the screen with the rest of the sisters. Invisible," she gives a short, ironic laugh, "like Saint Eufrosyna herself in her monk's habit. Though I did wonder, at Candlemas..."

Candlemas. That sense that she was watched, then, was not merely a trick of her conscience, a stirring of what modesty she has left. She feels the blood boiling up her neck until her cheeks are a cauldron of shame. "If you summoned me here to chide me, it is no more than I deserve."

But Edith merely laughs. "My dear, I have long given up taking a partisan view of these things. It cannot bring my lord back from the dead nor my children from exile, so what is the point of it? Besides, I knew long before I saw you with...your lover."

Gytha flinches, but Edith seems not to notice. "There you were, expensively dressed, coming to church with your attendants like a great lady, and living at Winterbourne which I knew to be in Bishop Odo's tenure. I am no mathematician, Gytha, but I can add two and two. No, I did not ask you here to appeal to your patriotism but merely for your company. I am lonely. Most of those I loved are dead or gone abroad." She pauses for a moment, making a space in which Gytha, too, remembers, then goes on in a determined way, "I was thrilled to see you alive and well and obviously prospering, and near enough for you to visit me. I just wanted someone to talk to. The sisters mean well but they are rather dry and do not quite approve of me."

"Yet you live by the Rule?"

"Oh no, this," wafting a pale hand around her habit and headrail, "is just for appearances. So Mother Abbess cannot be accused of harbouring an improper woman. And for my own protection. As you did not know I was here, so I am also kept hidden from others who may wish me ill."

"I understand. I will be discreet."

"Will you, my dear? Even in your pillow talk? My presence here must be kept strictly *sub rosa*."

"I promise." But he must know, he knows everything. Surely one of those men who come and go with sealed scrips and caches of jewels hidden in cloaks must have told him that Godwinson's concubine was masquerading as a nun less than half a day's ride from his border. So why has he never said anything? Does he trust her so little? Does he really not know? She wants to believe it, but she fears his silence on the subject has more complicated roots. Yet if she is sworn to secrecy by Lady Edith she cannot ask him. There is a worm in this rose.

"Now." Edith rises to stir the fire. "There is a jug of wine on that little table behind you. And some honey cakes. Pour us a cup each and let us indulge in some gossip. We can both confess our idleness later, as we both have close access to a priest."

"My lord is at court," says Gytha, unable to suppress a giggle as she hands wine and cakes to Edith.

"You must tell me all about how you came to meet, and how he tolerates your stubbornness, for I doubt it is due to his saintly nature, but first," leaning forward, dropping her voice to a conspiratorial whisper, "tell me something I am dying to know. Is it true Norman men kiss with their tongues?"

Gytha holds the shining, cornflower gaze for a moment, then looks down at her hands. "Yes, madam."

Edith wrinkles her dainty nose. "That must be...unpleasant?"

The thought of Odo's tongue laps Gytha's face and neck, his saliva sweats between her breasts though her mouth feels parched. Oh for one of his kisses, his deep, hungry cardamom kisses. "Not really," she says, in a voice which is little more than a dry whisper. "I suppose you get used to it."

Edith lets loose a peal of laughter. It's true, thinks Gytha, what Earl Harold used to say, that she has a laugh like a wood pigeon, something between a coo and a hoot, altogether too comical to issue from those pale pink lips, that delicate breast. "Oh Gytha, you dissemble no better than you ever did. And there was I, surmising the Bishop was merely a strategy for survival."

"Far from it, madam. On the contrary, I once believed he would be the death of me."

"You are like two people, Gytha, one who speaks and one who

acts. Be yourself, don't try so hard. If I, of all people, do not reproach you for loving Bishop Odo, why should you reproach yourself? Besides," she takes a bite out of her cake, licks crumbs from her fingers, "he is appealing to women. I always thought so. Does he remember you from that time he came to my house? When was that? Not long before Harold's embassy to Normandy, I think."

"He has never said so."

"Well I'm not surprised. I seem to recall he had set his cap at Trudy that night? I wonder what happened to her?"

Trudy, of course. Trudy with her cool, Nordic beauty, icy looks that made men burn to warm her. Trudy, married to one of Earl Harold's thegns, already in his dotage and flagrantly cuckolded by his bored young wife. All Lady Edith's male guests beat a path to Trudy's bed eventually, just as they went to watch the illuminators at work in the great school founded in the reign of Athelstan, or walked up Saint Giles' hill to admire the view. Why should she expect Odo to have behaved any differently? Did she believe him to have been a model of priestly virtue before they met? Of course not. There is John, and also the delicious, disquieting certainty that what he knows about pleasuring women could not have been learned merely by poring over proscribed texts in the library at Bec or playing the catamite to some older monk.

"And I don't doubt he was successful," she says, trying to sound as though she does not care one way or the other.

"Lesser men were," replies Edith with a shrug.

It is after Sext by the time Gytha leaves. All their conversation has been in the same vein, remembering life in Winchester before Harold became king, gossiping about love affairs, recollections of people they knew then, always ending with the same refrain: I wonder what happened to..? Their chatter is enjoyable, undemanding, and the time passes quickly, but when the cakes have been eaten and the wine drunk, and Edith rises to bring an end to their meeting, Gytha cannot help feeling that something remains unsaid. She is both delighted and apprehensive when Edith invites her to visit again, as often as she likes.

Life at Winterbourne settles easily into its new routine. The continual comings and goings of Odo's spies and messengers are replaced by the static industry of the women at the embroidery frames, the whispered bartering of information by inconsequential conversations about needles and colours, menstrual aches, Leofwine's teething and the comparative weight gain of the house piglets.

Sometimes Gytha herself works on the hanging, though only when she can show some justification for it, if one of the others is ill, or a scene is being embroidered which she worked on before. Just before. Nobody ever specifies what before, and that is part of the trouble. Seated at her frame alongside the other women, she is nevertheless apart, her rich gowns and jewels, her head often uncovered in the privacy of her own house contrasting with the grey and white of the atelier livery. A skilled seamstress but proven dispensable, she is envied and at the same time despised. She is mistress of this house and its demesne, but then again, where is its lord? Gone to London and left her in the charge of his dwarf.

Turold flirts shamelessly with the women, though Emma is his favourite. Because she can't answer back, says Judith, making her the most receptive target for his barbs. What else could it be? No man could find Emma attractive, not even a dwarf. But dwarves, queries Margaret, who seems quite restored since their arrival at Winterbourne, surely they aren't men, not in that sense? Turold wags his beard at her, Sister Jean's pale stare flies arrow straight above the cloth and parchment landscape of her master plan spread over the hall table. One of the Saint Augustine's women giggles and pinches Turold's rump; puffing out his barrel chest, he emits a deafening cock crow.

Gytha, working opposite Margaret on a little dog in the Fable of the Wolf Who Reigned, left unfinished the day she went to Odo to appeal for his mercy for Alwys and never came back, keeps silent, but knows exactly what Turold sees in Emma. Himself. A mistake, an incarnation of sin, or carelessness. Careless loving.

"Put me in your hanging," he pleads with Emma now. "Go on, his lordship won't object. It will amuse him."

Yes, thinks Gytha, *it might*.

Her smile is intercepted by Agatha, who goes across to where Emma is sitting, the dwarf on tiptoe, peering over her shoulder. Emma lays down her needle; her twitching begins almost immediately; the dwarf lays a soothing hand on her shoulder, her spasms travelling up his arm, shaking his shoulder in turn.

"Here is space enough for Turold," says Agatha. "A little place in history." Above and to the right of Judith's plough horse, at one of the turning points, where Agatha has devised scenes to run right to left rather than left to right in order to accommodate the corners of the rooms in which the embroidery will hang. She sketches in a diminutive figure holding the panting mounts of the messengers sent by William to Guy of Ponthieu to order him to hand over Godwinson.

"Put my name," pleads the dwarf, capering on his bandy legs, making the women laugh. "Please put my name. I can recognise it, you know."

"You are a clever manikin. Here, then, tell me if I have it right." Agatha forms the letters and the dwarf nods his approval. He has his place in history.

Leaving the dog still unfinished, after the day meal, Gytha escapes to visit Edith. She has been three or four times now, and she enjoys their meetings, the cakes and wine and gossip. She is grateful to Edith for helping her pass the time, which hangs heavy in Odo's continuing absence, his silence, his embroidery colonising her hall, reminding her, if she cares to think about it, how they are each drawn according to different designs, intertwined but never united. Yet her sense of the unsaid persists, it hangs around the edges of her conversations with Edith like a curtain.

Edith delights in Gytha's clothes and jewellery. She tries on her bracelets and necklaces, unties her hempen cincture and replaces it with Gytha's various girdles set with precious stones and lozenges of silver or gold. A ritual has evolved whereby Gytha removes her shoes so Edith can sit with them in her lap, stroking the soft leather. Happy to talk for hours about Odo, she refuses to listen to anything Gytha has to say about him as he is today, but always as she remembers him on the several embassies he made to Harold during the later years of King Edward's reign. If memory is a house, as Gytha has heard it described sometimes, a many roomed palace undergoing perpetual adaptations and alterations, then Odo is merely an anteroom to Harold in Lady Edith's mind.

Edith's gaiety and contentment are no more substantial than the sugar crust on the macaroons she so much enjoys, and sometimes, in the silences which can flow between them like an unfordable stream, Gytha sees again the shut off face of the woman who returned from their failed mission to the Bastard to plead for Harold's corpse. Now, suddenly, she interrupts the story she has been telling of some escapade to throw Trudy's husband off the scent of a new lover and says, her fingertips gliding more rapidly along the high fronts of Gytha's shoes,

"His feet smelt terrible, you know, Harold's." She pins a pleading look on Gytha, as though pressing her for some justification. "However often I washed them for him."

Gytha thinks of long, morning kisses when bodies are indolent and lascivious, still imprinted with dreams, the intimate mingling of sleep sour, morning breath, hair catching in stubble. Where is Odo? Surely he should be back by this time. It cannot be long before the papal legate arrives and he has to go to Winchester. "But he could run as swiftly as any man," she says, "and dance better than most, so what does it matter?"

"Oh, dancing. Didn't we dance, Gytha? I remember mornings when I could scarcely put a foot to the floor after dancing all night. And how my lord used to laugh when we performed the *mal mariee*." Letting Gytha's shoes slip from her lap, Edith rises to her feet. "How does it go?" She closes her eyes and begins to hum, then to sway in time to the rhythm of the song impressed on her body's memory even if its words elude her mind. Gytha knows the words, summons them up from the deep cauldron of words simmering inside her, the snatches of Ovid and Virgil, her mother's fairytales, Aesop's Fables strung out along downward sloping lines of script.

"Fat lot I care, husband, for your love."

"Now that I have a friend," she begins, but Edith is not listening. Edith bends and turns, twists and straightens, her hands and feet inscribing the air and the white oat straw covering the floor with patterns only she can see, lines converging, diverging, multiplying, bringing her to Harold, splitting them apart, scattering their children to foreign courts from Ireland to Denmark.

Stealthily Gytha picks up her shoes, removes her cloak from the hook by the door and creeps out, steadying the door with her outstretched hand so her mistress' memories are not disturbed. As soon as she regains Winterbourne, she goes to her bower and takes Odo's Christmas letters from the box in which she keeps them. How fortunate that she did not read them all when they were sent, that some remain with their seals still unbroken, to see her through this famine. She has heard from him, but sporadically, often by messenger or in letters written by a scribe, the sort of letters a man writes to his wife, in which she must try to interpret his affection between the lines of instruction about the management of the estate.

On the Feast of the Annunciation, the entire household attends Mass at the convent church. Walking back from the service, under a canopy of uniform, pale grey cloud which seems to trap moisture in the air, so their clothes feel damp and the going is sticky, Margaret asks Gytha,

"How long have we been here now?"

"Since soon after Valentine's, I think. That's," she counts off the intervening saints' days on her fingers, "more than a month."

"Tom must be better by now."

Glancing sidelong at the girl's cast down profile, Gytha slips her arm through Margaret's. "I'll tell you what," she says, "why don't I send

Fulk to Canterbury to find out for you?" Odo could be in Canterbury too.

Margaret beams at her like a child given a new toy. "Would you?"

"Of course. He can be there and back in less than two days and set your mind at rest. Tom is probably digging over Brother Thorold's herb garden this very minute, happy as a lark."

"Not this very minute," laughs Margaret, jerking Gytha's arm as she gives a little skip. "He'll be coming out of church, just like us."

A lad is walking two strange horses around the yard when they arrive back. The animals have been ridden hard; their heads are low, mouths foam-flecked, sides heaving like bellows. Though Gytha does not recognise them, the saddle on one, and the hilt of the sword protruding from its elaborately stamped and scrolled scabbard, are as familiar to her as the backs of her own hands. Dropping Margaret's arm, she rushes indoors.

He is there alone, his short riding cape draped over one shoulder, spurs clanking as he prowls among the embroidery frames wearing a dark, mutinous expression.

"My Lord." Though the muscles in her throat and mouth stretch and contract to form the words, she is nevertheless surprised to hear her voice. "We did not know to expect you." She yearns to run into his arms, but is impeded by the frames. Is that why he makes no move towards her either?

He glares at her. "What is going on here?"

"Have you no greeting for me, My Lord?" She intends to sound indignant, but her voice is plaintive, querulous, thin with apprehension.

"You will answer my question, mistress."

"I will not," she retorts, stung to anger by his intransigence. "You must ask your sister. She is just outside."

He hesitates. "This is not the homecoming I had looked forward to," he says softly. He looks exhausted, his eyes dark ringed, his skin powdered with the dust of the road. She thinks he must have ridden all night, and still been on the road while she was in church celebrating Our Lady's Annunciation, one of his favourite festivals. Compressing her lips into a hard line to keep back the remorseful sobs gathering in her throat, she waves him towards the door. She refuses to carry the blame for his inability to keep control of everything, or for Sister Jean's determination to behave as though she is a man, free to come and go as she pleases.

The chatter of the women in the courtyard, pushing back their hoods, straightening caps, shaking mud from their shoes, fades to silence as the Earl emerges from the shadows of the doorway with a look like thunder on his face.

"Your grace." Sister Jean kneels, followed by everyone else except Gytha, and Thecla, who, catching sight of one of the piglets, starts running towards it.

"Get up," says Odo with an impatient wave of his hand. "Sister, explain..." but as he approaches Sister Jean to demand her explanation, the piglet hurtles across his path at a determined gallop with Thecla in precarious pursuit, almost tripping him up. "Melusine!" he bellows, as though the piglet might be subject to the same discipline as a puppy.

"That's not Melusine," snaps Gytha from the doorway, "that's Thor."

How can he possibly do what William has asked, he wonders, adoring the defiant set of her chin? Alright, his brother had said, bring her to court. It might do us some good to have one of Swan Neck's women dancing to our tune. Odo had tried to explain, that Gytha loved him for himself, not his part in the overthrow of Harold Godwinson, that she would probably love him better, in fact, if he were merely the Vicomte de Conteville, unrelated to William other than by ties of vassalage. That she dances to no tune but the one in her own head. William had laughed at that. She's living at your expense, brother, isn't she, eating your bread, wearing your jewels? Sleeping and God knows what else in your bed? Hadn't she better do as you say? He was right, but he didn't know Gytha.

"Thor?" he queries, scooping up Thecla and balancing her on his hip where she fiddles contentedly with the clasp of his cape.

"You can tell by the black patch at the side of his nose. Like a beauty spot. And Melusine is fatter."

He must be in Winchester the day after tomorrow. Even if he knew where to begin trying to persuade her, there is no time for it now. He will have to sort out this business of the tapestry before he leaves, and he does not want to waste the precious hours remaining to him quarrelling with Gytha. He will simply tell her he is taking her with him to Winchester and explain his reasons later. Besides, it will be harder for her to resist once she is there, at the heart of William's court. Setting Thecla back down again, he holds out his arms to her.

She cannot make a scene in front of the women, under the glare of Judith or Sister Jean, so she submits to his embrace, laying her cheek against his chest, slipping her arms around his waist.

"And is my woman fatter?" he whispers, sliding one hand between them to pat her belly.

"Really, My Lord, Rome wasn't built in a day." His hand seems to pass right through her flesh, she dissolves in the heat from his palm.

"But if the builders had been as enthusiastic in their work as we are, it might have been."

She laughs, a muted chuckle. "You have no shame at all, do you?"

"None." And as if to prove it, he tilts up her face, cupping her chin between thumb and forefinger, and kisses her, his tongue pushing against her teeth, his erection pressing into the pit of her stomach, until her will to resist is undermined. Winding her fingers among the curls at the nape of his neck, pulling his face to hers, she kisses him back. Greedily. In full view of them all. Unpleasant? You might as well describe Noah's Flood as a slight change in the weather.

When he opens his eyes, the yard is deserted, thank God, except for the groom walking the two blown horses.

"We have melted them all away," he murmurs, stroking her flushed cheek.

"I have almost melted away myself. Whereas you..." She brushes his cock with her fingertips; he shivers.

She takes his hand and leads him towards her bower, where the great bed awaits them like a procuress and they tumble together among the fur and feathers, a sweating, salivating chaos of hands scrabbling at buckles and laces, of twined limbs and mingled fluids, prayers and obscenities, all the tangled threads and tender violence of lovers.

Dusk is falling before he dresses, slowly, with many delays and false starts due to his mistress' hands straying as she helps him with his clothes. He resents the precious time he will squander talking to his sister, but she must be ordered back to Canterbury as quickly as possible. It horrifies him to contemplate his tapestry set out in the smoky hall of this undefended house, with dogs and children, even piglets, it seems, weaving their games among its panels and logs spitting on the open hearth. And the journey, dear God, it is a miracle they met with no accidents or highway robbers. Crossing the yard towards the hall, he shouts for Fulk, who appears from behind the kitchen with an axe in his hand, cooking smells clinging to his clothes.

"I want you to go to Canterbury, Fulk, and collect an escort sufficient to get all the women safely back there. Come with me now and I'll write an instruction to Lord Hamo. I don't suppose there's a scribe in this house, is there?"

Fulk looks around as though a scribe might be found in the cattle byre or the brewhouse. "No, My Lord," he concludes.

In the hall, work has finished for the day. The women stand in little groups, stretching, rubbing tired eyes, chattering in low voices. Odo notices Turold the dwarf among them, his head resting against Emma's hip, a serene, foolish expression on his face which irritates his master, who does not keep a dwarf for his gentle heart but for his sharp wits and the ease with which he can walk on his hands. He will take Turold to Winchester, away from the influence of women. Looking sidelong at Fulk, he wonders if he might detect evidence of any similar softening. They take our hearts and pound them as though they are tenderizing meat, he says to himself.

"I might do better to take one of the horses you brought with you, My Lord. They're both better than anything we have here save Mistress Gytha's roan."

Odo slaps Fulk heartily on the shoulder. "Can she ride it yet?"

Fulk shrugs, caught between tact and honesty.

"Like that, is it?" Odo laughs. "Take which horse you like, though for myself I'd favour the bay. He has an ugly eye but his wind is good."

Agatha, engrossed in putting her worktable in order for the night, looks up in response to the draught from the door sifting through her parchments and the abrupt hush of the women.

"A word, Sister, if you please."

She straightens up, but remains behind the table, contemplating her brother's florid, well-fed handsomeness, his big hands and easy manner.

"But first," he adds, "do you have a clean piece of parchment to write on, and a pen?"

"How clean?" She offers a slightly irregular square, pumiced on one side but with a sketch on the back. Odo nods, smoothes the parchment over a vacant patch of table as Agatha pushes an inkwell with a quill sticking out of it towards him. "Does the ink need slaking?"

Shaking his head, he begins to write, standing at the table, one leg stretched behind him, the other bent at the knee, his left forearm holding the parchment steady. Watching him, Agatha is transported back to the summer after the Conquest, scenes in fields and tents and half built keeps, following one another the way the scenes in the embroidery do, comings and goings of men and horses, Odo writing, dictating to his scribes, consulting with his officers. Daylight, candlelight, voices raised or lowered, groups on foot or on horseback, Odo's distinctive hand gestures, the sign language of the monastery liberated, expanded to fill the great spaces in the outside world.

"Damn," says Odo, straightening up and stretching his hands in front of him. "Fulk, my seal is on its way to Winchester so I mean to give you a ring Lord Hamo will recognise, but I think I must have left it in the bower. Go and ask Mistress Gytha to find it. Now, Agatha," as if he has not noticed Fulk's blush or the determined way in which Agatha resumes her tidying up. "The letter to Hamo orders him to send you an escort. As soon as they arrive you will pack up and return to Canterbury. Honestly, woman," casting a dismayed glance around the hall, "what were you thinking of?"

"There were rumours of plague. I thought it safer."

"But you did not think to consult me?"

"I tried, but no-one knew where you were. I did not want to waste time sending messengers to chase you round the country."

"Well there is no plague in Canterbury. We're scarcely into spring yet, hardly the season for plague." Softening his peremptory tone to one of mild enquiry, he continues, "As a matter of fact, what would you have done if you had brought the infection here? To Gytha's house?"

"I weighed the risks. As you would have done."

"Not quite."

"Oh, I think so. You have courted fame a lot more assiduously than Mistress Gytha."

Fulk remains just outside the entrance to the bower while Gytha, dressed now, but with her hair still unbound, rummages among tousled bedclothes for Odo's ring, finding it eventually wedged under the lip of a candle holder on the floor, half under the bed.

"Really," she teases, handing him the jewel, which is set with a large ruby, "it's just the same colour as your face." And winks at him, but will not permit him to flee to the hall as he is inclined to do, pleading Lord Odo's impatience. "Fulk, there is a commission you can do for me in Canterbury as well." Briefly, she explains her promise to Margaret. "And Fulk," she adds as he turns to go, "there is no need to tell Lord Odo about this." He nods, though whether in agreement, or mere acknowledgement, she is unsure. "And Fulk," she calls finally, interrupting his retreat, "be sure we shall take good care of Thor in your absence. By the time you return, he will be bigger than Melusine."

Odo should not have let Agatha's last remark go. By calmly folding his letter to Hamo, saying nothing, he has demeaned himself and insulted his mistress. But the fact remains that Agatha spoke truly. And if he now orders Gytha to accompany him to Winchester, without telling her why, letting her believe he is prepared to defy William on her account, he will have compounded the insult.

"I will do your hair," he tells her, returning to the bower and finding Freya there, her mouth full of pins, combs and ribbons arrayed on the bed, now tidied, discreet as a loyal servant, which the two women sort through like torturers choosing their instrument. Freya leaves them and Gytha, with a sigh of contentment, submits herself to her lover's ministrations. For a little while he works in silence, seated beside her on the bed, her back turned to him as he lifts and separates the heavy ropes of hair, combs out knots, divides, braids, smoothes. From time to time he pauses, kisses her shoulder or the nape of her neck, breathes in the salty warmth of the skin beneath her hair, knowing that what Agatha said is both true and not true, that it is complex, many stranded, but there is a way of plaiting it together.

"Which ribbon?" he asks when he is ready to bind the single, fat braid he has made.

"You choose."

He selects a gold one; he always likes to see her dark hair set off with gold. "You know," he says, "there may be a way around William."

She laughs. "As though he is a wreck in a harbour mouth."

"A wreck sometimes," admits Odo. "He ails greatly in his belly."

"It is his greed."

Odo gives an exasperated sigh, but having begun, he might as well continue. "I mean, I might take you to court, if you could be...if it could be seen that you were not unfriendly towards us."

"I don't understand. When have I ever shown myself unfriendly to you, My Lord?"

"Not me, Gytha, us. The Normans. William." Absorbed by the elaboration of his new notion, he does not notice a change in the quality of her stillness, a tensing of muscle which squares her shoulders and sets her jaw. "There are a number of Englishmen at court, you know, perhaps people you knew once. My brother Mortain is to get an English wife. I signed his request to the Pope for an annulment myself while I was in London, the present countess being clearly barren."

"Poor woman," she says, with an intensity which catches him off guard.

"She will not go empty-handed. I didn't think you cared for her."

"I don't, except that she is a woman, as I am."

He shrugs. He has no time now to embroil himself in the contrary business of women's likes and dislikes. "So will you do it? Come to court with me? Give William a chance?"

"William," she says with icy deliberation. "Let me see what I can recall of my one and only encounter with your noble brother. But on second thoughts," turning to face him, letting a note of dawning revelation enter her voice, "I don't have to, do I, as you have reviewed it so often in your dreams? Perhaps *you* are better equipped to remind *me*."

"It is possible my brother regrets...certain of his actions." He fiddles with the ribbon, weaving it between his fingers, then drawing it out and starting again.

"You mean," still that false dawn in her tone, "that, although he is quite content to have defeated King Harold, usurped his throne and let him be chopped into pieces like dog meat, he is now very sorry he declined to let Lady Edith have what pieces could be found to give them Christian burial. Surely, My Lord bishop, I do not have to tell you that

314

there can be no forgiveness without genuine remorse."

"Gytha." Discarding the ribbon, he tries to take her hands, but she twists them out of his grasp and stands up. "All I want is to find a way for us to be together. I love you, I'm proud of you, I want you to be acknowledged as my, what do you call it? My handfast wife, as your precious mistress was to Godwinson. Surely a form of words…if that's what it would take. Surely my love is worth that much. And it would be your chance to help put an end to the strife between our peoples."

Now she laughs, a harsh, strident sound, without humour. Though her cheeks are flushed, the skin around her mouth and at the corners of her nostrils is white as bone. "So now I am to cry your wares like a market trader, am I? Roll up, roll up," she assumes the dipping and rising, singsong notes of a peddler, "Odo fitz Huerluin's universal dispensations, only three a penny…I tell you, My Lord, there was no such bargaining between my lady and King Harold. They didn't weigh love in a scale."

"I had no idea you were so unworldly, mistress. I hadn't noticed you refusing any of my gifts to you." He picks up the pearl and ruby necklace from the nightstand, but she dashes it out of his hand then swipes at the stand, sending everything flying. Jewels shower the floor, a water jug smashes, its contents darkening the oat straw from white to dull yellow.

"Take them back then!" she shouts, her mouth contorted with rage. "Everything. They're probably all stolen anyway. Everything you have is stolen from us. You're a fraud, Odo. You're nothing but what we made you."

"I am nothing but what William made me," he says quietly, beyond anger. "If you cannot accept that, then there is no hope for us."

"I can't accept it because I don't believe it." She had her hand on the door latch but her vehemence propels her back into the room. "How could I hold you in any esteem if it were true?"

For a moment he believes she is going to drop to her knees and plead with him for it not to be true. But it is. There is no escaping it. He shakes his head sadly. "If it weren't for William I wouldn't even be here. We would never have met." With a rueful laugh he adds, "Not even in my dreams. The whole thing is built on William, don't you see?"

"If you really think that, then there is no hope." With her hand on the door catch, she looks at him. The regret in her eyes is immeasurable, but that it is there at all gives the lie to what she has said. There is always hope.

"Let me finish your hair," he cajoles, picking up the gold ribbon again.

"Why? For whom?" Behind him, among the dark folds of the bed hangings, a woman is dancing, a woman clad in grey and white whose hands describe a ghost, a memory, a lost ideal. Gytha shivers, folds her arms tight across her midriff, pinching the flesh over her ribs to make sure she is real.

Sensing a softening of her mood, Odo holds out his arms to her. "I can only stay tonight. The King believes I am already on my way to Winchester. Please let us be kind to one another."

"It's Lent, your grace."

"That didn't seem to trouble your conscience earlier."

"But now I am repenting of my sin. Surely you should give thanks for it." Pushing open the door she goes out into the yard. "Bishop," she flings back over her shoulder as she leaves.

VIRGINS OF THE MIND

ANNUNCIATION TO EASTERTIDE 1072

From the hall entrance, Agatha surveys the courtyard through swirls of dust whisked up by a stiff, cold breeze. Winter is not quite done with them yet. Her eyes water, making the figures in front of her shimmer, giving a false impression of fluidity in their composition. Freya is reaching up to Fulk, who bends from his saddle to take a package from her. Food, no doubt. She is always feeding him and, young and big as he is, he is always hungry. Leofwine sits in the dust with a grubby fist in his mouth, Thecla staggers, tugging at her mother's skirts to keep her balance.

Although the convent bells are only now ringing Prime, carried intermittently to the ears of the people in the yard by the vagaries of the wind, the smith is already at work, the glow from his fire splashing warm orange into the grey of dawn, the clang of hammer on iron competing with the bells. Odo's horse threw a shoe earlier, that is the only reason he is still here, the only reason he sits on the horse now, with the new shoe gleaming on the rim of its hoof, in the middle of the dusty, rutted yard, his man at arms a few, respectful paces away, and stares at Gytha, who stares back as though they are both mute.

Failing to find the smith asleep in his forge, he had gone into the hall looking for him, and although he had tried to keep quiet, prowling among the wool stands and embroidery frames and the blanketed mounds of sleepers on stockinged feet, peering into the piss and stale-breath-smelling gloom without the aid of a candle, she had awoken; had sat up quickly, hugging her knees under her blanket, the plait he had so carefully made earlier frayed like a worn rope.

"I'm looking for the smith," he had whispered quickly, in case either of them believed he had any other purpose in being there.

"Try the kitchen," she replied, then lay down once more with her back to him, the carapace of blanket hunched up to her neck.

Yet once the smith was roused and the horse shod, she appeared in the yard, her cloak fastened over her chemise, her ankles bare above her unlaced shoes, an uncompromising set to her mouth which was at odds with something much more equivocal in her eyes.

"God grant you a safe journey, My Lord," she says now, fitting her words carefully into the silence.

He nods his endorsement. "Shall I write to you, Gytha?"

"As you please."

Nothing is as I please, he wants to tell her, nothing has happened as I planned. I thought of everything, foresaw every eventuality; I memorised Caesar and Tacitus, studied Bede, rode through the shipyards at Avranches with saws rasping their secrets in my ears and tar fumes stinging my eyes to tears; this venture stretched and pierced me the way the sailmakers stretched and pierced their canvas, I was as bent and nailed by it as the planks and clinkers for the hulls. Yet I remained unprepared, hopelessly unarmed; I never expected to fall in love, with you or your damned country. I am a practical man; I do not believe in comets or wicker men and I know the age of miracles long ago gave way to the age of reason; I have no idea what to do now.

When he looks out of the open gate, over the narrow bridge, to the broadening rim of nacreous light on the eastern horizon, his mind escapes the mists to take refuge in thoughts of Winchester and the fight to come. It will be close, but he is certain of winning it. York's claim to the disputed bishoprics is supported by a mass of evidence, not to mention three hundred years of custom and William's preference for maintaining English practice wherever feasible. And as for the oath, he can hardly wait to see the look on Lanfranc's face when he is compelled to accept Thomas' allegiance merely to his person, for his lifetime, and not to his holy office in perpetuity. All Odo has to do is bide his time and let nature take its course; once Lanfranc is dead, with Thomas' support, he can make his own move on Canterbury. And by the time the court assembles for Easter, Gytha will have come to her senses, and he will send for her to join him. With a nod to his man at arms, he kicks his horse into an easy trot, out of the gate towards the bridge, taking the lane south, towards the London road and thence to Winchester.

Gytha remains in the courtyard long after he is lost from view, dipping beneath the hill sloping away from her gate, obscured by the dust of Fulk's departure. Her face turned to Freya as she gathers up the children and goes into the kitchen, she smiles, but sees nothing, is unaware of Agatha, still watching from the hall doorway. Her skin feels clammy, her back aches as though she has been kicked by a mule at the base of her spine, a pain easier to concentrate upon than that of her heart. The backache, at least, is a blessing, for she knows it heralds her courses, another month safely got through.

She must consider what to do next. She cannot stand here forever, while her blood chills and congeals, looking for the silhouettes of Odo and his companion against the brightening sky once they breast the hill. She cannot stay here at all; if she is to be a whore, she will at least be an honest one rather than playing happy families with a Norman bishop. Judith has been right all along, and she has been so blinded by foolish love she could not see it. She wonders if Judith's understanding is a matter of her age; being past her fertility, her perceptions are no longer scrambled by the demands of her body. What a release that must be, to dry up, no longer to crave the warmth of a man inside you.

How long before Fulk returns, and the escort arrives to take the women back to Canterbury? Four days, five at the most? Fulk, travelling alone, may well make the journey more quickly. Plenty of time to instruct her...Odo's steward and pack up the little she will take with her. She will go to Saint Eufrosyna's where she can re-enter Lady Edith's service. No, too easy for him to find her. On the other hand, what makes her think he will even bother to look? Now he has discovered she cannot be manipulated as easily as a cartoon embroidered on linen, even though she would be a lot simpler to transport from house to hall to cathedral nave and put on display? And even if he did come looking for her, he would hardly violate holy sanctuary, even for her. Especially for her.

Practical matters, simple questions with simple answers; if she sticks to those, everything else will take care of itself. In time. "Will you carry on with the work until the escort gets here," she asks Agatha on her way back inside, "or pack up and wait? So no harm can come to the hanging?" She gives the nun an ironic look, one eyebrow raised a little higher than the other.

She could destroy it, she realises. How easily sparks might fly from the hearth, or a hot coal go astray, how effortlessly Odo's lies and pretensions be reduced to dust, mingled with earth and straw and the scorched bones of her house. Then the villagers would come, scrape among the ashes for the odd coin or pewter vessel, and content themselves with the least damaged planks and palings to repair their fences. No doubt the steward, fearful of his master's anger, would order a few hands lopped off here and there, some confiscation of grain or livestock to set an example. Though Odo's place in history might be compromised, hers would be assured. Oh, that was in the year the Earl's madwoman burnt the manor down, they would recall. That dish? Part of my mother's wedding portion the year the old hall was destroyed. Look, there's a burn mark on its base I could never polish out...

"I think it best to carry on," Agatha is saying. "Or the devil will find work for idle hands. Will you join us today? I'm inclined to think you need something to occupy your thoughts, other than..."

"We wouldn't want the devil to find any more work for my hands, would we?" cuts in Gytha with a strained laugh. She looks for Margaret, who is helping a young lad lift the shutters down from the hall windows, and is already making her way towards her as Agatha, screwing up her eyes at the white light angling across dust motes, remarks that she is late with her prayers.

"Meg." Waiting for Margaret to lower her side of the wattle oblong to the floor, she then slips her arm through the girl's and draws her aside. "Fulk has gone this morning," she tells her. "He will be back in a few days with news of your brother."

"Gone?" Margaret repeats, collapsing on to an upturned half barrel the smith keeps outside his forge, to sit on when he needs the cooler air.

"The day after the Annunciation, apparently," says Gytha. "Brother Thorold couldn't persuade him to stay. But Fulk only just missed him, he can't have gone far, especially if he's still not completely recovered."

Margaret looks up, naked trust beaming from her broad face. "That's true." Then she frowns, her features folding in on themselves. "But if he isn't at Christ Church, how can I go after him? Sister Jean will never let me."

As the two women consider this problem in silence, Alwys appears in the yard, carrying Leofwine on her hip, Thecla trailing from the end of her stump as though the best adults were designed with stumps for little girls to hang on to. They meander across the yard at Thecla's pace, Alwys with her face turned up to the buttermilk sun pouring over the jumbled roofs of the outbuildings whose shadow holds Margaret and Gytha in its depths. Margaret wonders if Alwys would have any more idea who Tom is than he would of her. How their family has unravelled as Lord Odo's embroidery takes its inexorable shape.

"I think she might be persuaded," says Gytha, "if you don't mind stretching the truth a little."

Glancing from the empty dish of her sister's face to Gytha, whose features seem to be fighting for space in their pinched, heart shaped frame, Margaret is certain she does not object to tearing the truth to shreds if it will give her the chance to save Tom. "Tell me," she says.

"Let's walk." Gytha takes Margaret's arm and guides her around to the south side of her house where vegetables and herbs grow in strips and squares divided by plank walks, rocking and wobbling beneath their feet exactly as they do beneath Sister Jean's stout hide shoes when Margaret, a short time after listening to Gytha's plan, asks Sister Jean if she can speak privately with her, and Sister Jean suggests a walk in the garden.

"So, Fulk has brought you news of your brother?"

"Yes, Sister. He is fully recovered, Saint Dymphna be praised. Brother Thorold told me he had gone home, though he had no memory, apparently, of my visit to him, and that he has since sent a gift of preserves to the abbey with a message that our father is dangerously ill and that God's providence worked through Brother Thorold to enable him to be reunited with his son before he dies. Sister, please may I go to him? I know it will make difficulties for you, but surely you can bring in someone to replace me for the time being. Besides, I cannot work well if I am thinking about my father dying." God forgive her, but the lies come so easily, bubbling up inside her like a brook of clear water through rock.

Agatha surveys the garden, its rows of crinkled spring cabbages and beanstalks entwining bowers of hawthorn and hazel. The rosemary is dotted with pale blue stars of blossom and chives nod heads of tousled purple. New sage leaves sprout silver green among the brittle, frost-browned remains of last year's growth. *Lily of the valley*, she thinks, that will be out in the cloister garden at Saint Justina's by now. As the end of her task draws closer, time seems to move more and more slowly, so that her hopes of one day returning to Falaise, to the order of the community and the immutability of its stone buildings, seem as remote as ever. What must it be like for a young woman who has just learned her father is dying?

"Of course you must go," she says. "You will have an escort from among the men Lord Odo is sending us. Will two weeks be sufficient? I will expect you back by the second Sunday after Easter, or you must send word by then if your father is still sick."

"Thank you, Sister." She smiles at Sister Jean, at her powdery skin crazed with fine lines like a sheet hung to dry without being properly shaken out, at her shrewd, blue eyes and her clean, deft hands. Excitement fizzes and ferments inside her as she thinks of her plan. She may never see Sister Jean again. One thing is for certain, if she finds Tom and succeeds in taking him home, she is never going to embroider another stitch as long as she lives. Not even shirts for her husband when she gets one.

At the beginning of Holy Week, a party of men from the garrison at Canterbury arrives at Winterbourne to escort Lord Odo's tapestry back to its rightful place. Of course it is sensible, as the danger of contagion has passed, thinks Agatha, of course the work will go better in the light of the great windows, where smoke and sparks are sucked up a chimney and the women can sleep soundly in their own beds instead of chattering all night in the den of cushions they have made around Gytha's hearth. Yet it is comfortable here, a chaotic peace prevails among children and piglets, removed from the iron grid of watch changes and chapel bells ringing the hours. And when they leave, it will be without Margaret.

Of course they must go, Gytha tells herself, as she must. She has already made a bundle of the few items she will need – an extra gown, a change of linen, the small leather pouch containing her bronze locket and her white rosette, all rolled in her second best cloak which is perfectly serviceable. She has removed her jewel case from beneath the bed linen piled in the chest at the foot of her...*his* bed, and hidden her bundle there instead. The jewel case, smelling faintly of camphor, his mother's ring added to the treasures it contains, is now stowed behind a loose brick at the back of the bread oven, a place decreed as a *secretum* should the household ever be under threat. Briefly she wondered if she should take one of her necklaces or bracelets with her, as a dowry offering to the nuns, but she will not. She has no wish to contaminate the next stage of her life with what has gone before, no intention of incurring any further debt to Odo. She will take the roan mare, simply because it would raise suspicion if she left the house on foot or on any other mount, but she will have a groom from Saint Eufrosyna's bring her straight back again as soon as she arrives.

Margaret is the first to leave, mounted on a jennet which seems too small for her between the tall horses of her escort. They are crammed into a corner of the courtyard, now filled once again by the two great carts, serviced by a revolving stream of men carrying boxes, frames, trestles, stands out of the hall, then returning empty handed for more. Soon the hall will be empty, no more trace of the embroidery than the body of a dead moth dismembered by ants.

At the jennet's head stand Freya, with a basket of provisions, and Sister Jean, handing up last minute advice on the proper conduct of a young woman travelling unchaperoned at this busy time of year when pilgrims are making their way to the great religious centres for Easter. Margaret nods each time Sister Jean pauses in her speech, she accepts Freya's basket with an eager smile, but her eyes rove the yard until they light on Gytha, standing at the gate.

"Good luck," she mouths as the little party rides past her, taking the same direction as Odo had done, and holds up her right hand, the middle and index fingers crossed. For a blessing, for the triumph of earth over water, life over oblivion.

By early afternoon, the loading of the carts is complete, covers lashed down, the oxen, to the accompaniment of much whooping and hooting, shouldering, shoving, warning flicks of the whip above broad, pink muzzles, backed into the shafts. In response to the women's complaints about the hardness of the benches running down either side of the wagon in which they are to travel, Gytha has invited them to help themselves to the cushions spread around the hearth.

"There are plenty more," she reassures them, returning Agatha's curious gaze without blinking, "His lordship will probably never notice they have gone. At any rate, they will be restored to him in Canterbury."

As one of the guards bolts the tailgate behind the last of them, Agatha mounts her mule, eschewing the offer of a leg up from another of the soldiers. Watching, Gytha is reminded that she is only a year older than Odo, a woman in the prime of her life, yet shrivelled by her self-imposed drought. *In time*, she thinks, both relieved and disbelieving, *I shall become the same, sexless, invisible. Free. If I can find the strength for it.*

"Gytha..." Speaking quietly, Agatha leans down from the saddle so Gytha can hear her. Gytha's face is composed to receive the thanks due to a hostess, a modest smile, a distance in the eyes measuring the extent to which she is thinking, no longer of her guests, but of clearing up after them. "Love changes, that is all, it is a shape shifter." The composition crumbles, plaster flaking from a damp wall in a bathhouse. "The challenge lies in continuing to recognise it."

Gytha reaches up to take both Agatha's dry, bird-boned hands in hers. "Goodbye, Sister."

The silence in the hall seems much greater than the space it has to occupy. The sounds of daily life – one of the children crying in the yard, chickens clucking, the cloying persistence of a blackbird's song, the byre door banging in the wind (how many times has she asked Fulk to see to it?) – drop into it like pebbles into a deep lake. The floor strewing is crushed in a repeating rectangular pattern, as though the trestles are still there but have become invisible. How can nothing take on shapes? Embroidery shapes, Meg shapes, Agatha shapes? The maimed form of the flirtation between Emma and Turold, the courting dance of two birds with broken wings, cut short by Odo's order to Turold to accompany him to Winchester. Love shapes. Odo's shape.

"I'm sorry," she whispers to the empty hall, but, struck dumb with grief, it gives nothing back. She crosses the yard to her bower, intending to make herself ready for her own departure, but finds herself instead lying down on the bed, its mattress now worn into unfamiliar contours by the sleeping twists and turns of Agatha and Judith. She bleeds heavily, with pain balanced like a burning stone in the bowl of her pelvis, as though her body is still purging itself of the accumulation of humours dammed up in her during the time when she did not bleed at all. Drawing up her knees, curling herself around the precious ache, which means she is free, yet can still be caught, she closes her eyes, tells herself she is merely gathering her strength for her journey. The scent of rosemary and sandalwood is in the air, light and distinct as a distant note of music.

When her eyes open they are hot and sore, as though she has been weeping, yet dry. So dry. Looking at her eyes, she sees dark stones, salt scratched, tossed up above the tideline. Then she looks at what her eyes are watching. Flames. Orange fingers, blue tongues, licking, caressing, probing, making love to the figure of a man. A tonsured man with familiar hands. His hands speak, they remonstrate with the fire, they soothe it and mould it until it goes to sit on the hearth and glowers like a whipped dog with acrid breath. Then the man laughs. *Do what you will*, he gasps between guffaws. *After all, I am only made of wool.*

She must have slept for an hour at least, to judge by the angle of the buttery sunlight falling through the open bower door when she wakes. Thoughts jostle her, pushing her off the bed before she has a chance to order their clamour. *What time is it? Will there still be enough daylight to see her safely to Saint Eufrosyna's? Her bundle?* Check. Still where she put it, at the bottom of the linen chest. *The jewel case? Let them guess. Surely they will guess. They will not think...he would not believe her capable of theft.*

Damn him, oh, damn him. When she thought of burning the embroidery, what stayed her hand was the thought of so many years of hard work, such an investment of skill, being destroyed. Not Odo's story, but the stories between, the Fables, Alwys' blood, Judith's plough horse. What she believed she had envisioned, making her shudder with revulsion, were shipbuilders, seed sowers, cooks, men carrying dogs into the sea, soot blackened and curling at the edges, frayed, distorted, silenced. Yet all along, her most deep rooted fear had been the fear of burning Odo. However late it is, she must go. Now.

Fulk has made a better job of teaching her to ride than he believes. Once clear of Winterbourne, she kicks the little roan into a gallop and manages to keep her seat even when the mare breaks her stride and gathers herself to jump a tree which has fallen across the track leading up to the summer pastures. She climbs the hill, following the path of the stream, letting the mare slow to a walk as the way grows steeper. This is not the direct route to the convent, but she needs time to compose herself after her disturbed sleep and heart-in-the-mouth departure, saddling the mare herself with fumbling fingers, leading her out of the wicket giving straight on to the sheep pasture behind the house to avoid being seen.

Her spirits begin to lift at the antics of the lambs, the sight of clusters of violets and primroses studding the stream's banks, the songs of skylarks bubbling up through bright blue air. He has played her like a fish, letting her run then reeling her in, but this time is different, this time she will escape. She can feel the surge of the sea in her veins, see it sparkle in the grass. From the top of the hill, facing east, with the evening sun warm on her back, she can almost smell it, almost glimpse the flat, mud silvered, oyster-crusted shores of her childhood. As the roofs of the convent, green gold thatch and dark slates shot through with gleams of lead, come into view in the valley bottom, just where the stream now rushing down the hill beside her widens and slows enough to accommodate a mill, she starts to sing. A ditty her mother used to sing to her whose beat she fits to the rhythm of the mare's sway-backed downhill jog. It was nonsense to her ears, though her mother told her it was in the language of the Celts and had a meaning for those prepared to hear. Well, she will hear nothing but English from now on; she has had her fill of foreign tongues.

It is almost dusk by the time she reaches the convent gate, the last rays of the sun striking gold and gems from the stained glass chapel windows. The sisters being at Vespers, she is admitted by a groom who recognises her horse though looks a little disconcerted by her arrival so late in the day.

"I am here at Sister Cygnea's request," she assures him, unfastening her bundle from the back of her saddle and rubbing the mare's nose as she hands her into the groom's care. He has pimples, she notices, and a cock as stiff as a branch under his homespun tunic. The music, she wonders, the dense, sweet mesh of women's voices drifting across from the open chapel door? Or some novice he whiles away his evenings imagining in her shift? Possibly the horse; she had a client once who could only maintain himself at attention when thinking about a favourite horse.

"They're all in church," says the boy sullenly.

"I know where to go. I will wait for her."

She is glad, she thinks, glancing at a bronze medallion bearing a likeness of King Harold as she sets down her bundle just inside the door to Lady Edith's bower, that she possesses no image of Odo. She would not care if she never set eyes on a man's face again, and ignores the contrary voice inside her telling her, better a man than his likeness. A devil's voice, a little, run-of-the-mill devil who will soon give up if she takes no notice.

"My dear, what a lovely surprise. I had not expected you again so soon. I was told you had a house full of guests." Edith, fragrant with incense and beeswax, holds her arms wide and Gytha subsides into her embrace with a sigh. Edith takes her by the shoulders, holding her at arms' length as she peers into her face. "But you look tired, and this is a late hour for a visit. They will lock up before Compline."

"I...I have come to stay, madam."

"Overnight? Well, of course, my bed is plenty big enough. I imagine Winterbourne is rather crowded. You wanted some peace and quiet, is that it? Sit."

"No, madam, I want to stay for good, in the convent. I don't suppose I can take orders, I have no dowry and no calling, but I can be of service, as you know. I have brought with me what little I have, a few clothes...perhaps they can be given to the poor or..."

"Wait." Edith raises an imperious white hand. "You go too fast for me. Sit down, I command it, and tell me what has happened."

Gytha takes her customary stool beside the fire, though there are no wine and honeycakes on the table behind her this evening, only Lady Edith's missal, flung there as she came in. She stumbles through her account of Odo's proposal for her acceptance at court, and she can see from the puzzled frown on Edith's face when she comes to the end of her account, that her old mistress has not understood her.

"It would be a betrayal, don't you see?" she adds, to make herself plain, "of you and Lord Harold...everybody. Even Trudy." She laughs, but Edith's expression remains troubled, at odds with her round, cornflower eyes and pink lips; she looks like a not quite pretty doll, or a portrait of herself done by an artist with no feeling for her gaiety.

"Frankly, Gytha, I don't see. What is more important, your sense of honour or Lord Odo's love and protection? You are a woman, not a knight, not even a noblewoman. Your duty is to your lord, not to me, certainly not to Harold who is dead."

Gytha stares. "I thought you would understand."

Edith, who has been sitting opposite her, rises as though to bring their meeting to a close. "I neither understand nor condone." She starts to pace about the room, tangling and disentangling her fingers, her hands sometimes at her sides, sometimes steepled in front of her mouth. "Gytha, do you not imagine there were people who had dealings with Earl Harold of whom I did not approve? There were many. I kept quiet. When he married Ealdgyth, I kept quiet. Keeping quiet, that is women's strength."

"But Odo was not asking me to keep quiet."

Edith kneels in front of her, taking her hands. "Oh my dear, I think he was. If you would but smile and curtsey to the king, I feel sure Bishop Odo would be content."

"For the moment," retorts Gytha, snatching back her hands. "You do not know him as I do. He is never content for long."

Edith rises and stands considering Gytha, her head on one side, cheek cradled in her palm. She sighs with the air of having made a decision. "You may stay tonight, but then you must go back."

Gytha shakes her head.

"You cannot stay here. What if he comes looking for you?"

"No doubt you know the story of Saint Eufrosyna better than I do, but did she not deliberately hide herself in the very monastery her father was accustomed to visit, because it was obvious, and therefore the last place he would look for her? If I cannot be of service to you, madam, I'm sure Mother Abbess can find some use for me – if embroidering the tale of the Conquest for Lord Odo has not made my fingers unfit to stitch vestments or altarcloths in her eyes. Even if it has…"

Though Edith says nothing, Gytha stops, feeling she has been interrupted. Edith draws a sharp breath and plunges into the crevasse which seems to have opened between them, floundering momentarily, slipping down a scree of words. Gytha sweats and turns cold, all at once. It's nothing, just her monthlies playing tricks.

"There is something I have to tell you, Gytha. I swore not to, but it seems where you are concerned, neither your silence nor anyone else's has any currency. So I shall forswear myself, may God forgive me." She sits, straight backed, drawing Gytha's attention to the marked difference in their height so she begins to feel like a child, a foolish little girl. "You have seen our chapel?"

Where is this going? "Yes, madam, you know I have."

"It is fine, is it not? Stained glass windows, the reliquary for Saint Eufrosyna's hair. And we burn beeswax candles at every hour between Vespers and Prime. Have you ever thought it surprising that so small a house should be so well endowed?"

"I have never thought about it at all. I suppose, if I did, I would assume that you had been generous to those who gave you sanctuary."

"Generous?" Edith gives a bitter laugh. "You saw the way I was taken from Winchester, my dear. Don't imagine I was left with much, in the way of moveable wealth anyway. No, someone else's generosity made it possible for me to come here and remain undisturbed. Bishop Odo paid my dowry and returned enough of my things to me to ensure my comfort."

Everything starts to spin away from her. "Odo? Are you sure?" As though, by asking the question, she might create the possibility of a different answer.

"Certain. When I was recovered enough to ask Mother Abbess how I came to be here, and to be concerned that I had no way of repaying her hospitality, she showed me his letter. It had his signature upon it as well as his seal. Perhaps she should have been more discreet, she was certainly most anxious that I shouldn't try to contact him myself, but she was so excited about the windows and the reliquary, she could scarcely contain herself."

"But you did not see him." Gytha gropes after an acceptable solution. "Perhaps the letters were forgeries, made by someone of Lord Harold's camp who wanted to keep you safe."

Edith shakes her head. "I know of no-one who might try such a thing and get away with it. Do you?"

Gytha considers the strongbox in which Odo keeps his seals, its padlocks with keys secreted in many different places, and how it is guarded, even at the heart of a military stronghold such as Canterbury. Hope flees with a soft sigh. "But why?"

Spreading her hands in a gesture of ignorance, Edith says, "That I was hoping to learn from you. I have no idea. I have had no direct dealings with him myself, and I cannot imagine what he hoped to achieve by placing me under his protection."

"So that is why you sent for me?"

"Oh my dear, not entirely. I was lonely, and I have enjoyed, I *do* enjoy our talks, but yes, I admit it, I hoped you would drop some hint about him that would make it clearer to me. I felt it was lucky for me when he brought you here."

"Luckier for you than me, madam. Why didn't he tell me? How could he let me live so close to you in ignorance?"

"Don't reproach him. To be honest, he's probably forgotten I'm here."

Gytha gives a sceptical laugh. "Odo? He never forgets anything. He should have told me."

"Why? Men like to escape politics when they're with their mistresses, not embroil them in the same mire."

"And the mistresses? Are they not permitted a view?"

"Frankly, Gytha, he probably chose to say nothing because he thought it might lead you to do something stupid. As it has done."

Gytha stands. "Don't worry, madam, I'm going." Crossing the room to the door, she unwraps her cloak from around her bundle of belongings, and extracts the leather pouch which she fastens to her girdle. "You need have no more fear I shall jeopardise your good name with Bishop Odo."

"But where will you go?" Edith hurries after her. "It's dark, the gate will be locked." Each phrase a hand plucking at her sleeve.

Gytha remains in the doorway for several seconds, fastening the clasp on her cloak, her dark eyes disconcertingly fixed on Edith. Edith blushes, looks away, picks at an imaginary speck of fluff on her skirt.

"Do you think I would tell you?" Gytha asks finally. "You might go and do something stupid."

The truth of it is, she has no idea where she can go. As she goes in search of her horse, she glances up at the rising moon. A perfect half moon, an idiot gape repeated to infinity in all the panes of glass in the south wall of the chapel, mocking her as she creeps into the stableyard. *What now?* asks the moon, *where to next?*

"I don't know." The sound of her voice, a hoarse whisper, almost a muffled shout, surprises her. Hooves thud and scrape softly, ears flick as she approaches the long barn where the horses are tethered, easily picking out the roan by the way the moonlight shines on the grey hairs among the red, making her look like a chestnut which has been imperfectly whitewashed.

She belongs nowhere. She cannot, will not, go back to Winterbourne, to the games Odo plays with her the way Thecla plays with her dolls. Not wishing to run the risk of waking the grooms, she takes the first sidesaddle and bridle she finds on the rows of pegs set into the barn wall; they are not hers, but she consoles herself with the thought that what she leaves behind will probably be of superior quality to what she takes.

"Hey." Too late. With much rustling and cursing, a heap of straw in a corner of the barn resolves itself into the oversexed, pimply youth of that afternoon. Hoping she is not too much in shadow, Gytha plasters her most helpless, feminine smile to her face and contrives to stumble slightly beneath the weight of the saddle.

"I didn't want to disturb anyone," she breathes.

"What are you doing?" The boy scratches his head, then his arse.

"I have to leave."

"Now?"

"Urgent business." A slight emphasis on the word, urgent; another spoon of honey in the smile. "Can you help me?"

The boy pauses, weighing the situation up.

"I'm not sure this is my saddle. It's terribly heavy." She drops the saddle. Now. Just right. The boy lunges to retrieve it. His face comes within inches of her breasts as he straightens up.

"It's not," he says in an anguished whisper. He returns the saddle to its peg, then peers among the rest of the tack until his eyes pick out by moonlight the scrollwork on the backrest of Gytha's saddle. "I don't think your mare'd like that bit much either," he adds with a smile, slipping the bridle from her outstretched fingers. His breath smells of sour milk and whistles through the gap where his two upper front teeth should be. He walks down the horse line gingerly, holding the saddle over his crotch.

He backs the mare out of the line quietly enough, pulling her ears and whispering to her, just the way Fulk does, and...but she is not going to think about Odo. But just as he is leading her towards the mounting block, a commotion of loud swallows, followed by a hooting yawn and a succession of grunts, explodes from somewhere in the depths of the barn.

"Oh Mary Mother of God," the boy exclaims, "that's the head groom."

Thankyou, Mary, Mother of God, thinks Gytha. "Go," she whispers, "quickly, and thank you."

"There's a gap in the wall," he throws back over his shoulder as he runs towards the barn, "behind the smithy. Turn left through there and you'll soon find the path to Winterbourne."

He'll probably get his ears boxed, she supposes, as she sets the mare towards the right, but no doubt he'll find some way of consoling himself. Her path winds gradually uphill, meandering among stooks of trees sheaved by giants, the mare picking her way steadily around clumps of bramble and juniper. The moon is fully up now, the black outlines of bud-knobbed branches, clawed thorns and heart-shaped ivy precisely cut out of sheets of silver. The evening is chilly, but it is a spring cold, not dense enough for frost.

A fox barks, followed by a brief crescendo of scratchings and scurryings in the undergrowth. The mare flicks her ears and tenses a little but Gytha urges her on, chats to her about the foolish stable boy, her voice sounding eerie and alien in this monochrome night-world of silent plants and animal intelligences. Once she catches sight of a barn owl, a brief glimmer of white swooping beneath the dense canopy of some pine trees.

"The wisest of birds," she says to the horse, "who knows everything and tells nothing," and starts to laugh, her laughter running off among the trees like a wood sprite.

She continues to ride because there is nothing else to do. As night deepens, the moon retreats behind cloud. A thin, cold drizzle begins to fall, seeping through her clothes, making the reins stiff and slippery between her aching fingers. From time to time she dozes and the mare stumbles, jarring her back into wakefulness. All she wants in the world is to sleep. She begins to dream of a bed of leaf mould and pine needles beneath the trees, so exhausted even the threat of wild beasts seems worth the risk if only she can dismount, escape the endless swaying of the horse, the hard saddle, the burning strain in her thigh muscles. Besides, if she is torn to pieces by wolves, or her brains are eaten away by an earwig creeping into her ear while she sleeps, at least it will bring an end to this utter desolation. She will be done with the world of men and all its rich disappointments.

She rides deeper into the woods. Without even bothering to tether the mare, she rolls herself in her cloak and closes her eyes. The last thing to enter her mind as she falls asleep is the face of the woman in the ruined church in Winchester, the face she thought was Death.

"Gone?" Fulk scratches his head.

"Her bed hasn't been slept in and that leather pouch is gone, the one she keeps that locket in, and..." Freya's speech tails off; she knows about the cockade in the leather pouch, but she is not sure she wants Fulk to. "I don't know what he's done to upset her. You could have cut the atmosphere around them with a knife the evening before he left for Winchester. Why they can't just settle down and live like normal people beats me. You'll have to go and tell him, Fulk. If his lordship doesn't find out from us, he might think we had something to do with it, and then what?"

"Maybe she's just gone to the convent, she's been going there a lot recently."

"Without you or I? Without even telling us?"

Freya is content at Winterbourne. Until now, her mistress has been so taken up with the Earl she scarcely seems to have noticed how her household is run, as long as it runs smoothly, and the steward concerns himself only with estate matters, leaving Freya a free hand to exercise the authority of housekeeper. It is Freya who keeps count of the candles and spice boxes, supervises the laundry and dairy and scolds the rest of the servants. She is particularly proud of the way she was able to rise to the challenge of Sister Jean's arrival, with all the other women, and the embroidery; she would defy any of them to complain they had gone short of anything, whether straw for bedding or wine to warm their bellies.

She has her man by her every day, and at night a good quilt and a clean hay mattress in the warmest corner of the hall. There is no shortage of food even now, on the cusp of winter and spring, for a small household with all the resources of the Earl of Kent at its disposal, so her milk remains abundant and the babies are thriving. She has no intention of letting any waywardness of Gytha's threaten the life she has made for herself here.

"You have to go this morning," she insists. "You can be there by tonight. I'll go and pack up some food for you so you don't have to stop. And Fulk..."

"Yes?"

"Don't mention the convent. We wouldn't want his lordship thinking we'd let her go out alone."

As soon as she begins to recognise the country they are travelling through, Margaret suggests to her two escorts that they stop to eat the food prepared for them by Freya. She leads them in among paths crisscrossing the woods close to her home, ways known to her since childhood when she used to go poaching with her brothers. She was never much good with snares or slingshots, but came in useful for winding her curls coquettishly round her fingers and melting the hearts of the forest wardens whenever they were caught. Excusing herself to answer a call of nature, she slips away through the trees to join another path which will put her back on the main road.

She has no clear idea how she is going to set about finding Tom, but this does not trouble her. Although yesterday's blue skies have been replaced by a layer of high, white cloud, the day is dry, full of sparkle and lark song. She walks easily along the road, which is in better repair now than it probably has been since the Romans left, carrying nothing but a little money given to her by Sister Jean, about which she might feel guilty if the day were not so fine, revelling in her health and strength, and the freedom to be out of doors instead of cooped up in the atelier like a goose being fattened for Christmas.

The way is crowded with Easter pilgrims, making her feel safe among their numbers. There are monks, and penitents travelling barefoot with their heads uncovered to the sun. The sight of a tooth puller, wearing the trophies of his trade strung on a macabre necklace, makes her shudder and turn away, catching the eye of a young mason, his tools hanging from his belt, who grins at her appreciatively. She stares ahead; she has no time for dalliance.

From time to time parties of knights cut a swathe through the slow moving throng with their riding whips and once she sees a closed litter, draped with embroidered curtains, escorted by liveried men at arms. There is hymn singing and singing of a more profane nature, peddlers cry their wares and prostitutes, wearing coloured ribbons on their hoods instead of pilgrims' badges, solicit openly for trade, leading their clients in among the trees bordering the road. Gytha would be proud of her, she thinks, carrying through their deception so cleverly. Everything is full of hope, the days are growing longer, the sun has some warmth in it, a smoke of pale green blooms among trees and bushes, birds shout for their mates. The travellers push back their hoods, square their shoulders and smile at one another. Another winter ended, another year survived.

Before long, Margaret's stomach is griping with hunger. The sun, at its zenith now, is strangely hot for so early in the year; she has tried keeping her hood raised to protect her head, but her cloak is heavy, and covering her thick hair and couvre chef with yet another layer makes her dizzy. Sweat runs freely down her sides, between her breasts, and chafes her bare thighs as she walks. She wishes she had kept the jennet, or at least that her shoes had thicker soles, her feet are so bruised by ruts and stones in the road, and she is aware of a blister forming on her right heel, making her limp to try to prevent it bursting. Bright spots dance before her eyes, her head aches, she feels sick. She should have eaten before giving her escort the slip. What use is Sister Jean's money and her small, almost empty water flask now?

Catching sight of a group of men and women seated on a flat patch of grass beside the road, emboldened by hunger and exhaustion, she asks if she might share the food they have spread on a cloth in the centre of their circle. She has money, she tells them, and will pay whatever they ask. Two of the women look to a man who seems to be their leader, whose hostile expression softens at the mention of money. He nods and they shuffle sideways to make room for her; one has a child in her lap.

"Hello," says Margaret, but the little girl buries her face in her mother's breast.

"She's shy." The mother's voice sounds familiar, making Margaret look at her cautiously. It is not unusual to meet people you know travelling at this time of year, particularly close to a great pilgrimage centre like Canterbury, but Margaret knows of no-one she would want to catch her on this journey.

"Oh, but it's still Lent." She hesitates to eat the cheese accompanying the hunk of bread passed to her by the woman on her other side, convinced by the gurgling in her stomach that it is a heathen even if she is a good Christian.

"Dispensation for pilgrims," says the woman with the child, "and you look as though you could do with it."

"Hawise!" exclaims Margaret as the two women face each other. Hawise holds her daughter in front of her like a shield. Seeing the hard, watchful expression in the servant's small eyes, like currants in a pudding Little Walter used to say, Margaret's smile shrivels.

"Miss Margaret." Hawise expresses neither surprise nor curiosity.

"Are you making a pilgrimage, Hawise?" Both women look at Hawise's little girl. *No*, thinks Margaret, taking in the child's broad face, its small features grouped around a snub nose, *there can be no doubt*. Hawise does not bother to reply.

"And you, Miss?"

"I..? No, I..." She is unsure if she should trust Hawise, the girl seems so unfriendly, evasive even. It must be something to do with the child. Margaret does not believe her father would have thrown Hawise out over a child, but perhaps Lord Vital sees things differently. Lord Vital, of course. There is a way of ensuring Hawise's co-operation after all. "It's Tom," she says. "I've found out he's alive, but he's..."

Hawise runs her fingers through her daughter's sandy curls. Solemnly sucking a grimy thumb, the child stares at Margaret with eyes the colour of gooseberries.

"Of course." Margaret puts down the bread and cheese, suddenly not hungry. "But Hawise, if you knew, why didn't you do something?"

"Keep your voice down, Miss. I don't want the whole world knowing my business."

"Sorry. Is it the child? I might...I mean, there may be a way of settling things."

"It's not her, she doesn't deserve this." Hawise casts her eyes over her poor clothes and bare feet, the others in the company, some of whom, Margaret now notices, have whores' cockades pinned to their hoods. The man who gave her permission to join them wears a bracelet Margaret could swear she had last noticed several miles back around the wrist of a lady on a white palfrey, escorted by a liveried man at arms. "It's him. If you've seen him, you'll know. He's as mad as a basket of ferrets, and I'm not going back to your father's house in case he comes looking for me there."

"How dare you speak that way. He's not mad, he's just lost his memory. If I can just get him home, and he can see Christine and their little boy, everything will be alright, I know it will."

Hawise gives a sceptical snort. "I know what I know. And Mistress Christine's child is all the more reason to keep him away."

"Hawise, you must tell me where he is."

"Not me, Miss."

"So you do know?"

Hawise shrugs. "I might."

"Then tell me."

"I'm not your servant now, Miss."

"Do you know where Alwys and I have been?" Margaret draws herself up straight, trying to imitate her stepmother's demeanour when disciplining any of the servants. Hawise gives a sullen shake of her head. The little girl, bored by grownups whose conversation claims all their attention, squirms out of her mother's lap and runs off to play. The man with the bracelet dangles a string of pearls in front of her, repeatedly hoisting it out of her reach as she tries to grab hold of it.

"Since the second spring after the invasion, we've been employed at Canterbury Castle. As embroiderers for the Earl of Kent. D'you know who he is?"

"Can't see how it concerns me."

"He's the King's brother, and I know him very well." No harm in a little exaggeration. "And I'll tell you what else, my father's new overlord is one of his tenants in chief."

"So?"

"So, if I were to tell the Earl I'd found one of his serfs on the run..." She pauses, watching the meaning of her words sink in. Hawise's currant eyes seem smaller and blacker than ever, her mouth twists between her doughy cheeks in a way that reminds Margaret of Gird pinching patterns on the tops of loaves.

"You're on the right road," she whispers. "About half a day from here, there's an ale counter by the roadside with a cottage at the back. Ask for Martin. After that you're on your own."

"Thank you." Margaret hugs Hawise to her with one arm and kisses her cheek. "Go home, Hawise. Everything will be fine, you'll see. Here, for the food." She presses a coin into Hawise's hand, but she is gone before she can see Hawise pass the money to the man in the bracelet.

"Left." It is not a question. Lord Odo scarcely seems surprised, let alone angry, thinks Fulk, relieved. He has ridden hard as much to prevent himself thinking about the consequences of the message he is carrying as to reach Winchester quickly. But when he dares to look at the Earl, he is fearful. The man is as white as a corpse. He has begun to sway, so Fulk is afraid he is going to faint and wonders, should he put out a hand to support him, or call Osbern? The etiquette of such a situation is beyond him. Eventually, after what seems an eternity of indecision, he takes a step towards Odo, but Odo, recovering himself, extends one hand, palm towards Fulk in a preventive gesture.

"There can be no doubt? She has not simply...gone to visit neighbours or something?"

Fulk shakes his head, torn between his duty to his lord and Freya's exhortation not to mention the convent. If Mistress Gytha is at the convent, Freya will have found out by now and will send word in such a way they will not look blameworthy. Freya is better than he is at understanding complicated situations. Silence, he concludes, is the policy least likely to make matters worse.

Odo groans and drops his head into his hands, fingers pressed into his forehead so that, when he looks up again, their tips have left bloodless prints on his skin. "I knew it. Fulk, you must go from here straight away. Tonight. Take food and a fresh horse. I will give you orders to turn out the garrisons at Rochester and Dover. Tell their commanders she must be found. Whatever it takes, she must be found. Do you understand me?"

"Yes, My Lord."

"Go now. Tell Osbern to bring a scribe to me on your way out. Come back for my orders as soon as you have all you need for your journey. And Fulk..."

"My Lord?"

"Never fear, I shall get her back. I shall turn this country upside down until I do."

"Yes, My Lord."

When Fulk has gone, Odo's knees give way and he has to hold on to the table he has been working at for support. Gone. The word seems to toll like a bell inside his head. Gone where? How? Why? No, he knows why. He looks around the room he is in, at the tapestries on the walls, the fire in the brazier, the candles in silver stands on his worktable. He looks at his hands clutching the table edge, the rings and bracelets, the clean, square tipped fingers against the dark, polished wood. He runs his tongue around his dry mouth, feels the smooth backs of his teeth and the arch of his palate she says makes her think of a tiny cathedral nave. He looks at the camel in its gold frame studded with topaz and yellow sapphires to represent the colours of the desert. He has given her everything. How is he going to get her back again?

The rat-faced man puts down his mug on the counter and approaches Margaret. Nobody notices him; inconspicuousness is a skill he cultivates, it is the talent God gave him, and then God gave him Sebastian, into whose service he has put his talent. He sidles up to the girl and touches her sleeve.

"You are enquiring about Sebastian," he says. Margaret looks down at him. Her candid gaze seems to burn into the shadows of his own shuttered, suspicious features.

"Yes. Do you know him?"

"Do you wish to join his congregation?"

"I suppose so, yes."

She has one of those voices that cannot help but carry and he does not want to be overheard. "Step aside with me a moment," he says, nodding to the ale wife, then leads Margaret around the back of the bar and into the cottage. The room is lit by a single lamp, its flame shielded by a sooty horn shade.

When Margaret's eyes adjust to the gloom after the blue, spring twilight outside, she sees a beaten earth floor and an untidily thatched roof from whose beams hang cured meats and sausages in greasy nets.

A man sits at the table in the centre of the room, knife in hand, food and drink before him.

"This is Martin," says Margaret's escort, and disappears.

Martin waves his knife at Margaret, which she takes as an invitation to come closer. She is not afraid, she tells herself; the rapid beating of her heart, the lightheaded feeling, are caused by hunger and tiredness, not fear. She has travelled non-stop since she left Hawise and her party to get here before nightfall. Her mouth floods with saliva at the sight of the food on the table, though it is not much, a hunk of coarse, grey bread and some hard boiled eggs.

"You've been asking a lot of questions," says Martin, looking at her critically, "not something to be encouraged in a woman." He has startlingly pale hair, still showing the remains of a tonsure, and almost colourless, pink rimmed eyes. His voice is soft and sibilant. "Tell me what your interest is in Sebastian."

"I want to join him."

"I see. And why would that be?"

"Because..." She struggles frantically to remember some of Tom's ravings in the Christ Church infirmary. "Because the Tyrant of the Last Days is at hand and men must be ready for his signs and lying wonder. He will make war with the saints..."

"Enough. I am satisfied you know your Bible, but what do you know of Sebastian?"

She had expected this meeting to be a mere formality, not unlike her first meeting with Sister Jean when she and Alwys had answered a few practical questions, shown a piece of needlework each, and been told to fetch their travelling clothes and be ready to leave within the hour. *If all else fails, tell the truth.*

"I have seen him, and I love him."

At this, Martin smiles, a smile of disconcerting, almost frightening, sweetness. "Well, woman, I think we must trust each other. There aren't many young women who would take to the road all alone as you say you have done. Sebastian will be impressed by your dedication. Wait here with me, and I will take you to him once darkness has fallen. My people tell me they have seen military patrols on the road since Sext. Kent's men. I don't suppose you know anything about that? Do you?" He slices an egg in half, sliding his knife blade with slow precision through slippery white and crumbling yoke so they do not separate.

Sweet Mary, Mother of God, her escort must have found their way out of the woods and back to Canterbury. She will be discovered. She will end by leading poor Tom straight into a trap. But what can she do? If she admits to knowing the reason for Lord Odo having turned out his soldiers, Martin will never take her to Tom. He might even kill her. On the other hand, he must be well used to evading detection by the authorities. If she pretends ignorance, they both stand a better chance. She shakes her head and shrugs.

Martin smiles again, mashed egg yolk cementing the gaps between his front teeth. "You look hungry," he says. "Sit down."

The sacristan closes the chapel door softly behind him, and at last, Odo is alone. He kneels at the foot of the altar steps, raising his eyes to the Crucifix but letting them slip out of focus so that all he sees is a cross shaped blur, shimmering dark gold in the glow of the two remaining candles either side of the altar. He prays that his mind might be emptied of its troubles and become a space fit for God to enter, that God will guide and fortify him and grant his soul peace. Then he places his palms flat on the floor and lowers himself until his body is prostrated, knees, hips, ribs, forehead pressed against the stone, and stretches his arms out to his sides in imitation of Christ on the Cross.

To begin with, he is afraid it is not going to work. His body clamours for his attention. The cold makes his head ache, as though the stone had entered his skull. His ribs hurt when he breathes. The muscles in his neck and chest begin to burn in protest at their enforced immobility. Far from emptying, his mind seethes, going over and over the litany of his preparations the way Osbern checks off items on his fingers when they are planning a complicated journey.

His orders have gone out to every soldier under his command in the east of England. His officers must stop at nothing to find her; those who do will be well rewarded, any who shirk their duty will quickly know what it means to disobey, or even misunderstand him. She is to be taken to Dover, the strongest of his castles, and held there until he arrives. He has explained to the King that an urgent matter of internal security has arisen on his Essex border, necessitating his immediate departure from the conference. He hopes the matter will be resolved quickly. In the meantime, Thomas of York has his proxy. Lanfranc was also present at their meeting, tugging his beard, his black eyes darting from Odo to William and back again. Lanfranc's face was a mirror in which theirs appeared superimposed, William's wary and puzzled, his own haggard, pulled out of shape by his lies. William believed him, he is certain of it, because he wanted to, and because he could never understand what Gytha means to him. William does not have those kinds of dreams.

Images come to him. As night settles on the castle and the cold of air and stone slows his blood, they float into the empty spaces in his mind. William and his father, facing one another across the corner of the high table in the hall at Conteville. His father's stricken expression. William is talking. He cannot hear what William is saying, but he knows it is something terrible and unexpected, and about him. A phrase: he's the clever one, the Church is the best place for the clever ones. Agatha, crying, but her clothes are wet so perhaps it's just rain, or river water. His mother, so small in the great bed. He prays, but his sisters place the pennies on her eyes. His tears are purple, no, blood red. Unstoppable. They will all drown in his tears. He gulps down air, his ribs grinding against the chapel floor. A dark woman stands beneath the apple tree, a small, still, dark woman. Watching him.

Peace. His breathing steadies, slows, deepens until the stone feels like waves rocking him. The door to the chapel opens, he feels the draught stirring the hairs on the back of his neck. Footsteps are coming towards him, the muted thud of soft leather on stone, familiar footsteps, a long stride, heavy, not quite as long as his own. Rising stiffly to his knees, he smells fresh wax like the scent of morning; they are preparing for Matins, then, screwing fresh candles into the tall, gilt iron stands flanking the altar. He rubs his forehead, flexes fingers and toes. His arms, released from their discipline, feel as light and tremulous as wings.

"Damnably uncomfortable way of spending a night," comments William, genuflecting awkwardly beside his brother, knee joints cracking, his bulky torso appearing to topple forward from the hips. Odo stands up, then helps William to his feet, a hand beneath the older man's elbow.

"I find it...consoling, from time to time."

"All the same, I expected you to be away by now, seeing this border security matter is so urgent."

Odo shrugs. He wants to keep the tone light, light enough to blind William to the heart of the matter. "Travelling in the dead of night seemed more likely to exacerbate the risk than curtail it. I will be gone before Lauds."

"And back when?"

"As soon as I can. Thomas of York knows my mind. I am satisfied my absence need not hold you up, God willing."

"God? Something in my water tells me God's will has little to do with it."

"God's will, your grace, is expressed in everything. But for His will there would be no earth nor men put upon it."

"Don't you go playing the bishop with me, Odo. Best you remember by whose will you hold that holy office. Besides, it's not men that concern me but the other half of creation."

The two deacons have completed their preparation of the chapel and retreated to the sacristy. Any moment now the bell will start to toll, summoning the faithful and the sleepless to prayer. He is wasting time; as the night thins and the stars grow pale, she is slipping away from him. He must go, but William must not learn the extent of his desperation.

"Animals?" he enquires, injecting a note of humorous surprise into his voice, smiling his downturned smile.

William pushes himself away from the pillar against which he has been leaning. By the light of the newly lit candles, Odo observes an unhealthy flush creep up the bolster of flesh between William's collar and his hairline. Better not overdo it; he feels William's health is not all it used to be. "Sorry," he says, ducking his head so William can look down to meet his gaze.

"It's the woman, isn't it?"

Odo fights the impulse to look away.

"I thought as much. Why did she not come here with you?"

"She was reluctant to set herself up as mistress in the house where she once served. She's...sensitive that way."

William gives him a shrewd look. "Nonsense. The place is hardly recognisable. You've had masons and carpenters crawling all over it ever since it fell into your possession."

"Alright," Odo concedes. "She refused. She wouldn't accept your terms."

"It's not up to her." William's sandy brows knit in an uncomprehending frown. "She's yours, she must do as you require."

Odo shrugs but says nothing. He will never make William understand, and he has no time to waste trying.

"Beware, brother," William continues, "she has completely turned your head. How many times did I beat you at chess at Christmas? I swear Mortain would have made a stronger opponent. But chess is one thing, this...I should forbid you to go. For your own good."

Now he stands up straight, arms folded, balanced on the balls of his feet like a prize fighter. "It is your prerogative to do so."

William makes himself comfortable against the pillar once more, flexing his back against the pitted stone as though using it as a scratching post. "Tell me about her."

Keep it brief. Thank God for Matins; the chapel will fill up soon and the service begin, preventing William from detaining him longer.

"What do you want to know?"

William spreads his hands. "Is she pretty?"

"Not especially. Small. Like Matilda, and *Maman*."

"And wilful, it seems. Must be good in bed then. Can't imagine what else a man would want with a bloody minded woman unless she was pleasing on the eye."

"Presumably you don't expect an answer to that."

"I'm your king, Odo, I always expect answers."

The clergy are assembling, William's chaplain, assorted priests and deacons attached to the Papal legacy, gliding along the nave and side aisles to converge on the door to the sacristy where they jostle briefly for precedence; everyone feigns ignorance of the King and his brother.

"Very well, this is my answer. I love her. That's the best I can do."

William makes a dismissive gesture with one hand. "Oh if I had a penny for every time I've heard you say that..."

"You'd be a poor man."

William's pale eyes, their whites bloodshot in the candlelight, remain fixed on him for a long moment while he wonders desperately if his brother has any more to say or if he can simply leave. His feet tingle, yet he feels bound by William's look, as though it is boring into his heart, searching for what is written there. "Go on," says William finally, "go."

"Thank you, your grace." Odo bows, to give himself cover while he composes his features into the right expression of respect and affection with which to take his leave. He is angry at the time wasted but William, he thinks, is disappointed, which makes them even, but is troublesome nonetheless.

"I want you back by Lauds on Easter morning, Odo. I fancy we will have the play of Our Lord's appearance to Mary Magdalene, as we do at Rouen. Eh?"

Odo smiles, holding William's gaze. Reassurance, he tells himself, trustworthiness, loyalty, love; marshalling these emotions in his eyes as though preparing an assault. He backs away a few steps before turning and fleeing towards the door at the north end of the transept.

"You've still got dust on your forehead," William shouts after him. "And, Odo, remind her she has no choice but to accept my terms, same as all the English."

The eyes worked, thank God. You cannot perjure yourself with a look. Today is Holy Tuesday; even if his men find her today, he has no intention of leaving her to return here in time for Easter. He will contemplate the mystery of the Resurrection in the arms of his own Magdalene. Her rapt gaze will make the miracle plain to him.

Though everything is set for a quick departure, a fast horse and two of his knights equally well mounted awaiting him in the castle's outer court, he finds his trials are not yet over. When they reach the city gate, the officer of the watch is reluctant to open up for them.

"In the name of the Earl of Kent," barks one of Odo's men, doling out his words slowly and deliberately, as though talking to an idiot or someone hard of hearing. The officer stands his ground, a torch held in front of him so Odo cannot read the expression on his face. With a momentary failure of nerve, he wonders if, after all, William has sent orders to have him detained in the city. No, of course not, William never changes his mind. He spurs his horse forward into the wavering circle of light cast by the officer's torch and pushes back his hood to reveal himself.

"You know me, I think," he says to the man, who glances from his face to the amethyst on his left hand and back again.

"I do, My Lord."

"Then open the gate."

"It's not as simple as that, My Lord. There's a rabble outside been clamouring to get in since before the watch changed."

Odo's horse stamps impatiently; letting the animal have its head just enough to trample the ground a little in front of the officer's thin shod feet, he says, "A rabble? I hear nothing. No shouting, no clash of arms. What sort of rabble?"

"The holy sort, My Lord. They've probably got a chap on a donkey and a stack of palm fronds for all I know."

"Watch your tongue, man, and the minute you get off watch find yourself a priest and make confession. Now get that bloody gate open. Surely the might of the Norman army is equal to a few hedge preachers."

The officer shrugs off any further responsibility for what may happen next and orders his men to open the gates. A muted soughing reaches Odo's ears from the other side of the dense oak barrier as two of the watch remove the pegs holding the latches down and heave the bar free of its iron rest, a sound like wind in the upper branches of the trees bordering the road. Yet the night, in this hour between Matins and Lauds is still, holding its breath.

His knights loosen their swords, hands hovering nervously over hilts. Retreating to flank their officer in the entrance to the guardhouse, a lightless room hollowed like a rectangular cavern out of the city walls themselves, the two men of the watch seem determined to do nothing more. Odo walks his horse into the wedge of night sky filling the narrow gap between the gates, seeing nothing but the black outlines of trees and stars fading as the darkness is suffused by the blue glow of coming day. His scalp prickles where the hair, if he were not tonsured, would stand on end. *He descended into hell.* What is this rabble? A host of the undead sinking back into the earth at his approach? He crosses himself. Perhaps the last days are truly at hand. He signals to one of the knights behind him to bring up the officer's torch.

"But this persecution flames up today and tomorrow blows away, today burns hot and cools tomorrow." The voice is not loud, but resonates, as though the air in which it hangs is a sounding board, a drumskin stretched over the void. It is a voice he has heard before. Faces appear, flickering in and out of his vision, distorted by the play of fire and darkness, noses fantastically elongated or eyes evaporated from their sockets, gaping mouths, teeth of flame.

Odo's horse, responding to its master's fear, baulks at the gate and rears. Unprepared for the sudden uprush of muscle, he is thrown forward, forced to cling to the animal's mane like a boy at his first riding lesson. He would have fallen were it not for the tall man stepping forward from the mad jostle of silent faces, calmly reaching for the reins flapping about the horse's neck, oblivious, it seems, of thrashing hooves or bared teeth, the sheer weight of the beast should he come down on him. He talks quietly to the horse in a rhythmic murmur, like the chant of gentle waves on a shore, until it steadies. As the animal comes to rest, blowing softly through its nose, head low in submission to the man now scratching it between the ears, Odo's own feeling of powerlessness increases, condenses to a cold sense of the inevitable located somewhere which may be his forehead or deep in his chest, but is anyway his centre.

"You again," he says, gathering his reins and looking into the unreadable lizard eyes of the latterday Sebastian. "It seems I am indebted to you."

"God has appointed me to give succour to souls in torment, Norman." Odo's knights are drawn up on either side of him now, the torch held aloft by one lending its glow to the red blond hair cascading over Sebastian's shoulders. The other has his sword drawn.

"I have no time to debate the state of my soul with you now." And no time to arrest you and have you flung in gaol as I should. But you will keep, Saxon. He kicks his horse forward, forcing Sebastian aside, but cannot accelerate above a slow, disjointed walk as the preacher's followers mill about him. A pathetic bunch, barefoot, ragged, mostly, it seems, young women with babies and small children. Pretty, some of them, once. Fearing they may try to cut him off from his escort, he calls out behind him, "Trot on. Don't be nice about it. If some get in the way, it's a few souls to keep the devil off our backs," and takes the whip to his horse's rump.

"I shall see you again then," Sebastian shouts after him as the horse leaps into a canter, but Odo does not hear him, nor the curses of a young mother as she snatches her child from under its hooves, nor the crunch of bone in the foot of someone less nimble. His senses are ahead of him now, rushing towards the lightening horizon, to Dover, to his love. Nothing else is real.

Margaret, Martin and the rat-faced man do not leave the cottage until well after dark. Martin leads them away from the road, through scrubby woodland at first and then deeper into a forest where Margaret thinks the light probably never penetrates even when there is any. The moon has not yet risen and she cannot see an arm's length in front of her, stumbling over tree roots and brambles, hawthorn and holly tearing her clothes. Her arms and legs are scratched raw, yet Martin is adamant they cannot risk a light if the Earl's men are abroad. He himself moves as quietly and sure footedly as a lynx, pausing often to let the other two catch him up.

"Albino," pants the rat-faced man eventually. "Half blind. Prefers the dark. Take my hand if you like." His fingers brush her arm, the skin exposed by a tear in her sleeve. She gasps. The rat-faced man laughs, a hoarse, high pitched sound like the bark of a fox. "Don't you fear, girl. Martin guards Sebastian's new disciples very close, especially the women."

Margaret has no idea how long they have been walking when her straining eyes pick up a flicker of light between the trunks of trees. At last. But Martin says nothing and they carry on, the light sometimes just visible, sometimes lost to them so she is sure they cannot be going straight and begins to fear a trick, despite the rat-faced man's assurances. Her heart beats in her throat as though a live bird is stuck there. She is dizzy with exhaustion. Somewhere, beyond this forest, it must already be morning, but she will never see light again and her ears are condemned to hear nothing but the rasping breath of the rat-faced man and the occasional death shriek of some forest creature taken by a wild cat. *Wolves*, she thinks, *bears*, without light what defence do they have? Will even her bones be found? Surely bears eat bones, sucking out the marrow they way she might suck the green sweetness from a grass stalk. God has deserted her. She has gone down to Hell, and the world will close over her like water over a stone.

Then suddenly the lights are all around them, torches, a cooking fire, lamps glimmering through the walls of makeshift shelters. What was it the midget fortune teller said, at the Pentecost fair when she was still quite a little girl? *The fruits of your labours will endure for a thousand years.* Of course the world is not finished with her yet. She wipes her face with the back of one hand, smoothes her hair, pulling out leaves and bits of branches, pats and picks at her skirt, trying to pleat the ragged edges of torn cloth with her fingers.

"That's better," says the rat-faced man, not unkindly.

"Where is Sebastian?" she asks Martin. "I must see Sebastian." She does not want to stay here any longer than she has to. She looks around her.

It is an untidy camp, as though a giant child has left her toys lying just as they were when she was sent to bed. There are shelters of scrub and animal hides, a few mangy looking horses, some clothing spread to dry in the lower branches of trees, a dented cauldron set over a loose fire. A juggler is practising his art with three wooden spoons. The cook perhaps? Sitting on the ground at the edge of the clearing with her back against a tree is a heavily pregnant woman, a young girl squatting beside her holding out a bowl and spoon. A group of men dressed as friars, but unkempt, in patched habits and bare feet, are carrying a large box, supported by poles at each corner, across the clearing. It reminds her of something. The oath, that's it. Alwys embroidered a reliquary very similar, though much more ornate, for the scene where King Harold stood on the shore at Bayeux and swore fealty to William of Normandy. Now Alwys refers to it as the Ark of the Covenant and frequently tells Sister Jean that God wishes a rainbow to be added to the scene. There is no sign of Tom.

"All in good time," says Martin, flinching as another woman emerges from one of the shelters and comes towards them carrying a torch. He takes a piece of black cloth from somewhere in the folds of his clothes, shakes it out and pulls it over his head, a hood with blinkered eye pieces, similar to those you sometimes see on horses in races or tournaments. "This is Irene," he tells Margaret. "She will take care of you now."

Irene smiles, showing two upper teeth missing, one in front and one at the side. Once a handsome woman, with strong cheekbones and a pointed chin like a cat's, she looks worn out, her skin slack and grey, her mouth, in repose, disappointed.

"My, my," she says, clicking her tongue against the roof of her mouth the way Margaret remembers her stepmother doing when she had been out with the boys and dirtied her clothes. "We shall need to tidy you up a bit before Sebastian will see you."

"Will he see me tonight? How late is it?" Irene? There is something about Irene and Saint Sebastian. She wishes she had listened more to her grandmother, who used to tell them the stories of the saints before bed each night when they were small.

"So many questions. There's no need to be quite so impatient. I don't expect the Antichrist to appear before morning." Smiling again, Irene takes her arm and leads her towards one of the shelters, a large tent of hides spread over withies. Inside it is warm and cheerful with a shallow pit full of glowing embers and some boxes set on their sides to make shelves for cups and plates, spoons, combs, children's toys. Piles of brush covered with blankets serve as beds, though none of the tent's occupants is asleep. Several women are grouped around the fire pit chatting quietly, one suckling a baby, another plucking a primitive, three stringed lute. Some have pieces of needlework in their laps, though the light is far too poor for sewing. They sit idle, but alert, as though waiting for something. The smell of milk and blood and sweaty hair reminds Margaret of the atelier, and she has to blink away sudden tears.

Irene. The woman who found Saint Sebastian left for dead by his executioners and nursed him back to health. She must know. If he calls her Irene, she must have been there when whatever happened, happened.

"This is...tell us your name, girl," says Irene. Margaret opens her mouth, but something stops her. She does not want to give her name to these people. What might they do with it? If the Earl's soldiers are hunting for her, they might give her up before she has a chance to speak to Tom. Hawise. She should never have told Hawise. But it's too late to remedy that now, she must simply be more careful from now on.

Irene laughs. "Then we shall call you Zoe, after the Christian woman to whom the saint restored the power of speech."

Margaret nods and smiles.

"A lot who come here leave their old names behind," continues Irene.

"Did you?"

Irene takes a little iron cup, in which she mixes a handful of herbs and water from a jug standing beside the entrance to the shelter, then sets it to warm over the embers. "We don't talk about the past. It's the future that matters."

"I just thought," Margaret persisted, "as you're called Irene. But perhaps it's just a providence."

"We're all here thanks to providence, and God's grace."

"And William of Normandy," adds the woman with the baby.

"Hold your tongue, Frieda." Irene lifts the cup from the embers, the trailing end of her head scarf wrapped around her fingers, and sets it down on the lip of the fire pit. "Sit down and drink this. It will help you sleep."

The women shuffle round to make room for Margaret, who sits down next to the nursing mother.

"What's your baby called?"

"Sebastian," the woman replies, as if it is a stupid question.

Margaret takes a sip of her drink. Its bitterness sets her teeth on edge but she dare not spit it out.

"I'm going out to check on Goda. I'm sure it'll be tonight," announces Irene. As soon as she is gone, the atmosphere in the tent relaxes.

"Tell me about her," says Margaret to the nursing mother.

"Oh, Irene's the spiritual leader of the women. She was Sebastian's first disciple."

"How did they meet?"

"They say he was left for dead at Hastings and she found him. Just like the real Irene. He was buried under a mound of corpses, apparently, that's what saved him. The Normans didn't take prisoners. She still looks after his wounds. They never heal, you know. It's a miracle."

Something in the woman's tone puzzles Margaret. "Why are you here?" she whispers.

The young mother glances cautiously at her companions, but no-one is paying her any attention. The lute player has begun a song, one Margaret recognises as a hymn to her own patron saint for women in childbirth, and several of the rest join in.

"I was a priest's wife. When we got a new bishop sent from Normandy, he said priests couldn't marry, it was an abuse of the sacrament and if my husband wanted to keep his living he would have to get rid of me. Shall we say he saw the error of his ways?"

"Is that his child?"

The woman looks down at her baby, who has fallen asleep. Pulling the front of her dress closed, she says, "He always does that, leaves me with one empty and one full to bursting." She leans to kiss the baby's head then gives Margaret a hard, searching look. "You know nothing about what goes on here, do you? Take my advice, get out. Now, before…"

But it is too late. Irene comes back into the tent, letting the flap fall behind her, sealing them into the drowsy warmth. "Nothing yet," she says, then looks sharply at Margaret and the young mother. "Drink up. You'll need your beauty sleep for tomorrow."

There is nothing for it. She gulps the remainder of the drink down in one, shuddering as the bitter herbs hit the back of her throat. Within minutes she is sound asleep, oblivious as the women half drag, half carry her on to the brushwood bedding and cover her with a blanket.

The sun is already well up by the time she wakes, and the tent is empty, only the lingering, sour smell of sleeping bodies and the cold ash in the fire pit as evidence of its previous occupation. She gets up and goes outside. It is another bright day. Her head feels sluggish and the sunlight striking through tree branches stabs behind her eyes. She rubs them, noticing as she does so that her hands are covered in dried blood, her nails filthy and broken. Not an embroiderer's hands. What would Sister Jean say? She looks around. The camp seems deserted, though the cooking fire is lit, the cauldron suspended over it from an iron tripod giving off a wholesome aroma of boiling mutton, and some of the horses have been hobbled and turned out to graze in the surrounding woodland. She notices a stream running alongside the clearing and, kneeling on its bank, splashes her face with cold water, tasting bracken as she swallows a mouthful. She cleans her hands as best she can, then dips a corner of her skirt in the water and rubs it over her teeth. Feeling better, though hungry, she sets out to explore before they all come back. She supposes they have gone to hunt, empty traps, gather berries.

Incongruous among the makeshift shelters is a military tent, the kind used by officers, big enough to be divided into two chambers, the hides painted with designs in red and blue. Standing before its entrance is the portable altar from the night before, now covered with a piece of linen embroidered in whitework, looking suspiciously like a priestly vestment. There is also a cross made from a broken arrow. Deciding the tent must be Tom's, she is about to lift the flap and go inside when she is distracted by a commotion on the edge of the clearing.

A procession of people comes towards her at a kind of dancing march, the juggler of the night before turning cartwheels alongside. Somebody is singing to the accompaniment of the three stringed lute. At the head of the procession is Tom, ruddy cheeked, his hair loose and pouring down his powerful back like water over iron bearing rocks. He has a holly garland on his head and wears a fine woollen gown beneath his cloak of light. His beauty makes Margaret catch her breath and wonder, for a second of insane exhilaration, if he has been right all along.

"I have a new son," he announces, "a new soul to welcome Our Saviour when He comes among us." His voice is not loud, but it seems to make the air quiver and stun the birds into silence; it contains echoes of Tom's voice, but something more, fired into his chest with the Normans' arrows. Balanced on his outstretched arms he carries a small bundle of wool and linen from which the occasional cry hiccups. Seeing the way his lizard eyes soften and crinkle at the corners each time the baby makes a sound, Margaret remembers Christine and Little Tom, and hope rises in her.

In the middle of the crowd, among whom Margaret recognises Irene, the rat-faced man and some of the women from the night before, though Martin is nowhere to be seen, the new mother is carried on a litter. She too wears a wreath, of ivy studded with woodland flowers, wood goldilocks, windflowers and herb robert. Swathed in sheets, she grips the sides of the litter to keep her balance, her round, very young face split by a dazed grin. Margaret assumes she must be Goda, whom Irene spoke of the night before.

The litter bearers deposit their burden beside the fire. Tom, making his way through the crowd of his followers, the men all slapping him on the back, some of the women touching his sleeve and smiling at him, kneels beside the litter and places the baby in his mother's lap. She strokes his head. Tom unlaces the front of her gown, exposing her breasts, which he begins to fondle, his fingers circling and squeezing her nipples. Smelling his mother's milk the baby begins to root frantically and then to cry, high, thin wails of desperation as Tom now kisses the woman's mouth, pulling back her head with one hand entangled in her hair, now her throat, now closing his own lips over her breasts, one then the other, while she smiles and rolls her eyes ecstatically and no-one takes any notice of the baby. When he finally rises and starts to walk towards his tent, his chin is shiny with spilt milk and some spots of blood have soiled his gown, just where the fabric bulges over his groin.

Sickened, Margaret makes a run for the forest behind the tent, praying he has not seen her, that no-one will notice she has gone. She hopes Martin is right about the Earl's soldiers. She will find them and tell them everything, she no longer cares what happens to her. She is so ashamed, nothing the Earl could do could hurt or humiliate her further, no torture he can devise could be more than her foolishness deserves. Thank God the other boys are dead and Alwys out of her senses so they do not have to witness Tom's degradation. Beloved Tom with his bold eyes and his broad grin, who always insisted she was his favourite sister even though Alwys had prettier hair and quieter manners. How proud she was when he danced with her at May feasts and harvest suppers, the village girls looking on in envy. Remembering how his bright plaits used to swing around his head as they skipped and whirled, she is overcome by grief and starts to cry noisily. She is the only one left, and now…

"Not so hasty, my girl." Strong fingers clamp her arm, her flesh grinding against bone. "You wanted to meet Sebastian. Well, now's your chance," hisses Martin, his voice muffled by his hood. She struggles, but Martin is very strong for a man so slightly built. Twisting her arm up into the small of her back he holds her facing him. "Do you not find him beautiful?" he asks, and though she can see nothing but dark hollows where his eyes hide behind their blinkers, she can feel the calculating, knowing way he looks at her. "Most women do. He gives most of them that itch between the legs." He makes a couple of obscene thrusts with his groin. Margaret lowers her eyes. "And then he scratches it," Martin continues, thrusting his face close to hers so she can feel the warmth of his breath through the hood, "as you're about to find out."

Margaret struggles frantically, twisting her arm this way and that until her scratches start to bleed again and she can feel the sticky blood gluing her skin to Martin's. She must tell him, make him believe her. After all, she and Tom are not unalike, with their red hair and green eyes, their height, the freckles on the backs of their hands. But her throat is clenched with fear; she cannot squeeze the words out. Then Martin laughs, a laugh of such pure spite it makes her angry and frees her voice.

"He's my brother," she shouts, using her weight now to try to break free of him, but he is like a cat with a mouse, loosening his grip only to tighten it again when she squirms.

"We are all brothers and sisters in Christ," he replies imperturbably.

He doesn't care, she realises. He is simply there to gratify his master's appetites; he does not look gift horses in the mouth.

"So what's in it for you? Surely you can't be content with his leftovers?" If it has to happen, please God let it be anyone other than Tom.

"What he has consecrated can satisfy any hunger. How could I disdain to eat from God's holy vessels? And we are all charged with the duty of bringing new, unsullied souls into the world to greet Our Lord when He comes again in glory."

Margaret gives up. Martin staggers as she goes limp in his grasp. These people are so steeped in sin it has no meaning for them. As Martin leads her towards Tom's tent, where Irene stands holding the entrance flap open, she prays to God to understand that this is not her will.

A Turn of the Wheel

Eastertide 1072

Odo knows what his officer meant. It was obvious from the way he refused to meet Odo's gaze, and cleared his throat before coming out with the word. Attacked. He felt as though he was watching the man from the opposite side of an unbridgeable ravine rather than across an average sized room whose only obstacles were a few unopened packing cases. As a commander, he encourages honesty among his officers; a soldier who cannot speak his mind is like a fire burning unseen in the foundations of a castle. But in this he is not a commander, he is a victim.

"Give me a few moments," he says, "then bring her to me."

"My Lord." The officer bows and hurries away.

Odo stays as he is, arms folded, leaning against the deep, narrow window embrasure. No wide casements here at Dover; it is nothing but a fortress, a stone tower dominating the cliffs above the town, squinting at the sea through arrow slits. Besides, he can hear the view from this room, the boom of the water in the mill race like the heartbeat of the sea, gentle today, breathing steadily as the tide creeps up the beach to tickle the feet of the cliffs. Knowing the mill is there behind him, the sea around it tamed, put into his service to grind flour from which he will profit, in money or labour or kind, gives him some consolation. It helps him confront what he must confront before she is brought up to him.

Attacked. Raped? Or simply reverted to her old ways like those lickspittle Christians who keep Norse idols on their altars? You might own every pig in Christendom and all the silk worms in Damascus, but you still can't make a silk purse out of a sow's ear. He has been a fool to try. He hears footsteps on the stairs, two pairs of men's shoes and a kind of bumping and shushing sound. Bare feet dragging against the edges of the steps. How dare they? What has happened to her shoes? A hard knot of anger forms in his chest and settles against his windpipe, making it difficult to breathe. He sees her feet, small as a child's, the way her little toes curl in under the ones next to them and have a thin ridge of hard skin where they meet the ground. He imagines the fine, high arched bones bruised and splintered. Looking up, he presses his folded arms hard against his ribs to stop his hands shaking.

"That's not Mistress Gytha, you bloody fools." He shouts, but his anger has dissolved. He shouts from relief, the way parents do when telling off a child for playing dangerous games.

The two soldiers look flummoxed. "But she said she was one of the embroiderers. From Canterbury. She recognised your livery, sir," says one, too surprised to remember protocol.

And well might he be surprised, thinks Odo. It is an extraordinary coincidence that two of the women from his atelier should be roaming the country unescorted. It is too much of a coincidence to be true. "Explain to me how you found her."

"We came across her in some kind of encampment, in the forest near Rochester, My Lord. One of your verderers tipped us off. Said there were too many for his men to deal with on their own. They fled when we raided them, just left two women behind, this one bleeding and another very weak, blathering on about them taking her baby. We didn't pursue them. We thought we'd found what we were looking for."

"Where is Gytha?" he asks, addressing himself to Margaret. "Did she get away?" Did she make no attempt to help the girl?

"Gytha?" repeats Margaret. "Is she not with you, My Lord?"

Her stupidity irks him. "Clearly not, girl, or I would not be asking."

Margaret shrugs and shakes her head. One of her guards casts Odo an enquiring glance. He nods. The guard slaps her across the face. She flexes her jaw, probes with her tongue for loose teeth and spits a couple out. Tears spring to her eyes and tremble on her lower lids as she stares at the teeth, tiny parcels of blood and bone among the floor rushes. Odo can see her trying not to blink.

"Answer His Lordship when he asks you a question," says the guard.

"Try again," says Odo with icy patience. "Surely you do not expect me to believe you have no knowledge of her."

Again the wretched girl shakes her head, eyes widening in fear as the soldier raises his hand a second time, but Odo makes a gesture of restraint. No point in frightening her witless.

"Sit down, Meg," he says, more kindly, and to the men, "Let her go."

The girl looks about for somewhere to sit.

"You," he commands one of the men, "bring her a chair. Yes, that one. Where are your manners, man?"

The soldier lifts the chair with some difficulty; it is a heavy object, high backed with carved arms. He puts it down behind Margaret. The other soldier pushes against her shoulders until she sits.

"Leave us," Odo orders, then, seeing panic flit across Margaret's features, adds, "Find a woman."

"A woman, My Lord?"

"A woman. Presumably you know what one looks like. From the kitchens, anywhere. It will make the girl more comfortable." He smiles at Margaret. "I don't think she wants to be left alone with me."

The soldiers leave. For a long time Odo remains as he is, with the window at his back, saying nothing. He knows she cannot read his face, blinded by the light shining behind him, in whose beam he can see everything he needs to see of her. She no longer looks like much of a catch for young Guerin, her exposed calves and the backs of her hands covered in scratches and bruises, bits of leaves and twigs entangled in her hair. Her head is uncovered, her feet bare, and she is wearing a white robe of some stuff that leaves little to a man's imagination, stained with blood and semen.

As he shrugs off his long surcoat, she flinches and begins to tremble like an ill-treated dog. He crosses the room and holds the garment out to her. "Put it on, make yourself decent."

She grabs the surcoat and tucks it around herself as though it is a blanket, staring at him over the embroidered hem with great, vacant eyes. He moves away and sits on the edge of a bench beside a long table littered with the usual paraphernalia of his office – seals, pens, blocks of wax, parchment rolls, a silver sand caster. He picks an apple from a wooden bowl, but the flesh feels pappy beneath the wrinkled skin so he gives it to Juno, sitting with her muzzle in his lap. Pushing her away, he leans forward, resting his arms on his knees.

"So," he says, in the voice he keeps for penitents, "tell me what happened." He wonders if she will speak to him alone, but calculates he stands a better chance than with the two soldiers present. She knows him, she knows he has no interest in any woman other than Gytha. And he cannot wait for his men to unearth some other female from wherever women are to be found in this barracks. Every moment of ignorance puts Gytha at greater risk.

The beginning of Margaret's story is clear enough. With only a little prompting he finds out about her seeing Tom in the infirmary, how she deceived Agatha about her father and how her chance meeting with Hawise led her to Tom's camp. Then everything becomes hazy. She starts sentences, but stops half way through, leaving meanings suspended in the air, broken bridges going nowhere. She speaks in riddles, of blind friars and men with rat's heads, a ditch full of corpses and a wedding. She becomes agitated, squirming in her chair, tossing her head from side to side, stiffly, as though it is being yanked by some outside force. The words are stuck inside her. Arrows, she says. A heart stuck full of arrows like a pin cushion. Buried. Suffocating. Tearing open. Lungs, legs. Parting her thighs, she scratches at herself, then starts to sing. A hymn to Saint Margaret.

He is appalled, but dare not interrupt for fear of silencing her altogether. A discreet cough reaches his ears from the other side of the hide covering the entrance to the room. Slowly and quietly he crosses the room, lifts the curtain aside and nods to the woman standing there to come in and sit on the bench where he had been, where Margaret can see her. She is respectable, neatly and plainly dressed, with floury hands and the aroma of fresh bread clinging to her. His men have chosen well. He himself goes back to the window and leans against it, keeping his face in shadow. They are like figures in a tableau, he and the two women, no-one moving or speaking. But something happens; as he had hoped, the atmosphere becomes more relaxed; Margaret shifts a little in the chair, making herself more comfortable, then looks straight at him. With a silent prayer that he will be forgiven for any abuse of his estate, he fingers his cross with the hand that bears his bishop's ring.

"Confess me, Father," she says, taking his bait. Good. Now he will get the truth out of her. Glancing at the other woman, she beckons him closer, so he positions himself to one side and little behind the chair, knowing it will be easier for her if she does not have to look him in the eye.

"Go on, child. God is listening."

What she tells him nauseates him, makes him sweat and shake like a man with an ague. Her words make him want to hit her, or throw himself to his knees before her and beg her to tell him she has made it all up. It is not the fact that she has been raped by this ranting imbecile, nor that, in some curious, convoluted way, she seems to have enjoyed the experience. Odo has been in the world a long time, longer, he thinks, since the invasion, than his years make possible. Very little surprises him, he expects no more or less of human nature than is offered, and he can adapt himself to feast or famine as he finds. Now, though, he has surprised himself. All he can think, over and over, images as vivid as fever dreams burning his mind, is that this might have been Gytha, could still be Gytha, on her knees in the mud like a bitch in heat, ploughed half senseless by some hedge preacher who cannot tell the difference between earthly lust and religious ecstasy.

"Forgive me, Father."

What? She cannot have finished, she has not yet made any mention of Gytha.

"Are you sure you have told me everything?"

She pauses, frowning, then says, "Sure, Father."

"But what about Gytha? Tell me about Gytha, Meg."

The room seems suddenly very quiet; he realises the mill has stopped working.

She turns to look at him. "Only the first bit was her idea."

"The first bit?"

"The story about my father being sick. But you shouldn't be angry with her. It was me carried the deception through. On my own," she adds, a note or pride entering her voice.

"When you left Winterbourne she was not with you? You were alone?"

"Except for the soldiers."

"Yes, yes." He waves his hand impatiently. "The soldiers of course. But not Gytha?"

"No, My Lord." She snivels, wiping her eyes and nose on his surcoat. Their eyes meet briefly. He knows she is telling the truth.

He makes the sign of the cross on her forehead. "*Ego te absolvo.*"

"Please, My Lord, can I have a bath?" she whines, rubbing her eyes.

"This is a barracks, girl." He shakes his head wearily. "Tomorrow I will have you taken back to Canterbury. No doubt you can have a bath there. Now get out of my sight, both of you." He can no longer bear to have them near him, these women who are not his love.

When Osbern wakes him, the first sound he hears, above Osbern's urgent whisper and the long sighs of the sea, are the bells ringing in the town's churches. Matins? Lauds? It is pitch dark outside the circle of light cast by Osbern's candle. Matins.

"What is it? What's happened?" He sits up, swallowing stale saliva, disentangling himself from a dream in which he had been running along a beach, but then the sand turned into skeins of wool snagging his ankles, and the sea was a sheet of white linen, flapped up and down by mummers playing the pageant of Noah. He is astonished, and feels guilty, that he was asleep.

"A party's just ridden in from the west, sir. I think they've found her."

He leaps out of bed, wrapping himself in the fur-lined gown Osbern holds out to him. He does not even wait to put on his shoes, running barefoot down the two flights of spiral stairs, across the great hall and out into the inner court, Osbern lighting his way as best he can. At first all is chaos. The yard is full of men and horses, gigantic shadows leaping up the high walls and guard towers as their torches flare and gutter. A wind has got up and blows grit into his eyes, making them water and blurring his vision. Striding out into the melee, he is oblivious of stepping on stones or mounds of dung; every sense strains towards her. Where is she? Is it another mistake, another spiteful twist of fate?

Then he recognises the little roan mare, her neat head alert despite a night on the road, and his heart lurches, seems to crash against his chest like a drunk colliding with a wall. He shoulders his way through the commotion to where the mare is standing, her front feet performing a nervous tattoo, between two taller horses with cavalrymen on their backs. He takes hold of the mare's bridle and rubs her nose, and looks up into Gytha's face, flickering in and out of shadow. He waits for her expression to change, for a smile or a frown, even a blink of her eyes or a movement of her hands resting on the pommel of her saddle. Nothing.

Her stillness and her blank stare curdle the hope in his heart, wither the words of love and relief and welcome set to pour out of him. She mocks his vulnerability, or worse still, she does not care.

He sees himself prostrated in the chapel at Winchester. He is haunted by Thomas of York's dismayed expression and the suspicious narrowing of William's pale eyes when he told them he was leaving. He knows a clerk has come from Lanfranc with the charter for him to sign, granting jurisdiction over the three bishoprics to Canterbury, though so far he has managed to avoid seeing the man. The messenger he could not evade was Fitzosbern's. Fitzosbern has never trusted him and was reluctant to believe that his army's incursion over his neighbour's borders during the search for Gytha had been an accident. Unable to eat or sleep, he is at odds with his brother's best friend, making concessions to Lanfranc, ashamed to think he stood by and let his man strike Margaret, whom Agatha loves, whom he should protect, and Gytha cannot bring herself even to acknowledge his existence.

All these days of waiting, he has tried to convince himself, with a picture so vivid he could feel her lips, her tongue, her arms around his neck and the tug of his curls wound around her fingers, that there would be a joyful reunion, an outpouring of pleas, confessions and absolutions, the abscess of grief and fear swelling inside him lanced. Instead the abscess hardens, grows hotter, erupts into blind fury. He drops the mare's reins and turns on his heel, kicking a dog as he makes his way back inside. Its yelp brings temporary relief, but all he knows, all he can see through the hot fog in his brain, is that he must get away, out of the crowd, put distance and doors and walls between Gytha and himself before he strikes her, or worse. His body tenses, fists clenched, veins and sinews pulled taut, the muscles in his throat clamped around his windpipe so he thinks he will suffocate with rage. A great, inarticulate roar tears itself from some deep place where he is at one with wolves and bears, the mandrake ripped from the earth, Adam in the wilderness.

When he comes to himself again, he is standing in the middle of his parlour, sweat soaking his forehead and temples, suddenly cold in his armpits and between his shoulderblades. He shakes like a man with an ague, his teeth chatter, he cannot make his arm obey him as he tries to raise it to wipe his face on his sleeve. As his eyes come back into focus, he sees the room looking as though it has been in a fight, the carved chair smashed into kindling, the table overturned, parchments scattered, ink oozing between the floorboards, quills bent and broken. Juno's yellow eyes consider him watchfully from a dark corner where she lies with the half eaten apple between her paws.

Like the man from whom Christ cast out devils, he knows he has been in some dark, indescribable place, but now he is purged, empty and clean. Sheepishly, he picks up the embroidered camel from the floor, caressing its dented frame with the ball of his thumb, pressing a loose topaz back into its setting. Calling Osbern to clear up, he goes back down to the hall where his men are now holding Gytha, awaiting his orders. She is seated on a bench close to the door, where the lowest members of the household sit, condemned to tolerate the draught. Hunched and muffled in her cloak, she looks small and defeated and he can no longer imagine how she could ignite such rage in him. Dismissing the soldiers, he squats beside her, lightly touching her knee. A shudder runs through her, unleashing a rush of pity in him so overwhelming he can scarcely restrain himself from folding her in his arms. But his instincts, sharpened by his love, warn him against it.

"Come with me," he says, his voice quiet and even. She says nothing, but rises stiffly to her feet then suddenly smiles, a flicker of recognition in her eyes so brief he thinks he must have imagined it, but knows he did not. She is looking, not at his face but down at his hand, still clutching the camel in its bent frame. He smiles back.

Osbern has wasted no time setting the room to rights. He invites her to sit, which she does, on a faldstool brought in to replace the smashed chair whose severed limbs are now piled beside the brazier, smoothing her skirts under her the way he remembers, with a lurch of his heart into his sore throat. The lamps are all lit, and by their light he considers her.

Though she has not removed her cloak, she has pushed back her hood to expose features pinched with exhaustion. She might veil her feelings, but she cannot conceal the greyness of her skin, the frown lines between her brows, her lank hair gathered into an untidy bunch at the back of her neck. Her eyes look dull and dry, yet she never seems to blink. He does not know if she is looking at him, or beyond him, at things he cannot imagine. A momentary terror grips him. Perhaps, like Margaret, she has lost her mind. Perhaps, like Margaret... But no, she was sane enough when she recognised the camel, and she seems to have no cuts or bruises, no signs of misuse. And if any man had attempted such a thing she would have fought, surely, out of love for him. Wouldn't she? There are so many words inside him his chest aches with the effort of containing them, yet he has no idea what to say to her. Perhaps he should simply fling himself at her feet and beg her forgiveness.

"I'm sorry," he says, but makes no move towards her, telling himself it is because Juno is now sitting on his feet, and Gytha will not like it if he kicks the dog out of the way; in an abstract way, she is sentimental about Juno.

"Why didn't you tell me?" she asks. Her voice has a husky, cobwebbed note to it, as though she has not used it for a long time.

"What?"

And simultaneously she says, "What for?" A brief flicker of humour kindles between them, then she looks away again, twisting her fingers in her lap.

"Tell you what?" he repeats.

"About Lady Edith?"

Swan Neck? It had been a gamble to leave her at Saint Eufrosyna's when he decided to set Gytha up at Winterbourne, but he had believed she would keep silent. She owed him that much, he thought, chiding himself immediately for being so trusting of an Anglo Saxon. "How did you find out? Both she and Abbess Biota were sworn to secrecy on pain of losing Edith's dowry."

"Her ladyship sent for me," she replies, her voice gaining strength and clarity, "after seeing us together at Candlemas. It seems you were…careless, My Lord. Or perhaps you just assumed that, having told her to keep quiet, she would simply do as she was bidden. You forget how curious women are. Must I remind a bishop to consider Eve and the serpent?"

"And must I remind you how women continue to be punished?" His words hang in the air like a foul smell, float like scum on bad water. He does not even have to look at her for confirmation of his arrogance, his tactlessness, his want of any feeling save the fury of self loathing swelling in his throat. Her very silence on the matter of her children should have been enough to warn him, that and the four locks of hair he discovered, in a moment of curiosity of his own, in the cheap locket she keeps under her pillow. Is he really the same man who stood on the dais in the great hall of Rouen castle and preached the crusade against the English with such conviction, in phrases so exquisitely constructed, even William had tears in his eyes as his vassals, hard nosed realists the lot of them, fell to their knees in waves, like scythed grass, to pledge their allegiance to his great enterprise? Yet this mere woman, this little English seamstress, has the power to tie his words in knots, to jumble and break them until he vomits them up like a spiteful imbecile.

This time he does kick the dog, which scurries, whimpering, to Gytha's side, where it leans against her leg, its head in her lap. He glowers at them, this alliance of motherhood, wondering how many times he has sat with the bitch during whelping, worried because she has such slender hips, stroking her, singing to her, even on one occasion having Wulfric, his master of the citole, play to her. They look back, woman and dog, mute and uncomprehending of his cruelty. Damn them, damn their invincible vulnerability.

He draws a deep breath, sucking the cold, smoky air down into his lungs to damp down his emotions. "Is that where you went? To Edith? Yet that is not where you were found. I would have made the connection if Saint Eufrosyna's had been mentioned."

She looks away again, wiping her eyes with the back of one hand.

The dog, he tells himself, just the dog, making them water. Her nails are black and broken, his mother's little ring is missing.

"She said all the wrong things too. She is so grateful to you for your protection, so loyal. She counselled me to be quiet and obedient. Like a good wife. But Odo..." Something in the way she uses his name gives him hope, his name in her mouth like the balm of a kiss, a declaration of love. He smiles at her. The dog stretches out, still pressed against Gytha's foot, but with her snout pointing towards her master. "I don't want to be your wife."

"Well you never will be, barring some highly unlikely shift in the Church's interpretation of Saint Paul."

Ignoring his attempt at levity, she goes on, "Then why do you entertain that notion, of presenting me at court as if I were?"

"To show how I respect you, that you are more to me than just a..."

"Whore?" Her eyes take on a hard glitter. "Is that it? Your little indulgence? Worth burning down the odd village for, though. I expect I should be grateful for that."

"The damage will be repaired. It will be better for the people in the long run. They will have stone churches and granaries."

"You still speak English like a foreigner," she accuses. "At the place I was staying, at Terce the day your men...I left, a woman came to the gate. She had three small children, one a babe in arms, and nothing but what she stood up in. She begged the porter for charity, said the Earl's men had killed her husband for trying to stop them burning down his cottage. What use is a stone church to her? As for me, dear God, Odo, I was so ashamed."

"Of me?"

"Of myself. My...of the English, what we have let you make of us."

"Don't let Edith colour your view of me, Gytha. Do me the courtesy of hearing my justification for the behaviour of my own soldiers. Can't you see it's a measure of how much I love you? How afraid I was for you?" He thinks of Margaret with a shudder of distaste.

She rises and begins to walk up and down the room with Juno at her heel, passing so close to where he is sitting all he has to do is reach out his hand to touch her. He strokes Juno's head, pressing down so hard the dog ducks away from him with a whimper and follows Gytha to the window.

"It's getting light." Pushing back her cloak, lifting her hair clear and shaking it down her back, she leans her elbows on the sill. As if on cue, the bells begin to ring for Lauds and the mill wheel grinds into life with a sound like a giant's bones cracking as he stretches himself. "What's that?"

"There's a mill in the harbour mouth."

"No. Really?" She turns to him, incredulous, her reserve dispelled by curiosity. "What about storms?" She pauses, listening, perhaps, to the high pitched moaning of the wind around the tower. "And ships coming in and out?"

Suddenly he is filled with the beauty of the mill, tall and square between the jumble of rocks supporting the causeway leading out to it and the grey surge of the sea, milky on the harbour side, wave faceted on the other, as though the mill wheel itself had alchemical properties of turning mud to silver. "Every time I come here, I am badgered by some deputation or other begging me to take it down. But it's stood through three winters and there have been no more wrecks than usual in the harbour entrance. I love it."

"How unwisely you love, My Lord." In the following silence they do not look at one another, but he can hear their memories conversing and feel the thread which joins them tightening until it begins to sing.

"Why did you do it?" he asks softly.

"To show you I am yours of my own free will."

Am yours, she says, and with such tenderness, such a tremor in her voice. Not was, or have been, or even, will be again, but am, now, in the present which has no end or beginning. At last he feels he has permission to look at her, absorbing into his heart the way she hugs her dark cloak around her body, her watchful eyes, her sad, inward smile, how pale she is in the watery dawn light beginning to trickle through the narrow window.

Her gaze wanders away from his face to rest on the camel in its jewelled frame, which he has replaced on the table by his elbow. Frowning, she continues, "Just once, let me teach you something."

"Go on."

"As I see it, there's not much difference between a whore and a wife. They're both one side of a business transaction." Seeing he is about to protest, she holds up her hand to prevent him. "Lovers are different. They come together, and stay together, or not, because they want to. Free will. You see?"

It is a pretty notion, and he would like to believe it, but the law says otherwise. Everyone belongs to someone else, that is how society is bound together. He belongs to William as Gytha belongs to him, tied by duty and dependence. Why else would she work for him, or he protect her? Love makes no difference to such matters.

Then the image of a horse-drawn plough comes to his mind, followed by other pictures from his tapestry, flaring up and disappearing at random, as though he were trying to view the work by the light of a frequently extinguished candle. A portable shrine like nothing he has ever seen, a filigree of crosses and arches balanced on poles. A row of empty stitch holes leading like tiny footsteps to the eye of a knight fallen under a Norman sword. A crow perched in a fantastically curlicued tree with a wolfish fox beneath. His tapestry, but not his pictures. His story, but not the way he has told it to himself. How orderly his life was once, neatly segmented by prayers and bells, collects and canticles, everything in its place and a place for everything. Now he flails at each day just as the mill's arms wave at the immensity of the weather, and he knows a time must come when he and it will both be engulfed by his ambition, that life is short and God is unimpressed.

"I have behaved very badly towards you, in all sorts of ways," he says humbly, "and I don't deserve to hear you say such beautiful things." Thinking the time has come when he might take her in his arms and kiss away their misunderstandings, he crosses to the window, but she turns to look out at the broadening daylight.

"We're so high up."

He surveys the segment of courtyard and walls, and beyond them the sea, trying to see through her eyes. He sees foreshortened figures of herdsmen driving their cattle out to pasture, a guard on the crenellated wall, a small fleet of fishing boats crawling past the mill. This elephant skin sea bears no resemblance to the vision of the women in his atelier, who set William's ships, and Godwinson's, afloat on waving ribbons of ochre, teal and ultramarine, rebellious, unpredictable colours. The party escorting Margaret back to Canterbury will be leaving soon, he thinks, and wonders if he should tell her about Margaret, and thinks he will not.

"You should get some rest. I suppose you were on the road most of the night?"

"Yes."

"Where..? After Saint Eufrosyna's?"

"I'm tired, Odo. Ask your officer." She turns to him with a bashful smile. "To be honest, I don't rightly know. Isn't that stupid?"

He shrugs. "Sometimes places don't matter, sometimes they're everything. It just depends." He moves away from her, towards the table, where he stands with his back to her, fiddling with the camel in its frame. "You may sleep in my bed. I...have matters to attend to before...I'll send Freya to you."

"Freya? Why is she here?"

"She came with your clothes and things. I decided that when...if... that I'd take you to Normandy."

"Oh, I see. I suppose I'm less likely to run away there, where I can't speak the language and don't know the roads."

"I hoped you would be less likely to run away if you really knew who I was." He speaks with the voice he uses in debate, courteous, carefully modulated, attractive as thin ice under a canopy of snow. "To know is to love, or so we are taught. The harbour master tells me the tide will be with us late tomorrow afternoon. Your belongings are in my bed chamber. It's not as comfortable as...some others you have slept in, but I expect Freya has everything you need." Pausing at the head of the stairs he adds, "You took very little with you."

"Odo?"

"Yes?"

"Why did you save Lady Edith?"

He does not reply immediately, not because he does not know the answer, but because the answer touches his core in a way even Gytha has not, until now. Because it led him to Gytha, but could as easily snatch her away again. "It was a debt of honour," he says eventually, then runs down the stairs before she can ask him anything more.

It is a relief when he goes, a wrench also, but she scarcely notices the hurt. She has felt as though her heart were a block of ice burning her chest since she left Lady Edith, she does not know how many days ago now. Pushing herself away from the window frame she goes through to his bedroom, her legs shaking, so tired she feels like a ghost. She does not wait for Freya. Removing her cloak and shoes, loosening the laces either side of her gown, she falls on to the bed, not bothering to cover herself or draw the curtains.

But sleep eludes her. Once she lies down, her body feels so heavy she has the sensation of falling through the mattress. Every time she begins to doze, some noise outside jolts her awake, the sudden cackle of geese, men shouting as a party rides out of the castle, the shrill whinny of a horse. She has bites in all the most inaccessible parts of her body, clamouring to be scratched; she is certain the pallet she has been sleeping on had an infestation. Even after she has closed the bed curtains, too much light seeps through, hammering against her closed lids the way the turning of the mill thuds in her head. The curtains are thin, the mattress filled with a mixture of wool and straw, crunching and crackling whenever she moves. It is a soldier's bed, almost a priest's bed, narrow and austere. She cannot lie here as she lies in the bed she thinks of as theirs, enfolded in feathers, hearing nothing but the rhythm of her lover's sleeping breath in their own world bounded by the blue silk hangings.

Her lover. When her wind-scalded eyes had picked him out, making his way through the throng of men and horses towards her, her body seemed to cave in on itself. She had not been aware until that moment how her teeth were clenched so hard her head ached, and her hands on the reins gripped like a prize fighters' fists. He would not have approved. She smiles to herself now as she imagines the lecture he would have given on the sensitivity of horses' mouths.

Her mind, like the courtyard itself, was half lit and seething with impressions. Odo's bare feet in the dust, so close to her horse's hooves. The glint of his amulet in the open neck of his gown, his nakedness beneath, fur slipping over skin. Shivering as she watched the strong curve of his fingers scratching the mare's muzzle, she waited for him to lift her out of the saddle, the way he did every time they rode together, and hold her for a moment, kissing her forehead before putting her down. Yet just as she had convinced herself he would do this, as though nothing had changed, he turned on his heel and strode back indoors, Osbern scurrying after him with a smoking candle, extinguished by the wind. Not a word, not a touch.

Still not a touch, though she thought she had seen the intention in his red rimmed eyes when he came to stand beside her at the window and his sleeve brushed her little finger. And he has not struck her, though no doubt he feels himself entitled. She wishes she had spoken what was in her heart when she had the chance. She did not mean to be shrewish or evasive. She longed to tell him how it felt to be with him again, how it feels now to lie like a leveret in a form, in the indentation left by his body in the mattress. Inhaling his perfume, remembering his mouth, his hands, his taste, his belly pressed against hers, the luscious, slippery abandonment when he is inside her. It is as though, by some unnameable magic, the vessels of their bodies are fused, and each carries the other's blood in their veins like an extra humour.

When he tried to ask her where she had been, why could she not simply answer him? That she has been in a priory, whose monks found her sleeping in the woods when they brought their pigs out to graze. Not in the guest house, packed with Easter pilgrims, palm crosses and spring lilies pinned to their hats, but in a cell alone, the menstruating woman kept apart for fear of curdling milk or sending dogs mad. The brooding, silent woman at odds with the joy of the Resurrection. She did not know it was Easter Day until she heard the friar charged with waking his brothers for Matins shouting, "Hallelujah! Christ is risen!" outside her door. She remained unaware of any activity beyond the agitation of her own mind, going over and over his words and Edith's the way an ant dissecting a cockroach treads the same route backwards and forwards, each time carrying what it can, until the prior himself came to her and told her a detachment of soldiers with orders from the Earl of Kent were waiting for her in the courtyard.

"Forgive me, daughter," he had said, plucking nervously at the sleeves of his habit, "for revealing your presence here, but they have done a great deal of damage round about and now they are threatening to plunder my church and have the brothers whipped one by one until I surrender you to them. I have exacted the officer's promise not to harm you."

"Don't worry, Father Prior, the Earl's men won't hurt me."

"I thought not." She had not, it seemed, travelled far enough from Winterbourne for the prior to be in ignorance of her identity.

The Earl's mistress. Odo's lover. All the time they were together in the next door room, the sea below them turning from pewter to pearl to diamonds as the sun rose above the shoulder of the cliffs, a voice inside her was pleading with him to understand what lay beneath the words she spoke. I love you, said the voice, I love you, over and over. Why could she not simply speak the words out loud? Humble herself to say the true, simple thing instead of always taking pride in clever obliquity.

And now it is too late. He is going to imprison her in Normandy, where she will be completely dependant on him. She must ask him, when he takes Winterbourne back, if he will make a gift from the estate to the priory where she stayed, for she had nothing to give when she left, only the horse she needed to ride and her locket, which she could not part with. She must remember to tell him her jewel case is safe, and that Fulk and Freya had nothing to do with any of it. She hopes he will take care of Freya. She will ask him, in honour of the love he once bore her, to let Fulk and Freya marry.

A debt of honour? Mentally, she turns away from the phrase with a shrug of incomprehension. Honour is for men, a pretty thing of little practical use.

"Madam? Wake up, madam."

In the second between the return of consciousness and coming fully awake, she thinks it is him, he has come after all. Then she is aware of being shaken quite roughly by the shoulder. She opens her eyes on Freya, sharp-featured with impatience.

"His lordship says the ships will be ready to sail in an hour."

"An hour?" Gytha sits up, rubbing her eyes and the back of her neck, greasy from her hair which badly needs to be washed. "I can't be ready in an hour."

"Of course you can. The wind and the tide are right and that's that. His lordship gave orders not to wake you sooner. Your boxes have gone on board so you'll have to go as you are. I dare say, with a bit of a brush..." Freya looks her up and down with a sigh and a shake of her head. Meekly, Gytha swings her legs over the side of the bed and stands up, keeping silent as Freya brushes her dress, tightens her laces, straightens her garters and re-does her hair, all to the accompaniment of a sustained tirade against her mistress' feckless behaviour.

"That poor man loves you to distraction," she concludes, stepping back to consider her handiwork. "It's plain to anyone."

"So you think I've forfeited my right to fart through silk as you once so beautifully put it?"

Freya lays hold of a strand of hair which has escaped Gytha's braid and yanks it into place. Gytha sucks her breath sharply through her teeth, but says nothing.

"He's a decent man, madam, fair and loyal. You should count your blessings in him."

He is waiting for her in the outer ward, already mounted, alone except for several dogs and a groom holding her roan mare's head. Looking composed and well rested, he makes her a slight bow, an air of mischief playing about his freshly shaven face. She feels he is somehow mocking her, with his clean shirt and his sable lined cloak newly brushed. The groom squires her on to her horse then Odo dismisses him with a curt nod.

"I have something for you." He does not ask how she has slept. Biting back the urge to remind him she is not to be bought, she smiles and thanks him, and he hands her a tin disc stamped with the image of Saint Christopher bearing the Child on his shoulder.

"For a safe journey," he says as she turns the medal about, examining it from all angles. Her smile broadens; it is a poor thing, crudely made, the sort of trinket you might buy from any market miracle seller with his horsehair crosses and Bleeding Heart pin cushions.

"There is a ribbon if you wish," he adds, fishing in the money purse he has hanging from his belt. "I hope the colour is to your liking."

"Yellow. You have always said it was my colour. Will you tie it on for me?"

He takes the medallion, threads the ribbon through a small hole stamped near its rim and manoeuvres his horse until he is in a position to fasten the ribbon around her neck, his fingers skimming her flesh as he lifts her couvre chef. She shivers but he gives no sign of having noticed.

"Yellow has the virtue of faithfulness. And," he adds, squinting up at the sky, itself glowing primrose in the remains of the late afternoon sun, "it's the colour of spring. Hope. April, the month God made man."

And jealousy, she thinks, *what of jealousy?*

"Come on. Have you ever seen horses being loaded on to ships? It's usually quite a pantomime." He sets his spurs lightly to his horse's flanks and she follows suit, riding beside him down the hill to the harbour.

He has commissioned two ships, one to carry their luggage and the horses, one, smaller and deeper keeled, for themselves and Turold who, Odo says, will help to distract him from the nausea sea voyages always induce in him. How can a descendant of Rollo the Viking suffer from seasickness, she teases. Perhaps he is a changeling. They hand their mounts over to Fulk and board the smaller ship; two sailors with their shirts kilted up to their thighs link hands to make a lift to carry her through the idle waves. She remembers how, as a little girl, she would swim out to the fishing boats wearing only her chemise, alongside the men and boys who were tall enough to wade and carried her dress for her, holding the bundle high above the spray. She looks at Odo, sitting on a bollard, fastening his shoes. A sailor hovers nearby with a coil of rope, but he appears oblivious.

She turns to watch Fulk, soaked with sweat and sea water, coaxing the horses into the other boat. It lies broadside to the shore, the shore side gunwale tilted until the water is just beginning to lap it, enabling the animals to step on board without jumping. Most of them look as though they have done this before, needing little more than a few words and a slap on the rump to encourage them, but the roan mare shies, whinnying and kicking out at the side of the boat. By the time Fulk has calmed her, with his French nonsense and a handful of oats from a pouch on his belt, and she is standing in the hull with the others, her head poking just above the deck, the sun is nothing but a rosy fingertip above the western horizon, staining the sea pink and violet between furrows of indigo. The thrashing, whinnying chaos gives way to a litany of orders and responses as anchors are weighed and the two ships get underway.

Gytha does not like the set of their sails; with the wind from this quarter, just east of north east, she thinks, it will bring them too close to the mill. But Odo already has the inward expression of a man preoccupied with the question of whether or not he is going to vomit, so she watches the Kent coast recede in silence. Already most of the town is in darkness, only the cliffs glimmering pale green in the twilight and the silhouette of the castle dark and sharp above them. It is a long way from the coastline she used to know, flat and shifting, the iron grey sea ribbed with sandbars, the boundary between sea and water always uncertain.

Odo's stomach feels like a wineskin turned inside out and scraped with a blunt knife. Lying propped against the gunwale somewhere near the stern of the ship, cursing William for having chosen to conquer an island rather than France, or Burgundy, or Anjou, he watches Gytha moving among the seamen, clambering over coils of rope and stacked oars, ducking under the boom, twisting around sheets tautly angled from masthead to cleat. He marvels at her knowledge of fishing lines, hooks, net gauges, the surest bait for cod or bass, how you must never eat a petrel because they carry the souls of the damned down to hell, and keep silent near herring gulls because they are gossips. She talks to the men about tarring and sail mending and the best way to season hemp for rope-making. When the wind veers further to the west, it is Gytha who tells him, sparing the captain, that they may have to spend a second night at sea or put ashore before reaching Arromanches.

Dipping the hem of her skirt in a bucket of seawater, she mops his face as though he were a small boy being made ready for an important visitor.

"Why did you come?" She sounds exasperated. "You could have sent me with one of your officers, or even just Freya. She has your interests well at heart."

"Gytha, what are you talking about? I'm in no condition for riddles."

The captain gives the command to go about. Odo groans and shuts his eyes.

"Don't close your eyes, it'll only make it worse. I'm afraid we shall be in for a lot of this. It looks as though the captain's decided to make short tacks into the wind to try and make headway west." She glances up at the sky, the map of the heavens flawless with neither moon nor cloud to obscure the spheres and the fixed stars, not glimpses of heaven, or dead gods, or the light in lovers' eyes, but a tool, a fine, functional part of God's creation.

"Even your words make me feel sick. Couldn't we dispense with the seafarer's jargon?"

"Sorry." She sits beside him silently, her knees drawn up to her chest for warmth; the temperature has dropped sharply since sunset. The sailors bring the ship about, the rattle of loose canvas and the slap of the sea against the hull momentarily overwhelming the delicate notes of Turold's lute. On the other side of the ship Osbern, who appears to know better than to try to do anything for his master, is grinding the oyster shells left from dinner with cardamoms to make tooth powder. The breeze carries the minty scent of the spices and she parts her lips to catch the familiar, beloved taste on her tongue.

Despite her situation, she feels a deep contentment, a sense that everything is in order. It is the way she always feels at sea, underlying whatever else may be in her mind the way the sinews of water flex and twist beneath the boat. Perhaps she is really a mermaid. Perhaps she will jump overboard, and her legs will fuse into a muscular, silvery tail, bearing her into the depths, far below the reach of men's nets.

"Are you serious?" he asks suddenly. "Do you really think I intend to imprison you in Normandy?" She gives a sheepish laugh but says nothing. "Because I was, when I said to know is to love. You only know half of me, not even that. I want to show you where I was for the first thirty years of my life. You know this...king's brother. But until I was about eleven I didn't even know I had an older brother." William, he remembers, his big hands gripping Odo's shoulders. 'Your father tells me you know Caesar, lad.' '*Gallia est omnis divisa in partes tres,* your grace.' That anxious, eager treble. 'It's a damn sight more than that nowadays, Odo.' "I expected to become *vicomte* when my father died."

he resumes, coming back to the present. "Marry. Farm. Have children. Campaign for my overlord when needed. I thought my years would turn on seedtime and harvest rather than Advent and Easter. But William had other ideas. Gytha, look at me."

She turns towards him and he takes her hands, prising them from around her knees. They are freezing cold. Pulling her close, he tucks them inside his cloak, and she slips them up under his arms, his ribs ridged like plough furrows under her fingers.

"I had never been on a battlefield before I came to England. And I'd never...I belonged to God and William, and now I belong to you as well. My trinity."

"Oh, so John was your immaculate conception, was he? Perhaps he was born out of your mouth like a crocodile."

"Eggs."

"What?"

"According to Isidore of Seville, crocodiles lay eggs, though I don't know if he ever actually saw a crocodile, so..."

She starts to shake, her chest heaving, her breath coming in a series of small, hot explosions against his skin beneath his clothes. Afraid she may be crying, he tilts her face up into the fitful light of the ship's lamps. Seeing his earnest, troubled expression she can restrain herself no longer and breaks into fits of laughter, kneeling between his legs to cover his face with kisses between convulsions. At first he is tense, then he starts to kiss her back, mouth seeking mouth in the dark, the muscular dance of tongues, and she does not care that he tastes of sickness as he tugs at her clothing, rocking her back against the deck, covering her with the dark wings of his cloak. She reaches for his sex but he takes her hand away.

It is his turn to unwrap her, peeling away layers of wool and linen and silky, slippery skin, and as he does so, and finds what he is looking for, he watches her face. There is no treasure more precious to him than what lies between her thighs, nor any map more perfectly executed than that of her face, every flutter of her eyelids and flare of her nostrils, every gasp that escapes her parted lips, swollen with kissing, showing him the way to possess her. As the waves gather and break inside her, tossing her body against his, fearing she may cry out, he puts his free hand over her mouth and she bites into the soft mound of flesh at the base of his thumb, then falls away from him with a long sigh, stretching, pressing her thighs together as though closing her lips on a secret.

"What are you thinking?" She has such a grave expression as he smoothes her hair out of her eyes. She catches hold of his sticky hand and draws it to her face, breathing in fish and onions, rosemary, sandalwood, salt and iron.

"That I'm not a mermaid," she says, licking his palm where her teeth have left their imprint.

"I might be, though. Turold's disappeared and even so, I don't feel sick any more."

"Then I am good physick?"

"I shall become a quack and hawk you round markets. Odo fitz Herluin's universal remedy."

She smiles, acknowledging his reference to their last conversation at Winterbourne, though it seems to her that it cannot have taken place between these same tired, tender lovers, swaddled in the intimacy of his cloak, their private world bounded by the dark and the indifference of the stars. "I wonder how you would look without a tonsure?" She runs her hand over the dome of his skull, stubble grazing her palm.

"I can't imagine."

It is too hot in the atelier to concentrate, the urine and lanolin stench of the wool unbearably pungent. Some of the dyes have not set properly because of the unusually hot weather, and smudges of madder and woad appear like bruises around recently worked figures. Tempers run short and mistakes are frequent as the women struggle to keep control of their needles with sweating, slippery fingers. The work is getting behind; Agatha has been unable to replace Alwys and Gytha because she is reluctant to leave Canterbury for the long period needed to find embroiderers good enough, and now Margaret has failed to return or send word about her father. Nevertheless, at None she dismisses the women, irritated by their interminable carping and twittering, like being shut in a cage of finches.

Remaining behind to inspect the day's work and note corrections to be made in the morning, she nevertheless sits on at her work table, doodling listlessly. A tall priest dancing with a small woman, a man with a sad clown's mouth perched in a grapevine. She knows, if she does look at the embroidery, all she will see is the last piece of work Margaret did before she left, a scrolling figure of leaves and vines, repeated to form the borders above and below the scene in which Odo blesses the feast at Pevensey. Borders full of symbolic beasts in balanced pairs, gryphon speaking to gryphon, lion to lion, a pair of cranes fishing symmetrically among letters instructing the literate that, after the feast, William ordered the building of a fortified camp. Her own designs, elegant, neat, predictable, a hymn to the order of God's universe.

Who will ever bother to look at them? She throws down her charcoal, suddenly annoyed with the image of the dancing priest and the woman. Merciful heaven, she has even begun to write a legend for it. *Ubi unus clericus et Aelfgyva...* Where a priest and Aelfgyva what? She stands up, wilted as the seedlings of tender herbs some of the women have been attempting to grow on the window sills, now burnt by the sun. *A coffin*, she thinks, running her fingers under the edges of her headcloth where it is bound tight around her forehead and beneath her chin, a glass coffin. Life goes on outside, but in here is nothing but an old tale of dead men.

Looking down into the courtyard she sees a party of men at arms filing through the gate and is about to turn away for want of any distraction in that, when she is overcome by a powerful sense of déjà vu. She crosses herself and mutters an *ave*, but rather than passing, the sensation crystallises into a memory, so vivid she shivers with cold, feels her wet clothes clinging to her skin and Odo's heartbeat pounding through her shoulder. She knows it is Margaret she is looking at in the midst of the new arrivals, and that she is alone in the saddle, and her clothes are not soaked with moat water, yet it is herself she sees, the same unformed, girl's features registering nothing but blank incomprehension, the aura of waiting, as though the explanation must surely come. Life cannot be determined by random accidents.

As she makes for the stairs, she hears spurred feet running up them. A messenger appears and hands her a scroll bearing Odo's seal.

"Where have you come from?"

"Dover, madam. We left before Terce."

"I had understood my brother to be at Winchester, for the council of bishops."

"He has been at Dover for several days, madam. Perhaps the council is over."

"Perhaps." But she knows it is not, for Lanfranc is still in Winchester. No doubt his letter will contain an explanation. She breaks the seal and unrolls it. "Does his lordship expect a reply?"

"I was not told so."

"Then you may leave me."

The messenger bows, but hesitates on the threshold. "What about the girl, madam?"

"I will come down directly."

So this is a pretty kettle of fish, she reads in conclusion, after skimming the rest of his letter to get the sense of it. *The girl clearly cannot be betrothed to Guerin, or anyone else, now, without a dowry far in excess of her value. I suppose we must consider giving her to God, who forgives all, and I fancy Abbess Clothilde would be happy to take her for the right sum, compensation, perhaps, for the fact that you came to Saint Justina's without any dowry. Though, Agatha, if this is my decision, as indeed seems most practical, I caution you as Paul cautioned the Romans (1:26) and refer you for elucidation to Saint Ambrose's commentary, also Theodore of Tarsus and, now we are good Englishmen, the Venerable Bede himself.*

Ripping off the bulky seal, she stuffs the letter in her sleeve. She will destroy it as soon as she has the chance, but for now will keep it close. Though it is as clear as day the men who have brought Margaret from Canterbury know what has happened. There is an insolence in their manner towards her as infuriating as it is hard to define. Nothing is said or done out of order, but Agatha notices they do not keep their eyes averted as they should, and the one who helps her to dismount holds on to her arm a fraction longer than necessary. Dismissing them abruptly, she then wishes she had not for, left alone with Margaret, she has no idea what to do or say. It would be easier if the girl were to cry, or look remorseful, or show signs of pain. She has a bruise across one cheek, but it does not seem to trouble her. Agatha feels like an actor stranded without a cue.

"My brother has told me what happened to you, Meg," she begins, taking Margaret's arm and guiding her towards the atelier, "and I grieve for you, but if you pray, God will forgive you for He knows you did not act of your own will." Margaret looks at her strangely, almost contemptuously. Puzzled, she goes on, hoping her talk will smother her confusion. "But for now, you must rest, and..." Suddenly, with the sensation of a fist closing around her bowels, she thinks, *what if there is a child? Conceived in such a welter of sin?* There are ways, she knows, but how can she find out? Who can she ask? Freya would be able to help her but Freya is not here. Juniper. She thinks juniper may be involved, but how? Taken internally or applied to..? "And I will get whatever physick you need, if you feel...unwell."

"I feel perfectly well, thank you, Sister."

Dare she consult Brother Thorold? She wracks her memory for innocent medicinal uses of juniper. Worms. Haemorrhoids? Oh God, prevention against plague. If she asks Brother Thorold about juniper without giving straightforward reasons, he will think there is plague in the castle after all.

At the dormitory door, Margaret turns to face her. "I shall be alright now. A short sleep and I'll be back to work as if I'd never been away." Her smile is brightly formal.

"Of course you will. You won't be disturbed. The others have gone out walking, to escape the heat. Rest now, and I will pray for you."

"Thank you," says Margaret, still barring the doorway.

"Yes, well." Agatha clears her throat uncomfortably and turns to leave. Margaret closes the door behind her, the wind of its passage lightly disturbing Agatha's hood and habit.

She is unable to pray. Odo's letter presses against her arm, trapped beneath the sleeve of her chemise, the creases in the parchment digging into her flesh. When she tries to contemplate the cross all she sees is a juniper bush, though perhaps, she tells herself in a wry attempt at consolation, it might be possible to see the spiky leaves and white flowers as emblematic of the Crown of Thorns and the purity of Our Lord's spirit.

Purity. She'll give Odo Saint Paul's Epistle to the Romans, and Saint John Chrysostom's gloss on Ambrose, and Saint Augustine's letter of instruction to his sister on taking holy vows. Does he imagine she has not pored over, studied, meditated upon all these texts and more over the years? But what armour are words against the world? As long as men govern it, and as long as men keep their brains somewhere lower than their heads, there is no recourse for women like her other than to shut themselves away. Odo should have known that; he did know it once. He could not give her hope, but he had, at least, given her his protection.

Oh, the relief of arriving at Saint Justina's and being handed, numb with cold and shock, into the care of the novice mistress there. She had been stripped of her soaked clothes and bathed in warm water, the colour gently sponged back into her lips and feet and finger ends. Women with assured, capable, loving hands had dressed her in her novice's habit, brushed and braided her hair, laced her shoes. They had wound the black headcloth around her face and neck, and with it the aspiration to the white worn by the sisters who had made their full profession. So safe had they made her feel that she did not realise until morning that Odo had left without saying goodbye or giving her a chance to thank him. She had asked for writing materials, only to be told that the sending and receiving of letters by novices was permitted only at Christmas and on Saint Justina's feast day. To help you sever your attachments to the outside world, explained the novice mistress. As, later, her sisters severed her connection with her womanhood by shaving off her hair.

TRIUMVIRATE

PENTECOST 1072

"Left the country, you say?" The King frowns, more, it seems to Lanfranc, for the benefit of others present than due to any real puzzlement or disbelief. Nor does he appear to be angered by Lanfranc's news; his anger rarely expresses itself merely by frowning. Or perhaps it was spent on the journey back from Scotland, where his army is in the middle of a campaign against King Malcolm. "I don't recall him asking my permission. Do you, Mortain? My Lord Archbishop? And it seems an odd thing to do if there is drought in Kent, as you say there is, Lanfranc."

The three men are seated at a table in an upper chamber of the King's tower beside the Thames. It is hot and still, the sun almost directly overhead, a smell of mud and sewage and rotting fish drifting up from the river.

"No, Your Grace, but..." says Robert. He is sweating heavily.

"Then he must be got back. Are there many with him?"

"It seems to be merely a private trip, Your Grace," says Lanfranc. "Members of his household and a small personal guard only, and...the woman, of course."

"Ah yes, the woman." The King scratches the back of his neck where the shaved hair gives way to greying orange stubble. A mosquito whines, disturbed from feasting on the royal blood. "D'you remember, Robert, that odd couple we had at court once? Great, tall woman. Husband said she was a fairy. He'd come across her dancing in a fairy ring in a wood at night. These English are as bad as the Bretons for their tales."

"If I may venture an opinion, Your Grace."

"You are my brother, and the only one remaining with any sense. Speak freely."

"Well, to start with, Mistress Aelfgytha isn't tall. Quite the opposite, in fact."

"Do you mock me, Robert?"

"No, Your Grace, only the superstitions of the English. Sire, clearly my lord of Kent means no harm. As the Archbishop says, he has gone to Normandy in his private capacity, to Conteville, in fact..."

"So you were privy to his plans, were you?"

The sweat trickles down Robert's temples. He smears a broad, slightly grubby hand across his face. "Insofar as he asked me for use of the house at Conteville. It is his home as much as mine. I would not have refused him."

"And you did not think to advise him to stay put and attend to his estates?"

"I assumed he had your leave, Your Grace, but even so, I see no harm in his taking Mistress Aelfgytha on a private visit. He has reliable men under him in Kent. And surely you can't imagine he intends any ill will towards you. He's devoted to you."

"His devotion, even if it does exist outside the pages of that execrable flatterer, William of Poitiers, doesn't excuse irresponsibility or disobedience to the law. Splendour of God, Robert, he wrote most of it, surely he can remember what it says about leave to go abroad. And consider this. He has made over property to that woman, who was once close to Godwinson, I understand...

"Really?" says Robert.

"Some sort of waiting woman to Swan Neck, I'm told."

"Learnt her trade from an expert, then."

The Archbishop clears his throat.

"Pardon, Your Reverence," says Robert.

"Now, where were we?" the King resumes. "Yes, property. And then there are the complaints from Fitzosbern about encroachments on his territory. And now my brother of Kent has left the country secretly, in the middle of a drought. I'll tell you what I think, Robert." He emits a grim laugh. "I think no good can come of a man with an interest in embroidery."

"Oh, I don't know," says Robert. He takes the King's point, but is pleased by the way he is depicted in Odo's hanging, sitting in council with his brothers at Pevensey, an eager, visionary expression on his face, his hand ready on his sword hilt as he listens to Odo expounding some scheme or other. "Anyway," he continues, "I don't think you can levy a charge of secrecy against Odo. You and I both know that if my lord of Kent wants to keep secrets, he usually does it more efficiently than this.

"William, I beseech you, don't order him home as if you were whipping in a hound. He's done nothing to deserve such humiliation. If he's allowed to indulge his passion for the woman, I dare say he'll get over it the sooner and be back in his senses. You turned a blind eye to Adeliza, even after John was born, surely you can do the same again."

"Adeliza was a boy's folly. And he did the right thing, married her off and stepped out of the picture as soon as the child arrived. It's not the fact of the woman that troubles me. God aid, with an uncle like Mauger of Rouen, you might expect me to be tolerant of churchmen's tarts, and I have allowed for the fact of his being born in Scorpio. No, it's the obsessive nature of his attachment. What of his haring off after her in the middle of the council at Winchester? A more fanciful man than I am might almost say she had bewitched him. Eh, Lanfranc?"

"It is possible, Your Grace."

"Frankly, I'm disappointed. When you were at Caen, Lanfranc, you and Odo were good neighbours. Competitive. That worked well in the interests of the duchy. I had hoped for some of the same spark here, and all I'm getting is a damp squib, a mooning lover more suited to my minstrelsy than my council chamber. Tell me, Lanfranc, what's to be done?"

Lanfranc tugs at his beard, as though teasing out a solution from among the grey hairs straggling over his chest. "I believe my lord of Mortain gives good counsel, Your Grace, as always."

"Oh come, Lanfranc, speak plainly, what do you really think?"

Leaning his elbows on the table, lacing his fingers together with slow deliberation, Lanfranc glances at Mortain and then at the king. William jerks his chin dismissively at his brother. "Robert, go to the mews. Make sure the birds are ready if we're hunting this afternoon, there's a good fellow."

"Your Grace, William," pleads Robert as he prepares to leave them, "remember who we're talking about. You know how Odo loves you."

"I do, Robert, I know just how he loves me."

"You can't fall out with him over a woman."

"No," says William thoughtfully, "of course not. Ridiculous. You're absolutely right."

Mollified, Robert goes to find the falconer, William's pale eyes and Lanfranc's dark ones following his bow-legged progress to the door.

"Now," resumes William when the curtain of painted leather has swung down behind Robert's back, "tell me what is in your mind, my friend." He pours a cup of wine and pushes it in front of Lanfranc, who sips sparingly.

"I think Mortain is right, though for the wrong reasons."

"As is so often the case. Odo, on the other hand, is frequently wrong for all the right reasons. If I had but one brother as sharp as Odo and as loyal as Robert."

Lanfranc shrugs, spreading his hands out to his sides so he looks like Christ Pantocrator, though older. "We must do our best with the tools God gives us. And it seems to me Odo's harlot might just be one such."

"How so?"

"Don't order him back. Let him stay in ignorance of what is going on in Kent..."

"Odo stays in ignorance of nothing for long. He has more spies about the place than even I do."

"But spies are of no use if their reports cannot get through. That can be arranged. In the meantime, perhaps a suggestion to my clergy that the drought signifies God's disapproval of Lord Odo's mistress, even that she has somehow bewitched him, or the weather, or both, might give the woman enough rope to hang herself."

"And you would have them preach such a thing to their congregations?" William thumps his fist on the table enthusiastically. "Splendour of God, old friend, I like it." Then, leaning towards Lanfranc, fixing him with a shrewd, wary gaze, he adds, "and you would keep my name out of it? I want Odo back in the tent pissing out not outside pissing in."

"It would be a matter of dogma, Your Grace, a matter of reminding our flock that what some of them may see as an an all-embracing church has become morally lax and reprehensible and is in grave need of reform." Lanfranc gives an ironic, implacable smile. "Church and state are not one and the same, are they? When it comes to the Word of God."

The Fall

Ascension to the Nativity of the Blessed Virgin Mary 1072

In Odo's new palace, Gytha is given apartments so spacious that she and Freya, wandering about soundlessly on thick turkey rugs, marvelling at the glazed windows with their deep, cushioned embrasures, agree neither of them has ever lived in anything to match them.

"Most houses aren't this big," says Freya, gazing at the painted ceiling of the bed chamber, in which Adam and Eve sit in naked bliss beneath the shade of the tree of knowledge, oblivious of the serpent coiled around its trunk, looking cunningly like bark.

"Most houses aren't as big as this bed." Gytha sits down on the edge of it, reluctant to disturb the embroidered coverlet thrown over the furs and quilts. She unpins her couvre-chef and removes the linen cap beneath it, while Freya pulls off her shoes. Tugging a strand of hair from her head, she knots it with her small, deft fingers and pushes it under the mattress. Freya, kneeling, with the mud splashed shoes in her lap, gives her a hard look. Brushing vigorously at the muddy hem of Gytha's gown, she says, "I hope his lordship's apartments aren't far away, or he'll never be able to find you in the dark." The two women giggle, unaware that there is some truth in Freya's apprehension.

Odo has never lived in this house, has never spent more than three or four weeks in it at a time. It has been built since the conquest of England, an unaffordable luxury before he acquired his English estates, and he does occasionally lose his bearings among its galleries and cloisters, its lobbies and anterooms leading through gilded doors to inner chambers ornamented to impress and enchant with treasures collected from all over the world. A bishop's palace decked out like the house of a Jew, some say. Odo is known to be a man of catholic tastes, delighted by objects of beauty and splendour, intrigued by what is rare or strange, and wealthy enough to pay handsomely for what takes his fancy. Merchants, pilgrims returning from Jerusalem or Compostela, speculative investors and ambitious thieves are never far from his door. He is buying paradise piecemeal, an ebony table here, a filigree censer there, a book of hours encased in ivory for his library, a crucifix studded with pink freshwater pearls to adorn the altar of one of his two private chapels.

He does not plan to remain long in Bayeux on this visit either. To his clergy he explains,

"I'm not really here. This is a private visit. I wish to keep business to the minimum." And his clergy are understanding. Some of these men have served the diocese since Bishop Hugh's time. They kept their counsel when the boy bishop was imposed upon them; at best, it was an honour to serve the duke's brother, at worst, unwise to protest. Most were pleasantly surprised by the lad. No saint, perhaps, but quick witted and eager to learn, shrewd, but compassionate in his judgements. As Abbot Robert of Saint-Vigor, much admired for his commentary on the Song of Songs, has said of his bishop, he shows his love of God in his love for the world God made. Which includes a love of luxury, of fine wine and falconry, good horses and the art of soldiering, and, from time to time, the love of a woman.

He takes Gytha to see his cathedral, walks with her up the nave whose arches still soar like the fingers of God into the open sky, so high that the men working above the clerestory and triforium, throwing across the roof trusses, look as though they are crawling across the blue face of heaven. Standing with their backs to the glittering slab of white marble destined to become the high altar, looking towards the west door and the rose window above it which, she thinks, empty of glass, looks like a giant pastry cutter, he bids her imagine the tapestry, stretched between the columns of the nave, lit by hundreds of candles, scented with incense, shivering a little in air vibrant with music. Complete.

Another thought comes to him from the same treasure house of the mind in which he keeps the tapestry. That he would like to make love to her here, in this petrified forest, to the accompaniment of the builders calling to one another and the booming, rhythmic songs of the serfs treading the wheel which hoists the crane, under the unseeing eyes of cherubim and gargoyles, the stone effigies of his parents, of John and Adeliza, and Adeliza's first husband, and the men who carried his crozier before he did. To doubly consecrate his church. To make a child dedicated to God.

He demands she sit for his master mason. He wants her to appear as the Magdalene at the foot of the Cross in the pieta to be carved on the front of the altar. She taunts him for his lack of originality.

"She is the woman most loved by Christ," he counters, "what more do you want?"

"I don't think they had a relationship quite like ours, though."

"No two human loves are ever the same. Christ was a man. It's only later commentators who invite us to believe in His humanity and at the same time deny that He ever laughed or drank wine or admired a pretty woman. *Homo est animal rationale, mortale, risus capax.*"

"What?"

"Man is a rational, mortal animal, capable of laughter."

"There's a true blasphemer hidden under all that episcopal purple, isn't there? Do you never worry that God is listening to you?" She plucks at his clothing with teasing fingers.

"You're tickling me," he says, catching hold of her hands and kissing her palms.

"D'you suppose Mary Magdalene used to tickle Jesus?"

"I'll set up a council to consider the question."

The sitting is to take place, not in the tracing house, but at the master mason's home, an old, but substantial, stone house close to the city walls.

"I have business to attend to," he tells her on the morning she is due to go there, "so Osbern will escort you. He knows the house well." And, curiously, Osbern smiles. She looks doubtfully from one to the other, suspicious of some joke at her expense.

"Shall I tell her, Osbern, or will you?"

They are sitting in the palace garden, having breakfasted outdoors in the hour before Prime. The day promises to be hot, but for now is pleasantly warm, the sun benevolent behind a haze of high cloud. Osbern has come to clear away the remains of the meal, lying between them on the stone bench in the middle of a large, triangular bed of white roses. Gytha throws a handful of breadcrumbs among the flowers, flapping her hands to ward off wood pigeons.

"No! That's for the little birds," she shouts. "They're such bullies. They all ought to be in a pie."

Odo laughs and pats her knee. "Always championing the underdog. Go and see about the horses, Osbern, we'll be along shortly."

"What is all this mystery about the mason's house, then?"

"Walk with me." He takes her arm, pressing it against his side so she can feel his heart beating against the back of her wrist, and leads her along one of the three paths crossing the rose bed, each built of thirty-three stones to represent the Trinity, across a square of camomile lawn which releases its apple sweet scent like a gift to their nostrils as they tread over it, along the edge of the west facing cloistered terrace where they often sit in the evenings.

"Osbern used to be a soldier, a very good one. The year of the French invasion, he was part of my personal bodyguard."

"What happened? Was he hurt?"

"No, I found out he was a skilled midwife."

"Now you're talking in riddles."

"The mason's house. It's where Adeliza used to live."

"Oh." She withdraws her arm from his.

"You mustn't mind. She hasn't lived there for a long time. She married again, a merchant from Rouen. But...John was born there. His mother was the widow of my last master mason. I suppose that's why I wanted you to see it."

"And yet you will not come with me? You send me with your servant. Who I think doesn't like me."

"It is his desire."

"And since when have the wishes of servants been your concern?"

"Osbern is different. He serves me, not out of loyalty to me or because I pay him well, but out of love for my son. He safeguards me for John's sake. You see, it was Osbern who brought John into the world."

They have reached the end of the terrace. Odo takes her hand to prevent her walking on towards the stables and they stand for a moment, awkwardly. He has never told the story of John's birth before, and he is afraid his words will be inadequate to convey the mystery of it, the mixture of fear and elation, the remembered, yet oddly unfamiliar image of himself cradling his son in his mail clad arms.

Gytha wishes he would not go on. She knows it is not his fault, he knows nothing about her children, the pain she knots into the hairs she tucks beneath their mattress. But somehow she expects him to understand and is irritable with him that he does not.

"Won't you be late?" she asks.

"For what? I have no-one to see, just accounts to go over, that sort of thing." He sits down on the edge of the terrace and takes a deep breath, savouring the perfume of camomile and sun-warmed stone. "I was twenty," he begins, "I had Henry of France encamped on my doorstep and a message from William ringing in my ears that

I was to hold Bayeux at all costs. One half of me knew it would be straightforward. William had already cut a swathe through Henry's forces and their supply lines were stretched to breaking point. But the other half was in a spin. I hadn't the vaguest idea how to conduct a siege, every word I had ever read on the subject had gone right out of my head, and all I could think of was Adeliza, in that house right under the city wall with her child – my child – due any day." He pauses, looking up at her with that self-deprecating smile of his, then continues,

"The second time I lost my place during prayers for the safety of the city, my chaplain, who was a practical man, told me to send some good men to fetch her to the palace and then put her out of my mind till we had dealt with the French."

"I sent Osbern and a couple of others, but before they could return, Henry had launched his assault. And, thank God, I was busy enough with our defence to stop thinking about her until the French were beaten off and I went out to inspect the damage, where one of the other men found me and begged me to come straight to the mason's house. It seemed to take forever to get there, the streets were full of people celebrating, all stopping me to thank me, press wine on me and so forth. I was…I felt…as though I was the only man in the world ever to have achieved something so extraordinary as becoming a father, and at the same time ashamed. Because all these people believed I was their hero and really, I had done nothing. Henry had brought about his own defeat entirely.

"Anyway, I found Adeliza safe and well, sitting up in bed nursing her child, and Osbern beside her feeding her a broth of fennel which, he told me with great assurance, would help bring down her milk."

Until now, Gytha has listened to him without comment. Now she gives a curt nod of affirmation.

"It was the strangest thing," he goes on, misled by her silence. "Adeliza put the baby in my arms and when I looked at his face, I…recognised him. I can't put it any better, even though I know it's nonsense." Lost in his memories, his senses once again filled with the scent of his son, clean linen, milky breath, the perfection of his ears and fingernails, his lashless eyelids and the tiny, moist sound of him sucking his bottom lip in his sleep, he does not notice Gytha turn away, digging her nails into her palms.

"It was your idea, wasn't it? The mason didn't ask for me to go there, you wanted it."

"Well, yes, I admit it would please me."

"I can't go."

"Why? Because of Adeliza? I've told you, she's been in Rouen for years."

"Not Adeliza. I wish you would understand. It's John. I can't go because of John." She starts to walk away from him, in the direction of the stables. She longs to flee to her own room, but is unsure of being able to find it.

"John?" He follows her, attempts to take hold of her hand but she twists it out of his grasp. "Gytha." Lengthening his stride, he overtakes her easily as she crosses the stableyard.

"You may unsaddle that horse," she tells the groom holding her mare beside the mounting block, "there has been a change of plan." The groom remains motionless until Odo repeats her instruction; her French is still incomprehensible.

"Gytha." Hands on her shoulders this time, bearing down, fingers digging into the web of flesh beneath the bone. "Stop. This has something to do with your children, hasn't it?" His tone is that of a man to whom a mystery has been revealed. "Are you afraid we shall not have any?"

"Please don't ask me about my children."

"Because you mustn't be. I know I've never made any secret of the fact that I should like more children, but I won't love you any the less if God sees fit to deny me."

"Oh well, if you and God are content, why should I worry?" She scratches the black nose of a stallion, tethered on his own in the far corner of the yard. "Are you enjoying yourself, horse? We humans are a pretty spectacle, aren't we?"

Odo stands next to her, arms hanging helpless at his sides. "Tell me, Gytha," he pleads, "tell me what happened?"

"I can't talk about it, not even to you."

"Careful," he warns as she begins to scratch the horse harder. "He has an awful temper, this one. Don't make him bite you." He summons a careless sounding laugh to conceal his hurt. "You are honoured. He doesn't usually let anyone near him except his groom. I keep him for stud. He's a pure bred Turkey, a gift from the Patriarch of Alexandria."

"Do you not place your soul in peril, accepting gifts from an excommunicate?" Her tone is sulky, but there is a spark of curiosity.

"Just because he believes one thing about the Trinity and I another doesn't mean we should fall out over important matters like horse breeding. I call the horse Filioque, to remind me that good may come even of schism."

She smiles, but she still feels the souls of her children plucking at the frayed threads of her heart. "Odo, what do you believe?"

"I believe in God, the Father Almighty, Maker of heaven and earth..."

Now she laughs. It is not his fault they died; priest he may be, but he cannot take all men's sins and shortcomings on himself, and he cannot bring her children back. Go, she tells them, sit quietly, behave yourselves until I can be with you again. The horse, as if jealous, tosses its head, butting Odo in the chest. "Be serious," she orders. "You are never serious. Even the horse thinks so."

"Alright. I believe God made me to love you. Seriously. Now perhaps the damned horse will not knock me over."

She does agree to sit for the master mason, though in his tracing house rather than at his home, an arrangement more suitable to them both as the light is better there. While the master prepares his sketching tools, she occupies herself leafing through a pile of drawings on his work table.

"Your son?" she asks in her hesitant French, pausing over the image of a round faced boy with a shock of hair falling into one eye, and a broad grin which reveals the absence of both top front teeth. He must be six or seven years of age, she thinks.

"Master John," replies the mason, glancing over her shoulder, "just before he was sent away."

"He is not very like his father."

The mason shrugs. "Might be by now. Boys change." He taps his own front teeth. "These will have grown for one thing. He hasn't been back here in years, now my lord bishop has so many commitments in England."

She lays the drawing aside with a polite smile. Though she understood nothing of the master's reply except the word *Angleterre*, his disapproving tone was unmistakable. And the gesture with the teeth was not polite. Perhaps he dislikes the English, or perhaps the fact that his bishop has a son, in which case...

"Are you ready to begin?" she asks, suddenly anxious for the sitting to be over as quickly as possible. The master looks surprised but nods his assent, then shakes his head vehemently as she turns her head to the light. Picking up the sketch of John from the table, he places it in her lap where she is sitting close to the open north side of the tracing house, the pure, pale spring light bathing one side of her face while the other remains in soft shadow.

"This is better," he explains slowly. "Your expression is right when you look at the picture. So...look, please."

The master takes the finished drawing to Odo with a light heart. It is the best he has done, the agony of loss and powerlessness so perfectly captured in that slight, concentrated frown, the sad, grave curve of the bowed neck. She is, he comments without a trace of irony, the perfect Magdalene at the foot of the Cross. Odo agrees, though he looks more exasperated than gratified.

He takes her outside the city walls to the handsome new abbey he has built to the glory of Saint Vigor, on land which still bears the scars of forest clearance but where he can already see, in his mind's eye, lawns and a herb garden and white cattle grazing.

She is among the congregation gathered to witness he and Abbot Robert bestow their blessing on a party of knights setting out for Jerusalem to do penance for the murder of a neighbour's two sons during a border dispute. In Chapter she sees a young oblate, no more than eight or nine years old, handed over to the monastery by his parents; when he is presented to Odo, Odo raises him from his knees and kisses his pale cheeks, causing the boy's father to puff out his chest like a fighting cock. A murmur runs around the chapterhouse in response to his unusual gesture, and he glances up as if to quell it, but she knows he is looking, not at the assembled community, but at the fresco behind them, depicting him, baculum in hand, conducting the defence of Bayeux from the top of the city wall. He is measuring the distance from schoolboy to hero, son to father.

After Chapter, he shows her his tomb in a side chapel of the abbey church, dedicated to his patron saint, whose familiar image gazes down sternly from a niche in the wall beside the altar. The tomb stands before the altar, finely wrought of the same pale Caen stone he used to build his atelier in Canterbury, its sides decorated with friezes, only the lid left plain, waiting for the effigy of the bishop himself, the unimaginable postscript to this unforeseeable life. Stilled heart, petrified breath. He takes her hand.

"I recognise him," she says, pointing to a relief of Turpin, four spears sticking out of his body, decapitating a fantastically bearded infidel.

"You know the Song of Roland, then. I always thought it a very Norman preference."

"Strangely enough, it was a great favourite of King Harold. I have heard it sung many times, though I understand it poorly. But who is this?" she asks, indicating a muscular carving on the front of the tomb depicting a haloed saint slaying a dragon.

"It's Saint Vigor himself. He was a dragon slayer."

"It makes me think. The Godwinson family emblem was a dragon."

"And are there not dragons to be found in Wales?"

"I believe so, My Lord, though I have never been there."

"Well, if there are, I dare say my brother's armies will make short work of them."

"I think Welsh dragons may be more easily tamed by kisses than the sword, My Lord."

"You think the saint should kiss the dragon?"

"If he dares. It would take more courage than to slay him."

"Gytha?"

"Yes?"

"Will you lie with me here? When we are both dead? 'Flesh of my flesh, bone of my bones'?"

Standing on tiptoe, she kisses his cheek. "Don't be maudlin. What a thing to think about on such a beautiful day."

Conteville is an old house, though house is not the right word for it. It is a muddled agglomeration of buildings, some wood framed, some stone, a rough patchwork of tow-coloured thatch, red tiles, dark moss and buttery clay interspersed with shadowy courtyards and sudden patches of garden. Odo reveals it to her, leading her along twisting passages, in and out of doors which then seem to disappear, like the doors to a labyrinth, with the eager delight of a boy showing off a treasure of conkers and pheasant feathers and odd-shaped stones. He shows her the irregular row of notches on the kitchen doorpost which mark his and his brothers' and sisters' growth, pointing out with a pride not entirely ironic that, actually, he is about half an inch taller than William. And the lumpy patch of ground in the orchard where generations of de Conteville dogs and falcons lie beneath a miniature forest of mouldering wooden crosses.

"Full funeral Masses, the lot of them," he tells her. "Such an advantage, having a bishop in the family."

On a morning of high winds and driving rain, he leads her up a winding stair to a small, octagonal room at the top of the lookout tower.

"What's this?" The room is bare, except for a narrow bed whose moth-eaten hangings look as though spiders have attempted to darn them with cobwebs, and a plain linen chest which reminds her of the dormitory in the atelier at Canterbury. He does not answer immediately and his expression, when she glances at him to prompt his reply, is ruefully humorous. "I know. This is the bed where you lost your virginity."

He shakes his head. "This is where Agatha spent the night before her wedding."

"Her wedding? But…"

"Precisely. Come here." He leads her to one of the seven arrow slits cut into the walls, one overlooking a patch of muddy ground between the house and the moat. Rain blows through it, condensing into a steady trickle of water down the wall underneath. "Down there, there used to be a brew house. A small person could squeeze through this window, drop on to the brew house roof, then down onto the barrels stacked outside, and then to the ground. And if you could swim, well…"

"So you knew all along. And you helped her?"

"She told me. Wrote to me, in fact, when William made the match. Some man with land on the Breton border, married a girl from Anjou in the end. I dare say it still rankles with William."

"I dare say."

"But I couldn't…You see, I already knew how it felt to be forced into William's mould. He still had Muriel and Mathilde at his disposal, and Robert of course. I didn't see why Agatha shouldn't get away, if the thought of marriage was so distressing to her. I tried to persuade William she had a vocation. I was wonderfully eloquent, almost believed it myself by the time I'd finished, but William would have none of it. He'd had to come back from Flanders to sort matters out, right in the middle of his negotiations for Matilda's hand, so he wasn't in the best of tempers."

"I can imagine." She clears her throat. "My lord and lady used to make some very unflattering jokes about…the King's…courtship methods. Is it true he favoured a horsewhip?"

Odo laughs. "Is there no-one from whom that is hidden?"

"You must remember Lord Harold was family. One of his brothers was married to the Queen's sister."

"Yes, well, apparently that was all Agatha's fault as well. When William discovered her escape, he was so mad even the ride back to Baldwin of Flanders' court wasn't enough to calm him. And then Matilda refused him again, and made the mistake of raising his bastardy as her reason. So he clouted her with his riding whip, which appeared to do what no amount of presents or flattery or orders from her father could achieve, and she agreed to have him."

"So really, he has cause to be grateful to you and Agatha."

"It did help to bring him round. He has never known the truth. He still believes Agatha was called to God, and, being William, he sees it all as part of God's plan for him. He doesn't understand why she agreed to come to England to oversee the tapestry, or why she refused to stand for election as Abbess when the old one died. Maybe those bits are part of God's plan for me."

A gust of wind buffets the tower, whining through the narrow windows, dislodging some of the cobwebs from the bed posts.

"Let's go down." Gytha shivers. "I'm not sure God approves of us second guessing His plans like this."

"It'll be fine this afternoon, you'll see. It always is when the wind's in this direction. I shall take you to visit my old nurse."

She is an ancient woman, small and hard as a walnut, with seamed lips folded over toothless gums so that her smile, which is ready and frequent, looks like a row of untidy stitching. It is hard to imagine her wizened body could ever have nourished a child. Her flat chest beneath the coarse, shapeless garment she wears makes Gytha acutely aware of her own body, of the ache in her womb with its sewn up mouth, of her breasts which her lover suckles in the insatiable hunger of his passion the way he used to suckle this old woman.

Odet, she calls him, still using his childhood nickname, and shows no surprise, no pleasure or alarm, at all the adventures that have befallen him. He might be a bishop and the brother of a king, but to her he is still the boy who, scratched and sweating, wielded a scythe beside the villagers every harvest, made solemn visits with his parents on the occasions of births and deaths and broke his collarbone twice in one year falling off his pony. She tells, at least as Odo translates her tale, how Guy, her son, Odo's foster brother, spiked Odo's cider one harvest supper, and how he was sick all over the priest when the man tried to take him home, slung across the shoulders of his mule. And another occasion when he took a fledgling hawk into church, hidden in his clothes, but the bird escaped and shat on the altar cross and the priest had to consult the bishop about the need for a rededication. And look at him now, she says, gesturing with her clawed, arthritic hand, tonsure, crucifix, amethyst and all.

"Does she realise who I am?" Gytha asks Odo when their visit is over and they are walking back to the house, across the grass common around which the village is built. He nods a greeting to a woman tethering a goat, stops to admire a saddleback sow in the charge of a small, dusty boy carrying a dead rat tied to a stick.

"Most certainly," he replies. "That's why she was so anxious to make sure you know who I am."

At Pentecost he preaches in that same church, though thanks to his generosity, the old statue of the Virgin no longer has to suffer the indignity of rain dripping on to her through a hole in the roof, wearing a groove in her cheek down which the water flowed like tears, and the altar cross in question has been replaced by a much more impressive ornament of chased silver set with garnets and lapis lazuli. She cannot understand what he says to his congregation, because he speaks in French, but she sees the way their eyes follow his every move as he crosses and recrosses the space before the altar, makes gestures of head or hands for emphasis, his body dedicated to the message he wants to convey, his brow wreathed with flowers to signify the descent of the Holy Spirit. Several times he makes them laugh, and when he goes among them to exchange the kiss of peace they crowd around him, enmeshing him in their love, holding him fast in his place.

They sleep in his parents' bed, the bed in which he was conceived and born, in which his mother laid out the body of her husband, and was in her turn prepared for burial by her daughters. It is the bed in which Robert spent his wedding night and to which Odo crawled for comfort on the eve of his departure for Bec, his mother stroking his curls until his father, sensing an extra presence beneath the quilts, kicked him out and sent him back to the pallet he shared with Robert at the other end of the chamber, telling him to stop snivelling like a girl. And lying next to him, their limbs and nightclothes entangled in an effigy of their passion, listening to bats squeak and the ghostly conversations of owls, the rustle of mice in the stack of pallets kept for visiting kin and honoured guests, Gytha too is seduced by a sense of belonging.

They lead the life of a vicomte and his lady, riding and hawking, practising at the butts, making and receiving visits from neighbours. They hold a feast, at which the men stay up all night playing dice, and a boar hunt during which they lose a young de Conteville cousin who returns long after dark with leaves and brambles in his hair, swearing he has seen a fairy in the woods. They do not sleep together on Wednesdays or Fridays or the eve of festivals. Odo tours the estate with Robert's steward, viewing frankpledge, updating the rolls, noting repairs to be made, births and deaths among the villein families likely to affect the number of days' labour due to their lord.

When Lammas comes, the villagers celebrate with fire-leaping and the distribution of loaves made from the first barley, and the consumption of heroic quantities of liquor made from last year's crop. Gytha pleads with him to join in, but he shakes his head, fiddling his amethyst ring around his finger, and confines himself to remarking that there will be a fine crop of babies presented for baptism come spring. The night is close and she cannot sleep so, wrapping herself in her dressing gown she goes outside and stands looking across the moat at the shadows leaping up the bleached mud walls of the cottages, dancing to the relentless rhythm of drums and an eerie, high pitched singing. The fire flares and sinks back in showers of sparks; laughter gusts then dies; voices surge into song and as suddenly fade away.

Gytha's heart drums in her chest, her bare feet tingle with remembered steps, she is dizzy with scents of cow parsley and wild garlic and hot earth. The goddess sends her a memory, of Lammas in the last year of King Edward's reign, of watching Harold and his two younger brothers, Gyrth and Leofwine, leaping the fire, flashing white grins at the women, their long hair alive with lights of tawny and gold and redcurrant. It seems to her now that they were like the comet crossing the night sky, from the dark disgrace of Harold's journey to Normandy to the dark, damp earth where the remains of all three now lie. A brief, sparkling trajectory of glamour. Not real. She turns her back on the celebrations and returns indoors.

"Now harvest is over," he mutters sleepily, turning to put his arms around her as she climbs back into bed, "I think we might plan a trip to Liege, to see John."

Fruit picking begins; in the kitchens, when she is not tending Fulk's burnt feet, Freya supervises the serving women as they clean bottles and cut fine linen sieves for preserving; in the woods, the lovers feed each other blackberries and lick the rich, dark juices from one another's lips. They bring home baskets of elderberries and sloes for wine-making, and in every barn the cider press is cleaned down, greased, and set up to await the bitter apples for which, each autumn, Norman farmers do battle with legions of wasps. It is not so different from home, remarks Gytha to Freya as they sit in the last of the afternoon sun, outside the kitchen house, stoning plums. Freya hands a plum to Thecla, who throws it for a passing wolfhound pup, and smiles.

In the evenings, unless they have company, she and Odo often dine alone, in what used to be his mother's solar, while the sun sets beyond the open window shutters, staining the moat silver rose. Gytha fishes the moat when she has the opportunity, sitting on the jetty, thinking of Agatha and her desperate swim. When darkness falls and the lamps have been lit, Odo attempts to teach her to play chess, or they sing part songs to Turold's accompaniment. Odo is surprised by the quality of her voice, high and true, but fragile, as though it comes from some other source than her speaking voice, which is deep and slightly husky.

On other evenings, she does her needlework and he simply watches her, seeing in the angle of her head, the arc of her needle as she pulls it up through the fabric, the woman he first saw in the atelier at Canterbury, in the dark dress and white cap, mimicking Agatha's monasticism. He is touched and amused that she darns his chausses and patches his shirts, although he does not wear the mended clothes; he gives them to Osbern and tells him to be discreet about where he distributes them. Their talk is domestic, inconsequential. They discuss the life of the estate, the forthcoming visit to John, for whom Gytha is embroidering a set of shirts, and their plans for Winterbourne when they return.

Late one afternoon near the Feast of Saint Augustine, they emerge from a woodland ride into a broad water meadow. The sun is low, spilling apricot light across a narrow band of clear sky between the meadow and a mass of cloud the colour of Toledo steel. Rain has fallen, and the standing water in the meadow forms patches of luminous gold from which grass and wild flowers emerge as delicate silhouettes. They stop to admire the view, and a family of storks grazing, rising and falling with great, slow flappings of wings and an occasional splash. With their narrow beaks and thin legs trailing, the birds look unfinished, skeletons only half fleshed out. Gytha laughs at their antics.

"D'you know," says Odo, "when I was little, my mother told me that new babies were left by storks in the well, ready for us to fish out. So whenever we knew she was expecting another child, I'd spend ages peering down the well to see if I could see it. Hoping it'd be a boy. As I could never see the babies, I started to believe they must be transparent, and only take on the colour of flesh when exposed to the air. Like those stones that are translucent under water but turn opaque when they're dry.

"Then I got to worrying about families who didn't have their own well. If the babies were left in a communal well, how did they know which ones belonged to who? I expect she wished she'd told me the truth in the end, she must have got so fed up with my questions."

"Did she have a lot of children?"

"The five of us living, and two others, two boys. One died at birth, but Richard I just remember. He came between Muriel and Mathilde. He died when he was about two. He fell into the kitchen fire."

She reaches for his hand, prising his fingers from the pommel of his saddle. "I was an only child. I had some cousins, boys, fishermen, but most of the time I used to talk to my doll, till I dropped her in the fire. She was straw, with her eyes and mouth stitched in wool and a blue dress. She burned so fast I couldn't even think to put my hand in to pull her out. I can remember it so clearly, the way her mouth curled up and shrivelled, as if she was smiling, then crying, one after the other. It's an odd sort of coincidence, isn't it? Do you think it has any meaning?"

"Gytha," he says, ignoring her question, as the storks finish feeding and flap idly away into the setting sun whose fiery face is streaked with wisps of dark cloud, "please tell me about your children. Before we go to Liege. I do so want the visit to go well."

She looks at him for a long time without replying, moved by his pleading, his concern for his son, feeling as though she has never seen him properly before. As though, in all the time they have been together, her eyes have been out of focus, seeing double, seeing a blur. She studies his face, committing to her heart's memory all the features she thought she knew but did not, his sanguine complexion, his wide mouth and short nose and curly hair which make her think of a Roman bust, the disconcerting softness of his eyes with their curling lashes. She finds herself wondering how much John resembles him by now.

She notes the tiny, unconscious adjustments his body makes in response to the movements of his horse, and the fact that the nail on the little finger of the hand she is holding is broken. She considers the damaged bone in his left wrist, the way he attempts to disguise it by wearing bracelets, whose opulence usually only serves to draw closer attention to it. Today's is silver, studded with great lozenges of polished amber. She disentangles her fingers from his. It has been so long since she spoke any of their names aloud, she is not sure her voice will be able to form the right sounds.

"Matthew, Mark, Luke and Johanna," she begins, "not very original. We didn't have a lot of time to think of names. Mark was the most poorly. The midwife had to baptise him, though that was one good thing. I couldn't see the others baptised because I hadn't been churched."

Odo has never considered this before, the feelings of mothers when their infants are borne away for baptism. How had Adeliza felt, in the solitude made all the more absolute by the knowledge that, as her son was to receive his baptism during the Mass to give thanks for the city's deliverance from the French, almost everyone in Bayeux would witness it except she herself?

"He lived less than an hour," Gytha continues. "He was so tiny. His skin and bones were so thin you could see his heart beating. Fluttering, like a little bird in his rib cage.

"Johanna lived the longest. Four days. She had this determined look. I used to watch her while she was feeding. She never blinked, hardly moved, except for those little jaws working away. I thought I was willing her to live, but afterwards, I wondered. You see, I was never...happy with Adam, the way I am with you. I couldn't...in bed...it didn't work. So I wonder if it was my fault they were all so weak. Johanna died very quietly. I woke up in the night to feed her and there she was, cold beside me, a little stiff bundle between me and Adam." And how my breasts ached, and how quietly I wept for her, so as not to disturb my husband.

Odo, who had deliberately looked away while she was speaking, as he would when hearing confession, turns back to her. She is staring at her hands, fiddling with the reins of her horse. Her head is uncovered but her hair, fastened in two loose braids, shields her face from him. He looks for evidence that she is weeping, for sniffs or shaking shoulders, and finds none. He wishes she were crying, then he would know what to do.

"But I loved them, Odo," she says with sudden vehemence. "I do love them. I can still feel them. Here." She lays a hand over her belly. "They kick me sometimes. And I've kept locks of their hair. They all had dark hair like mine. So I can stay in contact with them. I worry. I mean, how do they manage without me? Heaven must be such a busy place. So many souls. Who knows they're special?"

Odo dismounts. "Come here," he says, lifting her from her saddle and folding her in his arms. He holds her for a long time, until the sun has dropped below a starless horizon and the water underfoot has soaked through their shoes. A fierce anguish grips him, yet he holds her tenderly, as though he is in danger of crushing her.

Then he lifts her on to his own horse and rides home with her cradled in the crook of his arm, her head against his shoulder, her breath warm against his throat, the mare's reins tied to his pommel. She does not cry; she is so still and quiet he thinks she may have fallen asleep. Though when they arrive back at Conteville she dismounts without assistance and stands, smiling up at him as he unties her horse. In answer to his anxious enquiry, she assures him she is perfectly well and will go, if he will excuse her, to dress for dinner.

"You'll need to hurry, madam," says Freya, who is in the bedchamber laying out Gytha's clothes. "You're late back this evening. Had his lordship forgotten there are guests?"

"Probably. Freya, I need your help." At first she had felt simply relieved to have told him, anyone, about her children, wondering how she could have been so afraid to do it sooner. It is an ordinary story; all women lose children, as his mother had done, and hers, and no doubt

Adeliza and the old nurse, and perhaps Freya. Think of Leofgeat, and the others who die. At least the winding sheet, neatly folded in her linen chest at the beginning of each pregnancy, had remained there, to do service for Adam, in the end. What arrogance had possessed her, that she imagined her experience to be any more painful than any other woman's? Now she is almost delirious with joy. Her happiness fizzes and ferments inside her, she is drunk with it, with him, alight with the revelation that she loves him. She really loves him; whatever life brings, she is in it with him, for good or ill. "Quickly, before his lordship comes in from the stables."

He likes to see the horses bedded down for the night. Fulk complains of it endlessly. Does his lordship think him incompetent? He has been around horses all his life. Fulk prefers it when his lordship has less time on his hands to play the peasant.

"What am I to do, madam?"

"I want you to help me lift the mattress. I want to get rid of the knotted hairs."

"What's happened? Has the charm not worked?"

"As far as I know it has," says Gytha, taking hold of the bottom corner of the mattress. "I've changed my mind, that's all."

"About time." Freya grasps the top corner and together they lift the mattress clear of the bed frame, though it is heavy and ungainly, flopping back down every time they attempt to wedge it on its side. Eventually, Gytha holds up her corner while Freya brushes her sleeve in wide arcs across the base of the bed, then Freya lifts her corner and Gytha sweeps, raising clouds of dust and feathers and knotted strands of black hair which float to the floor, unnoticed among the rushes and lavender sprigs. As they pummel the mattress back into the box frame and smooth the bed clothes, Freya remarks,

"I have a tincture of rose petals, with a few other bits and pieces mixed in. Ask him to anoint you with it, breasts and women's parts. It brings a most intense pleasure."

"What else is in it?"

"A little laurel and galingale, cloves, nutmeg."

"It sounds more like something to eat."

"It sharpens the appetite, madam." The women exchange conspiratorial smiles.

"His lordship will be up to dress shortly." Osbern, who makes no secret of his opinion that the living conditions at Conteville are not up to the standard he and Lord Odo are accustomed to, bustles into the room with a velvet surcoat draped over his arms and lays it on the bed. His hard eyes dart suspiciously between the laughing women.

"You may leave us, Osbern, I will attend his lordship," says Gytha, taking pains to make herself understood. Osbern tuts softly as he withdraws, followed by Freya.

"I'll bring you the tincture, madam."

"Thank you, Freya."

The master of the house comes late to table, but his mood is so charming and expansive, and his hospitality so generous, that he is quickly forgiven by his guests.

Odo is out when the monk from Christ Church arrives, and Gytha spends a difficult hour with him, watching him sit, then stand and pace about, all the time giving her sidelong glances which make no attempt to hide his embarrassment or disapproval. Eventually she excuses herself and takes refuge in the kitchen with Freya and the children. Odo finds her there, sitting at the long table in the centre of the room with Thecla in her lap. Thecla is pummelling small rounds of pastry with her fat fists; both of them are covered in flour and Gytha has a smudge of some dark purple fruit juice on her cheek. The scene makes him laugh, but there is more to his good humour than delight in domestic harmony.

"Freya," he says, "I want you to pack for your mistress. We are returning to England as soon as we can find a ship. I want to set out for Bayeux before nightfall. You will all follow."

"What's happened? What about our visit to John? Is it that monk? Did he bring news?" asks Gytha.

"He most certainly did. Excellent news. But I'm afraid it means John will have to wait."

Odo has just seen the man on his way, unable to persuade him to accept any refreshment in that house, only by appealing to his compassion for God's lesser creatures able to press a fresh mule upon him. Nor had it been easy to get the man to talk at first, though once he started, what he had to say came out in a torrent.

"I cannot keep silent any longer, Your Reverence," he finally began, standing before Odo in the small room adjoining the great hall to which men with private business to discuss are in the habit of withdrawing after dinner. His hands trembled and his right eye was afflicted with a tic, improbably resembling a conspiratorial wink. "I have come straight to you from Worcester where I was cataloguing the library for my lord Archbishop. I made up my mind and took ship from Gloucester."

"Sit, man, and tell me what led you to make such a journey." Odo leaned back in his chair, arms folded, a mild, smiling expression on his face.

"It is the Winchester Council, Your Reverence." Looking about him for somewhere suitable to sit, the monk drew up a stool and perched on the edge of it, his knees pressed together like a girl's, a slim leather satchel clutched in his lap.

"Go on."

"The papal letters the Archbishop produced to support his claim to the three bishoprics. They were...they were forgeries, Your Reverence."

Odo's smile intensified. "God bless my soul. And how do you know this, brother..?"

"Ealdred, Your Reverence, Ealdred of Malden."

"Malden? That is near to Colchester, is it not?"

"It is, Your Reverence, though I was given to Christ Church as a small boy, in the year Archbishop Robert fled to Rome."

"Then you have seen many changes there. But we stray from the point, Brother Ealdred. You were telling me about these forged documents."

"Yes, Your Reverence. I forged them."

Odo laughed, slapping his thigh. "By heaven, that's good. That's very good. And did Archbishop Lanfranc know what you had done?"

"No, Your Reverence, he would not have countenanced it, but I felt, in all humility, Your Reverence, that the dignity of my house was under threat and that…"

"Naturally. I understand. Christ Church has been your home all your life. You are loyal, you love your community, your family of brothers. You did not wish to see it impoverished by some nouveau riche such as myself."

The shutters were closed and the room stuffy. Ealdred's sweating face paled to the exact sheen of the underbelly of a trout, the watery white beneath the flash of silver as you pull it from a stream. "That's not for me to say, Your Reverence," he muttered.

"There is no need. I have said it myself, more than once. But tell me, if your conscience troubled you, why not go to Archbishop Lanfranc and tell him what you had done? Why come to me?"

"Because I do not like what the Archbishop is doing at Christ Church, Your Reverence. His reforms are too stringent. Many of the older members of the community are upset by them. He is trying to make us…uniform. In the scriptorium, for example, we are obliged to conform to Norman practice in calligraphy and illumination. We are losing our own ways. You, on the other hand, employ English embroiderers, and are known to be a benefactor of Saint Augustine's, where the old ways are allowed to continue. And I am told you can speak our vernacular. His Grace the Archbishop has no English to speak of. And besides, you are the wronged party. And besides, also, such letters may well have existed before we lost all our records in the fire during the second Advent of King William's reign."

"The Archbishop's English may be wanting. Between you and me his French leaves something to be desired as well, but being Italian, he is a great Latinist. Have you considered that he may already know what you did and have chosen to disregard it?"

"It is possible, I suppose, though unlikely, I think. I am a scribe. I copy manuscripts for our library. God has granted me great skill in calligraphy. The Archbishop is a fine writer, in the intellectual sense, but he is no calligrapher."

"Also, he is an honest man, a scrupulously honest man." No, there could be no doubting Lanfranc's sincere belief in Canterbury's right to the three bishoprics and the other disputed properties; he would be incapable of supporting what he knew to be a lie with such conviction.

"Well, Ealdred. And you are prepared to give evidence before a council of your trickery?"

"I have brought a written deposition with me, Your Reverence." Ealdred withdrew a folded parchment from his satchel and handed it to Odo, who scanned it briefly then placed on a low table beside his chair.

"Good, although you may still be required to give evidence in person."

"I had hoped for your protection, Your Reverence."

"The only way I could protect you, Ealdred, would be if I punished you myself for your transgression. I cannot give anyone grounds to believe that I connived in your crime."

"I understand that, Your Reverence, but I do not think I can return to Christ Church."

"Very well. You know I could have your eyes put out for this?"

Ealdred swallowed hard.

"But you have done me a service, so I shall be lenient. Instead, you will lose only your right hand, the instrument of your sin, as Saint Matthew tells us, and then I will arrange for you to be taken into the community of Saint-Vigor outside Bayeux, where you will be cared for and suitable work found for you."

"But Your Reverence," said Ealdred, sounding ashamed, "I am left handed."

420

"Ealdred, Ealdred." Odo stood up and clapped his hands on Ealdred's narrow shoulders, feeling the young monk flinch at his touch. Had Ealdred dared to look, he would have seen that Odo was grinning broadly. "Your honesty does you great credit. Besides, I have a special affection for left handed people. You may go with my blessing. Take my greeting to Abbot Robert at Saint-Vigor and ask him, has he had any more thoughts about the Queen of Sheba's legs."

"Your Reverence?"

"He will know what I mean. Now, get out of my sight before I change my mind."

Gytha does not wait for the household at Conteville to be packed up ready for the return to England, but goes immediately, with Odo and a small military escort headed by Fulk. Having, as she explains it to herself, found him at last, she cannot bear to be parted from him, even for a few days. What if he were to meet with some accident on the road, or be shipwrecked? He could be hurt, or killed, and she would not know, would not be there to nurse him or say goodbye, or accompany him into the afterlife. As he has become so precious to her he has also come to seem endangered, the earthly space he occupies precarious and rare.

There is a dreamlike quality to the progress of their journey, in the way in which nothing impedes them. Great men such as Odo can cut swathes through the world like Moses cleaving the Red Sea. Changes of horses appear as if by magic. A ship is found which can carry them to Rochester within an hour of their arrival in Bayeux, catching the evening tide which might have timed itself expressly for the bishop's convenience, and the wind, though it carries a cold breath of autumn, is brisk and south westerly, blowing straight on to the Kent coast.

The devil, as always, is in the detail. The ship, a cog carrying Flemish wool and wine from Burgundy, and a white bull tethered in the hull, is shallow keeled and overloaded, so that despite the tail wind their progress is slow and accompanied by a yaw sickening even to Gytha.

She dozes fitfully, in a palpable nightmare of seaspray gluing her clothes to her chilled and aching limbs, the feeling that even her stomach, her veins and her head are full of salt water, sloshing and swaying around her body. The mournful lowing of the bull is like a bass note to the delirious music in her head, and the smell of its shit is everywhere.

When she opens her eyes it is to the baleful, yellow gaze of a remote, three quarter moon and Odo, incessantly, irritatingly energetic, oblivious to seasickness as he dictates letters to a scribe who shields his tablet with his cloak, or rehearses the arguments he is going to put to Lanfranc and considers from which garrisons he can most efficiently move troops into the disputed areas to back them up, or plans uses for the land and income which will be restored to him as a result of Brother Ealdred's conscience.

They make landfall around dawn. Gytha sits her horse in an exhausted stupor while Odo dispatches messengers to Thomas of York, and the bishops of Worcester, Lichfield and Dorchester, and to the castellan at Rochester Castle explaining his haste to set out for Canterbury. In the cold, clear morning she dreams of soft mattresses and the enveloping warmth of her lover's arms. One of the soldiers brings her a mug of small beer and some rye bread.

"Has My Lord breakfasted?" she asks, staring at the food and drink as though she is not quite sure what they are for.

"He tends to forget such matters when this mood is on him," the man replies, not unkindly, though Gytha hears his words as a reproach. You don't know him, the soldier seems to say, not as we do, in this man's world of action and politicking.

"I am not hungry."

"He won't stop again before Canterbury."

"Nevertheless."

The soldier shrugs and, grumbling under his breath, takes the food away. Gytha looks up the beach to where Odo stands at the centre of a flurry of activity, scribes squatting in the wet sand with their tablets balanced on their knees, messengers already mounted, their horses dancing and flicking their ears nervously after the confinement of the sea crossing. He himself is uncharacteristically still, reading something, his attention concentrated regardless of all that is going on around him.

She looks away, thoroughly awake again now, at the men unloading the ship, rolling barrels up the beach under the watchful eye of the harbour master and the white bull, at a small shoal of fishing boats putting out into a sea like a sheet of pale yellow silk. The wind has dropped and the sun just below the horizon floods the cloudless sky with the same luminous primrose. A fine day, thank God, her clothes will soon be dry and her bones warmed. She slips her feet out of her stirrups and flexes them, trying to get their circulation going.

"Witch!"

So close she feels, rather than hears, the accusation, how the shout makes the air vibrate seconds before her startled horse rears, staggers backwards and loses its balance as its hind legs crash into a stack of barrels. She is thrown clear and lands, winded but unharmed, on her back on the beach. As she lies trying to catch her breath she sees, out of the corner of her eye, a shadow, all bony, etiolated limbs, a dark skeleton, flit away up the beach and disappear among the alleys between the warehouses lining the shore.

Then Odo is kneeling beside her, cradling her head in his arm.

"Deep, steady breaths, that's it. Does it hurt when you breathe? Did you hit your head?"

"The mare is done for," says another voice. "Must've broken its leg when it fell." And she becomes aware of an unearthly screaming and the sun breasting the horizon, its beams seeming to fracture against her eyeballs, then silence, blue darkness, a sighing sleep.

"She's fainted. Fulk, stay with her. I'll see to the horse myself."

He hates this, but he feels responsible for the little mare; he broke her in himself for Gytha; it is as though he is her godfather. She is lying where she fell, on her side, wine from the shattered barrel spreading a purple stain out from under her flank. She lifts her head as Odo kneels beside her, but the effort forces a groan from her which goes right through him. He wonders if, as well as the broken leg, the splintered timber has pierced her body somewhere. All the time, as he removes his short cape and blindfolds the horse with it, as he draws his dagger and strokes the animal's neck to find the vein, he tells her what a good, brave, wonderful horse she is. He thanks her for not falling on Gytha and tells her how much God loves her for sparing her mistress, and what a fool he is to be talking this way. He makes the cut quickly, with certainty, and holds the mare's head in his lap until her legs stop twitching and her blood has flowed to join the wine soaking into the dull gold sand.

His men watch him silently as he goes down to the shore, washes his hands in the lazy tongues of water, then addresses the harbour master.

"Can you take care of it?" he asks. "I am anxious to get on my way."

"My Lord."

"Good." Odo fishes in the purse he carries attached to his belt and offers the harbour master a gold coin which, to his surprise, the man declines.

"With respect, My Lord, the horse itself will be more use to us here than your gold. We've had no rain since heaven knows when and the harvest has failed. People have very little to eat."

"What?"

"I think you have been abroad for some time, My Lord."

That should make no difference. Why has he heard nothing of this until now? He rubs his hands over his face, trying to remember the last time he had any word from Hamo or any of his other lieutenants in Kent, but he cannot. Time spent with Gytha is a slow, endless river of bliss, the days flowing into weeks, into seasons. He might have received their despatches the day before yesterday or three months ago. "Do as you see fit with the horse," he says, feeling suddenly weary and foolish.

He is sceptical, to begin with, of Gytha's account of the accident, thinking she must have imagined her accuser. She has gone a day and a night without sleep, it is more than a woman's constitution can be expected to bear, it is his fault, he should have insisted she remain behind and travel later, with Osbern, Freya and the rest. She accompanied him at her own insistence, she reminds him, and she is as sure as she can be that she has imagined nothing. What could possibly spark such an incident in her imagination? Many prelates keep mistresses and none she can think of has ever been condemned as a witch. No, she is certain everything happened as she described, but doubtless the perpetrator was some lunatic or simpleton, harmless, deluded, probably mistaking her for someone else. They should think no more of it but make haste for Canterbury where she, for one, will be glad of a good night's rest.

As they ride on, however, Odo starts to believe her. Everywhere it is the same. The dust from the roads parches their lips and sticks in their throats, but the streams are dry and the wells they stop at contain little more than brackish sludge. At one, he fancies he sees wolves, slinking like wraiths back among the trees bordering the road, raising the hairs on the back of his neck. Slowing their pace as they pass through villages, they are greeted by sullen, lethargic people lounging in doorways or sitting listlessly on bare commons, men and women who should be harvesting at this time of year, children whose skin is grey and wrinkled from malnutrition, making them look like ancient midgets. They pass dead cattle by the roadside, hides draped stiffly over bones picked clean by carrion crows, and living cattle in a little better state, bags of bones with shrunken udders. In the orchards, the trees are shrouded with a grey, friable mould, the fruit rotted and wizened.

In one village, only three or four miles from Canterbury, part of Odo's personal fief, in which he is well known, their progress is halted by a funeral procession. They wait uncomfortably as the mourning party, which seems to consist of almost the entire population, crosses their path on its way to the church. No-one takes any notice of them, they cannot conjure rain out of clear skies or bring the dead to life. The body bound in the white winding sheet is small, a child. Gytha averts her gaze and, in doing so, meets Odo's, full of concern and something else, a hesitancy she reads as guilt. He reaches for her hand. A woman among the mourners, distracted by his movement as he leans from his saddle, stops and looks at them.

"It's her!" she shrieks, stooping to pick up a stone and hurling it in Gytha's direction. Her arm is weak and the stone falls harmlessly, several feet in front of Gytha's horse, which is too tired from the journey to do more than stamp its feet a little. Within seconds, their escort has surrounded Odo and herself, swords drawn. The villagers whirl and break against the tight box of cavalrymen like a sea of dusty ghosts.

"Whore!" says the woman who threw the stone, her mouth a bright, moist gash, an oasis in the desert of her face, and again, "Witch!"

Odo orders his men to put up their swords and rides out in front of the escort.

"Who is in charge here?"

"Not you, I reckon, My Lord," comes a man's voice from the crowd. There is a ripple of laughter, quickly silenced as Odo raises his riding whip and walks his horse forward.

"Where is your priest?" He addresses the pall bearers, standing helplessly with their burden sagging between them, the winding sheet becoming smeared with dust. "For pity's sake, men, carry the body into the church and fetch me your priest."

The priest, who, notes Odo with distaste, looks a lot less hungry than his parishioners, though the same dust as shrouds the rest of them clings to the hem of his somewhat grubby alb, is thrust forward, through the crowd, from his place beside the church door. Odo, without dismounting, proffers his ring to be kissed.

"Explain to me the meaning of what I have just witnessed," he says.

"The woman is mad, Your Reverence, out of her head with grief. It is her child we have come to bury."

"But the child did not die of witchcraft, I think."

"No, Your Reverence, of a flux, from eating berries before they were ripe."

"Which she wouldn't have been eating if we weren't all starving," interjects the mother.

Odo ignores her. "And these people believe that the drought has come about through witchcraft, do they? Good God, man, what do you preach? 'The Lord thy God is a jealous God'. Beware you do not set up rivals to Him in determining the weather."

"I preach as instructed by My Lord Archbishop, Your Reverence," announces the priest in a clear voice.

My lord Archbishop? So Lanfranc has directed his clergy to preach witchcraft against Gytha? Odo is unsure whether to laugh or despair. If he is so far out of his senses then retirement to Caen in favour of a more capable man cannot be long. But if he is not out of his mind, if he believes such a tactic can be of use to him, then Odo has overestimated his own strength and Gytha may be in real danger.

Sidling closer to Odo's horse, emboldened by his silence, the priest goes on in a more confidential, obsequious tone. "Your Reverence, the people are simple. They see your lordship acting against the ordinances of Holy Mother Church, and then their crops fail, and guided by their prayers, they make a simple connection…"

The priest is abruptly silenced by Odo's whip coming down with great force across his cheek. He looks at Odo in disbelief, putting a plump hand up to the blow, a gash of white through the pink flesh, rapidly assuming various shades of purple and red as the blood flows back into it. There is a gasp from the mourning party, a backward stepping and stumbling. Odo leans down close to the priest's ear.

"Listen to me," he says quietly, "Mistress Aelfgytha is more to me than my life, and certainly more to me than yours, or any of your halfwit congregation. If you value your hide you will never even think such things as you have implied to me, let alone say them. I am your lord after the King's Grace, and I will have you out on the road like a mendicant in the time it takes to match that stripe on your cheek with another if I ever, ever hear such talk from you again."

"But Canterbury is my bishop," retorts the priest.

"Aye, and you may repeat all I have said word for word in his ear, as I will make sure to tell him all you have told me, you fat bastard travesty of a man of God." He digs the point of his whip into the man's paunch, up under his ribs. The priest chokes and splutters.

"Fulk."

"My Lord?"

"Take a couple of men into the priest's house. Whatever food and drink you find there, give to the people. Now, priest." Odo removes his foot from his stirrup and gives the priest's arse a sound boot. "Go and bury your dead. But first," he continues, raising his voice as the priest stumbles away, "let the mother come forward."

She emerges from the crowd and stands trembling in front of him, her head bowed almost as though she can already feel his whip across her shoulders.

"Here," he says gently, holding out a coin. "Take it. For Masses for your daughter's soul."

The woman shakes her head. "We can't eat your money, My Lord."

"Woman, we must nourish the soul as well as the body. Would you deny your child the sustenance of prayer?"

She looks up. She has hard, pale, implacable eyes. "I never denied her anything, My Lord. Perhaps if I had she might still be alive."

Odo sighs and returns his money to his purse. "Very well. Tell me your daughter's name and I will have the Mass said for her myself, on this day, every year, by the brothers at Saint Augustine's. And I promise you this, I will do everything in my power to alleviate the situation in which Kent finds itself. And you know that, saving the King's Grace, no-one in this land has more power than I do."

"My daughter was called Aelfgytha, sir."

"Then I will not forget it. Pray for me too, Aelfgytha's mother."

WITCHCRAFT

OUR LADY OF SORROWS 1072

"Dried peas again." Margaret pushes the yellow, glutinous mass around her plate with a small piece of bread. "As if taking our land wasn't bad enough, they have to grow peas on it." She still surprises herself by talking this way, although the others seem to have become used to it. It is almost as though she has grown to fill the space left by Gytha's departure, the way everything in nature shapes itself to the place God has allotted it. She wonders, with an apprehensive tightening in her stomach, what will happen now that Gytha has come back.

Margaret has not seen her yet, at least, not to speak to, though she saw the earl's party arrive from the workshop windows, and Gytha, elegantly dressed in a plum coloured gown with gold embroidery, leaning heavily on Odo's arm as they made their way towards the inner court and the private apartments. She never so much as glanced in the direction of the atelier. No-one has seen them since, and there have been rumours that Gytha is under some kind of house arrest, as she was, apparently, in Normandy. Margaret is somehow afraid it all relates back to the garden at Winterbourne, and the plan Gytha hatched to help her get away to look for Tom; everything has been so hazy since then, like fighting her way through lines of wet sheets hung out to dry, the clear view glimpsed then snatched away by heavy slaps of linen.

"They say she was deceiving him all along, getting close then plotting against him," said one of the Saint Augustine's women as they peered down from the great windows.

"Nonsense," replied Judith, "he's just doing what great men do when they tire of mistresses who know too much about them."

"'And the kings of the earth who have committed fornication and lived deliciously with her shall bewail her and lament for her when they shall see the smoke of her burning,'" chanted Alwys, drawing a sharp look from Sister Jean as she summoned them back to their frames. Sister Jean did not hear what Margaret heard, Judith whispering to Alwys,

"The Whore of Babylon. Good girl. Quite right."

Looking at the peas, pus coloured and lumpy, suddenly makes Margaret feel sick. She pushes her bowl away.

"That girl's looking peaky," comments Hamo, glancing down the hall. "Are you sure all is well in your workshop, Sister? There's a lot of sickness about."

Agatha has been much occupied with sick visiting in recent weeks, though there has been little she can do to help those suffering from bad air, brackish water and failing crops, and nothing she can say in response to the mumbled imprecations against Odo and his woman.

The hall is gloomy, lights being kept to a minimum because of the risk of fire. Agatha envies Hamo his eyesight, though she is relieved to be spared too clear a picture of the women seated below the empty hearth. The atmosphere in the atelier has become scarcely bearable. In the early days, there was grief and anger, but they laughed more as well. All of them, not just Agatha, were infected by the excitement of the project, its novelty, its enormous scale and ambition. Perhaps it was because, even if as individuals they did not grasp the overall plan and purpose of the work, they knew that Sister Jean did. Sister Jean gave them all a sense that they were making history, that they were important in the new, Norman scheme of things, more than heads to be counted in Lord Odo's assessment of his holdings, more than pawns in whatever game Harold of Wessex and William of Normandy had played with the English crown.

But four years have passed. The miraculous windows are dusty, the cat has died, entangled in the spokes of a cartwheel, the linen is grimy and overworked, and the conquest of England, the history of which they fancied themselves a part, is all but finished. Typical of Margaret to discover resistance just as everybody else has given it up. And that is not all Margaret has discovered since she was brought back from Dover. Dis-covered, Agatha says to herself, how appropriate. There is Guerin, of course, and Gird, the widowed baker, and who knows how many more in this castle full of soldiers. She has heard the whispered jokes about bed and bawd, and what's sauce for the goose.

"We are all well, God be thanked" she replies to Hamo's enquiry, "but the heat is oppressive. It does tend to sap the appetite." At high table, the peas have been leavened by the addition of a large eel, but the flesh is dry and chalky. Probably it would have been thrown back if the need were not so pressing and Agatha, chiding herself for her ingratitude for God's bounty, wonders if everyone might not be better off if it had been. If it does not call down more bad luck upon them, it may well poison them.

"All the same, we can't afford to waste food. She'll live to regret it, a bonny girl like that one."

Bonny once, perhaps, but now she has begun to dress carelessly, she has pimples on her chin as though even her skin is reflecting some wantonness in her attitude. Her flesh is slack and blowsy, arrayed about her big bones like an ill-fitting gown imperfectly pressed. The girl is a slut; glancing sidelong at Hamo, she wonders if even he has been dipping his wick in that particular cresset of oil. And who is to blame him for taking what is offered? After all, he would merely be following his overlord's example.

Odo is solicitous, but preoccupied. He has not told her what the priest said about Lanfranc's directions to his clergy on preaching the causes of the drought, or worse still, the cure implied in those causes. No point in upsetting her further with such obvious nonsense, but he is rattled by it in spite of himself. He will not rest easy until he knows what he is up against, whether Lanfranc has lost his wits or has launched a serious campaign against Gytha.

"Rub my back for me," she pleads, "I am stiff as a corpse from my fall."

"I thought I might try and get to see Lanfranc this evening. You don't mind, do you?"

Yes, yes, I mind. Today I have been twice accused of witchcraft and nearly killed falling from my horse for you. "No, but I think you're being hasty. You haven't slept for nearly two days. Even your powers of persuasion must be at a low ebb by now. Go in the morning."

Contemplating her face, pinched with anxiety, her eyes huge with pleas she will not utter because she doesn't want him to know how afraid she is, he yields to her advice. Though he does not expect to sleep; he is apprehensive himself, if not afraid. He does rub her back, and her round buttocks, and the arches of her feet whose sinews make him think of the roof vaults of his cathedral, slender and strong. He kisses a bruise emerging like a stain on the creamy skin of her thigh, and makes love to her with great tenderness, but a distraction which makes her certain he is hiding something from her.

She lies beside him pretending to sleep, while he sits with his long legs stretched out on top of the white fur coverlet, ankles crossed in a parody of relaxation, turned a little away from her towards the light of the cresset on his night stand, pretending to re-read Ealdred's deposition. Listening to the too perfect regularity of her breathing, he knows she is awake. When she steals a glance at him under her lashes, she sees he is not looking at the parchment in his hand but into the dark beyond the tallowlight, his eyes red with the reflection of whatever he sees there.

Eventually she puts a hand out from under the covers and touches his arm lightly.

"Come to bed, Odo. It'll all look better in the morning, whatever it is."

Giving her a wan smile and a nod, he stands, placing the deposition on the nightstand and shrugging off his fur-lined gown. The deep, simple joy of watching the gown slip away from his fair skin, the play of muscle and bone in the smoky light as he unties the bed hangings before climbing into bed beside her, consoles her like drinking mulled wine on a winter day. Her love sparkles in her fingers and the tips of her toes. With a contented sigh she surrenders to the curve of his body around hers, the damp heat of his breath on the back of her neck, the perfect seclusion of the world bounded by the bed curtains.

He remembers the first time he lay with her this way, her small frame curled inside his like the sweet kernel of a nut, and how she had been talking about Aristophanes and his theory of wholes. *That's it,* says a voice which may be inside him or may be the voice of God, *the power of the perfect whole.* Whoever, or whatever, is trying to prise them apart cannot succeed; they are fused together by love, tempered and shaped by it into a single, indissoluble being. Lanfranc's hints at witchcraft and divine retribution are powerless against them as long as they are together. Besides, if the people have been so easily swayed by words, how much more easily can he persuade them by deeds, by importing grain to feed them and engaging dowsers to find them water? The bishoprics and Brother Ealdred's intriguing revelations, those are what set him on this course and he will not be deflected.

Lanfranc, approached by one of the abbey servants as he makes his way from chapter to Terce the following morning, knows before the man opens his mouth that he has come to tell him the Earl of Kent is here in person and is asking for an audience. The only surprise is that he did not come last night, although he will admit to having been caught off- guard by the abruptness of Odo's departure from Normandy. He is as certain as he can be that no word could have reached him about the drought, and positive that, had he received reports of sermons being preached against Gytha, he would not have brought her to Canterbury but would have kept her out of harm's way in some more peripheral corner of his empire.

The man looks bewitched, he thinks, as Odo is shown into his office, or at least like a man in whom the humours are catastrophically out of balance. A fire burns in his eyes which Lanfranc has not seen since the meetings in Rouen at which the conquest was planned. His embrace, as they exchange the kiss of peace, is brief and wary; even Odo's skin feels as hot and dry as the parched fields beyond the city walls where the corn lies stunted and shrivelled, taunting the hungry. Yet his smile is as it always is, broad, ironic, self deprecating as only the smile of a supremely confident man can be, and his grip on Lanfranc's shoulders is firm, perhaps a little too firm. And when he opens his mouth, what he says is mundane enough.

"I've come to set your mind at rest about some lost property,"

Gytha wakes to find him gone. Closeted with Lord Hamo for a good hour before Terce, explains the serving girl who brings her her late, lady's breakfast, complete with flowers, and now departed for Christ Church. Drawing back the bed curtains, Gytha looks out of the window. The sun, whose heat here seems malevolent, is already high, approaching its late summer zenith she estimates, squinting up into the dense blue of the sky. He must return soon. Dismissing the girl, she settles back among the pillows to wait. She nibbles at the white rolls, picks at the preserved damsons and almonds toasted with honey, leaves the wine because there is insufficient water in it for breakfast. She is not very hungry, but her meal helps to pass a little time while she plans how else to occupy herself.

Sext is rung and still he does not return. She rises and dresses herself, deciding against summoning Countess Marie's maid, who has been lent to her until Freya arrives, because, without assistance, she can spin out the process for as long as she wishes. Having left Normandy so precipitately, she has only the gown she travelled in. She brushes it carefully, with an ebony brush inlaid with mother-of-pearl, then spits on her shoes and rubs them with a corner of the bed sheet. She arranges her hair in a fantastic elaboration of twists and plaits, then takes it all down again because, she thinks, *it looks more like a fancy loaf than hair.* Looking at her reflection in the mirror, she notices a small tear in her skirt, a result, no doubt, of being thrown from her horse yesterday.

And realises there are no sewing materials in Odo's apartments. She will have to find the maid and have her bring some up. Very well. She leaves the bedroom and crosses the parlour to the door giving onto the head of the stairs, and stops with her hand on the latch. She cannot do it, cannot go out into the household, knowing what is being said, knowing what they think of her. She should have stayed in Normandy, come back with Freya as any sensible woman would. Any decent woman.

She is being stupid. She has Odo's protection, whatever they are thinking they will not dare say it to her face. But they did yesterday, the starving, the grief stricken, the ones whom he could not protect. Here, though, in the castle, it is different. No-one is starving here, and everyone knows her. They will not accuse her of bewitching him. But perhaps she has. *I believe God made me to love you,* he told her. Perhaps even he believes himself to have been bewitched, and that is why he has become so cool. She stares at her hand on the latch, her left hand. She snatches it back as though the latch has burned her. The tear will have to wait, it doesn't matter, no-one is going to see her.

This is the place to begin, with Brother Ealdred and his revelations, catch the old man off-balance and only then make mention of the sermons against Gytha.

"And I wonder what I can have lost that has come to you?" asks Lanfranc, his tone warmed by relief.

Odo snaps his fingers at the clerk he has brought with him. The clerk steps forward and hands his master a document. "A few days ago," says Odo, "I received a visit from a Brother Ealdred of Malden."

Lanfranc starts tugging at his beard.

"It's a conundrum, isn't it?" Odo goes on pleasantly. "What do we do with troublemakers? Get them out of the way? Or keep them close."

"Brother Ealdred was at Worcester on my proper business."

"If you cast your eye over this," Odo puts down the document on Lanfranc's desk, smoothing it out over the grey hairs scattered there by the old man's nervous tugging, "I think you'll find he wasn't. He was at least premature in pricing up Worcester's library on your behalf."

The silence tightens between them as Lanfranc reads. "You must give me time to consider my reply to this, Odo. You understand I knew nothing, absolutely nothing, of it. Are you sure it's genuine?"

Odo shrugs. "Why should it not be? Ealdred's motives seem plausible enough to me. He is a man of strong convictions."

"Oh yes," says Lanfranc ruefully. "May I keep this?" He waves the parchment at Odo.

"Be my guest. It is a copy, of course, but exact in every particular save Brother Ealdred's hand, which is uniquely fine, I think."

"Uniquely, it seems."

"I have written to His Holiness, of course."

"Of course." Oh, of course. "I will write to him myself immediately, to remind him of what other authority exists for Canterbury's claims, Bede and so forth."

"I also referred His Holiness to the transcripts of witness testimony in Cardinal Hubert's possession, though I do not think it was conclusive on either side, do you?"

"Perhaps not so far as you heard it. I imagine I do not have to remind you that you left Winchester before the council ended."

"I have since seen all the papers."

"And signed the agreement."

"Hardly binding if a major part of its legal foundation turns out to be fraudulent."

"I will speak to you again on this matter in a week, Odo."

"Take as long as you like, Archbishop. But a word of warning. In case you thought to take comfort from the fact that Thomas can do little from as far afield as York, be sure I already have troops on the borders of all three dioceses. I have only to tighten the noose a little and my 'hangmen' are already on their way."

"A week," repeats Lanfranc, in a tone designed to bring an end to their interview, but Odo seems to have other ideas. Drawing up a stool, he sits down opposite Lanfranc.

"You may go," he says to his clerk. "Wait for me outside. Well, Lanfranc," he continues once the clerk has gone, "whatever have you been up to in my absence to bring down the wrath of God on us so with this drought?" Acutely aware, although he cannot see it, of the squat outline of the new cathedral rising confidently beyond the cloisters, he adds, "Is it what Saint Anthony condemns as the lust of building, do you suppose?"

"Not my lust, brother." Lanfranc watches him for his response, his black eyes beady as a magpie's when it has some glittery thing in sight.

"Who can know the mind of God? I simply suggest it as a possibility, an example I might use in my own preaching. The shepherd who became so absorbed in building the finest fold ever seen that his back was turned when the wolf came and took his sheep. Rather fine, don't you think?"

"I have done what I could."

"You have done nothing," Odo shouts, rising from the stool and slamming his hands down flat on the desk. "Absolutely nothing. How many lives do you think you have sacrificed just to give my mistress a bad name? Hamo says you have blocked him at every turn. You may believe I am destined for hell, Lanfranc, but I'll wager you'll be there to greet me."

"My concern is all for the good of your soul, Odo. Your welfare is of particular interest to the king, your brother, and therefore to me."

William. Suddenly he finds the thought of William's solicitude cold comfort. Turning from the thought of it, he takes a deep, calming breath and smoothes the frown from his face. "I'm arranging to have grain brought in from my estates elsewhere, Normandy if necessary, and I'm lifting the hunting restrictions till Saint Andrew's day. My verderer is overseeing the cutting of firebreaks round the town, and by this time tomorrow I'll have guards on the wells and dowsers out all over the county hunting for underground water courses. Seeing as a rule it hardly ever stops raining here, there must be whole seas under our feet. I'll be the apple of their eye again in no time, you'll see." He pauses, then adds as if it is an afterthought, "Extraordinary how I knew nothing of all this until I returned to England." He gives a light, chilly laugh which does not fool Lanfranc for a moment. "I'm obviously not paying my spies well enough. Tell me, what is the going rate now? Clearly it has risen since my departure."

"I don't know what you mean." Stealthily, Lanfranc draws his hands into his sleeves, slides his frail, lawyer's wrists away from Odo's broad hands.

Odo raises his hands and shows Lanfranc his palms in mock surrender. "Ah well, perhaps the messengers all met with accidents. The Channel is a cursed stretch of water even in the middle of summer and the roads are not that safe whatever my brother would have us believe. What's done is done. I just wanted to be sure you knew that I know what has been done. I will leave you now. I have given you a great deal to think about."

"One last question."

Odo waits with his fingers on the latch.

"Brother Ealdred?"

"He is safe."

Gytha used to be fascinated by these apartments, enthralled by Odo's possessions in all their lavish eclecticism and opulence. The dragon's lair, the cave of the robber baron. But now she knows he has entire houses like this, in Rouen and Caen, London and Rome, as well as his official residence in Bayeux. What is moonstone when you can look at the moon, or gold in comparison with the sun? She picks up books, but puts them down again unopened, put off by bindings of ivory and filigree and gilded leather studded with gems. Letters and pictures do not breathe nor silks serve any better to cover the body than woollens, and idleness passes the time more slowly than work.

Her gaze falls on the flowers left by the girl who brought her breakfast. Broom, dyer's greenweed, goldenrod and lady's bedstraw. Every one yellow. She stares at them. Fleabane, and the daisy called goatsbeard. Yellow. For a moment it seems as though her heart stops beating and the blood stills in her veins. Yellow flowers to ward off witches, golden wands and haloes to protect against the powers of darkness. Is this the fate she decreed for herself when she threatened silly Trudy with the dark arts if she attempted to change Lady Edith's gown? She picks up the vase, of blue, semi-opaque glass, and flings it and its contents into the empty fireplace. The glass shatters and water seeps into the ashes, precious water, holy water. Better to go thirsty than leave a witch to flourish. Ash tarnishes the flower petals, only hedgerow flowers, humble and hardy enough to withstand drought, yet she would not touch them. Holy Mother of God protect her, she could not touch them. Cannot stay here where their tawdry eyes stare at her from the empty hearth.

She runs out of the parlour, slamming the door behind her so that people going about their business in the great hall glance up and see her running down the stairs from the private apartments, struggling with the latch on the wicket until someone, hearing the frenetic rattle, opens it from the outside. She flees the bailey, slipping on the crumbling motte, down through the inner gate, past the guards who stand aside for her in amazement, across the outer ward to the atelier. Where else can she go? They know her in the atelier, that she has a sharp wit and a tongue to match, but she is not a witch. Sister Jean will help her.

Once inside the building, she heaves the door shut behind her and leans against it, heart pounding against her breastbone, breath rasping in her throat. She closes her eyes, then opens them again, letting them gradually adjust to the interior light after the glare outside. She becomes aware of Sister Jean's drawings, their curled edges touched by dusty sunlight and lifting a little in the draught she has created as she came in.

She starts to walk slowly down the hall towards the dormitory, pausing occasionally to look at the drawings. So many memories. How many yards of grey and indigo wool looped and twined into rings of mail since the first time she saw these pictures, confused and troubled as to how the beautifully executed images could relate to the brutes she had witnessed, with their short cropped hair and their ugly language that made them sound as though they were being strangled, looting, burning and raping her country?

This sad, supplicant woman, standing outside her burning house, holding a small boy by the hand. What has she to do with the smell of charred flesh or the burning sensation of a Norman prick rammed into a dry, shrinking cunt? Colonising the country with a whole generation of Norman bastards. And what can that possibly have to do with the tides of fire flooding her nights with Odo, melting them together until she no longer knows where he ends and she begins?

This man hiding in the vine, looking as though he has seen a vision of eternity nevertheless knows nothing of the mundane, messy, pain-ridden way he will get there. This comet, more like a toppled weathervane than the falling, feathered star whose awful loveliness set King Harold's chaplain rifling through the Revelation of Saint John by its fractured light. And the name of the star is called Wormwood: and the third part of the waters became wormwood: and many men died of the waters, because they were made bitter. She shudders, acknowledging the truth there may be in signs.

"So, here you are."

"Sister Jean." Turning aside from the wall, Gytha makes a little curtsy which Agatha acknowledges with a bow of her head.

"I wondered when you might come to see us. I heard the door and then, silence."

"I…was on my way up. I got distracted. Reminiscing."

"I felt it was the first time I'd heard your own true voice, when you exclaimed over these. I felt it vindicated my decision to bring you here, though I always knew you'd cause me trouble."

"Never as much as I intended, I assure you."

"Then I must be thankful that my brother disarmed you."

She acknowledges Agatha's wordplay with a brief laugh.

"And now you've come to see how we're getting on without you? How much we have sacrificed for My Lord's peace of mind?"

"The tapestry is his, Sister, so I suppose the sacrifice is his also."

"Listen to you, calling it a tapestry. You haven't been able to prevail upon him to give it its proper designation, then?"

"When he talks about it, he clearly has in his mind's eye something quite other than the wool and linen that are its component parts. He makes a magical transformation."

"And expects that we are doing the same. Do you think he'll be disappointed?"

Gytha smiles, only realising as she does so how tense the muscles of her face have become in their effort to keep the mask of unconcern in place. "I know he won't. How is it going? Are you close to finishing? Odo expects the roof to be over the cathedral nave before winter, and then the work will go much quicker."

"Whenever I think the end is in sight there is a new development. Because life goes on, I suppose, and finds its way into the embroidery. Meg, for example…"

"Meg?"

"Have you not heard? I cannot believe my brother said nothing."

"Nothing. Why? What has happened?"

Agatha tells her everything, from the discovery of Tom in the Christ Church infirmary to the discoveries since made by Guerin and the rest, in the guard posts on the wall, the woodstore behind the bakehouse, even, according to one rumour, the sacristy of the chapel with one of the sub-deacons.

"And all of it finding its way into the embroidery. Piles of dismembered corpses and…other bodies. When I tried to chide her about one particularly lewd image, she just stared at me and said, 'It's true, like Judith's plough horse. How could I argue? How would I know?" she finishes with an uncharacteristically silly, sheepish laugh.

Gytha lays a hand on her arm. "When we were at Conteville, Odo told me…he showed me the room that used to overlook the brew house. This must be very hard for you."

Agatha stares unseeing at the comet, willing her eyes to remain dry, her mouth working as though she is trying to choose between many possible, but inadequate, words.

"Gytha, will you talk to her? She always took notice of you."

"If you think I can do any good, but there is something I must speak to you about first."

Agatha looks at her in surprise. "Of course. Shall we go into my parlour?"

Agatha shows her into the room where, by the remorseless light of the afternoon sun pouring through the window, she sees how pale Gytha looks. Her dark eyes shift restlessly around the familiar room. Her face has lost its characteristic hardness, which makes her both more beautiful but more troubling to look at.

"Are you truly glad in my brother's company?"

"Now, yes. I have nothing to reproach him with. He treats me with every courtesy and generosity."

"So I see." Agatha takes in the richness of her dress, the garnets and pearls around her neck. "But you have a tear in your skirt."

"I took a fall from my horse yesterday, and everything else is still on its way from Normandy. I hoped maybe you could find me a needle and thread."

"I think that might be possible." Agatha gives an ironic smile.

Gytha, twisting her fingers together, seems unaware of her attempt at humour. "Was it a bad fall? Did you hurt yourself?" Agatha persists.

"No, but the horse…" She remembers recovering from her faint to see Odo, a splash of blood on his sleeve, cleaning his dagger on the maram grass bordering the beach, and bursts into tears. The poor horse, the poor, dumb horse. Agatha sits her down in a chair beside the empty hearth and stands in front of her, hands folded under her scapular, the novice mistress, all brisk compassion and common sense.

Gytha composes herself quickly. She sniffs. "Sister Jean, they're calling me a witch. They say I'm responsible for the drought. That was why I fell, someone shouting at me and startling my horse. And there was another incident just before we arrived here, and then, this morning, the girl who brought my breakfast brought me a posy of yellow flowers."

"Yellow flowers?"

"Yes. We believe yellow flowers ward off witches."

"I see. I haven't come across that belief before."

"We don't believe storks leave new babies at the bottom of wells, though," adds Gytha with an attempt at a smile. The two women's eyes meet in an exchange of understanding.

"Perhaps our mother told us that tale to comfort her daughters, but only the boys were taken in by it."

"What am I to do, Sister? What if it's true?"

"That you bewitched him? Of course it's true."

Gytha gives a little gasp, almost a sob, and starts for the door. To her utter chagrin and disbelief, Agatha merely laughs.

"As women are always bewitching men, and babies their mothers." *As Meg bewitched me.* "In the convent from time to time we have had Sisters who fall into ecstasies. They have dreams, speak in tongues. They are bewitched by the love of Jesus. It seems to me that witchcraft has acquired the reputation it has because it is the means whereby we ensure that someone stronger than us will protect us. People have been turned against you by simple envy, Gytha. Because you were not born to the life you are living now, you show them the possibility of dreams or aspirations coming true. That's what makes you dangerous, and if you are to remain with my brother, believe me, you must get used to it."

"I couldn't leave him. I love him." There, she has said them, the simple words.

"I know you do. I have known since his name was first mentioned between us in Winchester. Some fate has been drawing you two together as surely as a needle draws thread since you were specks in your mothers' wombs. I feel it."

Gytha peers at her curiously; this is an aspect of Sister Jean she has not seen before, this aptitude for sentimental clairvoyance.

"Now dry your eyes and come and see how we're getting on. We miss you, you know. No-one laughs as much, and Aesop is gathering dust."

"No, I couldn't. What if they all think the same? I can't face anyone. I wish we could have stayed at Conteville."

Oh yes, amen to that, thinks Agatha. Forever, drawing and dancing, fishing and farming, hawks in the air, game in the forest, babies in wells, a world away from William and his ruinous ambition.

Gytha looks out of the window. "I wonder if it will rain soon?"

"It must eventually. And in the meantime, will you stay walled up in your tower like Saint Barbara? Beware of looking as though you have something to hide, either of you."

"Thank you, Sister." Gytha stands and holds out her hand. Agatha, grasping it firmly in her own, dry and delicately bony, kisses Gytha's cheek as though they are kin.

"We are fallen beings, my dear, and we experiment with all kinds of methods of redemption, but love is the only one. It is worth the pain to achieve it. And remember, true love is not always recognised, even in the Church. Consider all the heretics and schismatics who lay claim to the truth."

And Odo, with his idiosyncratic theology? "I wonder if it exists at all outside the heart of God."

"Who, being pure spirit, has no heart."

"Then how does He love us?"

"With extreme difficulty sometimes, I should imagine."

Only as she is crossing the outer court on her way back to the keep, head lowered to avoid the curious looks of the castle community, does she remember the tear in her skirt.

As soon as Odo has gone, leaving behind that perfume of his like a sniggering, triumphant wraith, Lanfranc tries to put his thoughts in order; their meeting scratches at his conscience as though his conscience skulks inside him like a scrofulous beggar. He must remember his duty. His duty is to God and the king. He must concentrate on the good of Odo's soul. Odo has spoken and acted throughout at the prompting of the Devil. Lucifer was once God's favourite angel; he can perform righteous anger and steadfast love with infinite conviction. Lanfranc must pray.

Rising from his desk to go to the prie dieu in the adjoining bed chamber, his sleeve catches on a pile of papers, scattering them on the floor. As he stoops to pick them up, his gaze happens to focus on one of them. And immediately he knows it is not chance, but the hand of God which has directed his vision. The document contains his response to a question put to him some months ago by Odo, concerning his plans for the marriage of one Judith of Harbourne to a vassal of his, an older man with several sons looking, not for more heirs but for more land to share between the ones he has. Odo had been afraid, however, that an issue of consanguinity might arise through some shared cousins in the female line, and wanted a second opinion before sanctioning the match.

Their discussion comes back to him with perfect clarity, as though he is watching it happen again, at Winchester it had been, before Odo's sudden departure precipitated everything which has happened since. The woman was one of his embroiderers, Odo had explained, the widow of a Saxon thegn with substantial holdings in Kent. She had no sons, but a couple of grandsons living in Denmark, and it would be necessary to scotch any hopes they had of inheriting well before either came of age. He could wait for the woman to die, of course, for she was far from young, but in his experience, a lot of women who came safely through their childbearing years had a tendency to want to live forever. So marriage to one of his own people seemed the ideal solution, and this man, in whom the desires of the flesh were diluted by his years and a brood of strong, hungry sons, was as keen to make the match as his lord.

As soon as he can do so without Odo getting wind of it, he will have a little conversation with Judith of Harbourne, and he will have Gytha watched as close as he can. He wants to know everything about her, when she sleeps or wakes or beds her lover, when she eats, drinks and visits the privy, where she goes when she leaves the castle and how well she is guarded. He will have her monthly cycle monitored. That especially, for you can never be sure in situations of this sort when a pregnancy might intervene to alter the balance of everything.

"Margaret." Agatha looks at the girl with something close to despair. Her skin is sallow, the hair escaping from her creased cap is dull, like cheap gilt or copper left out in the rain. She sits motionless on her stool, her spine curved, a mark of interrogation. Her needle lies on the rump of a dun coloured horse, its tail of wool disappearing into the tail of the animal.

"That's Gytha's work," she says, pointing listlessly at an improbable tableau in the lower margin of her work piece, a man, stark naked, impressively endowed and visibly aroused, reaching for an equally naked woman who holds one hand over her pudenda and covers her face with the other. Agatha knows she is lying; several of these suggestive images have appeared recently in the borders. They are Margaret's work, and it angers Agatha that she should so clumsily try to pass them off as anyone else's, particularly Gytha's. She knows she should have the girl thrown out of the castle, but some rebellious ghost of her former affection prevents her. Besides, the girl can sew, and the embroidery must be completed.

"Judith says it's right, what everyone's saying. She says that's a charm, a spell she cast on Lord Odo. She says when he came to her house, he was seemly and modest and he'd never..."

"That's enough, girl. I want you to do something for me."

"Yes, Sister. Sorry, Sister."

"Mistress Gytha was here, not an hour since, looking for needle and thread, but forgot to take them with her. Can you go up to Lord Odo's apartments with them for her?"

"Me, Sister? Oh no, I couldn't, I'd be too afraid."

"Afraid, girl? What on earth of? Lord Odo? Gytha, who you worked with for four years? Listen to your own heart, Margaret, not malicious gossip." Not, she calculates, that Margaret's heart will have anything much to say. "Now do as I ask without any more fuss."

When Gytha returns to their apartments, Odo is there, in the wide solar window seat. He turns as she enters, but cannot erase the anxious expression from his face quite quickly enough to conceal it from her. And why is he there, gazing out of the window when he has so much to do he was out of bed and gone from her almost at dawn? She sits beside him and takes his hands.

"So," she begins, determinedly cheerful, "I expect the Archbishop was put nicely out of countenance by your news?"

He smiles absently, nodding a brief assent. "Gytha, I think you should go to Winterbourne."

"Without you, My Lord?"

"I will come as soon as I have sorted matters out here."

"But that could be weeks. Longer. Who knows when it will rain?"

"You would be safer there, and make less mouths for the castle to feed."

"By that reckoning, you should not stay here yourself. You know others will be deprived to put food on the high table."

He gazes at her, at how beautiful she is in her dismay, and how

447

marvellously right in drawing his attention to something he would never otherwise have considered. How firmly she is rooted in the flesh and blood reality of the people who, for him, represent battles won or lost, weights of crops harvested, sheep sheared, pigs bred, masses sung for the numberless dead. He can hardly bear to be parted from her, yet Lanfranc's almost casual reference to William is like cold rain dripping down the back of his neck. It was a warning, he is certain of it, a scrap tossed by the Archbishop to his conscience.

"I will make sure that is not the case," he assures her gently, touching her cheek with his fingertips. "Thankyou for reminding me of it."

"I won't go." She takes his hand and replaces it firmly in his lap, stroking the fingers flat against his thigh.

"Oh, won't you, madam. We have been apart before and managed. Why should it be any different this time?"

"Odo…" Playing with his fingers now, lifting them one after the other, entwining them with her own, "since we were at Conteville, and I told you about my children…"

"I know. You don't have to say anything. I feel it too, whenever I make love to you. It's as though…you've finally begun to trust me. But don't you see? That's why it's more important to me than ever to keep you safe."

"And why I would rather face any peril at your side than be cosseted like a jewel in a padded box anywhere else. So what shall we do?"

"You will do as I say." He keeps his tone light, teasing, but he can tell as soon as he looks at her that she knows he is serious and has no intention of doing as he says.

Yet she bites back the temptation to rise to his bait; if they quarrel, then those who wish them ill will have won. "Consider this," she says. "If you send me away, won't it make you look guilty? Surely we should just carry on as though we have nothing to hide."

"We do have nothing to hide."

"Exactly."

Margaret dawdles. Although the afternoon is well advanced, the day's heat has stagnated between the buildings, thick with dust, heavy with odours of dung and rotting meat which make her feel queasy. The sound of the air is the sound of flies buzzing. Her clothes stick to her skin, her belly feels bloated, due no doubt to the diet of peas. She almost forgets the purpose of her errand but then, passing the chapel, remembers what Sister Jean has asked her to do, and tells herself not to worry. Sister Jean is a holy bride of Christ; whatever Gytha's magic, Sister Jean's is stronger. Besides, she and Gytha were friends, Gytha will not bear her any ill will. And she vaguely recollects that there was something she wanted to ask Gytha. And if her nerve fails her, she can always leave the needle and thread with one of Lord Odo's guards; none of them would give her away to Sister Jean; they love her too much.

When she reaches the door to Odo's apartments, curiosity triumphs. She has never been into these rooms, though Gytha used occasionally to let drop some remark about books and precious ornaments and window recesses full of silk cushions. And, remembering the gown of primrose silk, the emerald necklace and green satin slippers, she longs to see what Gytha is wearing, what jewels she has, how her hair is dressed.

She is shown into the solar. Gytha and his lordship are seated in one of the window embrasures, holding hands, their heads bent close together as they talk quietly. As Gytha springs to her feet, Margaret feels like a thief caught in the act of breaking into a house.

"Meg." Gytha embraces her warmly, kissing her cheek. She smells faintly of the earl's perfume. The earl rises and gives her a courteous greeting, as though he has no recollection of their last meeting in Dover. She tries not to flinch from Gytha's kiss and hopes her voice will not fail her as she tries to answer the earl's questions about his tapestry.

"Well," he concludes, stretching like a great cat, "if you ladies will excuse me, I'll leave you to gossip. I have letters to write." Planting an uxorious kiss on Gytha's proffered cheek, he adds, puzzlingly, "Alright, nothing to hide."

Gytha gives him a warm smile, touching his sleeve as though he is a talisman.

"When you return to the atelier, Margaret, warn my sister I shall come tomorrow to see how you are getting on. Give her time to evict all the young pikemen and cover up the books of dirty stories."

"What did he mean?" asks Margaret, aghast, when he has gone.

"Just a joke."

The two women stand looking at one another. Margaret is disappointed. Gytha is still wearing the same travelling dress she arrived in. Her head is uncovered and her hair falls down her back in a single plait without even a ribbon in it, she wears stout shoes and little jewellery. She looks tired.

"I brought you these," says Margaret, hurriedly putting down the sewing materials on a small table, next to the camel in its frame.

"Thank you. You couldn't sew the tear for me, could you? It's an awkward angle for me to reach unless I undress."

"Oh no, I mean, Sister Jean said to go straight back."

"Oh, come on, take a little break. What can she do? Besides, I want to hear all the gossip." And Sister Jean will be disappointed in her if Margaret returns too quickly. Margaret does not look well, though perhaps that is just a consequence of the drought. She also looks, realises Gytha, with a tightening of her chest, panic stricken. "You believe them, don't you, Meg, the people who say I'm a witch?" She sits down suddenly in the window seat she had been sharing with Odo. There are fires burning somewhere; a blue pall of smoke veils the trees beyond the Roman wall. "You're afraid of me."

"Judith says..." Margaret begins, in a whining tone aimed at deflecting blame.

"Judith." Gytha cuts across her contemptuously. "Judith just wants the head of her Holofernes."

"What?"

"She's jealous, Meg, and disapproving. Thinks blue bloods should stick together."

"But she has evidence."

"Evidence? What evidence?"

Margaret says nothing; the deception over the naked figures has gone too far.

"You see?" Gytha continues. "Nothing. Because there is none."

"Freya," says Margaret suddenly. "Freya knows spells, and she's your maid."

"Freya knows no more than most women, a few charms to protect infants and mothers in childbirth. Hardly enough to cause a drought."

"Gytha." A pleading note in Margaret's voice, together with her own slight unease about Freya, makes Gytha look up at the girl. Two oily tears run down either side of her face, channelled between her cheeks and the sides of her nose, into the corners of her mouth. She licks her lips. Gytha folds her hands in her lap and waits. Margaret struggles, twisting her fingers together as though what she has to say is captive in her hands and she cannot make up her mind whether or not to let it out. She sniffs noisily and blurts out,

"I think I might be pregnant. I don't know, but I haven't bled for ages and I can't eat, but maybe that's the peas..."

Hardly surprising, if all Sister Jean told her is true. "Have you tried any remedies?" She will not condemn Margaret's behaviour; that is Sister Jean's responsibility. "Some swear by motherwort and honey, or feverfew boiled in wine. I suppose you can still find both, despite the drought. They grow anywhere."

Margaret shakes her head dumbly.

"Well, what about the father? Could it be Guerin? He'd marry you, I'm certain of it, and if he hesitated, I'm sure Odo could...persuade him."

Margaret stares at her, then bursts into noisy sobs, shaking her head, her tears and snot leaving a silvery trail up her sleeve as she wipes her face. "You don't understand. I know who the father is. I can't marry him."

Tom. What mischief has she done in her zeal to help Margaret?

Almost before she has cast herself in the excusable role of misguided well-wisher, she has snatched it back, torn it up and scattered the pieces to the wind. The only person she had sought to help was herself, sacrificing Margaret on the altar of her spleen as surely as a true witch might sacrifice a goat or a cat or a newborn child. And what if she herself had not run away? Presumably Margaret would never have been found and returned to Canterbury. She might have had the child and lived well enough among the heretics, strong and willing with her blithe, unquestioning good nature.

Or died giving birth in some dank forest somewhere, or lost her child. Her brother's child, destined to be born in mortal sin, a monster, deformed perhaps, or wicked as the Black Oppressor of the tale of Peredur. Her mother's stories come back to her, always in the identical words her mother would use, as though reciting charms. *A big, black, one-eyed man who lost his eye to the Worm of the Barrow, who is greed.*

"How can you be so sure? By all accounts there have been others since."

Margaret shrugs. "I just know."

Gytha has heard other women say this, usually when the putative father was a man of sufficient wealth to have some to spare to keep a bastard and its mother. But she has changed since those days, she has learned to listen to her body, to be aware of all the minute signs of its cycles. She nods.

"I'm scared, Gytha. What will Sister Jean say, or his lordship? Where can I go?"

"Let me worry about Sister Jean and his lordship. I'll think what's best to do and speak to you again in a few days." How easy it is to take charge, to reassure this great, stupid girl. "Now dry your eyes and go back to work, and try to eat, it's important for your health."

"Shall I do your skirt first?"

"Thank you. Now tell me, how is your sister?"

"Oh, mad as ever, though quite happy. A walking Book of Psalms.

452

The cat died, you know, caught in a cart wheel, poor little thing."

"And I should be sorry?"

"Of course, I'd forgotten, they make you sneeze. Fancy my forgetting that."

"It's been some time, Meg. I'd say a lot of water under the bridge if it didn't sound like a bad joke, the way things are."

Lanfranc seizes his opportunity when Odo is called to Dover on some matter of coastal security. He uses the truth insofar as it serves him, instructing his messenger to tell Sister Jean he wishes to question Judith on a matter connected with Lord Odo's plans for her marriage. He suspects Judith has no inkling of Odo's intentions. Why should she? All the better. The walk from the castle to the abbey will give her just enough time to reflect on the implications for her grandsons and become rattled. An agitated mind will grasp quickly and uncritically at any opportunity to soothe itself.

Awaiting her arrival, he feels like a poacher skulking around his snares, a sensation not lessened by Judith's trapped, baffled air when she is brought before him. Dark sweat patches stain the underarms of her gown, her horse face has a shiny pallor, when she kneels to kiss his ring she is shaking so hard she almost loses her balance. Staring at her quivering couvre chef, Lanfranc is suddenly overwhelmed with loathing, so strong it feels like nausea, washing bile into the back of his throat. Of her, of himself, but mainly of Odo and William for entangling him in their complex and obsessive relationship, their rivalry and jealousy and total inability to keep out of one another's business. Something snags at his memory. Was there not some incident during William's courtship of Matilda, some upset involving Odo and Agatha that brought William hurrying back from Flanders? He thinks of his cathedral and sees himself and Agatha as capstones, set to prevent their arch from falling. He wonders how Mortain stands it.

Raising Judith to her feet, he tells her she may sit and does the same himself, steepling his hands over the document which says he can find no prohibitive grounds of consanguinity between her and her proposed bridegroom.

"You know why I have sent for you, daughter?" he begins, which unleashes a torrent of protests from Judith. She knows, but His Grace must be mistaken. It contravenes everything the Earl of Kent promised her, and surely the Earl is a man of his word.

"I assure you," he says smoothly, as soon as he can get a word in, "I am not mistaken. Lord Odo discussed the matter with me some months ago. He was very clear, save in the matter of consanguinity."

"Consanguinity?" Judith repeats, staring at him, her manners quite forgotten.

"Yes. His lordship was concerned there might be a prohibitive relationship between yourself and the man he has in mind for you. He asked for my opinion. I have looked into the matter and..." He springs the trap. "I can find none." Snaps it shut. "But..."

"Yes?"

"These matters are seldom clear cut. I might be persuaded to look into it again. If you could see your way to doing me a small service."

"Anything," sighs Judith, her bony chest suddenly curved and hollowed out with relief.

It is not difficult to find a time when Gytha is away from the castle, for wherever Lord Odo goes, she likes to ride with him, distributing alms to the weakest, inspecting firebreaks, watching the work of dowsers and well diggers, the sluggish progress of grain barges up the exhausted Stour to unload under heavy guard at Fordwich. A cynical exercise, some say, to make the people associate her with the remedies for the drought rather than its causes, but seeing them together, riding hand in hand, the way he kisses her as he lifts her from the saddle in the outer court, the laughter blooming between them as they climb up to the bailey shoulder to shoulder, hip to hip, it seems to be something much simpler and more reckless.

The difficulty lies in finding the Earl's apartments unattended.

Freya seems always to be there, and the sinister Osbern, and the outer door is guarded night and day because the Earl keeps his treasury and his great seal in those rooms. Sometimes Judith is tempted just to give up and accept her destiny. Then she sees them together, Gytha in her fine gowns and jewels with her doting lover in attendance, the pair of them utterly careless of the spectacle they make with their nuzzling and fondling, and her determination to smash their charmed circle, their wilful conspiracy of oblivion, clenches like a fist in her belly. She thinks of the Earl's casual treachery and her resolve to repay him in bitterer and more heartfelt coin is hammered down against the anvil of her heart.

Bearing her grudge before her like a shield, she climbs the stairs to the private apartments one afternoon when the heat has cast a spell of torpor over the castle and even Lord Odo's guards are dozing at their posts, lolling over their pikes. Although she knows Lord Odo himself is out, having seen him ride away between Terce and morning mass in the company, God be praised, of Osbern, and she has observed Gytha, accompanied by Freya and two guardsmen encumbered with a faldstool, a blanket and a sewing box, setting out after the day meal to walk in the meadow in front of the castle. Sister Jean thinks she has gone to the privy, so she doesn't have long.

"Mistress Gytha sent me to fetch something for her," she announces, her voice strident and uncertain. The men look her up and down without interest and stand aside. It is so easy she is almost resentful, her courage hanging in the air like a half finished sentence. She steps confidently through the door one of the soldiers pushes open for her, only to feel herself almost knocked senseless by the overpowering opulence of Odo's rooms. The hot air is nearly solid with the scent of that perfume he wears, the colours hammer her eyes, weak with age and years of close work, the clutter strewing the floor seems to rise up deliberately to trip her as she wanders around, wondering where to start, stumbling over discarded clothes and scattered cushions, barking her shins on book chests.

Evidence, the Archbishop had insisted, anything to help prove a case against the woman. But what? Judith had pleaded. She was not the sort of person to know what constituted evidence of witchcraft. The Archbishop had merely shrugged his shoulders as if to say nor was he.

"We must release my brother of Bayeux from her spell," he had said, rising to draw their interview to a close. "Only then can we hope to make him see the injustice he has done you."

We. It had been flattering at the time, but now she wishes the Archbishop were more than a sleeping partner in the hunt. *The bedroom*, she thinks, catching sight of the great bed beyond the archway, its hangings tied back to reveal the rich fur coverlet. She approaches the bed cautiously, as though it were a large beast of uncertain temper. It gives off a sickly odour of stale sweat, fallen roses and something else that brings unbidden to her memory the image of her husband, toiling over her stiff, inert body, his sweat dripping and chilling against her skin. She prods at the bedclothes, arm extended to its limit, recoiling from their telltale rumples, the dents in the pillows, one with a long, dark hair snaked across it.

And the tip of a leather thong peeping out from under it, a lace, perhaps, or a drawstring. Something hidden, a secret, this is what she has been looking for. Heart wedged in her throat, she grabs the thong and tugs. The pouch, the one containing Gytha's white cockade. Well that on its own might be of use to the Archbishop, but wait, there's something else. A hard disc, a medallion of some kind. Cramming the pouch into her sleeve she turns her back on the bed and flees, but as she is crossing the parlour, dodging its snares, she hears voices on the other side of the door.

"Ma'am," says one of the guards smartly, then a drumming of feet, scrape of iron on wood as the men come to attention. Judith scans the room in a panic. Nowhere to hide; even the space beneath Lord Odo's worktable is stuffed with locked chests. She scurries behind the door; if the guards close it from the outside, then Gytha, for it must be Gytha, may not see her. If she does...if she does...

The door opens. She is accompanied by Freya, the two of them in deep conversation, their heads inclined at a conspiratorial angle which alerts Judith to the importance of what they are saying.

"So you can do it?" asks Gytha. "You know someone?"

"The same as gave me the charmed stones for Leofwine. I never paid her properly that time. One of your trinkets should cover both debts nicely."

"Good, but it must be quick. If it happened around Easter time..." Gytha holds up one hand and begins to count on her fingers, folding each one down as she says the numbers. "One two, three, four. It's a wonder it doesn't show yet."

"Lucky people only see what they're expecting to see."

"Come through to the solar. My jewel case is there. Let's see what we can spare without his lordship noticing."

Judith waits until she is sure they have crossed the bed chamber and gone into the solar beyond, then opens the door quietly and slips out of the Earl's apartments, head high, wilfully disregarding the idly inquisitive stares of the two guards. But now what? The Archbishop told her what she was to do when she had news for him, but the implications of the conversation she has just heard are so enormous they have driven everything else out of her head. She can scarcely resist the urge to run straight to the abbey and tell him, the witch is with child and is trying to procure a miscarriage. The witch is with child, the witch is with child. It sounds like the refrain of a song.

Once outside the great hall door, she forces herself to take a deep breath and walk with measured steps back across the inner and outer courts to the atelier. As her heart stops jigging and the words cease whirling around her mind, she remembers the code she agreed with the Archbishop. Composing her features into a mournful expression, she tells Sister Jean she has developed a mighty sore head and wonders if a remedy might be sent for from Brother Thorold, who has a particular powder she always finds efficacious.

"Surely you can work till Vespers," retorts Sister Jean, surveying her depleted workshop in exasperation.

"If the powder could be sent for, once I have taken it I could work all night, Sister, if you wished it."

"Very well. Go to your place and I will find someone to send."

"You have done well," says the Archbishop, leaning back in his chair, hefting the battered leather pouch in his cupped palm, but he does not invite her to sit, and his preoccupation seems deeper than when she was orignally summoned before him, as though the first time was only a rehearsal. "Have you looked inside here?" He picks up the bronze and enamel locket in his free hand, letting the chain slip through his fingers.

"No, your grace," she lies, because she could not see that the locks of hair might serve any useful purpose.

"It contains four locks of hair. From a small child, or a baby, or possibly four different babies. Does that suggest anything to you, Judith?"

The woman looks blank, compounding Lanfranc's sadness.

"It suggests to me," he goes on, feeling as though he is wading through mud, "a woman who uses the hair from infants, possibly other parts also, teeth, nail parings and the like, in unchristian practices. And in conjunction with the conversation you overheard and reported to me, a woman who might go to any lengths, even with the fruit of her own womb, to do the bidding of Satan. I believe the...er...products of miscarriage are much sought after by practitioners of the black arts."

"So you think...?"

"I think," he interrupts, his voice welling with passion, "that woman is very dangerous indeed and Odo is risking his soul more than I could begin to imagine when I started my enquiries. She must be stopped before she kills him. Where will they go?"

Judith looks shocked. "I don't know, your grace."

"I might be able to guess," he says, half to himself. There's a woman with an assart in the middle of woodland belonging to the abbey who is rumoured to provide such a service, though he has never been able to catch her out. Perhaps this is his chance to kill two birds with one stone. As soon as he has dismissed Judith, he calls his captain of guards and instructs him to put a discreet watch on the place.

Gytha had not intended to accompany Margaret to the cunningwoman's house. As soon as she had explained the situation to Freya, Freya had taken charge and Gytha had hoped that would be the end of her involvement. Odo will not let her outside the castle compound without an escort. Her presence would only complicate matters. But Margaret was adamant; she mistrusted Freya, she would not go to the wise woman unless Gytha went with her. Gytha judged that Margaret must be three months gone at least; there was no time for persuasion. Fulk could accompany them; he was trustworthy.

Even so they had some difficulty in persuading Margaret to enter the forest. She seemed to become delirious, struggling even against Fulk, muttering some nonsense about men with pink eyes and rats' heads and the murder of the firstborn. Finally, Fulk picked her up and carried her over his shoulder, with Gytha walking where Margaret could see her. Although the path to the cunningwoman's assart is clearly marked for those who wish to see, by scraps of cloth tied to branches, corn dollies and little dishes of bark and leaves and flower petals, Gytha does not think they were observed, despite Margaret's fuss.

Fulk is outside now, while Gytha waits with Margaret in the main room of the house for Freya and the wise woman to conclude their negotiations. The room is dark, its shutters closed and little light entering through the doorway from the overcast day outside. A small fire burns, despite the oppressive heat, mingling the fragrance of pine logs with pungent scents of burning herbs. She smells rosemary, the fragrance of her love, fenugreek seeds smelling of burnt apples, sage to stimulate the mind and catnip to cure the ague, juniper to promote miscarriage. Gytha's sweat breaks, sticky in her armpits, creeping down her spine in a slow, reptilian caress, plastering her gown to her back. The storm's first lightening rips through the mellow firelight, momentarily blinding her.

When her eyes adjust, she sees a long table in the centre of the room, patched with dark stains and scarred with knife cuts, a pile of folded sheets at one end. In the middle of one of the dark patches are two flies fucking. If that's what flies do. Shelves house rows of stone jars, pestles and mortars, neat stacks of muslin strainers and a shallow dish in which various implements of metal and bone gleam fitfully as the light of the fire dances on their polished surfaces.

Freya and the cunningwoman rejoin them. As the cunningwoman lifts the greasy woollen curtain dividing this room from a smaller one at the back, Gytha catches a glimpse of a bed and a large basin standing beside it.

"My Lady will pay you," says Freya.

As she holds out her hand for the gold brooch Gytha has brought, a piece she does not like and never wears, the woman reminds Gytha of the wife of the bathhouse manager in Winchester, who used to collect the girls' rent, fleshy, respectably dressed, with her hair concealed beneath a voluminous matron's head cloth. Her hands are very clean, smooth and plump as a child's. "And the waste, of course."

"The waste?"

"The foetus and the afterbirth. They are very useful and in short supply."

Gytha glances at Margaret, still standing close to the door, looking slowly around her with stunned, vacant eyes. If she has heard what the wise woman said, she has not understood it. She responds to nothing but the thunder and lightening which produce an involuntary shuddering, as though her skin is creeping with parasites.

"Freya," whispers Gytha urgently.

"What is it?"

"What day is it?"

"I don't know. Why?"

"Thunder on a Monday, a woman will die. If it's Monday, we must come back another time."

"Don't worry. She won't take any unnecessary risks."

"Now." The cunningwoman rubs her soft hands together with a dry whisper of skin, looking from Margaret to Gytha and back again, "which of you is the patient? For I think you are both with child."

For a moment Gytha feels as though she is standing on a precipice. She holds her body so still it is as though even her heart has stopped beating, while terror and elation war inside her. She wants to dance and scream, but wills herself not even to smile.

"It is not you, is it, my dear?" the cunningwoman says to her. "Your baby will be a girl child, born under the sign of the Twins who govern the arms that bind in love and obligation. Her stone will be pearl, symbolising wealth." Your baby will be."

"Excuse me," says Gytha in a small, tight voice, and goes outside.

She leans against the wall of the house and takes several deep breaths. The coming rain whispers like gossip in the tops of the trees surrounding the assart. Cupping one hand over her belly, she wonders if it can be true. Her cycle is erratic, but she is sure it hasn't been that long; Odo would have noticed, probably even more quickly than she would herself. And she does not feel different, no nausea, none of that exquisite tenderness of her breasts that used to melt her with the lust for motherhood before fear took over and she simply wished to miscarry quickly rather than lose another child brought to term. Only the seasickness on the way back from Normandy, unusual for her. But what of her fall from her horse in Rochester? She is bound to miscarry this time.

Yet the wise woman was so matter of fact, so certain in her detail. Should she tell him? Not yet. She needs a little time alone with the new life swimming in her womb, her little mermaid, the two in one, an interlude of privacy before Odo takes possession of his child and makes up their trinity. They will be parted soon enough, the fish salter's daughter and the King of England's niece, in the inevitable social replication of birth. The cord of mother love severed, a husband will be found, and her daughter will be made to submit to the partial, imperfect nurturing and grooming of a stranger, a mother in law only, a woman to whom she represents limitable things: money, power, prestige, heirs, ambition. She remembers her own mother-in-law, binding her breasts with strips of linen to curtail the supply of useless milk and quicken her restoration to fertility, tightening the bandages until Gytha cried out in pain. No, she will not tell him yet; she will luxuriate in the freedom to love in secret for just a little longer, to imagine a life for this daughter, unconfined, impossible. She goes back inside.

Freya and the wise woman take Margaret through to the back room, each holding her by one arm.

"Where's Gytha?" she keeps asking, "I'm not going without Gytha." Her legs drag.

The two women push and pull, handling her as though she were a heavy sack, *a load of dumb bad luck*, thinks Freya, *a bag full of rotten seed*. Hardly worth the risk, if doing nothing could not be construed as a slur on her professional reputation. "Come on, Gytha will be back in a minute. The sooner we get started, the sooner it'll be over."

"Will it hurt?"

"Oh no, just a little sting," the wise woman assures her breezily. "Now, up on to the bed with you. Legs apart, bend your knees. A bit further. That's it, lovely. Good girl."

Margaret lies as instructed, staring up at the roof, the thatch pushing between beams festooned with bunches of herbs and leather pouches with labels attached to their drawstrings. It reminds her of the room where she met Martin, and her mind floats back to that time of hope and clarity, the last time, it seems, when she understood anything properly. Since then, it has been as though the effects of Irene's strange teas have never worn off, as though she exists on one side of a semi-transparent curtain and the rest of the world on the other. The only time anything makes sense, when she catches glimpses through a tear in the curtain, is when she is with the men who love her. Even now she exults in her secret courtships, the furtive smiles, the rolling eyes and jerks of the chin, teasing fingers, dark corners, muffled cries. How lucky she is to have so many suitors, the merest thought of whom floods her with passion.

"That's it, dear, you relax, it will make it easier." The cunningwoman emits a small, effortful grunt followed by a sigh. Margaret's body jolts with the sudden stab of the long needle. Pain burns in her belly, her thighs, the base of her back, explodes hot red in her brain. Sweat breaks all over her body, needling her pores, prickling her hair. Her stomach heaves, flooding her mouth with bile. Hands pull her roughly on to her side; the last thing she remembers is the curiously pretty sight of her vomit, yellow and green with specks of red, cascading on to the earth floor.

"Perhaps you shouldn't go in there just yet," says Freya, as Gytha re-enters the house, "not," she adds with a knowing look, "in your condition."

"Has it worked?"

"We shan't know that for a while. She'll be given something to help it along, when she comes round. She bled a lot, though, which is a good sign." Seeing how the colour drains from Gytha's face, she continues, "Look, madam, why don't you go now? It will be an hour or two until Meg can be moved. We don't want his lordship sending after you. Let Fulk take you back and I'll wait here."

Gytha demurs, and goes back outside, where Fulk is nowhere to be found. She calls him once or twice then, thinking perhaps he has moved out of earshot, or stepped behind a tree to relieve himself, then sets out alone, expecting he will catch her up. She has just rounded a bend in the path and is out of sight of the assart, when two men at arms in Lanfranc's livery approach and fall into step on either side of her. One places his hand lightly on her shoulder; she stops. The rain has begun, slow, fat drops smacking against the leaves, spreading dark stains the size of pennies in the dust.

"What day is it?" she asks.

"Monday, madam," one of the men replies. Gytha reaches around the back of her neck to untie the medal of Saint Christopher, which she has not removed since Odo put it there before their voyage to Normandy. Lanfranc's soldiers are clearly nervous; one's hand darts to the hilt of his dagger in response to her movement, making her laugh bitterly.

"Have no fear, I shall come with you quietly. I have nothing to hide from you. But please…" She puts on a wheedling tone, dangling the medal, still warm from its place between her breasts, in front of the soldiers. "Let me tie this to the oak here. It is a sacred tree."

The men exchange doubtful glances, then the one who appears to be senior nods his assent. Wearing the Archbishop's livery is no certain guarantee of salvation.

"I do not know the right words," whispers Gytha to the spirit of the tree as she fastens the medal on its yellow ribbon in one of the lower branches, "but if my gift pleases you, guard poor Meg from the curse of thunder on a Monday." She turns back towards the soldiers. "I will go with you now." Where is Fulk? Perhaps his disappearance is her just desert for being so careless of Margaret.

"He's not here," says Osbern. "He's gone out with Lord Hamo to inspect the firebreaks." As lightning sheets across the square of sky framed by the parlour window and gleams on Fulk's soaked hair, he adds, "I dare say they'll be back sooner than my lord expected."

Fulk brandishes the rolled parchment he is carrying; Lanfranc's seal dangles from the ribbon appending it to the letter. "All the same, I'll go after him. He needs to see this."

Fulk would rather do almost anything than deliver this letter to his master. He thinks of using the storm as an excuse to await the Earl's return, and give him the letter then. He thinks of simply taking a decent horse from the stables and setting out for the coast; back home in Normandy he could lose himself easily enough. But then he thinks of Freya, his ice princess with her winter blue eyes and her spun glass hair, Freya like a pale, polished gem, a diamond or…or…he doesn't know the names of any others, found half buried in mud. He has seen what value his lordship puts on the lives of Saxon women and children, and he doubts the mere fact of Mistress Gytha being a Saxon would save Freya or Thecla if he were to fail in his duty. Or if he succeeds.

Odo and Hamo, oblivious to the rain, are deep in a discussion about replanting some of the breaks with low growing bushes to provide cover for game birds when they hear hoofbeats and, seconds later, Fulk's horse slithers to a halt in front of them, mud and leaf slime spraying up around its fetlocks.

"My Lord." Fulk delves in the breast of his tunic and produces Lanfranc's letter. "An urgent message. From the Archbishop." He sounds panicky, yet Fulk is not a man to frighten easily. Telling himself it is merely that he is breathless from his ride, Odo takes the letter, breaks the seal and reads it. His hands, he observes with irritation, are shaking.

"Do you know what this contains?" he asks Fulk.

"I have an idea, My Lord."

"A lot of men would have balked at bringing me such a message, Fulk, yet you have done it. Twice in a very few months. It begs the question, who is the more foolhardy, you, or Mistress Gytha?"

"I couldn't say, My Lord."

"No." He sighs, drawing the wet, warm air into his lungs. He feels as though his arteries are full of frost, his mind as sharp and dead as an icicle. He bears Fulk no ill will; he knows he cannot afford to waste energy on futile emotions. "Well," he continues, "we had better go and get her back again. Again. Hamo, go back to the castle and bring twenty good men from the garrison to join me at Christ Church. Quick as you can."

"At the abbey, My Lord?"

"Yes, man, the abbey. This is no time for scruples. Now, Fulk, let's go and get even for your black eye, shall we? Were there a lot of them?"

"Three, My Lord," Fulk replies as they coax their horses into a stiff legged gallop in the slippery mud, "and a hulking great smith from the mint. I didn't make it easy for them."

"I'm sure not."

She will say nothing. Odo must come soon and then they will let her go. For now, she will simply keep silent, even if the Archbishop himself tries to question her. He has been down to this room where they are holding her, some kind of strongroom, it seems, beneath the Mint Yard, the only light entering through a narrow, barred window at ground level. Perhaps, usually, coins are kept here, or the ingots of gold and bronze and silver from which they are wrought. He had smiled, displaying long, yellow, irregularly spaced teeth, greeted her courteously and asked if she wanted for anything. Glancing up as a pair of clogs attached to bare, mud spattered ankles passed the window, he had apologised for the rain beginning to drip through it and the absence of anywhere for her to sit. He had not offered any explanation as to why she was there, and she had not asked. She must wait for Odo, surely it cannot be long.

When they reach Christ Church, Odo tells Fulk to wait at the gate to the Archbishop's house. Voices are audible from the chapel adjoining Lanfranc's apartments, singing a psalm.

"Afternoon Mass," says Odo. "If I haven't sent word to you by the end of the service, you must come after me. Hamo should have arrived with the other men by then."

"Yes, My Lord. Good luck, My Lord."

Odo dismounts and knocks on the gate with the butt of his riding whip. The gate swings back with a creak of hinges and a swish of water which has gathered in the hollows worn in the entrance by generations of passing feet. Lanfranc himself is standing in the middle of the courtyard, his cowl pulled over his head, looking, thinks Odo, as lightning flares, like Death's plump assistant.

"I heard the knock," says Lanfranc. "I expected it would be you, though not alone."

"Do I need an army, then?"

"Come inside."

"Afraid I might be struck by a thunderbolt?"

"Simply getting rather wet."

They go into Lanfranc's office where a servant crouches over the hearth, hastily laying a fire in response to the sudden change in the weather. Lanfranc dismisses him; he scuttles past the two men without igniting the fuel. Lanfranc then begins hunting for a tinder box.

"Should be on the desk, I don't know."

Odo contemplates Lanfranc, acting out the part of a querulous old man. Lanfranc is trying to rattle him, and he is succeeding. He attempts to compose some witticism about fire, never where you want it when you want it, always where you least look for it.

"Where is she?" he demands, giving up.

Lanfranc abandons his pantomime and sits down at his desk. "She is here. Safe."

Odo shivers slightly. Cold? Relief? Fear? "What possessed you?" he asks.

"I am directed by my duty. Perhaps it would be best if we kept clear of such words as possessed."

"Don't tell me you really believe she's a witch. You've seen her, she's just a woman, not even a very remarkable one, unless you know her. Good God, man, she doesn't even like cats. They make her sneeze."

He speaks with such a warmth of affection that Lanfranc falters momentarily. "Let us not speak of witchcraft, Odo, it is a crude concept. Perhaps, though, she is your fatalitas, your...what do you say in French, your fairy?"

"Fatalitas, fate. Without doubt she is my fate, but fate is not magic or chance, fate is what we choose. Let me see her, let me take her home. The weather's broken, by tomorrow this will all be forgotten. If, as you say, she has come to no harm, I will not fall out with you over it. We are no more immune to the pressures of hunger and thirst than other men, and such pressures may affect our reason."

"Alas, Odo, I do not think this is as straightforward as you imagine."

"What do you mean?"

"Sit down."

"What do you mean?" Odo repeats, ignoring Lanfranc's invitation. He stands in front of the desk, leaning forwards, gripping its edge with both hands. Let the old man get a stiff neck looking up at him.

"Do you know where we found her?"

Odo shakes his head.

Lanfranc sighs. "My men followed her from the house of a cunningwoman in the forest by Saint Augustine's."

"So? Women are always consulting such people. She probably wanted a charm against toothache or..." He stops himself before saying something that might be offensive to the elderly monk, or give Lanfranc too intimate a glimpse into the life he shares with Gytha. "It's the way their minds work."

"This woman has a particular reputation, Odo. She is an abortionist."

His mouth goes dry, a fist seems to clench around his bowels, he wants to shut his eyes but he just goes on staring at Lanfranc, at his pious, pitying expression, his self righteous, simpering mouth behind that wretched beard which is never properly trimmed.

"You can't bear it, can you?" His voice is very quiet, almost a whisper. He is surprised it works at all; his mouth is so full of words he thinks they may choke him. Lanfranc leans forward to hear him better. He bends further over the table and Lanfranc sits back again. "You're eaten up with envy for men like me. You wouldn't recognise passion if it bit you in the arse, it's all prayer and self denial and dry intellectual puzzles for you. Well, fine, I'm glad, I need your prayers, I need everyone's prayers. But it was your choice to immure yourself in your monastic tomb, your fatalitas. Don't take your revenge on me."

"You're upset, Odo, of course you are..."

"Upset?" Shouting now, pushing himself away from the desk

and prowling around the room, running one hand repeatedly over his tonsured crown as though trying to brush it away. "Upset? What are you talking about? I'm Our Lord turning over the tables of the moneylenders. I'm Moses breaking the tablets. I am the Wrath of God. Never forget it." Borrowed words. Whose?

Lanfranc crosses himself. "Consider what you say, Odo, ask God's forgiveness."

"Oh, God will forgive me, God always forgives me. You know why? Because He loves me, I keep Him entertained. You think God gave us our desires to be triumphed over? That He was setting us some kind of obstacle course? Avarice, gluttony, coveting thy neighbour's ass. Jump through all the hoops and there you are. Heaven. I'm closer to Heaven than you'll ever be, Lanfranc. You know how? Fucking and fighting, Lanfranc, fucking and fighting. That's how a man transcends the earthly and touches the heart of God. The moment you look Death in the face and Death smiles back is the moment you're truly alive." Breathing hard, he turns his back on Lanfranc and presses his forehead against the damp window frame, listens to the rain drumming into the ground outside and the roar of the blood in his veins.

Lanfranc considers him, his broad, powerful silhouette against the liquid grey light, his well cut clothes and long boots in the slightly rakish, Palestinian style. The man talks dangerous nonsense, yet he is probably right. God probably does love men like Odo, the lost sheep, the prodigal sons, more than He loves those who proceed cautiously along the straight and narrow path. All the more reason they should be silenced. "Your heart is dark, Odo, I shall pray for its enlightenment."

"And yours is empty, and I don't think it's worth my praying for its fulfilment. Now let me see Gytha."

"I do not think it wise."

Turning back to face the Archbishop, Odo fixes the older man with his sweetest smile. *What now*? wonders Lanfranc.

"Brother Ealdred," says Odo. "He might not be quite as safe as he believes. One must preserve a healthy scepticism. The margin between a true document and a good forgery is very fine. Perhaps his testimony should be subjected to further scrutiny. If you would like to appoint someone to examine it…"

Lanfranc shakes his head, though there is an element of regret in his gesture which gives Odo hope. He waits, but Lanfranc says nothing.

"I could lose it," he says bluntly, "if you'd let her go. Thomas of York isn't going to starve for the want of three revenues."

"I can't," Lanfranc replies.

Odo is across the room almost more quickly than Lanfranc can think, on the Archbishop's side of the desk, his right hand resting on the hilt of his dagger, his left lightly but firmly gripping the folds of the older man's cowl. "And don't tell me I wouldn't dare, or that the place is crawling with your soldiers. Mine will be there too by now. I'll do what I have to, it doesn't matter to me."

"So there is nothing left, not even the respect you once had for the rule of law?"

"We're playing by your rules today, My Lord Archbishop. The evidence on which you're holding my mistress is barely circumstantial. Now, I suggest you let me see her and then release her on my parole while you try to scrape together a case against her."

"The charges are too serious for any parole, but you may see her, provided you will hold your own men in check. Perhaps it will serve to convince you of the heinousness of her crimes. "

The door of the strongroom is thick, solid oak armoured in iron, muffling the sound of approaching footsteps so Gytha has no time to prepare for his arrival. She looks up when she hears the bolt slide back outside the door to see him standing in front of her, head slightly bowed in the low entrance, like a wish come true.

"Oh, Odo." She feels as though some external force, some energy compounded of relief, love, fear and simple, physical attraction propels her across the room towards him. Before he has even stepped over the threshold her arms are around his waist, her cheek against his chest, feeling his heart beat through the bones of her skull, steady, calming, the steps to freedom.

Instinctively he holds her, strokes her hair, murmurs soothing nonsense to her as he might to a child in the throes of a nightmare. Then he remembers what Lanfranc has told him. His body stiffens. He prises her arms from his waist and holds her away from him. She is a pitiful sight, her face streaked with tears and now full of dismay and confusion. She is so small. He knows that, of course, his body knows the precise spot where the top of her head habitually makes contact with it when he hugs her, cushioned by the tendons linking his shoulder and breastbone, the exact soft place at the base of her belly that will yield to his erection. Would. If. But he has never properly considered her vulnerability before, how easy it would be to twist her head that little bit further, bend her body into a slightly deeper arc. And snap her spine.

She has seen this implacable expression before, on the battlefield at Senlac Ridge, though then it was not directed at her, and his face, younger, less heavyset, seemed to hold more potential for redemption. Then he was her enemy, but now she fears him more. Archbishop Lanfranc has told him, then, how and where she was found.

"Get out," he says to the two men accompanying him. They hesitate. "Oh for heaven's sake," Odo continues wearily, "where am I going to go from here, with you outside the door? Through that little window? I'm a priest, not a miracle worker. Now go. Lock us in if it makes you feel better." Panic flickers in her eyes. Good.

"What have you done?" he asks when the men have gone, sliding the bolt back into place behind them. She wonders if it will happen now, if they have sealed her into her tomb. "Don't deny anything. Lanfranc has told me where his men found you."

Even if he could command the guards to unlock the door and she were to walk out of the abbey beside him, she is trapped, enmeshed as surely as a fish in a net by what she knows and cannot tell. She remembers One-Eyed Peg in Winchester, and imagines, with a welling up of nausea, in itself both wonderful and terrifying, Margaret, cowering, bruised, flayed, beaten by the whips and stones and hypocritical tongues of the righteous men who rule the world. She knows she was the only one taken, the only bait of interest to Lanfranc's men, and she cannot give Margaret away. Already weighed down by her responsibility for the poor, stupid girl's plight, she cannot bear the burden of exposing her to a punishment she does not deserve.

Yet she will not lie to Odo so she must simply keep her mouth shut. Yet he, and Lanfranc, will take her silence to be an admission of guilt. The sharp ache of his breaking heart is hers also as she thinks of the cunningwoman's words. Your child will be. If she is right, she must also be wrong, because the child cannot live without her mother, and she is certain Odo will not let her live if he believes she has aborted his baby. She is stretched between the witchcraft Lanfranc accuses her of, and the witchcraft Agatha knows she has accomplished. The choice is stark – Margaret, or herself and her child, love or duty, self indulgence, or self respect.

She looks at Odo, willing him to read her conflict in her eyes but it is like looking at a stone.

"Speak," he says, in a flat, emotionless tone which takes her straight back to the trials following the riot in Winchester after the child was killed by his horse.

"I have nothing to say." It is as though the words have come from someone else, though she feels the air vibrate as she pushes them out of her throat. How can this be happening to them, these two whom Sister Jean says have loved each other since before they were born? It's impossible, but it's not, because love is not the answer to everything.

"Then," he says, almost conversationally, "you may rot here until the Devil sees fit to take you, madam. I only pray, for the ease of my brother, Archbishop Lanfranc, it is not too long." He knocks on the door and the bolts slide back with fat, well oiled clicks.

He wonders how he manages to get back outside without stumbling, so overwhelmed is he by grief and incomprehension. He cannot bear to return to Lanfranc with 'I told you so' plastered all over his sanctimonious face, but stands, for how long he has no idea, in the Mint Yard, letting the rain cool the fever in his brain and mask his tears. Tipping his face to heaven, muffled now in impenetrable layers of cloud, he yells at God, "Is it so much to ask? Is it? Just a woman and a child like other men have?"

She hears him through the grate, below which water leaks down the wall, his hoarse, fretful shouting above the steady thunder of the rain, the heavy splash as he falls to his knees in the mud. Curled up in a corner, trying to make herself the smallest possible target for sorrow, she moans to herself, the same phrase over and over until she falls into a merciful trance, "I'm sorry, Odo, I'm so sorry."

Somewhere in the deep, dark time between Compline and Matins, Odo awakes in need of a piss. Shivering in the cold air the rain has brought in its wake, a memory overwhelms him, of climbing back into bed beside her some night, somewhere, and how she had hooked her knee over his thigh, and the warm, wet kiss of her secret mouth against his flesh. Such a simple thing, deep, direct and true. Desire hits him like the flat of a sword in his midriff, forcing the breath out of him in a great sob, which brings Osbern in from the next room. He thinks of making Osbern share his bed, for warmth, but the prospect of a body other than hers beside him is too painful to contemplate. You cannot lie to yourself in the darkest, loneliest hours of the night.

"It's nothing, Osbern, go back to sleep."

It is his fault. He has not loved her well enough to make her trust him. If she had truly believed their child might live she would never have done such a heinous, cruel thing. He should have realised, should have understood the strength of her conviction that she could not bear a healthy child. If only they had gone to see John, and she had been able to weigh him in the balance against her dead babies, if only he were not so hungry for power, if only, if only...

Believing they had a lifetime in front of them, nothing he has said or done has been sufficient. He has not asked the right questions, nor given the right answers. Not a single gift he has given her, of jewels, or horses, of words or land, or his own body, has adequately expressed his need, his hunger, his adoration. He has not possessed her, she has slipped away from him to a place he cannot follow. If his heart were to be removed from his chest and held up to the light, her image would be plainly visible, not written with a pen of iron or the point of a diamond but tattooed with woad, the way of the elusive Britons. He will never possess her, there will be no children, no heirs. It is a love destined to die in infancy, never to be more than a memory, a romance, a morality tale.

Gytha does not sleep, yet nor does she believe she is really awake. Her consciousness seems to have slipped sideways. Hugging herself to ward off the cold, her hands are no longer her own. She feels her skin, its down of fine hair, the way it stretches over her bones and slackens in the hollows of her body, as though touching some substance other than herself. Her hands, cupping her breasts, registering the erect points of her cold hardened nipples against their palms, running up the insides of her thighs, are Odo's. His curls she strokes, his lips parting under the pressure of her fingers, his name in her mouth.

Then, as she speaks his name aloud in the darkness, suddenly she sees him again as he was when she first laid eyes on him, in the company of Harold and Lady Edith, in that house which no longer exists. All of them, herself included, are like the illuminations in one of Odo's books, tiny, bright, intricately lovely, yet unreal, stylised representations of themselves which no longer belong in this world of flesh, blood and bone. Turning on to her back, she stretches herself flat against the straw they have tossed her to lie on, sensing the cold, damp earth of the floor beneath, smoothing her clothes over skin that feels as cold and dead and empty as clean vellum.

The storms continue unabated. From the window of Odo's bedchamber it looks as though the bailey on its mound is afloat in a sea of yellow mud, a precarious web of planks spread over the deepest puddles. Thunder grumbles in the distance and from time to time lightning throws a sudden wash of silver and blue over the grey and brown and the unearthly stillness of Odo's features. He has not moved from his bed since the night after Gytha's arrest, indeed, he has scarcely moved at all but lies, on his back, unshaven, in his night gown, which is beginning to stink, staring up into the indigo depths of the bed canopy. The last time he spoke was to let fly a string of invective against his physician, sent for by Osbern several days ago. Osbern does not think he has even seen his master blink, though he moves one hand from time to time, languidly stroking Juno, who cowers beside him with only her snout and terrified eyes visible under the bedclothes. The dog has thwarted all Osbern's attempts to rouse Lord Odo, even to wash or shave him, baring her teeth and snapping as though only she can comprehend what is going on in his mind. If anything.

He is not ill. Hovering just beneath the canopy, he looks down on himself lying in bed and knows he must rouse himself. He has to hold courts, hear petitions, take action to minimise the damage done by these storms just as he dealt with the drought before. He must inspect the atelier, make certain there are no leaks in the workshop roof and that the women have not lit braziers or candles against the descent of this permanent seeming dusk. He must give orders for the mares in suck to be brought into the hall before their foals drown, if Hamo has not already done so.

But before all that, he must decide what he is going to do about Gytha, and he cannot. Every scrap of physical and mental energy he possesses has been sucked into the vortex of his indecision where possible solutions whirl past too quickly for him to grasp or even see clearly. Often he dozes and in the seconds after waking, before he knows he is awake, the answer will be clear to him, only to dissipate as dreams do, as all the other things he has to think about crowd back in on him. *Simple*, says the man's body in the bed, soaked in cold piss and dog saliva, *you love her, forgive her, get her out of there and start again. Simple,* answers the sprite swinging from the cobwebs stretched between blue satin pleats, *she betrayed you, she did the worst thing a woman can do to a man, let Lanfranc condemn her. Forget her.*

Forget her? Don't be absurd, says his body. *Think about something else,* his mind pleads, like a choirmaster trying to bring discipline to a disorderly set of responses and antiphons.

Before long, Gytha loses track of the time they have kept her in this room, with its sodden floor and sweating walls, and sudden, magical glitters of gold dust when people come in with candles, which they do sporadically, throwing food at her from the door as if she is a dangerous beast. The days and nights leak into one another, the compartments formed by bells or meals, light and dark, breaking down as she drifts in and out of a torpid, dream-like inertia. Sometimes people speak to her, her guards, the novice who throws the food, the Archbishop, she thinks, his prophet's beard wagging, his scalp pink as a baby's bottom under his sparse hair. She doesn't listen to any of them.

All she does is ask for Odo, all she hears is the silence which follows her pleas. If her mouth so much as forms the full moon shape of his name, if she even thinks of him, it seems, they shake their heads and turn away. So she gives up speaking, which only exacerbates the cracks forming in her lips, and tries to give up thinking, but her mind will not stay empty, he fills it, and Meg, and the baby. The baby. What did the cunningwoman say? What did she really say? what is her body telling her when there is nothing else to listen to but the scrabbling of rats and the soggy rustle of soiled straw? *Your child will be.*

THE MIRACLE

SAINT GERMANUS TO ALL SOULS 1072

Odo awakes from a sleep that has descended like a gauze over his brain, fuzzing but not quite cutting out the remorseless round of arguments between the sprite in the cobwebs and the body on the bed, to find himself looking, not at the bed canopy but up into the face of his sister. Her features appear strangely pulled forward, cheeks, brows, lips all bunched around her sharp nose like a curious configuration of sails about a mast. He starts to laugh, though Agatha shows no sign of wishing to join him.

"You are awake? Aren't you?" she demands. "Because I need to speak to you." Juno growls. Agatha looks as though she may growl back. "This can't go on, Odo. What with nursing Margaret, and Judith suddenly worse than useless...the workshop isn't functioning and I need you to do something about it." She has tried to be patient with him, but if he is not ill, what is the meaning of this extraordinary lassitude, with Gytha imprisoned, the little of what remains of the livestock drowning in mudslides, the grain brought in from Normandy at such expense rotting in sodden granaries, and his workshop full of idle hands and poisonous gossip? Determined to bring him round, she will tip him out of bed and scrub him head to toe with cold water herself if need be. Watching a sullen frown settle between his eyes, she realises he is just a small boy in a sulk.

"Nursing Margaret?" he queries, prompted by what he will think of for the rest of his life as some kind of guardian angel. "What's wrong with her?"

Agatha's strangely distorted face recedes, then reappears looking more like Agatha as she perches on the edge of the bed and stares at her hands, wrangling in her lap.

"Freya says it's…a miscarriage. I suppose I shouldn't be surprised, considering…"

"A miscarriage?" The vortex stops spinning, the sprite clambers nimbly down the carved bedpost and slips back into his body, smooth as a knife. He sits up, elbowing the dog out of the way. "Margaret," he says, smiling at Agatha, a gleam in his eyes which comes as a relief to her after the eerie sensation that he had somehow gone missing from himself, though she cannot imagine what it presages. "Thankyou." He squeezes her hands, quickly and fiercely, then everything is a whirl of activity. Flinging back the bedclothes, he almost tips his sister off the edge of the bed. As he shouts for Osbern to have the bath filled, bring shaving things, find him a clean shirt, he is already stripping off his nightclothes regardless of her presence in his bed chamber.

"Christ, I stink!"

"The workshop, Odo."

He gives her a blank look then waves her irritably away. "Yes, yes, later. Go and find Freya for me. Send her to me, and tell them to saddle me a horse."

"And three bags full, sir," says Agatha with a bow, but her teasing is lost on him so she shrugs and goes to relieve Freya at Margaret's bedside.

Freya looks momentarily panic-stricken when Agatha delivers Odo's summons, but recovers her usual, glacial composure almost immediately, handing over care of the invalid with calm efficiency.

"I've just changed her cloth, but she's still bleeding quite heavily, and you should give her another spoonful of the syrup when they ring the bell for Sext. I'll be happier when her fever goes down."

Taking up a bowl of rosewater and a linen rag, Agatha begins patiently to mop the girl's brow, dipping, ringing out, dabbing at her broad, pale forehead and freckled temples, tidying the damp coils of hair which have escaped from her coif. Soothed by the rhythm of her actions, she begins to hum the tunes of old rhymes remembered from her childhood, until Margaret's eyelids flutter down over her gooseberry green eyes and she seems to sleep. How strange, reflects Agatha, as her fingertips make contact with the girl's clammy skin, that dreams may come true, but only when you have stopped wanting them to as though only by ceasing to be dreams can they become realities. How fitting that her career, founded on her revulsion from the violence of the sexual act between men and women, should come to this, to tending its casualties.

When Freya is shown into Odo's parlour, he is rummaging in a jewel case, clad only in shirt and chausses, Osbern standing behind him with a long tunic of dark brown velvet draped over his arms. She tries to convince herself that he has sent for her merely to ask her to take something to Mistress Gytha, but she cannot deceive herself so easily. Why not go himself? And what could her mistress want with jewellery in the abbey prison?

"Freya." As soon as he becomes aware of her presence, he closes the jewel case and fixes his attention on her, drawing her gaze to his despite Osbern helping him on with the tunic, tying its gold laces, fastening a belt set with turquoises and some green stones she cannot identify about his hips, fussing with a clothes brush and several pairs of shoes. "You must tell me all you know about your mistress' visit to the cunningwoman, Gunhild."

He is impressed that her gaze does not falter, she does not blush, or fidget, or even pause before replying. Almost as though she has anticipated his question and has been rehearsing her reply.

"The truth," he impresses upon her, "not whatever story you may have concocted between you should I ask."

"She should have told you herself," responds Freya bluntly. "What on earth has she said to you?"

"Nothing. Literally. She would not open her mouth."

Freya pushes an exasperated blast of air down her nose. "So proud, that one," she mutters.

"I beg your pardon?"

"She came to me for help, sir, knowing I have some...expertise." She darts Odo a cautious glance, but he bids her continue with a gesture of his hand. "Told me some long, involved tale about Margaret and a hedge preacher who had raped her but was really her brother, so..."

"Her brother? Good God."

"Yes, but he doesn't know it, apparently. He's quite mad and believes he's Saint Sebastian."

Odo turns very pale and sits down suddenly.

"Are you ill, sir?"

"No. Go on."

"Well, Mistress Gytha felt responsible, because she had helped Meg get away to try and find her brother and persuade him to go home to his wife and child, but then this happened, and Meg came to my mistress saying she was sure she was pregnant and sure her brother was the father."

"How could she be so sure? By all accounts she's since acquired a taste for barnyard behaviour, however nasty her initiation."

Freya shrugs. "Women just know these things, My Lord. We feel it. I can't say more."

"So you and Gytha took the wretched girl to this Gunhild, and I suppose Gytha wouldn't talk because she was afraid of getting either of you into trouble. Of all the women I should fall in love with, why must it be one with such a contrary head on her shoulders?" And there, he thinks, is a question with its own answer hidden inside it.

"There's more," says Freya. God knows, the Earl must be as grieved and anxious as any man about his mistress, but Gytha's misplaced heroics have spoilt things for her and Fulk also. By telling his lordship everything, Freya sees her chance to strengthen Gytha in his favour and restore her own position at Winterbourne.

"Yes?"

The wise woman said Mistress Gytha was with child also. She asked which of them had come for her help, for she thought they were both expecting. She said…" But before she can finish he has bounded across the room like an affectionate puppy and, seizing her face between his hands, plants a resounding kiss on her forehead.

"After the Holy Virgin and my beloved Gytha," he says, "you are the most wonderful woman that ever lived," and is gone, running down the stairs to the hall with Osbern in pursuit.

"Your cloak, sir, it's still raining."

"Is it, Osbern?" he shouts back over his shoulder. "It feels like the first day of spring to me."

He will have their bed made with clean linen, scattered with bunches of mint and lavender, ready for her return, he thinks as he gallops through the narrow streets, a couple of guardsmen clearing a path for him through the shopkeepers and their customers, herdsmen with small flocks of soaked sheep and mud caked pigs, an enterprising fellow hawking squares of oilcloth with head holes cut in them to make rain capes. She will have every care and consideration. She will be kept away from dogs and needles. She will not eat pork nor ride, especially not ride, after her terrible fall at Rochester, when she must already have been carrying the child. He crosses himself at the memory of it. She must not stoop or bathe or sit to the left of a monk.

He will kiss her eyes and hold her in his arms, but he will not make love to her, and he will sprinkle her with holy water and pray for her daily. He will make her presents of jewels set with jasper, moonstone and chrysolite, all known to have special virtues for pregnant women. Six grains of pearl powder ingested daily will ensure the quality of her milk. The child will be born and will live, and there will be more, a dynasty, a whole string of brothers for John.

The abbey community is at None when he arrives, his horse skidding through the cautious crack in the gate with which the surprised porterer responds to his torrent of knocking and shouting. Flinging himself out of the saddle and tossing the reins to one of his guards, he makes straight for the chapel, where the singing of the psalm falters, then recovers as he slams the north door open and strides the short distance to the middle of the transept where the Archbishop's throne stands, the monks' voices mirroring the guttering of the candles in the sudden blast of damp air.

With the briefest of bows to the altar, he confronts Lanfranc.

"I need to see her," he says in an urgent, careless whisper heard by all.

Let not mine enemies triumph over me, chants the congregation. Lanfranc signs him to be patient, patting down the air with the flat of his hand.

"Now," he hisses. One of the novices at the front of the congregation steals a quick glance in his direction and receives a withering stare from the novice master for his pains.

Thou art the God of my salvation, the monks sing.

With a sigh, Lanfranc rises from his throne and leads the way back out of the north door. Odo's spurs clank behind him, an incongruous accompaniment to the psalm. As Odo closes the door, Lanfranc rounds on him, the lappets of his mitre whipping furiously in the wind which has risen as the rain abates to a needling drizzle.

"What is the meaning of this?" he demands, as though Odo had been summoned before him at Bec to answer some charge of stealing books or raiding the kitchens during the Great Silence. But Odo is no longer a boy in his charge, and it is his mistake to keep forgetting it.

"You must let her go." His handsome face is disfigured by a triumphant sneer.

"I must do nothing of the sort," Lanfranc replies testily. It is cold out here, the wind beginning to snarl around the corners of the buildings and slap the face of the abbey fish pond on the far side of the monks' burial ground where they are standing among hummocks and headstones. He sniffs.

"She is innocent," crows Odo. "She never intended to procure herself an abortion. You got the wrong end of the stick, old man, and I have witnesses to prove it."

"Do you have the cunningwoman then? I could not find her anywhere."

"No, of course I don't. Neither of us will find her, she'll be too well hidden. People value such women, they take care of them, they believe in Christ, but they like some insurance."

"Nevertheless, I shall continue to look." But not too hard, he adds to himself, because if she doesn't reappear, I can take back her assart which clutters up my forest.

"As you please. She is of no interest to me. I have other news which changes everything. Mistress Gytha is pregnant, so even if you try her you cannot carry out any sentence until after my child is born." My child. His collarbones ache with joy and impatience.

Lanfranc tugs at his beard. Perhaps it would be wisest to let Odo see the woman. Obviously he has not had this information from her directly, or even from the cunningwoman, who is no doubt prone, like most of her sort, to making such predictions, so it is always possible he is wrong and she will tell him so, and it must be her who tells him; he will not believe anyone else. If he is right, though, if he is right... He looks at the younger man's flushed cheeks and shining eyes and shudders. He is as certain as he can be, since seeing the locket, that the woman is engaged in some diabolical practices involving the killing of infants. The thought of what she might do to a child of Odo's shrinks his vitals, if, indeed, the child is his and not the spawn of the devil himself. "Come, then, I will take you to her."

A rage like a whirlwind descends on him as the guard unlocks the door to the strongroom and stands aside for he and Lanfranc to enter, sucking everything out of him but a boiling fury whose heat stings his eyes and dries his mouth and leaves his body trembling like the last, desiccated leaf on a winter tree. He turns to Lanfranc to protest, but his voice has shrivelled to no more than a dry whisper and his words are jumbled, meaningless. Not that he needs them; as Lanfranc's gaze shifts from him to the figure cowering in the corner and back again, he sees that he is understood by the shame and mortification in the Archbishop's face.

"How could you?" he manages finally, "How could you treat her this way? I thought you were a Christian."

But she is not, Lanfranc wants to reply, though considering the confined space they are in and the knife in Odo's belt, he thinks better of it and says nothing, merely bows his head beneath Odo's contempt. A frightened whimper comes from the corner, tugging Odo around to face his mistress. His anger dissipates as quickly as it came, dissolved in pity as he drops to his knees in the filthy straw and gathers her into his arms, burying his face in her hair, breathing in its loved, familiar musk through all the other smells of her imprisonment. Wet cloth, piss, shit, sweat; loneliness, starvation, fear of the dark. He raises her face and kisses her, feels with his tongue that she has lost a tooth in her upper jaw, near the back. Tracing the lines of her small bones with his fingertips, he conjures warmth back into her skin, desire as he touches her breasts and she squirms against him with a little sigh, then falls still as he cups his hand over her belly and contemplates his child, their child, their miracle.

"Freya told me," he whispers.

It is just another dream. Her dreams have become almost unbearably vivid since her imprisonment, as though her mind is trying to fight the solitude and boredom by filling her cell with visions. Sometimes its workings are too rich for her so she awakes retching and vomits up the little they give her to eat. She feels her lover so deeply and intensely inside her she fears her heart may tear, she hears the singsong lilt of her mother's stories with such clarity the words flay her like tiny knives. When Adam comes to her, she believes she is one of his barrels, strapped tight in iron bands, stuffed full of salt fish, her father's raw red hands reaching in to turn and sort and weigh and value. The best dreams are of her children, because they have the same calm reality she feels now, and she only knows she is dreaming when she realises the children are no longer babies but grown, playing, squabbling, helping with the chores. And that there are five of them.

"Odo," she says sleepily and smiles, and closes her eyes, her cheek resting against his chest. He lets her stay that way for a moment, cradling her carefully in his arms, afraid, suddenly, that she has lost her mind, not wanting to wake her in case it is true. But he must. Lanfranc's gown rustles as he shifts his footing. The oblong of muddy light afforded by the grating blurs and wanes. He cannot let her spend another night like this. He must persuade her to speak, so Lanfranc can hear it from her own lips.

"Why did it have to be Freya?" he asks, his voice still soft, but with an insistent edge.

It seems an age before she replies. Holding her gaze, he tries to prompt her by the force of his will. He dare not say more in case Lanfranc accuses him of putting words in her mouth. Then all of a sudden it is as though she has come back into focus.

"I was afraid for..." She darts a scared look at Lanfranc and falls silent.

"But more afraid for her than for our baby?"

"I didn't think..."

"You convinced yourself the child would die, didn't you, the way the others did? So you thought to save...the girl rather than yourself."

She nods miserably. He is careful to shift his weight so Lanfranc can see her.

"But he won't die, darling. He'll grow like John, you'll see. He'll be bigger than me one day."

With a curious smile, both loving and vexed, she says, "She, Odo. The wise woman said the child would be a girl, that she would be born under the sign of Gemini and her stone would be pearl." Her eyes hold some inner light, like phosphorescence on the sea.

"A daughter." His voice is full of wonder. Raising his right hand, he makes the sign of the cross with his thumb on her forehead. "God be praised. She will be as precious to me as Our Lady to Saint Anne. You hear that, Lanfranc?" he asks, rising to his feet. "Now, my love," raising her also, his hands beneath her arms, feeling how close her bones cleave to her skin, "I'm going to take you home."

"Wait." Lanfranc steps into the doorway, raising his hand as though bestowing a blessing. "What the woman says is hardly proof. She must be properly examined."

Odo feels Gytha shudder against him.

"And how can we know the child is yours...?"

"What?" He laughs in disbelief.

"...and not some trick of Beelzebub," finishes Lanfranc.

"If she were the devil's handmaid, don't you think she would have escaped your clutches by now, old man? Or at least made sure she kept herself clean and well fed, as Lucifer tempted Our Lord in the wilderness?"

"If she does not flinch at the Cross, she has the power to resist miracles. This is her means." Lanfranc is imperturbable "You are her instrument."

She senses his withdrawal in a slight tensing of his muscles, the opening of a little space between their bodies as he straightens up. The fear he dispelled begins to trickle back like a cold sweat between the shoulderblades, a sickness, the nagging whine of a wheel that needs oiling. He has fallen for Lanfranc's plausible logic. He doubts, he does not love her, he too believes their daughter will die. Though her throat does not contract to form sobs, tears begin to spill out of her eyes, catching on her lashes, at the corners of her mouth, on the sharp edge of her jaw. Her nose runs. She should make some effort to wipe her face, but she is so tired, so desperate for peace and order and freedom from dreams.

He understands. He is drawing his knife now for her, to put her to rest like the little roan mare on the beach at Rochester. Yet he is not looking in her direction but at Lanfranc. He takes a step towards the Archbishop, pulling her with him then, in a whirl of movement too complicated for her to follow, suddenly he has his free arm braced across Lanfranc's chest and his knife at the old man's throat.

"And you are my instrument," he hisses between his teeth.

The guard who let them in makes a half hearted attempt to rescue his lord, but he has only to adjust his grip on his pike for Odo to jerk the knife up under Lanfranc's chin, the blade pressed against his windpipe, well enough honed to shave a few hairs from his beard.

"Stand aside," says Lanfranc, sounding like a strangled cat, "he will not harm me."

"Keys," says Odo to the guard. He hesitates, Odo gives the knife another jerk, the guard holds out the keys. "Take them," says Odo to Gytha. "Lock him in. Get inside," he orders the guard, and Gytha locks the door behind him, dropping the keys on the ground. Odo kicks them down the passage. "Walk," he tells Lanfranc, "to the main courtyard."

His luck is with him. The service of None is still in progress, and they see no-one as they make their way through the maze of stairs and passages, the Archbishop frequently stumbling because Odo has forced his head up at such an angle he cannot see where he is putting his feet, Gytha almost running to keep up with her lover's long stride. Coming to a side door which leads into the great court, Odo kicks it open with the flat of his foot and pushes Lanfranc out into hazy evening sunlight lying like spilt honey in the ruts and puddles. A couple of link boys hurry past with their torches, going to light the lamps in the refectory, but the group approaching Odo's two men at arms and the three horses is just a tarry mirage to them, veiled by heat haze from their flambeaux, and they carry on chatting together as they do every evening.

Odo's men approach, leading his horse between them. Eyebrows are briefly raised, but they know better than to ask questions and the elder of the two, who has been in Odo's service for twenty years or more, remembers he once had the Duke's uncle, Archbishop Mauger, at knifepoint over a disputed game of chequers.

"Help Mistress Gytha to mount," Odo orders the man, "and be careful with her." The guard dismounts, takes Gytha around the waist and lifts her bodily on to Odo's horse, then remounts and the three animals walk towards the gate, the two soldiers bunched protectively either side of Gytha, who clings to the pommel of Odo's saddle. The horse is the tallest she has ever ridden, and a sudden, irrational notion enters her head that this must be what riding a camel feels like, and she thinks, when we get home, *I shall tell him*.

Seeing Bishop Odo and the Archbishop enter the court, the porter comes out of his lodge to open the gates. Then looks again, and hesitates, his hands braced under the bar, his mouth agape like a baby bird's.

"Open it," Odo tells him. The porter's eyes fly to the Archbishop's face. Lanfranc nods as well as he is able with Odo's dagger wedged under his jaw and the porter lifts the bar. Once the gate is fully open, Odo releases Lanfranc, sheaths his knife and mounts his horse behind Gytha.

"Good day, Lanfranc." His smile, as he turns the horse and spurs it through the gate, is very broad and full of mischief.

Only much later, when Gytha has bathed and eaten, and he sits watching her sleep, her hair tangled around her heart shaped face, her lashes casting long, blue shadows across her pale cheeks, her body so frail and infinitely precious beneath the lavender scented sheets and the fox fur coverlet, does he begin to wonder what he has done. What act of love began the work of creation going on inside her? Some long night of lazy passion, or one of those intense encounters that glitter like jewels in his memory, on beds of leafmould or in the dark turns of deserted stairs?

And what sort of world will this daughter be born into, now that he has made an enemy of Lanfranc, his brother's most loyal friend? He has ordered the castle guard doubled. No-one is to go in or out except on his personal authority. Even now they are bringing up crates of swords, bows and halberds from the armoury to be kept in readiness in the hall, and the fletcher and his boys are hard at work increasing stocks of arrows. He has told Agatha to dismantle her workshop, and despatched men to carry the chests containing the embroidery and all Agatha's plans up to the bailey also. When his love awakes he will have to tell her it is not safe for her to leave the tower, that she has simply exchanged one prison for another, albeit one with fine food and a feather mattress. But the air here is poisoned by his guilt, it cannot do his child any good.

He creeps out of his apartments, instructing Freya not to stir from her mistress' side, and goes in search of his confessor. Compline has been sung and by rights his household should be settling itself for the night, but everywhere is bustle and restlessness, the hall packed with soldiers and the women from the atelier who would normally return to their homes in the town at night, light spilling from the forge, the armoury and the fletcher's workshop, torches snaking up and down the motte. It is as though the entire castle is infected by a fever.

He finds his confessor at the horse lines with Countess Marie; they are trying to persuade one of her daughters there is no need to take her pony up to the hall. Prising the man away from the distraught child and the countess, who has a mutinous, volcanic look about her, he goes with him to the chapel, where he tells him, without sparing either of them, how, incensed by Lanfranc's accusations against his mistress, he drew a knife on the Archbishop and held him hostage for her safety.

"I did wonder what all this was for," he says, with the familiarity born of his peculiar intimacy with his lord's soul, when he has pronounced absolution. *He's stalling*, thinks Odo, *he can't decide what penance I deserve*. But repentance was not the true purpose of this confession. What he wanted was to clear his mind; by confessing his actions he has put them in order and stacked them up outside himself, like a housewife clearing her rooms for spring cleaning. And knows exactly what he must do. He must go to William, get to him before Lanfranc does, and tell his side of the story. There can be no question of Lanfranc presiding over a fair trial, since he has clearly already made his mind up that

Gytha is a witch. There might as well be no trial at all until the child is delivered, since no corporal sentence may be carried out on a pregnant woman, and by then, he will have spirited her away somewhere safe.

"What you have done is grievously sinful, My Lord," the priest continues when Odo makes no response, "but as no harm came to the Archbishop, other than a stiff neck, perhaps, which is not exactly an injury, I see no need for a physical penance. On the other hand…a pilgrimage. A long one. To Compostela, or even Jerusalem."

Odo gives an absent-minded nod of concurrence. A pilgrimage to Westminster first, he thinks, shouting for Osbern over the hubbub in the courts.

When Odo arrives at the king's palace, the high, hammer-beamed hall is full of people. A court is in noisy session just inside the great door, before a judge unknown to Odo, drowsing fitfully over a dispute as to milling rights on one of the city's many rivers. A merchant, surrounded by rolls of carpet, awaits an audience with the king. Odo recognises William, Bishop of London, who breaks off from conversation with a group of other priests to greet him, but responds with no more than a curt nod as he makes his way towards his brother, seated at a long table on a dais with a number of plans spread before him. Standing looking over his shoulder is a man whose dusty hair and leather apron proclaim him to be a mason.

Odo steps on to the dais and kneels on one knee, head bowed. The curious eyes of everyone else in the room burn the back of his neck; he feels the sweat break and prickle his skin. But everything must be done properly. He has taken care to leave his men at arms outside the palace gates, and his swordbelt in Osbern's custody at the entrance to the hall, though he is still wearing the shirt of light mail he thought it prudent to put on for the journey.

"Odo," says William, dismissing the mason with a nod of his head. He does not sound surprised. Surely no messenger from Lanfranc can have reached him already, though one of his own spies possibly…

490

"Your Grace." He kisses William's proffered hand.

"Get up, man, no need to stand on ceremony. I've been expecting you. Drink?"

Both men rise and embrace, exchanging the kiss of peace. William dispatches a servant to bring wine and clear the hall, though the crowd is slow to disperse. *Carrion crows*, thinks Odo savagely. They sit with the wine jug between them, William in his high backed chair at the head of the table, Odo across its corner from him, on the end of a padded bench. The lamps smoke, logs settle in the fire, a sudden flurry of wingbeats draws their attention briefly, away from one another and towards a knot of sparrows roosting in the beams.

"Well?" says William eventually.

Odo pours wine for them both. "It seems you know why I'm here."

William drinks. "It has to do with the woman, I suppose."

He doesn't know, no word has come from Lanfranc. Odo feels almost more shaken by relief than by the prospect that William was already familiar with the facts as Lanfranc wished to present them. "Something new has come to light," he says. The wine beckons but he dare not lift his cup for fear William should see his hands trembling.

"Oh yes?"

"She is pregnant, William, she is expecting my child." He pauses. Best not to divulge Gytha's conviction she already knows the sex of the child. "Your niece or nephew." He watches William absorb the news. A brief flicker of pride lights his lonely eyes, marooned among the folds of fat developing around his cheeks and brows, before their look of old ice or glass pebbles returns and his mouth turns thin and mean.

"How do you know? It could be a trick."

"She would not lie about such a thing, you must take my word for that."

"Your word, Odo?" He gives a harsh laugh. "Show me proof and I will listen."

Clinging to the thought of that brief, arctic glow in William's eyes, he says coolly, with just the right note of masculine camaraderie in his voice, "Proof, brother? Diagnosing pregnancy is hardly an exact science. If I tell you she is sick, bursts into tears over foolish songs or finches in cages, has a yearning for lambs' liver with honey and has missed two courses, will you call that proof?" He leans towards William and glares at him. "Or perhaps you must have some quack poke and prod her till she miscarries and you can see the foetus for yourself." He waits, a fervent prayer repeating itself in his head. That the symptoms he has described, remembered from Adeliza's pregnancy with John, will come true. That he has sowed enough doubt in William's mind to make him hesitate.

"You wish me to order Lanfranc to postpone the trial?"

"Yes."

"But what guarantees can you offer me that the woman will not miraculously disappear before she comes to term, she and my niece or nephew?"

"William, I implore you. I have seen how Lanfranc keeps her, it is as though he has already tried and convicted her in his own mind. She will die if she is left there, she and the child, and I could not live without her. My heart would be dead. So you would lose us both, brother and nephew."

William stretches his legs, leaning back in his chair and clasping his hands behind his head. "It's a funny thing," he says reflectively, "dying. I remember a letter I received from King Edward, when he was in his last illness, in which he wrote that he was dying piecemeal. His feet were dead for he could no longer feel them, and his bladder, he was certain, was already in paradise because his piss smelt of honey."

"The feet and the bladder are one thing, the heart quite another."

"That I grant you, but I do not think it is your heart that will die of her death. Unless your heart is in your prick and not your chest."

"I am born in Scorpio. It's possible, I suppose."

"An inconvenient affliction for a churchman."

"Perhaps you should have consulted your astrologers more carefully before making me one."

"Perhaps you should meditate more upon the love of God than of this woman. I tell you, Odo, though you cannot see it, she has bewitched you. Everything points to it."

"I am in love with her, William. Were you never in love?"

William purses his lips. "I do not call this monstrous, puffed up thing consuming you love. Possession, more like."

Possessio mea. What he says is true, merely their construction of the words differs.

William leans across and gives Odo's thigh a hearty pat. "I'll tell you what I'll do. I'll send her to Matilda in Rouen. She'll have her taken care of until the child's born and then we'll see what's to be done. Perhaps she can be made to repent, then she could go into the Abbaye aux Dames at Caen and atone for…everything." William smiles, the smile he wears on the rare occasions he beats Odo at chess.

Rome, thinks Odo, *Rome*, where figs and lemons grow in his garden, and the stone is warm, and the worldly ambitions of priests are understood. He will take her to Rome.

"That is my decision, Odo, and I think it is more than you deserve. I suggest, if you love her as much as you say you do, you persuade her to acquiesce. If she is inclined to listen. Listening is not her strong point by all accounts." He stands up, signalling an end to the audience. "Splendour of God, Odo, how did we ever come to this?"

Odo rises also and looks at his brother, measuring the fractional difference in their height. "We gambled, William," he says softly. "One can never anticipate all the consequences."

"You're back so soon," she says, greeting him at the door to the private apartments. Her smile, the way it seems to spread over half her thin face and warm her grave eyes, almost breaks his heart. Without waiting for the door to close behind them, she winds her arms around his neck, pressing herself against him, giving little moans of pleasure as his mail shirt grazes her tender breasts.

She has missed him, but in the poignant serenity of knowing he would return with William's blessing, that they are together again, that Lanfranc may have tarnished the magic of their shared life a little but now it is bright again, brighter than ever, shiny as a silver spoon for their daughter's baptism. Feeling him stiffen, she kisses him, thinking to herself she must disabuse him of this notion he has that lovemaking is dangerous for the child. There is an irrational sentimentality in men which is, in its way, as cruel as violence. Now, already, he is pulling back from her, licking her kiss from his lips, unwinding her arms from his neck.

"I must speak with you," he says, in a tone which makes her search his face anxiously. He is drawn, serious, his skin grey with the dust of the road, his eyes bloodshot, their long lids pleated with weariness.

"What's wrong?" She follows him into the parlour, feeling suddenly sick. Good, she tells herself firmly, that means the baby's taken well. He lets Osbern divest him of his chain mail then dismisses him and Freya.

"Sit," she says, "let me pour you some wine. Let me take off your boots."

"For Christ's sake stop fussing, woman." He waves her away as if she were an irritating insect, then immediately holds out his arms to her. "I'm sorry," he says, pressing her cheek to his heart. "Tell me how you have been?"

"A little tired and sick, but that's all to the good."

"I told you, I make my children tough. Which is just as well." He moves away from her, twisting his rings around his fingers. "Because we're going to have to go on a long journey."

"To get away from Lanfranc? I thought…"

"To get away from William."

"William?" She had pinned her hopes on William. He won't jeopardise the child, Odo had assured her, his conscience won't let him, not his own flesh and blood.

"He has proposed sending you to the court at Rouen, into Matilda's safekeeping until the baby arrives."

"Is that so bad? You could visit me. Perhaps I could go to Conteville."

Odo shakes his head. "I'll tell you how it would be, Gytha. You wouldn't be out of Matilda's sight for a moment till the cord was cut, and the minute that was done, she would take the baby and you'd be packed off to her nunnery at Saint Etienne in Caen. That's William's deal. He gets our child, we get nothing, not even each other."

"So what are we going to do?"

"We'll go to Rome. I have a house there, you know, on the Tiber. It has a garden with figs and lemons in it, and an olive grove. Have you ever eaten olives? They taste like hot sunshine."

She looks at Odo, at the play of hope and anxiety over his beloved features. She imagines olives, like miniature suns, burning her tongue. She imagines Rome, full of mysterious white ruins, broken pillars and eyeless statues such as you would suddenly come across in the landscape of her childhood, rounding the shoulder of a low hill or a bend in a lane. She imagines dark, glossy creepers, stone drapery, hot, spicy air and making love in gardens, by starlight, like Ovid and Corinna.

But the lover of her imagination is not Odo. He is some eyeless man, beautiful, marble, with broken arms. She cannot see Odo in Rome, so far from his home, his roots, his schemes and ambitions, his family. She thinks of John, sequestered in Liege, and of their cancelled visit to him, and of this unborn daughter in her belly. In Odo's world of dangerous aspirations and shifting alliances, loving one's children means keeping them at a distance, cloistered in a monastery or subject to a husband. Loving one's children is making the best use of them. That is why his meeting with William has left him so disappointed, because William intends to deprive him of a counter to play in his power games, not because he intends to part him from her.

"And what are you going to do in Rome?"

"Oh, I don't know. Write, teach, be a farmer. Become Pope. Does it matter?"

It would be so easy...Perhaps he's right. Doesn't he have relatives in Sicily? She isn't sure where Sicily is, but she is certain it is even further from here than Rome. It may even have camels. She glances up at his profile, the candlelight glimmering ruddy gold on his chin stubble.

"The half finished angel," she murmurs.

"What?" He is somewhere else. *Good God*, she thinks, registering the absence in his eyes, *it wasn't a joke, he* can *see himself on the throne of Saint Peter*. He is already calculating the sacrifice he must make to keep her in terms of the benefits it might bring him. There is, she realises, no escape for him from William because they are too much alike.

"You look so tired," she says. "Sit. We don't have to go this minute, I suppose."

"Within the day, to be safe." But he does sit, and allows her to pull off his boots. Sitting back on her heels she rubs his feet, tracing the fan of fine bones with her fingertips then drawing her thumbs hard along the arches so she does not tickle him. He sighs with pleasure and closes his eyes, resting his head against the chair back.

"Odo…"

Her tone makes him sit up straight. "What is it?"

"Running away to Rome isn't the answer, is it? Wherever you go, William will find you, and you'd miss…everything you've achieved here."

He gives an uncertain laugh. "I never thought to hear you say such a thing. Perhaps I would miss some of it, but it's a price worth paying to keep you safe."

"Not if it fails." Prising his knees apart, she kneels between his legs, resting her arms on his thighs and considers him in silence for a long time. "You know, don't you," she says finally, "that the only way to keep your daughter free from William, the only foolproof way, is for me to disappear."

"Disappear? Rubbish. I have a lot of friends in Rome, there are a great many Normans there. I'm not without influence among them, and I was at Bec with His Holiness. William would soon give up, he's only going to risk so much for one little girl."

"But for you, Odo? It seems to me he would risk a great deal to have you back in the fold. I think he not only loves you, but fears you, and that is a potent combination."

"Darling Gytha." Leaning forward, he encases her hands in his own, loving how they curl like nestlings in his broad palms. How could she disappear? There is no place on earth remote enough to hide her from him, were she to shroud herself in the holiness of Jerusalem or go to the far south where men stand on their heads and shield themselves from the sun with their single foot shaped like a hood. No desert is so featureless nor forest so dark he would not find her in it. The attraction between them is as elemental as that of stone for the earth or the soul of man for God. "Don't trouble yourself about William. Trust me."

Yet he is curiously withdrawn, displaying little interest in Freya's packing or Osbern's preparations for their journey, content to leave the selection of horses, the stowing of wagons and calculations of winds and tides to others. When Gytha retires, he does not join her, saying he will inspect the guard before turning in, then he has last minute business to discuss with Hamo and perhaps he will hear Matins.

He walks on the walls for half a watch or more, prowling among the guards, sunk in thought, apparently oblivious to the crunch of their footfalls, the occasional chink of arms on mail, the odd, smart, "Good night, sir," as he passes. Tonight is Toussaint, when the universe wears thin and the different orders confront one another through a veil. As a priest, he should be keeping vigil, placating the souls of the dead with his prayers, yet he feels more like one of those spirits his office commands him to fight than a soldier of Christ on earth. His body is here, feeling the cold, damp air settling against his skin like the breath of a sea serpent, but his heart is somewhere far from these men with their mundane jokes, the small comforts of their smoking fires and jugs of ale and mittens knitted by their women. His heart is howling in a desert with no-one to hear it but sand and stones.

She is right, he knows it. He cannot barricade the truth behind an edifice of maps and packing cases and messengers bearing complicated gifts to cardinals in Rome, the way he has sealed their love inside this castle where it will suffocate. And if not here, in another fortress, always running, hiding, fighting petty rearguard actions, patching up breaches in walls, holes in purses and cracks in hearts. That is no way for his daughter to live, like an outlaw, under the protection of a father who is a fugitive from himself. Gytha is right; if their child is to have any chance at all, she must be dead to him.

At least until William himself dies, then who knows? Neither Curthose nor Rufus shows much aptitude for kingship and though Henry is a bright lad, he is barely eight years old and might be moulded to any shape if he survives childhood. Yes, he would miss England, she is right about that too.

He goes down to the atelier, where the women still sleep even though the embroidery languishes in its chests in the overcrowded hall, and wakes Agatha, creeping into her chamber and shaking her by the shoulder himself, as she has refused any other servant since Leofgeat died. He remembers, with a yearning that pricks like needles behind his eyes, scenes like this at Conteville, summer nights of darkness fine as a moth's wing or thick with the scent of windfalls mouldering in the orchard, when the children of the household, in varying combinations, would rise from their pallets like ghosts and go hunting for adventures.

"Agatha, wake up." When real adventures come, with heroes and villains and damsels in distress, he thinks, as his sister stirs, mumbles, opens her eyes and sits up in confusion, they are a long way from what you have come to expect from those far off, barefoot, heart-in-mouth nights.

"Odo? What is it? Are Lanfranc's men here?"

"No. But I want you to get dressed, wake Margaret, and come up to the hall."

"Why?"

"You have to leave here. Tonight. William is coming and you and the girl must be away from here before his people arrive."

"William?"

"It was all William, Agatha, all along. He's used Lanfranc as a smokescreen."

"And you? Gytha?" She is out of bed now, pulling on her habit in the dark just as monks and nuns do every night in every corner of the Christian world as the Great Silence ends and the bell summons them to Matins.

"I shall be alright. Gytha…Take Meg to Saint Justina's. I'll give you money for a dowry for her and a letter to Abbess Clothilde. She can travel? Well, even if she can't, there's no alternative. William's people mustn't get their hands on her, do you understand?"

"Not entirely. Why is Meg such a risk to you?"

"Her miscarriage, Agatha, it wasn't a miscarriage as such, and Gytha…helped." He tells Agatha everything, about Sebastian, and the cunningwoman, and all that she said to Gytha, while Agatha unwinds and rewinds her headrail, gets it wrong and appeals for Odo to help. He has to light a candle, by whose light he contemplates his sister's bare head, the bones and nodes of her skull beneath the close-cropped grey hair, the sharp planes of cheek and jaw. His blood, all iron and intellect.

"I'm sorry," he says, his hands on her bird-boned shoulders, "you were right. I should never have brought you here."

"What will happen to the embroidery?"

He shrugs. "It doesn't really matter any more. Go and get Meg and I'll meet you in the hall shortly." He smiles, but his smile does not reach his eyes.

Once back inside the bailey, he wakes Freya and orders her to make her mistress ready to travel immediately, with only what one mule can carry. Fulk, she tells him in answer to his enquiry, is on watch on the horse lines, probably, she adds with a wan smile, under the personal command of Lord Hamo's daughter who is still most anxious about her pony. He kicks a small boy hunched under a threadbare cloak by the great door and sends him to find Fulk.

He does not return to his apartments until he has bidden Agatha farewell, standing at the hall door, watching her small, upright frame as she pulls Margaret, stumbling and blowsy, down the motte and into the outer court, lighting their way with a smoking torch. Trying to shake off the irrational conviction that he has seen his sister in this life for the last time, he climbs the stairs to his parlour where he finds Gytha and Freya rummaging among the packing cases, turning out clothes, jewel boxes, comb cases, books and bundles of quills in a frenzied hunt, Osbern following in their wake, putting everything back again.

"I can't find my leather purse," explains Gytha, "you know, with my locket in it."

"We have to go," says Odo firmly. He knows what the locket means to her, with its freight of baby curls, but they must look forward now, to this new life growing inside her. They cannot delay out of nostalgia.

"But…" It seems an ill omen to her, to leave without those few precious possessions she has carried with her through everything which has befallen her since the Bastard's arrival in Winchester so long ago it seems like another life.

"Now."

Then again, perhaps it is a good thing. The locket, the cockade, a gritty lump of unpolished amber with a fly trapped inside it from an east coast beach, these are the symbols of her past, and without her past, she is no-one. Which is what she must become from now on. Odo takes her mantle from Freya and settles it around her shoulders, then they go quietly down into the hall where Fulk meets them with Thecla asleep in his arms. Gytha forbids herself a backward glance; the joys she has known in those makeshift rooms have been superseded now by a greater joy and a graver responsibility. She takes Odo's hand and lets him lead her away, only pausing for a space between heartbeats to contemplate the cedar chests, fire orange in the glow of the embers from the great hearth, in which she knows the embroidery is stored. She feels a little surge of pride, almost as though her daughter is dancing in her belly, at the hand she had in it. Her future may contain other silk hung beds, gilded chairs and jewels fit for a queen, but she knows that tangle of truth and lies, real life and make-believe, stained with sweat and blood, unpicked, restitched and probably covered with cat hair, is unique, a miracle of human endeavour in all its savagery and devotion.

Odo guides their small party to a hunting lodge he has in a densely wooded stretch of forest some miles to the west of the city. He has chosen it for its concealment, also because it is a place he often uses and knows he can find his way to in darkness, and, which he keeps to himself, it will serve his plan for it to be known he took a forest path at night. The sky is covered by thick cloud, so even though many of the trees are leafless as a consequence of the drought, their path is lit by little more than the gleam in Juno's eye at the prospect of game. They travel at a cautious trot, their horses' hooves, and those of the mule carrying Gytha's belongings, bound in rags to mute their sound. The two women are flanked by Fulk and Odo, both with swords drawn, eyes and ears straining in the darkness to catch anything more than the loom of bushes and trees, the rustle of foxes and badgers and the small creatures of the night fleeing the scent of men and horses. Gytha leads the mule. At one point Thecla awakes and starts to cry, until her mother tucks her inside her own cloak and sings to her softly. Odo snaps at her to shut up, and feels Gytha's eyes upon him through the dark, and is glad she cannot see his face.

They reach the lodge, a low stone building with a thatched roof, without incident. Though he had been sure none of William's men could be in the area yet, Odo is relieved to have been left unmolested by Lanfranc's. A great jurist and churchman he might be, but the Archbishop is no tactician. As he dismounts, he glances up at the sky. He can sense the thinning of the night, the light pushing at its fabric like the wind filling a sail. A pheasant starts up from the ground with a cacophony of chinking calls and a clatter of wings which make the horses start and send Juno off in pursuit. No fire, Odo commands, pushing open the door, they will not be there long enough to make the effort worthwhile, and no light. He and Fulk take the animals around to the back of the building while Gytha and Freya go inside, groping their way in darkness imbued with the smells of damp earth, stale smoke and rank meat. Gytha stumbles over a stool, rights it and says, "Come towards me, Freya, there's a stool here. You can sit with Thecla."

She hears the swish of Freya's cloak along ground covered with drifts of dead leaves as she negotiates her way to the stool and sits, her breathing suddenly loud, close. Though she says nothing, her resentment is like another person in the room.

"I'm sorry," says Gytha. "This is hardly what you can have expected from waiting on a royal mistress."

Freya makes some non-committal murmur of demur.

"I shall make it up to you as soon as I can, I swear to you."

As soon as the men come in, Odo tells Fulk to take Freya and his daughter to the small room adjoining the main body of the lodge which is, on happier occasions, used to prepare the game. He longs to be alone with Gytha, yet once Fulk and Freya have left them, he is suddenly overwhelmed by dread. There is nothing more to do now than say goodbye. As soon as it is light she must go. He is grateful for the fact that the lodge's shutters are closed, for the density of the woods and the cloud obscuring the sun, for anything which will postpone the coming of day.

Though she cannot read the expression on his face, the shadowy outline of his body, where he stands on the other side of the narrow trestle table in the centre of the room, tells her all his pain and grief, the ache of loneliness opening up between them. She waits for panic, or tears, or a flood of regrets and retractions to choke her, yet all she feels is a profound calm. Walking around to his side of the table, she slips her arms around his waist and presses her face against his chest, breathing him in, committing each scent to memory. Rosemary, sandalwood, horses, saddle soap, sweat and earth and cardamoms.

"I love you," she murmurs, but her words are stifled and he knows them only as a change in the rhythm of her breathing, warm through his clothes.

"What?"

She disengages herself and smiles up at him; their breath mists and mingles in the cold air between them. "Nothing." She takes his hands, turning them palm up and smoothing her thumbs over the callouses at the base of his fingers. It was the wrong thing to say. If she truly loves him, she must do all she can to make this easier for him.

Dismayed, he realises her features are becoming clearer to him by the second as the sun advances towards the eastern horizon. Why isn't the tree canopy denser, the shutters stouter, the cloud thicker? Disengaging his hands from hers, he starts to prowl about the room, peering into the fading shadows as though whatever words there are for a situation like this may be hidden there. A scratching comes at the door. They freeze. Fulk bursts through from the game larder, sword drawn.

Then suddenly, Odo starts to laugh. "Juno," he announces, opening the door a crack to let her in then slamming it shut hastily on the ragged autumn dawn chorus beginning outside. Fulk retreats, and they hear low conversation followed by a chuckle from Freya. Their eyes meet, and each knows how the other longs to be in the next door room, in the world of the ordinary, uncluttered by the wills of great men or the obligations of history.

"I wish William was dead," says Odo suddenly, bringing his fist down on the table with ferocious savagery.

"No you don't. If you wished that you wouldn't be you. Oh do stop prowling around like a performing bear, you make me nervous."

"I can't stay still, it hurts too much."

Stepping into his path, she puts her arms around him again. "It's cold. Hold me."

He hesitates. "I don't know…"

"Only hold me." She shivers and he yields, enfolding her in his sable cloak, pushing back her hood and kissing her hair which smells of salt and apples.

She feels him harden against her belly, thinks of their daughter, growing there between them in her watery sanctuary. She lifts her face and lets him kiss her mouth, her mouth telling him of the extent and difference of her love for him, her body bent to him, muscle and bone, while her blood flows into the life of her child. Her love is not less, but it has changed direction, reordered priorities. They have made this baby together, out of a sweetness most people never know, a blessing unsought and undeserved, but the child is hers now, her responsibility. Yet his mouth is so lovely, with its cardamom taste and its agile tongue, and the syrupy warmth in the pit of her stomach so seductive. Surely a moment of forgetfulness can do no harm.

They kiss for a long time, holding themselves very still, almost self-contained, as though their kiss is frozen in isolation from the working of the rest of their bodies. They are like a pair of virgins on their wedding night, he thinks, uncertain how to answer the promptings of their flesh. How do you make love, in the knowledge that it will be the last time? Where do you begin?

And suddenly he cannot bear it, the realisation that they are not one, can never be one on this earth, hopelessly divided by what most draws them together. Pulling away from her, tenderly contemplating the slight, pink rash his stubble has left on her chin, he says,

"Please don't make me be parted from you. How can I live?"

She caresses his cheek with her fingertips. "Think of John. You will live for him, and our baby." She takes his hand and lays it on her belly, but he feels, not the way it is beginning to distend, the fabric of her gown stretched across the little hard mound, but her stillness, her inwardness. "And new loves, other children."

What she says is so appalling he fails to hear the brittleness in her voice, like a fine layer of ice smoothed over a pool full of deep currents. He shakes his head emphatically. "No," he says, "never. Never, as I live and breathe."

"Oh, nonsense. Women admire you, I see it in the way some of them have treated me. And you have wealth and power, the most effective love potions."

"Yet not sufficient to keep you."

"A new mistress would be the best way of forgetting us. There is nothing deader than an old love when a new one comes along. Find someone you can take to court. Live contentedly, Odo, stop fighting."

"How can I?" The question escapes him on a sob.

Disentangling herself from his arms, she is full of pity as she considers which words to speak and which to keep to herself. His face is as wan as the autumn morning knocking at the shutters. The image of Lady Edith, dancing alone to a tune heard only in her head, twists on to the horizon of her memory. "Because..." she begins, lowering her arms to her sides.

"Yes?"

"When I...ran away from you, and went to Edith, I suppose I had some notion that we could simply take up where we had left off, she and I. Then when she told me about you, and I realised there was no escape, I knew."

"Knew?"

"That there was no place left for me, nowhere I belonged any more. You see, Odo, I don't belong with you, even now, I never have. Think about it. The very first time you held me, we were at odds over the representation of King Harold's death. We fell in love in spite of ourselves, didn't we?"

"But my dream..."

"If I had not been so close to the man your brother usurped, I would never have been in your dream. I don't believe that dream shows we were meant to live together at all."

"And the child?"

"Is mine. Unless you want to hand her over to William and me to the gallows."

"It wouldn't come to that," he scoffs. "The worst they'd do is send you on a pilgrimage or something. You did what you did from the best of motives."

"They'd kill me, that's what they've intended from the beginning and you know it, or we wouldn't be here. My time is over, Odo, but yours is just beginning. It's an age for men like you, law makers, organisers, men with an eye for the perpendicular. Do you know the meaning of my name?"

He raises his eyebrows. Now where is she going? "I believe it means elf-gift. Aelfgytha."

She nods and looks up at him. *Looks like an elf-gift*, he thinks, her eyes huge above the sharp, delicate bones of her cheeks, all light and darkness. *Spirit. Sprite.*

"But where are the elves now, Odo?" she asks softly. "All imprisoned in stone crypts? If you love me, you must let me go. It is my choice."

Silence. Odo, the preacher, the persuader, is at a loss for words. *Credo ut intelligam* the brothers at Bec used to insist, not the other way around, and after so many years of struggle, the truth of Anselm's dictum is revealed to him by the daughter of a Saxon fishmonger. Love first, understanding second, if you're lucky.

Suddenly, she smiles and reaches out to him. "Come here, we haven't long. Let's not be miserable. Tell me, what are you going to do about the hanging now you've sent Sister Jean away?"

He tells her he has no intention of finishing the hanging, he no longer has the heart for it. He will send the rest of the women back to their families and pull down the atelier; the stone can be used in the building of the new castle. "And besides," he adds, "I'm not the man who wanted it. I no longer find it so easy to see reasons to celebrate or commemorate what we did. Perhaps I'm a relic also, whatever you say."

"You can't not finish it," she bursts out. "What a betrayal. You prised us all out of our lives to do it for you, and look at the price some of us have paid. Margaret, Alwys' hand. Me, I suppose, though perhaps you might say I got what I paid for. And another thing, once it is finished, you look at it very carefully and then decide what you think it celebrates. It may not be as straightforward as you imagine."

"Oh, stop it, Gytha, please. What do I care about the bloody tapestry?"

"You must care!"

"Well, I don't. At the moment I feel...as though I'm being eaten from the inside out by a manticore."

"Oh really," she teases, "anyone else might come up with a wolf, or a bear. For you, a manticore. Remind me how one is made."

"With the body of a lion, a man's head and a scorpion's tale, and spines, like a porcupine."

"A devil's hedgehog."

He laughs.

"That's better," she says. "When you start work again on the hanging, have one put in it."

"A devil's hedgehog. I like that. I shall remember..." Suddenly one of the horses outside wickers nervously. Odo's right hand flies to the hilt of his sword. "Fulk? What's out there?" He runs through to the larder and peers cautiously around the rear door, Fulk just behind him, to see the horse nose to nose with a startled looking badger, no doubt disorientated by the daylight. The two men laugh with relief. Fulk swings his daughter up in his arms and deposits her in the doorway to look at the sight, and only then does Odo realise the cloud has dispersed, and shards of sunlight are piercing the forest from the east, casting a tangle of long, blue shadows across the clearing where the lodge stands.

"Get ready," he says to Fulk. Gytha, standing in the arch adjoining the two rooms, raises her hands to tighten the clasp at the neck of her cloak.

"No," says Odo, taking her by the elbow and guiding her back into the principal room. "I mean for you to have this." He removes her cloak, then his own, which he drapes around her shoulders, pulling it solicitously close over her chest. Its weight makes her stagger. "There are jewels sewn into the seams," he explains. "No coin, for that would make you too easy to identify, but enough stones and pearls to keep you and...our daughter until...until..." He falters. Until what, he cannot bear to imagine. He ploughs on, clinging to what he knows and can control. "You must take the horses Fulk and Freya rode here. You ride the chestnut. I know she's big, but she's the most docile mare in my stable, she will take good care of you. Freya can double up with Fulk, or you, or…"

"Odo, my darling, I think we can manage to sort out two horses and a mule between us."

"Which way will you go?"

"I'm not telling you that."

"No, of course not. I shouldn't have asked. Habit. I'm sorry." He turns away from her abruptly. "I feel so ashamed."

"Ashamed?" She touches his shoulder.

"That with everything I have I couldn't protect you." His head hangs, and his arms, as though the sinews have snapped, leaving him powerless over his body. He hears again the wisdom of the anchorite. *In the end, you know, we are all like Saint Peter. We betray what is nearest to us and to God.*

"But you could. I never doubted it. You would have fought off everyone, William's men, Lanfranc's. We *decided* this, remember, we *chose* to do it this way, for the baby. Standing here, you're ten times braver than any great lord defending a castle." Grabbing his upper arms she turns him to face her. His eyes are dark ringed and swollen with tears. He looks so lost, but what can she do? "Kiss me," she entreats him after a pause, but instead of taking her in his arms, he starts to unbuckle his sword belt. She frowns at him.

"I'm not going to kiss you with a sword between us, only the baby, what joins, not what severs." He lays the sword on the table then turns and puts his arms around her, his movements slow and deliberate, as though he is under water. She lifts her face to him, eyes closed, wanting only his smell, the length of his body against hers, his erection pressing into the base of her belly. Can the baby feel it, she wonders? His curling eyelashes and shaky breath. His lovely mouth. Carrying her back to a staircase in another life, a private world caught between gossiping embroiderers and a grumbling army, a first kiss that was meant to be a camel. Hugging him close, her fingers digging in between his ribs, she yearns to be one flesh with him, indistinguishable, indivisible, then her daughter says, whispering through the cord that binds them, *that's my prerogative, if you let me live.*

Gently, she lifts her hands to his face and prises their lips apart with her fingers. Though she can still feel the pressure of his mouth the way, she thinks, Alwys must still feel her missing hand. "The sun's up, I have to go."

He nods. He does not want to break the spell of their kiss by speaking. He releases her from his arms, hands lingering on the rise of her hips.

"Odo?"

"Yes?"

"There's one more thing I want to say. We're true lovers, aren't we? So I'll always be with you. Sleeping, waking, wherever you are and whoever else you're with. I'll be in your heart and soul and dreams. You can always talk to me and I'll always answer, and one day, when you can, you'll find me again. It's just that...what we have...had...it's like the comet, a wonderful, beautiful moment of light that shoots across the sky and disappears, and then comes back, but changed. Am I making any sense?"

He shakes his head. "Not really, but I love listening to it. I wish..."

Putting her fingers to his lips again, she says, in a low, unsteady voice, "No more wishes."

"No more wishes, but..." Raising his arms, he unhooks the chain holding the Tear of the Virgin and fastens it around Gytha's neck. "For your safety, with your journey, and the birth and everything, and for our little girl. A christening gift."

"What shall I call her?"

"She's your daughter, you choose."

When Gytha and her small party are mounted ready to leave, she turns to face him, standing in the doorway to the lodge. Everything falls away, birdsong, the sigh of wind in the upper branches, the horses champing their bits, Thecla grizzling with exhaustion, the soft slap of Juno's tail slapping her master's leather gaiters as she stands at his side, wagging hopefully. They are alone, and the look they exchange contains nothing but themselves. It is without questions or answers, without desire, despair or joy, past or future, doubts or promises, but a look present, essential and unwavering, not distracted by the tiniest curve of a lip or arch of a brow. Not a muscle moves, not a breath is drawn, neither to mist over the past or give life to a future. And after a space of time which is perfect, neither sentimentally long nor brutally short, she gathers her reins and kicks her horse forward, feeling the sun on her back.

Odo does not immediately move from the doorway. A part of him fears she may glance back over her shoulder, and if he goes inside he will miss it. But he knows better and, roused by dew dripping from the thatch down the back of his neck, he ducks under the lintel to do what has to be done to put the next part of his plan into action. Drawing his dagger from his belt, he picks up Gytha's discarded cloak from the table and begins to cut and tear at the fabric, disciplining himself to take no heed of the loved, perfidious scent lying in wait among its folds to ambush his heart, holding it up from time to time to inspect his effort. He becomes so absorbed in his task, the work of hand and arm as he grasps the knife, raises it, plunges it into the cloak and rips down, untangles the loose threads and begins again, that Juno's sudden outbreak of frenzied barking makes him jump as though he has just awoken from a deep sleep.

Boar perhaps; he noticed scrapes on their way here, shallow nests of earth surrounded by broken branches and uprooted brambles. Or an inquisitive buck. Clamping one hand over the dog's muzzle to silence her, he creeps towards the open door, knife poised, keeping out of the wedge of sunlight that ripples over the uneven floor. Footsteps, men's footsteps. Unmistakable, a cautious crunching of small twigs and acorn cups, then a pause, as Juno stops barking and the stranger is obviously wondering what has silenced her. William's men already? Or Lanfranc's? Or perhaps just one of his verderers doing his rounds. Odo wishes the steps would start up again, then he would know how many of them are out there. No horses anyway, other than his own, still tethered at the back of the building. He waits, holding his breath, feeling his body's tension, muscles knotted between his shoulderblades and in the backs of his calves, the quivering, velvety muzzle of the dog under one hand, the smooth grip of the knife perfectly worn to the contours of the other.

Finally the stranger starts to move again, obviously satisfied the barking dog was somewhere else in the forest, the proximity of its voice a trick of the crowding trees. Tree sprites are known to gather sounds and toss them from one to another like children playing with a ball. Odo detects only one set of footsteps and relaxes a little. Not soldiers, then, for they would not come singly. Just one of the woodsmen, or a poacher who is going to get a very nasty surprise when he comes face to face with his landlord. Odo steps out from behind the door, his dog at his heels.

"Norman."

"Good God in heaven. You."

The cloak of white lambskins has lost the strange, inner luminosity he remembers but instead seems grubby, dirt patched, the hem stuck with twigs and dead leaves. The Saxon has a gaunt, neglected air, more common vagabond than resurrected martyr. Only his eyes, dense as moss in the oblique forest light, still have the power to make Odo's soul shudder in his skin. He adjusts his grip on his knife. Surely this meeting was meant; just as his love affair with Gytha was preordained, so is this encounter with its nemesis. It is so perfectly opportune his heart lifts to think of it, shaking off the mire of grief and loneliness which had threatened to engulf it. This is a sign from God, the ram caught in the thicket, the burning bush.

Odo is quick for a big man; his agility always catches his enemies unawares because his body speaks to them of immoveable solidity, of the need to besiege rather than attack first. Before Sebastian can make any move to defend himself, Odo runs at him, hooking one heel around the back of his ankle and shouldering him in the chest to knock him off balance. He intends his spur to slice through Sebastian's Achilles' tendon, ensuring he won't get up again, but instead it becomes entangled in his cloak, pulling Odo down on top of him. The two men crash to the ground with a crunch of bone and the whump of air forced out of Sebastian's lungs. Odo's knife flies out of his hand and skitters along the ground out of his reach. His sword, he realises, furious with himself, is still lying on the table in the lodge.

And what if Sebastian's followers are near at hand? Though his instincts tell him the man is alone; he lacks the confident bearing of a well supported leader, and the forest remains locked in its particular brand of rustling, sighing, chirruping silence. As likely as not his men dispersed Sebastian's flock so effectively when they found Margaret they took fright and never reassembled. That is the way of these marginal groups, without the proper social structures to hold them together.

Before his opponent has a chance to catch his breath, Odo clamps his hands around his neck and presses hard on his windpipe with his thumbs.

"Where are your disciples now, Sebastian?" He spits out the name with all the sarcasm he can muster. But Sebastian seems oblivious to it, clawing frantically at Odo's hands, his ragged nails tearing at the sinews between his thumbs and first fingers. They struggle silently, Odo's eyes locked to Sebastian's as he presses inwards, the pulses in his thumbs beating, he believes, exactly in time with that in Sebastian's throat. Suddenly he no longer fears those eyes, those enamelled irises you can't see into, but hates them, the power of his hatred flowing into his hands as he squeezes Sebastian's neck.

From somewhere, Sebastian finds a surge of strength. Grasping Odo's wrists, he manages to drag the stranglehold from his throat and, coughing and gasping for air, rolls over and pinions Odo beneath him, his knee pushed into Odo's chest, his foul breath and the stench from his wounds like the stink of hell in Odo's nostrils.

"While the devil strangles, he is killed, Norman," he pants.

For a moment Odo thinks, *oh, let him, what does it matter?* Then, with a fierce uprush of joy and rage, he remembers his daughter; no girl so fine, made of such love, is going to live with the shame of a father killed in a brawl with a common hedge preacher. Twisting under Sebastian's weight, which is less than the man's big frame leads him to expect, he manages to throw him off and lunges across the forest floor after his knife, Sebastian at first clinging to his ankle then letting him go with a sharp cry as Odo's spur cuts into his palm.

"While he wins, he loses, Saxon."

Sebastian jumps to his feet, followed by Odo, gripping the recovered knife. Sebastian attempts to run, but encumbered by his cloak and at the limits of his endurance, he cannot outpace Odo, who catches hold of his plait and yanks his head back until he hears the cracking of vertebrae and a hoarse bark of pain from the preacher. They are some way out of the clearing, in a dense copse of beech where the low winter sun does not penetrate. Odo shivers, the sweat cooling under his arms and between his shoulderblades. Sebastian slumps to the ground, whether through exhaustion or because his neck is broken, Odo cannot tell. He continues to hold up the Saxon's head by his plait, coarse as hemp, as a hangman's rope.

But it's over; the fight has gone out of his enemy. He yanks Sebastian round to face him, bracing himself for those lizard eyes, but sees only their whites, lumpy, a dingy yellow in the pond-light of the copse. His hatred fills him the way a drowning man fills with water, precise, steady and cold. He loathes everything about the man from his dramatic looks to his blasphemy, his mad eyes to his improvident prick. Sebastian's eyes roll back into place, the irises slipping out from under the lids like plates of verdigrised bronze.

"I can't feel my legs," the man whines.

"Then you won't feel what I'm going to do to you next, Tom. A pity." Odo's words falls into the immense stillness of the forest with no more significance than the squeaking of a shrew or the unheard creak of a pine cone opening to release its seeds. For a second he imagines comprehension in Tom's eyes, even remorse, but it is only his imagination, his priest's liking for stories with morals. The man's soul is as rotten as his arrow wounds.

"If you kill me, it will be a kindness," Tom pleads.

Good. "Oh, I'm not going to kill you, Tom. We don't have a death penalty in England any more, you know. Besides, I want to give you a taste of what I am condemned to, thanks to you and your inability to resist poking any cunt you can get your hands on, even your own sister. No, there is a punishment on the statute for men like you, but it isn't death." He lets go of Tom's plait and he falls back heavily against the forest floor. Unwinding the strapping from one of his gaiters, he rolls Tom over on to his side, his knee in the small of the Saxon's back. Tom groans. "You should have killed me, you know," Odo continues in a light, conversational tone as he binds Tom's wrists with the leather thong, "when you had the chance. For a minute there, I wouldn't have resisted, but now...well, things change. Fortune's wheel turns."

"What are you going to do to me?"

"Cut your tongue out if you don't stop that whining." He lets Tom roll on to his back again and lifts his tunic to expose his genitals. Tom whimpers and starts to shake his head. "That's right, preacher. The Book of Deuteronomy. *He that is wounded in the stones, or hath his privy member cut off, shall not enter into the congregation of the Lord.*"

"*A bastard shall not enter into the congregation of the Lord,*" says Tom between gritted teeth, "tell that to your bastard brother, Norman." While Odo thinks about this, Tom tries to squirm away from him, but with his arms bound behind him and his legs dead he achieves nothing but an ineffectual flapping of his body, like a landed fish.

"Your thegns undid his bastardy, Saxon. They all cheered when he was anointed king. Like a bunch of silly children cheering a conjuring trick. He's as legitimate as you or I now, and I dare say the Lord likes him better. Now, hold still and it'll be over quicker."

Straddling Tom's chest to hold him down, Odo begins to cut, through the slack, goose-pimpled scrotum with its scattering of coarse, blond hairs. His skin crawls as he takes hold of Tom's penis, wrinkled and intimately clammy. Feeling sick, he hesitates, the barbarity of what he is doing, and its pointlessness, as clear to him as though he were watching himself from the upper echelons of one of the trees.

Then he remembers what Tom has done, how he has cut at the root of Odo's own masculinity, leaving him powerless to protect his woman and their child, and his mind darkens again, the dark swelling like a plague boil, leaving no room for reason. Adjusting his grip on his knife, his hand slipping a little on a slick of sweat, he makes a final upward cut, severing Tom's organs from his groin, momentarily rapt by the welling of blood into the shallow reservoir between the Saxon's lifeless legs. Then, twisting round to face Tom, he holds up the penis, the testicles dangling from it like a couple of pearly, purplish plums.

"The source of life, Saxon," he gasps between gusts of laughter, afraid he is beginning to rave but helpless to prevent it. Tom seems to have fainted. Clambering off his chest and kneeling beside him, Odo slaps his cheeks hard. Tom's eyelids flicker. "God is such a fucking joker!" he shouts, angry that such a fine insight should go unappreciated. Blood and urine trickle down Tom's thighs. Odo cleans his knife on the grass then holds the blade over Tom's mouth to see if he is still breathing. Just. A thin mist on the blade, a scarcely perceptible rise and fall of his scarred chest. Odo does not think he will last long. His skin already has the waxy bloom of a corpse, his blood dark, his mouth lolling open. Odo feels a mild, sentimental regret at the prospect of his death, which will deprive him of the consolation of company in his enforced chastity.

He forgets to say the comfortable words, which annoys him later, when he remembers, because he would have enjoyed the luxury of considering, and then rejecting, the idea. There might be something satisfying, he reflects, in stuffing the man's mouth with his genitals, making him a mirror image of his foresworn king in death. But what is the point? His followers have clearly deserted him, there is no-one to appreciate the irony but the odd fox or badger. Besides, Tom is beyond feeling the pain of that damned battle and what it did to the men who fought in it; all such a gesture would achieve would be to remind himself of it.

He turns away from Tom and starts back towards the hunting lodge, realising as he walks that he is very hungry, with a good, pure hunger like that of a man who has purged himself through fasting. Whistling up Juno, he takes down a bow from a hook in the lodge wall and goes looking for breakfast. His heart feels oddly light and insubstantial in his chest as he prowls around the forest paths hunting for small game. He even sings, and talks nonsense to his dog, as he might have done on any day's hunting in the company of friends and vassals, knowing his mistress was waiting for him at home with a long kiss and a cup of wassail. The forest itself confers a sense of unreality, enmeshing him in its shadows and silences, its sudden, eerie eruptions of birdsong and the whispered parliaments of trees. He is nothing in this ancient landscape, steeped in the consolation of indifference, so how much less is his pain?

He shoots a good, fat wood pigeon, and Juno takes a couple of wild rabbits, which makes him think, as he tucks their hind paws into his belt, he must have a word with his warrener about the improvement of the pillow mounds. He finds some late blackberries, sweet with must, and a fairy ring of mushrooms. As he picks them, he thanks the fairies for their bounty, then laughs sheepishly at himself, putting his hand to his throat without thinking, to touch the Tear of the Virgin. Its absence opens a chink in his serenity, and he whips his hand back as though the sensation of his shirt lying flat against his skin has burned him.

"Come on dog," he says heartily, "breakfast."

He gives one of the rabbits to Juno then, waiting for his fire to heat up sufficiently for cooking, he prepares the rest of the meat. He dips the frayed edges of Gytha's torn cloak in the blood. He himself is plausibly bruised and bloodied from his encounter with Tom. Spreading the cloak out on the table, he then examines it critically as the room fills with smells of roasting meat, walking around the table, standing back occasionally, with his head on one side, as though he is admiring a tapestry or an illumination in a book.

The food tastes delicious, the meat, the mushrooms fried in the fat from the pigeon, spring water, all have the holy taste of the sacrament on his tongue. He knows there will be pain to come, but for now, with work still to do, in a world rid of Tom, he feels strong and serene. He wonders if this is how expectant mothers feel, if this is what accounts for their tranquillity in the face of all the terrors of childbirth.

Once he has eaten, he kicks earth over his fire, catches his horse and spurs it to a fast gallop, carrying Gytha's cloak bundled roughly over his pommel. Reaching the castle as dusk is falling, he flings himself out of the saddle and pounds on the gate with both fists as though all the devils in hell are after him. The shocked, fearful features of the guards as they open up to him fill him with satisfaction, though he is careful to keep an anguished expression on his bruised and scratched face and to exaggerate his breathlessness when he speaks, making wild, sweeping gestures with his bloodstained hands.

"Wolves," he gasps and, "Toussaint," letting his haunted eyes do the rest. Then, when he can see the men have filled in the gaps for themselves, that before morning it will be all round the castle that the witch's escape attempt was thwarted by ghosts in wolfskins, and only he managed to escape with his life, he shows them the cloak, torn and bloodstained, which they all recognise as Gytha's. Humbly, he begs leave to sit awhile in the gatehouse. He will take a cup of ale and try to recover himself, but he bids them summon Osbern, because he does not think he has the strength to take another step unaided.

He realises how thoroughly his play acting has succeeded when he sees Osbern's face, stricken and drained of colour as a souling mask. Full of solicitude, he cups his hand under Odo's elbow to help him to his feet.

"Come along, My Lord, let's get you to your bed."

As soon as they are clear of the guardhouse, in the outer court, deserted at this hour, Osbern sees his master somehow grow in stature, the broken man mend himself. He is afraid, for a moment, that Odo too is a ghost, a further elaboration of whatever hideous spell has been worked by the spirits of the forest in this season of mischief. But when his master speaks, in a voice on the strained side of normal, he is reassured; whatever has happened, it has not involved any congress with the other side.

"Have men arrived from the king, Osbern?"

"Only this evening, sir, around Vespers. Lord Hamo managed to impress upon them that it was too late to go after you tonight."

"Good. And no nonsense from the Archbishop?"

"Quiet as a mouse, sir. I suppose he will leave it to the king now?"

"And we, I trust, will slip in between the two of them."

"We, My Lord? Do I take it Mistress Gytha got away then?"

They are just outside the hall door. Putting a finger to his lips, Odo nods, then says loudly, as he precedes his servant through the wicket, "Have my bath filled, Osbern."

While he bathes, he debates sending some men to bury Tom in the morning, but thinks better of it. Let the forest take care of its own, let the earwigs have his brain and the worms his mad eyes, boar take his flesh and wolves his great bones. Odo has had enough of him, and his men have better things to do. He closes his eyes and tries to believe the world is nothing but this cocoon of fragrant steam he is wrapped in, and the delicious tingling of his skin as Osbern scrubs it with a stiff brush until he glows like a bridegroom.

He grants William's officer a brief audience, clad only in his shirt and dressing gown, during which he listens to nothing the man has to say but manages to persuade him he is almost out of his mind with shock and grief, drawing quite coldly on whatever resource drove him to disfigure Tom as he did. If, he tells himself, he harbours a lunatic inside his skull, then he might as well learn to turn this strange affliction to his advantage. So he speaks in disjointed phrases of wolves and hobgoblins and peering through the fabric of the universe to the other side. He crosses himself frequently, contriving to make his hand shake as he does so, and continually breaks off in the middle of sentences to stare distractedly into the gloom beyond the wavering circle of light shed by his single candle.

Disconcerted by the Earl's ravings, the officer withdraws as soon as he decently can, satisfied the task he was charged with by the king has been done for him by some other agency whose nature he would prefer not to dwell on. Osbern, with a conspiratorial glance over his shoulder as he sees the officer out, mouthing obsequious apologies as he does so, expects to be reassured by a smile or a wink from his master, but instead sees him slumped in his chair staring moodily into the heart of his fire. Though surely the blankness in his eyes is just a trick of the poor light.

Once Odo is alone, and Osbern in his usual position, rolled in his blanket across the threshold to his lord's bedchamber, he kneels at his prie dieu and hopes for prayer to enter him, if not to drive out his tormentor, at least to silence it for the night. He recites the *Nunc Dimittis* but the words cannot exclude him from the life of the castle around him, the tramp of the guards' feet on the wall, his household packed into the hall and the great chamber above this room, many, no doubt, too nervous to sleep, staring up into the dusty dark between the roof beams or into the glimmering eyes of lovers. He thinks of the baker and his boy, and baby Leofwine, curled up beside the ovens which never go cold, of the smith whose night breath blows ash across the embers in his forge, of the fletcher, the armourer, the grooms and pigmen and cattleherds, the dairy women and the laundresses with their forearms like prize fighters, of Master Pietro stroking his great belly as if it were his mistress and Turold, probably stroking the mute, Emma, while he turns over new jests in his hard mind, of Hamo pretending to sleep while the countess berates him for some imagined slight or other.

Of his great hanging, packed away in boxes, all its figures, the soldiers and lovers, kings and shipwrights, the horses and dogs and wolves and falcons, his brothers, himself, holding their breath, waiting to dance, to ride down an enemy, to pursue a destiny. *You must finish it,* she had said, *look at the price some of us have paid.*

Not some of us, all of us, he answers her now, from the dark heart of his castle whose walls bristle with the armed men he has interposed between himself and William. *Nothing,* he thinks as he climbs shivering into bed and flexes his toes against the hot stone wrapped in flannel Osbern has placed at the bottom of it, which is as cold as a cold love. And tries to hate William for forcing him to replace the warmth of his love's embrace with hot stones. But cannot.

Because there is a new bond between them now, the bond of solitude.

PEARL

THE FEAST OF SAINT ODO 1072 TO THE SOLEMNITY OF PETER AND PAUL 1073

"But where are we going?" Freya asks this several times a day, as though it is the refrain to the long song of their exile.

"I shall know when we get there," Gytha replies, an inadequate response, plunging Freya back into a hostile silence, but it is the best she can do. Fulk, riding beside Gytha, with Freya and Thecla a little way behind on the overloaded mule, says nothing. He is torn between his sympathy for his woman and her longing for a destination, a place where she can establish a household and bring up their child, and his solemn promise to Odo to watch over Gytha as if she were his own flesh and blood. In such circumstances, where women are concerned, he thinks it wisest to keep silent.

Gytha is uncertain how long they have been travelling, though she knows there have been two Sabbaths, when the roads were quiet, the fields deserted, the doors of houses more firmly closed. Despite their good horses, stout shoes and warm clothes, the conditions of their journey have been wretched due to the need for discretion. *They are out of Kent now, in the honour of William de Warenne*, Gytha thinks, or

possibly Fitzosbern. Every other Norman seems to be called William.
Whichever lord it is, like Odo, he keeps the main roads in good order,
potholes filled, verges cut back, troops of liveried soldiers barracked at
regular intervals, inns and way stations where the price of bread and
ale is strictly controlled. These are the routes leading from London to
the south coast, the king's communications links with Normandy and
his buttress against invasion from France or Anjou, and for this reason
Gytha keeps away from them.

She insists on taking by-roads and sheltering at night in remote
granges or byres, even caves, sometimes, in preference to risking
identification in a manor hall or abbey pilgrim house. They are
permanently soaked to the skin and plastered in mud, it seems, from the
rain driven through their clothes by the bitter November winds or from
fording streams that have burst their banks. They have to make frequent
stops for Fulk to gouge packed, sodden earth from the horses' hooves
before their feet rot or bruise. Thecla whines incessantly, exhausted
by nights without fires when it is too cold to sleep and, sometimes, a
shortage of food if Gytha thinks it unsafe to exchange any of Odo's
jewels for supplies. His generosity has been too ostentatious; she must
find somewhere, far enough away for no-one to ask questions, or at
least, not pertinent ones, where she can change showers of diamonds,
uncut emeralds and rubies, veined lumps of turquoise and smoky quartz
the colour of his eyes in a summer dusk, into small coins to buy bread
or herrings or bacon. She will not sell the pearls, though, she will keep
them for her daughter.

She banishes all considerations but practical ones. Her heart is
hardened against Freya's complaints and Thecla's misery; it will not
even listen to Fulk's silence. She knows they struggle to understand her
behaviour, but how could they? They have each other. They may have
wet feet and frozen hands, but not the chill she feels, in her spirit, in
the marrow of her bones, the cold of pennies on her eyes and soil in
her mouth. Her only concern is to stay alive for the child, his child, the
ember glowing in her belly. Curled around that nugget of hope, looking

always inward, she becomes oblivious to everything outside her own body, its needs and changes.

It is no longer possible to doubt the cunningwoman's prediction. Her breasts are swollen and tender, she is sick almost every morning, craves certain foods yet, when they are put in front of her, her stomach revolts. But cruellest of all is her almost permanent state of arousal, which gives her no peace, and makes her believe Odo was right when he said God had a sense of humour, though it disturbs her that it seems to be such a bitter one. Sometimes she touches herself for relief, but the respite is brief and hollow, and carries the danger of memories she dare not admit to consciousness. Sometimes, to her shame, she finds herself eying up men they pass on the road, or even Fulk, speculating, wondering, dismissing, spurring her horse ahead with a flush scalding her neck and cheeks.

Before she fell in love, she could lose herself in bed in the consolatory power of her imagination; if she kept her eyes closed and her head averted from panting breaths that stank of onions, or tooth rot, or other women's kisses, any man might be a prince in one of her mother's tales. Now, however, there is no substitute for her real prince, even though, or perhaps because, he is a Norman, a bishop and tends to heaviness. Often, when she does succeed in deceiving her body into a brief and troubled sleep, enfolded in Odo's sable cloak, she dreams of being at sea and wakes with her eyes full of tears and the scent of rosemary and sandalwood, and salt and iron, in her nostrils. She will sell the cloak, she tells herself firmly.

She feels better when she crawls out of a barn one morning to be sick, and finds the cloud has lifted to reveal the first day of sunshine she can remember since riding away from the hunting lodge, however long ago that was. The simple beauty of the scene before her, rolling pasture dotted with trees and, in a fold in the hills half submerged in white mist, a village huddled around a long hall and a church, its cultivated strips fringing it like a striped skirt, has the effect of settling her stomach and giving her a sense of hope. But the wind has risen and veered to the east, bringing the temperature down sharply, and it is not long before Freya has followed her outside with straw stuck to the back of her shawl and a mulish look on her face.

"Thecla has a cough," she announces. She squats down beside Gytha, who is sitting on a grass hummock, taking deep breaths of the clean air to scour out the residue of nausea and the terrible nostalgia of her dreams. "Madam, we can't go on like this. Whatever you decide, I must think of my daughter."

"And I of mine."

"Then you should be taking better care of yourself. What do you think his lordship would say if he could see us now? He would be horrified."

"But he can't. It's up to me to do what I think best. If I am found by some man anxious to do William Bastard a good turn, I shall most likely be killed."

"And this way you're likely to die of cold or hunger."

"Watch your tone with me, girl." Part of her knows Freya is right, but another part asks, if you are warm and comfortable and well fed, what then is to distract you from thinking about the past? She is too worn out arguing with herself to argue with Freya as well. She glares at Freya, and Freya, who has never pretended her relationship with Gytha was anything so straightforward as that between servant and mistress, glares back.

"You'll find out what it is to be a mother soon enough," she hisses, and in the ensuing silence they hear Thecla racked by coughs and the low, rumbling tones of Fulk attempting to soothe her.

"Alright," says Gytha. "We'll go down to that village." She points to where the mist is thinning around the jumble of walls and thatch, and the squat stone tower of a Norman church. "We'll ask for lodging in the manor for tonight. But just tonight, mind. We haven't gone nearly far enough yet."

The master of the house is away, explains his wife, on a trip to sell their surplus sheep at the market at Horsham, before the winter sets in properly and there is no more grazing. But she would be heartily glad of company, as her two sons have gone with their father, and her youngest daughter is recently married and moved to live with her husband's people, and her daughters-in-law, well, you know daughters-in-law, always criticising, aloof...And more of the same, as she ushers the women into her hall, then breaks off to tell Fulk where to put the horses and to recommend a tincture of liquorice root pounded with common horehound, taken before bed, for the little girl's cough.

"A couple of nights back I had a troupe of acrobats here, would you believe," she tells them as she settles them beside the fire, orders them to take off their wet shoes and plunges a hot poker into a jug of ale. "I can't imagine what my Eric would have said, but the place feels so empty with all the men away except old Joseph and those two sour-faced girls occupying themselves with their children. They never let me near them, you know, as if I hadn't raised six of my own, though poor Eadric died of the smallpox two winters back. Terrible, it was, we're lucky we didn't lose more. Joseph's daughter lost all three of hers, not one over five years."

Gytha feels her eyes beginning to droop under the influence of the fire and the warm, spiced ale, the breathless chatter of their hostess, like a single, winding, endless word, vowels and consonants rising and falling, strident or confidential, proving a surprisingly effective lullaby. So she awakes with a jolt, her chin jerking up from her chest, when she hears the woman say, 'Canterbury'. Drawing a mask of polite attentiveness over her features, nodding from time to time as she listens, she feels every nerve strained towards the opening and shutting of the woman's mouth, the wobble of her jowls, the quick, emphatic gestures of her square hands, the barely perceptible breathing spaces that make sense of what she is saying.

"...all that way at this time of year to perform at the Earl's birthday feast, only to find everything shut up and his lordship gone to Normandy with the king. They say," dropping her voice to a whisper, "he's gone travelling to heal a broken heart. Apparently some woman he kept with him was taken by the spirits at All Souls." The goodwife gives a theatrical shudder. "Nothing left of her but a bloodstained cloak. Such goings on among the high and mighty. Makes you glad not to be one of them, doesn't it?"

"Doesn't what?" asks Fulk, coming in from turning out the horses, his face ruddy and beaming with health beneath the shock of tow coloured hair. *Nothing touches him*, thinks Gytha with a sudden glow of affection. Freya looks at Gytha, waiting for her to speak, but she cannot trust her voice.

"We were just hearing how the Earl of Kent's mistress was spirited away by ghosts at All Souls. Apparently some travellers who passed by here a few days ago had been in Canterbury and heard it," says Freya. Fulk's good natured face broadens in a smile. "My husband is a down to earth sort of man," explains Freya hurriedly. "He says he never believes such things. I expect you'd say she'd just run off with a handsome woodsman, dear, wouldn't you?"

Fulk goes to the hearth and helps himself to ale, aware that this is another occasion on which it would be best to keep quiet.

"He's a bishop, isn't he?" enquires the goodwife of no-one in particular. "I suppose some might say he should never have kept a mistress in the first place. Mind you, the priest here has a wife and fifteen children. Everyone complains of it, us because the tithes are so high, and the abbot of Saint Leonard's because he never gets his due because the children need breeches or shoes or some such, so perhaps it would be best if he'd never married. Then again, I like a priest who understands what worries ordinary folk with mouths to feed."

Gytha smiles, the slow smile of a lazy cat, then stretches and yawns.

"My mistress is with child," says Freya, "not three months gone yet. The difficult stage." She and the goodwife exchange looks of knowing sympathy. "If she might lie down for a while..."

"Certainly. You may take my bed, my dear, for God knows I have little use for it while my man is away. So tell me," she continues, leading Gytha towards a platform at the far end of the hall where there is a box bed with a wool mattress and a sheepskin thrown over a feather quilt, "why are you travelling in your condition?"

"My husband is a knight in the Count of Mortain's service. I am going to stay with my mother while he is away fighting rebels in Yorkshire."

Freya's approving look turns steely at Gytha's final embellishment.

"Sensible girl. Your mother'll be far more use to you than your husband when your time comes. I'll tell you something for free, by the time that baby's born you'll never want a man near you again."

I hope you're right, oh I so hope you're right, thinks Gytha as she stretches out on the bed and her hostess tucks the quilt around her. She falls into a deep, dreamless sleep, *the sleep of the dead*, she says to Freya later, with a strange laugh.

Odo counts. He counts the days and nights since she left, how many psalms he has sung and prayers he has recited to mark the passing of the hours; how many candles he has burned when he cannot sleep. How many breaths he has drawn of air which is empty of her. How long does it take to draw a breath? He tries to calculate that also. Still, when he awakes in the middle of the night, or in the morning, he reaches for her. His body expects her, like some dumb, domestic animal waiting to be fed. He counts the months they have spent together and marvels, considering them as a proportion of his life, a tiny fraction of the months he has spent on earth, how behaviour so recently learned can have become so habitual, so fundamental, so necessary.

Sometimes he stands in the empty workshop, counting the motes of dust dancing in the light from the great windows. He listens to the sift of ash in the cold fireplace and wonders how many stitches her little left hand executed during how many hours of working there, head bowed over her embroidery frame. How many roof tiles, links of mail, hawks, saddles, bridles and bits? How many fables, how many broken promises? How many yards of wool, how many needles? He tries to measure the distance between the man who commissioned this work and the creature he has become.

His heart hibernates, his soul as cold and dark as the winter around him, an empty grate full of mourning ash. In one of his libraries, he cannot remember which, is a book of hours containing an illustration of the fall of Lucifer in which the archangel and all the rebel angels are shown in blue robes, with golden wings, twisting and tumbling into the fiery mouth of hell. Their wings look like leaves caught in an eddy. He feels the same, sere, insubstantial, falling, burning, ash.

Although he continues to function, administering his estates, conducting the business of his diocese and overseeing the coastal defences, it is plain to everyone that he is, quite literally, out of his mind, absent from himself. His brain and body work as they always did, but his spirit, they believe, must have been taken by the hobgoblins along with his mistress. It quickly becomes clear to William, who plans to spend Christmas in Normandy quelling signs of revolt among his two elder sons, both of whom are more interested in becoming King of England than Duke of Normandy, and neither of whom seems to consider the fact that their father is still living, and in fair health, an obstacle to his ambition, that leaving Odo as regent is unthinkable. He orders his brother to accompany him. Perhaps it will give them an opportunity to mend fences. Perhaps home will have a healing influence on Odo.

With the messenger who carries his summons across London to Odo's palace beside Saint Giles' Gate, where he is busy consulting his lawyers about Brother Ealdred's forgeries, William sends a brief note in his own hand. *We grieve for you, brother*, Odo reads, in William's ponderous, smudged script, *though we are certain in our heart that our servant Canterbury acted wisely and lawfully in apprehending the woman, we would have wished the outcome otherwise. Be assured of our prayers.*

From your lord and loving brother
William Rex

Odo crumples the parchment in his fist and tosses it into the fire. William's pious platitudes make him feel mutinous, but he will go. One day, he will find his love, and his daughter, and he is not so foolish as to risk his estate for the short term release of lancing his resentment against William. What use can he be to his daughter if he has no dowry to confer on her, no influence to wield in finding her a husband? How could a man who would throw away everything for pride be worthy of Gytha's love?

Before answering William's summons to meet him at Tilbury on the commemoration of Saint Spatius, martyr of Bayeux, Odo returns to Canterbury. He does not expect to be in England again for some time. He has his own interests to pursue regarding William's sons and their ambitions, interests in which, perhaps, John may have a part to play also. The boy is growing up; the time is coming when he should take his place in his father's world. He is also mindful of his promise to undertake a penitential pilgrimage, and has decided he will go to Jerusalem. It is not that Compostela would be insufficiently arduous to expiate his sin, but that in Jerusalem he is more likely to find camels. It might be a year or more before Kent sees him again, and he has loose ends to tie up before he leaves.

The greatest of these, if he is not to fatally endanger everything he has won for himself since the Conquest, is Lanfranc. Having thought of little else on the journey from London, two days of mud-stuck tedium in the rain which never seems to have ceased since the drought broke, he concludes that a straightforward request for an audience is not the answer. Better to seize the moral high ground from the Archbishop before he even realises it is under attack.

The same day he arrives back in Canterbury, he enters the Archbishop's chapel during Vespers, clad in nothing but a shirt of plain linen, his feet bare and his head scattered with ash. Prostrating himself before the kathedra, his forehead pressed to the stone floor, he begs

Lanfranc's forgiveness in a loud, clear voice, just as the candles are being lit and the choir is preparing to sing the Lucernal psalms. Lanfranc will not be able to resist him.

As if at his direction, the Archbishop stands, then stoops to raise Odo to his feet and embraces him in the kiss of peace, all to the accompaniment of a somewhat ragged rendition of the psalms. He then insists Odo remain beside him for the rest of the service, which he does, keeping his teeth clamped and his fists clenched to prevent himself shivering in the November cold, all of which seems to be condensed in the space of the chapel, despite the warmth of the congregation's packed bodies and the steam of their breath, gilded by the evening candles.

When the service ends, Lanfranc instructs one of his novices to find Bishop Odo a habit to wear and then conduct him to the Archbishop's private office.

"You look in need of this," he says, pouring mulled wine as Odo enters, wrapped in a habit which is too wide and too short for him, leaving his ankles exposed above a pair of sandals with a strap missing, the skin of his face still grey with ash over the grey of loneliness.

"Thank you." He takes a deep draught of the wine, feeling its effect like a colour, like the flaring of the Vespers candles, the light growing and intensifying as each one is lit, warming the cobwebbed recesses of churches in every corner of the world at this hour.

"That was a gracious gesture, Odo. In the circumstances, I would not have expected it."

"I treated you dishonourably, your grace. That is neither in my nature nor my training. Such things are designed to withstand the death of love, I think. They have more weight, more substance." The lunatic lover inside Odo's skull watches the man of affairs make his pretty speech; he sees the curl of his lips around the words, the articulation of his jaw, he even appreciates the well moderated melodiousness of his tone, but what he says makes no more sense than if he were speaking Greek. He feels as though someone has taken a sword and cut his brain in two, and somehow, by some black miracle, he has stayed alive.

"I am very sorry things ended as they did for Mistress Gytha. It was far beyond my intention that she should die. I mourn the loss of any opportunity to bring her to repentance."

"That responsibility is in the hands of a higher authority than you or I now, Lanfranc."

"I pray for her soul."

"As do I."

"And for yours."

"As do I."

"So," continues Lanfranc, turning away from the gaunt intensity of Odo's stare, "you are going abroad."

"To Normandy and then…I don't know. I should like to see something more of the world. I have never travelled further than Rome."

"A man does not need to." Lanfranc affects the air of a sophisticate, but succeeds only in appearing foolish and vulnerable, like a child dressed up in his father's clothes.

"All the same. I intend to make a pilgrimage to Jerusalem, and I think I shall go to Alexandria. The Patriarch once sent me a very fine stallion. I should like to see if he has more of the same."

"You serve the aim of reunification very worthily, my son." Then, letting the ironic smile die from his lips, Lanfranc leans towards Odo across his desk. "A change of air will do you good, it will heal you. When you pray in the holy places, meditate upon the teaching of our brother Anselm."

"Which particular teaching of Anselm's did you have in mind, father? If I meditate upon them all, I shall run out of holy sites for my reflections."

"That the clergy may help themselves to resist sexual temptation by conjuring the image of the object of their desire after she is dead. *Place yourself with her in the bed where she now lies. Gather her worms to your breast. Embrace her corpse. Kiss closely her naked teeth, for the lips have now rotted away.*"

So absorbed is Lanfranc in trying to recall Anselm's words exactly, he does not notice the mischievous smile which flits across Odo's face as he says, "Believe me, Lanfranc, if I could lie in the bed she lies in now, I would."

The Archbishop crosses himself fervently. "Her power reaches you even from beyond the grave."

Before Odo can reply, they are distracted by a soft coughing outside the door.

"Come," calls Lanfranc. A young monk sticks his head cautiously into the room. "What is it?"

"If you please, your grace, Brother Mark needs the key to the plate room and the Prior can't find his."

"Very well." Lanfranc unlocks a small chest standing on his desk, with a key on the end of a chain around his neck. Rummaging among its contents, he eventually withdraws a much larger key with a fancy, trefoil head, but has some trouble disentangling it from a bronze chain with a locket on the end of it. As he holds out the key to the young monk, the locket swings from it, its enamel patterning nearly as familiar to Odo as the back of his own hand. Or hers.

"Where did you get that?"

In his haste to disentangle the jewel and return it to his box, Lanfranc is simply making matters worse. There is no possibility of pretending Odo has not seen it, or that it is anything other than what they both know it to be. Time to throw a sop to the wolf.

"One of Sister Jean's women brought it to me. She was troubled by what it contained."

Odo looks puzzled. "It has some locks of hair in it. Most lockets do, it's what they're for."

"Infants' hair, Odo. It is well known that witches will take the souls of infants who die unbaptised to be their familiars."

"All those children were baptised, Lanfranc." Odo speaks with icy precision, his power of self control stretched to its limit. "There were four of them. Matthew, Mark, Luke and Johanna. None lived more than a few days. What more would you like to know? Perhaps Mistress

Gytha's attachment to her dead children bordered on the idolatrous, but I've seen worse, even among men, whose minds are known to be stronger. Which of those foolish mares of Agatha's brought it to you? No, let me guess. It was Judith, wasn't it? You have based your whole case against Gytha on that woman's spite."

Lanfranc continues his futile fiddling with the locket while the young monk shuffles nervously in the doorway.

"Oh give it to me," says Odo, snatching the key and its burden from Lanfranc. He unwinds the chain easily, and hands the key to the young monk, who flashes him a grateful smile and flees. "You know," he goes on, dribbling the locket chain from hand to hand, "her hatred of Gytha was not even born of her pride in being the widow of one of Godwinson's leaders. That might have made them allies. Oh no, it was nothing but jealousy, that Gytha was loved, not only by me but by all sorts of people, and had pretty dresses. And you know I intended well by the woman, she had not even anything to be jealous of."

"In God's name stop your fiddling," snaps Lanfranc. Has Odo guessed the bargain he struck with Judith? If so, he is as much shamed by her mean spiritedness as she is herself.

"Did you really believe Judith thought Gytha was a witch, old man? Seems to me the only witch you have had dealings with is Judith herself." He rises, pulling the ill fitting habit into place and tucking the locket into his scapular.

"I burnt the hair," says Lanfranc defiantly.

"No matter." Odo gives him a glacial smile. "She is with her children now." *With the one that counts anyway,* he adds to himself, *the one who is going to live.*

Secure in the knowledge of her death, Gytha is content to travel openly once they leave the village near Horsham. They purchase an extra horse with a topaz taken from the store hidden in Odo's cloak, and call it Topaz, though it never answers to any name other than Maud. They take to the main roads and spend the nights in manor houses or priory guest houses. Everywhere they elaborate their story of Gytha's absent husband and her mother in the west a little further, which is why they avoid any great households or prominent abbeys where they might encounter those who could put their fabrications to the test. He is an older man, named Alain, in his fifties, to whom Gytha has been married for two years, having been widowed during the invasion. This will be their first child, though there is a grown up son from a previous marriage who regards her with suspicion. Regarding Sir Alain's estate, they do not have to rely on imagination, but on memory, and they recreate Winterbourne in every particular, even giving Sir Alain an aptitude for rearing orphaned piglets.

Though the weather worsens towards Advent, they continue to make good progress, travelling steadily north west as the character of Gytha's mother develops and it becomes clear to them she lives near Brysheiniog. *Brysh...what?* queries Freya when Gytha first comes up with it. Where is this unpronounceable place, for she has never heard of it? Gytha thinks she may have made it up, but she knows she hasn't, and on Christmas Eve, as they are returning from Mass in the company of their hosts, a family of wool merchants in Oxford, the sky ablaze with stars and the ground silvered with frost crunching beneath their feet, the memory comes to her.

It is as if the cloud of her breath forms itself into her mother's face, and the singing of the ice in tree branches and the eaves of the tall, stooping houses takes on the likeness of her voice, describing bony hills with their peaks bitten off by the dragons who live in the caves above racing streams which draw breath in deep, clear pools where the dragons cool their noses and read the future. There are sheep in the hills, of course, but also wild ponies, shaggy as goats, too wild even to be ridden by Lleu Llaw Gyffes who was raised to ride every horse, and they crop the grass so well that in the spring it is as green as seaweed. From then on, she knows where she is going and the character of her journey changes. No longer an escape, it becomes a running towards.

Days before his birthday, Odo makes the short journey to Saint Augustine's, on a visit to his old friend Scolland, who receives him warmly, coming out in person to the abbey gate, accompanied by a young novice bearing a bowl of water and towels with which the abbot washes his visitor's hands before kissing him with an affection much more enthusiastic than courtesy requires.

"My dear boy, you have been in difficult times. We remember you in our prayers."

"For which I thank you." Looking about him, at piles of timber and scaffolding, a wagonload of rough hewn stone awaiting the attentions of a mason, he asks, "How does the rebuilding of the church progress?"

"Excellently well. Blither, my master mason, is a treasure, and we are very grateful to you for the grant of Fordwich. We would be paying you so much import duty for the stone otherwise, we wouldn't be able to afford to build on the scale we are doing. You must let me show you round."

"I am glad to be of help. I should like to do more, though this time, I fear, I have come to ask you a favour. Two favours, actually. First, that you will have masses said here for...Aelfgytha."

They are crossing in front of the chapter house towards the abbatial lodging. It is mid-morning, between Terce and Sext, and the abbey's public spaces are almost deserted, the monks and abbey servants all at their work. Odo can hear a chorus of boys' voices reciting their lessons in the cloister, which makes him smile, though he notices that Scolland, as he links arms with him, is frowning.

"I cannot pretend to be happy about it."

"Why not?" asks Odo, all innocence. "She is but a child who died during the drought. I made a promise to her mother."

Scolland looks relieved. "Ah, I thought..." He opens the door to his house and stands aside for his guest to enter the austere vestibule with its lime washed walls and a great ebony crucifix before which Odo briefly bows his head.

"It's a common enough name among the English. Your confusion is understandable." Turning to Scolland, he seizes him by his arms. "Pray for her, Scolland, of your compassion, or just because I ask it if that makes it easier for you. Write what you will in your necrology, but when you say the Mass, let it be for her. And for me with her. My sins are many times greater than hers, and I feel…just as dead. I will pay handsomely, of course."

God knows, the abbey needs the money; when Scolland first arrived there from Mont Saint Michel, the place had been falling down. Shortly after his arrival a monk was killed in the church itself, struck on the head by a lump of falling plaster. It was heart-breaking to think that this place, one of the great sites of Christian pilgrimage, should have fallen into such neglect. And whether Odo means the child, or the woman of the same name, who is he to decide who is deserving of God's mercy and who is not? "Of course we will pray for her. I will have a scribe sent for to enter her into the roll."

"Later. I must come to my second favour first." They climb the stairs to Scolland's parlour where they sit beside a window overlooking the church, the old building dwarfed by scaffolding. "I want you to finish my tapestry. A lot of your people have already worked on it. Your workshop is one of the best in the country, whereas mine…well, let us say I underestimated the difficulties." Gazing out at the workmen swarming over the scaffolding, their tools between their teeth or strapped to their backs, he casts his mind back to his interview with Judith the day after his penitential visit to Christ Church. Watching her turn more and more pale and agitated as he swung Gytha's locket in front of her weasel snout like an enticing titbit, he had calmly announced that the man he had had in mind for her had been smitten by the charms of a young woman, the virgin daughter of one of his neighbours, and had begged leave to marry her with such urgency Odo had not the heart to refuse.

"Love is a powerful persuader, I find," he had commented equably, watching the woman's lips purse till they resembled nothing so much as a dog's arse. So, he continued, he had made arrangements for her to enter a convent which held land from him near Thetford. The abbess was, as Judith could surely imagine, delighted at the dowry she would bring of an entire estate in Kent.

What he did not tell her, seeing no reason to distress her further, was that he had also sent word to his man at the Danish court to seek out the grandsons of the thegn of Harbourne and ensure some accident befell them. Like those who are doubtless still harbouring Gunhild, he is easier in his mind if he has insurance.

"I have all my sister's notes and drawings," he continues, recollecting himself. "It shouldn't be difficult for your master to pick up where she left off."

"I thought, when Sister Jean returned to Normandy, that you had decided against continuing with it."

"Briefly. But I changed my mind. No, don't look at me like that. It's not my vanity. It's an important record. Time passes, people forget. You and I probably feel as though we've lived this way, one foot in England, one in Normandy, forever, but we haven't. We shouldn't take it for granted. And besides, so much work has already been done. It would be a pity to let it go to waste. It should be finished, for remembrance." He pauses, looks out at the church, then continues, "I thought, with your agreement, it might be appropriate if I were to sponsor a chapel, dedicated to Saint John the Baptist, say, in gratitude."

"There's a perfect spot at the eastern end. I could show you now, if you like."

Gytha knows she has reached the place when the people around her all seem to speak English with the same accent as her mother, a pattern of speech that reflects the hills they live in, a dizzy plunge into the vowel sounds followed by a climb up crumbling consonants. She knows because her daughter begins to dance in her belly the way bees dance at the mouth of the hive to thank God for a safe homecoming.

"Feel," she says to Freya, eyes shining above ruddy cheeks. "The baby moved."

They are standing beside the horses in the square of a small market town tucked into an elbow of river, the broader channel of which forms one boundary of the square and, swollen with meltwater from the mountains they can see in the distance, has overlapped its banks and turned trampled earth into syrupy mud. It is near dusk on an afternoon during Lent and Fulk has gone in search of lodgings for the night.

"With good food," Freya had called after him. The Lenten fast is hard enough without being in the company of a pregnant woman whose condition exempts her from its rigours. Now she lays her hand over Gytha's hard little belly and waits, looking into Gytha's eyes where the image of the Earl is still discernible, but fainter, as though sunk very deep in a pool of dark water. Within a moment she feels it, not only the flutter of tiny legs and arms but something more, a life force disproportionate to the strength of this five month child who has known nothing but persecution, flight and deceit almost since the moment of her conception.

"Strong," she says to Gytha, removing her hand.

Gytha beams at her. "It's because she can smell the air from the mountains. That's the place, Freya." Freya's gaze follows hers to the western horizon where the mountains are heaped up behind a barricade of strangely sculpted, dark green hills, the sun waning from primrose to apricot as it sinks behind them. "That's where we're going."

"But madam," says Freya, gripping Thecla's hand tight in dismay, "there'll be nothing out there except sheep and bandits."

"It'll be alright, I know it will. You must trust me."

For all the glow of her physical well being, as though her body is alight with the life of the child inside her, Freya thinks her mistress must have lost her mind. Perhaps the Earl chose unwisely in his tale of wolves at All Souls, conjuring spirits which have colonised Gytha's senses the way the baby has taken over her body. Perhaps the child is an incubus after all. Turning her back on the darkening mountains she says impatiently,

"Where is Fulk? This child needs her bed."

"Not," protests Thecla, who is very taken with a curly coated red and white heifer being led across the square, planting her feet daintily in pools of mud. The women laugh and Freya tells herself she is being ridiculous.

"You don't have to accompany me, you know. There's more than enough here," she touches a seam of the sable cloak, "to set you and Fulk up for life as well as for me and the baby."

"Oh no. The Earl would never stand for it."

"We're a long way out of his jurisdiction now, Freya. Over there," she nods towards the mountains, "even King William's writ doesn't run."

"His eyes watch it though." Rising on a motte above the town is a keep, whose like they have seen, and steered clear of, all over the counties they have passed through on their journey. A cylinder of dusty, dun coloured stone, scored with lead lined drains, it regards the town and the surrounding country through deep arrow slits. "You know what it looks like, don't you, stuck up there on its mound?"

They are still laughing when Fulk returns, a troubled look on his face as he glances up at the keep. "You know who the lord is here?"

"Well no, of course we don't," snaps Freya. "All we know is our feet are wet and our bellies are rumbling. What have you done about it?"

"Fitzosbern," says Fulk, ignoring her. "Only the king's oldest friend, so they say."

"It's true," says Gytha. "We mustn't stay here, not even one night. We must go on before they shut the gates. He's not here himself, is he? There's no standard on the keep."

Fulk shakes his head. "Held for him by a man called Neufmarche. Mistress is right, though. It won't be dark for a while yet, especially going west. Here." Fulk unwraps his short cape, which he has been using as a makeshift bag. "Some bread and cheese. Till we find somewhere for the night."

They find the mountains neither as high nor as deserted as they looked from the town square. Having passed the first night tolerably comfortably in the hay barn of a farm a mile or so downriver, where Thecla was spoiled with hot milk and honey, and griddle cakes smeared with damson jam, and they learned the town was called Y Gelli by the local people, though Hay by the English and God knows what by its latest masters, and the river was the Wye, they set out once more towards the heart of Brysheiniog, keeping the river to their back and the mountains ahead of them. Every climb is rewarded by the unfurling of immense views, hills and mountains shaded from rock black to the most delicate violet, every descent brings them into meadows where the yellow winter grass is giving way to new growth, scattered with clover, buttercups and spikes of purple orchids. The country is crisscrossed by streams full of spotted trout, still sluggish in the icy water, which Fulk catches in his hands and they cook even in the middle of the day with a clear conscience, fish being acceptable fare during the fast. They pass through hamlets where neither English nor French is spoken, though the language of Odo's jewels is well enough understood, until one morning, looking down from the track they are following along a ridge strung between two peaks like a washing line, they notice a roof emerging from a fold in the shoulder of the further hill.

Not much of a roof, they discover, as they climb down towards it, leading the horses over a scree of loose earth and boulders, the thatch caved in completely in parts and broken beams pointing at the sky like fingers with ragged nails. The building beneath, however, seems sound enough, a dry stone structure of the local granite, a stubby L shape, perched on a ledge of close bitten grass with a brook cutting through the flank of the hill on its southern side, followed by a sheep track. About a mile away, in a valley still in shadow this early in the day, they can just make out some kind of fenced settlement, one large building with a timber roof and several smaller thatched ones grouped inside a palisade.

While Fulk lets the horses drink from the brook, and Freya, saying it looks like rain, rummages among the mules' packs for something to wrap Thecla in, Gytha goes inside the building. The longer arm of the L is a bare room, its earth floor spattered with desiccated bird droppings and its corners thick with spider webs. The shells of last year's swallows' nests cling to the broken rafters. A high, thin wind carries the ghosts of their songs, lifting the loose thatch and whipping up eddies of dust. Poking at one of the old nests with a stick she finds lying on the floor, Gytha wonders when this building was last used by men.

She walks through a low arch with the remains of a curtain pole fastened above it into the smaller room beyond. Once again, its only ornaments are webs and dust and empty nests, but in the middle of the floor is a standing stone, intricately carved. In the pearly light filtering through the holes in the roof, the stone glitters slightly as she stoops to examine the decorations. It is covered on all sides except the top, which is smooth and greasy with old tallow, with dense geometric patternings of circles and crosses giving way on one side to an image, framed by trails of stone ivy, of a haloed saint striking with a lance at the breast of a winged serpent.

"A saint slaying a dragon," she mutters to herself with a rueful smile. *And are there not dragons to be found in Wales?* he had asked as they stood before his tomb at Saint-Vigor. What had she answered? Something about dragons more easily tamed by kisses than armies? "Well, Odo, it seems I have found my tomb. It may not be the one you intended, but at least it has a saint and a dragon." Straightening up, pushing her fists into the small of her back, which is beginning to feel the strain of carrying her growing infant up and down so many steep hills, she notices for the first time an arched doorway in the wall opposite the stone's saint and dragon face. The hinges screech as she pushes open the door, which sags, gouging a fan of earth out of the floor, then promptly falls down with a loud thud which startles the horses and makes Thecla cry. Stepping over it into the grassy court formed by the two arms of the L, Gytha announces, "This is it. I shall live here."

Fulk and Freya exchange eloquent looks.

"You know what I said to you in Y Gelli, Freya."

"Yes, madam."

"I meant it."

"Thankyou, madam."

"Roof'll need completely replacing," comments Fulk, reaching up and snapping off the end of a rafter where it overhangs the door. "Rotten. But you could do alright. Couldn't grow much at the back, too much shade. But there's room for a pig there." His face brightens. He scuffs up the soil with the toe of his boot. "Beans, peas, grow anywhere they will. Don't know what we'll do for bread though. Need something to trade. Honey maybe. We could keep a couple of hives. Plenty of clover in the valleys. Fish. Water parsnip I shouldn't wonder…"

"Oh Fulk do shut up." Freya glares at him, colder than the brook rushing past his feet.

"I am confident I can find a way to live," says Gytha, "but first I suppose we should find out if it belongs to anyone. I think the smaller room may be a chapel of some kind." By silent consensus they all look down at the settlement below them. "I shall change. Freya, help me."

It is late morning by the time they ride up to its gates, the sun almost at its zenith, an indistinct glow of pale pewter behind a veil of cloud. Though nothing is visible behind the double palisade of sharpened poles, it is obvious this is not a village but the stronghold of some local chieftain. One gate opens a chink as they approach and a small man with inquisitive eyes and delicate hands appears in it, flanked by two others, not much taller, but considerably broader than himself, both armed with bows charged. Gytha urges her horse forward, Fulk a few paces behind, his hand on the hilt of his sword.

"My name is Aelfgytha," she says to the small man, speaking slowly to be sure she is understood. "My mother was Aranrhod and she came from these parts. My father was an Englishman. I wish to speak with the master of this house."

The small man takes in Gytha's gown of yew green Flemish wool beneath the sable cloak, the jewels in her ears and on her fingers, the quality of her horse. "The master of this house is Owein ap Llwyr," he replies, in a voice unexpectedly resonant for so dainty a frame, "but he is away now at his daughter's wedding. I am Gereint, his steward. How may I be of service?" His English, mercifully, is fluent, though richly accented.

"Firstly by offering us kinder hospitality than a chink in the gate and drawn bowstrings. We have been on the road a long time."

"Forgive me." Satisfying himself that they are no more than one man, a couple of women and a child, Gereint signals his men to lower their weapons and shouts an order in his own language which elicits much creaking of ropes and a widening of the opening in the gate. "We are obliged to be cautious since the Normans settled themselves in Y Gelli."

Trusting that Fulk's Norman origin will be sufficiently concealed by the length of his hair and the beard he has grown since they left Canterbury, Gytha gives Gereint a conspiratorial smile and says, "We understand completely, believe me."

They ride into a spacious, well-kept courtyard bordered on one side by a long, low hall with an undercroft and on the rest by the usual collection of kitchens, bakehouse, dairy, forge, armoury, women's houses, stables and mews. It is much as you would expect of any lord's establishment, except that the buildings are not in muted hues of wood and stone but are a conflagration of colour, every inch of plank or plaster covered with designs like those Gytha saw on the stone altar in a blazing discord of madder and ochre, weld and woad and a vibrant purple she thinks probably comes from the ground shells of certain kinds of shrimps. The people she sees going about their business in the courtyard are dressed, men and women alike, in tunics embroidered with similarly vivid swirls and crosses, the higher among them, such as Gereint, also wearing gold and silver jewellery of intricate workmanship. Even in the watery light of the pewter sun her eyes are dazzled. She begins to wonder if this is the root of her embroiderer's skill, which was always more than simply having small hands well suited to close work, if it came from her mother and the bright visions of her people among their black rocks and seaweed grass.

Fulk helps her down from the saddle and Gereint leads her into Owein ap Llwyr's hall, which seems sparsely furnished to eyes used to Odo's magpie excesses, though the walls are hung with many bright tapestries and paintings on hides, and the roof beams elaborately carved with mythic beasts and goblin heads with their tongues sticking out and heads wreathed in ivy, some gilded, some painted in the same colours as the outside walls. She becomes anxious when she sees Fulk and Freya taken off to some other part of the compound, but she will not show it for fear of insulting Gereint by mistrusting his hospitality. Seating herself on the stool he offers, she casts her eyes down and folds her hands over her belly.

"Your husband," says Gereint, standing before her with his back to the fire. "Where is he?"

"Dead, sir."

"I am sorry. Have you no family you could go to?"

"None, sir, but my two servants and their daughter. But I have not come to you for charity. I do not lack substance. Rather, I desire to fulfil a promise made to my husband on his deathbed, to ease his passage to heaven by dedicating my life to God."

"A worthy notion, though I fail to see how Owein ap Llwyr can be of service to you."

"There is a chapel, in the hills about a mile from here, fallen into neglect. Is it in Lord Owein's gift?"

"Saint George's, you mean. It is, but as you say, in a parlous state. There was a hermit there, but he was killed in Fitzosbern's raids three summers back. There has been no-one there since. Surely you would be best pursuing your goal in a convent. If you are set on this part of the world, I'm sure my lord could recommend you to a place."

"I am a naturally solitary person, sir. My own resources are sufficient to me."

"But the child?"

"I believe I know enough to raise and educate her."

"Her?"

544

Gytha gives a self-deprecatory smile. "Just a fancy I have."

"I understand," says Gereint warmly, "my wife is just the same. We have five sons and she was convinced every one of them would be a girl. Preparing me for the worst, I suppose. Well, I cannot think Lord Owein would make any objection."

"I have means. I will make Lord Owein a gift in exchange for the chapel and the hermit's house." Opening the purse hanging from her girdle, she takes out an uncut sapphire the size of a robin's egg and holds it on the flat of her hand while Gereint inspects it with something close to wonder in his shrewd, black eyes.

"That is very…impressive," he says.

"I have more."

"Two such and it's yours."

That is robbery, she thinks, but then again, *is any price too high to pay for perfection? And was there ever a steward who did not like to line his own pocket as well as his master's?*

"Done." She draws a second stone from the purse, a ruby this time, and slightly larger. Gereint sweeps them from her palm as though they might be withdrawn, or even disappear in a puff of coloured smoke, if he fails to act quickly.

"For that you may have roofing materials and whatever else you need to make the place sound."

"I thank you. I will send my man to discuss our requirements with you, once we have assessed everything. And now, if you will forgive me, I should like to make a start."

"Will you not at least break bread with us and set out after the day meal?"

Thinking of Fulk and Freya, she demurs, but sits through the meal in an agony of impatience. All the time she endures Gereint's wife's counsels on childbirth, a vision shimmers in her mind of her new home and how it will be when the roof is sound and the beans planted, the hearth swept and a couple of these prettily carved stools before it, when there are stout hides at the windows and bees in the hives and a silver cross upon the altar to draw out the glitter in the granite dragon's eyes.

They work unceasingly throughout the spring, Fulk and a couple of men from Owein ap Llwyr's household. Though Freya is clearly minded to take up Gytha's offer of freedom, Fulk will not hear of it until the hermitage is restored and a decent sow chosen. He is Lord Odo's man before he is Freya's, he tells her, with the uncomfortable suspicion that it is more complicated than that, though he could not say how.

By the time Owein ap Llwyr returns from his daughter's wedding in Ireland, the hermit's room is weatherproof and they are working on the roof of the chapel. Having chided his steward severely for letting the lady live up there in such conditions, and heard Gereint's reply that she had refused all offers of hospitality, accepting only the services of the two workmen, a plain cross of silver forged by the smith and the carpenter's offer to make her an oak table, a set of stools and a crib, Lord Owein mounts his pony and goes up to Saint George's to see the mad Englishwoman for himself. Suspecting she may be genuinely holy, for how else to account for her behaviour, he takes with him a mule laden with two sacks of flour, a barrel of wine, some Welsh onion sets and a bag of bean seed.

Her new landlord puts Gytha in mind of nothing so much as a goat. Though tall for a Welshman, he is a head shorter than Fulk, with a black beard which curls to a point like a goat's and yellow goat eyes. His legs are bowed, but he is nimble, and so quick Gytha, now well into her sixth month, can scarcely keep pace as he tests the soundness of a rafter with the point of his knife, or praises the stonework around the hearth, or wonders that she can be content with so plain a cross, or frets about the safety of her child. His speech bubbles like the brook over stones, and occasionally falls into reflective pools, at the bottom of which Gytha suspects a cool, analytical intelligence lurks like an ancient and wily pike.

Once he has satisfied himself that the work is progressing to an acceptable standard, he asks Gytha to accompany him to a rock ledge overhanging the brook a few paces down the track from the hermitage's eyrie.

"Permit me," he says, taking her arm with a smile of stained goat teeth glimpsed through the glossy curls of his moustache, "the path is very rough."

"And I am very ungainly," she replies gallantly.

"I used to come here, you know, when I was a boy. Old Dafydd would hide me from my father when I'd displeased him, which was often. I would fish from this ledge and listen to Dafydd's wisdom while we cooked the trout. He was my Merlin, you might say, though I am no Arthur, for if I were, Dafydd would still be here and Neufmarche back in Rouen."

"Perhaps Dafydd's time had come, My Lord. The longer I live the more I see the futility of questioning God's will or the way He goes about achieving it."

"Then you are a wise woman and a worthy successor." He pauses. "I also have a son who fishes up here. It might be well if you would make yourself known to him."

"And do you suppose your father had this sort of conversation with Dafydd? Do you not think it wiser to let your son come to me of his own accord if he is minded to unburden himself? No doubt he has confidants more likely than me."

"But not ones to whom I may speak candidly."

"Which you believe you have a right to do to me because you have let me have your hermitage. I must take on the hermit's duties as well as his house. Even though I paid, more than fairly, I thought, for so small a plot."

"Gereint has shown me the stones. What's more, there are people in some of the villages between here and Y Gelli who have become suddenly and inexplicably wealthy. I will not ask how you came by your jewels, or your swollen belly...as long as you will do me this occasional favour. The boy is pleasant enough. You should not find it too onerous."

She looks into Owein's crafty, goat eyes, trying to read there if he is a man who will keep his word. She thinks he must, if it is a matter of his own son, but she wishes Odo were there. Odo has an instinct for these kinds of situations. Then thoughts of Odo lead her to see in her mind's eye the image of the saint and the dragon on the chapel altar stone, and she knows she has no choice but to trust Owein, because this is the place where her child must be born.

"I'm sure I shall not."

"Good, then we understand one another. I think we shall be fast neighbours, Aradrhon's daughter."

Though the weather in the hills is always changeable, it proves to be a kind spring, with few long periods when work on the hermitage is impossible. Under the inquisitive eyes of lambs and the occasional, lofty gaze of eagles, Fulk and his men complete the building and haul up the furniture from Owein ap Llwyr's carpenter's workshop. Helped by Thecla, the women plant out a vegetable garden, until Gytha can no longer bend to the work and occupies her time sewing baby clothes, hemming blankets for her bed and curtains for the crib, and embroidering a cloth for Saint George's altar.

She waits out her goose month almost in a trance, in which nothing seems real but her daughter, turning somersaults in her belly, clearly visible now beneath the taut stretched fabric of the gown she has made out of two of her old ones. Even the work going on around her seems to be happening behind a veil, immediate yet distant, all to her direction and yet somehow not her responsibility. Sometimes, especially when the baby moves, she thinks of Odo, but not as often as she had expected to, and not with the pain for which she braces herself. She feels guilty about this. Sometimes she talks to her daughter about it, as though the baby is a wiser soul than she is.

You know I still love him, don't you? she says, her voice soundless, merely a vibration of the cord that binds her to her daughter. *It's just that I have to think of you now. He would understand, wouldn't he?*

After all, you're part of him too. She tries to conjure up his face, but though she can list each feature, from the lazy cat curve of the smile that says, I want you, to his short nose and curling eyelashes, she cannot seem to put them together. He is a picture in her memory, without the spark of animation. She knows she should regret this, but does not, and that compounds her guilt until she begins her monologue of self justification all over again.

Her guilt becomes focused on Fulk, making her resentful of his obstinate loyalty to Odo, so that, in the end, she and Freya are working together to convince him he has done all he can for her. The day he puts the last straw in place on the ridge of the chapel roof, flailing at the swallows, newly arrived from their winter quarters and expecting to find their nests where they left them at the end of last summer, the three of them drink a toast to the future as the sun narrows to a bright diadem on the brow of the hill behind the hermitage. Then Gytha puts down her cup and goes into the chapel, where what remains of Odo's jewels, except the pearls, are concealed in a recess behind the altar which was once, she presumes, intended to house the Host. Grabbing a handful at random, she goes back outside.

"Hold out your hands," she says to Fulk, then pours the jewels into his cupped palms. "There. For you and your family. Go, lose yourselves, be happy. Keep the finest pigs in Christendom and give Thecla a tribe of brothers and sisters."

"But what about the baby, madam?" This time, perversely, it is Freya who appears reluctant. "It can't be long now."

"Freya, this will be my fifth child."

"Fifth? But I thought…"

"I have let you think a lot of things about me that were wrong. Forgive me. You believed I disliked children. I never disliked them, I was simply afraid. All my other four died, and it hurt me more than seemed reasonable or bearable."

"All the more reason…"

"But we know this one isn't going to die, don't we? We both heard what Gunhild said. I'm not afraid now, I haven't been since we...cleaned the bed at Conteville." Both women give Fulk a sidelong glance, but he is absorbed by the handful of gems and seems to have no curiosity about their conversation. "So please," continues Gytha, "have no concern for me, think of yourselves."

"His lordship..." ventures Fulk, wishing he had kept his mouth shut as the women turn on him.

"Oh for heaven's sake," snaps Freya.

"You have more than discharged your obligations to Lord Odo," Gytha insists. "He would be the first to say so. You have followed me beyond the grave, as it were, and built me a very fine 'tomb'. You could not have done more." She laughs, but Fulk looks doubtful and shivers as the sun disappears behind the hill.

"Before dark," she continues, "you will go down to Lord Owein's stables and take two of the horses and the mule. I said I would give him my mare in exchange for one of the mountain ponies. And I will never see you again. You will forget me and all the danger I put you in, though I will not forget you."

She kisses each of them, even Fulk, who flushes like a second sunset, and holds Freya for a moment by her upper arms in token of the secrets they have shared, but perhaps more because of the ones they have not. She watches them until a turn in the track takes them out of sight, Freya with her daughter on her hip, Fulk leading the way with their saddlebags slung over his shoulder. She watches until their foreshortened figures reappear outside Owein ap Llwyr's stockade, and the gate opens, and they disappear inside. Then she rinses the drinking cups in the brook, stoppers the jug of Lord Owein's wine, and carries everything indoors. She goes into her chapel and, finding kneeling difficult, sits cross legged in front of the saint and the dragon locked in their interminable combat.

"Well, George," she says, "here we are, you and me and the dragon." *And me*, says her daughter, feet drumming against the walls of her mother's womb.

One morning towards the end of May, she is certain something has changed the moment she opens her eyes. Her mattress still has the oily scent of freshly sheared wool and the room beyond her bed curtains smells, as it does every morning, of the dough put to prove the night before. Shards of sunlight pierce the false twilight of closed shutters, and outside, as always, skylarks bubble in competition with the brook. For a few moments she lies still, holding back the bed curtain and wondering. Then realisation dawns. The baby is not moving. Gytha feels no anxiety about this. She knows babies become still once they are ready to be born. Do they sleep, she wonders, gathering strength for the struggle ahead, or are they simply struck to stone by contemplation of the unknown world they are about to enter?

Heaving herself up from the bed on a surge of anticipation, she sets about making everything ready in her room. She spreads a clean sheet on the floor, and beside it puts twine, a knife, a cup of wine, and a linen envelope of powdered poppy seed Freya gave her for pain. Climbing cautiously onto a stool, she then fastens two lengths of rope over the rafters above the sheet. She wishes she still had her medal of Saint Margaret, patron saint of women in labour, that was tied to her left thigh during the births of her other children, together with eleven grains of coriander in a muslin bag. But the medal had been in her leather pouch and she has no coriander. She lights her fire, then goes out to the brook to fetch water, not bothering to dress but simply shoving her feet into her shoes and throwing a shawl over her night gown. Returning with her pail, she uncovers the dough, divides, kneads and shapes her loaves and puts them into the oven Fulk built for her beside the hearth.

Her mind is calm and clear, but her body is restless. She tries to sit, dragging a stool out into the morning sun, telling herself she must conserve her energy, but her feet twitch and her legs dance to a rhythm only they know. Her back aches and she knows she must be tired, up countless times every night to make water and then unable to sleep due to the baby's remorseless kicking, but sitting brings on heartburn so she decides to take a walk. She climbs the ridge behind the hermitage from where, if she looks to the east, she can see the dark smudge of Y Gelli, Neufmarche's tower shimmering over it this morning like the admonitory finger of some stone giant buried with his hand poking out of the earth. Just as she is perfecting this image to herself, the first pain creeps up on her, a stealthy shift of the ache at the base of her spine to some deeper, less definable location, vanished almost before she has registered what it is.

No harm in continuing her walk. It will be hours yet before anything happens. She goes on along the ridge in a northerly direction, trying to count the different shades of green and blue, mauve and grey in the vast, petrified sea of hills around her, watching the swoop and dart of swallows and wondering why it is you never see a skylark, as though its song forms a concealing cloud around it. When she reaches the pinnacle of the next hill, she returns the way she has come, gazing in delight at the neat, new thatch of her roof, the same, warm shade as amber, but so much more precious. *Like you, baby,* says the voice inside as another pain comes, sharper this time, more focused, *made, not found. The bread will be ready,* she thinks, clambering down the scree into her back yard where her little spotted sow grazes incuriously, her chain rattling as she pulls it through the iron eye in the pole she is tethered to.

"You wait till I get the boar to you," she says through gritted teeth. Definite pains now, sharp hammer blows to her abdomen, their rhythm growing quicker as though marking a Saint Vitus' dance. "Fifteen at least for you, not just one." But tiny, and with nice, narrow heads and neat, tucked in feet.

For the first time, bringing the loaves out of the oven with her hands wrapped in rags, taking care to leave the door open, for closed doors can obstruct the delivery of children, she feels a worm of fear burrowing into her. What if the baby is her father's daughter, with his great build, so she tears inside like Leofgeat and bleeds to death, and no-one finds the baby in time so she starves, or is taken by wild animals? She should have kept Freya with her. How stupid and selfish to let her go. How treacherous to Odo, what a waste of this perfect house. The next pain almost hurls the loaves out of her arms, as though their muscles are contracting in sympathy with her womb. She crawls on to the sheet, thinking she will try to rest a little, and lies miserably on her side, knees drawn up to her belly which no longer feels like part of her body but hard and smooth and indifferent as one of the great, flat stones in the bed of her stream. She is just a mind, floating free, utterly alone.

Until her body's work brings her back from her feverish doze to a howling, sobbing, self pitying consciousness. Turning on to her back, she notices the packet of poppyseed, but hesitates. How much? Too much and she may fall into a stupor and be unable to push when the time comes, but there is an iron band around her belly, and a torturer yanking it tighter.

"You bastard," she shouts at Odo, at his pompous purse-lipped image when he spoke so spitefully to her of the punishment of Eve, "you fucking, *fucking* bastard!" She'll take it all and die, serves him right.

Sitting up, she opens the envelope, licks her finger and dips it in the black, grainy powder then sticks her finger in her mouth. "Should have stuck to sucking," she says, with a mad laugh. "Just as much fun and fewer consequences." The torturer begs to differ, and tightens the band again. "Mary, a virgin, bare Christ," she mutters, casting about in her mind for the rest of the charm, clutching Odo's Tear of the Virgin, still fastened around her neck, "Elizabeth bore John the Baptist. I charge thee, infant...oooh, Christ, don't let me die!" Obviously not enough poppyseed, she decides, when the contraction is over. She takes another fingerful and a mouthful of wine which she promptly vomits back up, but some of the poppy must have stayed down because she begins to feel dreamy, dissolving, liquescent, slowly flowing out of her pain wracked body into cool, dark places made of sleep.

She becomes aware of being very cold. The room is dark and the fire has gone out, and the sheet underneath her is soaking wet. Her night gown is soaking wet, her legs, her feet as she struggles upright and puts them cautiously to the wet floor. *Waters*, she thinks, becoming aware of a pressing need to evacuate her bowels. Well, it will have to wait, she must build up the fire first. It may be June but the nights up here are still cold and she will have a baby to think of before long.

Oh God, she can't, she isn't ready. If she can just get this fire lit and have a shit, and put on some dry clothes, then she can think about the baby. She struggles across the room, bent as near double as a pregnant woman come to term can possibly be, the sodden gown clinging to her legs, and squats before the hearth, stirring the embers into life with a stick. She makes a careful heap of kindling over the glowing ash and, absorbed in her work, finds she has reached a brief truce with her body.

Stripping off her nightgown, she bundles it up with the wet sheet, which she replaces with another from her bed, and wraps herself in Odo's cloak which she takes down from a peg on the back of her door. Her teeth chatter. Taking a spill of kindling from the fire, she lights two candles and puts them at either end of her table, then throws a log on to the fire, sparks flaring up towards the smoke hole like a physical manifestation of the excitement inside her that makes her feel ready to explode. Finally she fills her iron pot with water and hangs it from the tripod straddling the fire, before lying down on the clean sheet.

Parting her legs, she probes herself with tentative fingers, suddenly shy, suddenly aware that this patch of wrinkled skin and damp hair she can feel is a new person, someone about whom she knows nothing. How can she bring her up, here, alone, in a Welsh mountain, the niece of a king? The king. Neufmarche's tower. They will find her, even here, and take her child. She should have continued to knot hairs. She should have taken Margaret's place on Gunhild's grubby bed.

But there is no time to answer her questions, no point in wishing she had made different decisions, because her touch has woken her body up again and she is overwhelmed by the urge to push, every last ounce of her strength bent to the task of forcing her child out into the world, the dumb act of love and violence. Squatting on the sheet, gripping the two ropes tied to the rafters until the grain of the twisted hemp eats into her palms, she bears down, sobbing raucously and uncontrollably as she thinks of Odo and how, for all these months, she has carried part of him inside her, treasured, nurtured and protected, only for them now, finally, to be wrenched apart in the appalling solitude of a Welsh mountainside.

She has not cried until now, on the whole of her long pilgrimage from Kent she has not felt so utterly abandoned and alone as she does now. Sobs well up from every fault line in her heart, as cracked and chipped as an old earthenware jug, so that when, with a final skin-tearing, heart-bursting, bone-cracking heave, she brings her daughter slithering into life, the first thing she says to her is,

"Well, you must think you have a monster for a mother. Just look at me." Wiping tears from her burning eyes, licking snot from the corners of her mouth, she holds up her baby, bloody and long limbed as a skinned rabbit, and a smile as uncontrollable as her tears spreads across her face.

"And just look at you." Wincing as a final contraction expels the afterbirth, she lays the baby carefully on a clean patch of sheet then ties off and cuts the cord before picking her up again and giving her a cautious shake. Her eyes fly open, she takes a tremulous breath, looks surprised for a second then lets out a long wail like the cry of a seagull.

"Pearl," she tells her daughter later, when they are washed and warm beside the fire, and she has the baby to her breast, feeling the sparkle of her milk in response to the sturdy suck. Once again, for the twentieth, or two hundredth, time, she unfolds the blanket and gazes at her daughter, pink and perfect in the firelight. She counts fingers and toes, marvels at her long eyelashes, her tiny nose, the way she sucks her lower lip, the dark curls plastered to her head like a mail hood, her indisputable female sex. "Pearl," she says again, contemplating opalescent fingernails and the sheen of her eyelids as she falls asleep with a drop of milk sliding down her chin. "Tomorrow, when we're all rested, I shall take you to my stream and name you Pearl."

The following afternoon, a herdsman scouring the hills for yearling ponies for Lord Owein's stables reports seeing the woman from old Dafydd's hermitage beside the stream with an infant. The following morning Gytha is roused from sleep by a knock on her door.

"Who's there?" she shouts crossly. She has been up half the night with Pearl, whose appetite and sleeping habits are already showing signs of resembling those of her father, and now she has slept late, and is all at odds with herself, her back aching, sunlight stabbing her eyes, damp shift stuck to sore nipples. Then she looks at the baby, tightly swaddled and sound asleep in her crib, pink cheeked and breathing regularly, and suddenly the morning is the most beautiful she has ever woken to and she exults in her body's pains the way she used to love the trail of scratches and bruises and bite marks left on her skin by Odo's passion.

"Lord Owein sent me," says a woman's voice, muffled by the door, "to see if you have everything you need."

"Yes, thank you." She does not open the door. She will not have these strangers in her house, invading its private space, set aside only for her and Pearl. If she had wanted other people, she would have kept Fulk and Freya by her, but when her four children by Adam were born, she was surrounded by people, hoardes of female relatives, neighbours, midwives, all regaling her with advice, exhortation, spells and prayers, sitting her up, lying her down, feeding her hot potions or ice water, and what good had any of it done? Other people are a plague to which she will not expose her precious daughter.

Silence. She can feel the visitor deliberating on the other side of the door, then she says, "Very well. Lord Owein sent some provisions. I'll leave them outside the door."

Gytha waits until the footsteps have receded, dislodging earth and stones which rattle down the path ahead of them, before going outside to see what the woman has left. A large basket covered with a muslin cloth stands on the doorstep, too heavy, Gytha decides, for a small woman who has just given birth to carry into the house. Squatting down, she begins to unpack eggs and cheeses, almond milk puddings, some blowsy cabbages with black earth clinging to their roots, and a box of strawberries to which she helps herself as she lifts out a parcel of tiny embroidered gowns wrapped in a crib coverlet made of lambskins from the bottom of the basket. Licking strawberry juice from her fingers, she holds one of the gowns up to the light to inspect the work. It is neat, though not as good as her own, but thankfully, no-one here knows she can embroider. No-one here must ever know the part she has played in embroidering history.

Her attention is caught by movement in the valley. The woman, in the company of a small boy, is re-entering Owein ap Llwyr's compound, her hand gripping the boy's shoulder as she follows him through the gate. So she is blind; the boy is a seeing-boy. True to his promise to make no enquiries about her wealth or the parentage of her child, Lord Owein sent a blind woman to her, who would be unable to answer any questions he might be tempted to ask about the appearance of the baby. Suddenly full of remorse, she regrets her unfriendliness. Perhaps, once she is fully recovered, once Pearl is stronger, she will take her down to the compound to thank her landlord in person.

"Well, Your Reverence, we have encountered the odd difficulty with interpretation," says the workshop master to Scolland in answer to his enquiry as to the progress of Bishop Odo's hanging. "It is very difficult to discern any order in the way the work has been done, almost as though Sister Jean did not wish her embroiderers to understand what was being asked of them. I suppose it's possible some of her notes and drawings became confused during the move."

More than possible, thinks Scolland, recalling the wagonload of collapsed frames, rolls of linen, boxes of needles, hanks of wool and chests of parchments. Above all, parchments. Drawings, notes, bills for dyeing, for needles, candles, firewood and dressmaking, many, he was told, found scattered about the workshop floor. He marvels his master embroiderer has managed to make any sense of it at all.

"We have found this, for example." Conducting the abbot to his work table, where the drawings lie pinned together in order, the master shows him a sketch which seems to have no bearing at all on the tale of William's conquest. It lies to the right of a scene in which William and Harold of Wessex parley in William's palace in Rouen. It shows an ornate doorway, with barley twist doorposts and pediments carved to resemble the heads of hounds, or bears, perhaps. Two figures stand in the doorway, a small woman and a priest, youthful and vigorous, long legged and fashionably dressed in a short, close fitting tunic. He has one hand extended towards the woman's cheek in a caress, or possibly a blow, the other on his hip, almost as though he is dancing. In the border immediately below squats a naked homunculus with his arm outstretched towards the priest and his lady, mirroring the gesture of the priest. Scolland shakes his head.

"Well, I cannot see that it has any bearing on the representation of King William's conference with Wessex, and I wonder at the...detail of the nude figure. Bishop Odo insists he wishes to display this work in his new cathedral. Can he be aware what it contains?"

"It is most vexing, Father."

"Wait." Scolland peers more closely. "Bring me a candle. Really, my eyesight. Thank you. Yes, I thought so. Look, there is an inscription: *Ubi unus clericus et Aelfgyva*. And there it stops."

"Aelfgyva," the master repeats. "Was that not the name..?"

"It was. Perhaps we should exclude it. And yet, the drawing is there, and Bishop Odo was most insistent that we follow Sister Jean's plan to the letter."

Nor is he here to be consulted, though Scolland has had letters from him aplenty, recounting his travels. He has been in Normandy with the king, thence to France and Flanders and Rome. Abbess Clothilde, he reports, is mightily pleased with the trophy Agatha brought her, an embroiderer of Opus Anglicanum, even if the girl does appear somewhat sickly. After visiting his cousin, Count Roger, in Sicily, he took ship for Alexandria where he learned to ride a camel, which confirmed his admiration for the horse, and purchased a Septuagint in Greek, though he has yet to find a translator for it. He has seen the great pyramids of the pharaohs glittering in the desert moonlight, and found the face of the Sphinx very reminiscent of the cathedral choirmaster at Rochester. He has prayed at the holy sites of Jerusalem, from where he sent Scolland a hair from the Baptist's beard in a gold reliquary to be placed in his chapel, and had cotton shirts made in Damascus. Once a man has worn cotton next to his skin, he will never want a linen shirt again.

He is travelling, thinks Scolland, *like a man trying to escape from himself.* "And Aelfgyva is a common enough name in this country," he adds, remembering the dead child for whom Odo ordered masses to be said. "Perhaps she is not who we think she is. Continue with it, Master, just as it is."

As it turns out, Gytha has plenty of opportunity to make up for her initial hostility to the blind woman, for she and her seeing-boy climb up from Owein ap Llwyr's compound quite regularly after their first visit. The woman, she finds out, is called Bronwen, and was blinded during childhood by a kick to the head from a mule. The seeing boy has no name, he is an orphan, as dependant on Bronwen, she says with a bleak laugh, as she is on him.

Sometimes they bring food and wine, or small beer, sometimes they come with tools over their shoulders and work among Gytha's vegetables. Lord Owein himself does not come, and nor does his son, though one evening she sees a young man with black curls fishing at the pool where she struck her bargain with Owein. She gives him a friendly smile, in response to which he packs up rod and net and moves downstream.

Though the seeing-boy gabbles in Welsh, Bronwen says little in any tongue, but Gytha can feel her listening, as though fine webs of hearing spread out from her ears to enmesh her in the life of the hermitage. She knows the state of the soil from the sound of a spade entering it and the growth of the little sow by the depth of her grunts. When rain is coming it whispers a warning to her, and when Pearl awakes, she is almost as quick to detect her snuffles and whimpers as Gytha herself. So it comes as a surprise to Gytha when, one afternoon near Lammastide, driving her spade into the earth at the very place between two rows of carrots where the afterbirth is buried, Bronwen says,

"Odd name, Pearl. Heathenish," she adds after a pause.

"It's her birth stone," says Gytha, thinking of the pearls, wrapped in a waxed cloth and buried in the earth floor beneath her bed. "Better than no name at all."

Bronwen shrugs.

Her remark rankles with Gytha, as her garden matures and the little sow fattens, and Pearl's dark eyelashes begin to curl. Perhaps Pearl really is no name, chosen on a whim, yet what other kind of name can she give the child if no-one is to know who she is? When William dies, when Odo finds them, he can name her. But what did he say? *You choose, she's your child.* Well, she has chosen. And if William lives ten more years, or twenty? There are all the poxes and fevers of childhood to be got through, there are plagues, droughts and freezing winters, and Pearl is not even baptised. One day a man may wish to marry her, but how can he marry a girl without even a name to bring him?

Once she has stopped bleeding, Gytha goes into the chapel to confide her anxieties to the saint, who is sometimes George, sometimes Vigor and sometimes, improbably, Odo. The cross glows against a backdrop of dark blue, luminous cloud, full of rain. Autumn is coming, she tells him, looking at stalks of honesty poking like fine bones from a vase on the altar, the seeing boy brought blackberries this morning. It will be very cold up here come winter. How far does Gunhild's prophecy extend? How safe is our daughter?

She should be properly baptised, cautions the saint. I am a bishop after all, adds Pearl's father, with his downturned smile.

"Please will you ask Lord Owein to send me a priest," she says to Bronwen as she and the boy prepare to depart one evening. Bronwen looks surprised, eyebrows arched above her milky, roaming eyes.

"It's time Pearl was baptised."

Bronwen nods. "Frost tonight," she says, sniffing the air. Gytha hugs her daughter close.

The priest comes on the following day, mounted on a shaggy pony, sure footed as a goat, his vestments and phials of oil and salt and holy water strapped to the back of his saddle. He is an old man, who used from time to time to give the Sacrament to Dafydd. He speaks no English, but his walnut face creases into a wide, toothless smile when Gytha addresses him in Latin. That, it seems, is enough to drive from his mind all the questions he might have thought to ask a woman living alone with a baby, two months old at least and still unbaptised, the questions Owein ap Llwyr has forbidden him to ask, though doubtless he will have a few of his own when the priest gets back.

"What will you name her?" he asks when he has finished his preparations. Gytha, still caught up in the memories evoked by the prayers for the ritual of clothing, does not reply immediately.

"Have you chosen?" prompts the priest.

"Oh...yes. She is to be named for her grandmothers. Aranrhod Herleva."

What harm can it do, naming her Herleva? It is not such an unusual name and besides, she doubts the Bastard boasts much of his mother, the undertaker's daughter content to open her legs out of wedlock for a man high enough born, when he had Duke Robert of Normandy for his father. And anyway, her child will never be known as Herleva. She is still Pearl.

Taking her from the priest's arms, she kisses her forehead, tasting the holy oil, and smoothes droplets of holy water from her downy curls with the flat of her hand. The baby fixes her dark blue gaze on her mother's face and begins rooting for the breast. Gytha feels her milk come in like a blessing, an affirmation of life and hope.

"I'll take my leave then," says the priest. "God keep you, daughter."

"Thank you, Father, and you."

It's true what Agatha said, she thinks, drawing a stool up to the fire and unlacing the front of her gown, at Winterbourne, when her life seemed on the verge of unravelling. *Love doesn't die, love endures; it merely changes shape.*

BELOVED GHOST

THE EVE OF SAINT VIGOR AND SAINT EXUPERY 1077

He still counts. Nine lengths of linen, four loops in the back of each, two at the top margin and two at the bottom, except the length stretched behind the altar, thirty two loops, thirty two hooks nailed into sixteen pillars. Twenty inches high, nearly two hundred and forty feet long, incalculable lengths of thread spun from inestimable numbers of fleeces. Eight dyes only, but he observes infinite variations and subtleties of colour because he looks at his tapestry with a lover's eyes.

The work was completed more than twelve months since, each finished piece then carefully washed and dried before they were stitched together and the borders hemmed. In order to avert any risk of the dyes running, the wool was not washed, and Odo has noticed dark edged needle marks and a few places where Agatha's original charcoal outlines show through the embroidery. He misses no detail, not even the faded, rusty stain of Alwys' blood, looking as though it has drained from the severed head of some Saxon Holofernes. The hanging was unpacked from the lead lined box it has been stored in since completion, its folds interleaved with cedar chippings to keep off moths, only this afternoon. Ten and a half years since he first disclosed his vision to Agatha.

Four years, seven months and a week since he started talking to ghosts. For that is how he thinks of them, Gytha and his daughter. For all he knows they could be dead, but if they are living, he has all the more reason to behave as if they are not.

"Pardon, Your Reverence," says the young deacon charged with the responsibility of locking up for the night. He only recognises his bishop, sitting on the steps leading to the high altar, by his robes, for he is new to Bayeux and has not met Odo before. "I didn't realise anyone was still here."

"Only me, I think. Give me the keys and I will lock up. I aim to share a moment of quiet reflection with Our Lady and all these other saints before the service of dedication tomorrow."

"The cathedral is magnificent, Father," ventures the deacon cautiously, aware of his bishop's reputation for a capricious temper, though he looks meek enough this evening, saintly even, the fringe of largely grey hair around his tonsured head like a halo by moonlight, his expression grave almost to mournfulness. The bishop smiles, a smile which does not reach his eyes, although their natural warmth conceals this from the deacon.

"A bride awaiting her husband," he says, a slight catch in his voice, an intimation of something in his tone which brings, unbidden, to the deacon's mind the memory of a little girl he used to play with before he was dedicated to the service of God. He clears his throat.

"The hanging, Your Reverence," he says, because there has been a lot of talk about the hanging in the deacons' dormitory, about its suitability or otherwise for display in a house of God. "It looks very well."

"Look at it carefully tomorrow, boy, in daylight. If I were a betting man, I'd wager you'd never seen anything like it before. The Council of Arras exhorted us to use hangings in our churches for the purposes of educating our congregations. So here is the first lesson of my hanging. Remember, it is not what we see but the way we look at it which matters."

"Yes, Father."

"Now give me the keys and get yourself to bed."

"Yes, Father. Goodnight, Father."

"God bless you, boy."

Odo continues to smile into the darkness, tossing the bunch of keys from hand to hand until the boy has gone, shutting the wicket in the great west door quietly behind him, sealing in the curiously sterile silence of a new, unconsecrated church. Everything has been brought from the old cathedral, the gospels and vestments, the mortuary rolls and calendars of saints, the reliquaries like miniature gold and silver palaces with windows made of crystal and precious stones. Yet what had life there seems, in these imposing surroundings, not dead, but waiting for the breath of the Holy Spirit that will come with consecration. The relics of the saints, bone splinters, twists of hair, flakes of dried flesh and threads of martyrs' garments, the reinterred bones of former bishops and benefactors of the diocese, are all, in Odo's imagination, sleeping beauties waiting for the kiss of their prince.

Now the boy has gone he is alone again with his beloved ghost. He puts the keys down on the top step. Turning towards the altar, his fingers seek out the contours of the Magdalene at the right hand edge of the pieta. He prefers this to looking, to conjure from touch and memory the exact curve of her cheek, her grave, ironic mouth and the candour of her look, rather than having to settle for cold, white marble which, however beautiful, has an unsatisfying glitter. Even in candlelight it is a poor approximation of all the subtle variations in shade of a woman's skin. In this midsummer moonlight, it is impossible. But it is what he has.

At first he used to dream about her repeatedly, terrible, vivid dreams from which he would awake breathless, heart-shaken, lathered in sweat and wasted semen. Profligate, murderer. He punished himself with scourges, ice water baths, prostrations clad only in his shift, stone striking his unruly heart and ungovernable sex through a veil of linen. In time the pain has eased. His heart has not healed, but he has learned to compensate for its wounds, like a man with one eye or a three legged dog. Sometimes, he is almost content.

"Well," he says to her, "what do you think? Is it how you imagined it would be? I haven't overdone it, have I? You know what a magpie I am." He gazes around the building, its construction thrown into elaborate relief by the light of the full moon pouring through the windows of nave and clerestory, a lattice of silver crisscrossing the expectant space beneath its vaulted ceiling. The light sings, glancing off the gilded scales of the dragon in the chapel of Saint Vigor and the spread, silver wings of the eagle which looks as though it has just this minute come to roost on top of the lectern, firing the hearts of gems, skidding over ivory and mother-of-pearl. The carved and painted faces of saints and angels smile down from the roof, the chevrons decorating the lancets vibrate with colour, viridian, lapis, cardinal red.

Perhaps a little, she tells him, directing his gaze towards certain pieces he couldn't resist, taken from the Holy Trinity at Bosham and one or two other churches close to the heart of Harold Godwinson, but she sounds, in the voice he gives her, absent-minded, like an adult humouring a child while thinking about something else. She really isn't interested in the gold and silver and precious gems, the statues and frescoes, the high bishop's chair, even the huge silver gilt corona hanging in the intersection of nave and transept, its arms straddling the high cross of air, or the ornate pulpit, intricate as lace, from which he will preach tomorrow, the feast day of his two holy predecessors, Exupery and Vigor. It will be the greatest sermon of his life, on God's gift of the Virgin as daughter to Anna and Joachim and the many miracles wrought by her...

Show me the embroidery, she says impatiently.

"The cope I shall wear, embroidered with the Life of Mary, with the Virgin at her lying-in placed so she and her Child will appear exactly between my shoulderblades? The haloes are done, I'm told, by something called underside couching, which will cause them to glitter when I move. My congregation will be dazzled by my back. I wonder what we may read into that? Aren't you impressed I've learnt the name of the stitch? For you."

Yes, yes, I know it. I have used it many times for just such a purpose. But stop teasing me. You know what embroidery I mean.

Stroking the Magdalene's cheek one last time with the tip of his finger, he stands up and starts to walk slowly down the nave towards the west door. His left hip pains him a little after sitting for so long. The work has been hung so Edward enthroned at Westminster, in counsel with Harold before his ill-fated voyage to Normandy, appears to the left of the west door. It is stretched between the pillars of the nave, barring the side aisles, across the choir behind the high altar, so that Odo blessing the feast at Pevensey is exactly aligned with a fresco of the Last Supper decorating the eastern end of the apse.

"Let's start at the beginning," he says.

All the best stories do, replies the ghost.

"Talking to yourself, brother?"

Preoccupied with listening to his ghost, his sight confused by the alternating shafts of light and dark, he has not noticed William come into the cathedral. William has advanced a little way up the nave and is peering closely at the other end of the hanging, which is not exactly opposite the first panel as the Pevensey blessing scene is not central to its length. He is bare-headed and the moonlight pouring through the rose window picks out the grey in his hair, giving its red a faded appearance.

"You're starting at the wrong end," says Odo, crossing the main aisle to join him. William, he notices, is wheezing slightly and smells like an old dog.

"Oh, I don't know. That's me, isn't it?" He points at the enthroned king, the towers of Saint Peter's abbey church at Westminster behind him, the mirror image of King Edward at the opening of the tale, if you were to ignore the variations in the lower border, where Edward is framed by pairs of dogs and pelicans, but William has flames licking his feet. "This is devilish tricky light to see in. What's that, some sort of…Splendour of God, flames. You might have glossed over that unfortunate detail."

"I might, Agatha clearly wouldn't. This part was done at Saint Augustine's, after…Agatha had gone home. I gave them instructions to follow her sketches absolutely. I hadn't seen it myself until earlier today, when they were hanging it. I like it. The more adversities, the greater the triumph."

William gives a sceptical grunt. "You're thinner," he says, "what's your secret?"

Odo makes a dismissive gesture with his hands. "I don't seem to have the appetite I used to."

"Fortunate for you. My physician's got me on a diet. All boiled chicken and lettuces. Enough to drive a man to an early grave. And that's you?" William has moved on to the next, or former, image, which shows himself standing with Odo kneeling before him, his hands between William's in the act of homage.

"Touching," William remarks.

"Why don't we start at the beginning?" asks Odo, ushering his brother across the aisle.

"Was this Agatha's notion?" he asks as they reach Harold's last supper at Bosham, pointing at the little figures of Aesop's fox and crow in the border below. "Or yours?"

Oh clever girl, he says to his ghost, *you clever girl*. "Neither," he says to William, with an abruptness which diverts William's attention from the hanging to his brother.

"Ah. You surprise me. For surely here we have Godwinson, the vain and stupid crow, dropping the prize into the waiting jaws of the wily fox, me."

"Or, the disingenuous and trusting crow being taken advantage of by the ruthless fox."

"Somewhat like this young woman here. Honestly, Odo, I wonder that you have the audacity to display this in a house of God." William frowns at one of Margaret's naked couples.

"The best love stories mingle the earthly and the divine," comments Odo.

"I wasn't aware this was a love story." William fixes a beady look on his brother. "I thought you were done with all that nonsense."

"Oh quite chastened. As you said at the time, it's just like striking your funny bone. But the memory lingers even after the pain has gone. As a warning, perhaps, to be more careful next time. Think of these," Odo waves a nonchalant hand at the little figures, "as characters in a cautionary tale if you like."

"Why am I always left with the impression that every word you utter has at least two meanings, Odo?"

Odo laughs and moves on, only a few feet, then stops, abruptly, like an animal reaching the limits of a tether. Here is something he has never seen before, surely he has never seen before, he would have remembered. If he had seen even the sketch for it, he would have said, no, it's private, irrelevant, leave it out. Yet he is glad that fate, or accident, or even God, has intervened to put it there. *Ubi unus clericus et Aelfgyva.* He touches the letters of her name, in its Latin spelling which he used to be so careful to avoid, as though they are a charm, as though their physical presence in indigo wool might somehow enable him to see what has become of her and the child.

"There you are," he says to her softly.

"What?" says William, coming up beside him. William, he thinks, is growing deaf.

"Nothing." *Our secret,* he tells his ghost. "I wish Agatha had come."

"That comet's a fine confection. Why didn't she?"

So, a comet may endure after all. "Oh, she's quite a recluse these days. She isn't even novice mistress at Saint Justina's any more. She lives in her own little hermitage, in a field of cows, I'm told. The only people who see her are her confessor and the servant who looks after her. Not even me, and I'm her bishop, if nothing else."

William sighs and shakes his head. "Women," he says. "I expect you miss her."

"Yes. Although part of me feels as though it has become a hermit with her."

"Why aren't these ships finished?"

The two men peer at the scene, a worried looking Harold listening to an adviser, the comet shooting overhead and in the lower border the empty hulls of ships, in pale yellow and whitework, suspended above a wintry sea.

"Damned if I know," says Odo, and his ghost says, of course you do. "Yes I do. They are finished. They're dream ships."

"Godwinson's nightmares," adds William, catching on.

"Or his dreams of Valhalla."

"Is there anything in this oddity that's simply what it seems to be?"

"As much as in me. Or you. It's been nearly ten years in the making. What do you expect?"

"What I like is things to be clear cut, unequivocal. Order."

"Ah."

The two men complete their circuit of the nave slowly and companionably. William admires the way Agatha has caught the syncopation of the horses at the beginning of a cavalry charge; his troops drill for hours a day to achieve such unity, good to see it appreciated. I know, responds Odo, seeing in his mind's eye the beach at Saint Valery, the squares and circles, the parallel lines of hoofmarks in the damp sand like a giant child's geometry slate. William teases him about the heroic representation of himself rallying the men when it was believed William had been killed. Whey-faced and knock-kneed as a virgin on her wedding night more like it. He considers Godwinson's death for a long time, searching his memory for any evidence of a shot in the eye, an unusual sort of injury, but it is years ago, and not important. The sea will have had the man's remains long since.

Then, with his hand on the latch of the wicket in the west door, saying he must get back to the palace before Matilda sends out a search party, he confesses something puzzles him.

"The oath," he says. "You've got yourself in all over the place, even the odd council I could swear you weren't at, but your biggest moment, when Godwinson swore on your relics and we thought we'd got him, well, where are you? You were certainly there, parading up the beach with your cope billowing out behind you and your swordbelt on like Saint Vigor himself."

Oh yes, he was there. He remembers the cloying softness of the sand, how the clergy carrying the heavy reliquaries, impeded by their skirts, struggled against it. He remembers the wind almost blowing his mitre off and whipping the words of the oath out to sea, so that William had to repeat them before Godwinson could hear what he was supposed to say. Silk vestments. Biting, salt cold. At least, with this grand new cathedral, there will be no more need to stage big events on the beach.

Ever since William came into the building Odo has been waiting for him to ask this question. Actually, he has been waiting for it, or something like it, for years. The pillars supporting the great arch of the west door are encircled by stone benches balanced on the spread wings of cherubim. Odo sits on one, William next to him. Their shoulders almost touch, yet they are facing away from one another due to the tight diameter of the bench. William is in darkness, shaded from the moon by the door recess. Odo listens to his brother's laboured breathing. He feels sick but deadly calm.

"Do you remember the Saint Exupery incident?"

William laughs. "You mean when you spent all that money buying what you thought were the saint's bones, only to find out they belonged to some peasant who probably couldn't even say his Creed?"

"People were punished," says Odo defensively, before reminding himself not to be distracted. "Well, I never did anything about the bones. They just stayed in the crypt at the old church, in the reliquary shrine I bought them in. So when it looked to me as though Harold was reluctant to commit himself to supporting your claim to succeed Edward, I switched the reliquaries and told him he wasn't binding himself to anything. He could swear, you'd let him take his hostages and go home, and then he could claim he was tricked, so his promise wasn't worth anything."

Ah, says the beloved ghost, *a debt of honour. Now I understand.*

"Splendour of God," says William in a subdued voice, "so he never was foresworn. And you really did it? You didn't just tell him you had?"

"Of course I did it. He watched me do it. He never would have sworn otherwise. You were treating him well enough, he'd profited from the campaign against Conan of Brittany, he'd have stuck it out."

"What made you so sure of him? I didn't see it."

"I knew him better than you. Remember, I'd visited him a couple of times, seen him on his home ground. And perhaps he was more prepared to talk openly to me. After all, I was just the bishop, the younger son sent into the church. None of Duke Robert's blood in my veins."

And do you remember seeing me, prompts his ghost, *through heat shimmer and wine haze, just one of the household women below the hearth? You never said you did.*

"*No wonder you wanted to disa*ssociate yourself. But why? Why make everything so complicated? The outcome would have been the same with or without the oath. Edward left the throne to me, Harold usurped it, even if he did pretty it up by getting himself elected king. Elected, I ask you. What nonsense."

"Because I wanted to be absolutely certain that, when the time came, you would act. I didn't want to risk your being undecided, or not getting enough support. The oath was my surety. You see," he goes on, rising from the bench and standing in front of William, "I couldn't bear the thought of spending the rest of my life here, going to waste in that dark, damp old palace, passing my time in councils on the appropriate vestments for baptisms or what's a suitable punishment for a priest who fails to maintain his tonsure, and grovelling to rich men who believe they can buy their way into heaven by paying to mend the cathedral roof. God gave me you, William, and then He reminded me that He helps those who help themselves."

William looks up at him. He speaks mildly, affecting hurt rather than anger. "I can't believe that you had so little faith in me, brother. Did you think I would let what was rightfully mine just slip away from me?"

"I doubted you'd get enough military support which, as it happens, was nearly true. You needed the Pope, and the notion that Harold had perjured himself lent weight to Lanfranc's argument in Rome. And I wasn't sure you were ruthless enough. There's a squeamish side to you, William, a tendency to draw back from the brink."

"Alencon?" William asks, still in the same conciliatory tone. *Me?* asks the beloved ghost. "I remember how much you used to like me to tell you that story when you were a boy."

"A fit of bad temper. Not ruthlessness. There's nothing rational in hacking off tens of men's hands and feet because they've insulted your mother."

Or driving out your brother's mistress because you're jealous of her place in his heart, scolds the ghost.

"I see." William clears his throat. "And the relics I wore during the battle? The false ones?"

"Oh no, of course not. I had them switched back. I wouldn't do that to you."

"You really are a very dangerous man, aren't you, Odo? More of Ganelon than Turpin in your make up. I must be grateful I have you on my side."

"I am your man, Your Grace, by blood and honour." He kneels before William, placing his hands between his brother's as if performing homage. His knees crack. Moonlight illuminates half his face.

"A pretty speech," says William, prising Odo's palms apart with his fingers so they are holding hands as they might have done if they had ever been children together. "I have heard you make so many over the years, inspired, I believed, by love of me. And now I find it was just your own ambition that fired you up."

Look into his eyes, Odo, commands the ghost, *and you'll see your own solitude mirrored there. His sons rebel against him and he cannot trust his wife not to side with them. You're not the only one to have sacrificed your heart on the altar of ambition.*

"It's the same thing," says Odo.

Odo frees his hands from William's grasp and stands up.

"Would you have wished it otherwise?" William asks.

"I don't waste my time wishing for what cannot be. I am a good and faithful servant. I use my talents to the best of my ability."

"Why do I not quite believe you?"

"What have I done that you should not?"

"Orchestrated a false oath?"

"In your interests as much as mine. Imagine, we could be sitting here now, under threat from England as much as France or Anjou, instead of preparing to celebrate the fact that we've drawn everybody's teeth. All the pregnant bitch's offspring," he adds, reflecting how that fable too appears in the margins of his tapestry. *Twice*, his ghost reminds him, *though the second time was not me.*

I understand, he replies, *yours was a warning to Harold, the other – whose? – was William's promise. Do not let Normandy get a foot in the door. If you do, he will give away everything you value.*

"Except that we wouldn't be here, in this spectacular cathedral, because you wouldn't have been able to afford it. Did you get what you wanted? Is this enough for you? I should think even God must find all this," he waves his arm at the spectacle of the cathedral, "hard to stomach."

Did you get what you wanted, asks his ghost, *is it enough?* He does not answer. He walks back slowly down the aisle, towards the glimmer of the white marble altar, with his tapestry in the corner of his eye, a strip of moony ribbon pierced and puckered with the story of his life, its lies and moments of truth, its fears, its compromises, its moments of shame and savagery, its loves. His great enterprise. It is not how he planned it.

A memory is vouchsafed him, something he has not thought about for many years, not lost, but disregarded, like an old sword at the bottom of a weapons chest, rusty but with an edge to nick the unwary hand. He remembers the dream that came to haunt him after Senlac, the four women beneath the tree, the mutilated beauty between his sheets. He used to think, when he thought about it at all, that perhaps it was a dream about the ambiguities of power, about the exhilaration of taking and the illusion of holding.

He finds himself staring at the embroidered image of a woman and child fleeing a burning house, and as he stares, the moonlight begins to play tricks with his eyes. He sees a meadow, very bright, almost luminous, studded with wild flowers the colours of gems, a filigree of silver water running through it. In the meadow are a woman and a small child in a linen bonnet, playing, laughing, their laughter dissolving in the sound of running water. As he looks, they become aware of him and wave, then the woman takes the child by the hand and they start to walk towards him.

"Yes," he says, a note of wonder in his voice, "yes, I did."

"Eh?" says William, pulling crossly at his earlobe.

"Get what I wanted," Odo explains, raising his voice slightly. He blinks, and the luminous vision is replaced once again by the embroidered image.

A dream come true, says the Beloved Ghost.

AFTERWORD

This is a work of fiction and as such, it would be inappropriate for me to give a full set of references. I am indebted to the research of Jan Messant for my re-imagination of the embroidery workshop. My speculations as to the interpretation of some of the more obscure imagery of the Bayeux Tapestry are partly my own and partly those of David J. Bernstein in his book, *The Mystery of the Bayeux Tapestry*.

I am sure I have committed many unintentional historical inaccuracies, but there also a few quite deliberate ones. Although Odo of Bayeux did have two sisters, Agatha is entirely a figment of my imagination. There is no evidence that Odo did attend the great monastery school at Bec, but it is plausible that he did, and there is no evidence that he did not. Odo's son, John, is his only recorded child and, as he was witnessing documents for his cousin, Henry I, as late as 1121, he was almost certainly born much later than 1056, which is the date I give for his birth in this novel.

One historical figure who I feel deserves an apology, because I have treated his reputation rather badly in this book, is Lanfranc of Bec. Lanfranc was a religious leader of good conscience, and an administrator so able that many of the structures he put in place as Archbishop of Canterbury govern the Church of England to this day.

As for Aelgyva, well, who knows? Perhaps she was just an "elf-gift" after all. Remember, if you translate Odo's surname, de Conteville, into English, you get Storyville.